THE COLLECTED
SHORT STORIES
OF LOUIS L'AMOUR

Bantam Books by Louis L'Amour

THE
COLLECTED
SHORT STORIES
OF
LOUIS L'AMOUR

FRONTIER STORIES
Volume 2

Louis L'Amour

BANTAM BOOKS
NEW YORK

2014 Bantam Books Mass Market Edition
Copyright © 2003 by Louis & Katherine L'Amour Trust

Excerpt from *Law of the Desert Born, A Graphic Novel,* by Louis L'Amour text copyright © 2013 by Beau L'Amour, illustrations copyright © 2013 by Louis L'Amour Enterprises, Inc.

All rights reserved.

Published in the United States by Bantam Books, an imprint of Random House, a division of Random House LLC, a Penguin Random House Company, New York.

BANTAM BOOKS and the HOUSE colophon are registered trademarks of Random House LLC.

Originally published in hardcover in the United States by Bantam Books, an imprint of Random House, a division of Random House LLC, in 2004.

ISBN: 978-0-8041-7972-0
eBook: 978-0-553-90078-1

Cover design: Scott Biel
Cover art: Frank Tenney Johnson. Courtesy of The Anschutz Collection. Photographed by William J. O'Connor

Photograph of Louis L'Amour by John Hamilton—Globe Photos, Inc.

Printed in the United States of America

randomhousebooks.com

16 15 14

Bantam Books mass market edition: September 2014

CONTENTS

THE COLLECTED
SHORT STORIES
OF LOUIS L'AMOUR

LAW OF THE DESERT BORN

S HAD MARONE CRAWLED out of the water swearing and slid into the mesquite. Suddenly, for the first time since the chase began, he was mad. He was mad clear through. "The hell with it!" He got to his feet, his eyes blazing. "I've run far enough! If they cross Black River, they're askin' for it!"

For three days he had been on the dodge, using every stratagem known to men of the desert, but they clung to him like leeches. That was what came of killing a sheriff's brother, and the fact that he killed in self-defense wasn't going to help a bit. Especially when the killer was Shad Marone.

That was what you could expect when you were the last man of the losing side in a cattle war. All his friends were gone now but Madge.

The best people of Puerto de Luna hadn't been the toughest in this scrap, and they had lost. And Shad Marone, who had been one of the toughest, had lost with them. His guns hadn't been enough to outweigh those of the other faction.

Of course, he admitted to himself, those on his side hadn't been angels. He'd branded a few head of calves himself from time to time, and when cash was short, he had often run a few steers over the border. But hadn't they all?

Truman and Dykes had been good men, but Dykes had been killed at the start, and Truman had fought like a gentleman, and that wasn't any way to win in the Black River country.

Since then, there had been few peaceful days for Shad Marone.

After they'd elected Clyde Bowman sheriff, he knew they were out to get him. Bowman hated him, and Bowman had been one of the worst of them in the cattle war.

The trouble was, Shad was a gunfighter, and they all knew it. Bowman was fast with a gun and in a fight could hold his own. Also, he was smart enough to leave Shad Marone strictly alone. So they just waited, watched, and planned.

Shad had taken their dislike as a matter of course. It took tough men to settle a tough country, and if they started shooting, somebody got hurt. Well, he wasn't getting hurt. There had been too much shooting to suit him.

He wanted to leave Puerto de Luna, but Madge was still living on the old place, and he didn't want to leave her there alone. So he stayed on, knowing it couldn't last.

Then Jud Bowman rode into town. Shad was thoughtful when he heard that. Jud was notoriously quarrelsome and was said to have twelve notches on his gun. Shad had a feeling that Jud hadn't come to Puerto de Luna by accident.

Jud hadn't been in town two days before the grapevine had the story that if Clyde and Lopez were afraid to run Marone out of town, he wasn't.

Jud Bowman might have done it, too, if it hadn't been for Tips. Tips Hogan had been tending bar in Puerto de Luna for a long time. He'd come over the trail as wagon boss for Shad's old man, something everyone had forgotten but Shad and Tips himself.

Tips saw the gun in Bowman's lap, and he gave Marone a warning. It was just a word, through unmoving lips, while he mopped the bar.

After a moment, Shad turned, his glass in his left hand, and he saw the way Bowman was sitting and how the tabletop would conceal a gun in his lap. Even then, when he knew they had set things up to kill him, he hadn't wanted trouble. He decided to get out while the getting was good. Then he saw Slade near the door and Henderson across the room.

He was boxed. They weren't gambling this time. Tips Hogan knew what was likely to happen, and he was working his way down the bar.

Marone took it easy. He knew it was coming, and it wasn't a new thing. That was his biggest advantage, he thought. He had been in more fights than any of them. He didn't want any more trouble, but if he got out of this, it would be right behind a six-gun. The back door was barred and the window closed.

Jud Bowman looked up suddenly. He had a great shock of blond, coarse hair, and under bushy brows his eyes glinted. "What's this about you threatenin' to kill me, Marone?"

So that was their excuse. He had not threatened Bowman, scarcely knew him, in fact, but this was the way to put him in the wrong, to give them the plea of self-defense.

He let his eyes turn to Bowman, saw the tensity in the man's face. A denial, and there would be shooting. Jud's right-hand fingertips rested on the table's edge. He had only to drop a hand and fire.

"Huh?" Shad said stupidly, as though startled from a daydream. He took a step toward the table, his face puzzled. "Wha'd you say? I didn't get it."

They had planned it all very carefully. Marone would deny, Bowman would claim he'd been called a liar; there would be a killing. They were tense, all three of them set to draw.

"Huh?" Shad repeated blankly.

They were caught flat-footed. After all, you couldn't shoot a man in cold blood. You couldn't shoot a man who was half-asleep. Most of the men in the saloon were against Marone, but they would never stand for murder.

They were poised for action, and nothing happened. Shad blinked at them. "Sorry," he said, "I must've been dreamin'. I didn't hear you."

Bowman glanced around uncertainly, wetting his lips with his tongue. "I said I heard you threatened to kill me," he repeated. It sounded lame, and he knew it, but Shad's response had been unexpected. What happened then was even more unexpected.

Marone's left hand shot out, and before anyone could move, the table was spun from in front of Bowman. Everyone saw the naked gun lying in his lap.

Every man in the saloon knew that Jud Bowman, for all his reputation, had been afraid to shoot it out with an even break. It would have been murder.

Taken by surprise, Bowman blinked foolishly. Then his wits came back. Blood rushed to his face. He grabbed the gun. "Why, you . . . !"

Then Shad Marone shot him. Shad shot him through the belly, and before the other two could act, he wheeled, not toward the door, but to the closed window. He battered it with his shoulder and went right on through. Outside, he hit the ground on his hands but came up in a lunging run. Then he was in the saddle and on his way.

There were men in the saloon who would tell the truth—two at least, although neither had much use for him. But Marone knew that with Clyde Bowman as sheriff he would never be brought to trial. He would be killed "evading arrest."

For three days he fled, and during that time, they were never more than an hour behind him. Then, at Forked Tree, they closed in. He got away, but they clipped his horse. The roan stayed on his feet, giving all he had, as horses always had given for Shad Marone, and then died on the riverbank, still trying with his last breath.

Marone took time to cache his saddle and bridle, then started on afoot. He made the river, and they thought that would stop him, for he couldn't swim a stroke. But he found a drift log, and with his guns riding high, he shoved off. Using the current and his own kicking, he got to the other bank, considerably downstream.

The thing that bothered him was the way they clung to his trail. Bowman wasn't the man to follow as little trail as he left. Yet the man hung to him like an Apache.

Apache!

Why hadn't he thought of that? It would be Lopez following that trail, not Bowman. Bowman was a bulldog, but Lopez was wily as a fox and bloodthirsty as a weasel.

Shad got to his feet and shook the water from him like a dog. He was a big, rawboned, sun-browned man. His shirt was half torn away, and a bandolier of cartridges was slung across his shoulder and chest. His six-gun was on his hip, his rifle in his hand.

He poured the water out of his boots. Well, he was through playing now. If they wanted a trail, he'd see that they got one.

Lopez was the one who worried him. He could shake the others, but Lopez was one of the men who had built this country. He was ugly, he killed freely and often, he was absolutely ruthless, but he had nerve. You had to hand it to him. The man wasn't honest, and he was too quick to kill, but it had taken men like him to tame this wild, lonely land. It was a land that didn't tame easy.

Well, what they'd get now would be death for them all. Even Lopez. This was something he'd been saving.

Grimly he turned up the steep, little-used path from the river. They thought they had him at the river. And they would think they had him again at the lava beds.

Waterless, treeless, and desolate, the lava beds were believed to harbor no life of any kind. Only sand and great, jagged rocks—rocks shaped like flame—grotesque, barren, awful. More than seventy miles long, never less than thirty miles wide, so rough a pair of shoes wouldn't last five miles and footing next to impossible for horses.

On the edge of the lava, Shad Marone sat down and pulled off his boots. Tying their strings, he hung them to his belt. Then he pulled out a pair of moccasins he always carried and slipped them on. Pliable and easy on his feet, they would give to the rough rock and would last many times as long in this terrain as boots. He got up and walked into the lava beds.

The bare lava caught the fierce heat and threw it back in his face. A trickle of sweat started down his cheek. He knew the desert, knew how to live in the heat, and he did not try to hurry. That would be fatal. Far ahead of him was a massive tower of rock jutting up like a church steeple from a tiny village. He headed that way, walking steadily. He made no attempt to cover his trail, no attempt to lose his pursuers. He knew where he was going.

An hour passed, and then another. It was slow going. The rock tower had come abreast of him and then fallen behind. Once he saw the trail of some tiny creature, perhaps a horned frog.

Once, when he climbed a steep declivity, he glanced back. They were still coming. They hadn't quit.

Lopez—that was like Lopez. He wouldn't quit. Shad smiled then, but his eyes were without humor. All right, they wanted to kill him bad enough to try the lava beds. They would have to learn the hard way—learn when they could never profit from the lesson.

He kept working north, using the shade carefully. There was little of it, only here and there in the lee of a rock. But each time he stopped, he cooled off a little. So far he hadn't taken a drink.

After the third hour, he washed his lips and rinsed his mouth. Twice, after that, he took only a spoonful of water and rinsed his mouth before swallowing.

Occasionally, he stopped and looked around to get his bearings. He smiled grimly when he thought of Bowman. The sheriff was a heavy man. Davis would be there, too. Lopez was lean and wiry. He would last. He would be hard to kill.

By his last count, there were eight left. Four had turned back at the lava beds. He gained a little.

At three in the afternoon, he finally stopped. It was a nice piece of shade and would grow better as the hours went on. The ground was low, and in one corner there was a pocket. He dug with his hands until the ground became damp. Then he lay back on the sand and went to sleep.

He wasn't worried. Too many years he had been awakening at the hour he wished, his senses alert to danger. He was an hour ahead of them, at least. He would need this rest he was going to get. What lay ahead would take everything he had. He knew that.

Their feet would be punishing them cruelly now. Three of them still had their horses, leading them.

He rested his full hour, then got up. He had cut it very thin. Through a space in the rocks, he could see them, not three hundred yards away. Lopez, as he had suspected, was in the lead. How easy to pick them off now! But no, he would not kill again. Let their own anxiety to kill him kill them.

Within a hundred yards, he had put two jumbled piles of boulders between himself and his pursuers. A little farther then, and he stopped.

Before him was a steep slide of shale, near the edge of a great basin. Standing where he did, he could see, far away in the distance, a purple haze over the mountains. Between there was nothing but a great white expanse, shimmering with heat.

He slid down the shale and brought up at the bottom. He was now, he knew, seventy feet below sea level. He started away, and at every step, dry, powdery dust lifted in clouds. It caked in his nostrils, filmed his eyelashes, and covered his clothes with whitish, alkaline dust. Far across the Sink, and scarcely discernible from the crest behind him, was the Window in the Rock. He headed for it, walking steadily. It was ten miles if you walked straight across.

"So far that Navajo was right," Shad told himself. "An' he said to make it before dark . . . or else!"

Shad Marone's lips were dry and cracked. After a mile, he stopped, tilting his canteen until he could get his finger into the water, then carefully moistened his lips. Just a drop then, inside his mouth.

All these men were desertwise. None of them, excepting perhaps Lopez, would know about the Sink. They would need water. They would have to know where to find it. By day they could follow his trail, but after darkness fell . . . ?

And then, the Navajo had said, the wind would begin to blow. Shad looked at the dry, powdery stuff under him. He could imagine what a smothering, stifling horror this would be if the wind blew. Then, no man could live.

Heat waves danced a queer rigadoon across the lower sky, and heat lifted, beating against his face from the hot white dust beneath his feet. Always it was over a man's shoe tops, sometimes almost knee-deep. Far away, the mountains were a purple line that seemed to waver vaguely in the afternoon sun. He walked on, heading by instinct rather than sight for the Window.

Dust arose in a slow, choking cloud. It came up from his feet in little puffs, like white smoke. He stumbled, then got his feet right, and kept on. Walking in this was like dragging yourself through heavy mud. The dust pulled at his feet. His pace was slow.

Thirst gathered in his throat, and his mouth seemed filled with something thick and clotted. His tongue was swollen, his lips cracked and swollen. He could not seem to swallow.

He could not make three miles an hour. Darkness would reach him before he made the other side. But he would be close. Close enough. Luckily, at this season, the light stayed long in the sky.

After a long time, he stopped and looked back. Yes, they were coming. But there was not one dust cloud. There were several. Through red-rimmed, sun-squinted eyes, he watched. They were straggling. Every straggler would die. He knew that. Well, they had asked for it.

Dust covered his clothing, and only his gun he kept clean. Every half hour he stopped and wiped it as clean as he could. Twice he pulled a knotted string through the barrel.

Finally, he used the last of his water. Every half hour he had been wetting his lips. He did not throw the canteen away, but slung it back upon his hip. He would need it later, when he got to the Nest. His feet felt very heavy, his legs seemed to belong to an automaton. Head down, he slogged wearily on. In an hour he made two miles.

———

THERE IS A time when human nature seems able to stand no more. There is a time when every iota of strength seems burned away. This was the fourth day of the chase. Four days without a hot meal, four days of riding, walking, running. Now this. He had only to stop, they would come up with him, and it would be over.

The thought of how easy it would be to quit came to him. He considered the thought. But he did not consider quitting. He could no more have stopped than a bee could stop making honey. Life was ahead, and he had to live. It was a matter only of survival now. The man with the greatest urge to live would be the one to survive.

Those men behind him were going to die. They were going to die for three reasons. First, he alone knew where there was water, and at the right time he would lose them.

Second, he was in the lead, and after dark they would have no trail, and if they lived through the night, there would be no trail left in the morning.

Third, at night, at this season, the wind always blew, and their eyes and mouths and ears would fill with soft, white filmy dust, and if they lay down, they would be buried by the sifting, swirling dust.

They would die then, every man jack of them.

They had it coming. Bowman deserved it; so did Davis and Gardner. Lopez most of all. They were all there; he had seen them. Lopez was a killer. The man's father had been Spanish and Irish, his mother an Apache.

Without Lopez, he would have shaken them off long before. Shad Marone tried to laugh, but the sound was only a choking grunt. Well, they had followed Lopez to their death, all of them. Aside from Lopez, they were weak sisters.

He looked back again. He was gaining on them now. The first dust cloud was farther behind, and the distance between the others was growing wider. It was a shame Lopez had to die, at that. The man was tough and had plenty of trail savvy.

Shad Marone moved on. From somewhere within him he called forth a new burst of strength. His eyes watched the sun. While there was light, they had a chance. What would they think in Puerto de Luna when eight men did not come back?

Marone looked at the sun, and it was low, scarcely above the purple mountains. They seemed close now. He lengthened his stride again. The Navajo had told him how his people once had been pursued by Apaches, and had led the whole Apache war party into the Sink. There they had been caught by darkness, and none were ever seen again according to the Indian's story.

Shad stumbled then and fell. Dust lifted thickly about him, clogging his nostrils. Slowly, like a groggy fighter, he got his knees under him, and using his rifle for a staff, pushed himself to his feet.

He started on, driven by some blind, brute desire for life. When he fell again, he could feel rocks under his hands. He pulled himself up.

He climbed the steep, winding path toward the Window in the Rock. Below the far corner of the Window was the Nest. And in the Nest, there was water. Or so the Navajo had told him.

When he was halfway up the trail, he turned and looked back over the Sink. Far away, he could see the dust clouds. Four of them. One larger than the others. Probably there were two men together.

"Still coming," he muttered grimly, "and Lopez leading them!"

Lopez, damn his soul!

The little devil had guts, though; you had to give him that. Suddenly, Marone found himself almost wishing Lopez would win through. The man was like a wolf. A killer wolf. But he had guts. And it wasn't just the honest men who had built up this country to what it was today.

Maybe, without the killers and rustlers and badmen, the West would never have been won so soon. Shad Marone remembered some of them: wild, dangerous men, who went into country where nobody else dared venture. They killed and robbed to live, but they stayed there.

It took iron men for that: men like Lopez, who was a mongrel of the Santa Fe Trail. Lopez had drunk water from a buffalo track many a time. *Well, so have I,* Shad told himself.

Shad Marone took out his six-shooter and wiped it free of dust. Only then did he start up the trail.

He found the Nest, a hollow among the rocks, sheltered from the wind. The Window loomed above him now, immense, gigantic. Shad stumbled, running, into the Nest. He dropped his rifle and lunged for the water hole, throwing himself on the ground to drink. Then he stared, unbelieving.

Empty!

The earth was dry and parched where the water had been, but only cracked earth remained.

He couldn't believe it. It couldn't be! It couldn't . . . !

Marone came to his feet, glaring wildly about. His eyes were red-rimmed, his face heat-flushed above the black whiskers, now filmed with gray dust.

He tried to laugh. Lopez dying down below there, he dying up here! The hard men of the West, the tough men! He sneered at himself. Both of them now would die, he at the water hole, Lopez down there in the cloying, clogging dust!

He shook his head. Through the flame-sheathed torment of his brain, there came a cool ray of sanity.

There had been water here. The Indian had been right. The cracked earth showed that. But where?

Perhaps a dry season. . . . But no; it had not been a dry season. Certainly no dryer than any other year at this time.

He stared across the place where the pool had been. Rocks and a few rock cedar and some heaped-up rocks from a small slide. He stumbled across and began clawing at the rocks, pulling, tearing. Suddenly, a trickle of water burst through! He got hold of one big rock and in a mad frenzy, tore it from its place. The water shot through then, so suddenly he was knocked to his knees.

He scrambled out of the depression, splashing in the water. Then, lying on his face, he drank, long and greedily.

Finally, he rolled away and lay still, panting. Dimly, he was conscious of the wind blowing. He crawled to the water again and bathed his face, washing away the dirt and grime. Then, careful as always, he filled his canteen from the fresh water bubbling up from the spring.

If he only had some coffee. . . . But he'd left his food in his saddlebags.

Well, Madge would be all right now. He could go back to her. After this, they wouldn't bother him. He would take her away. They would go to the Blue Mountains in Oregon. He had always liked that country.

The wind was blowing more heavily now, and he could smell the dust. That Navajo hadn't lied. It would be hell down in the Sink. He was above it now and almost a mile away.

He stared down into the darkness, wondering how far Lopez had been able to get. The others didn't matter; they were weak sisters who lived on the strength of better men. If they didn't die there, they would die elsewhere, and the West could spare them. He got to his feet.

Lopez would hate to die. The ranch he had built so carefully in a piece of the wildest, roughest country was going good. It took a man with guts to settle where he had and make it pay. Shad Marone rubbed the stubble on his jaw. "That last thirty head of his cows I rustled for him brought the best price I ever got!" he remembered thoughtfully. "Too bad there ain't more like him!"

Well, after this night, there would be one less. There wouldn't be anything to guide Lopez down there now. A man caught in a thick whirlpool of dust would have no landmarks; there would be nothing to get him out except blind instinct. The Navajos had been clever, leading the Apaches into a trap like that. Odd, that Lopez's mother had been an Apache, too.

Just the same, Marone thought, he had nerve. He'd shot his way up from the bottom until he had one of the best ranches.

Shad Marone began to pick up some dead cedar. He gathered some needles for kindling and in a few minutes had a fire going.

Marone took another drink. Somehow, he felt restless. He got up and walked to the edge of the Nest. How far had Lopez come? Suppose . . . Marone gripped his pistol.

Suddenly, he started down the mountain. "The hell with it!" he muttered.

A stone rattled.

Shad Marone froze, gun in hand.

Lopez, a gray shadow, weaving in the vague light from the cliff, had a gun in his hand. For a full minute, they stared at each other.

Marone spoke first. "Looks like a dead heat," he said.

Lopez said, "How'd you know about that water hole?"

"Navajo told me," Shad replied, watching Lopez like a cat. "You don't look so bad," he added. "Have a full canteen?"

"No. I'd have been a goner. But my mother was an Apache. A bunch of them got caught in the Sink once. That never happened twice to no Apache. They found this water hole then, and one down below. I made the one below, an' then I was finished. She was a dry hole. But then water began to run in from a crack in the rock."

"Yeah?" Marone looked at him again. "You got any coffee?"

"Sure."

"Well," Shad said as he holstered his gun, "I've got a fire."

THE TOWN NO GUNS
COULD TAME

Chapter 1

THE MINER CALLED Perry stepped from the bucket and leaned his pick and shovel against a boulder. He was a big man with broad shoulders and narrow hips. Despite the wet, clinging diggin' clothes, he moved with the ease and freedom of a big cat. His greenish eyes turned toward Doc Greenley, banker, postmaster, and saloon man of Basin City, who was talking with the other townsmen.

Perry's head and arms were bare, and the woolen undershirt failed to cover the mighty muscles that rippled along his back and shoulders. One of the men, noting the powerful arms and the strong neck, turned and said something to the others. They nodded, together.

"Hey, Perry," Doc Greenley called, "drift over here, will you? Me and these two gents want to make a proposition to you."

Casually, Perry picked up the spare pick handle leaning against the boulder and walked over, his wet clothes sloshing as he moved. He stopped when he reached the trio, and his eyes studied them, coldly penetrating. The three men shifted uneasily.

"Go ahead with it, then," Perry said shortly.

"It's like this," Doc explained. "Buff McCarty"—he nodded toward the larger of his two companions—"and Wade Manning, here, and myself have been worried about the rough element from the mines. They seem to be taking over the town. No respectable citizen or their womenfolk are safe.

And as for the hold-ups that have been raising hell with us businessmen . . ." Doc Greenley mopped his brow with a fresh bandanna handkerchief, letting the sentence go unfinished.

"We want you to help us, Perry," the heavy-set, honest-faced McCarty put in. "Manning, here, runs the freight line and I have the general supply outfit. We're all substantial citizens and need a man of your type for town marshal."

"As soon as I heard you were here, I told the boys you were just the man for us," Greenley put in eagerly.

Perry's green eyes narrowed thoughtfully. "I see." His gaze shifted from Doc Greenley, the most prominent and wealthiest man there, to the stolid McCarty, and then to the young townsman, Wade Manning. He smiled a little. "The town fathers, out in force, eh?" He glanced at Wade, looking at him thoughtfully. "But where's Rafe Landon, owner of the Sluice Box Bar?"

"Rafe Landon?" Doc Greenley's eyes glinted. "Why, his bar is the hangout for this tough crowd! In fact, we have reason to suspect—"

"Better let Perry form his own suspicions, Doc," Wade Manning interrupted. "I'm not at all sure about Rafe."

"You may not be," Greenley snapped, "but I am! Perry, I'm convinced that Landon is the ringleader of the whole kit an' caboodle of the killers and renegades we're trying to clean out!"

"Why," Perry said suddenly, "do you choose this particular time to pick a marshal? There must be a reason."

"There is," Wade Manning agreed. "You probably know about the volume of gold production here. Anyway, Doc has better than two hundred thousand in his big vault now. I have about half that much. There's a rumor around of a plot to loot the stage of the whole load."

"It's Landon," Greenley said, "that's who it is! An' do you know what *I* think?" He looked from one to the other, pulling excitedly at his ear lobe. "I think Rafe Landon is none other than *Clip Haynes,* the toughest, coldest gunman who ever pulled a trigger!"

Perry's eyes narrowed. "I heard he was down in Arizona."

"But I happen to know," Greenley said sharply, "that Clip Haynes headed this way—with the ten thousand he got from that stage job near Goldroad!"

Perry looked at Doc thoughtfully. "Maybe so. It could be that way, all right." He glanced at Buff McCarty, who was watching him from his small blue eyes. "Sure, I'll take the job! I'll ride in tonight, by the canyon trail."

The three men walked to their horses, and Perry turned abruptly back to the mine office to draw his time.

THE MOON WAS rising when the man called Perry swung onto his horse and took the canyon trail for Basin City. The big black stepped out swiftly, and the man lounged in the saddle, his eyes narrowed with thought. He rode with the ease of one long accustomed to the saddle, and almost without thinking kept to the shadows along the road, guiding his horse neatly so as to render it almost invisible in the dim light.

From the black, flat-crowned hat tied under his chin with a rawhide thong to the hand-tooled cowman's boots, his costume offered nothing that would catch the glint of light or prevent him from merging indistinguishably with his background. Even the two big guns with their polished wooden butts, tied down and ready for use, harmonized perfectly with his somber dress.

The trail dipped through canyons and wound around lofty mesas, and once he forded a small stream. Shortly after, riding through a maze of gigantic boulders, he reined in sharply. His keen ear had detected a sudden sound.

Even as he came to a halt he heard the hard rattle of hooves from a running horse somewhere on the trail ahead, and almost at the same instant, the sharp *spang* of a high-powered rifle.

Soundlessly, he slid from the saddle, and even before his feet touched the sand of the trail, his guns were gripped in his big hands. Tensely, he ran forward, staying in the soft sand where his feet made no noise. Suddenly, dead ahead of him and just around a huge boulder, a pistol roared. He jerked to a halt, and eased around the rock.

A black figure of a man was on its knees in the road. Just as the man looked around, the rifle up on the mountainside crashed again, and the kneeling figure spilled over on its face.

Perry's gun roared at the flash of the rifle, and roared again as a bullet whipped by his ear. The rifle fired once more, and Perry felt his hat jerk on his head as he emptied his gun at the concealed marksman.

There was no reply. Cautiously Perry lifted his head, then began to inch toward the dark figure sprawled in the road before him. A match flared suddenly up on the hillside, and Perry started to fire, then held it. The man might think him dead, and his present position was too open to take a chance. As he reached the body, the rattle of a horse's hooves faded rapidly into the distance.

Perry's lips set grimly. Then he got to his knees and lifted the body.

It was a boy—an attractive, fair-haired youngster. He had been shot twice, once through the body, and once through the head. Perry started to rise.

"Hold it!" The voice was that of a woman, but it was cold and even. "One move and I'll shoot!"

She was standing at one side of the road with a pistol aimed at Perry's belt line. Even in the moonlight she was lovely. Perry held perfectly still, riveted to the position as much by her beauty as by the gun she held so steadily.

"You murderer!" she said, her voice low with contempt. "Stand up, and keep your hands high!"

He put the boy gently back on the ground and got to his feet. "I'm afraid you're mistaken, miss," he said. "I didn't kill this boy."

"Don't make yourself a liar as well as a killer!" she exclaimed. "Didn't I hear you shooting? Haven't I eyes?"

"While you're holding me here," he said gently, "the real killer is making his getaway. If you'll put down that gun, I'll explain."

"Explain?" There was just a hint of hysteria in her voice. "After you've killed my brother?"

"Your brother?" he was startled now. "Why, I didn't—"

Her voice trembled, but the gun was unrelenting. "You didn't know, I suppose, that you killed Wade Manning?" Her disbelief was evident in her tone.

"Wade Manning?" he stepped forward. "Why, this isn't Wade Manning!"

"Not—not Wade?" her voice was incredulous. "But who is it then?"

He stepped back. "Take a look, Miss Manning. I don't know many people around here. I met your brother today at the Indian Creek Diggin's. He's a sight older than this poor youngster."

She dropped to her knees beside the boy. Then she looked up. "Why, this is young Tommy McCarty! What in the world can he be doing out here tonight?"

"Any relation to Buff McCarty?" he asked quickly.

"His son." Her eyes misted with tears. "Oh, this is awful! We—we came over the trail from Salt Lake together, his folks and mine!"

He took her by the shoulders. "Listen, Miss Manning. I don't like to butt in, you knowin' the lad an' all, but your brother came out here to see me today. He wanted me to be marshal here in Basin City. I took the job, so I guess this is the first part right here."

She drew back, aghast. "Then you—you're *Clip Haynes*!"

It was his turn to be startled now. "Who told you that?" he demanded. Things were moving a little too fast. "Who knew I was Clip Haynes?"

"Wade. He recognized you today. The others don't know. He wanted to see you tonight about something. He said it would take a man like you to handle the law job here."

Frowning thoughtfully, he caught up the boy's horse, grazing nearby, and lashed the body to the saddle. Then he mounted the big black, and the girl swung up on her pinto. Silently they took the trail for Basin City.

Despite the fact that she seemed to have accepted him, he could sense the suspicion that held her aloof. The fact remained that she had found him kneeling over the body, six-gun in hand. He could scarcely blame her. After all, he was not a simple miner named Perry. He was Clip Haynes—a notorious gunman with a blood price on his head.

"Who'd profit by this boy's death?" he asked suddenly. "Does he have any enemies?"

"Tommy McCarty?" her voice was incredulous. "Goodness no! He was just sixteen, and there wasn't a finer boy in Peace Valley. Everyone liked him."

Carefully, he explained all that had happened, conscious of her skepticism and of the fact that she rode warily, with one hand on her pistol. "But who'd want to kill Tommy?" she exclaimed. "And why go to all that trouble? He rides alone to the claim every morning."

Except for the glaring lights of Rafe Landon's Sluice Box Bar and Doc Greenley's High-Stake Palace, the main street of the town was in darkness. But even before they reined in at the hitching rail of the High-Stake, the body had been seen, and a crowd gathered.

They were a sullen, hard-bitten crew of miners, gamblers, freighters, and drifters that follow gold camps. They crowded around shouting questions. Then suddenly Wade Manning pushed through, followed by Buff McCarty.

One glance, and the big man's face went white. "Tommy!" his voice was agonized, and he sprang forward to lift the body from the saddle.

He stared down into the boy's white, blood-stained face. When he looked up his placid features were set in hard, desperate lines. "Who did this?" he demanded.

With the crowd staring, Clip quietly told his story, helped by a word here and there from the girl, Ruth Manning. When the story was ended, Clip found himself ringed by a circle of hard, hostile eyes.

"Then," Buff McCarty said ominously, "you didn't see this feller up on the hill, eh? And Ruth didn't either. How do I know you didn't kill Tommy?"

"Yeah," a big man with a broken nose said loudly. "This stranger's yarn sounds fishy to me. The gal finds you all a standin' over the McCarty kid with a gun, an'—"

"Shut up, Porter!" Manning interrupted. "Let's hear him out."

"Why should I shoot the boy?" Clip protested. "I never saw the kid before. I don't shoot strangers."

"You say you heard shots, then rode up to him." Buff rested his big hands on his hips, his eyes hard. "Did anybody but you an' Ruth come nigh him?"

"Not a soul!" Clip said positively.

"Then," Buff's voice was harshly triumphant, "how d'you account for *this*?" He lifted an empty leather poke, shaking it in Haynes's face. "That there poke held three thousand dollars when my boy left town!"

The broken-nosed Porter crowded closer to Clip. "You dirty, murderin' coyote!" he shouted, his face red with anger. "Y'oughta be lynched, dry-gulchin' a kid that way!"

"That's right!" another voice yelled. "Lynch him!"

"Hold it!" Clip Haynes's voice was hard. His greenish eyes seemed to glow as he backed away. Suddenly, they saw he was holding two guns, although no man had seen him draw. "Manning, you an' McCarty ought to know better than this! Look at those wounds! That boy was shot with a rifle, not a six-gun! He was shot from higher up the mountain. You'll find both those wounds range downward! You come out to Indian Creek to offer me the job of lawman around here. Well, I took it, an' solvin' this murder is goin' t' be my first job. But just to clear the air, I'm a-tellin' all of you now, my name ain't Perry—it's *Clip Haynes*!"

He backed to his horse, stepped quickly around and threw himself into the saddle. Then he faced the crowd, now staring at him, white-faced. Beyond them, he saw Doc Greenley. The banker-saloon man was smiling oddly.

"I'll be around," Haynes said then, "an' I aim to complete the job I started. You all know who I am. But if anybody here thinks I'm the killer of that boy, he can talk it out with me tomorrow noon in this street—with six-guns!"

Clip Haynes wheeled the big black and rode rapidly away, and the crowd stood silent until he was out of sight. Then quietly they walked inside.

"What d' you think, Wade?" McCarty asked, turning to the tall, silent man beside him.

Manning was staring up the road after Haynes, a curious

light in his eyes. "I think we'd better let him handle it," Wade said, "at least for the time. There's more in this than meets the eye!"

Doc Greenley walked up, rubbing his hands with satisfaction. "Just the man!" he said eagerly. "Did you see how he handled that? Just the man we need! We can make our shipment now when we want to, and that man will take care of it!"

Chapter 2

DAWN FOUND CLIP Haynes sitting among the boulders beside the trail from Indian Creek. Below him was the spot where Tommy McCarty had fallen the previous night. Opposite him, somewhere on the hillside, was the place where the murderer had waited. The very place of concealment was obvious enough. It was not a hundred yards away, in a cluster of boulders and rock cedar, not unlike his own resting place. That the murderer had waited there was undoubted, but why?

Clip Haynes pushed his hat back on his head and rolled a smoke.

First, what were the facts? McCarty, Greenley, and Manning, three of Basin City's most reputable business men, had hired him as marshal. But Rafe Landon, owner of the biggest mine, and the most popular saloon and dance hall, had not come along. Why?

Secondly, someone had killed and robbed Tommy McCarty. Obviously, the killer had not robbed him, for both Clip and Ruth Manning had been too close. Then, the obvious conclusion was that Tommy had been robbed before he was killed!

Clip sat up suddenly, his eyes narrowed. He was remembering the chafed spot on Tommy's wrist, dimly seen in the light from the High-Stake Palace. Chafed from what? The answer hit him like a blow. Tommy McCarty had not only been robbed, but had been bound hand and foot! He had escaped, and then had been shot.

But why shoot him afterward? That didn't make sense. He

already had lost the money, and if the thief had any doubts, he would have killed him the first time. The only answer was that Tommy McCarty had been mistaken for somebody else!

But who? Obviously, whoever had waited on the hillside the previous night had been expecting someone to come along. So far, Clip knew of only three people besides McCarty who might have come along. Wade Manning, Ruth Manning, and himself. But wait! What was Wade doing on the road so late? And why was Ruth traveling alone on that lonely trail?

There was always the possibility that Wade Manning, knowing Perry actually was Clip Haynes, had planned to kill him for the reward offered in Arizona. However, Manning didn't look like a cowardly killer, and the theory didn't, somehow, fit the facts.

Clip Haynes shook his head with disgust. If it was just a matter of shooting it out with some tough gunman, he was all right, but figuring out a problem like this was something he had not bargained for. It was unlikely, however, that anyone would want to shoot Ruth, or that anyone guessed she was on the road that night. That left Wade and himself as the prospective victims of the killer, for by now he would know his mistake.

Three men had known that he was taking the canyon trail to town—Doc Greenley, Wade Manning, and Buff McCarty. Clip's eyes narrowed. Why, since he had been riding slowly, and Tommy McCarty probably at a breakneck speed, hadn't Tommy passed him? Obviously because Tommy had come out on the trail at some point between where Clip had first heard his running horse and the point where he had seen the boy killed.

Mounting, Clip turned the big black down the mountainside to the trail. As he rode along he scanned the edges carefully. Suddenly, he reined in.

The hoof-prints of the big black were plainly seen, but suddenly a new trail had appeared, and Clip could see where a horse had been jumped from the embankment into the trail. Dismounting, and leading the black, he climbed the embankment and followed the trail. As soon as he saw it was plainly discernible, he swung into the saddle again and followed it rapidly.

Two miles from the canyon trail, at the end of a bottleneck canyon, he found a half-ruined adobe house. Here the trail ended.

Dismounting cautiously, Clip walked up to the 'dobe. The place was empty. Gun in hand, he knelt, examining the hard-packed earth of the floor.

The earth was scuffed and kicked as though by a pair of heels, such marks as a man might make in a struggle to free himself. But there were no ropes in sight, nothing. . . .

He froze. A shadow had fallen across him. He knew a man was crouching at the window behind him. His own gun was concealed from the watcher by his body. Apparently study-ing the earth, he waited for the first movement of the man behind him.

It could only have been an instant later that he heard the click of a cocking gun hammer, and in that same flashing split second, he hurled himself to one side. The roar of the gun boomed in the 'dobe hut, and the dirt against the wall jumped in an awkward spray even as his own pistol roared. Clip leaped to the door.

A bullet slammed against the doorjamb not an inch from his head, as he recklessly sprang into the open, both guns bucking. The man staggered, tried to fire again, and then plunged over on his face.

For a moment, Clip Haynes stood still, the light breeze brushing a lock of hair along his forehead. The sun felt warm against his cheek, and the silent figure on the sand looked sprawled and helpless.

Automatically, Clip loaded his guns. Then he walked over to the body. Before he knelt, his eyes scanned the rim of the canyon, examining every boulder, every tree. Satisfied, he bent over the fallen man. Then his eyes narrowed thought-fully. It was the big man who had been so eager to see him lynched the night before, the man who had joined Porter in his protests.

Clip's eyes narrowed thoughtfully, then he got to his feet.

He turned slowly, facing the shack. He stood there a moment carelessly, his thumbs hooked in his belt.

"All right," he said finally, "you can come out from behind that shack. With your hands high!"

Wade Manning stepped out, his hands up. His eyes glinted shrewdly. "Nice going," he said. "How did you know I was there?"

Clip shrugged, and indicated the big black horse with a motion of his head. "His ears. He doesn't miss a thing." He waited, his eyes cold.

"I suppose you want to know what I'm doing here?"

"Exactly. And what you were doing on the canyon trail last night. You seem to be around whenever there's any shooting going on."

"I can explain that," Wade said, smiling a little. "I don't blame you for being suspicious. After we talked to you at the mine that day, I decided I'd better go back out there and tell you I knew who you were, and to be careful around the men at the mine. And I didn't want you to jump to conclusions about Landon."

"What's Rafe Landon to you?" Clip demanded.

Wade shrugged, rolling a smoke. "Maybe I know men, maybe I don't," he affirmed, running his tongue along the paper. "But Rafe sizes up to me like a square shooter." He glanced up. "And in spite of what Ruth says, I think you are, too."

"Know this hombre?" Clip indicated the man on the ground.

Wade nodded. "Only to see him. He worked for Buff McCarty for a while. Lately he's been hanging around the Sluice Box. Name's Dirk Barlow. He's got a couple of tough-hand brothers."

Mounting, they started down the trail together. Clip Haynes glanced out of the corner of his eyes at Manning. He was clean cut, smooth, good-looking. His actions were suspicious, but he didn't seem the type for a killer.

Clip frowned a little. So Ruth didn't like him? Something stirred inside him, and he found himself wishing she felt differently. Then he grinned wryly. A hunted gunman like Clip Haynes getting soft about a girl! There wouldn't ever be any girls like Ruth for him.

He looked up, his mind reverting to the former problem. "How about this gent Porter back in town—the one who was so sure I shot Tommy McCarty. Where does he fit in?"

"A bad hombre. Gun-slick, and tough. He killed a prospector his first night in town. About two weeks later he shot it out with a man named Pete Handown."

"I've heard of Handown. This Porter must be fast."

"He is. But mostly a fistfighter. He runs with the surviving Barlow brothers—Joe and Gonny. They're gunmen, too. They've figured in most of the trouble around here. But they've got a ringleader. Somebody behind the scenes we can't decide on."

"Greenley thinks it's Rafe, eh?"

"Yes. I'll admit most of the gang hang around the Sluice Box. But I'm sure Rafe's in the clear." Wade looked up. "Listen, Clip. If you ride with the stage tomorrow, watch your step. There's three hundred thousand in gold going out."

Doc Greenley was standing with Buff McCarty on the walk in front of the High-Stake Palace when they rode up. He glanced swiftly at the body slung over the lead horse. Then he smiled brightly. "Got 'em on the run, boy?" he asked. "Who is it this time?"

"Dirk Barlow," Buff said, his eyes narrowing. "You'll have to ride careful now, Haynes. His brothers will come for you. They're tough as hell."

Haynes shrugged. "He asked for it." His eyes lifted to Buff's. "I back-trailed Tommy. I knew he cut in ahead of me last night, and if you looked, there was a chafed spot on his wrist. I knew he'd been tied, so I looked for the place. I found it, and this hombre tried to kill me."

"You think he killed Tommy?" Buff demanded.

"I don't know. He hasn't the money on him." He turned his head to see Ruth Manning standing in front of the post office. Their eyes met, and she turned away abruptly.

Clip swung down from the saddle and walked across the

street. When he stepped into the Sluice Box he saw Rafe Landon leaning against the end of the bar.

He was a tall man, handsome, and superbly built. There was an easy grace in his movements that was deceptive. He was wearing black, and when he turned, Clip saw he carried two guns, tied low.

"How are you, Haynes?" he said, holding out his hand. "I've been expecting you."

Haynes nodded. "What do you know about this McCarty killing?" he asked coolly. He deliberately ignored the outstretched hand.

Landon smiled. "An accident, of course. Nobody cared about hurting Tommy. He was a grand youngster."

"What d'you mean—an accident?"

"Just that. They were gunning for somebody else, but Tommy got there first." Rafe looked down at his cigarette, flicked off the ash, and glanced up. "In fact, it would be my guess they were gunning for you. Somebody who didn't want Clip Haynes butting in."

"Nobody knew I was Haynes."

Rafe shrugged. "I did. I'd known for two weeks. Manning knew, too. Probably there were others." He nodded toward the street. "I see you got Dirk Barlow. Watch those brothers of his. And look out for Porter, too."

"You're the second man who told me that."

"There'll be more. Joe and Gonny Barlow will be in as soon as they hear about this. Joe's bad, but Gonny's the worst. Gonny uses both hands, and he's fast."

"Why tell me this?" Clip asked. He looked up, and their eyes met.

Rafe Landon smiled. "You'll need it, Haynes. I'm a gambler, and it's my business to know about men. A word of friendly advice never hurt anyone—even a gent like you. Joe Barlow's never been beat in a gunfight. And like I said, Gonny's the worst."

"Porter? What's he like?" Clip asked.

"Maybe I can tell you," a harsh voice broke in.

Clip turned to see Porter standing in the doorway. He was

big, probably twenty pounds bigger than Clip, and his shoulders were powerful.

"All right," Clip said. "You tell me."

Chapter 3

PORTER WALKED OVER to the bar.

Glancing past him Clip could see the room filling with men. Come to see the fun, to see if the new marshal could take it. Clip grinned suddenly.

"What's funny?" Porter snarled suspiciously.

"You," Clip said shortly. "Last night I thought I heard you say I needed lynching. I suggested anyone who wanted to debate the matter could shoot it out with me in the street. You weren't around. What's the matter? Yellow?"

Porter stared, taken aback by the sudden attack. Somebody chuckled, and he let out a snarl of rage. "Why, you—!"

Clip's open palm slapped him across the mouth with such force that Porter's head jerked back.

With a savage roar, the big man swung. But Clip was too fast. Swaying on his feet, he slipped the punch and smashed a vicious right hand into the man's body. Porter took it without flinching, and swung both hands to Clip's head.

Haynes staggered, and before he could set himself, Porter swung a powerful right that knocked him sprawling. Before Clip could get to his feet, Porter rushed in, kicking viciously at Haynes's face, but the young marshal jerked his head aside and took the kick on the shoulder. The camel boot sent pain shocks through his body.

It knocked him rolling, but he gathered his feet under him and met Porter's charge with a jarring left jab that set the bigger man back on his heels and smashed his upper lip into his teeth.

Porter ducked his head and charged, but Clip was steadying down, and he sidestepped suddenly, bringing up a jolting right uppercut that straightened Porter up for a crashing right that knocked him reeling into the bar.

He grabbed a bottle and hurled it across the room, but

Clip ducked and charged in, grabbing the big man about the knees and dropping him to the floor. Deliberately, Clip fell with him, driving his head into the man's stomach with all his force, and then spinning on over to land on his feet.

Breathing easily, he waited until Porter got up. The big man was dazed, and before he could assemble his faculties, Clip walked in and slapped him viciously with both hands, and then snapped his fist into Porter's solar plexus with a jolt that doubled the bigger man up with a groan. A left hook spun him half around and ripped the skin under one eye. As he backed away, trying to cover, Clip walked in and pulled his hands away, crossing a wicked short right hook to the chin. Without a sound, Porter crumpled to the floor.

Turning on his heel, Clip walked quickly from the room, never so much as glancing back.

It was almost noon when he rode slowly down the mountain trail and tied his horse in a clump of mesquite. He glanced at the sun. In about fifteen minutes the stage should be along, and if it was to be held up, it would be somewhere in the next two miles. Carefully, he walked ahead until he found a place among the boulders, and then settled down to wait until the stage came along. From there on he could follow it.

Suddenly, he noticed a cloud of dust above the trail in the distance. The stage. He got up, and stood watching it as it drew nearer. He could see that everything was as it should be, and turning, he walked back to his horse. When he was about a dozen steps away, he halted in midstep, and drew back. There on the ground, over one of his own tracks was a fresh boot print, one heel rounded badly, and a queer scar across the toe!

His hand shot to his gun, but before he could draw, something crashed down over his head, and he tumbled forward into blackness. . . .

It was hours later when he opened his eyes. When he tried to lift his head a spasm of pain shot over him, and he groaned desperately. Then for a long moment he lay still, and through the wave of pain from his throbbing head, he remembered the stage, the boot print, the gold.

Desperately, he got to his hands and knees. The ground where his head had lain was a pool of blood, and when he lifted one hand, he found his hair matted with it and stiffened with sand. Crawling to his feet, he had to steady himself against a boulder. Then he retched violently, and was sick.

After he staggered to his horse and took a drink from his canteen, he felt better. Summoning all his resolution, he went back and examined the ground. The man had evidently followed him, waited behind a boulder, and as he returned to his horse, knocked him over the head. Quite obviously, he had been left for dead.

Clip walked back to his horse, checking his guns. They hadn't been tampered with. When he swung into the saddle and turned the big black down the trail, his lips were set in a tight, grim line. He loosened the big guns, and despite his throbbing head, cantered down the trail.

He didn't have far to ride. Only about three hundred yards from where he had waited, he found the coach, lying on its side, one wheel smashed. A dead horse lay in a tangle of harness, and sprawled on the ground was the stage driver. He had been shot between the eyes with a rifle.

About twenty yards away, evidently killed as he was making for the shelter of a circle of boulders, was the messenger.

———

IT WAS TWO hours before Clip Haynes rode up in front of the High-Stake Palace and tied the black to the hitching rail. His head throbbing, he stepped in.

At once the hard round muzzle of a gun jammed into his spine.

Clip stopped, his hands slowly lifting.

"Back up, an' back careful!" he heard Buff McCarty saying, his voice deadly. "One false move an' I'll drill you, gunman or no gunman!"

"What's the matter, Buff?" Clip asked. His head throbbed and he felt his anger mounting.

"You ask what's the matter!" Wade Manning snapped. Stepping up he jerked Clip's guns from their holsters. "We trusted you, and then you—"

"We found the money, that's what!" Buff snarled, his voice husky with rage. "The money you took off Tommy! We shook down your duffle bag an' found it there—the whole three thousand dollars you murdered him for!"

"Listen, men!" he protested. "If you found any money there it was a plant. Why—"

"I'm sorry, boy," Doc Greenley interrupted, shaking his head gravely, his usual smile gone. "We've got you dead to rights this time!"

Clip started to protest again, and then his jaw clamped shut. If they wanted to be like that, argument, he figured, was useless. He turned to walk out, and found himself facing Porter.

The big man sneered, and, for just an instant as Clip watched him, he saw the man's eyes flash a message to one of his captors. Then Porter was past, and Clip was being rushed to jail.

When the cell door clanged shut he walked across the narrow room, dropped on his bunk and was almost immediately asleep.

It seemed a long time later when he was awakened. It was completely dark, and listening, he knew the jail was deserted.

Clip walked across to the window, and took hold of the bars.

Then he heard a whisper. "Haynes!"

"Who is it?" he asked softly.

"It's me—Rafe. Stick your hand through the bars. I've got a key!"

Clip Haynes thrust his hand out, and felt the cold metal of a jail key in his hand. Then he heard Rafe speaking again. "Better make it quick. Porter's got a mob about worked up to lynching you."

In two strides he was across the cell. The key grated in the lock, and the door swung wide. Then he turned and stepped back, throwing the blankets into a rough hump to resemble a sleeping figure. Going out, he locked the door after him. His gun belts were on the desk in the outer office, and he swept them up, hurriedly checking the guns as he stepped outside.

Rafe Landon was waiting there. Surprisingly, Rafe had the black horse with him. Without a word, Clip gripped the gambler's hand, and then swung up.

"Listen," Rafe said, gripping his wrist. "Whoever robbed that stage today kidnapped Ruth!"

"What!" Clip jerked around, his jaws set.

"She rode out along the trail just before the stage left town. She told me she wanted to watch you. She hasn't returned yet, and Wade's just found out. There's only one place she can be—with the Barlows!"

"You know where they hang out?" Clip snapped.

"Somewhere back of the Organ. There's a box canyon up there, that might be it. Take the west route around the Organ and you'll find the trail, but watch your step!"

Clip looked down at Rafe in the darkness, his eyes keen. "Just what is Ruth Manning to you?" he demanded.

Clip thought he detected the ghost of a smile. "Does it matter? The girl's in danger!"

"Right!" Clip swung his horse. As he did so he heard someone shout, and glancing back, he saw a crowd of men spew from the doors of the High-Stake.

The big black stretched his legs and sprang away into the night, swinging around the town to the trail in tireless, space-eating strides.

Chapter 4

T HE HUGE PINNACLES of rock known as the Organ loomed ahead. For years during his wanderings, Clip Haynes had heard of them. Some queer volcanic effect had shot these hollow spires up into the sky, leaving them thin to varying degrees, and under the blows of a stick or rock they gave forth a deep, resonant sound. Around them lay rugged, broken country.

For a half hour he cut back and forth through the rocks before he located the box canyon. And then it was the horse that found the narrow thread of trail winding among the boulders. A few minutes of riding, and he sighted the dim light that came from a cabin window.

He dismounted and slipped a gun into his hand. Then he walked boldly forward, and threw the door open.

A startled Mexican jerked up from his seat on a box and dropped a hand for his gun, but at the sight of Clip, he reached for air. "Don't shoot, señor!" he gasped. "*Por dios,* don't shoot!"

Clip stepped in and swung his back to the wall. "Where's the girl?" he snapped.

"The señorita, she here. The Barlows, they go."

Clip stepped quickly across the room and spun the Mexican around. Picking up a handful of loose rope, he bound the man hand and foot. Then stooping, he untied Ruth.

"Thanks," she said, rubbing her wrists. "I was beginning to think—"

"No!" he exclaimed dryly.

Her face stiffened abruptly. Clip grinned at her. "You had that coming, lady. Let's get out of here!"

Suddenly, he stopped. In the corner was a heap of sacks taken from the stage earlier that day. Pausing, he jerked the tie string. The sack toppled slowly over. And from its mouth spilled nothing more than a thin stream of sand!

"Why—!" Ruth gasped. "Why, where's the gold?"

"I'll show you later!" Clip said grimly. "I suspected this!"

There was no talk on the ride homeward. Clip rode at Ruth's side, seemingly intent only on reaching town. It was almost daylight when they rode swiftly up the dusty street.

"Should you do this?" she protested. "Aren't they looking for you?"

"If they are, they better not find me!" he snapped. "I'm doing some looking myself. You ride to your brother, quick, and tell him about that sand. Tell him to bring Buff McCarty to the High-Stake just as quick as he can make it!"

His eyes narrowed. "And you," he went grimly, "will have a chance to drop by the Sluice Box and see your precious lover, who didn't have guts enough to come after you himself!"

Her eyes widened with amazement, but before she could

speak, he wheeled his horse and rode rapidly back up the street and dismounted. Then he walked into the Sluice Box, his face dark with rage.

Rafe Landon stood just inside the door. He walked up to Clip, smiling gravely. "I heard what you said to Ruth," he said. "I want to tell you just two things, Haynes. The first has to do with my want of—guts—as you put it. Once I offered you my hand, and you refused it. Will you take it now?"

Something in his manner seemed strange. Clip glanced down at the gloved hand. Then he took it. Amazement came into his eyes.

"Yes," Rafe said, "you're right. It's iron. The blacksmith in Goldfield made it, several years ago. I lost both my hands after a fire."

Clip looked up, his face tight. "Rafe, I—"

"Forget it. As for Ruth—"

The doors burst open, and Clip wheeled. Wade Manning stood in the door, Buff McCarty beside him. "The Barlows are coming!" he exclaimed, his face tense. "Both of them, Clip, and they've been bragging all morning that they'll kill you on sight!"

He stepped into the street, his steps echoing hollowly as he stepped across the boardwalk. He stopped in the edge of the dusty street and looked north.

The Barlows, Joe and Gonny, were standing on the porch in front of the old hotel building. Then they saw him, and started toward the steps.

Somewhere a horse whinnied, and in the saloon, a man's nervous laughter sounded strangely loud. Clip Haynes walked slowly, taking measured steps.

Joe Barlow's hand was poised over his gun. Gonny waited carelessly, slouching, a shock of hair hanging down over his eyes.

When they were fifty feet apart, the Barlows stiffened as though at a signal, and drew. Joe's hand moved; Clip Haynes shot.

The street broke in a thundering roar through which he found himself walking straight toward them, his guns hammering. He knew the first shot he had taken at Joe had been too quick. Suddenly it seemed as if a white hot branding iron had hit his left shoulder. He dropped that gun, feeling the warm blood run down his sleeve. His arm was useless—but his right gun kept firing.

Suddenly, Joe was falling from the steps, and almost as in a dream Clip saw the man straighten out, arms widespread, blood staining the dust beneath him.

Clip started to step forward, and realized suddenly that he was on his knees. He got up, feeling another slug hit him in the side. Gonny was facing him, legs spread wide, a fire-blossoming gun in either hand. A streak of red crossed his jaw.

Clip started toward him, holding his last bullet. Something slanted a rapier of pain along his ribs, and one of his legs tried to buckle, but still Clip held his fire. Then, suddenly, about a dozen feet away from Gonny, Clip Haynes turned loose his gun.

Almost before his eyes Gonny's gray flannel shirt turned into a crimson, sodden mass. The gunman started to fall, caught himself, and lifted a gun. They were almost body to body when the shot flamed in Clip's face. Something struck him a terrific blow on the side of the head, and he fell. . . .

Actually it was only a minute, but it seemed hours. Men were running from every direction, and as Clip Haynes caught at somebody's leg and pulled his bloody body erect, he heard Wade gabbling in his ear. But he didn't stop. It was only a dozen feet, but it seemed a mile. Step by step, he made it, fumbling shells into his gun.

Weaving on his feet, he stopped, facing Doc Greenley. His eyes wavered, then they focused.

Doc's face went sickly with fear. He opened and closed his mouth, trying to speak. Then suddenly he broke, and went for his gun.

It was just swinging level when Clip shot him. Then Clip pitched over on his face, and lay still.

He must have been a long time coming out of it because they were all there—Ruth, Rafe Landon, Wade Manning, and Buff McCarty—when he opened his eyes. He looked from one to the other.

"Doc?" he questioned weakly.

"You got him, Clip. We found the gold in his safe. He never moved an ounce of it, just sand. We made Porter confess. He robbed Tommy of the three thousand dollars, and later Doc Greenley made him plant it on you. One of the Barlows slugged you.

"We found the note you left in the jail. You were right. It was Doc who killed Tommy, trying to kill you. He didn't know you were Clip Haynes at first.

"I told him," Wade continued, "never suspecting he was the guilty one behind all this. He knew he couldn't fool you. Felt he'd given himself away somehow. He confessed before he died."

Clip nodded. "At first—at the mine. He said Clip Haynes got ten thousand. Only the law and the bandits knew it was that much." Clip paused, a wan smile twisting his features. "He was the one planned that job—not Haynes. I was the law. The express company hired me. When he said that, I was suspicious."

Clip closed his eyes, and lay very still. When he opened them again everyone was gone but Ruth. She was smiling, and she leaned over and kissed him gently on the lips.

"And Rafe?" he questioned.

"I tried to explain, but you ran away. He's my uncle—my mother's brother. He started Wade in business here, but no one knew. He thought it might hurt Wade if people knew a gambler backed him."

"Oh," he said. For a moment he was silent. Then he looked up, and they both smiled.

"That's nice," he said.

MAN RIDING WEST

THREE MEN WERE hunkered down by the fire when Jim Gary walked his buckskin up to their camp in the lee of the cliff. The big man across the fire had a shotgun lying beside him. It was the shotgun that made Gary uneasy, for cowhands do not carry shotguns, especially when on a trail drive, as these men obviously were.

Early as it was, the cattle were already bedded down for the night in the meadow alongside the stream, and from their looks they had come far and fast. It was still light, but the clouds were low and swollen with rain.

"How's for some coffee?" Jim asked as he drew up. "I'm ridin' through, an' I'm sure hungry an' tuckered."

Somewhere off in the mountains, thunder rolled and grumbled. The fire crackled, and the leaves on the willows hung still in the lifeless air. There were three saddled horses nearby, and among the gear was an old Mother Hubbard–style saddle with a wide skirt.

"Light an' set up." The man who spoke was lean jawed and sandy haired. "Never liked to ride on an empty stomach, m'self."

More than ever, Gary felt uneasy. Neither of the others spoke. All were tough-looking men, unshaven and dirty, but it was their hard-eyed suspicion that made Jim wonder. However, he swung down and loosened his saddle girth and then slipped the saddle off and laid it well back under the overhang of the cliff. As he did so he glanced again at the old saddle that lay there.

The overhang of the cliff was deep where the fire was built for shelter from the impending rain. Jim dropped to an ancient log, gray and stripped of bark, and handed his tin plate over to the man who reached for it. The cook slapped two thick slabs of beef on the plate and some frying-pan bread liberally touched with the beef fryings. Gary was hungry and he dove in without comment, and the small man filled his cup.

"Headed west?" The sandy-haired man asked, after a few minutes.

"Yeah, headed down below the rim. Pleasant Valley way."

The men all turned their heads toward him but none spoke. Jim could feel their eyes on his tied-down guns. There was a sheep and cattle war in the valley.

"They call me Red Slagle. These hombres are Tobe Langer and Jeeter Dirksen. We're drivin' to Salt Creek."

Langer would be the big one. "My name's Gary," Jim replied. "Jim Gary. I'm from points yonder. Mostly Dodge an' Santa Fe."

"Hear they are hirin' warriors in Pleasant Valley."

"Reckon." Jim refused to be drawn, although he had the feeling they had warmed to him since he mentioned heading for the valley.

"Ridin' thataway ourselves," Red suggested. "Want to make a few dollars drivin' cattle? We're shorthanded."

"Might," Gary admitted. "The grub's good."

"Give you forty to drive to Salt Creek. We'll need he'p. From hereabouts the country is plumb rough, an' she's fixin' to storm."

"You've hired a hand. When do I start?"

"Catch a couple of hours sleep. Tobe has the first ride. Then you take over. If you need he'p, just you call out."

Gary shook out his blankets and crawled into them. In the moment before his eyes closed he remembered the cattle had all worn a Double A brand, and the brands were fresh. That could easily be with a trail herd. But the Double A had been the spread that Mart Ray had mentioned.

It was raining when he rode out to the herd. "They ain't fussin'," Langer advised, "an' the rain's quiet enough. It should pass mighty easy. See you."

He drifted toward the camp, and Gary turned up his slicker collar and studied the herd as well as he could in the darkness. They were lying quiet. He was riding a gray roped from the small remuda, and he let the horse amble placidly toward the far side of the meadow. A hundred yards beyond the meadow the bulk of the sloping hill that formed the opposite side of the valley showed blacker in the gloom. Occasionally there was a flash of heat lightning, but no thunder.

Slagle had taken him on because he needed hands, but none of them accepted him. He decided to sit tight in his saddle and see what developed. It could be plenty, for unless he was mistaken, this was a stolen herd, and Slagle was a thief, as were the others.

If this herd had come far and fast, he had come farther and faster, and with just as great a need. Now there was nothing behind him but trouble, and nothing before him but bleak years of drifting ahead of a reputation.

Up ahead was Mart Ray, and Ray was as much a friend as he had. Gunfighters are admired by many, respected by some, feared by all, and welcomed by none. His father had warned him of what to expect, warned him long ago before he himself had died in a gun battle. "You're right handy, son," he had warned, "one of the fastest I ever seen, so don't let it be known. Don't never draw a gun on a man in anger, an' you'll live happy. Once you get the name of a gunfighter, you're on a lonesome trail, an' there's only one ending."

So he had listened, and he had avoided trouble. Mart Ray knew that. Ray was himself a gunman. He had killed six men of whom Jim Gary knew, and no doubt there had been others. He and Mart had been riding together in Texas and then in a couple of trail drives, one all the way to Montana. He never really got close to Mart, but they had been partners after a fashion.

Ray had always been amused at his eagerness to avoid trouble, although he had no idea of the cause of it. "Well," he had said, "they sure cain't say like father, like son. From all I hear your pappy was an uncurried wolf, an' you fight shy of trouble. You run from it. If I didn't know you so well, I'd say you was yaller."

But Mart Ray had known him well, for it had been Jim who rode his horse down in front of a stampede to pick Ray off the ground, saving his life. They got free, but no more, and a thousand head of cattle stampeded over the ground where Ray had stood.

Then, a month before, down in the Big Bend country, trouble had come, and it was trouble he could not avoid. It braced him in a little Mexican cantina just over the river, and in the person of a dark, catlike Mexican with small feet and dainty hands, but his guns were big enough and there was an unleashed devil in his eyes.

Jim Gary had been dancing with a Mexican girl, and the Mexican had jerked her from his arms and struck her across the face. Jim knocked him down, and the Mexican got up, his eyes fiendish. Without a word, the Mexican went for his gun, and for a frozen, awful instant, Jim saw his future facing him, and then his own hand went down and he palmed his gun in a flashing, lightning draw that rapped out two shots. The Mexican, who had reached first, barely got his gun clear before he was dead. He died on his feet and then fell.

In a haze of powder smoke and anguish, Jim Gary had wheeled and strode from the door, and behind him lay a dead and awful silence. It was not until two days later that he knew who and what he had killed.

The lithe-bodied Mexican had been Miguel Sonoma, and he had been a legend along the border. A tough, dangerous man with a reputation as a killer.

Two nights later, a band of outlaws from over the border rode down upon Gary's little spread to avenge their former leader, and two of them died in the first blast of gunfire, a matter of handguns at point-blank range.

From the shelter of his cabin, Gary fought them off for three days before the smoke from his burning barn attracted help. When the help arrived, Jim Gary was a man with a name. Five dead men lay on the ground around the ranch yard and in the desert nearby. The wounded had been carried away. And the following morning, Jim turned his ranch over to the bank to sell and lit a shuck—away from Texas.

Of this, Mart Ray knew nothing. Half of Texas and all of New Mexico, or most of it, would lie behind him when Jim reached the banks of Salt Creek. Mart Ray was ramrodding the Double A, and he would have a job for him.

JIM GARY TURNED the horse and rode slowly back along the side of the herd. The cattle had taken their midnight stretch and after standing around a bit, were lying down once more. The rain was falling, but softly, and Gary let the gray take his own time in skirting the herd.

The night was pitch dark. Only the horns of the cattle glistened with rain, and their bodies were darker blobs in the blackness of the night. Once, drawing up near the willows along the stream, Jim thought he detected a vague sound. He waited a moment, listening. On such a night nobody would be abroad who could help it, and it was unlikely that a mountain lion would be on the prowl, although possible.

He started on again, yet now his senses were alert, and his hand slid under his slicker and touched the butt of a .44. He was almost at the far end of the small herd when a sudden flash of lightning revealed the hillside across the narrow valley.

Stark and clear, glistening with rain, sat a horseman! He was standing in his stirrups, and seemed amazingly tall, and in the glare of the flash, his face was stark white, like the face of a fleshless skull!

Startled, Gary grunted and slid his gun into his hand, but all was darkness again, and listen as he could, he heard no further sound. When the lightning flashed again, the hillside was empty and still. Uneasily, he caught himself staring back over his shoulder into the darkness, and he watched his horse. The gray was standing, head up and ears erect, staring off toward the darkness near the hill. Riding warily, Gary started in that direction, but when he got there, he found nothing.

It was almost daylight when he rode up to the fire which he had kept up throughout the night, and swinging down, he awakened Dirksen. The man sat up, startled. "Hey!" he exclaimed. "You forget to call me?"

Jim grinned at him. "Just figured I was already up an' a good cook needed his sleep."

Jeeter stared at him. "You mean you rode for me? Say, you're all right!"

"Forget it!" Gary stretched. "I had a quiet night, mostly."

Red Slagle was sitting up, awakened by their talk. "What do you mean—mostly?"

Jim hesitated, feeling puzzled. "Why, to tell you the truth, I'm not sure whether I saw anything or not, but I sure thought I did. Anyway, it had me scared."

"What was it?" Slagle was pulling on his pants, but his eyes were serious. "A lion?"

"No, it was a man on a horse. A tall man with a dead-white face, like a skull." Gary shrugged sheepishly. "Makes me sound like a fool, but I figured for a moment that I'd seen a ghost!"

Red Slagle was staring at him, and Jeeter's face was dead white and his eyes were bulging. "A ghost?" he asked, faintly. "Did you say, a *ghost*?"

"Shucks," Gary shrugged, "there ain't no such thing. Just some hombre on a big black horse, passin' through in the night, that was all! But believe me, seein' him in the lightnin' up on that hill like I did, it sure was scary!"

Tobe Langer was getting up, and he, too, looked bothered. Slagle came over to the fire and sat down, boots in hand. Reaching down he pulled his sock around to get a hole away from his big toe; then he put his foot into the wet boot and began to struggle with it.

"That horse, now," Langer asked carefully, "did it have a white star between the eyes?"

Gary was surprised. "Why, yes! Matter of fact, it did! You know him?"

Slagle let go of the boot and stomped his foot to settle it in the boot. "Yeah, feller we seen down the road a ways. Big black horse."

Slagle and Langer walked away from camp a ways and stood talking together. Jeeter was worried. Jim could see that without half trying, and he studied the man thoughtfully. Jeeter Dirksen was a small man, quiet, but inclined to be nervous. He had neither the strength nor the toughness of Slagle and Langer. If Gary learned anything about the cattle it would be through his own investigation or from Jeeter. And he was growing more and more curious.

Yet if these were Double A cattle and had been stolen, why were they being driven toward the Double A ranch, rather than away from it? He realized suddenly that he knew nothing at all about Red Slagle or his outfit, and it was time he made some inquiries.

"This Double A," he asked suddenly, "you been riding' for them long?"

Dirksen glanced at him sharply and bent over his fire. "Not long," he said. "It's a Salt Creek outfit. Slagle's segundo."

"Believe I know your foreman," Gary suggested. "I think this was the outfit he said. Hombre name of Mart Ray. Ever hear of him?"

Jeeter turned sharply, slopping coffee over the rim of the cup. It hissed in the fire, and both the other men looked around at the camp. Jeeter handed the cup to Gary and studied him, searching his face. Then he admitted cautiously, "Yeah, Ray's the foreman. Ranch belongs to a syndicate out on the coast. You say you know him?"

"Uh-huh. Used to ride with him." Langer and Slagle had walked back to the fire, and Dirksen poured coffee for them.

"Who was that you rode with?" Slagle asked.

"Your boss, Mart Ray."

Both men looked up sharply; then Slagle's face cleared and he smiled. "Say! That's why the name was familiar! You're *that* Jim Gary! Son of old Steve Gary. Yeah, Mart told us about you."

Langer chuckled suddenly. "You're the scary one, huh? The one who likes to keep out of trouble. Yeah, we heard about you!"

The contempt in his tone stiffened Jim's back, and for an instant he was on the verge of a harsh retort. Then the memory of what lay behind him welled up within, and bitterly he kept his mouth shut. If he got on the prod and killed a man here, he would only have to drift farther. There was only one solution, and that was to avoid trouble. Yet irritating as it was to be considered lacking in courage, Langer's remark let him know that the story of his fights had not preceded him.

"There's no call," he said after a minute, "to go around the country killin' folks. If people would just get the idea they can get along without all that. Me, I don't believe in fightin'."

Langer chuckled, but Slagle said nothing, and Dirksen glanced at him sympathetically.

All day the herd moved steadily west, but now Gary noticed a change, for the others were growing more watchful as the day progressed. Their eyes continued to search the surrounding hills, and they rode more warily approaching any bit of cover.

Once, when Jeeter rode near him, the little man glanced across the herd at the other riders and then said quietly, "That was no ghost you saw. Red rode up there on the hill, an' there was tracks, tracks of a mighty big black horse."

"Wonder why he didn't ride down to camp?" Jim speculated. "He sure enough saw the fire!"

Dirksen grunted. "If that hombre was the one Red thinks it is, he sure didn't have no aim to ride down there!"

Before Gary could question him further, Jeeter rode off after a stray and cutting him back into the herd, rode on further ahead. Jim dropped back to the drag, puzzling over this new angle. Who could the strange rider be? What did he want? Was he afraid of Slagle?

A big brindle steer was cutting wide of the herd, and Jim swung out to get him, but dashing toward the stream, the steer floundered into the water and into quicksand. Almost at once, it was down, struggling madly, its eyes rolling.

Jim swung a loop and dropped it over the steer's horns. If he could give the steer a little help now, there was a chance he could get it out before it bogged in too deep.

He started the buckskin back toward more solid ground and with the pull on the rope and the struggling of the steer, he soon had it out on the bank of the stream. The weary animal stumbled and went down, and shaking his loop loose, Gary swung his horse around to get the animal up. Something he saw on the flank made him swing down beside the steer. Curiously, he bent over the brand.

It had been worked over! The Double A had been burned on over a Slash Four!

"Somethin' wrong?"

The voice was cold and level, and Jim Gary started guiltily, turning. Then his eyes widened. "Mart! Well, for cryin' out in the nighttime! Am I glad to see *you*!"

Ray stared. "For the luvva Pete, if it ain't Gary! Say, how did you get here? Don't tell me you're drivin' that herd up ahead?"

"That's right! Your outfit, ain't it? I hired on back down the line. This steer just got hisself bogged down an' I had a heck of a time gettin' him out. You seen Red an' the boys?"

"Not yet, I swung wide. Get that steer on his feet an' we'll join 'em."

Yet as they rode back, despite Ray's affability, Gary was disturbed. Something here was very wrong. This was a Slash Four steer with the brand worked over to a Double A, the brand for which Ray was foreman. If these cattle were rustled, then Mart Ray was party to it, and so were Slagle, Langer, and Dirksen! And if he was caught with these men and cattle, so was he!

He replied to Ray's questions as well as he could, and briefly, aware that his friend was preoccupied and thinking of something else. Yet at the same time he was pleased that Ray asked him no questions about his reasons for leaving home.

Mart Ray rode up ahead and joined Slagle, and he could see the two men riding on together, deep in conversation. When they bedded down for the night, there had been no further chance to talk to him, and Gary was just as well satisfied, for there was much about this that he did not like. Nor was anything said about the midnight rider. When day broke, Mart Ray was gone. "Rode on to Salt Creek," Red said. "We'll see him there." He glanced at Jim, his eyes amused. "He said to keep you on, that you was a top hand."

Despite the compliment, Jim was nettled. What else had Ray told Slagle? His eyes narrowed. Whatever it was, he was not staying on. He was going to get shut of this outfit just as fast as he could. All he wanted was his time. Yet by midday he had not brought himself to ask for it.

Dirksen had grown increasingly silent, and he avoided Langer and Slagle. Watching him, Jim was puzzled by the man, but could find no reason for his behavior unless the man was frightened by something. Finally, Jim pulled up alongside Jeeter.

The man glanced at him and shook his head. "I don't like this. Not even a little. She's too quiet."

Gary hesitated, waiting for the cowhand to continue, but he held his peace. Finally, Gary said, speaking slowly, "It is mighty quiet, but I see nothin' wrong with that. I'm not hunting trouble."

"Trouble," Jeeter said dryly, "comes sometimes whether you hunt it or not. If anything breaks around this herd, take my advice an' don't ask no questions. Just scatter dust out of here!"

"Why are you warning me?" Gary asked.

Jeeter shrugged. "You seem like a right nice feller," he said quietly. "Shame for you to get rung in on somethin' as dirty as this when you had nothin' to do with it."

———

DESPITE HIS QUESTIONS, Jeeter would say no more, and finally Gary dropped back to the drag. There was little dust because of the rains, but the drag was a rough deal, for the herd was tired and the cattle kept lagging back. Langer and Slagle, Jim observed, spent more time watching the hills than the cattle. Obviously, both men were as jumpy as Dirksen and were expecting something. Toward dusk Red left the herd and rode up a canyon into the hills.

Slagle was still gone, and Jim was squatting by the fire watching Jeeter throw grub together when there was a sudden shot from the hills to the north.

Langer stopped his nervous pacing and faced the direction of the shot, his hand on his gun. Jim Gary got slowly to his feet, and he saw that Jeeter's knuckles gripping the frying pan were white and hard.

Langer was first to relax. "Red must have got him a turkey," he said. "Few around here, and he was sayin' earlier he'd sure like some."

Nevertheless, Gary noted that Langer kept back from the firelight and had his rifle near at hand. There was a sound of an approaching horse, and Langer slid his rifle across his knees, but it was Slagle. He swung down, glancing toward the big man. "Shot at a turkey an' missed." Then he added, looking right at Langer, "Nothin' to worry about now. This time for sure."

Dirksen got suddenly to his feet. "I'm quittin', Red. I don't like this a-tall, not none. I'm gettin' out."

Slagle's eyes were flat and ugly. "Sit down an' shut up, Jeeter," he said impatiently. "Tomorrow's our last day. We'll have a payday this side of Salt Creek, an' then if you want to blow, why you can blow out of here."

Gary looked up. "I reckon you can have my time then, too," he said quietly, "I'm ridin' west for Pleasant Valley."

"You?" Langer snorted. "Pleasant Valley? You better stay somewhere where you can be took care of. They don't side-step trouble out there."

Gary felt something rise within him, but he controlled his anger with an effort. "I didn't ask you for any comment, Tobe," he said quietly. "I can take care of myself."

Langer sneered. "Why, you yaller skunk! I heard all about you! Just because your pappy was a fast man, you must think folks are skeered of you! You're yaller as saffron! You ain't duckin' trouble; you're just scared!"

Gary was on his feet, his face white. "All you've got to do, Tobe, if you want to lose some teeth, is to stand up!"

"What?" Langer leaped to his feet. "Why, you dirty—"

Jim Gary threw a roundhouse left. The punch was wide, but it came fast, and Langer was not expecting Jim to fight. Too late, he tried to duck, but the fist caught him on the nose, smashing it and showering the front of his shirt with gore.

The big man was tough, and he sprang in, swinging with both hands. Gary stood his ground, and began to fire punches with both fists. For a full minute the two big men stood toe to toe and slugged wickedly, and then Gary deliberately gave ground. Overeager, Langer leaped after him, and Gary brought up a wicked right that stood Tobe on his boot toes and then a looping left that knocked him into the fire.

With a cry, he leaped from the flames, his shirt smoking.

Ruthlessly, Gary grabbed him by the shirtfront and jerked him into a right hand to the stomach and then a right to the head, and shoving him away he split his ear with another looping left, smashing it like an overripe tomato. Langer went down in a heap.

Red Slagle had made no move to interfere, but his eyes were hard and curious as he stared up at Gary. "Now where," he said, "did Ray get the idea that you wouldn't fight?"

Gary spilled water from a canteen over his bloody knuckles. "Maybe he just figured wrong. Some folks don't like trouble. That don't mean they won't fight when they have to."

Langer pulled himself drunkenly to his feet and staggered toward the creek.

Red measured Jim with careful eyes. "What would you do," he asked suddenly, "if Langer reached for a gun?"

Gary turned his level green eyes toward Slagle. "Why, I reckon I'd have to kill him," he said matter-of-factly. "I hope he ain't so foolish."

Dawn broke cold and gray, and Jim Gary walked his horse up into the hills where he'd heard the shot the night before. He knew that if Slagle saw him, he would be in trouble, but there was much he wanted to know.

Despite the light fall of rain the night before, there were still tracks. He followed those of Slagle's bay until he found where they joined those of a larger horse. Walking the buckskin warily, Jim followed the trail. It came to a sudden end.

A horse was sprawled in the clearing, shot through the head. A dozen feet away lay an old man, a tall old man, his sightless eyes staring toward the lowering skies, his arms flung wide. Jim bent over him and saw that he had been shot three times through the chest. Three times. And the wound lower down was an older wound, several days old, at least.

The horse wore a Slash Four brand. Things were beginning to make sense now. Going through the old man's pockets, Jim found a worn envelope containing some tallies of cattle, and the envelope was addressed to *Tom Blaze, Durango, Colo.*

Tom Blaze . . . the Slash Four!

Tom Blaze, the pioneer Kiowa-fighting cattleman who owned the Slash Four, one of the toughest outfits in the West! Why he had not connected the two Jim could not imagine, but the fact remained that the Slash Four had struck no responsive chord in his thoughts until now.

And Tom Blaze was dead.

Now it all fitted. The old Mother Hubbard saddle had been taken from Tom's horse, for this was the second time he had been shot. Earlier, perhaps when the cattle had been stolen, they had shot him and left him for dead, yet they had been unable to leave the saddle behind, for a saddle was two or three months' work for a cowhand and not to be lightly left behind.

They had been sure of themselves, too. Sure until Gary had seen Blaze, following them despite his wound. After that they had been worried, and Slagle must have sighted Blaze the afternoon before and then followed him and shot him down.

When the Slash Four found Tom Blaze dead all heck would break loose. Dirksen knew that, and that was why he wanted out, but fast. And it was why Red Slagle and Tobe Langer had pushed so hard to get the cattle to Salt Creek, where they could be lost in larger herds or in the breaks of the hills around the Double A.

When he rode the buckskin down to the fire the others were all up and moving around. Langer's face was swollen and there were two deep cuts, one on his cheekbone, the other over an eye. He was sullen and refused to look toward Gary.

Slagle stared at the buckskin suspiciously, noticing the wetness on his legs from riding in the high grass and brush.

Whatever the segundo had in mind he never got a chance to say. Jim Gary poured a cup of coffee, but held it in his left hand. "Red, I want my money. I'm takin' out."

"Mind if I ask why?" Red's eyes were level and waiting.

Gary knew that Slagle was a gunhand, but the thought did not disturb him. While he avoided trouble, it was never in him to be afraid, nor did his own skill permit it. While he had matched gun speed with only one man, he had that sure confidence that comes from unerring marksmanship and speed developed from long practice.

"No, I don't mind. This morning I found Tom Blaze's body, right where you killed him yesterday afternoon. I know that Slash Four outfit, and I don't want to be any part of this bunch when they catch up to you."

His frankness left Slagle uncertain. He had been prepared for evasion. This was not only sincerity, but it left Slagle unsure as to Gary's actual stand. From his words Slagle assumed Gary was leaving from dislike of fight rather than dislike of rustling.

"You stick with us, Jim," he said. "You're a good man, like Mart said. That Slash Four outfit won't get wise, and there'll be a nice split on this cattle deal."

"I want no part of it," Jim replied shortly. "I'm out. Let me have my money."

"I ain't got it," Red said simply. "Ray pays us all off. I carry no money around. Come on, Jim, lend us a hand. We've only today; then we'll be at the head of Salt Creek Wash and get paid off."

Gary hesitated. He did need the money, for he was broke and would need grub before he could go on west. Since he had come this far, another day would scarcely matter. "All right, I'll finish the drive."

Nothing more was said, and within the hour they moved out. Yet Gary was restless and worried. He could feel the tenseness in the others and knew they, too, were disturbed. There was no sign of Mart Ray, who should be meeting them soon.

To make matters worse, the cattle were growing restive. The short drives had given them time to recover some of their energy, and several of them, led by one big red steer, kept breaking for the brush. It was hot, miserable work. The clouds still hung low, threatening rain, but the air was sultry.

Jim Gary started the day with the lean gray horse he had ridden before, but by midafternoon he had exchanged the worn-out animal for his own buckskin. Sweat streamed down his body under his shirt, and he worked hard, harrying the irritable animals down the trail that now was lined with piñon and juniper, with a sprinkling of huge boulders. Ahead, a wide canyon opened, and not far beyond would be the spot where he expected to find Ray with the payoff money.

The big red steer suddenly made another bolt for the brush, and the buckskin unwound so fast that it almost unseated Gary. He swore softly and let the horse take him after the steer and cut it back to the herd. As it swung back, he glanced up to see Langer and Red Slagle vanishing into the brush. Where Dirksen was he could not guess until he heard a wild yell.

Swinging around, he saw a dozen hard-riding horsemen cutting down from the brush on both sides, and a glance told him that flight was useless. Nevertheless, Jeeter Dirksen tried it.

Slamming the spurs into his bronc, Dirksen lunged for the brush in the direction taken by Slagle and Langer, but he had made no more than a dozen yards when a rattle of gunfire smashed him from the saddle. His slender body hit the ground rolling, flopped over one last time, and lay sprawled and sightless under the low gray clouds.

Gary rested his hands on his saddle horn and stared gloomily at the strange little man, so badly miscast in this outlaw venture. Then horsemen closed in around him; his six-guns were jerked from their holsters and his rifle from its scabbard.

"What's the matter with you?" The voice was harsh. "Won't that horse of yours run?"

Jim looked up into a pair of cold gray eyes in a leatherlike face. A neat gray mustache showed above a firm-lipped mouth. Jim Gary smiled, although he had never felt less like it in his life. The horsemen surrounded him, and their guns were ready. "Never was much of a hand to run," Jim said, "an' I've done nothing' to run for."

"You call murderin' my brother nothin'? You call stealin' cattle nothin'? Sorry, friend, we don't see things alike. I call it hangin'."

"So would I, on'y I haven't done those things. I hired onto

this outfit back down the line. Forty bucks to the head of Salt Creek Wash . . . an' they ain't paid me."

"You'll get paid!" The speaker was a lean, hard-faced young man. "With a rope!"

Another rider, a girl, pushed a horse through the circle. "Who is this man, Uncle Dan? Why didn't he try to get away?"

"Says he's just a hired hand," Uncle Dan commented.

"That's probably what that dead man would have said, too!" the lean puncher said. "Let me an' the boys have him under that cottonwood we seen. It had nice strong limbs."

Gary had turned his head to look at the girl. Uncle Dan would be Dan Blaze, and this must be the daughter of the murdered man. She was tall and slim, but rounded of limb and undeniably attractive, with color in her cheeks and a few scattered freckles over her nose. Her eyes were hazel and now looked hard and stormy.

"Did you folks find Tom Blaze's body?" he asked. "They left him back yonder." Lifting a hand carefully to his shirt pocket he drew out the envelope and tally sheets. "These were his."

"What more do you need?" The lean puncher demanded. He pushed his horse against Jim's and grabbed at the buckskin's bridle. "Come on, boys!"

"Take it easy, Jerry!" Dan Blaze said sharply. "When I want him hung, I'll say so." His eyes shifted back to Jim. "You're a mighty cool customer," he said. "If your story's straight, what are you doing with these?"

As briefly as possible, Jim explained the whole situation and ended by saying, "What could I do? I still had forty bucks comin', an' I did my work, so I aim to collect."

"You say there were three men with the herd? And the two who got away were Tobe Langer and Red Slagle?"

"That's right," Jim hesitated over Mart Ray and then said no more.

Blaze was staring at the herd, and now he looked at Jim. "Why were these cattle branded Double A? That's a straight outfit. You know anything about that?"

Gary hesitated. Much as he had reason to believe Ray was not only one of these men but their leader, he hated to betray him. "Not much. I don't know any of these outfits. I'm a Texas man."

Blaze smiled wryly. "You sound it. What's your handle?"

"Jim Gary."

The puncher named Jerry started as if struck. "Jim Gary?" he gasped, his voice incredulous. "The one who killed Sonoma?"

"Yeah, I reckon."

Now they were all staring at him with new interest, for the two fights he had were ample to start his name growing a legend on the plains and desert. These punchers had heard of him, probably from some grub-line rider or drifting puncher.

"Jim Gary," Blaze mused. "We've heard about you. Old Steve's son, aren't you? I knew Steve."

Jim looked up, his eyes cold. "My father," he said grimly, "was a mighty good man!"

Dan Blaze's eyes warmed a little. "You're right. He was."

"What of it?" Jerry demanded sullenly. "The man's a killer. We know that. We found him with the cattle. We found him with some of Tom's stuff on him. What more do you want?"

The girl spoke suddenly. "There was another rider, one who joined you and then rode away. Who was he?"

There it was, and Jim suddenly knew he would not lie. "Mart Ray," he said quietly, "of the Double A."

"That's a lie!" The girl flashed back. "What are you saying?"

"You got any proof of that?" Jerry demanded hotly. "You're talkin' about a friend of our'n."

"He was a friend of mine, too." Gary explained about Mart Ray. "Why don't you turn me loose?" he suggested then. "I'll go get Ray and bring him to you. Chances are Slagle and Tobe will be with him."

"You'll get him?" Jerry snorted. "That's a good one, that is!"

"Tie him," Dan Blaze said suddenly. "We'll go into Salt Creek."

RIDING BEHIND DAN Blaze was his niece, whom he heard them call Kitty. Jim Gary was suddenly aware, almost for the first time, of the danger he was in. The fact that it had been averted for the moment was small consolation, for these were hard, desperate men, and one of them, perhaps more, had been slain.

Fear was something strange to him, and while he had known danger, it had passed over him leaving him almost untouched. This situation conveyed only a sense of unreality, and until now the idea that he might really be in danger scarcely seemed credible. Listening to these men, his mind changed about that. He realized belatedly that he was in the greatest danger of his life. If he had none of their talk to warn him, the mute evidence of Jeeter's body was enough. And Jeeter had died yelling to him, trying to give him a warning so he might escape.

Now fear rode with him, a cold, clammy fear that stiffened his fingers and left his mouth dry and his stomach empty. Even the sight of the scattered buildings of the town of Salt Creek did not help, and when they rode up the street, the red of embarrassment crept up his neck at the shame of being led into the town, his hands tied behind him, like a cheap rustler.

Mart Ray was sitting on the steps, and he shoved his hat back and got to his feet. Beside him was Red Slagle. There was no sign of Tobe Langer. "Howdy, Dan! What did you catch? A hoss thief?" Ray's voice was genial, his eyes bland. "Looks like a big party for such a small catch."

Blaze reined in his horse and stopped the little cavalcade. His eyes went from Mart to Slagle. "How long you been here, Red?" he demanded.

"Me?" Slagle was innocent. "No more'n about fifteen minutes, maybe twenty. Just rode in from the Double A. Somethin' wrong?"

Blaze turned his cold eyes on Jim Gary and then looked back to Ray. "We found a herd of Slash Four cattle east of here, Mart. They were wearin' a Double A brand worked over our Slash Four. How do you explain it?"

Ray shrugged. "I don't," he said simply. "How does that hombre you got with you explain it?"

Kitty Blaze spoke up quickly. "Mart, did you ever see this man before? Did you?"

Ray stared at Gary. "Not that I recall," he said seriously. "He sure don't look familiar to me!"

"Blaze," Gary said suddenly, "if you'll turn my hands loose and give me a gun, I can settle this in three minutes! I can prove he's a liar! I can prove that he does know me an' that I know him!"

"There's nothin' you can prove with a gun you can't prove without it!" Blaze said flatly. "Whatever you know, spill it! Else you're gettin' your neck stretched! I'm tired of this fussin' around!"

Jim Gary kneed his horse forward. His eyes were hot and angry. "Mart," he said, "I always suspected there was a streak of coyote in you, but I never knowed you'd be this low-down. I don't like to remind anybody of what I done for him, but I recall a stampede I hauled you out of. Are you goin' to talk?"

Ray shook his head, smiling. "This is a lot of trouble, Dan. Take him away and stretch his neck before I get sore and plug him."

"You'd be afraid to meet me with a gun, Mart. You always were afraid!" Jim taunted. "That's why you left Red and Tobe with the cattle. You wanted the profit but none of the trouble! Well, you've got trouble now! If I had a gun I'd see you eat dirt!"

Mart Ray's face was ugly. "Shut up, you fool! You call me yellow? Why, everybody knows you're yellow as—!" He caught himself abruptly, his face paling under the tan.

"What was that, Ray?" Dan Blaze's face had sharpened. "Ever'body knows what about him? If you've never seen him before, how could you say ever'body calls him yellow?"

Ray shrugged. "Just talkin' too fast, that's all!" He turned and stepped up on the sidewalk. "He's your man. You settle your own war." Ray turned to go, but Jim yelled at him, and Ray wheeled.

"Mart, if I don't know you, how do I know you've got a

white scar down your right side, a scar made by a steer's hoof?"

Ray laughed, but it was a strained laugh. He looked trapped now, and he took an involuntary step backward. "That's silly!" he scoffed. "I've no such scar!"

"Why not take off your shirt?" Jerry said suddenly. "That will only take a minute." The lean-jawed cowhand's face was suddenly hard. "I think I remember you having such a scar, from one time I seen you swimmin' in the San Juan. Take off your shirt an' let's see!"

Mart Ray backed up another step, his face sharp and cold. "I'll be damned if I take off my shirt in the street for any low-down rustler!" he snapped. "This here nonsense has gone far enough!"

"Loose my hands!" Jim pleaded in a whisper. "I'll take his shirt off!"

Kitty stared at him. Her face was white and strained, but in her eyes he now saw a shadow of doubt. Yet it was Jerry who acted suddenly, jerking him around before anyone realized what he had done and severing the bonds with a razor-sharp knife and jerking the ropes from his hands. With almost the same gesture, he slammed guns in Gary's holsters. "All right! Maybe I'm crazy!" he snapped. "But go to it!"

The whole action had taken less than a minute, and Mart Ray had turned his back and started away while Blaze waited in indecision. It was Red Slagle who saw Jim Gary hit the ground. "Boss!" he yelled. His voice was suddenly sharp with panic. "Look out!"

Ray wheeled, and when he saw Gary coming toward him, chafing his wrists, he stood still, momentarily dumbfounded. Then he laughed. "All right, yellow! You're askin' for it! This is one bunch of trouble you can't duck! You've ducked your last fight!"

Furious, he failed to realize the import of his words, and he dropped into a half crouch, his hands ready above his gun butts. It was Jerry who shook him, Jerry who made the casual remark that jerked Mart Ray to realization of what he was facing.

"Looks like whatever Ray knows about him, he sure ain't heard about Jim Gary killin' Miguel Sonoma!"

Mart Ray was staggered. "Sonoma?" he gasped. "You killed Sonoma?"

Jim Gary was facing him now. Some of the numbness was gone from his hands, and something cold and terrible was welling up within him. He had ridden beside this man, shared food with him, worked with him, and now the man had tricked and betrayed him.

"Yes, Mart, I killed Sonoma. I ain't afraid. I never was. I just don't like trouble!"

Ray's tongue touched his lips and his eyes narrowed to slits. He sank a little deeper into the crouch, and men drew away to the sides of the street. Scarcely twenty feet apart, the two faced each other. "Take off your shirt, Ray. Take it off and show them. Reach up slow an' unbutton it. You take it off yourself, or I'll take it off your body!"

"Go to blazes!" Ray's voice was hoarse and strange. Then, with incredible swiftness, his hands dropped for his guns.

In the hot, dusty stillness of the afternoon street, all was deathly still. Somewhere a baby cried, and a foot shifted on the boardwalk. For what seemed an age, all movement seemed frozen and still as the two men in the street faced each other.

Kitty Blaze, her eyes wide with horror, seemed caught in that same breathless time-frozen hush. The hands of the men were moving with flashing speed, but at that instant everything seemed to move hauntingly slowly. She saw Mart Ray's gun swing up; she saw the killing eagerness in his face, his lips thinned and white, his eyes blazing.

And she saw the stranger, Jim Gary. Tall, lithe, and strong, his dark face passionless, yet somehow ruthless. And she saw his lean brown hand flash in a blur of movement, saw flame leap from the black muzzles of his guns, and saw Mart Ray smashed back, back, back! She saw his body flung sideways into the hitching rail, saw a horse rear, his lashing hoofs within inches of the man. She saw the gun blaze again from the ground, and a leap of dust from the stranger's shoulder, and she saw Gary move coolly aside to bring his guns better to bear upon the man who was now struggling up.

As in a kind of daze, she saw Jim Gary holding his fire, letting Ray get to his feet. In that stark, incredible instant, she saw him move his lips and she heard the words, as they all heard them in the silence of the street. "I'm sorry, Mart. You shouldn't have played it this way. I'd rather it had been the stampede."

And then Ray's guns swung up. His shirt was bloody, his face twisted in a sort of leer torn into his cheek by a bullet, but his eyes were fiendish. The guns came up, and even as they came level, red flame stabbed from the muzzles of Gary's guns and Ray's body jerked, dust sprang from his shirt's back, and he staggered back and sat down on the edge of the walk, and then as though taken with a severe pain in the groin, he rolled over into the street and sprawled out flat. Somewhere thunder rolled.

For a long moment, the street was motionless. Then somebody said, "We better get inside. She's rainin'."

Jerry swung from his horse and in a couple of strides was beside the fallen man. Ripping back the shirt, he exposed the side, scarred by a steer's hoof.

Dan Blaze jerked around. "Slagle!" he yelled. "Where's Red Slagle! Get him!"

"Here." Slagle was sitting against the building, gripping a bloody hand. "I caught a slug. I got behind Ray." He looked up at Blaze. "Gary's right. He's straight as a string. It was Ray's idea to ring him in and use him as the goat after he found him with us."

Dan Blaze knelt beside him. "Who killed my brother?" he demanded. "Was it you or Ray?"

"Ray shot him first. I finished it. I went huntin' him an' he busted out of the brush. He had a stick he'd carried for walkin' an' I mistook it for a gun."

"What about Langer?" Gary demanded. "Where's he?"

Red grinned, a hard, cold grin. "He lit a shuck. That whuppin' you gave him took somethin' out of him. Once he started to run he didn't stop, not even for his money."

He dug into his pocket. "That reminds me. Here's the forty bucks you earned."

Jim Gary took the money, surprised speechless. Slagle struggled erect. Gary's expression seemed to irritate him. "Well, you earned it, didn't you? An' I hired you, didn't I? Well, I never gypped no man out of honest wages yet!

"Anyway," he added wryly, "by the looks of that rope I don't reckon I'll need it. Luck to you, kid! An'," he grinned, "stay out of trouble."

Thunder rumbled again, and rain poured into the street, a driving, pounding rain that would start the washes running and bring the grass to life again, green and waving for the grazing cattle, moving west, moving north.

WHAT GOLD DOES TO A MAN

WE CAME UP the draw from the south in the spring of '54, and Josh was the one who wanted to stop.

Nothing about that country looked good to me, but I was not the one who was calling the shots. Don't get the idea that it was not pretty country, because it surely was. There was a-plenty of water, grass, and trees. That spring offered some of the coldest and best water I ever tasted, but I didn't like the look of the country around. There was just too much Indian sign.

"Forget it, Pike!" Josh Boone said irritably. "For a kid, you sound more like an old woman all the time! Believe me, I know gold country, and this is it. Why should a man go all the way to California when there's gold all around him?"

"It may be here," Kinyon grumbled, "but maybe Pike Downey ain't so dumb, even if he is a kid. He's dead right about that Injun sign. If we stick around here, there being no more than the five of us, we're apt to get our hair lifted."

Kinyon was the only one who thought as I did. The others had gold fever, and had it bad, but Kinyon's opinions didn't make me feel any better, because he knew more about Injuns than any of the rest. I'd rather have been wrong and safe.

Josh Boone did know gold country. He had been in California when the first strike was made, and I don't mean the one at Sutter's Mill that started all the fuss. I mean the *first* strike, which was down in a canyon near Los Angeles. Josh had done all right down there, and then when the big strikes came up north he'd cleaned up some forty thousand dollars, then he rode back east and had himself a time. "Why keep it?" he laughed. "There's more where that came from!"

Maybe there was, but if I made myself a packet like that I

planned to buy myself a farm and settle down. I even had the place in mind.

It was Boone who suggested we ride north away from the trail. "There's mountains yonder," he said, "and I've a mind there's gold. Why ride all the way to Californy when we might find it right here?"

Me, I was ready. Nobody would ever say Pike Downey was slow to look at new country. The horse I rode was the best in the country, and it could walk faster than most horses could trot. It weighed about fourteen hundred, and most of it muscle. It was all horse, that black was, so when we turned off to the hills I wasn't worried. That came later.

Josh Boone was our leader, much as we had one. Then there was Jim Kinyon, German Kreuger and Ed Karpe. I was the kid of the bunch, just turned nineteen, strong as a young bull.

Josh had been against me coming along, but Kinyon spoke for me. "He's the best shot I ever did see," he told them, "and he could track a snake upstream in muddy water. That boy will do to take along."

Kinyon calling me a boy kind of grated. I'd been man enough to hold my own and do my part since I was fourteen. My paw and maw had come west from Virginia in a covered wagon, and I was born in that wagon.

I'd been hunting since I was knee-high to a short beaver, and the first time I drove a wagon over the Santa Fe Trail I was just past fourteen. My rifle drew blood for me in a Comanche attack on that wagon train, and we had three more fights before we came up to Santa Fe.

Santa Fe was wild and rough, and I had a mix-up with a Comanchero in Santa Fe with knives, and I put him down to stay. The following year I went over the Trail again, and then I went to hunting buffalo in Texas. The year after I went all the way to California, and returning from that trip I got friendly with some Cheyennes and spent most of a year with them, raiding deep into Mexico. By the time I met Boone, I had five years of the roughest kind of living behind me.

Boone talked himself mighty big, but he wasn't bigger than me, and neither was Ed Karpe.

We rode up that draw and found ourselves the prettiest little canyon you'll ever see, and we camped there among the trees. We killed us a deer, and right away Josh went to panning that stream. He found gold from the first pan.

Gold! It ran heavy from the first pan, and after that there was no talking to them. We all got to work, but being a loner I went along upstream by myself. Panning for gold was something I had never done, but all the way back from California that time I'd traveled with one of the best, and he'd filled me to the ears with what was needful to know about placer mining for gold.

He told me about trying sandbars and little beaches where the stream curves around and throws up sand in the crook of the elbow. Well, I found such a place, and she showed color.

Wasting no more time on panning, I got my shovel and started digging down to bedrock. No more than four feet down I struck it. It was cracked here and there and, remembering what that old timer told me, I cleaned those cracks and went back under the thin layers of rock and panned out what I found. By nightfall I had a rawhide sack with maybe three or four hundred dollars in it.

All of the boys had gold, but none of them had as much as I showed them, which was less than half what I had. Jim Kinyon was tickled, but it didn't set too well with either Boone or Karpe. Neither of them liked to be bested, and in particular they didn't like it from me.

Kreuger patted me on the back. "Goot poy!" he said. "Das iss goot!"

We took turns hunting meat, and next day it fell to me. Mounting up, I took my Sharps Breech-Loader, and I'd buckled on my spare pistol. I had me two Army Colts, Model 1848, and I set store by them guns. I'd picked 'em off a dead Texan down east of Santa Fe.

That Texas man had run up on some horse thieves and out of luck at the same time. There'd been four horse thieves and him, and they had at it, and when I came along some hours later there they lay, all good dead men with a horse for each and six extry. There were their rifles, pistols, and a good bit of grub, and there was no sense in leaving it for the

Comanches to pick up or the sand to bury. In the time I'd been packing those six-shooters I'd become right handy with 'em.

They were riding my belt that morning when I rode out from camp. Sighting a couple of deer close to camp, I rode around them. I'd no mind to do my killing close by, where we might need the game at some later time. A few miles further away I fetched me a good-sized buck, skinned him out, and cut us some meat. Down at the stream I was washing the blood from my hands when I glanced up to see two things at once—only one of them was important at the moment.

The first thing I spotted was a full-growed Injun with his bow all drawed back and an arrow aimed at me. Throwing myself to one side I fetched one of those Colts and triggered me an Injun just as the arrow flicked past my face. He slid down off that river bank and right into the Happy Hunting Grounds, where no doubt someday we'll meet and swap yarns.

The other thing I'd glimpsed was upstream just a ways. It was only a glimpse, but I edged along the creek for a better look.

Under a ledge of rock, just above the water, was a hole. It was about crawling-into size, and didn't smell of animal, so I crawled in and stood up. It was a big cave, a room maybe twenty feet long by fifteen wide, with a solid-packed sandy floor and a smidgin of light from above. Looking up, I could see a tangle of branches over a hole, which was a couple of feet across but well-hidden by brush.

When I rode into camp to unload my meat I told the boys about my Injun. "I caved the bank over him," I said, "but they will most likely find him. Then they'll come hunting us."

"One more and one less," Karpe said. "A dead Injun is a good Injun."

"A dead Injun is the start of trouble," I said. "We'd better light out of here if we want to keep our hair."

"Are you crazy?" Boone stared at me. "With all the gold we're finding?"

"We don't need to leave the country," I protested. "But what does gold mean to a dead man?"

"The boy is right," Kinyon agreed. "We're in for trouble."

"We can handle trouble," Karpe said. "I ain't afeerd of no Injuns. Anyway, this just sounds like Pike talking big. I'll bet he never saw no Injun."

Well, I put down the meat I was eating and licked my fingers. Then I got up and looked across the fire at him. "You called me a liar, Ed," I said, mild-like. "I take that from no man."

He stared at me like he couldn't believe what he was hearing. "Now what about this?" he said. "The boy figures he's a growed-up man! Well, I'll take that out of him!" He got to his feet.

"No guns," Boone said. "If there are Injuns, we don't want to draw them nigh."

Me, I shucked my Bowie. Some folks don't fancy cold steel, and Ed Karpe seemed to be one of them. "Shuck your steel, Ed," I told him. "I'll see the color of your insides."

"No knives," he protested. "I fight with my hands or a gun."

I flipped my knife hard into a log. "All right," I said. "It makes me no mind. You just come on, and we'll see who is the boy of this outfit."

He come at me. Ed Karpe was a big man, all rawboned and iron hard. He fetched me a clout on the jaw that made me see lights flashing, hitting me so hard I nearly staggered. Then he swung his other fist but I stepped inside, grabbing him by shirt-front and crotch, swinging him aloft and heaving him against the bank.

He hit hard, but he was game and came up swinging. He fetched me a blow, but he was scared of me grabbing him and hit me whilst going away. I made as if to step on a loose rock and stagger, and he leapt at me. Dropping to one knee, I caught him again by shirt-front and crotch, only this time I throwed him head first into that bank. He hit hard and he just laid there.

When I saw he wasn't about to get up, I dusted off my knees and went back to the bone I'd been picking. Nobody said anything, but Josh Boone was looking surprised and sizing me up like he hadn't really seen me before. "You can fight some," he admitted. "That didn't take you no time at all."

"One time up in Pierre's Hole I fought nigh onto two hours with a big trapper. He'd have made two of Ed there, and he was skookum man, but I whopped him some."

After a bit Ed Karpe come around, and he come back to the fire shaking his head and blinking, but nobody paid him no mind. Me, I was right sorry. It ain't good for folks to start fighting amongst themselves in Injun country. Come daylight I went back to my shaft and taken one look. Whilst I'd been grub-hunting yesterday somebody had moved in and cleaned the bed-rock slick as a piano-top.

Sure, I was upset, but I said nothing at all right then. I went on up the creek to a better place and dug me another hole, only when I left this one I covered it with brush and wiped out the sign I'd left.

Kinyon had been hunting that day, and when he came in he was worried. "We'd better light out or get fixed for a fight. There's Injuns all around us."

They listened to Kinyon where they hadn't listened to me, so we dug ourselves some rifle pits and forted up with logs. I said nothing about my shaft being cleaned out.

Next day I went back to my brush-covered hole and sank her down to bedrock and cleaned up. This was heavy with gold, and the best so far. My method of going to the rock was paying off. It was more work than using a pan, and it was more dangerous.

That night when we all came in to camp Kreuger was missing. We looked at one another, and believe me, we didn't feel good about it. Nobody had seen the German, and nobody had heard a shot. When morning came I headed upstream, then doubled back to where Kinyon was working, only I stayed back in the brush. I laid right down in the brush not far from him, but where I could watch both banks at once.

"Jim?" I kept my voice so only he would hear me. "Don't you look up or act different. I'll do the talking."

"All right," he said.

"Somebody robbed that shaft of mine. Cleaned her out whilst I was hunting."

He wiped sweat from his face but said nothing.

"I've some ideas about German Kreuger, too."

"You think he stole your gold and lit out?"

"You know better. Nor do I think Injuns killed him. However, we better have us a look."

"Who do you think?"

"It wasn't you, and it wasn't me. And I'd bet every ounce I have that it wasn't that old German."

Pausing, I said, "You go on working. I'll watch."

He was canny, Jim was. He worked, all right, but he didn't get into a pattern. When he bent down he didn't lift up in the same place, but away from there. He kept from any pattern, so's if anybody planned a shot they'd have to wait until he was out in the open.

As for me, I almost missed it. Almost, but not quite. I'd been lying there a couple of hours, and my eyes were tired. The day was warm, and I'd been working hard the past few days and was tuckered. I must have been looking right at that rifle barrel a full minute before I realized it.

Only the fact that Kinyon was moving saved him. He was down by the water, partly hidden by some rocks, and he was digging sand from the low side of a boulder, preparing to wash it out. That rifleman was waiting for him to come up on the bank where he'd have no doubt.

Me, I didn't wait. Sliding my old Sharps Breech-Loader up, I just throwed a shot into that brush, right along that rifle barrel. There was a crash in the brush, and both me and Jim jumped for it, but the heavy brush and boulders got in the way, and by the time we got there that feller was gone. Nor could we make anything from the tracks except that he wore boots and was therefore a white man.

We tried to track him, though, and found nothing until we slid down among some rocks and there we found Kreuger. He'd been scalped. "No Injun," Kinyon said, and he was right. That was plain as day to any old Injun fighter.

"We've got a murderer in the outfit," I said.

"Maybe," Kinyon said doubtfully, "but there could be somebody else around, somebody we don't know about."

After a pause he said, "We've not much gold yet."

"No one of us has," I agreed, "but for one man it's a healthy stake, if he had it all."

"Injuns around," Kinyon said, that night at the fire. "Today I was shot at."

"I've been afraid of that," Karpe agreed. "We'd better watch ourselves."

Josh Boone glanced over at Karpe. "It ain't Injuns that scares me," he said, but if Ed Karpe noticed he paid no attention.

For the next two days everything went along fine. I worked with an eye out for trouble, and every now and again I'd quit work and scout around the area to make sure nobody was closing in on me. On the bottom of the shaft I'd sunk, I broke up the layers of bedrock where there were cracks, and made a good cleanup. Even me, who'd been doing well, couldn't believe how rich the find was. When I sacked up that night I had more than I'd had in my life, more than I'd ever seen, in fact.

Kinyon met me at an agreed-upon place on the creek bank. "Let's go higher," I suggested, "and sink a shaft together. We'll work faster, and this ground is rich enough for both of us."

Ed Karpe came up to us. He looked from one to the other. "I'd like to throw in with you boys," he said. "I'm getting spooked. I don't like going it alone." He looked at us, his face flushing. "Maybe I've lost my nerve."

"Why do you say that?" I asked.

"I feel like somebody's scouting me all the time."

Boone joined us just then, carrying his rifle in the hollow of his arm. "What's this? Everybody quitting so soon?"

"We're going to team up and work together," I said. "We figure it will be safer. Less chance of Injuns sneakin' up on us. I think we should get what we can and move out while our luck holds."

Josh Boone stared at me. "You runnin' this show now? I thought I was elected leader?"

"You was," Kinyon agreed. "It wasn't any idea of leading that started Pike talking. He figures we'd all do a lot better working together on shares than each working by himself."

"Oh, he does, does he? I don't see he's done so durned well."

"I got more than four thousand in gold. If any of you has over a thousand I'll cook chow this night."

"Four thousand?" They just stared. Jim was the one who said it, then he spat into the dust. "What're we waitin' for? I ain't got five hundred."

That settled it, but it did not settle Josh Boone. He was sore because they all listened to me now. Even Karpe listened, although I was keeping an eye on Karpe. He kept his gun close and his eyes busy, but mostly he was watching me. I saw that right off.

We were edgy, all of us. Here we were, four men out miles from anywhere or anybody, hid out in the Black Hills, but we watched each other more than we watched for Injuns.

German Kreuger was gone, so our little world was lessened by one, our total strength less by twenty percent, our loneliness increased by the missing of a face by the fire at night.

Somebody, either Karpe, Boone, or some stranger had killed Kreuger, and had been about to shoot Jim Kinyon. Only we had found no stranger's tracks, nor even the tracks of any Indian at the time.

Our meat gave out, and Karpe was the hunter. He did not like it very much and he hesitated, about to say something which his personal courage would not let him say. My father, who had been a reading man in the few books he had, often quoted the Bible or other such books, and he was one to speculate on men and their ways. I thought of him now, and wondered what he would say of our situation. Since my father's death I have had no books and read but poorly. It ain't as if the idea wasn't there.

Karpe took his rifle and went out alone, and the rest of us went to work.

It was hot and the air was close. Jim paused once, leaning

on his shovel. "Feels like a storm coming," he said, and I did not think he meant only in the weather.

Taking off my guns, I placed them on a flat rock close at hand while I worked. Folks who've never packed pistols can't imagine how heavy they are. Pretty soon Josh Boone got out of the hole and traded places with Kinyon. Jim, he put down his rifle and went to work.

All of a sudden, and why I turned I don't know, I turned sharp around, and there was Ed Karpe standing on the bank with his rifle in his hands. He was looking down at Boone and I'd have sworn he was about to shoot him.

Boone, he was on his feet, his own rifle ready, and what would have happened next was anybody's guess, when suddenly an arrow smacked into a tree within inches of Karpe's head, and he yelled "Injuns!" and ducked for cover.

He took shelter behind the bank while Jim and Boone made it to the fort. Me, I squatted down in the hole where I was, and when the Injuns rushed us I opened up with both Colts. Karpe had turned to fire on them, and what he or the others did I didn't know, but I dropped four men and a horse. Then I caught up my rifle, but they were gone, leaving behind them several horses and some Injuns. A couple of them started to crawl away, and we let 'em go.

Boone went out to gather up what guns he could find and to catch up horses and bring 'em in. Whilst he was collectin' them, I saw him throw something into the bushes. At the time I thought nothing of it. My guns reloaded, I watched the boys come together again. Nobody had more than a scratch. We'd been ready, as much for each other as for them, but everybody was ready to shoot when they showed up, and of course, we had our fort, such as it was.

"Lucky!" Boone said. "Mighty lucky!"

"They'll be back," Kinyon replied grimly. "Our scalps are worth more now that we've shown ourselves warriors."

Nobody knew better than I what a break we'd had. If the Indians had come at us easy-like, slipping up and opening fire from cover, we'd have had small chance. Indians have bad leaders as well as white men, and this one had been too confident, too eager.

Young braves, no doubt, reckless and anxious to count coup on a white man, and wanting loot, too, our guns and horses. But nobody needed to tell anybody what stopped them.

Josh Boone was staring at me again. "You handle them Colts like a man who knowed how to use 'em."

"Why d'you figure he carries them? I knew he was handy." Kinyon was smiling with some secret pleasure.

Karpe had a wry amusement in his eyes. "And to think I nearly got into a shootin' scrape with you!"

"This does it," Kinyon said. "Now we'll have to go."

Boone started to object, then said nothing. We slept cold that night, staying away from the fire and close to our horses. If they stole our horses and those we had of theirs, we'd never get out of here alive. It was too far to anywhere safe.

We slept two at a time, not taking a chance on having just one man awake, because we didn't know who the murderer was.

At daybreak we slipped away from camp. We'd covered our holes, hiding our tools and what gear we did not want to carry. We kept one pan for taking samples downstream, and then we took off.

What the others were thinking I had no idea, but as for me, I was worried. One of us was a murderer and wanted all our gold. It wasn't enough that we had to watch out for Injuns, but one amongst us as well.

We hadn't gone three miles before Kinyon, who was in the lead, threw up a hand. "Injuns!" he said hoarsely. "Must be thirty or forty of 'em!"

That about-faced us, you can bet! We turned back up-creek, riding fast, and then turned off into the woods. We hadn't gone far before we heard 'em again, only this time it was another bunch already spread out in the woods. A gun thundered somewhere ahead of us, and then an arrow whistled by my head, and as I swung my horse I took a quick shot with the Sharps and saw an Indian fall.

Then I was riding Hell for leather and trying to load whilst we ran.

There was a yell behind us and Karpe's horse stumbled,

throwing Ed to the ground. He lit running just as a couple of Indians closed in on him.

One swung a tomahawk high, and I shot without aiming, then shoved the Sharps into the boot and went for a six-shooter. Boone and Kinyon both fired, and Ed came running. He still had his rifle and saddlebags.

"No use to run!" Jim yelled. "Too many of 'em! We've got to stand!"

There were rocks ahead, not far from our old fort, and we hit them running. My horse ran on, but I was shooting soon as I hit the ground, and Kinyon beside me. Boone and Karpe found good places, and they also opened fire. The attack broke off as quick as it began.

Karpe had a bullet scratch along his skull, and a burn on his shoulder. "You boys saved me!" he seemed amazed. "You surely did!"

Our horses were still with us. Mine had run on and then circled back to be with me, or with the horses he knew, I did not know which. We had our horses, but we had Indians all around us and no help nearer than three or four hundred miles. At least, none that we knew of.

"If they wipe us out," Boone commented, "nobody will ever know what happened to us."

"We wouldn't be the first," Kinyon said, "I found a skull and part of a spine and rib cage back yonder when I was huntin' gold. The bones had a gold pan along with 'em."

We sat there waiting for the next attack and expecting little when I heard that stream. It was close by, and in all the confusion I hadn't thought of it. "Look," I said, "if we can hold on until dark, I think I can get us out of this!"

They looked at me, waiting, but nobody said anything. Right at the moment nobody thought much of his chances.

"If we can stand 'em off until dark, we can slip away upstream into a cave I've found. They'll think we've left the country."

"What about our horses?" Kinyon asked.

"Have to leave 'em," I said, although it went hard to leave my Tennessee horse.

"Maybe there's another entrance?" Jim suggested. "Where there's one cave there's sometimes others."

We sat tight and let the sun do its work. It was almighty hot, but we had to put up with it, for there was no more than an edging of shade near some of the boulders. The Injuns tried a few shots and so did we, more to let 'em know we were still alive and ready than with hope of hitting anything.

Boone was lyin' beside me and he kept turning his head to stare out over the rocks. "Think we'll make it?" he asked me. All the big-headedness seemed to have gone out of him. "I'd sure like to save my pelt."

They came on then. They came in a wave from three sides, riding low on their horses and again it was my Model 48s that stopped them. Not that I killed anybody, but I rained bullets around them and burned a couple, and they couldn't understand that rapid fire. They knew about guns, and had some themselves, but they had never run up against any repeating weapons.

The last Injun was riding away when he turned sharp in the saddle and let go with a shot that winged Josh Boone.

It hit him high but hard, and he went down. Leaving the shooting to Karpe and Kinyon, I went to Boone. His face was all twisted with pain, but when I went to undo the laces on his buckskin shirt he jerked away, his eyes wild and crazy. "No! Let me alone! Don't bother with me!"

"Don't be a fool, Josh. You've been hit hard. You get treated or you'll die sure!"

He was sullen. "I'd better die, then. You go off. I'll fix it myself."

Something in his voice stopped me as I started to turn away. Slamming him back on the ground in no gentle way, I ripped open the rawhide cords and peeled back his hunting shirt.

There was a nasty wound there, all right, that had shattered his collar bone and left him bleedin' most awful bad. But that wasn't all.

There was another wound through the top of his shoulder, which was all festerin' and sore. When I saw that I stopped. He stared at me, his mouth drawn in a hard line, his eyes ugly, yet there was something else, too. There was shame as well as fear.

There was only one time he could have gotten that wound. Like when a bullet comes along a man's rifle and cuts the meat atop his shoulder. It had been Josh Boone and not Ed Karpe who had tried to kill Jim Kinyon, and therefore it had been Boone who killed old German Kreuger.

He stared at me and said no word while I washed out the wound, picked away bone fragments, and put it in the best shape I could manage. I folded an old bandana to stop the bleeding, and bound it tight in place. By the time I finished it was fetchin' close to dusk, and the Injuns had let up on their shootin'.

Kinyon guessed right. There was another hole into that cave, just a big crack, like, but big enough to get a horse inside, even a horse as big as my Tennessee. Once they were inside we pulled a couple of pieces of old log into the gap and then we bedded down to wait it out.

Oh, they come a-huntin', all right! We could hear them looking for us, but we kept quiet and after a while they gave up and rode away. We sat it out for three days in that cave, and then Jim slipped out to scout around.

They were gone, thinking we'd gotten away, and we slipped out, mounted up, and headed back for the settlements. When we had buildings in sight and knew we were safe, I pulled up and turned to face them.

"Josh," I said, "German left a widder behind. She's up at this settlement waitin' for him. With German dead, she will be hard put to live. I figure you might like to contribute, Josh."

He sat his horse lookin' at me, and I knew he was left handed as well as right. He had a gun, a handgun I'd seen him pick out of the bushes after he'd taken it off a dead Injun. He looked at me and I looked at him. I put no hand to a gun and I knew there was no need. "You just toss me your poke, Josh," I told him.

His eyes were all mean-like, and he tossed me the poke.

"Now the other one."

Ed Karpe and Jim, they just sat watching and Ed couldn't

seem to figure it out. Kinyon knew, although how long he had known I couldn't guess.

Josh Boone waited, holding off as long as he could, but then he tossed me the other poke.

Pocketing the pokes, I then took a couple of nuggets and some dust from my own poke. "There's maybe a hundred dollars there," I said. "It's riding money, a loan from me to you."

"I'll owe you for that," he said. "I always pay my debts."

"I'll see no man beggared with a broken arm," I said, "but that's what I named it. Ridin' money. Now you ride."

We sat there watching while he rode away, back square to us, one arm hitched kind of high. He rode like that right out of time, because we never saw him again.

"Well," Jim said after a bit. "If we ain't campin' here let's ride in. I'm goin' to wet my whistle."

We started riding, and nobody said anything more.

HORSE HEAVEN

T HE HIGH WALL of the canyon threw a shadow over the entrance of the shallow cave where the two men stood, staring at the skeleton that lay on the sandy floor.

Only a few rags remained of the man's clothing, and the dried-out, twisted leather of gunbelt and boots. The front part of the head had been blown away by a bullet fired from behind. Another bullet could still be seen, lodged low down in the man's spine.

The taller and older of the two men lifted his eyes to his companion. "Are you sure it's him? There ain't much to go on, Jim."

Locklin's face was lonely. This was the last member of a once closely knit family who lay there, the brother he had loved and admired, who had pleaded with him to come west before the War.

"I don't need anything more, Nearly. See where the left elbow was broken? I helped set it in a buffalo wallow while we fought off a bunch of Comanches.

"That gunbelt was his own work. He did it himself. He was a good man, Pike, too good a man to be trailed here and murdered after he was wounded."

"My guess would be that bullet in the spine crippled him," Nearly Pike suggested. "Why d' you suppose he came here? Was he just huntin' a place to hide? Or did he figure you'd be along?"

"He sent for me, like I told you. This is where we were to meet, so he must have had some reason why he did not want me riding down to the place without seeing him first. He'd camped here on Savory Creek before he built down in the valley, so he'd told me all about the place."

"You won't have anything to go on," Pike observed. "There's no sign left after all these years."

"There's two things. His guns are gone, so somebody packed them off, and there's the ranch. Somebody will have it, and that somebody will have some questions to answer."

He turned away. "We will come back and bury him properly when this is settled. A few more days or weeks won't matter now. From now on we are hunting two ivory-butted guns, and each will have three grooves filed in the bottom of the butt."

The trail to Toiyabe was dusty and long. Clouds hung heavy with a promise of rain, but as the hours passed it failed to develop. Wise with the wisdom of forty years west of the Missouri, Nearly Pike knew the manner of man with whom he rode. Yet he was a man who wanted nothing more than peace, and saw little in the weeks ahead.

Ten years before, George Locklin, accompanied by his much younger brother Jim, was riding through this country heading home to Texas when they saw the V where Antelope Valley points back toward a notch in the mountains. There was water and grass, with lakes and timber in the nearby hills. It was then George told his brother he had found what he wanted, and he would come back and settle on this ground and make a home for them here.

As they spoke of their plans they were sheltered in the same shallow cave on Savory Creek where his bones now lay.

Jim Locklin had stayed on in Texas, but then came the note:

Come on out, Jim, I've bought you a place called Horse Heaven, up in the mountains. I bought it in your name and filed the deed in the court house at Jacobsville. Looks like a bit of trouble here and I could use a good hand. If you don't find me around look up a man named Reed Castle.

At the time the note came Jim Locklin had been trailing north with a herd, and as they were short-handed there was no way he could leave. The mention of trouble had not alarmed him, as it had not been emphasized and he knew George could handle trouble.

They would need money to develop their property, so he took on a job ramrodding a herd from Dodge City to Canada, and then he drifted south toward Texas, pausing long enough in Deadwood to strike it rich in a small way. Finally, back in Texas, he paid off old debts and banked the rest. Only then did he start west.

"They might have buried him," Pike commented. "A man deserves that."

"I'm glad they didn't. Now I know he was murdered. He was a good man, Pike. He asked nothing from anyone and gave all he could. He could be a hard man, but this is a hard country."

"We'd best say nothing about who we are," Pike commented, as they sighted the first buildings of Toiyabe. "If we listen we might learn something."

"Good idea. You round up some grub, and I'll roust around and see what I can hear. It's been a good while, but if we can get some old-timer to talkin' the rest should be easy."

Toiyabe was booming. In the bottom of its steep-walled canyon the town's few streets were jammed with freighter's outfits, the recently arrived stage, buckboards from the ranches, and horses lining the hitching rail. Aside from being the supply center for the ranches, it was also headquarters for miners and for the men who worked in the sawmill.

The Fish Creek Saloon was run by Fish Creek Burns, whose faded blue eyes had looked sadly upon a world that stretched from his boyhood in the Cumberland Gap country through Council Bluffs to the Platte and west to the Rockies and back again by way of Abilene, Dodge, El Paso, Tascosa, and Santa Fe. He was a man of many interests, few loyalties, and no illusions.

Now, suddenly, his hands stopped, utterly still, on the glass he had been polishing. A man rarely surprised, he was startled now to immobility; slowly then, after a moment, the hands began to move once more. Under the straw-colored brows, the eyes lost their momentary sharpness and assumed the faded, normal lack of lustre. Yet the mind behind them was busy.

The man who had come through the door was two inches under six feet, but broad in the chest and thick in the shoulders. He was a young man in his twenties, but compact and sharp, the lean, brown face holding the harsh lines of one much older. Fish Creek Burns never forgot a face or a loyalty.

"Rye," Locklin said mildly, "it's been a dusty ride."

"This time of year," Burns agreed, putting bottle and glass before him.

Down the bar was Chance Varrow, and behind the stranger was a poker table where one of the players was Reed Castle, of the OZ spread. Burns's eyes shifted to Locklin. "Driftin'?"

"Stayin'."

"Huntin' a job?"

"No, but maybe I'll have an outfit of my own."

Burns's tone was dry and casual as he picked up another glass. "That big man with the black mustache at the table behind you runs a lot of cattle in Antelope Valley, away back," his eyes met Locklin's, "where the valley notches the mountains."

Jim Locklin was immediately alert. What was the bartender trying to tell him? That ranch in the notch of the hills had belonged to his brother!

Burns's face was without expression. He was polishing another glass.

"Has he had the place long?"

"Three years or so. He's doing right well."

The last letter from George had been mailed just about three years ago. Jim wanted to turn and look but he did not. "Maybe he could use a hand. Does he have a name?"

"Reed Castle." Burns sighted through a glass. "He's the big man around here. A man who makes money fast makes both friends and enemies. Down the bar, the tall man in the white hat and the blue coat is Chance Varrow, and some say he could have a dozen notches on his guns if he wanted."

Varrow was taller than Locklin, with sharply cut features,

cold as a prowling fox. As Locklin looked, Varrow's eyes turned and stopped suddenly on Locklin.

"The big man in the black broadcloth suit," Burns continued, "is Creighton Burt, district attorney. A man with nerve, a man of integrity. He doesn't like Reed Castle."

Disturbed by the interest in Varrow's eyes, Jim leaned his forearms on the bar and asked Burns, "Do I look like somebody you know? Varrow acts like he's seen me somewhere."

Fish Creek kept his eyes on the glass in his hands. "Two or three years ago there was a man around here named George Locklin, and you're somewhat like him. Some said that Locklin and Varrow weren't friendly. Varrow hasn't been here long, either. Right around three years I'd say."

"Thanks. I would take it you were friendly to George Locklin?"

"He was one of the finest men I ever came across. However, I'd not speak his name about town if I were you."

"Thank you." He finished his drink. "By the way, there's a man travelin' with me. Tall old man named Nearly Pike. He may be in."

Jim Locklin managed a casual glance around the room that took in both Creighton Burt and Reed Castle. The former was large, fat, and untidy. Castle was big, and obviously prosperous. He wore a black mustache, and his face was strong-boned, a domineering face and a bold one, the face of a man who would ride rough-shod over obstacles. Jim turned and went out, letting the doors swing to behind him, turned quickly into the crowd and crossed the street. It would be a mistake to become a focus of their attention too soon.

Glancing back he saw Chance Varrow standing in the door, staring after him. Locklin went to the harness shop and, after a minute, out the side door to the alley and across to the general store where Pike was loading supplies into a couple of sacks.

Nearly Pike's Adam's apple bobbed in his scrawny throat. "Place in Hoss Heaven is lived on," he said, keeping his voice low. "Some gal moved on the place with an Injun. She's been havin' trouble with a man named Reed Castle."

Locklin was watching the street through the window. "What else?"

"Cattle range is sewed up slick and tight between four men. Reed Castle has Antelope Valley north to the mountains. John Shippey has the Monitor and Burly Ives the Smoky. Neil Chase has the Diamond outfit. They won't let anybody drive through or in."

"Get the horses around back and load up. I'm getting some ammunition." Leaving the older man, Locklin went over to the counter.

He loved the old, familiar smell of such stores, the smell of spices, freshly ground coffee, new leather, dry goods, and the sweetish smell of gun oil.

After buying a hundred rounds of .44 ammunition, he glanced at a new shotgun, a short-barreled gun of the express-gun type carried by shotgun messengers. "Give me that scatter-gun," he said, "and a hundred rounds for it."

The storekeeper, a short, stout man, glanced up. "You must figure to fight a war with all that ammunition. And a shotgun? Never cared for 'em myself."

Locklin smiled pleasantly. "Good for quail. I like bird-meat." He loaded the shotgun. "Only empty guns that hurt folks," he commented, smiling. "I like mine loaded." He thrust the muzzle of the shotgun into the grocery sack and gathered the top of the burlap around the trigger-guard, carrying it with the stock almost invisible behind his forearm. "As for wars, I never fight unless folks push it on me. However," he paused briefly, "I plan to go into the cattle business here."

The storekeeper's head came up from the bill he was adding. "If you figure on that you'd better double your order for ammunition. This is a closed country."

"Uncle Sam doesn't say so."

"Uncle Sam doesn't run this country. The Big Four run it, and that means Reed Castle."

Jim smiled. "Ever hear," he asked gently, "of a cowman named George Locklin?"

The fat man straightened slowly, staring at him. He half turned aside, started to speak and then said nothing. Locklin went to the front door and stepped out, calling back to Pike as he did so. He stepped out right into the middle of trouble.

Confronting him was a huge back, the top of the shoulders on the level with his eyes, the vest split down the back from the strain of huge shoulders and powerful muscles. The man wore a six-shooter, and his hand gripped the butt. Beyond him Jim could see a young Indian, straight and tall, his face expressionless. He was unarmed.

"You're a dirty, thievin' rustler!" the big man was saying. "Git! Git out of the country! We don't need your kind."

"I steal no cows."

"Don't you be callin' me no liar!" The big man's fingers grasped the gun butt tighter and he started to draw.

Locklin's left hand shot out and grasped the big man's wrist. With a startled grunt the big man began to turn, and Locklin let him turn but at the same time he shoved up and back on the gun wrist he held, pushing the elbow higher until the gun muzzle was back of the holster.

The big man struck viciously, but Locklin was too close, and the blow curled around his neck. At the same time he was shoving the big man back and keeping him off balance. The big man's back slammed against an awning-post, and Jim twisted hard on the wrist. The gun dropped from the man's fingers, and instantly Jim stepped back and drew the shotgun from the sack.

"The Indian wasn't armed," he said, "and I'll see no man murdered."

The flash of sunlight on the blue-black barrel of the shotgun had cleared the street behind the big man as if by magic.

Slowly the big man began to rub his wrist. "You'd no call to butt in, stranger. Nobody pushes Ives around."

"We've no quarrel," Locklin said, "unless you come looking for it, or unless you're one of those who murdered my brother and stole his ranch."

There was silence in the street. Somebody shifted his weight and the boardwalk creaked. "Who—? What did you say your name was?"

"My name is Locklin, Ives. Jim Locklin, brother to George

Locklin who was dry-gulched and murdered up in the Monitors about three years ago."

Ives backed another step, still rubbing his wrist. He glanced around hastily as if looking for a way out or for help.

Chance Varrow stood across the street; near him was Reed Castle. "Those are hard words, friend," Varrow said. "Before you make such a statement you'd better have proof."

"I have proof of the murder. As yet I do not have the murderers."

"You are mistaken," Reed Castle said carelessly, but speaking for the onlookers more than for him. "George Locklin sold his ranch to me and left the country. Whatever you think you know is a mistake. George left here under his own power."

Jim's shotgun held steady. "Castle," he replied, his voice ringing the length of the street, "you're a liar! I have a letter from my brother telling me of the trouble he was having and asking me to come out. He had no intention of selling out, and he did have plans for developing the ranch.

"As for your ownership, I am asking right now, before the town of Toiyabe, for you to produce a bill of sale. I want to see it in the office of Creighton Burt not later than the day after tomorrow."

There was no movement; the street held its silence. Nobody realized better than Reed Castle the position he faced. Since acquiring the Antelope Valley property nothing had stopped him. His personality and strength had drawn Shippey, Chase, and Ives to him and into the combine he formed. Other cattlemen had been frozen out or driven out, and Castle was building strong and deep.

In the town itself only Creighton Burt held out against him in the open, although Castle was well aware that many lesser men both feared and hated him.

Now he had been called a liar in the open street. He had been indirectly accused of murder and theft. Nor would the story stop with the borders of this small town. It would be told and repeated in Carson, Austin, and Eureka.

"We'll make it noon, Castle. Show up with your bill of sale, and if you have one the signature had better be valid!"

Coolly, he lowered his shotgun, picked up the dropped sack, and walked across the street. Nearly Pike waited at the corner of the alley, his rifle in his hands. "Wal, son, you sure laid down your argument. Now they've got to put up or shut up."

The ride to Horse Heaven was by a devious route. Neither man knew exactly where they were going, just a general direction and some landmarks to look for. They headed northeast when leaving Toiyabe, then turned back to the southwest through Ackerman Canyon. Daylight found them camped near Antelope Peak.

From there they turned back into the hills, climbing steadily through the pines and aspen, riding warily, for they understood their situation without discussion. The easy way out, perhaps the only way, was to have Locklin killed so he could not appear at Burt's office. If he did not appear it could be shrugged off as the talk of some loud-mouthed drifter. There would be criticism, but Castle could merely say that he had been there, ready with his bill of sale, and where was this so-called Locklin fellow?

The narrow trail through the trees ended in a long basin, a grass-covered basin scattered here and there with clumps of trees and brush. On the far side, nestled against a corner of the mountain, was a cabin. A lazy trail of smoke mounted toward the sky.

"You kicked into an anthill," Pike commented. "Castle will have men ridin' the hills huntin' you."

Locklin had been thinking of that, and now they drew up in the shadow of some pines and studied the cabin and its vicinity with careful attention. A saddled horse was tied near the corral, and three other horses were loose in the corral.

As they watched, two people came into sight, a girl from the cabin and an Indian from the rocks near the cliff. "That's the Injun you spoke for, Jim. I'd know that odd limp anywhere."

They had no sooner broken from cover than they were seen. The girl started toward the cabin, but something said by the Indian stopped her, and she turned back.

What he had expected he was not sure, but certainly not

what he found. She was a tall, beautifully shaped girl with dark skin, from which her gray eyes were both startling and lovely. She studied him carefully as he drew near, but she was by no means frightened. She had poise and manner, and seemed perfectly sure of herself. The Indian was wearing a gun now.

"Howdy, ma'am," Jim said. "I'm Locklin. I own this place."

"I know who you are. As to owning this place, that's a matter for discussion. Get down and come in, will you? Patch told me what you did for him."

Inside she busied herself putting food on the table and getting coffee started. "I'm Army Locklin. Army being short for Armorel, the Locklin because I was married to your brother."

"You were *what*?"

"We were married the day he disappeared. He got word of trouble at the ranch just after reaching town. He left me in town and rushed back to the place and right into an ambush. He was shot down, got away into the brush, and that was the last he was seen."

"I don't know what to say. George said nothing of you in his letters."

She smiled bitterly. "He did not know me then. I came to Toiyabe to marry Reed Castle, but we did not see eye to eye on several subjects, and I refused to go through with it.

"Reed became angry and threatened me, then he tried to get the people at the hotel to turn me out. George had had trouble with Reed, so when he heard of it he came to me and offered his assistance."

Her eyes turned to Jim. "I was alone in the world, and it had taken the last of my money to come here from San Francisco. I told George I did not love him, but if he really wanted me I'd try to become a good wife. We were married, but I never had a chance to be anything to him.

"Now," she added, "you know why I have no use for Castle, and why he wants me out of the country."

"How'd you meet him in the first place?"

"My father died, and he did not leave me very much. I had friends back east who knew Reed Castle, and they told him about me and sent him a picture. He proposed by mail. It all seemed very romantic, a handsome western rancher and all that."

"Why did you suggest I might not own this place?"

"You own half of it. I own the other half. I filed a claim on the land that lies alongside of your ranch.

"You see, George gave me money when we were married. He did not have all that much, but he did not want me to feel bound, and if I was unhappy I could leave whenever I wished.

"After George disappeared Reed came forward with a bill of sale and claimed the ranch. He said George had changed his mind about being married to me, had sold the ranch and skipped out. I did not believe a word of it, but I could prove nothing. Everybody was feeling very sorry for me, but after all, I had not known George but a few days, and he *might* have decided marriage was not for him. I could prove nothing."

"But you stayed on?"

"There was nowhere to go. George might reappear. And then, George had told me you were coming." She paused. "Did—did George ever mention a silver strike? Not far from here?"

"Silver?" He frowned, trying to think back. There had been a number of letters, early on. "No, I don't think so."

Then he indicated the bunkhouse where the Indian had gone. "What about Patch? Where does he fit in?"

"I don't know. I honestly don't. He rode in here one day on a flea-bitten roan pony, and wanted to work for me. I did need help, but had so little money. He told me he wanted to work for me and I could pay him when I wished. Since then he has worked hard, has been loyal, too, only when Reed Castle is around he always gets out of sight. I think he may be afraid of him."

"Why do you call him Patch? Is he an Apache?"

"He is, but he would give me no name, so I began calling him that."

There was no accounting for Indians. They had their own ideas, and followed them. Few Apaches could be found this far north and west, for they loved their southwestern desert country, but there were wanderers from all tribes.

Reed Castle was no fool. Crooked he might be, but he was also intelligent and shrewd, and the two were rarely the same thing. He would know that any bill of sale he might have would be an obvious forgery, so he must have other irons in the fire. Of course, he knew George Locklin was dead, and he had had nothing to worry about until now.

Jim Locklin wanted more than simply to recover the ranch. He wanted to face the man who had killed George. At this date the proof would be hard to come by, but the more he thought about it the more he wondered. George had always been a thorough man who left little to chance, and he had lived long enough to reach the cave on Savory Creek. As he certainly had not lived with that hole in his head, he must have received the spinal wound first, but had somehow kept going until he reached the cave.

He had undoubtedly been helpless when he was killed, but had he been helpless when he arrived? How much time had he before his lower limbs became paralyzed?

With a growing feeling of excitement, Jim Locklin got up and went to the bunkhouse. His brother had always been one to communicate. He always left messages behind him. One never had to guess with George. He always had a plan. There had been a hollow in the rocks on the old L Bar, and there had been a rock under a tree on the way to Toiyabe where they exchanged messages.

So why not now, of all times? If he had struggled to reach that cave with almost his last strength, it must have been done with purpose.

Excited though he was, he finally dropped off, and, tired from travel, he slept deeply.

He awakened to daybreak and angry voices. Hurriedly, he threw on some clothing and, grabbing his rifle, went to the door. His breath caught sharply as he saw Ives and several of his riders. Patch was nowhere in sight, but one of Ives's men had a rifle on Pike and Army.

Resting his rifle against the doorjamb he called out, "Looking for me, Burly? I'm right here!"

Ives turned sharply in his saddle, but only the rifle indicated Locklin's presence. And the rifle was aimed at him.

The bunkhouse walls were too solid to shoot through, and Ives was no longer in command of the situation. If shooting started it was quite obvious who would get shot first.

A rattle of horses' hooves distracted his attention, and when Locklin followed Burly's gaze he saw a half-dozen riders led by a square-built, oldish man with a white mustache. "What's goin' on here, Burly? You're not goin' to make trouble for that girl while I'm around!"

"Keep out of this, John! I came here to settle things with this here Locklin."

Jim put down the rifle and reached to the empty upper bunk for the shotgun he had left there. "If you want to settle things with me, why bring your whole outfit?" He stepped out into the yard. "Or do you think you need all that help to handle one man?"

"Put down that shotgun and I'll break you in half!"

Locklin handed the shotgun to Pike. "Get down off that horse and we'll see." He glanced at the white-haired man. "I take it you are John Shippey? Will you see that I get fair play?"

"You're durned tootin' I will!" He waved a hand. "Everybody stand back and let them have at it. Anybody who tries to interfere will settle with me."

Burly unbuckled his gun belts with great good humor and hung them on the saddle horn. Having little stomach for gunfights, he relished a chance to use his fists. That he had never been whipped helped him to anticipate the fight.

"He'll make two of you, son!" Pike protested. "Look at the size of him!"

Locklin ignored him. He was intent upon Ives now, and thinking only of him. He moved in swiftly. He circled warily. It was obvious from Burly's manner that he was no stranger to fighting, yet when the big man moved his first tentative blow was short. Locklin feinted a move, side-stepped quickly and smashed Ives in the mouth. The blow landed solidly, and blood splashed from badly cut lips. Locklin started to draw away and it was all that saved him. A hard right on the ear knocked him staggering, and Burly rushed, his greater height, weight, and reach driving Locklin back, off balance. Jim landed a couple of ineffective blows to the body.

Jim caught a hard blow and went down. Ives, carried forward by the impetus of his rush, tried a hasty kick and missed. Locklin came up fast, his head still buzzing from the blow he'd caught, and he went under a left and smashed both hands to the body. Neither man knew more of fighting than what they had learned by applying it, but both were skilled in the rough-and-tumble style of the frontier, which they had been using since boyhood.

Locklin bored in, went under a swing with a right to the body, then an overhand left that split Ives's ear and staggered him. Instantly, Locklin was on him, his blows ripping and slashing at the bigger man.

Ives struggled to get set, striking back with heavy, ponderous blows. Suddenly, Locklin ceased to punch and, diving low, grabbed Ives around the knees and upended him.

Ives hit the dirt with a thud, but he rolled over like a cat and came to his feet. Jim was set for him, and caught him with a hard right that cracked like a ball bat. Then Jim rushed in close and began to batter at Ives's body.

Ives was badly cut, and one of his eyes almost closed, yet Locklin was weary simply from punching and holding the larger man off.

He put his head on the bigger man's chest and punched at his body with both hands. Ives, an old river-boat fighter, stabbed at his eyes with a stiff thumb, but Locklin dropped his head to Ives's chest again and suddenly smashed upward with his head, butting him on the chin. Ives staggered, and Locklin swung with both fists for his chin, left and right.

Ives went down hard. He got up slowly, warily. Jim Locklin had backed off, gasping for breath. He started to circle, his foot slipped, and Ives grabbed him in a bear hug, forcing him back. Excruciating pain stabbed him, and Jim fought desperately to free himself, knowing the larger man was strong enough to break his back.

Suddenly, Jim deliberately threw himself backward. He hit the ground hard, but it broke Ives's hold, and Jim got to his feet. Ives dove at him to bring him down again, and Locklin met the dive by jerking up his knee into Ives's face.

The big man went to hands and knees, his features a blur of blood. Locklin waited, gasping. Ives started to rise, and Locklin moved in. A left and right, then a terrific right uppercut that snapped the big man's head back. He went down to his knees, then toppled over on the grass.

Jim staggered back, his jaw hanging as he gasped for breath, waiting for Ives to rise.

"Let him go, Locklin," John Shippey said. "He's whipped." Then he added, "I never thought I'd see the day!"

Seated in the kitchen, Army bathed Locklin's face, tenderly wiping the blood from his features. "You've got some bad cuts," she protested.

"They'll heal," he said. "They always did before."

Pike was explaining the situation to Shippey. He had gotten George Locklin's letters from a saddlebag, and showed them to the rancher. "Those were writ by no man who thought of sellin'!" Pike insisted.

Locklin pushed Army's hands gently aside. He got to his feet, staggering a little. His big hands were swollen and battered. "Shippey, I won't get into town in time. It would be a favor if you'd ride in and hold Burt an' Castle until I get there. Nearly Pike will ride with you."

"Where you goin'?" Pike demanded.

"I've had a thought, and if I'm right we'll have our killer." John Shippey nodded his head. "I'll do my best." He turned suddenly to Pike. "Where'd you get a name like that?"

"Wal, it was like this here, Mr. Shippey. My folks was named Pike. We headed west from Kentucky for Missouri. Bein' named Pike, we figured to live in Pike County, and I was to be born there. Well, we didn't make it. We had to stop some miles short, so they named me for it. Nearly Pike."

Army was looking at Locklin, an odd light in her eyes, a look of something close to fear. Women, Jim reflected, would never understand a man's fighting.

Ives got slowly to his feet, staggered a little, then stood erect. His face was a mask of blood and dirt. He leaned against his horse for a moment, then hoisted himself into the saddle. He said nothing until he had gathered the reins. "You're a hard man, Locklin," he said grudgingly, "I reckon I bit off more'n I could chaw."

Locklin watched him go, then turned to his horse, which Pike had saddled and ready. Army came to him. "Don't go, Jim! I'm afraid! And you're in no shape to go!"

He tried to smile, but his face was too swollen. He leaned over and put a hand on her shoulder. "You ride to town with them. Stay close to Pike. This is something I must do."

Jim Locklin rode toward Antelope Valley, then took a dim trail up to the bench. He rode through the pines, his face throbbing with every hoof-beat, his ribs aching from the bruises. His head ached and the sun was hot. At Butler Creek he dropped on his face and drank deep of the clear, cold mountain water. Then he bathed his face with it.

Rising, he glimpsed the tracks of two people across the narrow stream. Crossing on scattered rocks in the stream-bed he studied the tracks with care. Some were fresh, yet others were older. Obviously, whoever they were, they had met here several times. Some cowhand and his girl, no doubt.

He went back across the stream to his horse but as he started to mount the combination of sun and the fighting proved too much. He backed up and sat down on the grass. Then he dragged himself back into the shade and slept.

He awakened suddenly. A glance at the sun told him he had slept for all of an hour, yet despite the fact that his head still throbbed, he felt better. Later, he cut the tracks of one rider, heading toward Horse Heaven. The tracks were several days old.

He turned down into the canyon of the Savory, and almost at once was enclosed by towering walls, and the sound of the stream rose in volume. Then the canyon widened, and before him was a sandy shelf strewn with the gray bones of ancient trees. Beyond it, the cave.

Swinging down, he leaned against the saddle to still the momentary dizziness that beset him. Then he walked up to the cave.

He stopped then, quite abruptly, his mouth dry but his

brain sharply alert. He was looking into the peculiar white-gray eyes of Chance Varrow!

There was a taunting triumph in Varrow's eyes. "Took you long enough to get here. Long enough so I could beat you to it. Now you can die the way your brother died. Funny, you blaming Reed Castle. He had the idea, all right, but we beat him to it."

"You killed George?" Even as he spoke he was thinking less of what he was saying and more of his own swollen, battered hands and the gun-slick deftness of the man he faced.

"Sure! At least I finished him off. He was already down and crippled. Reed wanted that ranch, all right, and was trying to work out some way of gettin' it. Well, we wasted no time.

"He could have the ranch, because we knew of that silver strike he'd made, near Bald Mountain. We gambled on that, and now we've won."

"Are you sure?"

"Why not? Nobody knows I'm in this but Reed Castle, and he wouldn't talk. If he did nobody would believe him. Your coming upset things but that's ended now."

Locklin's mind was working swiftly. Who did he mean by "we"? How had Varrow known he would be coming to the cave?

Ives? Probably.

But why, in all this time, had they not taken possession of the silver strike, sold it, and skipped? The reason was obvious—they didn't know where it was!

"You're not killing me, Varrow. It's not in the cards, no more than your friend Ives could whip me. It's you who will die here in this cave, Varrow, right here on this sand.

"You've wasted your time and your killing. You've never laid hands on an ounce of that silver because you don't know where it is.

"I know where it is," he lied, "and if I die you will never get it. Why? Because nobody else knows, nobody at all!"

"I'm going to kill you, all right," Varrow's face was tight and cruel. "I'll gamble on finding the silver."

Locklin swayed on his feet, suddenly weak. "A thousand

have looked for it, and nobody found it until George, and he had a clue. He knew something nobody else knew. The same thing he passed on to me."

At the first sign of faintness Chance Varrow's hand dropped to his gun. Suddenly Locklin's knees buckled and he went to the sand. Then he sagged back on his heels. "Sorry, Varrow, I'm in pret—ty bad—" he lifted a trembling hand to his brow, yet even as the hand seemed to touch his face, it darted like a striking snake, spraying sand in Varrow's face!

The gunman sprang back, one hand clawing at his eyes, the other reaching for his gun. His gun came clear, but the moment's respite was all Locklin needed. He got his clumsy fingers on his own gun, swung it up, steadied it with the other hand, and fired!

Varrow's gun roared, but, blinded by the sand, he missed.

Locklin's bullet, at point-blank range, caught Varrow in the diaphragm, striking up and in. Varrow tried to swing his gun, but Locklin fired a second time, then a third.

Chance Varrow crumpled into the sand, his fingers relaxing their grip on the gun.

The gunshots echoed in the canyon and there was an acrid smell of gunpowder mingled with dusty dampness. Then the echoes died, and there was only the soft chuckling of water over stones.

Dusk was blending the shadows in the streets of Toiyabe when Jim Locklin cantered down the street and drew up at the hotel door. Pike rushed out and grabbed his stirrup leather. "You all right, boy? I been out of my skull with worry."

"Where are they, Pike?"

"Inside. What took you so long?"

"A bit of trouble." All eyes turned to him as he entered. Castle's looked pale, angry, and uneasy; those of Creighton Burt, John Shippey, and Fish Creek Burns indicated only sharp interest. Armorel Locklin stared at him, her eyes showing her anxiety. Patch, looking surly, sat behind her.

Locklin leaned his hands on the table. "Castle, I had you wrong. You are a thief, but you are not a murderer."

"I bought that ranch!" Castle protested. "Here's my bill of sale!"

"An obvious forgery. The trouble was, you had never actually seen my brother's signature. You didn't worry because nobody else had, either. I have several letters signed by him, and I also have his will. The will was written as he was dying, with the knowledge that he was dying, and he leaves the ranch and all property to me, including the mine on Bald Mountain."

"What about this young woman? She was his wife."

"That's just it," Jim's eyes turned to Army. "She never was his wife."

"I married them," Burt said quietly, "right in my own office."

"The marriage wasn't valid, because she was still married to Chance Varrow."

"What? Are you sure?"

"I am sure. The two of them were teamed up, trimming suckers out in Frisco, and when Reed came to town flashing money around and talking big about his ranch and mining interests, they latched onto him.

"Army came over here to marry him, then found out he had lied, and backed out. Chance had come along to enforce her claim, and he got wind of George's silver strike.

"They let Reed Castle keep the ranch to quiet him down." Locklin drew a deep breath. He was tired, very tired. He wanted this over, he wanted to be away from here. "She has takin' ways, this girl does, and I nigh fell for her myself. George left me a note telling me all about it.

"She found him alone and lonesome, buttered him up some, let him think he was saving her from Castle, and then, after they left town, she shot him in the back.

"That back shot puzzled me, for George was touchy about anybody coming up behind him. I couldn't see a man getting such a chance, but a woman might. As she shot him, Chance came out of the woods to finish him, but George got away.

"Varrow had to wait until daylight to pick up the trail, and by that time George had left his horse and crawled into the cave. His legs were paralyzed, but he wrote the details, then stuffed his notes, his will, what else he had, into a tin box he kept there.

"On that sandstone he scratched the old L Bar brand that would mean nothing to anybody but us."

"Where's Varrow, then?" Shippey demanded. "Let's get the sheriff and round him up."

Army's eyes were on Jim, wide and empty. She knew, and he could see that she knew.

"He was waiting for me at the cave. I left him there."

Jim dropped the notes and the will on the table before Burt. "There it is. There was enough to hang Varrow, and enough to send Castle away for a good long stretch."

Burt glanced at Patch. "Where does he fit in?"

"She my half-sister," Patch said sullenly. "She no good. Some white man bad, some Indian bad. She no good."

Locklin looked over at Patch, liking what he saw. "You want a job? A permanent job?"

"Uh-huh. I work good."

Army's eyes were sullen with hatred. Having them know she was a 'breed bothered her more than being accused of murder. Jim looked at her, marveling. When would people realize it wasn't race that mattered, but quality and integrity?

"How'd you work it out?" Burt wondered.

"The first thing was the back shot; then George's guns were gone. Later, I saw them hanging on a nail in her cabin. George's holsters and belt with his name carved into them were left; only his guns were taken.

"George took those guns off for nobody, and the holsters in the cabin weren't his. That started me on the right track.

"Then I found tracks where she and Varrow had been meeting over on Butler Creek. My head was aching so bad I could scarcely think; then it dawned on me where I'd seen her tracks before. Varrow's I did not know.

"My brother had seen her talking to Varrow one time, but did not want to believe there was anything between them."

Locklin got to his feet. "That winds it up." He looked over at Castle. "I'm moving onto the Antelope Valley place tomorrow. All your personal effects will be sent to town."

The door opened behind them, and a short, heavy man stepped into the door. "I'm Jacob Carver, of Ellsworth, Kansas. I'm holding six hundred head of cattle outside of town, but I hear you folks got this country closed up. Is that right?"

Shippey started to speak but Locklin interrupted. "No, of course not. There's some unused range up in Grass Valley, northwest of here. As long as a man is honest and a good neighbor we've room for him. Glad to have you."

As Carver left Locklin glanced at Shippey. "He's a good man. I knew his brand back in Kansas. This country can use his kind."

Locklin left followed by Pike. Fish Creek Burns glanced after him, then said, glancing from Shippey to Burt, "Things are clearin' up around here, and she looks like fair weather ahead."

He stood up. "Looks like we've got a new pair of pants in the saddle. It surely does!"

THE GHOSTS
OF BUCKSKIN RUN

F OR TWO DAYS they had seen no other traveler, not
even a solitary cowhand or an Indian. There had been
the usual stops to change teams, an overnight layover at
Weston's ranch, but no other break in the monotony of the
journey.

There was no comfort in the west-bound stage. The four
passengers alternately dozed or stared miserably at the un-
changing desert, dancing with heat waves.

No breeze sent a shaft of coolness through the afternoon's
heavy heat. Aloma Day, bound for Cordova, a tiny cowtown
thirty miles further along the trail, felt stifled and unhappy.
Her heavy dress was hot, and she knew her hair "looked a
fright."

The jolting of the heavy coach bouncing over the rocky,
ungraded road had settled a thin mantle of dust over her
clothes and skin. The handkerchief with which she occasionally touched her cheeks and brow had long since become
merely a miserable wad of damp cloth.

Across from her Em Shipton, proprietor of Cordova's
rooming and boarding establishment, perspired, fanned, and
dozed. Occasionally she glanced with exasperation at Aloma's
trim figure, for to her the girl seemed unreasonably cool and
immaculate. Em Shipton resembled a barrel with ruffles.

Mark Brewer, cattle buyer, touched his mustache thoughtfully and looked again at the girl in the opposite corner of
the stage. She was, he decided, almost beautiful. Possibly her
mouth was a trifle wide, but her lips were lovely, and she
laughed easily.

"I hope," he ventured suddenly, "you decide to stay with

us, Miss Day. I am sure the people of Cordova will do all they can to make your visit comfortable."

"Oh, but I shall stay! I am going to make my home there."

"Oh? You have relatives there?"

"No," she smiled, "I am to be married there."

The smile left his eyes, yet hovered politely about his lips. "I see. No doubt I know the lucky fellow. Cordova is not a large town."

Loma hesitated. The assurance with which she decided upon this trip had faded with the miles. It had been a long time since she had seen Rod Morgan, and the least she could have done was to await a reply from him. Yet there was no place in which to wait. Her aunt had died, and they had no friends in Richmond. She had money now for the trip. Six weeks or a month later she might have used it all. Her decision had been instantly made, but the closer she came to Cordova the more uncertain she felt.

She looked at Brewer. "Then you probably know him. His name is Roderick Morgan."

Em Shipton stiffened, and Mark Brewer's lips tightened. They exchanged a quick, astonished glance. Alarmed at their reaction, Loma glanced quickly from one to the other.

"What's the matter? Is something wrong?"

"Wrong?" Em Shipton had never been tactful. "I should say there is! Rod Morgan is an insufferable person! What can you be thinking of to come all this way to marry a man like that?"

"Please, Em," Brewer interrupted. "Remember, you are speaking of Miss Day's fiancé. Of course, I must admit it is something of a shock. How long since you have seen him, Miss Day?"

"Two years." She felt faint, frightened. What was wrong? What had Rod done? Why did they—

All through her aunt's long illness, Rod's love for her had been the rock to which she clung, it had been the one solid thing in a crumbling world. He had always been the one to whom she knew she could turn.

"That explains it, then," Brewer said, sympathetically. "A

lot can happen in two years. You haven't been told, I presume, of the murders in Buckskin Run?"

"No. What is Buckskin Run?"

"It's a stream, you know. Locally, it is the term used to designate the canyon through which the stream runs, as well as the stream itself. The stream is clear and cold, and it heads far back in the mountains, but the canyon is rather a strange, mysterious sort of place, which all decent people avoid like the plague. For years the place has been considered haunted, and there are unexplained graves in the canyon. Men have died there under unexplained circumstances. Then Rod Morgan moved into the canyon and built a cabin there."

"You—you spoke of murders?"

"Yes, I certainly did. About a year ago Morgan had trouble with a man named Ad Tolbert. A few days later a cowhand found Tolbert's body not far from Morgan's cabin. He had been shot in the back."

"And that was only one of them!" Em Shipton declared. "Tell her about the pack peddler."

"His name was Ned Weisl. He was a harmless old fellow who had been peddling around the country for years. On every trip he went into Buckskin Run, and that seemed strange, because until Morgan moved there nobody lived in the Run country. He had some wild story he told about gold in Buckskin Run, some gold buried there. About a month ago they found his body, too. And he had been shot in the back."

"You mark my words!" Em Shipton declared. "That Rod Morgan's behind it all!"

The fourth passenger, a bearded man, spoke for the first time, "It appears to me that you're condemning this young man without much reason. Has anybody seen him shoot anybody?"

"Who would go into that awful place? Everybody knows it's haunted. We warned young Morgan about it, but he was too smart, a know-it-all. He said all the talk about ghosts was silly, and even if there were ghosts he'd make them feel at home!

"We thought it was strange, him going into that dark,

lonely place! No wonder. He's deep, he is! With a sight of crime behind him, too!"

"That's not true!" Loma said. "I've known Rod Morgan for years. There isn't a nicer boy anywhere."

Em Shipton's features stiffened with anger. A dictator in her own little world, she resented any contradiction of her opinions.

"I reckon, young lady, you've a lot to learn, and you'll learn it soon, mark my words!"

"There is something to what Mrs. Shipton says," Brewer commented. "Morgan does have a bad reputation around Cordova. He was offered a good riding job by Henry Childs when he first arrived, but he refused it. Childs is a pioneer, and the wealthiest and most respected man in the country. When a drifter like Morgan refused such a job it aroused suspicion. Why would a man want to live in that canyon alone, when he could have a good job with Childs?"

"Maybe he simply wants to be independent. Maybe he wants to build his own ranch," the bearded man suggested. "A man never gets anywhere working for the other man."

Mark Brewer ignored the comment. "That canyon has always had an evil reputation. Vanishing wagon trains, mysterious deaths, and even the Indians avoid the place."

He paused. "You've only one life to live, Miss Day, so why don't you wait a few days and make some inquiries before you commit yourself? After all, you do admit you haven't seen the man for two years."

Aloma Day stared out over the desert. She was angry, but she was frightened, also. What was she getting into? She knew Rod, but two years is a long time, and people change. So much could have happened.

He had gone west to earn money so they could be married, and it seemed unlikely he would think of building a home for her in a haunted valley. He was, she knew, inclined to be hotheaded and impulsive.

But *murder*? How could she believe that of him?

"It doesn't make a man a murderer because he lives in a nice little valley like Buckskin Run," the bearded man said. "You make your inquiries, ma'am, that's a sensible suggestion, but don't take nobody's word on a man on evidence like that. Buckskin Run is a pretty little valley."

Mark Brewer gave the man his full attention for the first time. "What do you know about Buckskin Run? Everybody agrees it's a dangerous place."

"Nonsense! I've been through it more than once. I went through that valley years ago, before your man Childs was even out here.

"Pioneer, is he? I never heard of him. There wasn't a ranch in the country when I first rode in here. As far as Indians are concerned, Buckskin Run was medicine ground. That's why they never went there."

"How do you explain the things that have happened there?"

"I don't explain 'em. There's been killings all over the West, and will be as long as there's bad men left. There were white men around when I first came in here, renegades most of 'em, but nobody ever heard any talk of haunts or the like. Men like Tarran Kopp camped in there many's the time!"

"You were here," Brewer asked, "when Tarran Kopp was around?"

"Knowed him well. I was through this here country before he ever seen it. Came through with Kit Carson the first time, and he was the one named it Buckskin Run. Favorite camp ground for Kit, that's what it was.

"My name's Jed Blue, and my feet made trails all over this country. I don't know this man Morgan, but if he's had the sense to settle in Buckskin Run he's smart. That's the best growing land around here!"

Em Shipton glared at Jed Blue. "A lot you know about it! That valley is a wicked place! It's haunted, and everybody from Cordova to Santa Fe knows it. What about the wagon trains that went into it and disappeared?

"What about the graves? Three men buried side by each, and what does it say on their markers? 'No visible cause of death on these bodies.'"

The Concord rumbled through a dry wash, then mounted the opposite bank with a jerk, bumped over a rock in the trail, and slowed to climb a steep, winding grade.

Talk died as suddenly as it had begun, and Loma clenched

her hands in her lap, fighting back the wave of panic that mounted within her.

If Rod had become what they said, what would she do? What *could* she do? Her money was almost gone, and she would be fortunate if she had enough to last a week. Yet, what would have happened had she remained in the East? To be without money in one place was as bad as another.

Yet, despite the assurance with which they spoke, she could not believe Rod was a murderer. Remembering his fine, clean-cut face, his clear, dark eyes, and his flashing smile, she could not accept what they said.

The Concord groaned to the top of the grade, and the six horses swung wide around a curve and straightened out, running faster and faster.

Suddenly there was a shot, a sharp yell, and the stage made a swerving stop so abruptly that Loma was thrown into Em Shipton's lap. Recovering, she peered out of the window.

A man lay flat in the middle of the trail, blood staining the back of his vest. Beside his right hand lay a six-shooter.

To the left of the road were four riders, sitting their horses with hands uplifted. Facing the four from the right side of the road was a young man with dark, wavy hair blowing in the wind. He wore badly worn jeans, scuffed star boots and a black and white checkered shirt. There was an empty holster on his hip, and he held two guns in his hands.

"Now pick up your man and get out of here! You came hunting it, and you found it."

Loma stifled a cry. "Rod!" she gasped. "Rod Morgan!"

Her voice was low, but Jed Blue overheard. "Is that your man?" he asked.

She nodded, unable to speak. It was true then, she thought. He *was* a killer! He had just shot that man.

One of the horsemen caught the riderless horse and two of the others dismounted to load the body across the saddle. The other man sat very still, holding his hand on the pommel of his saddle.

As the other riders remounted he said, "Well, this is one you won't bury in Buckskin Run!"

"Get going!" Morgan said. "And keep a civil tongue in

your head, Jeff. I've no use for you or any of your rustling, dry-gulching crowd."

Loma Day drew back into the stage, her hands to her face. Horror filled her being. That limp, still body! Rod Morgan had killed him!

"Well!" Em Shipton said triumphantly. "What did we tell you?"

"It's too bad you had to see this," Brewer said. "I'm sorry, ma'am."

"That's a right handy young feller!" Blue said admiringly. "Looks to me like you picked you a good one, ma'am. Stood off the five of them, he did, and I never seen it done better. Any one of them would have killed him had they the chance, but he didn't even disarm them. And they wanted no part of him!"

The stage started to roll.

"Hey?" Blue caught at Loma's arm. "Ain't you even goin' to call to him? Ain't you goin' to let him know you're here?"

"No! Don't tell him! Please, don't!"

Blue leaned back, shaking his head admiringly. "Handy, right handy! That gent who was down in the road was drilled plumb center!"

Loma did not hear him. Rod! Her Rod! A *killer*!

———

As THE STAGE swung back into the road and pulled away, Rod Morgan stooped and picked up the dead man's six-shooter. No use wasting a good gun, and if things went on as they had begun he would have need of it.

He walked back to where his gray mustang was tethered, and swung into the saddle. A brief glance around and he started back up the canyon. There was so much to do, and so little time.

Perhaps he had been wrong to oppose the ingrained superstition and suspicion of the Cordova country, but working as a cowhand would never allow him to save enough to support a wife or build a home. Buckskin Run, from the moment he had first glimpsed it, had seemed the epitome of all he had dreamed.

The stream plunged happily over the stones, falling in a series of miniature cascades and rapids into a wide basin surrounded by towering cliffs. It flowed out of that basin and through a wide meadow, several hundred acres of good grassland. High cliffs bordered the area on all sides, and there were clumps of aspen and spruce.

Below the first meadow lay a long valley also bounded by sheer cliffs, a valley at least a half-mile wide that narrowed suddenly into a bottleneck that spilled the stream into another series of small rapids before it swung into the timbered land bordering the desert.

When Rod Morgan had found Buckskin Run there had been no tracks of either cattle or horses. Without asking questions, he chose a cabin site near the entrance and went to work. Before he rode out to Cordova on his first trip to town his cabin was built, his corrals ready.

In Cordova he ran into trouble with Em Shipton.

Em's entire life was ruled by prejudice and superstition. She had come to Cordova from the hills of West Virginia by way of Council Bluffs and Santa Fe. In the Iowa town she married Josh Shipton, a teamster freighting over the Santa Fe Trail. She had already been a widow, her first husband dropping from sight after a blast of gun-fire with his brother-in-law.

Josh Shipton was more enduring, and also somewhat faster with a gun, than Em's previous spouse. He stood her nagging and suspicion for three months, stood the borrowing and drunkenness of her brother for a few days longer. The two difficulties came to a head simultaneously. Josh packed up and left Em and, in a final dispute with her quarrelsome, pistol-ready brother, eliminated him from further interference in Em's marital or other affairs. But Josh kept on going.

Em Shipton had come to Cordova and started her rooming and boarding house while looking for a new husband. Her first choice, old Henry Childs himself, was a confirmed bachelor who came to eat once at her table. Wiser than most, he never came again.

She was fifteen years older and twenty pounds heavier than slim, handsome Rod Morgan, but he was her second choice.

"What you need," she told him, "is a good wife!"

Unaware of the direction of the conversation, Rod agreed that he did.

"Also," she said, "you must move away from that awful canyon. It's haunted!"

Rod laughed. "Sure, and I've seen no ghost, ma'am. Not a one. Never seen a prettier valley, either. No, I'm staying."

Em Shipton coupled her ignorance with assurance. Women were scarce in the West, and she had come to consider herself quite a catch. She had yet to learn that women were not *that* scarce.

"Well," she said definitely, "you can't expect me to go live in no valley like that."

Rod stared, mouth open in astonishment. "Who said anything—" He swallowed, trying to keep a straight face but failing. He stifled the laugh, but not the smile. "I'm sorry. I like living there, and, as for a wife, I've plans of my own."

Em might have forgiven the plans, but she could never forgive that single, startled instant when Rod realized that Em Shipton actually had plans for him herself, or the way he smiled at the idea.

That was only the beginning of the trouble. Rod Morgan had walked along to the Gem Saloon, had a drink, and been offered a job by Jake Sarran, Henry Childs's foreman. He refused it.

"Better take it, Morgan," Sarran advised, "if you plan to stay in this country. We don't like loose, unattached riders drifting around."

"I'm not drifting around. I own my own place on Buckskin Run."

"I know," Sarran admitted, "but nobody stays there long. Why not take a good job when you can get it?"

"Because I simply don't want a job. I'll be staying at Buckskin Run." As he turned away a thought struck him. "And you can tell whoever it is who wants me out of there that I've come to stay."

Jake Sarran put his glass down hard, but whatever he intended to say went unspoken. Rod left the saloon, his brow furrowed with thought and some worry. On this first visit to town he had come to realize that his presence at Buckskin Run was disturbing to someone.

For a week he kept busy on the ranch, then he rode south, hired a couple of hands, and drove in three hundred head of whiteface cattle. With grass and water they would not stray, and there was no better grass and water than that in Buckskin Run. He let the hands go.

But the thought worried him. Why, with all that good pasture and water, had Buckskin Run not been settled?

When next he rode into Cordova he found people avoiding him. Yet he was undisturbed. Many communities were clannish and shy about accepting strangers. Once they got acquainted it would be different. Yet he had violated one of their taboos.

It was not until he started to mount his horse that he discovered his troubles were not to stop with being ignored. A sack of flour tied behind his saddle had been cut open, and most of the flour had spilled on the ground.

Angered, he turned to face the grins of the men seated along the walk. One of them, Bob Carr, a long, rangy rider from Henry Childs's Block C, had a smudge of white near his shirt pocket, and another smudge near his right-hand pants pocket, the sort of smear that might have come from a man's knife if he had cut a flour-sack open, then shoved the knife back in his pocket.

Rod had stepped up on the walk. "How'd you get that white smudge on your pocket?"

The rider looked quickly down, then, his face flushing, he looked up. "How do you think?" he said.

Rod hit him. He threw his fist from where it was, at his belt, threw it short and hard into the long rider's solar plexus.

Bob Carr had not expected to be hit. The blow was sudden, explosive, and knocked out every bit of wind he had.

"Get him, Bob!" somebody shouted, but as Bob opened his mouth to gasp for air, Rod Morgan broke his jaw with a right.

Rod Morgan turned, and mounted his horse. From the saddle he looked back. "I didn't come looking for trouble, and I am not asking for it. I'm a quiet man, minding my own affairs."

Yet when he rode out of town he knew he had opened a feud with the Block C. It was trouble he did not want, and for which he had no time, but whether he liked it or not he had a fight on his hands.

When he returned to his cabin a few days later, after checking some cattle in the upper canyon, there was a notice nailed to his door to get out and stay out. Then his cabin was set afire and much of his gear burned.

Ad Tolbert picked a fight with him and got soundly whipped, but a few days later Tolbert was murdered in Buckskin Run. Rod Morgan took to packing a gun wherever he went.

As is the case with any person who lives alone, or is different, stories were circulated about him, and he became suspect to many people who did not know him and had never so much as seen him. Behind it there seemed to be some malignant influence, but he had no idea who or what was directing it.

Two things happened at once. A letter came from Aloma Day, and Ned Weisl came into the canyon. He had hesitated to suggest that Loma come west with the situation unsettled as it was, yet from her letter he understood what her situation must be. He had written, explaining what he could and inviting her to come.

Weisl was a strange little man. Strange, yet also charming and interesting. From the first he and Rod hit it off well, and so he told Rod about the gold.

"Three men came west together," Weisl explained. "Somewhere out in Nevada they struck it rich. The story was they had a hundred and twenty thousand in gold when they started back. They built a special wagon with a false bottom in it, where they hid the gold. Then, with three wagons in all, they headed east.

"They got as far as Buckskin Run, and there, according to the story, Tarran Kopp and his gang hit them. The three men were killed, and that was the end of it, only there was another story. With gold there nearly always is.

"One of Kopp's gang was a friend of mine years later, and when asked about it he claimed they had killed nobody in Buckskin Run, nor had they stolen any gold. At the time it all took place they were in Mexico, and he showed me an old newspaper story to prove it."

"So what became of the gold? And who did kill the people in Buckskin Run?"

"Nobody knows who killed them or how. Nobody knows what became of the gold, either. A hundred and twenty thousand in gold isn't the easiest thing to carry around in a country where people are inclined to be curious. According to the prices at the time, that would be right around three hundred pounds of gold. There are people who were right interested in that gold who claim it never left Buckskin Run!

"There's others who declare nobody went into the canyon from the lower end, and nobody knows who buried the three who died there. Markers were set over the graves, and on each one those words 'No visible mark of death on these bodies.'"

"What do you think?"

"That," Weisl said, smiling with puckish humor, "is another question. I've an idea, but it's a fantastic one. You hold the land now. Will you let me look around? I will give you one-third of whatever I find."

"Make it half?"

Weisl shrugged. "Why not? There will be enough for both."

Ned Weisl did not return to the cabin, so Rod had gone looking for him. He did not distrust the little man, but he was worried.

He found Ned Weisl—dead. He had been shot in the back.

Rod Morgan knew they believed him guilty of the murder, as well as of the killing of Ad Tolbert. No one accused him, although veiled references were made. Only today, on the trail, had he been directly accused.

He had ridden through the bottleneck and down to the stage trail, intending to ask the driver to let him know when

Loma arrived, although she could scarcely have had his letter by now.

The five riders had been about to enter the bottleneck. Jeff Cordell was leading, and one of the men with him was Reuben Hart, who had the name of being a bad man with a gun. He was the man Morgan watched.

"Howdy," he said.

"We're hunting strays," Cordell said. "We thought we'd come in and look you over."

"Are you asking me or telling me?"

"We're tellin' you. We don't need to ask."

"Then you've gone as far as you go. No cattle have come in here but my own. I've fenced the neck, so nothing can come in or out unless they open the gate. Any time you want a look around, just come and ask me when I'm home."

"We're going in now," Cordell said, "and if you're smart you'll stand aside."

"I'm not smart," Rod Morgan said, waiting. Inside he was on edge, poised for trouble. "I'm the kind of man who would make you ride in over at least three dead bodies. You decide if what you're doing is worth it."

Cordell hesitated. He was no fool, and Rod Morgan had already proved a surprise to both Bob Carr and Ad Tolbert. Cordell was a poker player, and Rod Morgan looked like he was holding a pat hand. He believed he could tell when a man was bluffing, and he did not believe Morgan was. He was also aware that if anybody died it was almost sure to be him.

"Let me take him." Reuben Hart shoved his horse to the fore. "I've never liked you, Morgan, and I believe you're bluffing, and I believe you're yellow!"

Reuben went for his gun as he spoke, and Reuben was a fast man.

Cordell and the others were cowhands, not gunfighters. They could handle their guns, but were not in the class of Reuben or Dally Hart.

Very quickly they realized they were not in the class of Rod Morgan, either, for he had drawn and fired so fast that his bullet hit Reuben even as that gunman's pistol cleared leather.

Reuben slid from the saddle and sprawled on the ground, and Rod Morgan was looking over his pistol at them.

Jeff Cordell noticed another thing. Morgan's gray mustang stood rock still when Morgan fired, and he knew his own bronc would not do that. Jeff Cordell put both hands on the pommel of the saddle. For a man with a horse like that and a drawn pistol, killing the rest of them would be like shooting ducks in a barrel.

The arrival of the stage saved their faces, and they loaded Hart into the saddle and headed for the home ranch.

Andy Shank expressed an opinion they were all beginning to share. "You know," Shank said, when they had ridden a couple of miles, "I believe that gent intends to stay."

Nobody said anything but Andy was not easily squelched. "Anyway," he added, "he seemed right serious about it."

But Andy had never liked Reuben Hart, anyway.

"He'll stay." Cordell's tone was grim. "Reub was never the gun-hand Dally is, and Dally will be riding to Buckskin Run."

Back on the ranch, Rod Morgan stripped the saddle from the gray and turned it into the corral. Carrying the saddle into the log barn, he threw it over a rail. Alone in the barn, he stood for a moment in the shadowed stillness.

He had killed a man.

It was not something he liked to think about. There had been no need to look his place over for strays. It was fenced at the opening and there was nowhere else a steer could get into the canyon. Nor did the Block C have any cattle running in the area. It was purely a trouble-making venture. They knew it, and so did he.

His cabin was silent. He stood inside the door and looked around. He had built well. It had four rooms, plank floors, good, solid, squared-off logs, and windows with a view.

Would Loma like it? Would she like Buckskin Run? Or would she be afraid?

Standing in the open door he looked back toward the bottleneck, a good six hundred yards away. Green grass rolled under the slight wind, and the run, about fifty yards from the house, could be plainly heard. The high rock walls made twilight come early, but the canyon was beautiful in any light.

He closed the door and began preparing his supper. He knew what would come now, and there was nothing he could do to prevent it but run, and he would not, he could not do that. All he had was here. His hopes, his dreams, all the money he had been able to get together, all his hard work.

The people he had talked to had told him about the Harts, watching his expression as they told him. Now that he had killed Reuben, there was no way he could avoid trouble with Dally. He hoped that would end it. And it surely would, for one or both of them.

The Block C had been against him from the start, and he had no idea why. Were they always so clannish against strangers? Were they offended by his refusing a job?

His thoughts returned to his talk with Ned Weisl. He had liked the little man, but he had brought questions. Who *had* killed the three men from Nevada? What had become of their wagons? What had become of their gold? And what became of the killers themselves?

A few things he had learned. Several of the stories about him, other than those from the malicious tongue of Em Shipton, had come from the Block C, apparently from Henry Childs, a man he had never seen. He was also aware that Mark Brewer wanted him off Buckskin Run. Brewer had even gone so far as to offer him a nice little ranch some distance from the Run, and for a very reasonable price.

He fixed the barest of meals and then sat alone to eat it, thinking of Loma. Where was she now? Had she received his letter? Would she come? Dared he bring her into all this? How would she react to what happened today, for example? In the world from which she came, the killing of one man by another was a crime, and even when done in self-defense it was somehow considered reprehensible. Yet soon all that would be over, and there would be peace on Buckskin Run. Or so he hoped.

His thoughts returned to the stories. Was there gold buried here? If so, he hoped it would soon be found, so people would stop talking about it and looking for it.

When morning came again he saddled the gray and rode to the upper end of the canyon, where a dark pool of water invited the flow down from the higher mountains. He had noticed the graves there before this, but had had no time to examine them. Yet they were tangible evidence that something had happened here in Buckskin Run.

Why had Weisl been murdered? Merely to cause trouble for him? That was ridiculous. Or was the peddler dangerously close to a secret no one wanted revealed?

What fantastic idea had Weisl had, there at the end? Rod Morgan wished, desperately, that he knew. That secret might lead to the solving of the mysteries, and an end to them.

He stepped down from the gray and walked over to the three graves. Side by side, and, what he had not realized, each was marked with the name of the man who lay there. Somehow he had gotten the impression their names were unknown.

NAT TENEDOU—HARRY KIDD—JOHN COONEY

"Well? What do you make of it?"

Startled, he looked toward the voice and saw a man seated on a rock beyond the pool, a long, lean man with a red mustache. To have reached that place unheard he must have moved like a ghost. Rod was sure he had not been there when he dismounted from his horse.

"Who are you? Where did you come from?"

The man jerked a thumb back toward the cliffs. "Come down from up yonder. I always intended to have a good look at this place, but I heerd you wasn't exactly welcoming strangers."

He indicated the graves. "Knowed that Kidd. Big man. Powerful. Don't do a man no good to be strong when a bullet hits him, I reckon."

"What are you doing here?"

The man grinned slyly. "Same as you. Lookin' for that there gold. I doubt she was ever taken out of this canyon. And those wagons? Three big wagons. I seen 'em."

"You seem to know a lot about this."

"Son, them days there wasn't much went on Josh Shipton didn't know."

"Josh Shipton? You're Josh Shipton?"

"I should reckon. Never heard of another. What d'you know about Josh Shipton?"

"There's a woman in town says she was married to you."

He sprang up so suddenly he almost slipped into the pool. "*Em?* You mean Em's here? Son, don't you go tellin' folks you seen me. Especially not her! That woman would be the death of a man! Nag, nag, nag! Mornin' until night." He spat, then squinted his eyes at Rod. "She married again? That's a marryin' woman, that one."

"Not yet, but I hear she has Henry Childs in mind."

"Childs? Reckon she'd think of him. She's money-hungry, that woman is." He chuckled suddenly. "Hee, hee! I reckon that would serve ol' Henry right! It surely would!"

"Do you know him?"

Shipton's expression changed. "Me? No, I don't know him. Heard of him." Then he added, "He ain't safe to know."

"He's just a rancher, isn't he?"

Shipton shrugged. "Maybe he is, maybe he isn't. Some folks get powerful unpleasant about those who ask questions."

Nothing was to be done with Shipton present, yet Rod was sure that somewhere in the vicinity of the basin he would find a clue to the mystery of Buckskin Run. Those wagons had to have gone somewhere, and it would have taken an army of men or many teams to hoist the wagons up the cliffs. That possibility seemed out of the question.

As for the run itself, those cascades could not be negotiated by a canoe, let alone three large wagons.

Mounting up, he waved a hand at Shipton and rode away. The man was a puzzle, but obviously knew more than he was letting on. Could he have been around at the time? It was possible.

By the time he arrived at the cabin he was sure of one thing. However those wagons had escaped, they had not come down this way. The wagons, he decided, were still there, and so was the gold.

Riding up to his cabin he swung down. Only then did he see the big, bearded man seated on the bench in front of the house.

"This looks like my day for visitors. Did you come with Shipton?"

"Shipton? You don't mean Josh is around? Now that does beat all! Wait until Em hears!"

"I promised I wouldn't mention it."

"Well, I surely won't. Any man who got away from that woman deserves his freedom, believe you me."

The man stood up. "My name's Jed Blue. I'm an old-timer here. Doubt if you heard of me, because I've been away for a spell. Trapped fur in this country. I come in with Carson, the first time."

"Had anything to eat?"

Blue glanced at the height of the sun. "Reckon it's gettin' on to time." He followed Morgan inside. "You've made a lot of enemies, son."

"I didn't ask for them."

"That was a neat gun job you did on Reuben Hart. Don't know's I ever saw it done better."

"You saw that? Where were you? On the stage?"

"I was. There were some other folks on it, too, including Em Shipton and a gent named Brewer. They'd been to Santa Fe, seems like." He glanced at Morgan. "There was a girl on that stage, too. Name of Loma Day."

"*Loma?* Here? But how—?"

"She said she'd come on without waiting for word from you. She had nothing back where she came from. My feelin' was she thought she'd better make the trip whilst she still had the money."

"But why didn't she say something? She must have seen me!"

Jed Blue was slicing some beef from a cold roast. "You got to think of her, and how it must've seemed. Women-folk are different than us, and she bein' from the East, and all.

"Em Shipton, she'd been tellin' her what a bad hombre you were and then she comes up when you've just killed a man.

"That killing seemed like proof of all they'd been saying

about you. She's down to Cordova now, and I figured I'd better break the news so you can plan on what to do."

He paused. "She may not welcome you with open arms."

"It can't be helped. I must see her!"

"You hold on. Just think about it a mite. In the first place, she's a mighty fetchin' young woman, and that Brewer may have some ideas of his own. He's a fine-lookin' man, and one who usually gets what he wants. You'd better set down and think this through before you go in there a foggin'.

"Also, you've got to remember there will be folks expecting you now. They know this girl has come out to see you. Em Shipton will tell ever'body in town. So they may just be waitin' for you, son. You've got to think about it."

Blue was silent for a moment and then he asked, "This here Brewer, now. Does he wear a gun? D' you know anything about him?"

"I never saw him with a gun, but I've only seen him once or twice."

"I was wondering. Reminds me somewhat of a man I knew one time, a long way back."

They were eating in silence when Rod suddenly looked up. "You didn't ride all the way out here just to tell me about Loma."

Jed Blue tipped back in his chair, his huge body dwarfing the table at which they sat. "Reckon I didn't, son. I was sort of lookin' over the lay of the land."

"In other words, you're gold hunting?"

Blue chuckled, plucking at his beard. "Right on the point, ain't you? I like that. I like a man who comes right out with it. So if I find it, what then?"

"You keep half."

Blue laughed. "You do speak out. What if I don't aim to give you none of it?"

Rod Morgan rested both hands on the table. He was not smiling. "Friend, I'm grateful for telling me my girl friend was in Cordova, but half of whatever you find is enough. The gold is on my land, but if you find it you keep half. You try to leave with all of it, and you'll have to shoot your way out."

Blue chuckled. "Of course, you might not find it so easy as

with Hart. I shuck a gun pretty good myself, and I've had a bit more experience." He cut off a slice of beef and placed it between two pieces of bread. "What you going to do with your half?"

"Buy cattle, stock this place, fix it up a mite, then hire a few hands."

Blue nodded approvingly. "Canny. Makes sense. Easy money is soon gone without a sensible plan." He looked up at Rod. "Don't want a partner, do you? I'd like to work into a setup like this, and I'm a top hand, even though I don't look it."

"I'd have to think about it," Rod said. He looked at the big man again, puzzled by something he could not define. There was more to this man than there seemed on the surface, but his impression was the man would be a square shooter. "It might be a good idea," he said, "but I wouldn't take any man in with me who didn't realize what he was getting into."

"Son," Blue said, "don't you pay that no mind. I've had wool in my teeth. I'm not one to hunt trouble, but I've stood alone many's the time. When I'm pushed I can back my play. You an' me together, we could show them a thing or two."

Rod shoved back his chair. "I'm riding to town now. Want to come along?"

Jed Blue picked his teeth with a straw. He shoved back his own chair. "Don't mind if I do," he said. "I reckon I might as well get acquainted."

As they passed through the bottleneck Blue gestured off toward the open country. "There's a passel of mavericks in the canyons and draws east of here. A couple of good men could build a herd real fast."

"That's a good way to get a chance to make hair bridles. You start that and they'd have us in a rockwalled garden."

"No," Blue said seriously, "most of this stock is over a year old and unbranded. It's for anybody. A few weeks of hard work and we could make a drive, sell out, and have some working capital."

They rode in silence, Rod preoccupied with thoughts of Loma. It had been two years since he had seen her, but now that she was near he was excited, eager to see her, but worried, too. He knew now that he wanted her more than anything in life, realizing how much he had stifled thoughts of her so he could build for their future. Now that she had come west, her mind had been poisoned against him, and she had seen him kill a man without knowing anything of what came before.

Cordova lay flat and still under a baking sun. The mountains drew back disdainfully from the desert town, leaving it to fry in its own sweat and dust. A spring wagon was receiving a load of supplies in front of the general store, and a half-dozen horses stood three-legged at the hitching rail of the Gem Saloon. Jed Blue glanced over at Rod.

"More than likely she'll be at Em Shipton's. It's about the only place a decent woman can stay. Want me to ride along?"

"Wait for me at the Gem, if you can stand their whiskey."

Turning the gray toward Em Shipton's, he felt all tight inside. He dismounted, stalling a little bit, afraid of what Loma might say. All his hopes, all his dreams were bound up in her. He walked up the slatted boardwalk and entered the boarding house.

Loma was standing at the end of the table in what seemed to be serious conversation with Mark Brewer.

"Rod! Oh, Rod!"

Yet even as he moved toward her he saw her eyes change as they fell to his gun.

He took her hands. "It has been a long time, too long."

Suddenly she seemed uncertain, she half turned from him. "Mark? Have you met Rod Morgan?"

"No, I'm afraid not." Brewer's voice was cool, but not unfriendly. "How are you, Morgan?"

Rod nodded. She had called him Mark. "Very well, thanks." His tone sounded less cordial than he intended.

"I am surprised to see you in town," Brewer commented. "You know, I suppose, that Dally Hart is gunning for you?"

"Is he?" Loma's hands had gone cold in his. She withdrew them gently. "But that isn't unusual in Cordova, is it? Hasn't someone been gunning for me ever since I settled in Buckskin Run? And I don't mean the Harts or any of the small fry."

"Just who do you mean?"

"If I knew that I'd go call on him and ask some questions. Now would you mind leaving us alone? I'd like to talk to Loma."

Mark smiled, but there was a taunting amusement in his eyes. "Now why should I leave you alone? Miss Day is to be my wife."

Rod felt as if he had been kicked in the stomach. His eyes turned, unbelievingly, to Loma's. Her eyes fell before his. Then she looked up.

"Rod, I want you to understand. I like you ever so much, but all this killing . . . I couldn't understand it, and Mark has been so kind. I hadn't seen you, and—"

"There's nothing to explain." He was in control again. "You are as bad as the rest of them. As for you, Brewer, you've done your work well. You've taken advantage of the fact that Loma doesn't understand the West, nor the situation here. You sneaked, connived, and probably lied."

"Don't try to bully me into a shooting, Morgan! I am not even wearing a gun."

Loma was coldly furious. "Rod Morgan! To think you would dare to speak like that! Mark hasn't lied. He has been honest and sincere. He told me not to believe all they said about you, but to wait and ask. He said I should see what men like Henry Childs thought of you, and—"

"Childs? Childs, did you say? Didn't you know it was Childs and the Block C who was fighting me?"

He looked over at Brewer. "You're welcome to her, Brewer. If she can go back on one man so easily, she will go back on another."

"If I was wearing a gun—"

"What then? If you like, I'll take mine off."

"I am not a cheap brawler. You had better go now. I think you have made Miss Day unhappy enough."

Rod Morgan turned sharply away, and started for the door. Behind him he half-heard a stifled cry as if she were calling out to him, but he did not turn.

He had just reached his horse when he saw Jed Blue. Without waiting for an explanation, he turned toward him, knowing what was about to happen.

"Son," Blue spoke quietly, "Dally Hart's over there. He says he'll shoot on sight."

"Let him! I'm in the mood for it! If he wants trouble, he sure picked the right time. I'm sick of being pushed around, and if I'm to have the name of a killer I might as well pay my dues."

"Watch yourself, son!" Blue said. "There may be more than one. I'll try to cover you, but keep your eyes open."

Rod Morgan started up the street, spurs jingling as he walked. Inside he was boiling, but he knew he must steady down, for Dally Hart was a dangerous man, much more so than his brother Reuben had been. Suddenly he found himself hating everything around him. He had come to the town a friendly stranger, asking no favors of anyone, and almost from the first he had faced dislike and even hatred. Someone, he was sure, was guiding the feeling against him, disclaiming the stories yet repeating them, and that person could be he who had killed both Tolbert and Weisl.

That person might also be the one who knew where the gold was buried, knew what had happened so long ago in Buckskin Run.

But who could possibly know? How could he know? He . . . or was it she?

At that instant Rod Morgan saw Dally Hart.

The gunman had been standing behind a horse; now he stepped into the open with his back to the sun, putting the full glare in Rod's eyes.

They were over a hundred yards apart, but Rod was walking swiftly. Sights and sounds were wiped from his world, and all he could see was the slim, tall figure with the high-crowned hat standing in the middle of the street.

Vaguely, he was aware that men had come from the stores and were lining the street, oblivious of the danger of ricocheting bullets. Dust arose in little puffs as he walked, and he could feel the heat of the sun on his face. His body seemed strangely light, but each foot seemed to fall hard to the ground as he walked.

He was going to kill this man. Suddenly all the hatred, the trouble and confusion seemed to center in the slim man with the taunting, challenging eyes and the hatchet face who was awaiting him.

He was sixty yards away, forty yards. Rod saw Dally's fingers spread a little. Thirty yards. The expression on Hart's face changed; his tongue touched his lips. Rod was walking fast, closing the distance.

Twenty yards, eighteen, sixteen—

There were men, he knew, who, proud of their marksmanship, preferred distance for their shooting, but as the distance grew less and less they became aware that at short range neither man was likely to miss. Luke Short, the Dodge City gunfighter, always crowded his foes, crowded them until they lost their poise and began to back up to get distance.

Fourteen yards—

Dally Hart's nerve broke and he went for his gun. Incredibly fast, and the gun lifted in a smooth, unbroken movement. It came level and flowered with sudden flame, then his own gun bucked in his hand, and bucked again.

Dally Hart wavered, then steadied. Something was wrong with his face. His gun came up and he fired. A blow struck Morgan. His legs went weak under him, and he fired again. Hart's face seemed to turn dark, then crimson, and the gunman toppled into the dust.

From somewhere behind him a gun bellowed and as from a great distance he heard Jed Blue saying, "That was one! Who will be the next to die?"

THERE WAS A rectangle of sunlight lying inside the cabin door, and beyond it Rod could see the green, waving grass of Buckskin Run. He could hear the muted sound of the stream as it boiled over the rocks, gathering force to charge the bottleneck.

He was home, in his own cabin. He turned his head. Everything was as he had last seen it, except for one thing. There was another bed across the room, a bed carefully made up.

The table was scrubbed clean, the room freshly swept. He wondered about that, wondered vaguely how long he had been here and who had brought him back.

In the midst of his wondering he fell asleep, and when he again opened his eyes it was dark beyond the door and a lamp glowed on the table. He could hear vague movements, a rustling as of garments, and he felt that if he lay still he would soon see whoever was in the room.

While he was waiting he fell asleep again, and when he awakened it was morning again and sunlight was shining through the doorway. Then he saw something else. Jed Blue was crouched near the window but well out of sight. The door was barred, and someone was moving about outside.

Rod started to lift himself up when he heard a voice he recognized as Josh Shipton's. "Halloo, in there? Anybody to home?"

Blue made no reply. It was grotesque to see the big man crouching in silence. What was he afraid of? What could Jed Blue possibly fear from Shipton? Yet it was obvious Blue did not wish to be seen.

After a while Jed Blue stood up and, standing first to one side and then to the other, peered out the window. After a careful look around, he unbarred the door. Rod hastily closed his eyes, then, after a bit, stirred on the bed and simulated awakening. When he opened his eyes the big, bearded man was standing over him.

"Coming out of it, are you?"

"What happened?"

"You killed Dally Hart, but he got two bullets into you. I was almighty busy for a few minutes, and had to pack you out of town before I could patch you up. You lost a sight of blood, and the trip back here didn't do you any good."

"You were in it, too, weren't you? I thought I heard you shoot."

"That Block C coyote Bob Carr tried to shoot you in the back. After he went down I had to hold a gun on the others whilst we rolled our tails out of town."

"How long have I been here?"

"A week or so. You were in a bad way."

"Any other trouble?"

"Some. Jake Sarran, that Block C ramrod, rode in here with a dozen hands. Said as soon as you could ride you were to get out, and they weren't warning you again."

"To Hell with that! I'm staying."

"Want a partner? My offer still stands."

"Why not? We're cut from the same leather, I think."

Rod was silent. He wanted to ask about Loma, but was ashamed to. He waited, hoping Blue would offer some hint as to what had happened to her. Was she married? Rod sighed, trying not to think of her. After all, she had thrown him over for Mark Brewer. Still, he had to make allowances. After all, she hadn't seen him in two years, then to hear nothing but bad about him, and then to see him kill another man—

His thoughts shifted to the vanished wagons and the gold, then to the strange actions of Jed Blue when Shipton came around.

Why had Blue not wished to be seen by Josh Shipton? Or had there been others outside, and Josh simply the bait to draw him out to be killed? It was possible.

Despite his curiosity he had no doubt there was a sensible explanation, and had no doubts about his new partner. After all, the man had saved his life, had gotten him out of town when they would certainly have either killed him or let him die. Few men would dare challenge the power of the Block C, and from the memory of the horses he had seen he knew the Block C had been out in force.

Lying there through the long day he tried to find an answer for the Block C's enmity for him; so much hatred could not stem from his original fight with Carr, nor even the shooting of Reuben Hart, which had been forced on him.

Behind it there had to be a reason, and he had a hunch the trouble stemmed from the man he had never seen—Henry Childs himself.

Hour after hour, as he lay in bed, he tried to find answers to the problem of the gold and the wagons. Three men had died and been buried, three wagons had vanished along with much gold and gear. It was not until the last day he was in bed that the idea came to him, an idea so fantastic that at first he could not believe it could be possible; yet the more he considered it, the more it seemed the only possible solution.

He was recovering rapidly, and when he could sit outside in the sun, even walk a little by favoring his bad leg, he could see many evidences of Jed Blue's work. Certainly the big man did not intend just to come along for the ride.

A comfortable bench had been built, encircling a large tree close to the house, a shady, comfortable place in which to sit. A new workbench stood near the log barn, and a parapet of stones had been built, fastened with some home-made mortar. This parapet faced the canyon entrance, and had loopholes for firing. It had been built, however, so it could not be used by anyone attacking the house, for a rifleman from the house could command both sides of it, because of the angle at which it was built.

A water-barrel had been moved into the house and kept full. Several steers had been slaughtered, and the meat jerked. It was hung up inside the house. Every precaution had been taken for a full-scale siege, if it came to that.

On a shelf near the door were several boxes of pistol and rifle ammunition. Obviously, Blue had been to town, so he must know what had become of Loma.

On the fourth day on which Rod could be outside he saddled the gray and, getting a steel hook from the odds and ends on the workbench in the blacksmith shop, he took an extra length of rope and rode up the canyon toward the basin. Blue had left early and Rod had talked with him but a few minutes. He supposed the other man had ridden to town, but Jed had said nothing about his destination.

Rod was quite sure he knew now what had become of the vanished wagons. Come what may, in the next few hours he would know for sure.

He understood something else. Both Weisl and Tolbert had been killed in the canyon, and both apparently after arriving at a solution or coming close to it. He would have to be very, very careful!

ROD MORGAN'S SUDDEN appearance at Em Shipton's had startled and upset Loma. Try as she might, she could not get his face from her mind, nor the hurt expression on his face when Mark told him she was to marry him, Mark Brewer.

She had been standing in the boardinghouse when she heard the shots, and she had rushed to the door, panic-stricken that Rod might have been killed or hurt. Mark Brewer caught her arm and stopped her.

"Better not go out! You might be killed! It is always the innocent ones who are hurt, and it is probably just Rod Morgan killing somebody else."

He had drawn her to him and kissed her lightly before turning to the door. She learned two things in that instant. She did not like to be kissed by Mark Brewer, and he had lied. He *was* carrying a gun. He was carrying it in a shoulder holster, for it pressed against her when she was in his arms.

She knew all about shoulder holsters because her uncle had been a plainclothes detective at a time when they were first beginning to be used in the East. She had not seen one since coming west.

Why had he lied? Was he afraid of Rod? Or did he merely wish to avoid trouble? Yet the lie worried her. There seemed to be something underhanded about that gun, for she had heard several times that Mark Brewer never wore a gun. Apparently no one believed he wore a gun, yet certainly he did.

The thought rankled as the days went by. She heard that Rod had killed Dally Hart and Jed Blue had killed Bob Carr. It was not until the third day that she heard that Rod Morgan had been seriously wounded and that Jed Blue had carried him out of town.

He might be dead! Horrified, she for the first time considered her own situation. She knew none of these people. Rod she had known for a long time. He had always been a gentleman and a fine man. Could he change so quickly? Or was something else happening here of which she knew nothing?

Coming downstairs from her room at Em Shipton's, she

heard Rod's name mentioned in the dining room and stopped on the steps.

The voice was that of Jeff Cordell, whom she knew as one of the four men who had faced Rod that day beside the stage.

"Got to hand it to him," Cordell was saying. "Morgan has plenty of nerve, and I've never seen a faster hand with a gun. Why, that day on the trail he could have got me sure as shootin' if I'd moved a hand. I'd lay odds he'd have gotten three or maybe all of us."

"Speaking of fast hands," said another voice, "what about that Jed Blue?"

"He's good, all right. Bob Carr never knew what hit him. You know, that Blue puzzles me. Where did he come from? Why did he tie in with Morgan? He claims he was in here with Kit Carson, but I know the name of everyone who ever rode with Kit, and none of them was named Blue."

Somebody laughed. "You always use the same name, Jeff? I doubt if Childs has a single rider who uses his real name. Hell, we've all had our ups and downs."

"What will come of it, Jeff?" asked the other voice.

"Morgan will be killed. You can't beat Childs. If he doesn't want a man in the country, he doesn't stay. Jed Blue will get it, too."

"Why? What's his idea?"

"Don't try. Don't even think about it. You're getting twice a regular cowhand's wages, so just do what you're told and keep your trap shut. Childs knows why, and Brewer knows. Personally, I think the two of them are land-hungry. This is good country, and they want to control it. Can't blame 'em for that."

Aloma had gone on to her room, and after she undressed and got into bed she could not sleep. What she had overheard disturbed her. There *was* a plot against Rod Morgan, just as Rod had implied. Childs *did* want him killed.

Why, Henry Childs was the wealthiest rancher anywhere around! Why would he be involved in such things? Mark Brewer and Em Shipton both spoke so highly of him, but on the other hand, who was it who gave her the first doubts about Rod? It had been Em Shipton and Mark Brewer.

Loma Day decided she must talk to Jed Blue. She recalled that he had defended Rod that day on the stage. Had he known him then? No . . . he had not. She remembered his comments at the time she recognized Rod.

It was the next day she saw Henry Childs for the first time.

She was talking to Jeff Cordell, for after overhearing the conversation in the dining room she had decided she must cultivate him and learn what he knew.

"Did you ever kill a man, Jeff?"

He looked at her quickly. "Why, I reckon I have, ma'am. I suppose there are a good many of us who have killed a man or two, not that we want to or are looking for it. These are rough times, ma'am, and a man can't always look to the law to defend him. He has to do it himself. Out here the law expects a man to do just that."

"How about that day on the trail when Rod Morgan killed Reuben Hart?"

Jeff gave her a sharp look. He knew enough of the gossip to know Loma had come west to marry Morgan. He also knew that now Mark Brewer was riding herd on the girl. He had his own opinion of Brewer, and it was not flattering. Jeff Cordell had rustled a few head here and there, and occasionally stood a stage on its ear for drinking money, but he had a wholesome respect for a decent woman.

"Ma'am, there's some would have my hide for saying this, but you asked an honest question, and you'll get an honest answer. If Rod Morgan had been a mite slower to shoot that day, he would have been killed. Reuben Hart was sent out there to kill him."

"Sent? By whom?"

Jeff Cordell had talked all he planned to. He was turning to leave when the door opened and a big man with white hair came into the room. He glanced at Jeff and then at her.

"Cordell," he said sharply, "they need you at the ranch."

"Yes, sir. I was just leaving."

He tipped his hat and walked quickly away. Loma knew instinctively that this was Henry Childs. He was not a bit as she had expected. He was a big, kindly looking man with white hair and gray eyes. His mouth was unusually small and his lips thin, but he was a handsome man.

Cordell turned at the door. "Boss?"

Childs turned sharply, impatience showing in every line of his face. "Cordell, I—"

"Boss, I found out who that other man was. The one we saw the other day. His handle is Josh Shipton."

Loma's eyes were on Childs, and she was shocked by the change. His mouth started to open, his features stiffened, and for a moment she thought he was about to have a stroke.

Childs seemed no longer aware of her presence. For an instant his face became cruel and harsh. "Jeff, tell Mark I want to see him. Find him now, and tell him. *Now,* do you hear?"

Em Shipton bustled into the room. "Did I hear somebody use the name of Shipton?"

"Yes," Loma said as Childs left, "it was Jeff Cordell. He said he'd seen a man named Josh Shipton."

"Why, that no-account blatherskite! I thought he was dead! If I get my hands on him, I'll—!"

She left the room suddenly, breaking off in mid-sentence.

Loma went out to the wide porch and sat in one of the rockers, spreading her skirt carefully. Too many things were happening too suddenly; there were too many tangled threads and too much that demanded explanation. Whatever else Cordell might be, she felt he was being honest with her, and she now doubted that any of the others were.

She must somehow arrange to talk to Jed Blue. That he had been to town several times since Morgan had killed Dally Hart, she knew. From where she sat she could see him if he returned to town today, and she meant to be ready.

She had been a fool to let Rod go away thinking she was promised to Mark Brewer. He had proposed, but she had not accepted. She had simply told him she needed time, that everything was so mixed up, that he would have to wait.

Fortunately, it cost little to room and board at Em Shipton's, and she had a little money left. Not enough to go home, but enough to go on to Denver. She had considered that, but nothing could make her forget Rod.

It was two days later that she saw Blue ride into town. He always avoided the Gem Saloon, where he might run into enemies, going straight to the supply store and buying what he needed. She was becoming sufficiently attuned to western life to see that he was always careful before entering or leaving a building. Now she saw him come out of the store and start for his horse.

No one was about, so she arose, walking down the trail toward the old well, where she occasionally went. Once out of sight of the boarding house, she caught up her skirt to keep from tripping and ran down the path. Panting and somewhat disheveled, she arrived at the trail edge just as he appeared.

She stepped into plain sight and waited until he rode up to her. "Mr. Blue? I must talk to you."

"Are you alone?"

"Yes."

He glanced around quickly, then walked his horse into the bushes across the trail, and she followed. She was surprised to find a small, rustic footbridge across the creek, and an old millpond, the mill no longer in use.

Quickly, she told him what she had learned, even Childs's shock on hearing of Josh Shipton. Blue chuckled grimly at that, and then she told him of Cordell's certainty that Rod would be killed.

"Mr. Blue, how is Rod? Oh, I wish I had it all to do over! I was such a fool! But it was all so different from what I'd known. I just wish I had listened to what you said on the stage."

"Rod's coming along all right, ma'am. I'm just afraid this trouble's all coming to a head before we're ready for it.

"You say that when Childs heard about Shipton he sent for Brewer? Now what do you know about that?"

"What's wrong?"

"Ma'am, you had better keep clear of Mark Brewer. As long as you know so much you'd better know this, too. Somebody has been doin' Childs's killin' for him, and I know he wants Shipton dead, so who does he send for? Mark Brewer!"

"Oh, no! You must be mistaken!" Even as she said it she remembered the gun. "Mr. Blue, I do know this, when he told Rod that he didn't carry a gun, he lied. He wears one in a shoulder holster."

Blue was pleased. "Now, then, ma'am, that's the best news you've given me so far. That little item might save my life or Rod's."

"Why should Mr. Childs want Josh Shipton killed?"

Jed Blue hesitated. "There's the question behind this whole affair. Only two men know what happened in Buckskin Run when that gold vanished. One of them was Henry Childs; the other one is Josh Shipton."

He smiled widely. "Trouble is, for them at least, that a third one has figured it out, and I'm the third.

"Ma'am, you go back and tell them you met a man on the road, and don't describe me, who told you to tell them that Tarran Kopp is back."

She was seated in the small sitting room at the boarding house when Mark Brewer came in. Before she could speak he went on up to his room, and when he returned he was dressed for the trail. He walked over and sat down beside her.

"I hear you met Henry Childs. Quite a fellow, isn't he?"

"He's big," she admitted, "and a fine-looking man." Then, giving her face a puzzled expression, she asked, "Mark, who is Tarran Kopp?"

If she had expected a reaction she was not disappointed. He started as if stung, grabbing her wrist in a grip that hurt. "Who? Where did you hear that name?"

"Please don't! You're hurting me!" She rubbed her wrist as he released it. "Why, it was nothing at all!" She spoke carelessly. "I get so restless here, so I took a walk over by that old mill, it is so quiet and peaceful there, and I met a man. He was very polite.

"Actually, he was just watering his horse there at the mill-pond, and he asked me if I wasn't living at Em Shipton's. I told him I was, and he asked me to tell Henry Childs that Tarran Kopp was back."

Mark Brewer got to his feet. "He said Kopp was back? What did he look like?"

"Oh, he was just a man. As tall as you, I think, but spare.

He was riding a black horse." The horse Jed Blue had been riding was a blue roan.

"This changes everything," Brewer muttered, talking more to himself than her.

"Who is Tarran Kopp? What is he?"

"Oh, he was just an outlaw who was active out here fifteen or twenty years ago. It's believed he was the one who robbed those wagons you've heard about."

He turned toward the door. "Look, if Henry Childs comes in, tell him what you just told me, will you? And tell him I need to see him."

———

BEFORE NOON, ROD Morgan reached the basin. After lying among the rocks for about twenty minutes while studying the terrain to be sure he was unobserved, he went down to the edge of the pool and, putting his rifle down beside him, he began to cast with the heavy iron hook. He would cast the hook as far out as possible, let it sink to the bottom, and slowly drag it back to him.

He worked steadily, tirelessly, taking occasional breaks to study the country around. He was well into his third hour, without finding anything but broken branches or moss, when the hook snagged on something. Twice it slid off before it held, and then hand over hand he drew in his catch.

A wagon tire!

An iron wagon tire, showing evidence of having been subjected to heat. So then, they must have burned the wagons, thrown the metal parts into the pool, and . . . what about the gold?

He was squatting beside the wagon tire when he heard the sharp, ugly bark of a rifle.

He hit the ground in a dive from his squat, grabbed his rifle, and rolled over behind a rock. He was lying, waiting for another shot, when he realized the bullet had come nowhere near him.

Starting to lift his head he heard two more shots, quick, sharp, fired only a breath apart.

Stones rattled, a larger one plopped into the basin, and then

Rod caught a fleeting glimpse of a man's body falling. There was a terrific splash, and the body sank from sight.

Peering up, he saw a shadowy outline, a man's figure, atop the cliff, peering down. Then the shadow disappeared and, jerking off his boots and gunbelt, Morgan went into the water. Its icy chill wrenched a gasp from his throat, and then he saw the body, only it was not merely a body but a man, still struggling to live.

Diving low, he slipped an arm around the man's body and struck out for the surface. It was a struggle to get him to the surface and out upon the shore, and the man was bleeding badly.

It was Josh Shipton, and one look at the wound in his side and Rod knew there was no chance.

Shipton's lids fluttered. "B—Brew—Brewer dry-gul—dry-gulched me." He waved a feeble arm. "Childs—gold—Childs." He seemed to be trying to point toward the graves; or was it only one grave?

Brewer had killed him, but what had he been trying to say? At what had he pointed? Or was it only a wild gesture from a dying man?

Horse's hooves pounded on the sod, a racing horse. Rod wheeled, rifle ready. It was Jed Blue.

"You all right? I heard shots." Then he saw Shipton. "Ah? So Brewer got him."

"How did you know that?"

Blue explained what Loma had told him, and what she overheard. He also added the bit about Mark Brewer's shoulder holster.

"What made Childs so afraid of Shipton?"

"They were afraid of what he knew. Shipton knew all three of the men buried there, and if he saw Henry Childs he would smell a rat, and rat is right."

"What do you mean?"

"Shipton was trying to point at one of the graves. The grave of Harry Kidd."

"Kidd? Childs? Are you telling me Kidd didn't die? That there's nobody in that grave?"

"Kidd murdered the other two, cached the gold, marked

the graves so people would grow superstitious about them, then left the country. Coming back later, he started a ranch and helped spread the stories about the ghosts of Buckskin Run."

"Smart," Rod admitted.

"Except for one thing. He accused the wrong man of the murders. He spread the story around that the three had been killed and the gold stolen by Tarran Kopp.

"Kopp killed a few men here and there, but all in fair fights. He never murdered a man in his life, and that story made him mad. I know, because I am Tarran Kopp."

From far down the canyon they heard a thunder of racing hooves, a wild cry, and then a shot. Both men turned, rifles lifting.

A small black horse was coming toward them on a dead run, and they could see a girl's long hair streaming in the wind. Behind her, still some distance away, a tight group of racing horsemen.

"It's Loma!" Rod said. "And the Block C riders!"

Dropping to one knee, he opened up with his Winchester. A rider threw up his arms and dropped from his horse, and the group split, scattering out across the small plain.

The black horse swung in toward their position and was reined in. Loma slid from the horse's back into Rod's arms. The black horse wheeled and raced off a few yards, tossing its head with excitement.

"Never figured on making a stand here," Rod said. "Jed? Have you got enough ammunition?"

"Plenty. How about you?"

"The same . . . *there's one behind that spruce!*"

He fired as he spoke and the man cried out, staggering into the open where a bullet from Jed put him down.

Bullets spattered on the rocks around them, but their position in the small basin around the pool was excellent. A man could stand erect alongside the pool and still be under cover. A ring of boulders almost surrounded the pool, and a stream of them fanned out downslope from them where the attackers were.

Rod turned to Loma. "Can you fire a rifle?"

"Just give me a chance! My father taught me to shoot when I was a little girl. Only, I—I never shot a man."

"You won't get much chance here. Those boys are pretty well snuckered down now, and they aren't about to get themselves killed. Just fire a shot in that general direction once in a while.

"Jed, I'm going to circle around and try to get whoever is leading this bunch. My guess is it will be Brewer."

"Or Childs. Don't forget him."

Rod slid back to lower ground, wormed his way through some brush, and descended into a small wash. All of this was on land he claimed, and over which he had ridden many times. He knew every inch of it.

There had been no more than eight or ten men in the original group, and at least two were out of action. Unless he was mistaken, the Block C boys had enough. Their loyalty was largely money loyalty, and nobody wants to die for a dollar, at least nobody in his right mind.

He moved swiftly and silently along the sandy bottom, his boots making no sound in the soft sand. He was rounding a boulder when he heard a voice. It was Mark Brewer.

"Think we've got 'em, Henry?"

"Got 'em? Oh, sure! We'll finish them off, send the boys home, and dig up that gold. It's high time we dug it up. Something always kept me from going after it before. Price on gold has gone up, so we'll have more money, Mark."

"You mean," Brewer's voice was so low Rod could scarcely hear, "*I'll* have more!"

Through an opening in the rocks, Rod could see them now. He saw the surprise and shock on Childs's face turn to horror as Brewer drew a gun on him.

"Very simple, Henry. I've been waiting for this chance. I'll have it all for myself, and everybody will blame Morgan and Kopp for killing you."

Childs's hand went to his holster, but it was empty. "Don't bother, Henry. I'm making it easy for you. I lifted your gun then waited until your rifle was empty. Now I'll kill you, let the boys finish off Morgan and Kopp, and I get the gold."

The two men faced each other across ten feet of green

grass, cut off from view of the Block C riders by trees and boulders and over fifty yards of distance.

Childs's small mouth tightened until it was scarcely visible. He was sullen and wary. "Well," he said casually, "I guess I've had it coming. I murdered good men for that gold and never got a penny's worth of it. Now you'll murder me. Of course, we're going out together."

His hand flashed in movement, and Mark Brewer's .44 roared. Childs swayed like a tree in the wind but kept his feet. In the palm of his hand was a small derringer. He fired, and then again.

Brewer's gun was roaring, but his last bullets were kicking up sand at Childs's feet. He went to his knees, then down to his face in the bloody sand.

Childs said, "I had a hide-out gun, too, Mark. I was half expect—"

He put out a hand for support that was not there. Then he fell, sprawling on the grass. Rod hurried to him.

His eyes flared open. "You got a mighty pretty girl there, son," he said. The two-barreled derringer slipped from his fingers and he was dead. Rod stood for a moment, staring down at him.

Without the stolen money the man had done well. He had built a ranch, fine herds of cattle, earned the respect of his community, and all for nothing. The old murders had ridden him to his death.

Rod walked around the bodies and through the trees. When he got where he could see the Block C riders he lifted his rifle.

"Drop your guns, boys! The war's over! Childs and Brewer just killed each other."

Jeff Cordell dropped his gun. "Damned if they didn't have it coming." He paused. "Mind if we look?"

"Come on, but don't get any fancy notions. Too many men have died already."

The Block C riders trooped over, and stood looking down at the derringer that had slipped from his fingers.

"Mark always said he never carried a gun except when he was out in the hills like this." He stooped and flipped back

Brewer's coat to reveal the shoulder holster. "His kind always want an edge."

Cordell started to turn away. "You can take them along, Jeff. Take 'em back down to Cordova and tell them the truth."

"Why not? All right, boys, let's clean up the mess."

When they were gone, Tarran Kopp came out of the trees. Loma was with him.

"We could have buried 'em where they fell," Kopp said.

Rod shrugged. "Maybe, but I want no more ghosts in Buckskin Run."

He glanced around at Kopp. "What name are you using from now on? If we're going to be partners I'd better know."

"Jed Blue. Tarran Kopp's a legend. He's from the past; let him stay there."

They walked away together to their horses. "We'd better dig up that gold, once and for all. We can buy cattle, fix up a place for you all, and I'll take the old cabin."

He glanced slyly at Rod. "You know where it is?"

"Where you'd expect to find it. Buried in the grave of Harry Kidd."

Together, they rode back down the trail to the cabin on Buckskin Run.

Jed Blue looked around at them, pointing at the cabin. "I never had no home before," he said, "but that's home. We're a-comin' home."

MCNELLY KNOWS A RANGER

HE RODE UP to Miller's Crossing just after sundown and stopped at the stage station. Stepping down from the saddle he stood for a moment, taking in the street, the storefronts, and the lighted saloons.

Turning abruptly he crossed the boardwalk into a saloon. The bartender looked up, swallowed hard, and then turned quickly to polishing the back bar. The loafers at the tables glanced at each other, and one picked up a deck of cards and began riffling them nervously.

Bowdrie's question warned them they had not been mistaken. "Where'll I find Noah Whipple?"

The bartender's Adam's apple bobbed. "He—they—they shot him."

"Killed?"

Bowdrie's eyes were cold. The bartender swallowed again and shifted his feet uncomfortably, staring in fascination at the man with the dimplelike scar under the cheekbone below his right eye.

"It was Aaron Fobes done it, Mr. Bowdrie. He's one o' the Ballards."

Bowdrie stood silent, waiting.

"About two this afternoon. They come ridin' in, five of them. Four got down an' come in here. The other'n stayed by the horses. They looked to be a purty salty outfit. They'd been ridin' hard by the look of the horses.

"They took a quick look around when they come in and paid no attention after. They seen everything with that first look. We all knew who they was, even without that holdup over at Benton where they killed the cashier. Everybody knows the Ballards are ridin' again and there ain't two gangs alike.

"The tall one I spotted right off. Had a blaze of white hair over his temple. That would be Clyde Ballard. He's a known man in Texas, from the Rio Grande to the Cimarron.

"The tall gent with the towhead, that would be Cousin Northup, and the slim, dark-faced youngster was Tom Ballard. The other two was Aaron Fobes and Luther Doyle."

"You seem to know them pretty well," Bowdrie commented. "Tell me more."

"Noah, he come in here three or four minutes before the Ballards got here. You maybe know about Noah. He was a good man, no trouble to anybody, but Noah was a talker. He hadn't paid no attention when the Ballards came in, just a glance and he went on talkin'.

"'Feller come through last night an' said the Ballards was ridin' again. Used to know that Fobes up in the Nation.' We tried to catch his eye but there was no stoppin' him. 'That Fobes,' he says, 'never was no account. Poison mean, he was, even then.'

"'Time's a-comin' when they won't let thieves like that ride around the country robbin' decent people.' Noah was just talkin' like he always done but Fobes was right there to hear him. Fobes tapped him on the shoulder. 'You talk too much, stranger,' he said, speakin' kind of low and mean."

Chick Bowdrie listened, seeing the scene all too clearly, and the inevitable ending. That was Noah, all right, always talking, meaning no harm to anybody, a decent, hardworking man with a family. At least, there was Joanie. Thinking of her his face tightened and he felt empty and kind of sick inside.

"Fobes, he said to Noah that maybe he'd like to stop the Ballards from ridin' the country? Maybe he'd like to try stoppin' them himself?

"Well, you know Noah. He might have been a talker but he was no coward. 'Maybe I would,' Whipple says. 'This country should be made safe for honest people.'

"Clyde Ballard put in then. 'Forget it, Aaron. He didn't know what he was sayin'. Let's ride.' Tom Ballard, he started for the door, Northup followin'. Noah Whipple thought it was all over, an' he dropped his hand.

"He never should have done it, but Noah was a habity

man. He was reachin' for a chaw. He chawed tobacco, an'
especially when he was nervous or bothered by somethin'.
He reached for his tobacco an' Aaron shot him.

"It happened so quick nobody had time to move or speak.
Clyde Ballard swore, and then they made a run for their
horses and rode off. Noah was dead on the floor, drilled right
through the heart, and him not wearin' no gun."

Chick was silent. He looked at the rye whiskey in his glass
and thought of Joanie. Only a few months before he had ridden up to their ranch as close to death as a man is apt to get,
with three bullet holes in him and having lost a great deal of
blood.

Joanie had helped him from his horse and she and Noah
had gotten him inside, then nursed him back to health. When
able to ride again he had started helping around the ranch.
He had not yet become a Ranger and the Whipples needed
help. There was only Noah, his wife, and Joanie. They had
two old cowhands but they were not much help with the
rough stock.

Ranching folks weren't inclined to ask questions of those
who drifted around the country. You took a man for what he
was and gave him the benefit of the doubt as long as he did
his share and shaped up right. Hard-faced young men wearing two tied-down guns weren't seen around very much,
even in that country.

Names didn't count for much and both Whipple and Joanie
knew that any man wearing two guns was either a man who
needed them or a plain damned fool.

He never told them his name. To them he was simply
Chick. Noah and his wife treated him like a son, and Joanie
like a brother, most of the time.

It had taken him a while to regain his strength but as soon
as he was able to get around he started helping, and he had
always been a first-rate cowhand.

Bowdrie walked outside the saloon and stood there on the
street. He knew what he had to do, and nobody had to ask his
intentions. It was the kind of a country where if you worked
with a man and ate his bread, you bought some of his troubles, too. The townspeople remembered him as a young cow-

hand who had worked for Noah, and they also knew he had come into the country in a dying condition from bullet wounds. Why or how he obtained the wounds, nobody ever asked, although curiosity was a festering thing.

He tightened his cinch, stepped back into the leather, and rode out of town.

———

TWO DAYS LATER Bowdrie rode back to Miller's Crossing. Folks working around town saw him ride in and they noted the brightness of the new Winchester he was carrying.

Bill Anniston, who ranched a small spread not far from the Whipples', was standing on the steps of the stage station when Bowdrie rode up. He had ridden with Bill on a roundup when the two outfits were gathering cattle.

"Bill, I'd take it as a favor if you'd ride over to the Whipples' an' see if they're all right." Bowdrie paused, rubbing the neck of the hammerhead roan. "I joined up with McNelly. I'm ridin' with the Rangers now."

"You goin' after the Ballards?"

"Time somebody did. McNelly said he'd send some men as soon as they finished what they were doin', but I told him I didn't figure I'd need no help."

As he rode away Bowdrie heard someone say, "I wonder why McNelly would take on a kid like that?"

Bill Anniston replied, "McNelly doesn't make mistakes. He knew what he was doing. Believe me, I've ridden with that boy and he's brush-wise and mountain-smart. He's no flat country yearlin'!"

Bowdrie rode south into the rough country. The wicked-looking hammerhead roan was a good horse on a long trail, a better horse than the Ballards would have. The roan liked to travel and he had a taste for rough country, a hangover from his wild mustang days.

The Ballards had not expected to be followed and their trail was plain enough. Once in a while they made a pass at hiding their trail, but nothing that would even slow Bowdrie's pace.

It was not new country to him although he had ridden it

but once before. South and west were some hills known locally as the Highbinders, a rough, broken country loved by Comanches because there was not a trail approaching them that could not be watched and there was ample water if one knew where to look.

Bowdrie thought as he rode. Clyde Ballard would be irritated. Clyde did not hold with killing unless it was in a stand-up fight or in the process of a hold-up. An outlaw had to have places to hide and if people were set against you you'd never last long. Often enough they were indifferent, but never if you killed a neighbor or someone they respected.

Aaron Fobes was another type entirely. There was a streak of viciousness in him. Yet Fobes would not want to cross Clyde Ballard. Not even Luther Doyle would consider that, for Clyde was a good man with a gun.

No one of them considered the possibility of pursuit. They had been a long way from Benton when the shooting took place and there was no marshal in Miller's Crossing.

With the shrewdness of a man who had known many trails, Chick Bowdrie could guess their thinking now. Clyde would be inwardly furious because the useless killing would make enemies and Miller's Crossing was a town they must avoid in future rides, and that meant some long, roundabout riding to get in and out of their hideout.

Bowdrie was in no hurry. He knew what awaited him at the ride's end and he was not riding for a record. It was almost ten days after the shooting before he rode up to the Sloacum place.

He drew rein outside the house as Tate Sloacum came striding up from the barn. "How's about some chuck?" Bowdrie suggested. "I've been thirty miles on an empty stomach."

"'Light an' set," Sloacum said. "Turn your hoss into the corral. There's a bucket there alongside the well if you'd like to wash off some dust."

When he had washed, he ran his fingers through his hair and went up to the house. He had no Indian blood but he looked like an Apache and sometimes there was hesitance from those who did not know him. There was food in plenty but nobody talked during the meal. Eating was a serious business.

Tate Sloacum was the old man of the house, a West Virginia mountaineer by birth. He had two sons and a hawk-faced rider named Crilley. His wife was a slatternly woman with stringy red hair and a querulous voice. A daughter named Sary served them at table. She had red hair and a swish to her hips. With brothers like hers she was a girl who could get men killed.

Bowdrie was uncomfortable around women. He had known few of them well. He took in Sary with a glance and then averted his eyes and kept them averted. He knew trouble when he saw it.

At twenty-one Chick Bowdrie had been doing a man's work since he was twelve, herding cattle, breaking the wild stock, and riding the rough string. There had been little softness in his life and few friends. Once, when he could have been no older than eight, a man had stopped by the house for a meal. It was wild country with Indians about, and few traveled alone. This man did.

When Chick walked out to the corral with him he watched the man saddle up and step into the stirrup. For some reason, he hated to see him go. There had been something about the man that spoke of quiet strength.

Looking down from the saddle, the man had said, "Ride with honor, boy, ride with honor."

He did not know exactly what honor was but he never forgot the man and he was sure what the man had said was important.

A member of the Ballard gang had killed a man who befriended him, and he needed no more reason for hunting him down, and wanted no more. He had enlisted as a Ranger because it was practical. The law was coming to Texas and he preferred to ride with the law. McNelly, a shrewd judge of character, had recognized him for what he was. This young man was destined to be a hunter or one of the hunted, and McNelly reflected dryly that he'd rather hire him than lose men trying to catch him.

"We demand loyalty," he suggested. "Absolute loyalty."

"I ride for the brand," Bowdrie replied. "I never take a man's money without giving him what he's paid for."

"Where is your home?"

"Wherever I hang my hat," Bowdrie said. "I got nothing, nobody." Then he added, "I can read an' write."

"Your home?"

"Got no home. I was born near D'Hanis. Folks all gone. Mostly Injuns killed 'em."

"D'Hanis? Are you French?"

"Some. Some other blood, too. I don't know much about it. I growed up where most of the youngsters spoke French an' German as well as English."

"I know the area. Do you speak Spanish?"

"I get by. I worked cows with Mexican riders. We got along."

That was how it began. Bowdrie thought back to it now, thinking he had taken the right turn, on the right side of the law, and he knew how easy it would have been to go the other way. Sooner or later he might have killed the wrong man.

"Need a place to hole up," he told Sloacum, "a quiet place where a man can rest and let his horse eat grass."

Sloacum gestured toward the hills. "We call 'em the High-binders. Used to be Comanches. Mostly they're gone now." He gestured toward the house. "Come up when you've un-saddled, and we'll have some grub on."

That was before he sat down. He ate well, simple food, well-cooked. The two boys disappeared when supper was over but Crilley lingered, stropping his knife on his boot sole.

"I seen you somewheres afore," he said to Bowdrie.

"I been someplace before, but I never seen you."

He did not remember ever seeing Crilley and did not care if Crilley had seen him. The cowboy might have seen him when he rode for Whipple and could take the information to Ballard if he wished. Bowdrie had to find a trail and Crilley might make it for him. Nor did he care if the Ballards were ready for him. He was ready for them, too.

He got up and Sloacum glanced at him. "You can sleep in the haymow. Ain't got an extry bed."

"I've slept in 'em before. Better'n most."

He left the house and went to the barn, where he found a big hayloft half-filled with fresh-smelling hay. He spread his blankets and bedded down, the big wide hayloft door open to the out-of-doors and showing a wide stretch of starlit sky.

He could have been asleep for scarcely more than an hour when he was suddenly awake, gun in hand. He could not have explained how the gun got there. It was one of those instinctive actions that come to men who live close to danger. Weapons become so much a part of their existence that they no longer seem remarkable.

Then he recalled what had awakened him. The sound of a horseshoe clicking against stone. Sitting up, he strained his ears to hear, and it came again, the muffled hoof-falls of a horse and a creak of saddle leather.

Keeping to the darkness away from the open door, he moved softly to where he could see out.

Chick Bowdrie had found little time for romance in his life or he, instead of Tom Ballard, might have been meeting Sary near the corral, but he witnessed their greeting, a healthy if not soulful kiss. If there was no delicacy in the kiss there was no lack of earthy appreciation in it.

Chick had not come to witness kisses, so he stood waiting. He had recognized Ballard from other days.

"Anybody been around?" Tom asked.

"Uh-huh. Stranger passin' through. Sleepin' in the loft right now. He was astin' Pa for a place where there was water where he could lay up for a while. Pappy thinks he's on the dodge."

"What's he look like?"

"He ain't no Ranger, if that's what you're scared of. Although he does have one of those new Winchesters like they carry. Looks more like a gunhand. Dark, narrow features. Nose like a hawk. Eyes blacker than a well bottom. Packs two tied-down six-shooters. Walks straight an' fast. He's ridin' a mean-lookin' strawberry roan."

Tom Ballard drew a breath. "Got a little scar, has he? Like a thin sort of dimple below his cheekbone?"

"That's him! Who is he?"

"Bowdrie, Chick Bowdrie. He's the man who killed Pete Drago a while back."

"Is he huntin' you?"

"I hope not. Why should he be? He's kind of on the outlaw side himself, from what I hear. Just ridin' through, most likely."

The rest was unimportant. Bowdrie tiptoed back to his bed and stretched out. He was fast asleep within minutes.

He was dipping his head in the water bucket when Sary appeared the following morning. He shook the water from his hair, then wiped his face and hands on the roller towel beside the back door.

"I'm huntin' a place to lie up for a while," he suggested. "I'd be obliged for any ideas."

"Nothin' around here." She eyed him with speculative eyes. "Would you come a-callin' if you was close by?"

Bowdrie admitted he was no hand with women but he knew a trail when he saw it. His bloodhound's instinct told him what to say. "Why else would an hombre want to stay in this country?"

Sary finished drawing her bucket from the well. "There's the Highbinders, them low, brush-covered hills you see out past the barn. There's water there, and a few deer. A body could kill him an antelope if he needed meat. Or even a steer, so long as it isn't one of ours. Nobody out here kills his own beef," she added.

At the table they ate thick steaks cooked well-done and drank black bean coffee. There were cookies, too. Ma Sloacum could cook and bake.

Crilley, Bowdrie noted before Tate Sloacum even spoke, was nowhere around. "Where's Joe? Ain't like him to miss breakfast."

"He got his coffee, then taken off to the hills before sunup," Ma explained.

———

ALMOST AN HOUR later Crilley rode into the canyon where the Ballards were holed up. He dropped from his horse at the cabin and glanced over at Aaron Fobes, who stood beside the cabin door.

"I got bad news," he said.

Clyde Ballard came to the door, Luther Doyle and Northup behind him.

"What news?" Fobes demanded.

"Chick Bowdrie's eatin' breakfast over at Sloacum's."

"What's that to us?" Clyde asked.

"Fobes here, he killed Noah Whipple over at Miller's, didn't he? Well, when Bowdrie rode in the other night I couldn't place him, then it come to me. He pulled into Whipple's a while back with some bullets in him. They nursed him back to health, an' he stayed on, ridin' for Whipple for a few months. I hear he sets store by that family."

Aaron Fobes looked sullen. "Bowdrie ain't got no call to come huntin' me. Anyway, I can take him or any two like him."

"You'd better hightail it, Aaron," Clyde suggested. "The way I hear it, he's somethin' to see with those guns of his."

"How'll he find me?" Fobes looked over at Crilley. "Unless you tell him."

"I ain't tellin' nothin' to nobody."

He knew Fobes and the thought did not make him happy. Suddenly he wished he hadn't been in so much of a hurry to ride over and tell him. He should have let well enough alone. Yet he liked Clyde Ballard and Clyde was a feudist—a fight with one of his men was a fight for all. Crilley had never liked Fobes. He was a mean, difficult man.

"He'll find you," Clyde said. "I've heard of him and he could trail a rattler across a flat rock, but if anybody is huntin' him they have to burn the stump and sift the ashes before they find him."

———

WHEN CRILLEY DID not appear for breakfast, Bowdrie decided there was but one reason for his absence. Obviously it was something of which the family knew nothing, and such absences were not the usual thing for Crilley, or no comment would have been made.

Why, then, had he gone? Only one thing out of the ordinary had happened at Sloacum's—his own arrival. The night before, Crilley had been sure he had seen Bowdrie somewhere before. Obviously he had remembered where and had ridden to inform the Ballards.

If he had ridden into the Highbinders, he would leave a trail, and where a horse had gone, Bowdrie could follow. A half-hour after breakfast he was in the saddle, riding east. When well out from the ranch, he swung in a wide circle until he picked up the sign of Crilley's horse.

He rode swiftly, making good time. Ahead of him the trail dipped into a dry wash and turned away from the hills. He followed until the trail came to a clear stream of water, less than a foot deep and flowing over a sand-and-gravel bottom.

Bowdrie swung down for a drink and let his horse drink, on the theory that a man never knew what might happen. He rode upstream first and was lucky. He found several hoofprints the water had not yet washed away. Riding or walking in the water is not always a means of losing one's trail. Bowdrie knew a dozen ways of following such a trail. Horseshoes could scar rocks even underwater.

Several times he reined in to study the country and the Highbinders, which were close now.

His thoughts returned to Joanie, clinging to his arm when he rode to town looking for Noah. She had not known about her father then, although her mother was worried that her husband had not returned as planned.

"Bring me something from town, Chick! Please!"

What did you bring a girl from town? That was more of a problem than Crilley's trail. He must find her something, some little knickknack. He would . . .

He saw a hoofprint in the clay bank where Crilley's horse had left the water. The trail turned back along the bank, weaving in and out of thick brush.

He never heard the shot.

A wicked blow on the head knocked him from the saddle, unconscious before he hit the ground. Something tore at him with angry fingers—and he hit, sagged, and hung.

When his eyes opened he was staring into a black, glassy

world. Something that moved, flowed, a glassy world that mirrored a face, his face.

He started to move, but brush crackled and he felt again that sagging feeling. Slowly he became aware. He had fallen from his horse and was suspended in the brush above the stream's edge. His foot felt cold, and looking down, he saw one boot toe trailed in the water. He lifted it clear.

Carefully he looked around. He had fallen into brush that partly supported his weight, but his gunbelt had caught on an old snag, which had helped keep him clear of the water, where he might have drowned, shallow though it was.

Nearby was a branch that looked sturdier than the others. He grasped it, tested it, and slowly, carefully lifted himself clear. Climbing out of his precarious position was a shaky business, but he managed.

He crawled higher on the bank. He had been dry-gulched. They had waylaid him and shot him from the saddle, leaving him for dead.

He still had his guns. One remained in its holster; the other had fallen on the bank. He picked it up and wiped the clay from it, testing the action.

It was almost sundown, which meant he had been unconscious for hours. Delicately his fingers felt the furrow in his scalp. The blood had dried and caked his hair. Better not disturb it. He knelt by the stream and washed the blood from his face, however.

Looking about, he found his hat and placed it gingerly on his head.

There was no sign of his horse but there was still enough light for tracking. When he had fallen, the roan had bolted. Weaving his way through the brush and then a grove of small trees, he suddenly glimpsed the horse standing in a small meadow, looking at him.

When the hammerhead saw him it nickered softly, and actually seemed glad to see him. His Winchester was still in the saddle scabbard. The horse even took a couple of steps toward him. When he had first caught the roan from the wild bunch, his friends advised him to turn it loose. "That's no kind of a horse, Chick. Look at that head. And he's got a mean look to him. Turn him loose or shoot him. That horse is a killer!"

They had been right, of course. The roan was such a savage bucker that when he threw a rider he turned and went for him with intent to kill. He was lean, rawboned, and irritable, yet Bowdrie had developed an affection for him. Pet the roan and he would try to bite you. Curry him and he'd kick. But on a trail he would go all day and all night with a sort of ugly determination. Bowdrie had never known a horse with so much personality, and all of it bad. Nor did the roan associate much with other horses. He seemed to like being in a corral where they were, but he held himself aloof.

Of one thing Bowdrie was sure. No stranger was going to mount the roan. As for horse thieves, only one had tried to steal the roan, for in a herd of horses the roan would be the last anyone would select. The one attempt had been by a man in a hurry and the roan was there.

The horse thief jerked free of the tie-rope and leaped into the saddle. The roan spun like a top and then bucked and the would-be rider was piled into the water trough and his screams brought Bowdrie and the marshal running, for the roan had grabbed the thief's shoulder in his teeth.

Bowdrie took the bridle, spoke to the horse, then mounted and rode away. The thief, badly shaken and bloody, was helped from the trough. Aside from the savage bite, he had a broken shoulder.

"What was *that*?" the outlaw whined. "What . . . ?"

"That was Chick Bowdrie an' that outlaw roan he rides." The marshal kept one hand on his prisoner while looking down the street after Bowdrie. "They deserve each other," he added. "They're two of a kind."

———

BOWDRIE FOUND THE camp by its firelight. It was artfully hidden but the light reflected from rocks and there was a small glow in the night.

On foot Chick Bowdrie walked down the grassy bank toward the fire. Aaron Fobes was talking. "No call for Clyde to get huffy," he complained. "I just got him before he could get me."

Meat was roasting over the fire, and the two men were doing a foolish thing. They were looking into the flames as they talked, which ruins the vision for immediate night work. There was no sign of the Ballards, nor of Northup.

"Maybe he didn't have a chance, but what difference does that make?"

"Get up, Fobes!"

Fobes started as if touched by a spark from the fire; then slowly he began to rise.

"You in this, Doyle?" Bowdrie's black eyes kept both men in view. "If you ain't, back up an' stay out!"

"I ride with him," Luther Doyle said.

Fobes had reached for his gun as he came erect, and Doyle, who had not quite made up his mind, was slower. Yet Doyle was the deadlier of the two and Bowdrie's first shot knocked him staggering and he fell backward over the saddles. The second and third shots took Aaron Fobes in the throat and face. Fobes fell forward into the fire, scattering it. Doyle got off a quick shot that knocked the left-hand gun from Bowdrie's grip, leaving his hand numb. Doyle fired again and missed, taking a slug in the chest. He fell forward and lay still.

Chick walked over and retrieved his gun, holstering it, rubbing his left hand against his pants to restore the feeling. Then he caught Fobes by the back of his shirt and lifted him free of the fire. The man was dead.

Bowdrie got his canteen from his horse and lifted Doyle's head to give him a swallow.

The wounded man's eyes flickered. "He wasn't worth it, but I rode with him. No hard feelings?"

"None," Bowdrie replied. "Next time you better choose better comp'ny. You could get yourself killed."

He opened the wounded man's shirt. The one low down on the left side looked ugly, but the other shot had hit Doyle's heavy metal belt buckle and glanced off, ripping the skin across his stomach for a good six inches, but the wound was only a bad scratch.

"Am I bad off?"

"Not too bad. You'll live, most likely. I'll patch you up some when I get time. Now we got comp'ny."

He thumbed cartridges into his guns, holstering the left one. His hand was still numb, but if necessary . . .

"What d'you plan to do?" Doyle asked.

"Take the Ballards," Bowdrie said. "I'm a Texas Ranger."

"Bowdrie? A *Ranger*?"

"Since Fobes killed Noah Whipple." He grabbed Doyle's handkerchief and shoved it into his mouth, but the outlaw spat it out. "I won't holler," Doyle said. "If I do, there'll be shootin'."

They waited in silence, listening to the approaching horses.

"Watch Northup," Doyle said. "I don't want Clyde shot up."

Three men rode into the firelight and started to swing down. One was on the ground before they saw anything amiss.

"Hold it, Ballard!" Bowdrie said. "This is Chick Bowdrie and I'm a Texas Ranger. I'm arrestin' you for the Benton bank job!"

Clyde Ballard stood very still. His brother was beside him, only a few feet away, and Northup was a good ten feet to their left. They were full in the firelight and Bowdrie was in half-darkness beyond the fire. Clyde could see Fobes's body, realizing for the first time that the man was dead, not sleeping. He could only see the legs of Luther Doyle but it was obvious the man was out of action.

Nobody had ever accused Clyde Ballard of lack of courage. He was hard, tough, and at times reckless, but even a child could see that somebody could die here, and Tom was only a kid.

"He means it, Clyde," Doyle said. "He's hell on wheels with them guns and we might get him but he'd get all of us. We can beat this one in court."

It was wise counsel, Clyde knew. It would not be easy to convict them of the Benton job, as they had all been masked. Moreover, it was miles to prison and they had friends.

"What about the Miller Crossing killing?" Clyde asked.

"Fobes did that. He's dead. As far as I'm concerned, that's a closed chapter. You can have it any way you want it. Doyle can live if we get him to a doctor."

Ballard hesitated. With a single move he could turn the evening into a red-laced bit of hell, but what the Ranger said was true and he had been careful never to buck the Rangers.

"You've got us cold-decked, Bowdrie. I'm dropping my guns." His hands went carefully to his belt buckle. "Tom?"

The guns dropped, and Tom's followed.

"Like hell!" Cousin Northup's tone was wild. "No damn Ranger is takin' me in!"

Bowdrie's gun was in his hand but he hesitated a split second as Northup's pistol cleared leather; then he shot him. The Ballards stood, hands lifted. Bowdrie looked at them for a moment, then holstered his gun.

"Cousin was always a mite hasty," Clyde said, and then added, "We might have gotten into that, but one of us would surely have gotten hisself killed, and there was Luther here. If we killed you, he'd have no show a-tall. An' we'd have nobody who knew we'd surrendered ourselves."

Bowdrie gathered their guns and hung the belts on his saddle.

"If we can get him to Sloacum's," Clyde said, "that ol' man's most as good as a doctor. He might fix him up until we can get help."

They got Luther into the saddle and started for the ranch. Bowdrie had three prisoners and a report to write up. He'd never written a report and did not know what to say.

And he would have to stop in town to buy something for Joanie.

"You fellers could help me," he said to Clyde. "If you was asked to buy something in town for a girl, maybe sixteen, what would you get for her?"

"Well," Clyde said, "I'd . . ."

It was a long way to town.

A JOB FOR A RANGER

THERE WERE TWO bullet holes in the bank window, and there was blood on the hitching rail where the cashier had fallen while trying to get off a last shot. Lem Pullitt had died there by the rail, but not before telling how he had been shot while his hands were up.

Chick Bowdrie stood on the boardwalk, his dark, Apache-like features showing no expression. "I don't like it," he muttered. "Either the hold-up man was a cold-blooded killer or somebody wanted Pullitt killed."

He glanced up the street again, his eyes searching the buildings, the walks, the horses tied at the rails. Many men kill, but killing a game man when his hands were up . . . it just wasn't the way things were done in Texas. And Lem had been game or he would not have stumbled out there, dying, trying for a shot.

The bandits had come into town in two groups. One man with a rifle dismounted in front of the Rancher's Rest while the others rode on to the bank. One then remained outside with the horses, and three had gone inside.

When shots sounded from inside the bank, men rushed to the street; then the man with the rifle opened fire. He covered the retreat of the four men at the bank, but what had become of the man with the rifle? He had not run the gauntlet in the street.

Henry Plank, clerk in the stage station, had stepped to the door and opened fire on the fleeing bandits. He claimed to have winged one of them. Bowdrie pushed his hat back on his head and studied the street, scowling.

A large man with a blond mustache emerged from the bank and walked over to where Bowdrie stood. His face was florid and he wore a wide, dusty Stetson.

"Are you the Ranger?"

Bowdrie turned his black eyes on the man, who felt a sudden shiver go through him. There was something in those eyes that made him feel uncomfortable.

"Name of Bowdrie. Chick, they call me. You're Bates?"

"Yes. They call me Big Jim. I am the banker. Or maybe I should say, I was the banker."

"Is it that bad?"

Bowdrie's eyes strayed up the street. That was the direction from which the bandits had come. They could not have been seen until they were right in the street, and when they left, it was in the opposite direction, which put them behind some cottonwoods within a minute or two.

On the side of the street where he stood were the bank, a livery stable, a general store, and a blacksmith shop. At the opposite end, standing out a little from the other buildings, was the Rancher's Rest. Across from the Rest were a corral, two houses, a dance hall, now closed, and the Chuck Wagon, a combination saloon and eating house. Directly across was the stage station.

"Yeah," Big Jim said, "it is that bad. I've got money out on loans. Too darned much. None of the loans are due now. A few weeks ago I loaned ten thousand to Jackson Kegley, and I was figurin' on loanin' him the ten thousand they stole."

"Who's Kegley?"

"Kegley? He owns the Rest. Got a big cattle spread west of town. Runs eight, nine thousand head of stock. His place runs clean up to West Fork. That's where the Tom Roway place is."

"Roway's the man you think done it? Something to that effect was in the report."

Bates shrugged. "I ain't seen Tom Roway but twice in five years. He killed a couple of men in shootin' scrapes, then went to the pen for shootin' a man in the back.

"Three years ago he came back and brought Mig Barnes along. Barnes is pretty tough himself, or so they say."

"Why did you suspect Roway?"

"Bob Singer . . . he's a puncher around here, seen that paint horse. I guess everybody else saw it, too. The gent who used the rifle was ridin' that paint. Sorrel splash on the left hip and several dabs of color on the left shoulder."

"Did you send a posse after them?"

Bates looked embarrassed "Nobody would go. Tom Roway is mighty handy with a rifle and he's fast with a six-shooter. Bob Singer is pretty salty himself, and he wouldn't go, and after that, people just sort of backed off. Finally Kegley, Joel, an' me went out. We lost the trail in the waters of West Fork."

"Joel?"

"My son. He's twenty-one, and a pretty good tracker."

Chick walked past the bank. There was a bullet hole in the side window of the bank, too. When they started shooting in some of these towns, they surely shot things up. He walked on to the Rancher's Rest and stepped inside.

Aside from the bartender, there were three men in the saloon. The big, handsome man standing at the bar had a pleasant face, and he turned to smile at Bowdrie as he entered.

A man at a card table playing solitaire had a tied-down gun. The third man was a lantern-jawed puncher with straw-colored hair.

"You'll be Bowdrie, I guess," the big man said. "I am Jackson Kegley. This is my place."

"How're you?"

Chick glanced at the straw-haired puncher. He grinned with wry humor. "I'm Rip Coker. That shrinkin' violet at the card table is Bob Singer. Better keep an eye on him, Ranger, he's mighty slick with an iron, either shootin' or brandin'."

Singer glared at Coker, and his lips thinned as he looked down at his cards. Chick noticed the glance, then turned his attention to Kegley.

"You know Roway. Do you think he done it?"

"I wouldn't know. He's a damn good shot. We trailed him as far as the West Fork."

Coker leaned his forearms on the bar. His plaid shirt was faded and worn. "Roway's not so bad," he commented, "and I don't think he done it."

Singer was impatient. "Nobody could miss that paint hoss," he suggested. "Ain't another in the county like it."

Coker gave Singer a disgusted glance. "Then why would

he ride it? If you was robbin' a bank, would you ride the most noticeable horse around?"

Bob Singer flushed angrily and his eyes were hard when he looked up, but he offered no comment.

"I'll look around some," Bowdrie said.

He walked outside, studying the street again. There was a suggestion of an idea in his mind, and something felt wrong about the whole affair. He went to the hotel section of the Rest and signed for a room, then strolled outside.

Something in the dust at his feet caught his eye, and he stepped down off the walk, running the dust through his fingers. He took something from the dust, placed it carefully inside a folded cigarette paper, and put it in his wallet.

Singer had come out of the saloon and was watching him. Bowdrie ignored him and strolled down to where his horse was tied. He was swinging into the saddle when Bates came to the door. "You ain't goin' after him alone, are you?"

Bowdrie shrugged. "Why not? I haven't seen any of his graveyards around."

He turned the roan into the trail. He was irritable because he was uneasy. There was something wrong here, it was too pat, too set up, and they were too ready to accuse Roway. "Personally," Bowdrie told the roan, "I agree with Coker. An outlaw using a horse everybody knew, that doesn't even make sense."

The trail was good for the first few miles, then became steadily worse. It wound higher and higher into rougher and rougher country. Skimpy trails edged around cliffs with dropoffs of several hundred feet to the bottom of dry canyons. Then, of a sudden, the trail spilled over a ridge into a green meadow, and that meadow opened into still another, each one skirted by borders of trees. At the end of the last meadow was a cabin, smoke rising from the chimney. A few cattle grazed nearby, and there were horses in the corral.

Chick Bowdrie rode up and stepped down. One of the horses in the corral was a paint with a splash of sorrel on the hip, a few smaller flecks on the shoulder. It was an unusual marking, unlikely to be duplicated.

"Lookin' for something?" The tone was harsh, and Bowdrie took care to keep his hands away from his guns.

The man stood at the door of his cabin not twenty feet away. He was a hard-visaged man with an unshaved face and cold eyes under bushy black brows. He wore a gun in a worn holster, and beyond him inside the door another man sat on a chair with a rifle across his knees.

"Are you Tom Roway?"

"And what if I am?"

Bowdrie studied him coolly for a long minute and then said, "I'm Chick Bowdrie, a Ranger. We've got to have a talk."

"I've heard of you. I've no call to like the law, but if you want to talk, come on in. Coffee's on."

The man at the door put down his rifle and put a tin plate and a cup on the table. He was a stocky man with a pock-marked face. "Ain't often we have a Ranger for chow," he commented.

Roway sat down, filling three cups. "All right, Ranger, speak your piece. What business do you have with us?"

"Have you been ridin' that paint horse lately?"

"I ride that paint most of the time."

"Did you ride into Morales Monday morning and stick up the bank?"

"What kind of a question is that? No, I didn't rob no bank and I ain't been in Morales in a month! What is this? Some kind of a frame-up?"

"Five men robbed the bank at Morales Monday morning, and one of them was ridin' a paint horse, a dead ringer for that one out yonder." Bowdrie gestured toward the corral. "Where was that horse on Monday?"

"Right where he is now. He ain't been off this place in a week." He looked up, scowling. "Who identified that animal?"

"A dozen people. He was right out in plain sight. Nobody could've missed him. One who identified him was Bob Singer."

"Singer?" Roway's eyes flashed. "I'll kill him!"

"No you won't," Bowdrie said. "If there's any killin' done, I'll do it."

For a moment their eyes locked, but Roway was the first to look away. Mig Barnes had been watching, and now he spoke. "Do you reckon Tom would be so foolish as to ride to a hold-up with the most known horse in the county? He'd have to be crazy!"

He gestured outside. "We've got a cavvy of broncs, all colors an' kinds. He could take his pick, so why ride the one horse everybody knows?"

"I thought of that," Bowdrie agreed, "and it doesn't look like anybody with a place like this would want to steal. You boys have got yourselves a ranch!"

"Best I ever saw!" Roway said. "Grass all year around and water that never gives out. Our cattle are always fat."

"Has anybody ever tried to buy you out?" Bowdrie asked casually.

"You might say that. Jackson Kegley wanted to buy it from me, and for that matter, so did old man Bates. Then some of Kegley's boys made a pass at running me off the place a few years back. We sort of discouraged 'em. Mig an' me, we shoot too straight."

The coffee was good, so Bowdrie sat and talked awhile. The two were hard men, no doubt about that, but competent. Nobody in his right mind would try to drive them off a place situated like this. Bowdrie knew their kind. He had ridden with them, worked cattle with them. Left alone, they would be no trouble to anyone.

Neither of these men shaped up like a murderer. They would kill, but only in a fight where both sides were armed and where they believed themselves in the right.

The idea persisted that the bank cashier had been shot deliberately, and for a reason. But what reason?

Bowdrie was not taking Roway's word for it as far as the paint horse went, but he did not have to. He already had some thoughts about that, and an idea was beginning to take shape that might provide an answer.

It was a long ride back to Morales, and Bowdrie had time to think. The sun was hot, but up in the high country where he was, the breeze was pleasant. Bowdrie took his time. Riding horseback had always been conducive to thinking, and now he turned over in his mind each one of the elements. When he arrived at a point where he could overlook the town, he drew rein.

Morales, what there was of it, lay spread out below him like a map, and there are few things better than a map for getting the right perspective.

The paint horse was too obvious. Rip Coker had put that into words very quickly, but Bowdrie had been quick to see it himself. To ride such a horse in a robbery meant that a man was insane or he was trying to point a finger of suspicion at its owner.

"What I want to know, Hammerhead," he said to the roan, "is how that fifth bandit got away. More than likely, if he rode around behind the Rest an' took to the woods, he had to come this way to keep from sight. He had to know a trail leading him up to the breaks of this plateau without using the main trail."

For two hours he scouted the rim, returning to town finally with the realization that there was no way to reach the top without taking the main trail in full sight of the town.

"And if he didn't use the main trail, he just never left town at all!"

Several men were running toward the bank as he rode into the street. Dropping from the saddle, Bowdrie tied his horse and went swiftly in the direction of the others. Hearing someone coming up behind him, he turned to see Jackson Kegley. "What's happened?" Kegley asked.

"Don't know," Chick said.

When they rounded the corner of the bank, they saw a small knot of men standing at the rear of the bank. Bowdrie glanced at Kegley. His face was flushed and he was breathing harder than what a fast walk should cause. A bad heart, maybe?

Bob Singer was there, his features taut and strained. "It's Joel Bates. He's been knifed."

Chick stepped through the crowd. He looked down at the

banker's son. A good-looking boy, a handsome boy, and well-made. Too young to die with a knife in the back.

"Anybody see what happened?" Chick asked.

Rip Coker was rolling a smoke. "He was investigatin' this here robbery. I reckon he got too close."

"I found him," Henry Plank said. He was a small man, bald, with a fringe of reddish hair. "I come through here a lot, going to Big Jim's barn. He was lyin' just like you see him, on his chest, head turned sidewise, and a knife in his back."

"When did you come through here last?" Bowdrie asked. "I mean, before you found the body?"

"About an hour ago. He wasn't lyin' there then. I walked right over that spot."

Chick squatted on his heels beside the body. The knife was still in the wound, an ordinary hunting knife of a kind commonly used. There probably were as many such knives in town as there were men. This one was rusty. Probably an old knife somebody had picked up. He bent closer, lifting the dead man's hand. In the grain of the flesh there were tiny bits of white. His hand looked much as it would if he had gripped a not-quite-dry paintbrush.

Bowdrie stood up, thinking. Joel Bates's body was cold, and in this weather it would not lose heat very fast. Bowdrie was guessing that Joel Bates had been dead for considerably more than an hour, but if so, where had the body been?

Big Jim, stunned by grief and shock, stood nearby. Only that morning Bowdrie had heard Bates speak with pride of his son, the son who now lay cold and dead.

Chick Bowdrie was suddenly angry. He turned to face the group.

"The man who killed this boy is in this crowd. He is the same man who engineered the bank robbery. I know why he did it and I have a very good hunch who he is, and I'm going to see him hang if it is the last thing I do!"

Turning sharply, he walked away, still angry. Perhaps he had been foolish to say what he'd said, and this was no time for anger, yet when he saw that fine-looking young man lying there . . .

He walked back toward the barn and entered. It was cool and quiet in there, and sunlight fell through a few cracks in the boards. There were three horses in the stalls and there were stacks of hay. At one side of the old barn was a buckboard. Chick was following a hunch now, and quickly, methodically, he began to search. His success was immediate—a pot of white paint hidden under sacks and piled hay.

"Found somethin'?"

Bowdrie glanced up, a queer chill flowing through him. So engrossed had he been in his search that he had failed to hear the man enter. His carelessness angered him. It was Bob Singer.

"Yeah," Bowdrie said, "I've found something, all right."

Gingerly he lifted the pot with his left hand, turning it slowly. On one side was a clear imprint of a thumb, a thumbprint with a peculiar ropy scar across it.

"Yes, I've found something. This is the paint that was used to paint a horse to look like Roway's skewbald."

"Paint a hoss? You've got to be crazy!"

Several men had followed them into the barn and were listening.

"Somebody," Bowdrie said, "figured on stickin' Roway with this robbery. He painted a horse to look like Roway's."

"And left the paint can here?" Singer said. "It must have been young Bates himself."

"It wasn't young Bates. You see . . ."—Bowdrie looked at Singer—"I've known that horse was painted from the first. He stamped his feet and some paint fell off into the dust up in front of the Rest. Young Joel must've figured out the same thing. Either that horse was painted here or young Joel found that bucket of paint and brought it here to hide.

"The man who painted that horse followed him here and knifed him. He left him in the barn until there was nobody around, then carried him out here, because he did not want anybody nosin' around the barn."

"Hell," Singer scoffed, "that bandit is nowhere around Morales now. He got away and he's kept goin'."

"No," Chick said, the dimplelike scar under his cheekbone seeming to deepen, "that bandit never even left town."

"What?" Singer's tone was hoarse. "What d'you mean?"

"I mean, Singer," Bowdrie said, "that you were the man on that paint horse. You were the man who murdered Joel Bates. You've got a scar on the ball of your thumb, which I noticed earlier, and that thumbprint is on this can of paint!"

"Why, you . . . !"

Singer's hand clasped his gun butt. Bowdrie's gun boomed in the close confines of the barn, and Singer's gun slipped from nerveless fingers.

"Singer!" Plank gasped. "Who would have thought it was him? But who are the others? The other four?"

"Five," Bowdrie said. "Five!"

"Five?" Bates had come into the barn again. "You mean there was another man in on this?"

"Yeah." Bowdrie's eyes shifted from face to face and back. Lingering on Bates, then moving on to Kegley and Mig Barnes, who had just come in. "There was another. There was the man who planned the whole affair."

He walked to the door, and some of the others lifted Singer's body and carried it out.

Jackson Kegley looked over at Bowdrie. "Singer was supposed to be good with a gun."

There was no expression on Bowdrie's hawklike face. "It ain't the ones like Singer a man has to watch. It's the ones who will shoot you in the back. Like the man," he added, "who killed Lem Pullitt!"

"What d'you mean by that? Pullitt was shot—"

"Lem Pullitt was shot in the back, and not by one of the three in the bank."

It was long after dark when Bowdrie returned to the street. He had gone to his room in the Rest and had taken a brief nap. From boyhood he had slept when there was opportunity and eaten when he found time. He had taken time to shave and change his shirt, thinking all the while. The ways of dishonest men were never as clever as they assumed, and the solving of a crime was usually just a painstaking job of establishing motives and putting together odds and ends of information. Criminals suffered from two very serious faults. They believed everybody else was stupid, and the criminal himself was always optimistic as to his chances of success.

The idea that men stole because they were poor or hungry was nonsense. Men or women stole because they wanted more, and wanted it without working for it. They stole to have money to flash around, to spend on liquor, women, or clothes. They stole because they wanted more faster.

Walking into the Chuck Wagon, Bowdrie took a seat at the far end of the table where he could face the room. The killer of Pullitt was somewhere around, and he was the one who had the most to lose.

Bates was not in the Wagon, nor was Kegley, but Henry Plank was, and a number of punchers in off the range. One by one he singled out their faces, and there were one or two whom he recognized. As the thin, worn man who waited on the tables came to him to take his order, Bowdrie asked, "Who's the big man with the red beard? And the dark, heavy one with the black hair on his chest?"

"Red Hammill, who rides for Big Jim Bates. Ben Bowyer used to ride for Kegley, but he rides for Bates now. They ain't tenderfeet."

"No," Bowdrie agreed, "Hammill rode in the Lincoln County War, and Bowyer's from up in the Territory."

Rip Coker threaded his way through the tables to where Bowdrie sat. "Watch your step, Ranger. There's something cookin', and my guess is it's your scalp."

"Thanks. Where do you stand?"

"I liked Lem. He staked me to grub when I first come to town."

Without having any evidence, Bowdrie was almost positive Hammill and Bowyer had been involved in the hold-up. Both men were listed as wanted in the Rangers' bible, both had been involved in such crimes before this. As wanted men they were subject to arrest in any event, but Bowdrie was concentrating on the present crime. Or crimes, for now another murder was involved.

There had been others. Was Coker one of them? He doubted it, because the man seemed sincere and also there had been obvious enmity between Coker and Singer, who had been involved.

Who was the man behind it? Who had planned and engineered the hold-up? He believed he knew, but was he right?

Bates opened the door and stepped into the room. His eyes found Bowdrie and he crossed the room to him.

"I guess my bank will hold together for a while. I am selling some cattle to Kegley, and that will tide me over."

"You gettin' a good price?"

Bates winced. "Not really. He was planning to stock blooded cattle, but he's buyin' mine instead. Sort of a favor."

Chick Bowdrie got up suddenly. "Coker," he whispered, "get Bates out of here, *fast*!"

He thought he had caught a signal from Hammill to Bowyer, and he was sure they planned to kill him tonight. There had been an appearance of planned movement in the way they came in, the seats they chose, the moves they made. He hoped his sudden move would force a change of plan or at least throw their present plans out of kilter.

"I'm hittin' the hay," he said to Coker, speaking loud enough to be heard. He started for the door.

He stepped through the swinging doors, turned toward the Rest, then circled out into the street beyond the light from the door and windows and flattened against the wall of the stage station.

Almost at once the doors spread and Red Hammill stepped out, followed by Bowyer. "Where'd he go?" Red spoke over his shoulder. "He sure ducked out of sight mighty quick!"

"Bates is still inside," Bowyer said, "an' Rip Coker is with him."

"It's that Ranger I want," Hammill said. "I think he knew me. Maybe you, too. Let's go up to the Rest."

They started for the Rest, walking fast. Bowdrie sprinted across to the blacksmith shop. Hammill turned sharply, too late to detect the movement.

"You hear somethin'?" he asked Bowyer. "Sounded like somebody runnin'!"

"Lookin' for me, Red?" Bowdrie asked.

Red Hammill was a man of action. His pistol flashed and a slug buried itself in the water trough. Bowdrie sprinted for the next building, and both men turned at the sound.

Chick yelled at them, "Come on, you two! Let's step into the street and finish this!"

"Like that, is it?" The voice came from close on his right. *Mig Barnes!*

Bowdrie fired, heard a muffled curse, but it did not sound like a wounded man.

A movement from behind him turned his head. Now they had him boxed. But who was the other one? Was it Roway?

He backed against the wall. The door was locked. On tiptoes he made it to the edge of the building, holding to the deepest shadow. He saw a dim shape rise up and the gleam of a pistol barrel. Who the devil was *that*?

A new voice, muffled, spoke up. "You're close, Tex! Give it to him!"

The shadow with the pistol raised up, the pistol lifting, and Bowdrie fired. "You're on the wrong side, mister!" he said, and ducked down the alley between the buildings, circled the buildings on the run, and stepped to the street just as Bowyer, easily recognized from his build, started across it. His bullet knocked the man to his knees. Red Hammill fired in reply, and a shot burned close to Chick, who was flattened in a shallow doorway.

He started to move, and his toe touched something. A small chunk of wood. Picking it up, he tossed it against the wall of the livery stable. It landed with a thud, and three lances of flame darted. Instantly Chick fired, heard a grunt, then the sound of a falling body. A bullet stung his face with splinters and he dropped flat and wormed his way forward, then stopped, thumbed shells into his right-hand gun, and waited.

Tex was out of it, whoever he was. Bowyer had been hit, too. Chick thought he had hit Bowyer twice.

He waited, but there was no sound. He had an idea this was not to their taste, while street fighting was an old story to him. What he wished now was to know the origin of that muffled voice. There had been an effort to disguise the tone.

He was sure his guess was right. They intended to kill Bates, too. Maybe that was where . . .

He came to his feet and went into the saloon with a lunge. There was no shot.

The men in the room were flattened against the walls, apparently unaware of how little protection they offered. Bates, his red face gone pale, eyes wide, stood against the bar. Rip Coker stood in the corner not far away, a gun in his hand. Red Hammill stood just inside the back door and Mig Barnes was a dozen feet to the right of the door.

Why his dive into the room hadn't started the shooting, he could not guess, unless it was the alert Coker standing ready with a gun.

Hammill and Barnes were men to be reckoned with, but where was Roway?

The back door opened suddenly and Jackson Kegley came in, taking a quick glance around the room.

"Bates!" Bowdrie directed. "Walk to the front door and don't get in front of my gun. *Quick!*"

Hammill's hand started, then froze. Bates stumbled from the room, and Bowdrie's attention shifted to Kegley.

"Just the man we needed," Bowdrie said. "You were the one who killed Lem Pullitt. You stood in an upstairs bedroom of the Rancher's Rest and shot him when his back was to the window."

"That's a lie!"

"Why play games?" Mig Barnes said. "We got 'em dead to rights. Me, I want that long-jawed Coker myself."

"You can have him!" Coker said, and Mig Barnes went for his gun.

In an instant the room was laced with a deadly crossfire of shooting. Rip Coker opened up with both guns and Chick Bowdrie let Hammill have his first shot, knocking the big redhead back against the bar.

Kegley was working his way along the wall, trying to get behind Bowdrie. As Hammill pushed himself away from the bar, Bowdrie fired into him twice. Switching to Kegley, he fired; then his gun clicked on an empty chamber. He dropped the gun into a holster and opened up with the left-hand gun.

Kegley fired and Bowdrie felt the shock of the bullet, but he was going in fast. He swung his right fist and knocked the bigger man to the floor. He fell to his knees, then staggered up as Kegley lunged to his feet, covered with blood. Bowdrie fired again and saw the big man slide down the wall to the floor.

Bowdrie's knees were weak and he began to stagger, then fell over to the floor.

When he fought back to consciousness, Rip Coker was beside him. Rip had a red streak along the side of his face and there was blood on his shirt. Bates, Henry Plank, and Tom Roway were all there.

"We've been workin' it out just like I think you had it figured," Henry said. "Kegley wanted a loan and got Bates to have the money in the bank. He killed Lem, just like you said.

"Kegley wanted to break Bates. He wanted the bank himself, and Bates's range as well. He planned to get Tom Roway in trouble so he could take over that ranch and run Bates's cattle on it.

"Mig Barnes apparently sold out to Kegley, but Lem Pullitt guessed what was in Kegley's mind, because he could see no reason Kegley would need a loan. Kegley was afraid Lem would talk Bates out of loaning him the money. Kegley hated Lem because Lem was not afraid of him and was suspicious of his motives."

"After you was out to my place," Roway said, "I got to thinkin'. I'd seen Barnes ride off by himself a time or two and found where he'd been meetin' Tex and Bowyer. I figured out what was goin' on, so I mounted up an' came on in."

Coker helped Bowdrie to his feet. "You're in bad shape, Bowdrie. You lost some blood and you'd best lay up for a couple of days."

"Coker," Bowdrie said, "you should be a Ranger. If ever a man was built for the job, you are!"

"I am a Ranger." Coker chuckled, pleased with his comment. "Just from another company. I was trailin' Red Hammill."

Chick Bowdrie lay back on the bed and listened to the

retreating footsteps of Coker, Plank, and Bates. He stared up at the ceiling, alone again. Seemed he was alone most of the time, but that was the way it had always been for him, since he was a youngster.

Now, if he could just find a place like Tom Roway had . . .

BOWDRIE RIDES
A COYOTE TRAIL

ONLY A MOMENT before, Chick Bowdrie had been dozing in the saddle, weary from the long miles behind; then a sudden tensing of muscles of the hammerheaded roan brought him out of it.

Pulling the black flat-crowned hat lower over his eyes, he studied the terrain with the eyes of a man who looked that he might live. His legs, sensitive to every reaction of the horse he rode, had warned him. If he needed more, he had only to look at the roan's ears, tipped forward now, and the flaring nostrils. Whatever it was, the roan did not like it.

Soft-footing it along the dusty trail, he approached the grove of trees with wary attention. He let his right hand drop back to loosen the thong that held his six-gun in place on the long rides. There was no change in expression on the dark, Apache-like face except that the scar under his right cheekbone seemed to deepen and his eyes grew more intent.

The trail he followed led along the base of a rocky ridge scattered with trees and boulders broken off from the crest of the ridge and toppled down the slope. The strawberry roan, stepping daintily, walked into the trees.

"Hold it, boy." He spoke gently as he brought the horse to a stand. A few yards away lay the sprawled figure of a man.

He sat his horse, his eyes sweeping the area with the attention of one who knows he may have to testify in court and would certainly have to file an account of his discovery.

The man beside the trail was dead. No examination was required to demonstrate that. No man could take a bullet where he had taken this one without dying. Also, he was lying on his back with the sun in his eyes.

No tracks showed near the body except those of the dead

man's horse, which stood nearby. From the size of the hole in the dead man's chest, the bullet had gone in from behind. Bowdrie turned in the saddle, measuring the distance, and his eyes found a large brush-covered boulder some fifty yards away.

The killer had not taken any chances. Chick still sat his horse. The killer had been smart to take no risks, as the man on the ground was no pilgrim. His was a good-looking face but one showing grim strength and the seasoning of many suns and the winds from long trails. He also wore two guns, and there were not many who did.

Bowdrie walked his horse closer, careful to disturb no tracks. He noted the chain loops hanging from the strap button of the dead man's spurs, looking from them to the horse, taking in the ornate Santa Barbara bit and the elaborate hand-tooled tapaderos that hooded his stirrups.

"California," Bowdrie said aloud. "He came a long way to get killed."

Dismounting, he walked over to the horse. It shied a bit, but when he spoke it hesitated, then reached for him with its nose, cautious but friendly.

"Your rider," Chick told himself, "must have been all right. You certainly haven't been abused."

He scratched the horse on the neck, his eyes taking in all the details. The rawhide riata suspended from a loop near the pommel attracted his attention.

"Eighty or eighty-five feet, I'll bet! I've heard of ropes like that. California, you were a *hand*!"

Texas riders stuck to hair ropes thirty-five to forty feet long and they worked close to a steer before making a toss. It needed an artist to handle such a rope, but he had heard talk of the California vaqueros who used ropes this long.

Walking over to the dead man, he went through his pockets. Dust was heavy on the man's clothing. He showed evidence, as did his horse, of riding far and fast. The horse was a tall black, heavier than most Texas cow horses, and was obviously well-bred and carefully trained. He was a horse who could stand long miles of hard riding, and by the looks of him he had done just that.

"Riding to see somebody," Chick guessed, "because from the look of you, you never ran from anything."

Making a neat pack of the man's pocket belongings, Chick tucked them into a hip pocket. Then he took the dead man's guns and hung them from his saddle horn.

The nearest town was too far away to carry a body, and there would be coyotes.

"I mean the four-legged kind." Bowdrie, like many a long riding man, often talked to himself. "You've already run into the two-legged kind."

He found a shallow place where the ground was not too hard, dug it out a little with a stick, and laid the body neatly in the trough he hollowed. Covering the rider's face with his vest, Chick scraped dirt over him, caved more from the bank above, then piled on juniper boughs and rocks.

When he swung to the saddle again he was leading the black horse. Starting away, he took a route that led past the brush-covered boulder.

A minute and painstaking examination told him little. He was about to leave when he saw the place where the killer's horse had been tethered. Something caught his eye and he studied the rough side of the rock, scowling thoughtfully.

The horse had waited for some time, judging by the hoof marks, and evidently had tried to scratch himself on the rock.

Bowdrie gathered several tiny fragments of wood from the rough surface. Dry and hard on one side, they were fresh and unweathered on the other. Carefully he picked off several of the bits of wood, scarcely more than shreds, and put them in a cigarette paper.

Hours later, when the shadows reached out over the little town of Hacker, Chick Bowdrie ambled the roan down the town's dusty main street to the livery stable. The black trotted behind.

Sitting in a chair tipped back against the outer wall of a saloon was a man who watched his arrival with some attention. As Bowdrie pulled up at the livery stable the man turned his head and apparently spoke to someone inside. A moment later the doors pushed wide and a man in a white hat stepped out and looked to where Bowdrie was stepping down from his horse.

Stabling the horses, Chick rubbed them down with care, fed and watered them himself. A stable-hand, chewing methodically, strolled over and watched without comment.

"Come far?" he asked, finally.

"Quite a piece. What's doin' around town?"

"Nothin' much." The hostler looked at Chick's lean, hard face and the two guns. "Huntin' a job?"

"Could be."

"Herman an' Howells are hirin'. If a man's handy with a six-shooter it won't hurt none."

"There's two sides to a fight. What about the other?"

"Jack Darcy. Pitchfork outfit. Young sprout, but he ain't hirin' gunhands. He's got no money."

The stable-hand's eyes went to the black. "You usually carry two horses?"

"It's handy sometimes." Chick straightened and his black eyes looked into the stable-hand's blue eyes. "You askin' for yourself or gettin' news for somebody?"

"Just askin'." He indicated the black horse. "You look to be a Texas man but that ain't no Texas outfit."

Chick smiled. "That'll give you something to keep you from sleepin' too sound. Somethin' to think about, Rainy."

Astonished, the stable-hand stared at him. "How'd you know my name?"

"Pays a man to keep his eyes open, Rainy," Chick replied. "When I rode up, you were diggin' tobacco out of your pouch. Your name's burned on it."

The stable-hand was embarrassed. "Why, sure! I forget sometimes it's there."

Bowdrie walked up the street, estimating the town. Quiet, weather-beaten, and wind-blasted, a few horses at the hitching rails, a stray dog or two, and a half-dozen saloons, a few stores. Only the saloons, a café, and the hotel showed lights in a town deceptively dead. He had seen many such towns before. A wrong word and they could explode into action.

The killing on the trail and the fact that at least one outfit was hiring gunhands meant there was more than was easily visible.

After booking a room at the two-story frame hotel, he went to the café. Ordering, he sat at a long wooden table and ate in silence. The slatternly woman who served him manifested no interest in the silent, leather-faced young man with the twin guns. She had seen them come and go and helped prepare a few for burial after they were gone.

He ate thoughtfully, turning over in his mind the problem that brought him here. Somewhere in the town of Hacker was a cow-stealing killer known as Carl Dyson. He was wanted in Texas for murder. Chick Bowdrie had been working out the man's carefully concealed trail for nearly a month.

He was sitting over his coffee when Rainy came in, slumping into a seat across the table. He had no more expression than Bowdrie. Picking up the pot, he poured a cup of coffee, black and strong.

"Couple of gents lookin' your gear over," he said without looking up. "Figured you might like to know. One of them is Russ Peters, a gunhand for the H&H outfit. The other was Murray Roberts, who ramrods for the H&H."

"Thanks." Chick pushed back from the table. "Where do they hang out?"

"Wagon Wheel Saloon, mostly. A couple of sidewinders, mister. Better watch yourself." Rainy's range-wise eyes dropped to the guns in their worn holsters as the stranger went out the door. "Or," he added, "maybe *they'd* better watch out!"

Several poker games were in progress in the Wagon Wheel, a few punchers were casually bucking a faro layout, and four men stood at the bar. One was a tall, fine-looking man in a white hat and neat range clothes. The other was shorter, heavier, and roughly dressed, with a brutal, unshaved face and a mustache. He wore a low-crowned sombrero with a crease through the middle.

He muttered something to his companion as Bowdrie came to the bar, but the bigger man merely shot a glance at Chick and went on talking.

"Darcy better sell while the sellin' is possible. At this rate he won't have anything left."

The man with the creased sombrero stared at Chick. "Right nice horse you led into town," he commented, "and a good many of us are wondering what became of its rider."

Chick turned slowly. His left elbow rested on the bar; his right hand held a glass of rye. He stared into the yellow eyes of the man in the creased sombrero, and somebody in the room swallowed audibly. Menace seemed to rise like a cloud in the smoke-laden air of the room.

Bowdrie's Apache face did not change. He lifted his glass and drank the rye, putting the glass back on the bar. Tension in the room was a living thing, and the studied moves of the young man at the bar awakened something in the minds of the onlookers.

"I said," the man in the creased sombrero repeated, "a lot of folks want to know what became of the rider."

Chick's eyes held steady, and then in a casual, almost bored tone he said, "The name is Russ Peters," making it clear he referred to the man he faced. "Used to call himself Rusty Padwill. Fancies himself a gunfighter but is always careful who he does his shootin' with. Ran with the Murphy-Dolan crowd in the Lincoln County War. Wanted in Colorado for stealin' horses, suspected of dry-gulchin' a prospector in Arizona. Run out of Tombstone by Virgil Earp."

Peters' mouth dropped open and he started to speak, but Chick Bowdrie continued.

"I might add that the man who rode that horse I brought in was dry-gulched, and I suspect everybody in town knows who is most liable to shoot a man in the back."

Peters had been startled into immobility by the quiet recital of his background. His face turned white, then red as a wild anger swept over him. "You pointin' that at me?" he demanded.

"When you throw a stone into a pack of dogs, the one that yelps is the one that got hit."

Overcome by fury, Peters lunged at him, but Bowdrie brushed Peters' grasping hand away and snapped a jolting right uppercut to the chin. Peters' knees buckled and he fell forward.

Bowdrie moved back a step to let him fall, then said to the astonished bartender, "I'll have one more. The riding across country was kind of dry an' dusty."

Peters pulled himself to his knees, shaking his head. Realization struck him and he lunged to his feet, grasping for his gun. He got his hand on it and stiffened. He was looking into the unwavering muzzle of Bowdrie's gun.

"I'm in no mood for a shooting," Bowdrie said, "and this ain't your night. You'd better mount up and head back for the home ranch."

Murray Roberts glanced over at Bowdrie. "That tip is appreciated, mister. We had no idea Russ was a wanted man." He glanced at the two guns. "You handle yourself pretty well. Where did you say you came from?"

"I didn't say."

"If you're huntin' a job, drop out to the H&H. We need men."

"If Peters is a sample of what you have"—he drained his glass—"I reckon you do."

Turning on his heel, he walked out, leaving Roberts staring after him, his features taut with anger.

Bowdrie had reached the hotel porch when a dark figure detached itself from the shadows.

"Hold it!" The man lifted a hand. "I'm friendly!" He was a short, blond man in worn boots, jeans stuffed into them.

"You're talking," Bowdrie said. "Shall we step inside?"

The young man wore a gun, a black-and-white-checkered shirt, and an unbuttoned vest. He had a wide, friendly face, very worried now. "You led a black horse into town? A California rig?"

"I did."

"What happened to the rider?"

"Shot in the back about ten miles south. Do you know him?"

"He was my friend, and I was expecting him. I'm Jack Darcy, of the Pitchfork. That was Dan Lingle, and he was coming in to help me."

Bowdrie was surprised, then irritated with himself. He

should have known the man. "That was Dan Lingle, the lawman? The one who cleaned out the Skull Canyon crowd?"

"That's him. What beats me is why they would shoot him. Nobody knew he was coming, nobody even knew I knew him. Lingle was my brother-in-law. Then my sister was killed."

"Killed? How?"

"Some hand she hired while Dan was away. She caught him stealing. He knocked her down. In falling, she struck her head, apparently, and died. Dan knew the man by sight, and he was hunting him."

"When did your fight begin here?" Bowdrie asked. "Tell me about it."

Darcy hesitated, then shrugged. "We were getting along all right, the H&H an' me. In fact"—he flushed—"I sort of was courtin' Meg Howells.

"Murray Roberts come in and hires out to Howells. Before long he's got Herman and Howells down on me. He showed 'em some doctored brands, and I never rustled a cow in my life! Then he started courting Meg, an' they wouldn't let me on the place.

"I'm no gunfighter. He drew on me, Roberts did, and I reckon he'd of killed me if Meg hadn't grabbed his arm. She claimed it was my fault and said I wasn't to come back."

Bowdrie sat down on the cowhide settee and motioned Darcy to join him. They were sitting so Bowdrie could watch both the window and the door without being seen. "How long has Roberts been here?" he asked.

"Six months, I'd say. His partner, Russ Peters, he showed up about a month ago, but he'd known Roberts before, I believe."

"Six months?" Disappointment was obvious in his tone. Rising, he started toward the stairway. "I'll be riding your way tomorrow, Darcy. Might put up with you for the night. Maybe I'm not the man Dan Lingle was, but—"

"Gosh a'mighty, man! Come ahead! I can use all the help I can get, but you're welcome, anytime! Fact is," he added, "it gets kind of lonely out there, with nobody coming by and me not seeing Meg anymore."

He turned to go, then stopped and looked back. "You didn't say what your name was?"

"I'm Chick Bowdrie."

"Chick Bowdrie, the Texas Ranger? I've heard of you."

Bowdrie went up the stairs, and the desk clerk, rising from his chair, watched until Darcy mounted his horse and rode out of town. The clerk came from behind his desk, glanced quickly around, then ran down the street.

Bowdrie came down the stairs and followed, keeping to the shadows.

A few minutes later, standing in the darkness outside an open window at the other end of town, he listened as the desk man told his story to Murray Roberts, Russ Peters, and a heavy-set man with a bald head.

"Chick Bowdrie, is it?" Roberts was saying. "That means we've got to kill him or we're through here."

"Then we'll kill him"—the fat man took the cigar from his lips—"and we can't waste any time. If he finds any evidence, he'll let McNelly know."

The fat man looked over at Roberts. "Who killed Lingle, Murray?"

Murray Roberts shrugged. "Not me!" he protested.

"Well, it wasn't me, either!" Peters said. "I'm damned if I know!"

"Murray, you ride back to the ranch. I'll keep Russ here. Ride herd on the old man. We can't let him start guessing or he might come up with some answers." The fat man paused and pointed a thick middle finger at Roberts. "You watch him, not that girl! Women will be the death of you yet!"

Chick Bowdrie returned to the hotel, slipped up the back stairs to his room, and went to bed. There were never any simple cases anymore. Maybe there never had been.

He had started hunting a killer with no accurate description except that he was carrying two diamond rings, a watch, and four beautiful Morgan horses—a stallion and three mares.

It had been a cold trail from the start, but one thing he knew. The killer had sold no Morgan horses. Wherever he was, he still had them.

"Better check those ranches tomorrow," he told himself.

He clasped his hands behind his head. Just to think! He, Chick Bowdrie, a Texas Ranger! No idea had been further from his mind a year ago. He'd grown up, at least part of the way, on a ranch not far from D'Hanis, a town near San Antonio. At sixteen he had killed his first man, a cow thief who was trying to run off some of his employer's cattle, but even that had not been his first fight. At six years old he had helped load rifles for his father and uncle as they fought Comanches, and by the time his sixteenth birthday came around, he had been in a half-dozen Indian fights.

His experience was not unusual for the time and the area. Indian fights and over-the-border raids were all too common, but skill with guns had come naturally. Like many another boy or girl of his time, he had been hunting meat for the table from the time he could hold up a rifle.

Yet the way things had gone, he might have wound up on the wrong end of the law. It was only chance and Captain McNelly of the Rangers that turned him around.

The H&H ranch lay six miles west of Hacker, and Chick Bowdrie made it by a few minutes after daylight. He reined in among some cedar at the end of a long hill and looked down upon the ranch.

It was enough to make a cattleman dream. Miles upon miles of green, rolling range spreading out like a great sea behind the cluster of ranch buildings. And there were cattle. As far as a man could see, there were cattle, scattered over the range or gathered along the stream that watered it.

Over against the foothills he could see what must be the Pitchfork holdings. Inquiries made before riding in here had told him what to expect. The Pitchfork cattle, or what he assumed to be them, ranged up the draws that led into the hills and along the flanks of the hills themselves.

Only within the past year had trouble arisen. H&H cattle had been missed, brands had been blotted, and Rack Herman had been led to believe that Darcy was rustling. Then Roberts had come in, was taken on as foreman, and complaints against Darcy multiplied. Then a Darcy hand was reported to have killed an H&H rider.

Chick studied the situation thoughtfully. He had grown up on the range, punching cows and riding the open range. He knew how range wars developed and on how little evidence accusations were often made.

Nobody had seen that H&H rider killed. He had been found near Pitchfork range, shot through the back. The H&H then killed a Pitchfork rider, and the H&H began hiring gunmen.

"It looks like somebody wanted trouble," Bowdrie surmised, but he was too experienced to draw any firm conclusions.

The trouble had started before Murray Roberts appeared, so he, apparently, was not the cause.

H&H hands were riding out on the range now. He sat his horse, watching them go. The fewer around, the better. Finally he started the roan and cantered down to the ranch yard.

A girl came running down the steps to drive some chickens from a flowerbed, her blond hair blowing in the wind. When she saw him she stopped, shading her eyes against the sun.

He drew up. "Howdy, ma'am. How's for a cup of coffee?"

"Of course. I am sure there's some left. We try to have coffee throughout the day for any of the hands who might ride in. Will you come in?"

He swung down and tied the roan to the hitching rail, and followed her into the house. The Chinese cook was just cleaning up after the cowhands. Seeing Bowdrie, he asked no questions but brought coffee, then some eggs and sliced beef.

"You will be Meg Howells," he said abruptly.

"Yes." She studied him. "How did you know?"

"Why," he said blandly, "I run into a feller who said you were the prettiest girl in these parts. He surely was no liar."

"Oh? You met Murray?"

He swallowed some coffee and used the fork on the eggs. "No, ma'am. His name was Jack Darcy."

"Oh?" Her voice was cool. "How is he?"

She tried to keep her tone disinterested, but underneath it he could detect not only curiosity, but interest.

"Looks mighty peaked, like maybe things were goin' bad at the ranch or maybe he lost his best girl or something." Before she could respond to that, he continued, "Of course, he did lose his best friend."

"Jack did? Who could that be?"

"Mighty fine man named Dan Lingle, a law officer from out California way. He was ridin' in here to visit Jack, and somebody dry-gulched him. Shot him from ambush and in the back."

"How awful! That's just terrible! And that's just how Jack's . . . !"

She hesitated, frowning.

"Jack's what?" Bowdrie asked.

He was no judge of women-folks. It was not like reading trail sign. Women made queer tracks, yet even he could sense that Meg Howells had something on her mind.

"Why, it just struck me that Jack's father was killed that way. He was following some rustlers. It was about eight months ago. He was found lying beside the trail and he had been shot in the back."

He sipped his coffee, and suddenly she turned on him. "Who are you? Are you looking for a job?"

"No, ma'am. I'm a Texas Ranger. I'm following a man who married a woman, murdered her, and then drove off her cattle. He told folks he was migratin' west, that his wife was sick in the wagon. After he was gone, they found her body. He'd taken the rings her father gave her, and four Morgan horses.

"There was another killing of a woman after that, but we're not sure the same man did it."

"Four horses?"

"Yes, ma'am. A stallion and three brood mares. Fine stock. Have you seen any such horses?"

"No. No, I haven't."

She seemed suddenly eager to be rid of him, so he pushed back his chair and got up. "Mind if I look around a little? You've a fine place here."

"Please do! Go right ahead!"

She was already hurrying from the room. He drained his cup of coffee and walked outside. Taking his time, he strolled toward the stable. When he saw the row of saddles on a railing, his lips tightened a little.

"Somewhere," he told himself, "you're going to find a saddle with wooden, California-style stirrups. Real old-time stuff, and some of the wood will have been rubbed off, just recently, on a rock."

No such saddle was in this lot, however. He was just turning away from them when a harsh voice cut into the silence, a voice that sent little prickles along the back of his neck.

"Who are you, and what are you doin', prowlin' around here?"

Chick's face was blank. "Just lookin' around," he said. "I asked Miss Meg if it would be all right."

"Well, it isn't all right." He was a short, enormously fat man with a thick neck rising from massive shoulders. Chick was suddenly wary. This man was not just fat. There was an ease and dexterity in his movements and the way he used his hands that belied his bulk. At least two inches shorter than he, the man must have weighed two hundred and fifty pounds. "Anybody who wants to look this ranch over comes to me!"

"I heard," Chick said mildly, "that the place belonged to Howells and Herman."

"That's right. I'm Rack Herman!"

"Yeah?" Something about the man stirred all the antagonism within him. "From the way you talked, I figured you were both of them."

Herman's features seemed to tighten. The easy-appearing fat man vanished and the face Bowdrie looked at was brutal.

"Think I'm just a fat slob, do you?" His tongue touched his lips, and into his eyes came a queer eagerness that made Bowdrie cringe as though he had touched something unclean. "I like to beat clever fellers like you!"

"Take it easy, boss." Murray Roberts appeared in the doorway behind Herman. "That's Chick Bowdrie."

Rack stopped in mid-stride, and the transformation was amazing. In an instant his face was all smiles.

"Bowdrie? Why didn't you say so? I thought you were some driftin' cowhand lookin' for something he could steal! Shucks, if I'd knowed you was the law . . .

"Come up to the house, will you?"

"Thanks, but I've some riding to do. However, if it is all right with you, I might stop by on the way back."

"Of course! Stop by anytime! Glad to have you at any time!"

Bowdrie walked to his horse and swung into the saddle. Turning his horse toward the Darcy range, he wiped the sudden sweat from his brow. "That, Mr. Bowdrie," he said aloud, "was a close one!"

Rack Herman was a new element in the situation, but the rancher was no tinhorn crook, but something more. He was a monster, a being of concentrated evil such as one rarely found on western range . . . or elsewhere, for that matter.

He was crossing the slope of a hill out of sight of the H&H when a movement caught his eye. It was Meg Howells on a small gray horse, approaching by a roundabout way and heading for the hills. Circling through the trees, keeping out of sight, he rode until he cut her trail; then he fell in behind. The girl was riding fast and she was going somewhere, obviously with a destination in mind.

Glancing down his back trail, he glimpsed another rider whose route had not crossed his. Hurriedly Chick Bowdrie pulled back into the trees until the horseman rode past. It was Murray Roberts.

The trail itself was dusty, so Bowdrie held to the grassy side of the road to raise no dust. It was simple enough to avoid being seen by keeping to low ground until suddenly Meg rode up a low hill and through a cleft in the rock wall.

Until now she had been riding a known trail, but she hesitated before going into the notch, obviously uncertain of what she might find. Hesitating from time to time, she rode on.

Pulling the roan to a stop, Chick watched Murray Roberts

allow the girl some time before he entered the cleft. He had the impression this was no new trail to Roberts.

Waiting approximately as long as Roberts had, Chick rode into the cleft.

It grew narrower and narrower, until at one point the sides of his boots rubbed the rock on either wall; then it widened again, and far ahead he could see the girl riding into a green and lovely box canyon. Beyond, there was a clump of cotton-woods and a small cabin. There was a corral, and in the corral, several horses.

Instinct told him what horses these were, and with that realization came a heightened sense of danger. Roberts was just ahead, spurring now to catch the girl.

Bowdrie turned sharply away from the notch and skirted the canyon, keeping to the brush but riding fast. He dismounted behind a ramshackle barn and eased himself to the corner. Peering around, he saw four horses in the corral.

The Morgan horses! Then Roberts . . . He heard voices, Murray Roberts' voice. "How'd you know about this place?" he was demanding.

"I saw you riding here. Later, I saw him coming here. I had no idea what was here, but I had to find out."

"Now you've found out, you'd better get, an' quick! If he finds you here, he'll kill you." He was silent for a moment, then added, "Meg, let's you an' me cut out. Nobody's got a chance with him around! He killed—"

"Who did I kill?"

The voice was so close that Bowdrie started as if stung. Then he realized the voice came from the barn behind which he was hiding.

"Rack!" Roberts was startled. "I thought—!"

"You thought I was back at the ranch!" Rack Herman moved out of the barn, walking toward them. "You didn't think I'd have a hideout without two ways in an' out, did you?"

He moved closer to them. "Murray, you're a weak sister! I've seen this comin' and knew I'd have you to kill. You're no good to me, anyway, and I've got the old man right where I want him, and it's time to clean house. I've already taken care of Peters, and now you."

Murray Roberts went for his gun and was too slow by half. Rack Herman put three bullets over his belt buckle before Roberts' gun had cleared its holster.

Rack Herman thumbed shells from his belt, but before he could load, Bowdrie stepped from behind the barn. "Drop it, Rack! Drop it right where you are and then move back!"

Rack let the gun slip from his fingers and moved back away from it. "If you didn't have that gun, I'd . . . !"

What made him do it, Bowdrie never knew, but he unbuckled his gunbelt and handed it to Meg. "Don't shoot unless it is to save yourself. Maybe I'm a damned fool, but I've got this to do."

She took the guns, and Rack moved toward him, sure of himself now. As they came together, Bowdrie stabbed a left to Herman's face, but the man took the blow and kept coming, very sure of himself.

A smashing blow caught Bowdrie in the ribs and a clubbing right caught his jaw and started bells ringing in his skull. He felt himself falling, heard Rack's grunt of satisfaction.

His knees hit the dust and then Bowdrie came up as Rack closed in. Bowdrie hooked hard to the side of the face, twisted away, and stabbed a left to the heavier man's mouth, drawing blood.

Herman could punch unbelievably fast. He caught Bowdrie with a left and right, but Bowdrie's right caught Herman on the chin. Yet how he got through the next few minutes, he never knew. Blows rained on his head, jaw, and shoulders, yet he stayed on his feet, taking them and fighting back. Through his befogged brain an idea penetrated. Battered though he was, Bowdrie realized that Rack was gasping for breath.

Powerful as he was, and amazingly fast for such a heavy man, Herman was carrying a huge weight and the sun was hot. Bowdrie, dried by desert suns and winds, was lean as an ironwood tree and just as resilient. No doubt Herman had won most of his fights with a blow or two, but Bowdrie had soaked up what punishment he could give and was still on his feet.

Through the fog in his brain and the taste of blood in his mouth, Chick knew he could win. Hurt though he was, he drew on some well of desperation within him and began to punch.

Left, right, left, right, blow after battering blow pounded the huge body and the brutal face. His arms were weary from just punching, but Herman's mouth was hanging open as he gasped for every breath.

Stepping away, he feinted, and as the heavier man's hands came up, he threw a low hard right to the midsection. Then, weaving to avoid the pawing blows, he threw blow after blow to the heavy body. Then there was nobody in front of him and hands were grabbing him.

"Stop it, man! You'll kill him! Stop it!"

They pulled him back, and Rack Herman lay on the ground against the barn wall, his face bloody and battered.

Jack Darcy and Rainy were there, holding him back from the man he had come so far to find, Rack Herman, the man who had once called himself Carl Dyson. Bowdrie knew he would have to look no further for the saddle he had hoped to find.

He shook his head to clear it of the last of the dwindling fog. He stared at Rainy. "What are you doing here?"

"I'd been wanting to marry Jack's sister," Rainy explained, "but Dan Lingle beat me out. He was a good man and I held no grudge, but I came on to find Darcy. I knew her murderer was somewhere around."

"That was only one murder. There was another in Texas." He took his gunbelt from Meg and slung it about his shoulders. "I'd no business doing this"—he gestured at Herman, who was being helped to his feet by Darcy—"but the man's arrogance kind of got under my skin."

"He had it coming," Rainy agreed, "but he'll live long enough to hang."

Holding their prisoner, they walked toward the corral. The Morgans were waiting, heads up, alert.

"After you get those horses back where they belong," Darcy suggested, "why don't you come back? There's a lot of good cattle country around here."

Bowdrie slapped the dust from his hat. "I'm a Ranger," he said, "and there's always work for a Ranger. Come to one trail's end, and there's always another. I kind of like it that way."

A TRAIL TO THE WEST

CHICK BOWDRIE STARED into the muzzle of the six-gun. His dark features showed no expression, but behind the black eyes there was an urge to draw and take his chance.

He had lived by the gun long enough to know that a wise man does not take such chances with the kind of man who was holding the six-shooter. He was a tall man with rounded shoulders and a narrow gray-skinned face, an unhealthy face on a man who had been out of the sunlight for some time.

"What's the matter, partner?" Bowdrie inquired. "What makes you so jumpy?"

"Who are you? Where you headin'?"

"Me?" Chick inquired innocently. "I'm just a driftin' cow-hand, ridin' the grub-line. I'm called Sam Dufresne."

"What are you ridin' up in the trees for? The trail's down yonder."

"Now an' again a man finds that trails aren't healthy. You know what I mean or you wouldn't be so touchy. I had an idea I wouldn't meet any travelers up here, an' it would give me a chance to have a look at who is ridin' the trail. Maybe see them before they saw me."

"Meanin' that you're on the dodge?" The man holding the gun was beginning to relax. He was puzzled but cautious.

"Now, that's a leadin' question," Bowdrie said, "but bein' behind that gun gives you the right to ask it. If you weren't holdin' that gun, you might hesitate to ask any such question."

The round-shouldered man's eyes glinted with sudden anger. "So?" The muzzle tilted just a bit, and Bowdrie was ready. If he died, he wasn't going to die alone. His own gun was only inches from his hand.

"Hold it, Hess!" The branches of a juniper pushed forward and a man came out of the trees to stand facing Bowdrie. Here was a danger, perhaps more deadly than the gun at his head. He also knew he had found who he was looking for.

The newcomer was big; a leonine head topped a thick, muscular neck and massive shoulders. He had small feet and hands for his bulk, and a square-cut face tight-skinned and tanned. His eyes were pale, almost white. This was John Queen.

"Howdy," Bowdrie said. "I'm glad you spoke up. I hate to get killed or kill a man this early of a mornin'."

John Queen studied him with cool, appraising eyes. "I would say if any killin' was done, he'd be apt to do it."

"Maybe," Bowdrie admitted, "but things ain't always the way they seem. He might kill me, but I'd surely kill him."

"You'd have to be a mighty fast hand with that gun," Queen said, "an' there's not many who could do that—if anybody could do it."

Queen glanced at the horse and saddle, and looked again at Bowdrie's twin guns. "You say your name is Sam Dufresne. I can count the men who could draw that fast on the fingers of one hand, and none of them would be named like you."

"Could be there's somebody new in the picture," Bowdrie suggested.

"You ain't Billy the Kid because you're too big and you don't have those two buck teeth. You're too slim and tall for John Wesley Hardin, and your hair's the wrong color for any of the Earps, but I'll come up with a name for you. Just give me time."

Turning to the other man, he said, "Put your gun away, Hess. I want to talk to this man." He motioned with his head. "Come on into camp, whatever your name is."

Three men sat around the fire when Chick Bowdrie stepped down from his strawberry roan. As he stripped the saddle from his long-legged, ugly horse he mentally cataloged them from his memory of the Ranger's bible, which carried descriptions of most of the wanted men in the Southwest.

The lean, hungry-looking man with the knife scar would

be Jake Murray, wanted in San Antone for a killing and in Uvalde for bank robbery. The other two were Eberhardt and Kaspar, rustlers and horse thieves from the Pecos country. Without discounting the danger in Eberhardt, Kaspar, and Hess, the real trouble here was in Jake Murray and John Queen.

He did not look around, for there would be danger in that. If the girl was here, he would see her sooner or later. Above all, he must not seem curious or even aware anybody else was here, if indeed she was here in this camp.

"Where y' headin'?" Queen asked when Bowdrie was seated with a cup of coffee in his hand.

"The Davis Mountains. Maybe Fort Stockton. If it doesn't look friendly, I'll just keep ridin' out to Oak Creek Canyon. I'm huntin' a place to lay up for the winter."

"You ain't Jesse Evans," Queen said, "although you've something of his look."

Bowdrie sipped his coffee. John Queen was too knowing, and if this continued he was going to come up with an answer. So far the Earps were the only peace officers mentioned, but if he started on Texas Rangers, he would not be long in coming up with an answer. Bowdrie was new to the outfit, but he had already made a name for himself.

"What the hell?" Bowdrie said. "You boys are all right. You've probably never heard of me, anyway. My name's Shep Harvey."

It was a gamble, of course. There was a possibility one of these men knew Shep Harvey, a gunman who had come from the Missouri River country and was riding with King Fisher's outfit. Harvey had come to Texas only a few weeks before, after killing a gambler in Natchez. He had been a cowhand and buffalo hunter in the Dakotas, had held up a stage on the Deadwood run, and killed a sheriff in Yankton who tried to make an arrest.

John Queen looked relieved. "No wonder I couldn't place you. How come you're down in this country?"

"Lookin' for a place to hole up for the winter," Bowdrie said. "I'm tired of runnin'. I want to put my feet under the same table for a while an' sort of rest up."

"Heard of you," Murray admitted. "Didn't you have some trouble in Laredo?"

"Some." Chick leaned back against a rock. He was riding a dangerous trail, he knew that. If these men discovered who he was, they would kill him without hesitation. They were all wanted men, and doubly so now. They had much to lose and nothing to gain by keeping him around. All they needed was an excuse. Somehow he had to locate the girl and get her away from them.

It had started three weeks earlier. Five hard-bitten men had ridden up to the lonely ranch of Clinton Buck on the South Canadian. Buck had gone to the door in answer to their hail, and died in a burst of gunfire. They had given no warning, no chance.

Old Bart Tendrel had come from the corral, only to be shot down in his tracks. Then they had taken the girl, what riding stock was available, and what money was in the house, and headed west, out of Texas.

McNelly had sent for Chick Bowdrie. "This is a job for a man who knows the outlaw trails, Bowdrie, and it's a one-man job. If we go after them with a bunch of Rangers, they will simply kill that girl. Somehow we have to get her away from them before the final verdict.

"We've got Damon Queen coming up for sentencing, and Judge Whiting is Jeanne Buck's uncle and he raised her from a baby whilst her father was off buffalo hunting. John Queen has gotten word to Whiting that if his decision is wrong, the girl dies. Clinton Buck was no kin to the judge, but the girl is. The old judge loves that girl like she was his own. You go get her back."

The wind whined through the junipers, moaning like a lost dog. "Sounds like rain," Queen said, "and we don't need that."

He looked over at Bowdrie. "How far to Oak Creek, Shep?"

"Not too far. There's a good hideout there. A friend of mine told me about a gent who has a ranch over thataway."

Eberhardt started dishing up the food and Jake Murray walked back into the trees, and when he returned, a girl was walking ahead of him. She was a shapely girl with auburn hair. She glanced at Bowdrie, then looked away.

"Friend of ours goin' west with us," John Queen explained.

Chick betrayed no interest. "Lots of folks movin' these days," he commented.

They moved out at sunup and there had been no chance for him to speak to the girl or to give her any hint that would have her alert and ready. One thing he discovered quickly. The girl had spirit. At breakfast it showed itself clearly when Hess idly dropped a hand to her shoulder.

Jeanne turned sharply, catching up the knife beside her plate. "Keep your filthy hands off me! You put another hand on me and I'll cut it off!"

Bob Hess jerked his hand back, and the other outlaws laughed. Hess's face reddened with anger and he started for the girl, when Queen spoke.

"Set down, Bob!" he commanded. "You asked for it. Now, you keep your hands to yourself!"

Jeanne resumed her seat, in no way disturbed, the knife ready at hand. She was reaching for the coffeepot when her eyes met Chick's. He lowered one eyelid and took a mouthful of beans. Then, in case he had been seen, he rubbed his eye.

Chick Bowdrie was a man virtually without illusions. His boyhood had been a hard one and he had narrowly missed becoming an outlaw himself. It was only Captain McNelly who made the difference. Unknown to him, the Ranger captain, always alert for promising material, had been watching him for some time.

A top hand on any outfit, Bowdrie was simply too good with a gun, and sooner or later he was going to kill the wrong man and become an outlaw. He had had several minor brushes with the law, none of them justified and none leading to gunplay, but there were too many around who thought themselves fast. McNelly knew from his own observations and those of some of his older, wiser men that Bowdrie was simply too good.

"Cap," one of his sergeants had said, "recruit the kid. He's one of the best trackers around, he's got good sense, nobody stampedes him, and he's so much better with a gun than any other man I know, that there's no comparison.

"He's instinctively a good shot, he's very cool, and he's been born with remarkable coordination and eyesight. He's got the makings for a Ranger if I ever saw one, and frankly, I'd rather have him on our side."

To use a gun well was one thing; to know when to use it was another.

Chick Bowdrie knew the odds were against him in every way. He was miles from Texas and the jurisdiction of the Rangers. Some law officers extended courtesy and worked with others; some resented any intrusion into their area. Whatever happened, he must handle himself.

Hess hated him. It was an instinctive and bitter hatred, and Bowdrie's certainty that he could get off a shot before Hess could kill him, rankled.

They rode out of the scattered junipers now and followed a long, grassy bottom toward distant hills. Chick was remembering a canyon north of their route where cliff dwellers had built their houses under the overhang of the cliffs.

It was something to remember. If he could get Jeanne Buck away, it would be only the beginning. They were almost five hundred miles west of the Texas line—he could only guess at the exact distance.

Once he got her away, if he could, he would have to exercise jurisdiction with a six-shooter and a Winchester.

Several times when he looked up he caught Bob Hess staring at him, eyes ugly with hatred.

Eberhardt and Kaspar seemed to have no great interest in him, but Jake Murray was a morose, silent man who went through life with a chip on his shoulder. Several of the killings for which he was known had simply resulted from minor slights that many a man would have passed over. He was extremely touchy.

Hess might bring danger upon him, but it was Jake Murray and John Queen whom he would have to face at the showdown.

The little cavalcade wound around the hills, in and out of the pines.

Queen saw an antelope.

"Fresh meat," he said, and throwing his rifle to his shoulder, he fired.

Queen made a beautiful shot. The antelope leaped straight up, then fell dead, but with the report Jeanne's horse bounded as if shot from a gun and broke into a dead run.

Instantly Bowdrie put spurs to his roan and went after her. It was a thrilling chase, but the roan was simply too fast for the paint, and closing in, Bowdrie seized the bridle.

It was a chance. They were off in the lead and might escape. He glanced back. Murray and Queen were sitting with their rifles up and ready.

"Not a chance," he told Jeanne. "He'd nail us just like he did that antelope."

She was staring at him with angry eyes. "That's the chance I've been waiting for!" she protested.

"You wouldn't have a prayer. Now, tell 'em your horse ran away with you, and act the same way you have up to now. I'm a Texas Ranger."

Hope leaped into her eyes, then sank into sullenness as she tried to assume her old manner. Chick took her bridle and waited for the other men to come up.

"Lucky you stopped her," Queen said. "She might have been killed."

He looked sharply at Jeanne. "How does it feel to be rescued? Doesn't that make Shep, here, a hero?"

"No hero would ride with a bunch of low-down thieves and murderers!" she flared.

"If it was me," Hess said viciously, "I'd slap those words right down her throat!"

"It ain't you," Queen replied mildly. "I like the gal's spunk."

Bowdrie's black eyes missed nothing. The big gunman was a shrewd judge of character, and Chick was sure the man suspected him. Also, he knew that every mile they put between themselves and Texas made the task more difficult.

This was Queen's country. He had ridden here before. He knew the land and the people, and they had come far from the Rangers and any chance of rescue.

Chick felt trapped. Every instant of delay drew him deeper and deeper into an entangling web of hills, and at any moment there could be a showdown. Bowdrie guessed Queen had seen the hurried conversation between Jeanne Buck and himself the day her horse ran away.

Yet the big gunman was agreeable, always pleasant, quick to smile. Then one night they camped some thirty miles south of San Francisco Peak.

When they finished eating, John Queen looked up suddenly. "Shep, you an' Hess might as well ride into the settlement with Kaspar. See if there's any strangers around, buy supplies, and you might as well bring back a jug of whiskey while you're at it. We're going to be holed up until the trial's over—"

"Trial?" Bowdrie looked surprised. "Who's bein' tried?"

He thought he made a credible appearance of ignorance, but a man could never be sure with John Queen.

"Oh? Didn't we tell you? Miss Buck here is sort of stayin' with us until we see how a trial goes back in Texas. We both kind of want to see it turn out right so's she can go home."

John Queen's smile faded. "Now, you boys just ride into town and get what we need. We'll be waitin' for you."

Chick's dark, Indian-like face showed no expression. He walked to his horse and started saddling up. It meant that for several hours she would be left alone with these men.

Not that they would molest her. If that had been a part of their plans, it would have happened long before this. What he feared was that Queen would spirit her away while he was gone. He might have decided who Bowdrie was, and be using this method to be rid of him. It was significant that Bob Hess had been chosen to accompany him. Hess was too volatile to trust to ride into a strange town when secrecy was imperative.

There was nothing to do but obey. There was a murmur of voices from the fireside, but Kaspar joined him and there was no way he could listen.

The time had come for a showdown, and he was sure Queen suspected him. In any event, he was not one of them, just a man on the dodge supposedly traveling the same route, and this was a good time to be rid of him.

As they headed for town, he was aware of the increasing silence on the part of his companions. It was a sullen, determined silence his comments could not invade. Bob Hess he did not expect to talk, but Kaspar was usually a talkative man.

Kaspar rode beside Bowdrie, Hess always half a length behind, and the danger of his position was obvious. Whether John Queen suspected him or not, he wanted no more of the man called Shep Harvey.

In town they trotted their horses to the hitching rail in front of the Frontier House. Inside, a half-dozen men were at the bar, and several gaming tables were active. Chick walked to the bar and bought a drink for Kaspar. Bob Hess lingered at one of the tables.

Suddenly Bob Hess's voice lifted over the noise and the talk. "Hey, Shep! Come here a moment!"

Chick Bowdrie turned instinctively, aware of the undercurrent in the man's voice. He straightened away from the bar, knowing if he went toward Hess he would put Kaspar at his back. As things stood, the two men were on the same side of him. "You come here," he said, "I've got me a drink."

There was a muttered exchange at the table, and then a man got up and started toward Chick. He walked beside Hess, and Bowdrie could see the triumph in Hess's eyes he was trying to hide.

The young man, scarcely more than twenty, had a hard, reckless face and he walked with a bit of swagger. When he was a year or two older, he would drop that. A tough man did not have to make a parade of it.

They stopped about twelve feet away and the young man said, "My name is Shep Harvey!"

Bowdrie felt his pulse jump, but he had half-expected something of the kind. His features showed no change. "How nice for you! It's a pleasure to know you."

Harvey hesitated. The announcement had been calculated to throw Bowdrie into confusion. Hess, too, was surprised.

"I hear you've been usin' my name."

"That's right. It sounded like a good name to me, and I didn't want these boys to know who I really was."

"I don't like four-flushers usin' my name. I don't like it one bit. I'm goin' to put an end to it right now!"

"My name's Bowdrie," Chick said, "Chick Bowdrie."

Bob Hess's face turned sick and Shep Harvey was caught flatfooted. He was good with a gun and liked being known as a fast man, but he had no stomach for facing men who might be faster. He preferred shooting, not being shot at. He took a step back, suddenly aware he was holding a busted flush.

"Go ahead, Hess," Bowdrie said. "You've wanted it, now you've got it."

Magically, the room behind them had cleared. Hess, panic-stricken, dropped a hand to his gun, and Bowdrie's flashing draw put a period to the moment. One shot only, and Bowdrie's gun swept past Harvey and shot into the slower-moving Steve Kaspar.

Kaspar took the bullet standing and continued his draw. As his gun came up, Bowdrie shot him again, and his knees gave way and he pitched to the floor.

Shep Harvey, his face a deathly white, held his hands high, away from his guns. It was the first time he'd had a chance to shoot it out with a really fast man, and suddenly all his appetite for gunfighting vanished. He stepped back, shocked, staring at the blood where Bob Hess lay dying.

"Drop your gunbelt, Harvey. Then get your horse and get out of town. But don't go back to Texas. We don't want you there."

Harvey stepped back, unbuckling his guns; then he ducked through the door, almost running.

Bowdrie glanced around the room, then gestured at the men on the floor. "These were Texas men. They abducted a girl after murdering her father. It is Texas business, and I'm a Ranger."

The bartender had both hands on the bar. "Far's we're concerned, mister, your business is cleared up. You probably saved Arizona the trouble of hangin' them."

The campfire was cold and dead when he reached the spot where he had left the girl and her captors. It was now too dark to find a trail, and much too dangerous. Moving back into the trees, he put down his bedroll and slept soundly until morning.

There was a faint chill in the air when he awakened. Obviously Hess and Kaspar had known where to go when they were rid of him. Some plan had been arrived at, either to tell him he was no longer wanted or to get him drunk and kill him. The accidental meeting with Harvey had probably seemed an easy way out.

If Hess and Kaspar had known where to go, it argued a hangout not too far away. If such was the case, no doubt the others awaited them there. Whatever was to be done must be done at once.

Trailing the horses proved simple enough. No effort was made to disguise their trail. They must be so close to home that it no longer mattered, or . . . The reason became obvious. The trail led to a large shelf of rock, then vanished.

He studied the situation with care. Shod horses do not cross rock without leaving tiny white scars, which often remain for days or until the next rain. However, in this case the rock was scarred by many comings and goings.

There were other considerations. In any hideout, water would be needed for themselves and their horses. Riding to the highest point he could safely reach, Bowdrie sat down and began a careful study of the country.

They would be in a draw, a hollow, or a canyon. At least, that would be the first choice. Otherwise they might choose someplace that would permit them to look over all the approaches. Seating himself against a rock, he studied the area before him. From this study emerged three strong possibilities.

He was still studying them when he saw a horseman. The rider, astride a buckskin pony, came from the direction of town and he was riding fast. Bowdrie gathered his reins and swung to the saddle, cutting diagonally across the mountain on a route that would bring him in behind the rider. "Nine chances out of ten, that feller is taking John Queen the news that I've killed his water boys."

Reaching the comparative concealment of a draw, he touched spurs to the roan and raced ahead. If he could round that rock right ahead before the rider reached it, he could be out of sight.

He heard the snapping whir one instant before the noose dropped over his head. He tried to duck—too late!

The loop dropped over his arms and tightened and he pulled in the roan but he was jerked from the saddle with a bone-jarring thud. The roan, relieved of his rider, whirled about and stared back, ears pricked.

Chick lunged to his feet, reaching for his gun.

"Hold it!" The harsh voice was Jake Murray, with a shotgun. "Better not try it, Bowdrie. John Queen wants to talk to you."

"You know me, then?"

"It was John Queen. He's got a memory for gunfighters. He never quit tryin' to figure who you was. He never bought that Shep Harvey story even a little. Last night it come to him."

Circling around behind him, Murray took his guns. "Where's the others?" he asked.

"Hess never liked me an' he got carried away by the idea. He ran into the real Shep Harvey and braced me with it. Hess started it an' Kaspar had no choice but to back him."

"What about Harvey?"

"A tinhorn. When shootin' started, he run up the white flag."

Murray tightened the rope and took another turn around him. "You nailed both Hess an' Kaspar, huh? You must be pretty handy. Can't say I mind about Bob Hess. He was troublesome. 'Bout as comfortable to be around as an irritated porcupine. But I better not tell the boss. He'd be apt to give you a gun so's he could kill you proper."

"Queen?"

"He's a hand, Bowdrie. Don't you forget it. To my thinkin', he's faster than Hardin or any of that bunch."

The route took them down through a rocky gorge into a long valley in the hills. At the far end there was a cabin, corrals, and a barn.

John Queen came to the door with a sleepy-eyed man in a

cowhide vest. "Got him, did you? What happened to Kaspar an' Hess?"

Briefly Murray replied, and John Queen looked over at Bowdrie. "You should have killed him, I guess, but I needed to talk to him. Bring him inside."

Jeanne Buck looked up as he came through the door with his hands tied behind him. Her lips tightened a little but she said nothing.

John Queen glanced at her. "Might as well settle down, miss. This here Ranger was tryin' to play the hero, but he stubbed his toe."

"Kill him," the man in the cowhide vest said. "No use to feed him."

"Ain't always a good idea to kill a Ranger. Them other Rangers don't take to it. They'll hunt a man down if it takes a lifetime."

"There ain't none of them this side of Texas!" the other man protested.

"Are you sure?" Bowdrie said.

"Are you suggestin' you weren't over here alone?" John Queen demanded.

"Figure it out for yourself," Bowdrie said. "If you were a judge in Texas and your favorite niece was kidnapped, would you send only one Ranger?"

"If there's more, why ain't they with you?" Murray demanded.

Bowdrie shrugged. "I got here first, that was all. I picked up your trail pretty easy, but that gunplay in Flagstaff will draw them like flies. They'll be all over this country, with all the local law helping them."

He looked over at Queen. "It was a fool play, John. You should have read the record a little. Judge Whiting wears a brand anybody can read, and he wouldn't ease up on a convicted man if you had his whole family. You've wasted your time.

"Also," he added, "you've made enemies of a lot of folks who might have been sympathetic until you kidnapped this girl. You know yourself there's mighty few outlaws will touch a woman, because they know what will happen. Well, you've got them down on you. There isn't an outlaw hideout in the West would let you in on a bet."

"Shut up, damn you!" Queen shouted, yet Bowdrie could see he was disturbed. He had acted in haste and now was repenting, although not at leisure. Queen had no way of knowing Bowdrie was acting alone and that he was the only Ranger who could be spared at the time.

"John?" he persisted. "Why don't you take this rope off, give us our horses, and turn Miss Buck and me loose? This is a game you can't win, so, being a good poker player, why don't you chuck in your hand now, while you can?"

"Do you think I'm crazy?"

"That's what I'm trying to find out, John. Why buck a stacked deck?"

John Queen made no reply, although Murray looked at him, a question in his eyes.

Bowdrie looked around the room from the chair where they had tied him. A huge fireplace covered the north wall, flanked by a cupboard on each side. There were bunks against both the east and west walls. Navajo rugs lay on the floor, Navajo blankets on the bunks. A rifle stood near the door, another on nails over the fireplace.

Jeanne sat on a bunk near the fireplace and Jake Murray sprawled on a bunk across from her. John Queen sat in a chair where he could watch the door, a big man, sullen now, in a black-and-gray-plaid shirt, staring into the distance.

The messenger from town was outside somewhere with Eberhardt and Peters, the man in the cowhide vest.

Murray sat up. "Seen a buck down by the stream when I rode in. I'm hungry for venison, so I'll have a try for him before it gets dark."

Queen made no reply. That he was worried was obvious. He did not like the thought that more Rangers might be coming, and he recognized the truth of what Bowdrie had said. Even outlaws were wary of annoying women, and in kidnapping Jeanne Buck he had transgressed an unwritten law. At the moment, he had thought only of saving Damon.

Jeanne's eye caught that of Bowdrie. Her hand was toying with the poker and she lifted it, showing a red-hot tip. Then she took her handkerchief from her pocket and threw it into the fire. At the smell of burning cloth, Queen looked around irritably.

"It's just my handkerchief. It was too dirty to keep. Next time one of your boys goes into town, he can buy some for me."

"You think that's all we got to do? Run errands for you?"

"You asked for it!" Jeanne replied. Queen gave her an angry glance, then resumed staring out the door.

Bowdrie's heart was pounding heavily. Her strategy was shrewd and evident enough now. With the smell of burning cloth in the room, Queen might not notice burning rope. Lifting the poker, she held it at arm's length to burn the ropes that bound Bowdrie's hands.

The smell of burning rope was in the room mingled with that of the handkerchief, but Queen, in a brown study, was unaware. Desperately Chick worked at the ropes.

Queen suddenly shifted on his chair and glanced at them, but Jeanne had the poker back in the fire.

"Light a lamp," he said to her. "It's gettin' dark in here."

Jeanne got to her feet and had just lighted the lamp and was still holding it when Eberhardt loomed in the doorway. He sniffed suspiciously. "Smells like burnt rope," he said. "What's goin' on?"

"Rope?" John Queen was suddenly alert. *"Rope!"*

Jeanne turned and threw the lamp at Eberhardt. He threw up a protecting arm, and the lamp shattered and he was drenched with blazing oil. He sprang back, cursing, and Chick lunged to his feet. How much the ropes had burned, he had no idea, but it was now, if ever. With a tremendous heave he felt the ropes give way as Queen turned on him.

With a quick motion of his foot he kicked the chair against Queen's legs, and the big man went down with a crash. Ripping the burned ropes from his hands, he sprang for his guns, but Queen grabbed his ankle and he fell against the bunk. Queen leaped at him, but he rolled away and came to his feet.

The big man was just as quick. As he struggled erect, he swung a powerful right that knocked Bowdrie back against the cupboard, but as he followed it in, Bowdrie kicked him in the stomach and drove him into the corner. They both came to their feet, and Bowdrie swung a left and right into the big man's midsection as they came together, then hooked a right to his ear.

There was a yell from outside, and Jeanne caught up the rifle near the door. She fired, and there was a cry of pain and shock from outside. Chick smashed Queen back with driving rights and lefts, taking a wicked blow on the cheekbone that staggered him, but he slashed a cut under Queen's eye with a lancing left.

Queen lunged at him, but Chick toed the chair in his path again and the big man went over it to the floor.

But the big gunman was tough; he came up off the floor. Bowdrie's knee flattened his nose, and he went down again.

Grabbing for his guns, Chick swung them about his hips and drew the buckle together. He sprang to the side of the door. "Where are they?" he asked.

"Eberhardt's in the barn, but he's burned pretty bad. Peters is out there with a rifle. I either wounded him or scared him."

It was dark now. Edging to the side of the door, Bowdrie ducked out the door, pulling Jeanne after him. They ran around the corner of the house. It was only a few feet to the corral where the horses were. "You run for it," Chick whispered. "I'll cover you!"

Jeanne dashed for the pole corral, out of the line of fire from either the barn window or door. Chick took a quick shot through each as the girl dashed, then thumbed shells into his gun. He heard John Queen moving inside, and ducked for the corral himself.

The roan was standing ready, and he threw his saddle on the horse, then saddled the gray for Jeanne. Somebody fired from the barn, but the bullet did not reach them. As he saddled the gray, he heard Queen trip and fall and heard him swear. They had a moment, at best.

As he led the horses out of the back gate, the man in the cowhide vest sprinted for the cabin. Letting him take two steps to get into the open, Bowdrie cut him down.

"We've got to circle around," Jeanne said as they swung into their saddles.

"No, we're going over the rim!"

"It can't be done! I heard Murray say so!"

"That's what they think!" He led the way into the trees. Ever since he had sat against the rock studying the country, he had begun to think there was something familiar about it. The trouble was, he had never seen it from that side before.

Winding through a maze of craglike rocks, he led the way to a rocky shelf, then rode straight at the edge. It dropped away into a black chasm.

"You'll have to lead your horse and feel your way. I'm goin' ahead. Once on this ledge, I think my horse will remember. He used to run wild in this country. I was here four years ago."

Leading the roan, he started down the trail. The roan snorted a couple of times but followed along, stepping carefully like the true mountain horse he was. Keeping one hand on the rock beside her, Jeanne followed.

They were halfway down when from above they heard somebody stumble and swear, then say, "Where d'you suppose they got to?"

For two days they rode steadily east, and Bowdrie kept an eye on his back trail. John Queen was not a man to take a licking and like it.

They were making camp on the Pecos when the time came. Jeanne was bending over the fire and Bowdrie was rigging a crude shelter. It thundered, and Bowdrie glanced at the sky. "Better get inside," he suggested.

"Let her wait and see this." John Queen stepped from the dark.

Chick Bowdrie walked away from the shelter. The drops were falling now, falling faster.

"You came a long way, John," he said. "You'd better call it off and ride back. I've got Jeanne Buck and I am taking her home. Damon Queen will be sentenced no matter what you do."

"I'll kill you," Queen said, "at the next crack of thunder."

Lightning flashed and thunder followed. Chick had been noticing the interval. Which of them drew faster, he never knew. He fired and saw Queen start toward him, but Chick Bowdrie fired his gun in a steady roll of sound, then did a border switch, tossing the right and empty gun to the left hand, the left-hand gun to the right.

Lightning flashed again, and Queen seemed to be no more than fifteen feet away. Bowdrie fired, and the big man went to his knees, struggled to rise, and went down again, sprawling on his face against the grassy slope.

Chick stared down at him, astonished. In a flash of lightning he saw five holes in the big man's vest. Five through the body, and he had kept on coming!

Turning, Bowdrie started back to the shelter, then slipped and fell. That was odd. Puzzled, he stared at the ground, then pushed himself up and staggered erect. He managed two staggering steps, then fell on his face.

When he opened his eyes, it was light. He blinked at the brightness of the light, then turned his head.

"Chick? Are you all right?"

He stared at the worried eyes. "I guess so. What happened?"

"You killed John Queen, then you passed out. You have a hole through your thigh and another through the muscles atop your shoulder. You've lost quite a lot of blood."

"And you've been caring for me?"

"Not exactly," she confessed, "although I helped."

"You mean that lazy Ranger has finally got himself awake?" Rip Coker thrust his head into the shelter. "McNelly was afraid you might need help, so when I finished that job in Tascosa, he sent me to look after you.

"Bowdrie, you disappoint me. Only five men? You must be losin' your grip!"

"Shucks," Bowdrie said lazily, "if I'd had another girl like Jeanne along, there wouldn't have been anything for me to do!"

He frowned suddenly. "Whatever happened to Jake Murray?"

"He went after that deer," Jeanne said, "and he never came back."

"It was him told me where you'd be," Coker said. "I met

him down the trail and he spotted me for a Ranger. He said you wouldn't need any help, but I'd find you up here."

"That all he said?"

"He just said, 'Enough is enough, and I've never been to Oregon.'"

There was a silence, and then Bowdrie smiled. "Rip, I'm glad you came along. Somebody has to take our horses back to Texas, and me being wounded like I am, I'll just have to ride back to Texas on the train, with Jeanne."

"That's just like him," Coker said, pretending disgust. "He's ridin' the cushions while I hit the saddle! He's nothin' but a red-plush Ranger, after all!"

THE OUTLAWS
OF POPLAR CREEK

MOBY FOSDICK KEPT the trading post at Lee's Canyon, and Moby was a hard man. It took a man with a cold eye and a ready hand to do business in the Poplar Creek country, and Moby had been there a long time.

The store was a low-roofed building built in a hollow of the hills just below the falls of Poplar Creek. Lee's Canyon, narrow and rock-walled, was mostly uphill until within two hundred yards of the trading post. Then it topped a rise and the trail slid down into the hollow with a creek to the north.

From the store you could hear the roar of the falls, perhaps a quarter of a mile away.

If you just rode up to the post, did your buying and then rode away, you would believe there was only one way in and one way out, both along the Lee's Canyon trail.

A knowing man could tell you there were at least two other trails out of the hollow and into the badlands. One led through a crevice in the rock wall, invisible until close up, an opening that barely allowed room for a man on a horse. If it were a heavy horse, the rider might have to push one stirrup well forward to slip through.

Across the wide spread of Poplar Creek the rock wall reared up for about three hundred feet, but downstream there was a gravel beach perhaps ten feet long.

Moby had often wondered about that beach. He was an old Indian fighter with an eye for terrain, and it looked like water had been running down through some crack in the wall after heavy rains, but no opening could be seen.

Moby planned to someday build a boat and have a look over there. If there was an opening it would be another way out. Busy around the place and with occasional customers, he just never found the time, but it lingered there, in the back of his mind.

The second of the unseen paths was up the face of the cliff itself, the trail beginning among some poplars across the hollow and maybe a half-mile from the post. It wound up the cliff, always hidden behind juniper and ponderosa pine.

Fosdick knew the trails, and the wild bunch knew them. At the head of the cliff trail on a little plateau there was a cave. Once, during an Indian attack when Jerry and Lily Fosdick were youngsters, they had holed up there with Moby and two other men until the attack was over.

Moby had windows overlooking the trail from either side, and nobody could enter the hollow without being seen. So when the rider on the strawberry roan topped the rise from Del Rio, he saw him.

His hard old eyes narrowed with speculation as they watched the shambling, loose-gaited stride of the roan. The rider was a stranger.

Few travelers came by way of Lee's Canyon, and most sought to avoid it. Nobody knew where the Tucker gang holed up, but there were rumors. Fosdick knew the wild bunch but he also knew most of the hands who worked on ranches west of him. The rider wearing the black flat-crowned hat was nobody he remembered seeing before.

Fosdick strode to the door and shaded his eyes against the setting sun. The trail was empty. He looked off to the south and the hidden road. Nobody there, either. The stranger was drawing near.

Moby took in the dark, Indian-like face and the two guns. Not many men carried two guns in sight. A lot of them had a hideout. He glanced at the rider's face as he stepped down from the saddle. There was something about that still, emotionless face that gave him a little chill.

He had known this time would come and now he had a decision to make. He had expected it would come with a dozen hard-riding men, not a lone horseman on a wicked-looking hammerhead roan. He looked again. That was probably the ugliest, meanest-looking horse he had ever seen.

"Howdy! How about some grub?"

"Come in! Come in! Lily, set another place. We've got company!"

Fosdick turned back to the rider. "You can wash up right outside the door there. Fresh towel an' soap. Put it out m'self, not an hour ago." He glanced at the roan. "I'll take your hoss around an' give him some hay." He paused. "Shall I take the hull off him or will you be ridin' on?"

"If you've room, I'll stay the night." The rider looked at Moby. "Treat that horse gentle-like, and be careful. He both kicks and bites on occasion. Give him the hay first so he'll know you're friendly."

Fosdick walked to the barn with the roan. Well, that settled it. Hell would break loose now and Jerry would be caught right in the middle. To protect his son he would have to warn the whole Tucker gang.

Jake Rasch was standing in the shadows of the stable. His greasy, unshaved face was suspicious. "Who's that in yonder? I seen him ride up an' figured I'd better play possum."

"Hit the trail, Jake. You get to Shad Tucker as quick as you can make it. Tell him there's a traveler down here who looks like a Ranger, and he looks pretty salty."

"One man?" Rasch sneered. "What's one Ranger goin' to do with all of us? Even with one of us?"

"You ain't seen him," Fosdick said dryly. "This gent's got the bark on! Rough! I can tell! You look into those black eyes and it's like lookin' into two six-shooters with the hammers drawed back."

Jake's expression changed. He grabbed Fosdick's arm. "Black eyes! Looks like an Apache?"

"That's him." Fosdick lifted the saddle from the roan's back and set it astride a rail. "What's the matter?"

"Chick Bowdrie!" Jake's face paled with excitement. "He's the one cleaned up the Ballard outfit!"

Resolution came to Fosdick. "Jake, you tell Jerry to meet Lily at the cave at sunup tomorrow. I've got word for him. Now, don't forget!"

"All right," Rasch said. "Bowdrie, huh? If I could only git him!"

"Are you crazy?" Fosdick's contempt was poorly concealed. "If you're smart you'll just forget that. You never saw the day you could match Clyde Ballard, and he wasn't good enough."

"I wasn't thinkin' of givin' him no even break. He's after us, ain't he?"

To kill Chick Bowdrie! As Rasch rode up the cliff trail, he sat hunched in the saddle dreaming of what it would mean. Why, he'd become one of the most famous men in the border country! In all of Texas! And to Jake Rasch, Texas was the world.

There'd be nobody to say how it was done. That girl in El Paso, she'd sure set up an' take notice of him if he got Bowdrie.

Three men lay about the fire at Cedar Springs when Jake Rasch returned to camp. Shad Tucker was a big, rawboned young man with features that betrayed the ugly savagery that lay beneath the surface. In a dozen years of outlawry he had come off scot-free in his brushes with the law. He claimed to have killed twenty men. Actually he had killed twelve, only three of whom had had an even break.

He was brutal, ignorant, and disdainful of the law.

"What's up?" he demanded, recognizing the excitement in Jake Rasch.

"Chick Bowdrie's down at the post. He's stayin' the night."

"Bowdrie?" His eyes turned mean as he saw the sudden apprehension in Buckeye Thomas's face. "If 'n he's huntin' us, he's askin' for it!"

"Stay shy of him," Frank Crowley advised.

Tucker spat. "He ain't so much! It's time somebody showed this Bowdrie a thing or two."

"Whar-at is Jerry Fosdick? I got word from the old man. He wants Jerry to meet Lily at the cave tomorrow at sunup."

Shad Tucker looked around at him. "You don't need to tell Jerry nothin'. I'll go to the cave."

Buckeye laughed coarsely and Jake's eyes showed his envy. Crowley looked up.

"You think that's wise, Shad? The old man's been a help, time an' again."

"He won't be no more. I been suspicious of him, an' he

never wanted Jerry to tie up with us. I reckon it's time we cleaned up Fosdick. We'll take his money and the gal and we'll git all he has in that store. He's got a rifle or two I've had my eyes on for months."

Crowley knew Shad Tucker hated Fosdick because he sensed the contempt Fosdick had for him.

"We'll send Jerry off somewheres an' tell him the Rangers done it."

They all knew about the iron box under the floor.

"Might as well git on with it. Jake, you go down there an' kill Fosdick. You can git him through a window. Then git back here. We'll handle that Bowdrie when he trails after you."

Jake Rasch's face was sweaty. He was chewing on a chunk of beef. "Better wait until mornin'," he advised. "Give Lily a chance to start for the cave."

BACK IN LEE'S Canyon Bowdrie accepted another plate of *frijoles* and cornbread. Lily, a slender, pretty blond girl, filled his cup with fresh coffee. "You're not very talkative, Mr. Bowdrie," she said, smiling.

"No, ma'am, I guess I'm not rightly a talking man. I've got lots of figurin' to do. Anyway," he added, "I know more about horses than folks, and the folks I know are mostly the bad ones. Gives a man a jaundiced opinion, I'm afraid."

"Don't you have a family?"

"No, ma'am. Once, when I was a youngster, but that's a long time ago. I went to work soon's I was able. Never had much time to get acquainted, me bein' out with stock all the time."

"Don't you have a girl?"

"No, ma'am. I've knowed a few here an' there, but there's not been many where I was. I don't even have one to dream about. There was a girl out in Tascosa, she was married to an Irish gambler, an' many's the cowpuncher rode miles just to look at her, she was that beautiful. I never rode that way when she was around."

He did have figuring to do. Fosdick had been too long taking care of the roan. Had there been somebody else out there? And where was young Jerry? At this time of night he should have been around.

Fosdick had looked anxious and irritated about something, and then Bowdrie heard somebody riding away. The horse did not go east or west or he would have heard the hoofbeats on the hard trail. He had heard three, maybe four hoofbeats, which meant the rider had crossed the trail, not ridden along it. The rider had ridden toward that apparently impassable wall of cliffs.

His deductions were wrong in one instance. Knowing Fosdick had a son, he assumed the rider was Jerry. Obviously he would be riding to warn the Tuckers, which implied a friendly relationship. Yet when Fosdick returned to the table Bowdrie could not reconcile the man's manner or his personality with what he knew of the Tuckers.

Chick Bowdrie's arrival was no accident. Tucker's gang had made a brief foray into Mexico, killing three people, one of them a woman, and stealing a bunch of horses. The Mexican government complained and McNelly sent Bowdrie to investigate.

So far the Tucker outfit had been confining their activities to the wilder, less-known areas, but emboldened by success, they had been striking at larger, richer places.

Getting a map of Texas, Bowdrie made ink marks to indicate the locations of the various raids. Then he calculated a probable location of their hideout as the various robberies seemed to radiate out from a given center, which could be Lee's Canyon. He had checked out several badland locations before coming to Fosdick's trading post.

Nobody had wanted to talk about the rough country south of Poplar Creek, although willing enough to talk of other places, so he deduced his search must begin there.

He took it for granted there was some kind of a working agreement or truce between the Tucker outfit and Fosdick. Otherwise he could not have existed there.

Obviously both Fosdick and Lily were disturbed by his presence. Shad Tucker would know Bowdrie was here and would resent his presence. So while he ate, he listened, every sense alert. Outside a coyote was howling.

Bowdrie was finishing his coffee when the coyote stopped howling. No coyote stopped howling suddenly on a moonlit night without reason. Somebody or something had disturbed that coyote. Chick lifted a forkful of beans, his dark eyes intent and aware. Lily's eyes were large and her lower lip was caught under her teeth.

Her brother? Or someone else? Chick's eyes sought her face, watching her expression. She had lived here, she knew the night sounds better than he. In that instant Jake Rasch's face appeared at the window. Neither Bowdrie nor Lily saw him, but Jake glimpsed the room, seeing what he wished to see.

Chick Bowdrie sat with his back to the door. Opposite him sat Moby Fosdick, and with luck Jake could get them both. His footsteps were catlike as he approached the door.

His heart was jumping like mad. It was the chance of a lifetime! To the devil with Tucker. If he could kill Bowdrie he'd be a big man, bigger than Tucker, and he could always tell Shad he just had to kill him. Yet Bowdrie's reputation was such that when Jake's hand touched the latch, it was trembling.

Six-gun gripped in his hand, he gripped the door latch with his left, and slamming the door back, he fired two quick shots into *an empty space*!

In the moment when Jake was rounding the corner of the house, Bowdrie got up and stepped to the corner for his saddlebags and Fosdick leaned over to get a light from the fire for his pipe.

Tense, every nerve on edge, Jake had fired at the place where the two men had been sitting. Only then did he realize they were gone. Pale with shock and sudden fear, he swung the gun, looking for Bowdrie.

Chick was standing, his saddlebags in his left hand, his gun in his right. He was standing casually, eyes alert, staring at Rasch.

The outlaw gulped, the sound loud in the room. The old clock ticked twice while horror mounted in Jake's breast. He found himself in the last situation he wanted to be in, facing Chick Bowdrie with an even break.

"Well"—Bowdrie was cool—"you came to kill me. Why don't you shoot?"

Transfixed with fear, Rasch forgot the girl in El Paso. He forgot about the important man he wanted to be. Suddenly the cost was enormously large. His mouth opened and closed. He tried to swallow. "You . . . you'd kill me! I wouldn't have a chance!"

"How much chance were you givin' us?"

Jake Rasch let his tongue touch his lips. Lust to kill was mounting past his fear. He took a step back toward the door, then another. Bowdrie's eyes were on him.

"No," he whined. "I was a fool! I was—"

He turned toward the door, then fired suddenly across his chest.

Bowdrie had been watching with the eyes of experience. The treachery in the man was obvious. He could see the fever to kill in the man's eyes. His gun was ready, and when he saw the man's knuckle move, his thumb on the hammer, Bowdrie killed him.

Jake's gun blasted, and there was a thud in the wall behind him. The gun slipped from Rasch's fingers and his legs seemed to melt under him. He sank to the floor, half in, half out of the door.

Moby Fosdick stared at the fallen man, then at the groove cut by Rasch's bullet in the surface of the table. Had he not leaned to pick that twig from the fire, he would be dead.

He realized what a fool he had been. There could be no tolerating of evil. One stamped it out or the evil grew worse. He had held on, hoping the Tuckers would leave the area or be killed. Now he knew that not only himself but his son and daughter were in danger.

"Lily, pack your things. Come daybreak we're gettin' out of here."

"Who was he?"

"Jake Rasch. He rides with Tucker."

Bowdrie knew the name. He was on the list of wanted men. "Who did he want? You or me?"

"I don't know." He looked at the groove again. "Looks like he wanted me, probably both of us."

———

DAYLIGHT WAS FILTERING into the hollow when Bowdrie rolled out of the hay, left the stable, and walked toward the house. A paint horse stood head down at the hitching post. Bowdrie considered it, reaching some agreement with himself. He was turning toward the door when it opened softly. Quickly he flattened himself against the wall and in the shadows of a tree.

Lily Fosdick slipped from the door, glanced fearfully toward the stable where she thought him to be, then hurried away across the clearing. Without stirring, he watched her enter the cedars near the cliff.

Moby was stirring around inside when Bowdrie entered. "Got some coffee on," he suggested. "Better have some."

"I'm going after the Tuckers this morning. Got anything you want to tell me?"

Moby straightened up from the fire. "I guess . . . not. They've got them a hideout, can't be more'n five or six miles off, the way they come an' go."

Bowdrie gulped hot black coffee and waited. Something was worrying Fosdick.

"Bowdrie, you've got a name for killin' men, but they say you're square. My boy's out there, Bowdrie. He ain't a bad boy, but it got kind of lonesome here and those fellers talked big about all they done. He sort of took up with Tucker. I don't reckon he's done anything wrong yet, ain't been time, and they ain't been away, so—"

"Any boy can get into trouble. No reason he has to keep on that road. I had a start that way myself but turned off before it was too late. As for killin', I don't do any more than I have to. Rasch there, he gave me no choice."

———

WHEN BOWDRIE HAD the saddle on the roan, he tied the reins of the paint horse to the saddle horn and said, "Go home, boy. You go home now."

The paint hesitated, trotted off a few steps, then headed down the trail. Whether the gelding understood or not, he remembered where the other horses were and where he'd been fed and watered.

There was no sign of Lily. He saw her tracks, then lost them as he followed the paint.

Almost an hour later Shad Tucker got up from the fire and saw the paint come trotting into the clearing. He stiffened, eyes narrow. "Frank? Look there!"

Crowley stood up. "Looks like Jake made a bad mistake," he commented dryly.

"Hey?" He dove into the brush, reaching for his rifle as he passed the rock where he had been sitting. "See those reins? Tied to the horn. I betcha that Ranger's followin'."

A short distance back along the trail, Bowdrie was puzzled. There should be some smoke. At this time of the morning somebody would be making coffee. He saw the paint had pulled up near a corral where there were other horses. He turned to look toward the left and saw the fire. He also saw two rifle barrels, and they were pointed at him.

"Jest set right still, Ranger. An' keep both hands on the pommel."

Chick Bowdrie swore softly. It would be madness to move now. At that distance they could not miss.

Shad Tucker came out of the brush. Behind him was Buck-eye Thomas. "Good man, Frank!" Tucker said. "We got him dead to rights!"

Thomas bared his yellow teeth. "The great Chick Bowdrie! Wal, Mr. Ranger, I reckon you got to be taught. I reckon so."

Tucker gestured at the maze of canyons and rough country. "This here's mine! You Rangers ain't needed. We'll just sort of make an example of you an' leave what's left for Rangers to find so they'll know what's comin' to 'em if they come into my country."

"There will be others," Bowdrie said calmly. "Others who are tougher and smarter than me."

"When they find you," Tucker replied, "they'll find you with no hands, nor will you have any eyes or skin on your chest. I'll keep you alive for all o' that, then leave what's left to the ants and the buzzards."

Crowley glanced from one to the other, worry in his eyes. Bowdrie could see that Crowley didn't like it. Robbery and killing was one thing, torture something else. "Shad, Lily will be down to the cave about now, won't she?"

Tucker slapped his thigh. "Damned if she won't! I almost forgot. I figured to keep that appointment she made with Jerry, so I better get down there."

Tucker reached up and flipped Bowdrie's guns from their holsters; then, grabbing him by the shirtfront, he jerked him from the saddle and threw a wicked punch to his belly. "How d'you like it, Ranger? You think you're tough, huh? Well, we'll see."

When Bowdrie was bound hand and foot, Shad Tucker swung to the saddle of his own horse and started down the trail. "Hold him for me. Don't do nothin' until I git back. This one's my meat."

"What about Jerry?"

"If he shows up, keep him here. Lily"—he grinned—"will be surprised to see me, but she'll get used to it."

Crowley looked down at Bowdrie. "You'd be dead if I had my way. This other idea is Shad's."

He walked to the fire and leaned his rifle against a log while he poured a cup of coffee.

Bowdrie, left alone for a moment, studied his situation with no pleasure. He was propped in a sitting position against a log, hands tied behind him, ankles bound together. Thomas was sprawled on a blanket across the fire, Crowley sipping coffee. The stump of a huge tree stood near Chick. In its edge were numerous gashes where an ax had been struck.

He heard the approaching horse several minutes before either of the others. The rider rode into the clearing, a clean-cut young man of nineteen with quick, nervous movements but a steady gray eye that Bowdrie instinctively liked.

"Snoopin' Ranger. Ketched him easy. Name of Bowdrie."

"Bowdrie?" Jerry Fosdick turned to look. "I've heard of him." He paused. "If you see Shad tell him I'm goin' down to the post to see Pa."

"You're to stay here," Thomas said. "Shad wants you here until he gits back."

Bowdrie had done what he wanted with his feet. He looked over at Jerry. "Tucker's gone to the cave to be alone with your sister. She thinks she's meeting you there. And Jake Rasch tried to kill your pa last night. Now Jake's dead. I killed him."

Buckeye jumped to his feet. "That's a damn lie!"

"Hold it!" Jerry's face was pale. "You said Lily thinks she's meetin' me? That Shad's gone down there?"

"Set down, kid." Thomas tried to be casual. "Ain't nothin' to it."

"Then why are you tryin' to stop me from goin' down there?" He swung his horse and Thomas dropped a hand to a gun. "You stay here, kid. When Shad wants him a woman, nobody butts in!"

Bowdrie had wedged a spur into a crack in the stump; he gave a quick jerk on the foot and it slipped from the boot. He lunged to his feet and threw himself at Crowley's back. The lunge sent Crowley sprawling against Thomas, and they both fell.

"Cover them, kid! Then cut my hands loose!"

Crowley, who had gotten up, dove into the brush. Jerry followed him with a quick shot; then, catching up a knife lying near the fire, he cut Bowdrie's hands loose. Chick grabbed up his guns, pulled on his boot, and ran for the roan.

"You watch him, kid! If he makes a wrong move, kill him! I'm goin' after your sister."

"I'm goin' too!"

"You stay here!"

———

LILY HAD WAITED anxiously, and when she heard the approaching horse, she stepped out of the cave. When she saw who it was, she drew back quickly, but not quickly enough. It was the first time she had seen Tucker when her father was not present. "Oh, I thought it was Jerry."

Shad hung a leg around the saddle horn and began building himself a smoke. He could see the mounting fear in her eyes and it was like wine in his blood. "You can quit expectin' him. I come instead."

"You mean . . . he's been hurt?"

"He don't even know you're here. I figured it would be more fun if I came alone. Anyway, I'm takin' you with us. Gits lonesome over in the badlands with no woman around."

"I'm going back to the post!" Lily said. "I'll see my father about this!"

Tucker dropped his foot back in the stirrup and brought his horse in front of her. "Jest sit tight, filly! We got business to do after I finish my smoke. You don't want your pa killed, do you?"

"Killed? Oh, you wouldn't dare!"

"Kill him? I aim to. He figures hisself too high an' mighty to suit me. As for that Ranger, don't you go to thinkin' he'll help. We got him back to camp, all tied up for skinnin'."

He swung down from his horse and tied it to a bush with a slip knot. Cut off from the trail, there was only one way for her to move. She darted into the cave.

She heard Shad's brutal laughter. "Like the dark, do you? I'll be right in!"

She stopped, looking around. It was even worse in the cave. Yet suddenly she remembered the opening she and Jerry had found. She ran on, stumbling in the dark. Behind her Shad Tucker's boots grated on rock.

Horror choked her. Behind her was Shad, his leering unshaved face, his broken-nailed hands. She ran into the dark. Then she could no longer run, for the floor was covered with fallen rock. She felt her way to the wall, waiting, thinking.

This cave had never been fully explored. She and Jerry had planned it, and had prepared torches for the purpose. Behind her, Tucker was fumbling about, growing more and more angry because of the trouble she was causing. He found a pile of the torches and lit one. The reflected light helped her.

She went on into an almost square room. The only escape was a dark opening, scarcely more than a crack, in the wall opposite. She paused, panting from her running and the close air. She went through the crack, and paused in amazement;

the faint reflection from behind her seemed to touch upon a forest of stalagmites and stalactites. Or was it merely the dancing shadows on the wall?

Frightened, she tried to fight back the terror. She must think, *think*! He was coming. She could hear his footsteps; then they faded. Had he turned another way? If she could only get back through the crack and outside! If she could—

He was there, before her, holding the torch. "Y' better git back the way you come," he said. "If this here torch goes out, we're both in trouble."

She felt around for some kind of weapon, a piece of stone, a broken stalactite . . . anything!

Coolly he wedged the pitch-pine torch into a crack in the wall, then turned toward her. "All right now, filly. The runnin's over. Come here!"

"Tucker?" Bowdrie's voice boomed in the cave. "You wanted me, now I'm here. Drop your gunbelts or start shootin'!"

Bowdrie took a quick step to the left to draw fire away from Lily, and his boot caught on a projecting rock. He tripped and fell, crashing to the rock floor. He heard the girl's quick scream of terror as he thumbed the hammer on the six-gun in his hand.

A lance of fire darted at him. His own crossed it. He heard a gasp and he scrambled to his feet. Across forty feet of torchlit cave the men faced each other.

Was Shad Tucker really hit? Or had his bullet only brought a startled gasp from the outlaw?

Lily shrank against the wall, and Tucker was bringing his gun up. Bowdrie shot from down low and the bullet ripped the gun from Tucker's hand. It fell, rattling among the rocks.

Turning swiftly, Tucker darted into the depths of the cave, running hard. Bowdrie sent a bullet after him, then, as the outlaw was no longer visible, he held his fire, moving deeper into the shadows.

They heard the running feet, then suddenly a wild, terror-riven scream. A scream that echoed again and then again in the vaulted room.

Lily Fosdick stared at Bowdrie. "What—?"

"Something happened," he said. He took the torch from

the wall and they started through the pillars of stone. Somewhere they heard water falling. Bowdrie stopped abruptly.

The cave floor ended suddenly, and before them gaped a great hole, a huge cistern within the cave. A mouth of blackness that gulped at their feeble light. Picking up a loose stone, he dropped it into the hole. Their eyes stared, listening, waiting. . . .

Then somewhere far, far below there was a splash.

Without a word they walked back to the cave entrance.

Jerry was waiting, gun in hand. He holstered the pistol when he saw them. Briefly Bowdrie explained.

"Got Thomas tied up," Jerry said. "Pa come along an' helped me. Crowley got away. Lit out."

Jerry cleared his throat. "I was goin' to ride with them, Mr. Bowdrie. I really was. Thought I was."

"Point is, you didn't. If you're restless here, ride up north to the XIT. Friends of mine up there, an' they're hirin' for the roundup an' trail drive. That'll be work enough to keep you out of trouble."

"Last night," Lily said, "after you went to the barn to sleep, I made a cake. Icing and all. I haven't even cut into it yet."

Bowdrie's head came up like a hound dog scenting a coon. "Now, that's something I haven't had in more than a year. Shall we ride a little faster?"

BOWDRIE FOLLOWS
A COLD TRAIL

PUFFS OF DUST rose from the roan's shambling trot, and Chick Bowdrie shifted his position in the saddle. It had been a long ride and he was tired. From a distance he had glimpsed a spot of green and the vague shape of buildings among the trees. Where there was green of that shade there was usually water, and where there were water and buildings there would be people, warm food, and some conversation.

No cattle dotted the grassland, no horses looked over the corral bars. There was no movement in the sun-baked area around the barn.

He walked the roan into the yard and called out, "Anybody t' home?"

Only silence answered his hail, the utter silence of a place long abandoned. The neat, carefully situated and constructed buildings were gray and weather-worn, and the gaping door of the barn showed a blank emptiness behind it.

It was strange to find no people in a place of such beauty. Trees shaded the dooryard and a rosebush bloomed beside the door, a rosebush bedraggled and game, fighting a losing battle against the wind, the dust, and the parched earth.

"Nevertheless," he said aloud, "this is as far as I go tonight."

He stepped down from the saddle, beating the dust from chaps and shirt, his black eyes sweeping the house and barn again. He had the uneasy sense of a manhunter who knows something is wrong, something is out of place.

The hammerheaded roan ambled over to the water hole and dipped his muzzle into its limpid clearness.

"Somebody," Chick muttered, "spent a lot of time to make

this place into a home. Some of the trees were planted, and that rosebush, too."

The little ranch lay in the upper end of a long valley that widened out into a seemingly endless range that lost itself against the purple of far-off hills.

The position of the house, barn, and corrals indicated a mind that knew what it wanted. Whoever had built this place had probably spent a lot of days in the saddle or up on a wagon seat planning just how he wanted it. This was not just a ranch for the raising of cattle; this was a home.

"Five will get you ten he had him a woman," Bowdrie said.

Yet why, when so much work had been done, had the place been abandoned? "And for a long time, too," Bowdrie told himself.

There were tumbleweeds banked against the side of the barn and caught under the water trough in the corral. This place had been a long time alone.

The dry steps of the house creaked under his weight. The closed door sagged on its hinges, and when he tugged on it they creaked protestingly, almost rusted into immobility. Yet when the door opened, his boot rested on the step and stayed there.

A man's skeleton lay on the floor; his leather gunbelt, cracked and dried to a stiff, dead thing, still clung to his waist.

"So that was it. You built it but never got a chance to enjoy it."

Bowdrie stepped into the room, glancing around with thoughtful attention. Here, too, was evidence of careful planning, the keen mind of a practical man who wanted to make life easier both for himself and for his woman.

The neat shelves, now cobwebbed and dusty, the carefully built fireplace, a washbasin built of rocks with a drilled hole from which a plug could be removed to drain off the water, all contrived to eliminate extra steps.

Bowdrie stepped over and looked down at the body. From the bones of the chest he picked up a bullet, partly flattened. "That was probably it. Right through the chest, or maybe even the stomach."

He glanced again at the skull. "Whoever killed you must have really wanted you dead. He finished you off with an ax!"

The skull was split, and nearby lay the ax that had been used. The man had been shot first; then the killer made sure by using the ax.

A gun lay not far away, evidently the dead man's gun, an old .44. The killer had used a .41.

In another room he found a closet, the warped door open. Inside were a few odds and ends of women's clothing. He studied the closet, some items hanging askew, some fallen to the floor. "Whoever killed you probably took your woman," he muttered, "an' whatever clothes he took, he just grabbed off the hangers an' the hooks. At least, that's what it looks like."

A man's clothing hung in another corner of the closet, a black frock coat and pants, obviously his Sunday best. In the inside coat pocket was a letter addressed to "Gilbert S. Mason, Esq., El Paso, Texas."

Dear Gil:

  After many days I take my pen in hand to address you once more. It is pleased I am to learn that you and Mary have found a home at last, knowing as I do how long you have wished for one. It will be a lovely place for little Carlotta to grow up. I am completing my business in Galveston, but before returning to Richmond I shall come west to see you.

                                                Your friend,
                                                Samuel Gatesby

Folding the letter, Bowdrie placed it carefully in a leather case he carried inside his shirt. He then began a methodical search of the premises.

Other than the clothing, there was no evidence of the woman or the child. If dead, their bodies had been disposed of elsewhere, but after another glance at the closet he decided they had been hurriedly taken away.

In a drawer of an old writing desk that he had to break

open he found a faded tintype. It was a picture of an attractive, stalwart young man and a very pretty young woman, taken, according to the note on the back, on their wedding day.

Gilbert S. and Mary Mason, and the date was twenty years earlier. In the drawer was an improvised calendar. Made from year to year, the dates were crossed off until a period in September, sixteen years ago.

In the kitchen he glanced at the skeleton again. "Well, Gil," he said, "you had a right beautiful wife. You had a little girl. You had a pretty home and a nice future, and then somebody came along. Gil, I'm goin' to make you a promise. I'll find who it was and what became of your family, even if it has been sixteen years."

The West was often a hard and lonely land where heat, cold, drought, and flood took a bitter toll in lives, but in this valley Gil Mason had made a home, he had found all a lonely man could dream of, only to lose it to a murderer.

"My guess, Gil, is that you didn't have horses and cattle enough, and not very much money. You were killed for your woman.

"You were a good-lookin' man who'd fixed up a nice home, so I'm bettin' she didn't go willingly."

He buried the bones, wrapped in a blanket and placed in a crude coffin slapped together from some extra planks stored in the barn. He buried them behind the barn, and from another section of plank he placed the name and added *"Murdered, September . . ."* and the year.

A month later, with other business out of the way, Bowdrie was loafing around a stage station called, by some, Gabel's Stop. There was nearby a general store, a saloon, and a few other activities. What Bowdrie had come to think of as Mason's Valley was only a few miles back in the country.

The stage station was operated, dominated, and had been constructed by Gabel Hicks. Tipped back against the wall of the station, Gabel Hicks spat a stream of tobacco juice into the dust of what he called a street. It wasn't often that he found a listener like this young sprout.

Chick Bowdrie, his own chair tilted back and his toes on

the porch on either side of the chair, listened absently. Hicks was an old-timer and a talker, but he had a lot to say, and had lived through it all. Bowdrie, long since, had learned that one learns a lot more by listening than by talking.

The sun warmed the street into dozing contentment. "Yep! Been here nigh onto forty year! Come west in a covered wagon. Fit Injuns all over these here plains and mountains. You youngsters, you think things is rough now! You should've been here when I come! Why, even twenty years ago! Now? The country's ruined! Crowded too much! Why, there's a ranch ever' fifty, sixty miles now! A body can hardly ride down a trail without runnin' into somebody else!"

"She must've been quite a country fifteen, twenty years ago," Bowdrie commented. "I'll bet this was wide-open, empty country back then! Not many riding the trails then."

"More'n you think." Gabel Hicks spat again, drenching a surprised lizard. "Some of them still around, like Med Sowers, Bill Peissack, Dick Rubin. They were all here. Old Johnny Greier, the town loafer, he was here. He wasn't no loafer then. He was a hardworkin' young cowhand . . . before he took to drink."

Chick Bowdrie let his chair legs down and picked up a stick. With a flick of his hand to the back of his neck he took out a razor-sharp throwing knife from under his collar and began to whittle. "Must've been a hell of a country then. Mighty little water, and no women around. Must've been right tough goin'."

"Women?" Hicks spat. "There was women. Even Johnny Greier had a woman when he came into this country. Purty, too, although not as purty as some. That Mary Mason, now, she was a humdinger!"

Chick Bowdrie's knife cut a long splinter from the stick. "Where'd they all get to?" he demanded. "I ain't seen a pretty woman since I hit town! Come to think of it, I haven't seen a woman!"

He inspected the stick. "Some of those pretty women must have had girl-kids, and they'd be about right for me now. What happened?"

"Sure they had kids. Some of them still around, but they

surely don't come down here, except to the store. That Med Sowers, now? He's got him a right purty daughter. Accordin' to what I hear, she's due to be comin' home soon. Been away to school most of her life. Boardin' school for young ladies. Med asked me to kind of watch out for her."

"Daughter? Well, maybe I'll just hang around and look."

"No chance for no driftin' cowhand! That Med's a wealthy man, although you'd never guess it to look at that place of his! Like a pigsty! Yessir, like a pigsty!"

He spat. "O' course, she ain't rightly his daughter, comes to that. She's his ward. I guess that means he has the handlin' of her."

Hicks's face turned grim. "He's had the handlin' of more than one woman. Can't say I'd want any gal of mine in his hands. He's a bad 'un."

Chick yawned and got to his feet; the knife disappeared as he did so. Hicks's wise old eyes measured him, the two guns, coupled with the hawklike face and the deep, dimplelike scar under the right cheekbone.

"Stayin' around long?" he asked.

"Maybe." Chick hitched his gunbelts into an easier position. "Might stay longer if I get a ridin' job."

"Averill's been takin' on a few hands."

Bowdrie grinned. "Not while I've got forty dollars!" he said.

Hicks chuckled. "Don't blame you none. When I was a young feller, I was just the same. If I had me an extry dollar, I was a rich man."

Chick Bowdrie walked across the street to the Lone Star. It had taken him nearly a month, but he was learning things. McNelly had been doubtful at first. After all, sixteen years was a long time. Finally he told him to go ahead.

Bowdrie had begun by using the Rangers' services to get information from Richmond and Galveston. Samuel Gatesby had been a respected businessman, a Southerner who had good New York connections and came back strong following the Civil War.

Gilbert Mason had been a major in the Confederate Army who married a childhood sweetheart and who had come west full of ambition and energy as well as love for his lovely young wife. The West, according to reports, had swallowed them.

Bowdrie checked further on Gatesby. The man had acquired large cotton and shipping interests, but had been a lifelong friend as well as a brother officer of Mason. Bowdrie paused under the awning of the Lone Star to reread the letter he had received a few days past:

Samuel Gatesby disappeared after leaving El Paso sixteen years ago. His two brothers, both wealthy men, offered rewards of several thousand dollars for information. Gatesby was never heard from again. Tugwell Gatesby wishes to be informed of anything you may learn. If necessary, he will come west to make identification.

There was a crude grave marked by an unlettered stone near the house in the valley. Bowdrie had a theory about that grave but did not believe it contained Gatesby's remains.

Johnny Greier looked hopeful when Bowdrie entered the saloon, as the rider in the black flat-crowned hat had been good for a drink several times in the past three weeks. Bowdrie took a seat at a table and gestured for Greier to join him.

Johnny hurried over, lurching a little, and the disgusted bartender heaved himself out of his seat at the far end of the bar and brought two glasses and the bottle. "Bring us a couple of plates of that free lunch," Bowdrie suggested, and dropped a coin on the table.

Waiting until the bartender had returned to his seat, Bowdrie poured a drink for himself, and after Greier had taken one glass, Bowdrie refilled it for him, then moved the bottle away.

Johnny looked up, hurt showing in his eyes. "You eat something before you have any more," Bowdrie ordered. "We've some talkin' to do."

"Thanks. Most folks don't 'preciate an ol' man, just because I take a drink now and again."

"Johnny, there's something I want to know, and you may be the only man in town with gumption enough to tell me."

Johnny's features seemed to sharpen, and the bloodshot eyes stared, then fell. "I don't know anything," he said. "Whatever I knew, the whiskey's made me forget."

"I think you do know, Johnny," Bowdrie said quietly. "I think that's what started you drinkin'."

Chick filled Johnny's glass again, but the old man did not touch it.

"Johnny, what became of Mary Mason?"

Johnny Greier's face went white and sick. When he looked at Bowdrie again, the alcoholic haze seemed gone from his eyes. Chick Bowdrie's black eyes were hard and without mercy.

"She's dead. Now, don't ask me no more."

"Johnny . . ." Bowdrie spoke gently, persuasively. "A man named Gil Mason built himself a home, something he always wanted, and he brought his wife out to enjoy it, and their small daughter was with them.

"I want a home too, Johnny. So do you. Every man west of the Brazos would like one, but Gil Mason made it. He realized his dream, and then he was murdered, Johnny. I want to know what happened."

"He'd kill me!"

"Johnny, most people around here take you for nothing but a drunk. I know better, Johnny, because I've looked into the past. You were a top hand, Johnny, one of the very best. You rode with all the good ones and you were one of them. It took a man to be what you were, Johnny, and it took a man to win the kind of respect you had. What happened, Johnny?"

Greier shook his head, staring at the full glass in front of him.

"Johnny, in a little while there's a stage coming in. On that stage, a pretty young girl will come in. She is Mary Mason's daughter and she is coming home to live on the ranch with Med Sowers. She's never seen him. She doesn't know what she's gettin' into. She's been away at school all these years."

Johnny stared at the glass, then pushed back a little from the table. "There wasn't many of us here then, an'

Med Sowers had all those gunmen around him, men who would kill you at the drop of a hat.

"There was no law here then. The country hadn't been organized. A man did whatever he wanted, and Med Sowers had the power."

Johnny stared at Bowdrie out of red-rimmed, bloodshot eyes. "I knew what happened. I seen it comin', an' I did nothing."

"What could you have done?"

"I dunno. Maybe nothing. I was nowhere as good with a gun as any one of that outfit. I seen Sowers watchin' her, and I could see what was in his mind. I started out to the ranch to warn Mason, but it was too late. That was the day they done it.

"Med will kill me for talkin', but I guess my time's about up, anyway. Med Sowers killed Mason for his woman."

He stared into the glass. "He taken her to his place an' kept her there. She lived a dog's life. He sent her girl away to school and held that over her, that if she didn't go along, he'd see the kid killed.

"Later he said he might as well raise him another woman. 'Let her grow up,' he said, 'and then she'll be mine.'

"First chance she got, Mary ran off. He followed her an' killed her. Afraid she'd do it again and talk to somebody."

There was a chorus of wild yells from the street, and the pounding hooves of racing horses.

"That's him. That's Med now, he an' that murderin' bunch of his. Dick Rubin, Hensman, Morel, and Lute Boyer. Rubin an' Boyer were with Med Sowers when he killed her."

Chick Bowdrie heard another sound above their yells. It was the incoming stage. Under the deep brown of his face, Bowdrie paled. His thoughts raced. What could he do? What could he legally do? There had been no law then, but there was now, and she was Sowers' ward.

The chances were that the girl on the stage was Carlotta, mentioned in the letter. Now she would face what her mother had faced, and there was as yet no evidence beyond the word of Johnny Greier, even if he lived to speak.

Bowdrie walked outside and leaned against the awning

post. It was the first time he found himself wishing he was not an officer of the law. He might walk out there, pick a fight with Sowers, and kill him.

He shook his head. That was no way to think. That was what the old Bowdrie might have done, the one before McNelly recruited him.

The stage rolled to a stop in a cloud of dust, the door was opened, and a girl got out.

Chick Bowdrie straightened with an indrawn breath. She was the image of the girl in the picture he had, a very pretty girl, every inch the lady.

Then his eyes shifted to Med Sowers. He saw the shock of recognition as the big man saw the girl's mother in her face. Then the shock faded, giving place to triumph and a sort of animal eagerness. Sowers pushed forward. His checkered shirt, far from clean, was open halfway down, revealing a massive hairy chest.

"Howdy, Mary!" he said. "I'm Med Sowers, your guardian!"

Mary? Why Mary?

She smiled brightly, but Bowdrie was close enough to see the dismay in her eyes.

"I am glad to see you," she said. "I do not remember you, of course. I was so very young."

"Think nothin' of it." He hitched his belt over the bulge of his stomach. "We'll make y' feel right t' home. You just wait'll we get to the ranch. You cost me a sight of money, but I reckon it'll pay off now."

"Thank you." She turned to the tall, good-looking young man standing slightly behind her. "Mr. Sowers, I would like you to meet Stephen York, my fiancé."

Med Sowers' hand stopped even as it started for the handshake. His face went dark with angry blood. "Your *what*?" he bellowed.

York stepped forward. "I can understand your surprise, Mr. Sowers, but we thought it best to tell you at once. Miss Mason and I wish to be married."

"Married?" Sowers was ugly with rage and frustration.

"I'll see you in hell first! I didn't spend all that money gittin' her eddication for you to take her away!"

Chick Bowdrie stepped into the center of the gathering crowd. "What did you raise her for, Sowers?" he asked.

Med Sowers turned impatiently, seeing Bowdrie for the first time, but realizing for the first time also that an interested crowd had gathered. "Who're you?" he demanded.

"Just a very curious bystander, Sowers." His eyes moved slowly over the faces of Rubin, Morel, Hensman, and Boyer. "I find it odd that you should be so mad because your ward has found her a young man."

Bowdrie indicated York. "He looked to me like a right nice young man who would do right by the girl, and also," he added, "one who would go a long way to protect her."

Med Sowers was aware of the waiting, somewhat puzzled crowd. Perhaps only one or two aside from Sowers and Bowdrie knew what was implied.

Sowers made up his mind quickly. "Well, no wonder I was surprised! Here I've had no word . . . you kind of sprung it on me, Mary. I guess I kicked up the sod, some." He grinned at York. "Better let her get out to the place an' git settled, then we can get acquainted. If you're the right man, I couldn't be more pleased." He turned, reaching for her suitcase. "Well, let's get out to the ranch!"

Chick caught the girl's eye and shook his head ever so slightly. Her brow puckered, but she turned to Sowers.

"Oh, please! I want to stay in town tonight! I am so tired! Anyway, I have some shopping to do, some things I need."

Sowers hesitated, fighting back the angry protest before his lips could shape it.

Bowdrie turned to walk away and found himself facing Dick Rubin. "Get out of town!" Rubin said. "Don't let me find you around after daybreak."

Rubin did not wait for a reply, but moved away into the crowd. As Rubin moved off, Bowdrie noticed the other passengers who had descended from the stage. They were city men. One was tall, gray, and handsome, the other a shorter man with a broad, tough jaw and a cigar clenched in his teeth.

The shorter man was already leading the way toward Bowdrie. "Chick Bowdrie? I'm Pat Hanley, Pinkerton agent. I'm employed by Tugwell Gatesby here. Do you have some news for us?"

"Not very much, Hanley, but if you would like to help, you can get at the records of the stage company. I think Sam Gatesby arrived here from El Paso, and was taken into the hills and murdered. I believe I know by whom. Can you check and see if he arrived here?"

Whatever happened, Chick knew, must happen quickly now. Sowers would not take defeat. Yet despite his wealth, whatever was done now must at least have the cloak of legality. Formerly there had been no law but Sowers' own; now the country was settling up and there were different standards.

Chick did not discount the danger to himself. He had interfered in a situation in which he had no part that they could see, as his status as a Texas Ranger was not known. Sowers could not know who he was or why he had asked his question, but the question itself was a threat.

Stephen York was in an even more precarious position. Chick was sure that before the night was over one of Sowers' men would pick a quarrel with either him or York, and try to kill whichever one it was . . . with maybe a stray shot to kill the other by "accident."

With Sowers and York, Mary Mason had gone to the two-story frame hotel. Morel, Hensman, and Rubin had gone into the Lone Star. Hanley had gone to the stage station and Gatesby to the hotel. Chick Bowdrie started to move toward the hotel himself, when he saw Lute Boyer watching him. As their eyes met, Boyer walked over to him. He had a lean, cadaverous face and eyes that always held contempt.

"I've been lookin' forward to runnin' into you sometime, Bowdrie," he said. "I nearly came up with you down around Uvalde, and again at Fort Griffin. I've heard you're good with your guns."

"Your friend Rubin warned me to get out of town before daybreak," Bowdrie said.

Lute Boyer drew the makings from his pocket and began

to build a cigarette. "Wait'll Dick learns who you are. He ain't even guessed, and you a Texas Ranger!"

"Lute, you ain't done all the guessin' that's comin' to you. Let me give you some advice. Don't you be the one they send to get Stephen York."

The Herrick House was not much of a hotel. A frame building with a large lobby and a rarely used bar. The Lone Star drew the town's liquor business. There were thirty rooms in the ramshackle old hotel. One of these was where Chick Bowdrie was staying. In others Gatesby, Hanley, York, and Carlotta Mason were staying. She was now known as Mary Sowers.

Med Sowers was seated in the lobby when Bowdrie came in. As he started for the stairs, Sowers sprang to his feet. "Don't go up there!" he said angrily.

Chick Bowdrie had found few people whom he disliked profoundly, but this man was one of them. He had never wanted to kill a man, but if ever one deserved killing, it was Med Sowers.

"Don't be a fool!" he said impatiently. "This is a hotel, and I live up there! Dozens of others do, too." He paused briefly. "Smarten up, Sowers. You aren't runnin' this country anymore. You've a lot to answer for, and your time's up."

He turned on his heel and started up the steps. He heard Sowers move, and he turned around. "I could kill you, Sowers. You'd better wait."

He went to Stephen York's room.

The tall young man was standing in front of the mirror combing his hair. His coat was off and he wore a shoulder holster, something rarely seen. He turned as Chick entered, and they stood facing each other.

"I'm glad she found herself a real man," Bowdrie commented. "She's going to need him!"

"You know about me?"

"It's my business to know. Two years back, some of the riverboat companies hired a special officer from Illinois and sent him to New Orleans to put a stop to the robbin' and murderin' of their passengers. In four months he sent thirteen thieves to prison, and there were several who chose to fight it out and were buried."

Chick pulled a chair around and sat astride of it; then he related the story of the Mason ranch, his quest for evidence, and all the indications that Medley Sowers was the guilty man. He revealed how Sowers planned to keep the daughter even as he had enslaved the mother.

He explained about the murder of Samuel Gatesby, and why Tugwell Gatesby and Pat Hanley were here. "Let's go see them," he said.

Hanley was explaining something to Gatesby as they reached the room. "Your hunch was right," he advised Bowdrie. "Samuel Gatesby arrived here three days after leaving El Paso. Hicks remembers him well. Gatesby rented a horse from Dick Rubin after inquiring as to the location of the Mason ranch."

"Something I was about to explain to Hanley when you gentlemen arrived. The man you call Sowers is wearing a Chinese charm on his watch chain that I gave Sam in sixty-seven. I recognized it this afternoon."

Bowdrie turned and left the room, walking down the hall to Carlotta's room. That was how he thought of her, despite the fact she had been using another name, that of Mary Sowers.

He tapped, there was no reply, and he tapped again more sharply. Hanley stepped into the hall and looked his way. Suddenly apprehensive, Bowdrie opened the door.

The room was empty!

"Hanley! York! She's gone!"

He hit the steps running and reached the lobby in time to hear a clatter of hooves. As he stepped into the street, he saw Sowers go by with Lute Boyer. The girl was between them.

As he ran out to the street, he saw Morel across the street in an alley lifting a rifle to his shoulder. His reaction was immediate, and as the rifle settled against Morel's shoulder, Bowdrie's bullet took him right between the eyebrows.

It was two hundred yards to the livery stable, and his own horse was unsaddled. A fine-looking black horse stood at the hitching rail, and without hesitation he loosed the slipknot and swung into the saddle. He was going down the street on a dead run when the others rushed from the door.

There was an outburst of shooting behind him and a bullet whined near his head. Ahead of him was the dust of the kidnappers of Carlotta.

If Sowers had time, there was no telling what he might do. Money and his followers had made him confident. For twenty years he had been the local power, and he could not grasp the fact that an era had ended.

Dick Rubin and Hensman were still in town. Between them they might wipe out York, Hanley, and Gatesby. With nobody to press charges, they might evade punishment and go on as they had.

If Sowers reached his ranch, where more of his outlaw hands waited, there was no telling what he might do. The townspeople had no idea of the evidence against him. With the witnesses eliminated and everybody believing that Mary Sowers was his ward, they could go scot-free.

The black horse had heart, and he loved to run. He ran now.

Yet Bowdrie saw that overtaking them would be impossible. They had turned from the trail into a maze of canyons, and with the coming of darkness Bowdrie could not hope to keep to a trail. Yet, details were beginning to appear that were familiar. He had ridden over this country when he first discovered the Mason ranch and the remains of Gil Mason.

Moreover, there was no water of which he knew, except for the ranch, and the chances were, Sowers was taking a roundabout route to that very place.

If he went directly there now, he would arrive ahead of them and with a fairly fresh horse.

It was completely dark when he rode into the ranch yard. Riding directly to it, he had been sure he would arrive before Sowers.

The buildings were dark and there was no sound. Chick watered the black horse, then led him back into the brush to a patch of grass seen earlier. There he picketed him. He walked back to the ranch yard and settled down beside a big cottonwood not far from the water trough.

He had dozed off, and awakening suddenly sometime later, he saw a man's head between him and the water. He recognized the shape of the hat.

"York!" he whispered.

York came back to where he was. "Bowdrie? They are coming in now. They must've stopped somewhere. Rubin's already here. There was some shooting in town. Rubin's wounded and Hensman was killed along with one other man. I think they ran into some more of their men who were on the way into town."

"Where are Gatesby and Hanley?"

"Close by. Unless they bother Mary, we'd better hang back until daylight."

It was hard waiting in the dark. Every sound was crystal clear, and they could hear movements and talk near the house, but words could only occasionally be distinguished.

"There's seven of them!" Hanley said as he came up.

Chick nodded. "They're holding the girl in the yard. They have her hands tied, but not her feet. I just saw them walking her over from the horses."

He turned. "Hanley, you an' Gatesby slip around and cover the out trail. Don't let them get away."

He touched York's shoulder. "You wait awhile an' then slip down an' get into the house. There's a back door. Get in if you can, and lie quiet."

"What about you?"

"I'm goin' down there an' get her out of there before the shootin' starts."

"That's my job!" Steve protested.

"I can move like an Indian. I'll do it."

Flat on his stomach, the side of his face to the ground, Bowdrie moved himself with his hands, elbows, or toes, inching along until he reached the hard-packed earth. He dared go no further by that means. His clothing would scrape against the solid clay, making too much sound.

He could see the girl lying on the ground, near her a guard. Bowdrie could see the glow of his cigarette in the dark. Seated with his shoulder against the corner of the barn, the guard would turn his head at intervals to glance all around him.

Chick worked his way to the side of the barn, and then, standing erect, he began to glide closer and closer to the guard. Once the guard turned, and Bowdrie froze to immobility, waiting, holding his breath. He saw the guard's elbow move, saw his hands come up—he was starting to roll a fresh cigarette.

He was still rolling it when Chick's forearm slipped across his throat from behind. Putting the palm of his right hand on the guard's head, he grasped his right arm with his left hand and shut down hard. The movement had been swift and long-practiced.

The guard gave a frenzied lunge and the girl sat up with a startled movement. Holding his grip until the man's muscles slowly relaxed, then releasing him, Bowdrie moved to the girl. Touching her lips with his hand to still any outcry, he swiftly cut her free.

Using the unconscious man's neckerchief and belt, he bound him tightly. It was not a good job, but all they needed was a minute or two.

Already it was faintly gray in the east. He had not realized they had waited so long, nor that so much time had elapsed since he began his approach to the girl.

He had Carlotta on her feet moving away when there was a startled movement. "Joe? What you doin' with that girl?" The man came to his feet. "Joe? *Joe?*" Then he yelled, *"Hey! You!"*

"Run!" Bowdrie hissed; then he turned, drawing as he moved.

Flame stabbed the night. Then a shot came from the stable, and he replied, rolling over instantly, trying for the partial shelter of the water trough.

At the first sign of trouble, Sowers lunged for the shelter of the house. Lute Boyer came up, gun in hand. *"Got you, Bowdrie!"* he yelled, and fired.

An instant late. Bowdrie saw Lute stagger back, blood running from his mouth as he tried to get his gun up. Bowdrie fired again, and Boyer turned and fell to his hands and knees, facing away from Bowdrie.

Hanley and Gatesby, their original plan foiled by the discovery, burst into the yard, firing.

Bowdrie ran for the front door, coming in from the side just as York tripped and fell, losing hold on his gun. York grabbed, got it, and rolled back from the door as Med Sowers started after him, firing. Sowers' concentration on making a perfect shot caused him to step without looking. The ball of his foot came down, something rolled under his foot, and he fell, catching himself against the doorjamb, half in, half out of the door.

Bowdrie fired as Sowers' body loomed in the doorway. The big man's body sagged and he slowly slipped to his knees on the step. He stared at Bowdrie, his face contorted. The gun slipped from his fingers, and slowly he pitched forward on his face.

Bowdrie walked closer, and stooping, took the pistol from Sowers' hand. It was a .41.

York came up. "He had me dead to rights. What made him fall?"

Bowdrie stooped and picked up a lead bullet, its nose partly flattened. "I dropped it when I was burying Gil Mason. He must have stepped on it."

Bowdrie took the bullet and rolled it in his fingers. "Fired from Sowers' own gun, sixteen years ago!"

In the gray light of morning, over a campfire a quarter of a mile from the ranch house, Carlotta looked across the small fire where they were making coffee.

"Steve has been telling me what you did. I want to thank you. I had never known anything about my parents. I was only three years old when I started living with Mr. Sowers' sister."

"He probably kept you first as a hold over your mother," Bowdrie said, "but when you got older and he'd seen some pictures his sister sent, he began to get other ideas."

"This was my father's place?"

"He built it for your mother and him. He put in a lot of

work. He was a happy man. He had the woman he wanted and the home he wanted."

Bowdrie got up. He should be back at the hotel writing up his report.

"It was built for two young people in love," he said.

"That's what Steve was saying—that care and thought went into every detail of it."

"No reason to waste it." Bowdrie accepted the reins of the horse Hanley led to him. "See you in town!"

MORE BRAINS THAN BULLETS

THE HAMMERHEADED ROAN stood three-legged at the hitching rail in front of the Cattleman's Saloon, dozing in the warm sunlight. Occasionally he switched a casual tail at a lazy fly or stamped a hoof into the dust.

Nearby, against the unpainted wall of the Bon Ton Café, in the cool shade of the wooden awning over the boardwalk, Chick Bowdrie dozed comfortably in a tipped-back chair. Hat low over his eyes, pleasantly full of breakfast and coffee, he was frankly enjoying a time to relax.

Fighting raiding Comanches and over-the-border bandits, as well as their own home-grown variety of outlaw, kept the Texas Rangers occupied. Moments of leisure were all too few, and to be taken as they appeared.

He had no family, so home was wherever he hung his hat. Had it not been for Captain McNelly, who recruited him, he might have been on the dodge himself by this time. He had been a top hand since he was fourteen, but too good with a gun, and there were too many around who thought to take advantage of a boy on his own, ready to steal stock in his care, steal his horse, or simply ride roughshod over him, and Bowdrie had met them a little more than halfway.

His family had been wiped out by Comanches when he was six, and for the next five years he had lived with his captors. Escaping, he was taken up by a Swiss family living near San Antonio. He attended school for three years, learned to speak French from his foster parents and a smattering of German from his schoolmates.

He had become a disciple of the old western adage that "brains in the head save blisters on the feet." A little rest and meditation often saved a lot of riding over rough country, and right now he had a lot to think about, when he got around to it.

Two men came out of the café adjoining the saloon. The man with the toothpick was saying, "Who else could it be but Culver? Only the two of us had the combination, an' I surely wouldn't steal my own money."

"The boy's a good lad, Lindsay. I've known him since he was a baby. Knew his pappy before him."

"We all knew old Black Jack Culver," Lindsay replied. "The boy does have a good reputation. Maybe he is a good lad, but the fact is, somebody opened that safe with the combination! Nothing damaged anywhere. No signs of a break-in, and that safe's a new one."

He spat. "Far's his pappy goes, he rustled his share of cows, an' you know it, Cowan!"

Cowan chuckled. "O' course I know it! I helped him! We all branded anything that was loose in them days, an' there's stuff runnin' on your ranch right now whose mamas wore another brand. You can't hold that against a man just because times have changed. Those days are past, and we all know it. We have the law now, and it is better that way. Besides, who knew in them days who a cow belonged to? Nobody branded for years, and of course, ol' Maverick never did brand any of his stuff.

"When you an' me came into this country, all a steer was worth was what you could get for hide an' tallow. After the Civil War, everybody needed beef an' things changed."

Bowdrie had not moved. If they were aware of him at all, they probably thought him asleep. "The fact is, Cowan, I'm in a tight spot for money. I can't stand to lose twenty thousand dollars just like that!" He snapped his fingers. "Six thousand of that was in payment for cattle I haven't delivered yet, cattle I sold to Ross Yerby."

"He buyin' more cows? He picked up a thousand head from me just t'other day."

"Don't I know it! You deposited that money with me, an' part of it was in that safe!"

"You don't say!" Cowan was suddenly angry. "Dang it, Lindsay! What kind of a bank you runnin', anyway?"

"It was you didn't want me to accuse young Culver. Looks different when the shoe's on the other foot."

The two moved off, still talking. Chick sat quietly. No bank robbery had been reported to the Rangers, yet this seemed to be an inside job, embezzlement rather than a hold-up. His curiosity aroused, he arose and sauntered back into the restaurant. "How's about some more coffee? I sure like your make of it. Strong enough to tan your boots!"

The ex-cow-camp cook brought a cup and the pot to the table. "I oughta know how a cowhand likes it," he said. "I've made coffee enough to drown a thousand head of steers!"

He dropped into the chair across from Bowdrie. He looked at the rider across the table, the dark, Apache-like face and black eyes—it was like looking into a pair of gun muzzles. "Huntin' a ridin' job?" Josh Chancy asked.

"Maybe. Anybody doin' any hirin' around?"

"Newcomer, name of Yerby, is buyin' a lot of stock. Plans a drive to Abilene in another month or so. Big man, pays well, free with his money. He's bought nigh onto four thousand head, an' payin' durn near what they pay in Kansas!"

"Might be a good man to work for. Newcomer, you say? What's he look like?"

"Big. Mighty good-lookin' man. Smooth-handed man, plays a good game of poker an' usually wins. White hat, black coat, black mustache. He's been courtin' Lisa Culver, seems like. Leastways he's been seein' her a lot."

"Culver? Didn't there used to be a Black Jack Culver?"

"He was her pappy. Good man, too. I worked beside him for more'n a year. His boy's a fine lad, too. He's no rider, but he's bright, got good sense. But that gal? She's the best-lookin' filly this side the Brazos!"

Josh liked to talk, and the place was empty but for Bowdrie. "Young Bill, he works over at the bank for Lindsay. He's been sparkin' that girl of Mendoza's. Don't know's I blame him, but she's a fancy, flirty bit, but she's got a temper worse than Mendoza's, an' nobody ever accused Pete of bein' no tenderfoot. He's a brush-wise old ladino, that Pete Mendoza is!"

The door opened suddenly and Lindsay stuck his head in.

"Josh, have you seen Yerby? Or Bill Culver? If they come in, tell 'em I want to see them, will you?"

Chick Bowdrie sipped his coffee. It might be a good idea to stick around a day or two, for the situation smelled of trouble.

He pushed back from the table and sauntered outside to resume his seat under the awning. The roan opened a lazy eye and studied him doubtfully, but when he seated himself again, the eye closed and the roan stomped at an annoying fly. They would not be moving yet.

Maravillas was a one-street town with a row of false-fronted, wind-battered buildings facing each other across the narrow, dusty street. The fourth building across the street had a sign: "MARAVILLAS BANK."

A girl came out of the bank and started up the street toward him. She was dark and her eyes flashed as she glanced at Chick. It was a bold, appraising glance. She had a lovely, passionate mouth and a free-swinging movement of the hips, and a body her clothing enhanced rather than concealed. A girl who, in this hot border country, was an invitation to murder.

A young man came from the bank and stared after the girl. Bowdrie could not see his expression. The young man turned and walked to a stable behind the bank. From where Bowdrie sat he could just see the edge of the stable door and part of a window. He saw Bill Culver swing a saddle to a horse's back.

Soon after, Bill Culver crossed the street and went into the restaurant, emerging with a small package.

A moment later Tom Lindsay went into the bank. Ross Yerby, or a man Bowdrie guessed was Yerby, came down the street and followed Lindsay into the bank. Instantly voices were raised in violent argument. One was Lindsay's voice, the other was Culver's. If Yerby was speaking, his voice could not be heard.

Bowdrie saw Yerby come from the bank and cross the street toward him. Chick stood up, pushing back his black flat-crowned hat. "Mr. Yerby? I hear you figurin' on makin' a drive to Abilene. You need any hands?"

Yerby had a quick, sharp eye. He took in Bowdrie at a glance, noting the tied-down guns. "I can use a few men. Have you been over the trail?"

"I've been over a lot of trails, both sides of the border."

Yerby hesitated, then asked, "Do you know the Nation? And the Cowhouse Creek just north of here?"

"I do."

"Stick around. I can use you."

Bowdrie dropped back into his chair. He was still seated there an hour later when he heard the shot. He was not surprised.

The sudden bark of the pistol struck like a whip across the hot, still afternoon.

Men burst from the café, the saloon, and several stores and stood looking and listening. Bowdrie remained sitting. From the grove back of the bank he heard the drum of horse's hooves, a sound that faded into silence.

Bowdrie slid from his chair and followed King Cowan into the bank.

Tom Lindsay lay sprawled on the floor. He had been shot through the heart at close range. The rear door of the bank stood open. Glancing through the door, Chick saw no horse in sight. His dark features inscrutable, he stood by as Wilse Kennedy, the sheriff, took charge. "Where's young Culver?" Kennedy asked. "He should be here."

A head thrust through the rear door. "His horse is gone, Wilse! Must've been him we heard ridin' away!"

"Culver had a motive," Cowan agreed. "Tom was tellin' me only this mornin' that twenty thousand dollars had been stolen from the bank, and that only him an' young Culver knew the combination to the safe."

"Must be him, then." Kennedy looked around from face to face. "Lindsay must have accused him of it, and Culver shot him down. He wouldn't have run if he wasn't guilty."

"Don't be too hard on the boy," Ross Yerby interrupted. "Bill's all right. I doubt if he'd do a thing like this. There's probably a good explanation for his not bein' here."

Bowdrie caught Yerby's eye and commented, "There's

somethin' to that. Can't never tell by the way things look on the surface."

"What's that? Who said that?" Kennedy looked around at Chick, his eyes narrowing. "Who're you?"

"He rides for me," Yerby explained. "I took him on today."

"You punch your cows"—Kennedy was sharp—"I'll do the sheriffin'." He turned to Cowan. "Did you say twenty thousand was missing? How come he had that much cash?"

"I paid him some of it," Yerby said, "and some may have been Cowan's. I bought cattle from him, too."

"Well, let's get after him!" Kennedy said. "King, you mount up and come along. I can use you, too, Yerby." Kennedy spoke to several others, ignoring Bowdrie, who stood looking down at the body. Familiar as he was with violent death, it never failed to disturb him that a man could be so suddenly deprived of life. Guns were something not to be taken lightly, but to be handled with care and used with discrimination.

Instead of following the posse outside, he went out the back door. He had a hunch and acted on it. Bill Culver had been accused of stealing twenty thousand dollars. He had been seen saddling a horse. The banker was killed after a quarrel with Culver overheard by a number of people, and now Culver was missing. It appeared to be an open-and-shut case.

Bowdrie's hunch was no more than that. Among other things, he was sure the posse had ridden off in the wrong direction, for he was sure Bill would ride around to see his sister. Moreover, if his hunch was right, there would be action in town before many hours were past.

Bill Culver's horse was gone, that was obvious. Chick glanced around, then walked behind the stable. In the dust lay the stub of a freshly smoked cigarette. He put it in a folder in an inside vest pocket. Then he went back across the street to the Bon Ton Café for coffee.

"You didn't ride with the posse?" Josh asked.

"No, I didn't. I think they're chasin' the wrong man, Josh. Culver sizes up as an unlikely killer."

"Ain't no better boy around!" Josh said belligerently. "I don't believe he done it!"

The door burst open and a lovely blond girl came in. "Josh! Is it true? Did Bill shoot Tom Lindsay?"

Bowdrie looked around. "They say he did, ma'am. They say he took twenty thousand dollars. He's gone and his horse is gone."

"He couldn't have!" she protested. "That's not like Bill! He wouldn't do a thing like that!"

The door opened and a short, thick-set man entered. He had a hard, swarthy face and black eyes that swept the room. "Lisa, where's Bill?" he asked.

"I have no idea, Señor Mendoza! They are saying he killed Tom Lindsay!"

"So? My Rita has gone. She has run away."

Lisa Culver was shocked. Chick took a quick swallow of his coffee, eyes shifting from face to face. They all had jumped to the same conclusion, that Culver had robbed the bank, killed Lindsay, and run away with Rita Mendoza.

Mendoza turned on his heel and left the room. Bowdrie stared after him. What would Mendoza do?

Lisa stood a moment in indecision, then fled. Chick sipped his coffee. "Busy little place," he commented. "Things happen fast around here."

He put his cup down. "Yerby buy cattle from anybody but Cowan an' Lindsay?"

"Huh?" Josh glanced around irritably, obviously upset by what had happened. "Oh? Yeah, I reckon he did. He bought a few head off old Steve Farago, over at Wild Horse. Five hundred head, I think it was."

Chick finished his coffee, then crossed to the bank. The white-faced clerk who had taken over was filled with importance. At first he refused Bowdrie's request point-blank, but at a flash of the Ranger badge, Bowdrie was given the information he wanted.

Swinging aboard the roan, Bowdrie headed out of town. Wild Horse Mesa was sharply defined against the horizon.

He would have preferred to stop at the Culvers', but decided against it. Later, returning from Wild Horse, would be soon enough.

Shadows were reaching out from the high cliffs of the mesa

when Bowdrie loped the roan into the ranch yard. "Hello, the house!" he called.

There was a sudden movement inside, a crash as of a broken dish. Bowdrie dropped from the saddle and started for the house, walking warily. There was no further sound. Nor was there any horse around but the three rawboned ponies in the corral.

Bowdrie hesitated on the doorstep, then stepped to the side of the door. It was black and still inside.

"Hey!" he yelled again.

There was no response, and no sound. Chick eased his right-hand gun in its holster and edged toward the door. A hinge creaked out back, and Bowdrie leaped through the door in time to catch a glimpse of a dark shadow at the back door. Then a gun flashed, and he hit the floor, losing the heel from one of his boots.

He did not fire. There was simply no target, and Chick Bowdrie was not one to blaze away on the sheer chance that he might hit something. He got to his feet and edged toward the back door. The ranch yard was shadowy and still, with neither sound nor movement. It was almost dark outside now, and looking for a man in that rough country in the dark would be suicide.

He turned back, and, his eyes becoming accustomed to the vague light, he peered around. He could see but a few things.

A chair lay on its side, and there was scattered bedding. He gambled and struck a light, keeping out of line of either windows or doors. Then he lit a candle.

The body of a man he assumed to be Steve Farago lay sprawled on the floor. His pockets were turned inside out. The old man had been murdered with two bullets through the chest, then thoroughly searched.

The bed had been upset and the mattress jerked off the wooden slats. Several pots had been opened, their contents scattered. Somebody had known that Farago had money and had murdered and robbed him. But had they robbed him? Or had Bowdrie arrived before the job was complete?

Chick dropped beside the body. He unbuttoned the shirt and unfastened the old man's belt. He found what he half-expected—a money belt. Unsnapping a pocket of the belt, Chick dug out a flat packet of bills. Hesitating only an instant, he took three bills from the packet, one from the top, one from the bottom, one from the middle. Returning the packet to the belt, he snapped the pocket shut, rebuckled the belt, and buttoned the shirt. Stepping around the can of spilled flour, Bowdrie blew out the candle, got into the saddle, and took the road for Maravillas, but switching to a roundabout route that would bring him down behind the Culver ranch, on the very edge of town.

Dismounting from the roan, he walked up through the yard. Two horses, bridled and saddled, waited behind the barn. One was the horse Bill Culver had ridden away from the bank.

Holding to the shadows, he got around the barn, ducking across the open yard to the wall of the house. Gently he lifted the latch on the door. It opened under his hand, and he went in on cat feet. The kitchen was dark. A crack of light showed under the door, beyond which he heard a murmur of voices. Suddenly there was a touch of cold steel behind his ear, and he froze in place.

"Now!" It was Pete Mendoza's voice. "You will open the door. One wrong move and this pistol, she speak!"

Chick opened the door with the gun at his back and stepped into the next room, his hands lifted.

Bill Culver started to his feet. The others in the room were Lisa Culver and Rita Mendoza.

"What's going on, Pete? Who is this man?" Bill asked.

"I don't know. He sneak in, so I catch him."

"If you'll put away that gun, we can sit down and talk. I'd suggest we get it over with before that posse figures out where you are."

"Who are you? What do you want?" Bill demanded.

"I'm Chick Bowdrie. I ride for the Rangers."

"Oh, Bill!" Lisa exclaimed. "The Rangers! What can you do now?"

"It won't make any difference! Rangers or no Rangers, I am not going to die for a killing I didn't do!"

"Suppose you all hold your horses," Bowdrie replied mildly. "I haven't said I was hunting you, have I? Don't make trouble for me and get the Rangers on your tail. You have trouble enough without that."

"If you don't want me, what are you doing here?"

"Oh, sort of figurin' things out, only I was afraid you'd run away before I got things straightened out. You ain't in no trouble now you can't get out of."

"No trouble!" Rita's eyes flashed. "What you call trouble? He is wanted for robbing and killing! We must run away to Mejico for the marriage!"

Bowdrie shrugged. "Must be mighty excitin' to have two such pretty girls worried over a man." He glanced at Pete Mendoza. "This marriage all right with you?"

Pete shrugged. "No, not at once. After I hear there is trouble, yes. My daughter is my daughter. If she wants this man, and if she marry with him, all is well. If they are in trouble? Well, I have been in trouble, too!"

Bowdrie glanced at Bill. "You can unsaddle those horses. There's no need to run away. Before sundown tomorrow, you will be a free man . . . or married," he added, smiling. "On the other hand, better keep the horses saddled. Pete and I can ride into town with you. We can all stay in the hotel until morning, and then we will get all this straightened out."

"They'd kill me!" Bill protested. "Yerby told me there was a lot of hard feeling in town."

"You saw Yerby? He wasn't with the posse?"

"He and King Cowan left the posse, then they split up. Cowan rode across country to see Farago, and Yerby cut back here to see me."

"What did he want to see you about?"

"He wanted to help. He thinks a lot of Lisa and he wanted to see if I had money enough to get out of the country. You see, he knew I was quitting the bank before the killing of Tom Lindsay. He's been pretty nice."

"All right, let's get into town." He turned to Lisa. "I'd come along, if I were you. I doubt if there will be trouble. We will beat the posse back to town."

When the girls and Bill Culver were safely in the Maravillas Hotel, Bowdrie turned to Mendoza. "Stay with them. I've work to do."

The street was dark and still. It was past midnight and the little cow town's people had found their way to bed. By six o'clock the next morning it would be awake and busy, stores would all be open by seven, and out on the range the cowhands would have been at work for two to three hours.

Bowdrie moved to the chair he had occupied earlier and settled down to wait. The chair sat in complete darkness, and from that vantage point Bowdrie could view the whole street.

The only place showing a light was the saloon, where the posse, which had ridden in shortly before, were having a few to "cut the dust," as the saying was.

Chick was tired. It had been a long day. Yet more was to come, and he had a feeling about it. He hitched himself around in his chair to leave his gun ready to hand. His eyes scanned the buildings across the street. The bank was dark and still, its windows staring with wide, blind eyes into the street.

Almost an hour passed before his ear caught a faint noise that might have been a hoof clicking on stone. He slid from the chair and crossed the street and vanished between two of the frame buildings.

At first he could see nothing; then his eyes caught a slight movement toward the rear of the bank, then a faint clink of metal. Bowdrie stepped forward quickly and inadvertently kicked a pebble, which rattled on a loose board. Instantly, flame stabbed from a gun at the rear of the bank.

Bowdrie fired in return, and glimpsed the dark figure of a man lunge toward the barn. Chick fired again, but as he squeezed off his shot, the running man stumbled and fell, rolled over, and vanished around the barn. Bowdrie followed, running. A hastily fired bullet kicked up dust at his feet; then there was a clatter of hooves and he rounded the corner of the barn in time to see a horseman vanish into the trees.

Limping because of his lost boot heel, Bowdrie went back to his chair. Toward daylight he got up and went to the hotel, realizing there was small chance the unknown man would return.

Dawn broke cool and cloudy over the town. Sleepy, and still tired, Bowdrie came down to the hotel door and scanned the street. Already there were horses in front of the saloon and the café. Then he saw Wilse Kennedy striding toward the hotel.

Chick drew back inside. Bill Culver, wide-eyed and pale from an obviously sleepless night, sat in a big hide-covered chair. Lisa was nearby, and beside Culver was Rita Mendoza, clutching one of his hands. Pete Mendoza, square-shouldered and thick-chested, leaned against a newel post at the foot of the stairs, his face somber.

Sheriff Kennedy shoved open the door and stepped in. "I heard you was here," he said to Culver. "I come after you!"

Josh Chancy, King Cowan, and Ross Yerby crowded into the door behind Kennedy. With them were several others.

"What are you doin' here?" Josh asked Culver. "I figured you'd be halfway to Mexico by now."

"He told me to stay." Culver gestured at Bowdrie. "He said he could prove I wasn't guilty."

Kennedy gave Chick an angry glare. "What business is it of yours? I thought you was ridin' for Yerby?"

"He hired me. I am quitting as of now. My name is Bowdrie."

"Chick Bowdrie?" Josh exclaimed.

"I happened to be in town," Bowdrie explained, "on some business of my own. It seems your bank trouble and my case are sort of tied together, so I declared myself in."

"We got a sheriff to handle our affairs," Cowan declared. "I've been a friend of that boy's since he was a baby, but if he steals and murders, he pays the penalty! We don't need no Ranger comin' in here to tell us our business!"

"You're damned right!" Kennedy said irritably. "And if he ain't guilty, why'd he run? And who could have opened that safe? He was the only one knew the combination."

"You've been so busy," Bowdrie replied, "that I've had no chance to report another crime. Steve Farago's been murdered."

"Farago?" Kennedy looked over at King Cowan. "If he's been murdered, you ought to know, King. That was where you were goin' when you left the posse."

All eyes had turned to the cattleman. His face flushed. "You ain't suspectin' me of killin' Steve?"

"Why did you go to see him?" Kennedy demanded. "You an' Steve have had trouble for years, off an' on."

"I needed to have a talk with him. Me an' Steve have had no trouble for months. Maybe a year. He did raise a fuss about some stock he thought was his, but he was an old sorehead, anyway."

"Did you see Steve? Did you get over there?"

"He was dead when I got there. He'd been shot, and the body was still warm."

"What did you do?"

"Got away from there as fast as I could. If folks found me there with him dead, they'd be thinkin' just what you all are thinkin' now. The trouble I had with Steve was no killin' matter."

"Plenty of men have been killed over rustled cattle!" Josh was skeptical. "An' if I hear right, Farago was carryin' a lot of money." Chancy turned toward Yerby. "Didn't you buy some cattle off him?"

"Yes, and I paid in cash. He wanted it that way. He said he could take care of his money as well as any bank could."

"Just like the old coot," Josh put in. "He never did care for banks!"

"We're gettin' away from the subject," Kennedy interrupted. "I don't see how that Farago affair could have anything to do with the bank robbery and the killin' of Tom Lindsay.

"Bill Culver, you worked for Lindsay. Who had the combination besides the two of you?"

"Nobody."

Lisa's cheeks were pale, and when her eyes turned pleadingly to Bowdrie, they showed her fear. Her lovely lips seemed thin and hurt.

"The safe wasn't blowed, was it?" Kennedy persisted. He was the center of attention and was enjoying it. His sharp little eyes were triumphant.

"No."

"Then how do you reckon that money was stole, if you or

Tom Lindsay didn't take it? And if Tom took it, he'd have to make it good out of his own pocket, wouldn't he?"

He paused, looking around, impressed with his own presentation of the facts.

"Now, where was you when the shot was fired that killed Tom?"

"I don't know," Bill protested. "I have no idea. I'd saddled my horse earlier and then went in to tell Lindsay I was quitting. Then he sprang that business about the missing money on me. He said I couldn't leave. He was having me arrested. I told him I did not steal his money and that I was leaving.

"Rita and I were getting married and we were going to El Paso. We'd postponed it several times, and she told me this was the last time. If I wanted her, it was now or not at all. Well, I wasn't going to have it postponed again, so I told Tom Lindsay to figure things out the best he could, and left."

"You just went out an' rode off?"

"That's right. I got my horse and rode away."

"Were there any other horses in that stable?" Bowdrie asked.

All eyes turned to him. Kennedy, irritated, started to interrupt.

"Not in the stable. There was a sorrel pony with three white stockings tied behind the stable."

"Whose horse was it?" Bowdrie inquired.

"I don't know," Culver replied. "I never gave it a thought."

"I seen that horse," Josh Chancy said. "That horse was stole from Jim Tatum two weeks ago."

Kennedy broke in angrily. "All this talk is gettin' us nowhere! The fact is, nobody could have done it but Culver, and I'm arrestin' him for robbery an' murder!"

Lisa jumped and cried out, but Pete Mendoza stepped forward. "You touch him over my dead body!"

Wilse Kennedy started to speak, then looked again at Mendoza, knowing all too well the Mexican could give him every break and still kill him. He started to splutter something about bucking the law, when Chick broke in.

"Hold your horses, everybody! Pete, you back up and sit

down. The law's in charge here, and you aren't helping one bit.

"I'll take charge now. Bill Culver is completely in the clear. The man who killed Tom Lindsay also killed Steve Farago, and robbed him as well."

All eyes switched to Bowdrie. Ross Yerby moved forward as if to speak, and King Cowan's face was stiff with apprehension.

"You are wondering what a Texas Ranger is doing here in town, anyway." Deliberately he scanned each face in turn. "I came here on the trail of a wanted man."

He paused. "That man doesn't even know he's wanted, but I've been tailin' him, and when I hit town, I had a hunch I wasn't far behind him.

"Matter of fact, I was close behind him, but I didn't expect there would be a killin'. That was somethin' neither me nor the killer reckoned on. He didn't know I was chasin' him, and he didn't expect anybody would even suspect him until he and his money were long gone."

Bowdrie's eyes dropped to Bill Culver. "The man I'm talkin' about figured on leavin' here fast!"

Bowdrie pushed his hat back. "As to that safe, it was no problem to the man I'm talkin' about. In the first place, he made a duplicate key to the front door, prob'ly from a wax impression from a key left on the desk. I've been in town only a few days, and I saw those keys lyin' on the desk in plain sight with nobody near.

"The thief came to the bank at night. That safe has a knob that could be unscrewed from the combination lock. I spotted it when I first walked in, knowing what kind of a safe it was. He slipped a piece of paper under the combination lock, and then screwed the knob back on. That way, every time the combination was twirled, it would leave a mark on the paper.

"All the thief had to do was take off that knob, get his paper, screw the knob back on, and open the safe. He could read the combination by the marks on the paper."

"If he could open that safe," Kennedy asked skeptically, "why didn't he just take the twenty thousand and go?"

"Wait a minute," Bowdrie replied, "I'm not through." He turned to Culver. "How often has Lindsay had that much in the bank?"

"That's the first time, so far as I know. He keeps about five or six thousand on hand, and that's enough for the business we do."

"And who knew he had more?" Kennedy said. "Culver, that's who!"

"He knew," Bowdrie said, "and the killer knew. I told you I came here trailin' a wanted man. This man thought he was safe, in the clear. He figured he would still be in the clear when this job was completed. He knew Culver was leavin' town and planned to hang it all on him.

"Only, he hadn't left the clean slate behind him he believed he had. He thought he had killed a man in New Orleans, but the man was not dead. He lived to give a description and to tell us his killer stole thirty thousand dollars in counterfeit money."

"Counterfeit?" Cowan exploded.

"That's right. That's why the bank was robbed, to recover the money before anybody knew it was counterfeit. That is why Lindsay was killed, because Lindsay found out! An' Farago was killed before he tried to spend any of it."

"But who . . . ?" Kennedy demanded.

Bowdrie was looking past him at Ross Yerby. "That's right, Yerby! You bought cattle with counterfeit money! You pulled the bank robbery to get it back, then you'd have had the counterfeit, six thousand extra, and the cattle, too!

"Two things you didn't count on, Yerby! That man in New Orleans livin' long enough to talk, and Lindsay takin' any of that money before night. Lindsay was short of cash, so he slipped a bill out of your bundle to spend for drinks, and recognized it as queer money."

"You're lyin'! You can't prove any of that!"

"I took three of the counterfeit bills from Farago's body before you had a chance to rob him. You have the rest of it in your possession now. Also, you have flour on your boot soles from where you spilled it last night in Farago's place!"

"Let's see those boots, Yerby! Turn 'em up!"

Yerby backed up. "That's nonsense!" he said. "This whole charade has been nonsense!" He glanced toward the door, but Kennedy was between him and the door. Cowan was on his right. "I'll have no more of this!"

He turned toward the door, but as Kennedy moved to stop him, Yerby's hand flashed to his waistband. As the gun was coming up, Bowdrie shot him.

Yerby backed up another step, and the gun slipped from his fingers. He slid down the wall to the floor.

"He's yours, Sheriff," Bowdrie said.

He took the three bills from his pocket. "These will match the ones from Farago's packet."

"About the safe? Was that how it was done?" Culver asked.

"It was. It's used quite a bit back East, with that brand of safe. If you run that bank, you'd better get you another."

He climbed the stairs, gathered up his blanket roll and haversack. For a moment he glanced around the room.

A bed, a chair, a stand with a white bowl and a pitcher, two pictures on the walls. How many such rooms had he seen? How many times had he slept in nondescript hotels in nondescript towns? And how many more would there be?

Some men would operate cattle ranches or stage lines or banks. While they got rich, he would be keeping the peace so they could make it, but it was a job somebody had to have; somebody was needed to hold the line against lawlessness.

He went down the steps. The lobby was empty. They had gone. Bill Culver and Rita to be married, Pete Mendoza and King Cowan to their ranches.

Lisa?

He hesitated. She had gone back to wherever she was when it all began.

As for him, there was a man down toward the border who had been losing cattle, and there was an outlaw killer who had just disappeared into the Big Thicket.

He strapped his roll behind the saddle and swung aboard.

Josh came to the door. "Cuppa coffee before you go?"

"It's a long trail, Josh! Another time! Come on, Crowbait," he said to the roan. "Move it!"

THE ROAD TO CASA PIEDRAS

CHICK BOWDRIE HOOKED his thumbs in his belt and watched the dancers. Old Bob McClellan and his two strapping sons were sawing away on their fiddles, lubricated by Pa Gardner's own make of corn whiskey.

Pa, flushed with whiskey and exertion, was calling the dances from a precarious platform of planks laid over three benches. Any platform would have been precarious, for Pa had been imbibing freely from his own keg of corn. Being the owner of the whiskey as well as the tin cup hanging from the spigot, he was the only one aside from the musicians who could take a drink without paying.

Emmy Chambers, blond and beautiful, whirled by Chick and smiled at him. A strand of her cornsilk hair had fallen over her eyes but she looked excited and happy. Chick couldn't see it himself, but womenfolks seemed to think a lot of dancing. Personally, he thought, it was better out on the sagebrush country with a good horse under him.

He never had been given to duding up, but lately some of the Rangers had been getting themselves some pretty slick outfits, so he followed the trend and had gotten himself up for this dance. He was wearing a black broadcloth shirt of the shield variety with a row of pearl buttons down each side, and for the first time in months he had his collar buttoned and was wearing a white string tie. It made his neck itch and he felt like he was tied with a rope halter.

His gunbelts were of black leather inlaid with mother-of-pearl and silver, likewise the holsters. His trousers were black, and he wore new hand-worked boots with California-style spurs with two-inch rowels, all shined up and pretty.

Emmy Chambers was the prettiest blond in the room, and Mary Boling the prettiest brunette. Mary was a dark-eyed girl with a hint of Spanish blood. This town was not his usual stamping grounds so he knew none of these people beyond a few names. He was about to leave when Emmy Chambers ran up to him.

"Chick, it isn't fair! Why aren't you out there dancing? Now, come on!"

"Now, ma'am," he protested, flushing, "I'm not a dancing man. I—" His words were cut off by the sharp report of a pistol shot, then another. An instant later they heard the pounding hooves of a racing horse.

Bowdrie caught up his hat and as he swung toward the door his eyes caught Mary Boling's. There was a strange brightness in them, almost a sort of triumph. Did that big cowhand affect her that way?

Chick stepped into the street, men and women crowding past him and around him.

Aside from the schoolhouse, where the dance was taking place, there was but one lighted window in the place, the stage station next door. With sudden realization, Bowdrie sprinted for the station. He was the first to arrive.

Shoving open the door, he saw John Irwin sprawled across his desk, his life's blood staining the clustered papers on which he had been working. His right hand dangled limply over the edge of the desk and his six-shooter lay on the floor beneath the hand. Irwin had died trying.

Bowdrie picked up the gun and sniffed the barrel. Then he checked the cylinder. The gun had been fired and one chamber was empty except for the cartridge shell.

"They got the money!" Ed Gardner exclaimed. "Twelve thousand dollars!"

Bowdrie glanced at him. "How'd you know that?" The fact that Irwin had the money in his safe was supposed to be known to but three men.

"When I stopped by before the dance, Irwin was countin' it."

Aside from Bowdrie himself, only Irwin, Sheriff Sam Butler, and Deputy Tom Robley were supposed to know the money was here. Butler and Robley had been at the dance. Bowdrie had seen them not three minutes before the shots were fired.

Bowdrie looked over at Butler. "You notify his folks, will you? No use doin' anything until morning. We'd just mess up whatever sign was left."

The crowd filed out and disappeared toward their homes. The dancing was over for tonight.

John Irwin had a cash deal for a herd of cattle, and as there had been several recent hold-ups, he notified the law that he would have the money on hand. Pa Gardner, who had seen the money, was not, despite his faults, a talkative man, yet somebody had known.

Bowdrie walked back to the schoolroom where the dance had taken place. A few couples stood around, reluctant to end the festivities or talking about the murder and robbery. Tom Robley was there.

"A pity," he said. "Irwin was a nice old man."

"Somebody else knew the money was there. If you come up with any names, let me know."

Tom stared at the knuckles of his big fists. He seemed unnaturally tense. "I will," he said, "believe me I will."

Mary Boling came over to them. "Hello, Tom!" Then to Chick, "You're the Texas Ranger, aren't you? I heard there was one in town."

Bowdrie's dark features were impassive. "You look mighty pretty in that dress," he commented.

She wrinkled her nose disdainfully. "This ol' thing? It's all right, but I'll have prettier dresses. I'll be going to New Orleans for my clothes. Or to New York."

"You'll keep some young rancher busted," Bowdrie said dryly. "Clothes are costly."

"Maybe the man I marry won't be just a rancher." Mary tossed her curls, smiling at both of them. Tom Robley looked miserable.

"Ranchin' ain't so bad," Robley protested. "Anyway, Al Harshman's a rancher, and Jim Moody's a cowhand."

She laughed at him, squeezing his arm. "And you're a deputy sheriff!" she said. "But you might become almost anything. As for Al, he won't always be a rancher. Al's got ambition."

"So've I," Robley protested. "You'll see."

TEN MILES OUT of town, Chick Bowdrie reined in the hammerhead roan, indicating the track on the edge of the shallow hole where rain had formed a pool.

"Headin' northeast. That track was made followin' the heaviest part of the rain, but before the last shower. Reckon he's our man, all right.

"Doesn't know the country too well. He's ridin' by landmarks. The trail's just a half-mile off to the east, but this gent is headed for Pistol Rock Spring, usin' that thumb butte over there for a marker."

"How d'you figure that?" Robley asked. He had believed he was a good man on a trail, yet he had seen very little since leaving town, while Bowdrie had ridden right along, only occasionally pointing out something he had seen.

"Twice he's swung too far west, and he's swung back until he's lined up on that butte. He's travelin' fast, so if he knew about that trail, he'd be usin' it. He wouldn't be afraid of meetin' anybody in this rain. Far as that goes, the trail isn't used much, anyway."

The three men rode on. Sam Butler had seen more than Robley, but not as much as Bowdrie. Tom's eyes were hollow from lack of sleep.

"He's got some help somewhere ahead," Bowdrie commented, "or else he's a damn fool. No man in his right mind would run a horse like he has his unless he knew there was another waitin' for him. He's headin' right into that wasteland of the Horse Thief Mesa country."

The sun lifted over the brow of the hill and threw lances of sunlight across the sagebrush levels. Ahead lay the waste of Tobosa Flat, a flat stretch of creosote bush, tobosa, and burro grass. Here even the showers of the previous night had not settled the dust.

It was very hot. Their passing raised a dust cloud. If the man they pursued was watching his back trail, he knew he was followed. Then Bowdrie spotted the bush and rode over to it.

"Tied his horse here. Prob'ly either a stolen horse or one he just got hold of. It doesn't like him and he doesn't trust it.

He tied fast instead of ground-hitching, an' when he started to get back into the saddle, it acted up. But let's see what he did when he got down from the saddle."

They trailed boot tracks to a nest of boulders on a low hill. There the man had knelt in the damp sand while watching his back trail. Had he seen them? They had not reached the dusty part at that time.

"Maybe daybreak, or right after. The first time he could see good, he stopped to look back." Bowdrie indicated a mark in the sand near where he had knelt. "Carries a rifle. Judging by the print of the butt plate, it could be a Winchester or a Henry, but that's just guessing."

He indicated the length of the man's stride. "Six feet tall, I'd say, weighs about one-seventy. Got a run-down heel on his right boot, and pretty badly run down. By the look of his tracks, I'd say he had something wrong with that leg. Else he's got an odd way of walkin'."

He went back to the bush where their own horses waited. He picked a black hair from the mesquite bush. "Black mane an' tail. From the stride I'd say about fourteen hands high. We'll have a picture of him real soon."

Butler agreed. Then he added, "You're like an Injun on a trail. Part of that trail back there I couldn't even see, yet you kept right on a-goin'."

"Instinct, maybe," Bowdrie said. "You pick up little things. Man on the run will usually keep to low ground until he wants to look back."

The desert became wilder and more barren. The mesquite thinned out and there was more burro grass. Even that became less and then they dipped down into a sandy draw littered with boulders. The man they followed had slowed to a walk here and Bowdrie did likewise. Pausing, he held up a hand for silence.

Nothing.

They rode up the slight incline and then the roan stopped suddenly, nervously.

Across the small, still pool of Pistol Rock Spring stood a bay horse; however, Bowdrie was not looking at the horse but at the sprawled body of a man. He had been shot three times through the stomach by somebody who could use a six-gun. The three holes in his chest might have been covered by a silver dollar.

The coffeepot lay on its side, most of the contents spilled into the sand. The dead man's gun was in its holster, and not far from the tethered bay was a saddle, but no rifle or scabbard.

"The man we followed must have killed this man for his horse," Butler suggested.

"No," Bowdrie said, "this is the man who killed Irwin. His partner waited here, shot him, and rode off with the loot.

"Look. See that run-down heel? An' the height and weight are about right. The other gent sat right over yonder. He let this man pick up the coffeepot in his right hand and then he shot him."

Bowdrie walked around the fire and the pool. There were the prints of boots, pointed toward the pool. The man had squatted here, his back against the rock, and from there he had killed the newcomer.

He glanced around. Tom Robley was staring at the dead man; he looked pale and shocked. "That's Jim Moody!" he said.

Butler came over and looked at the dead man's face. "That's Jim, all right. He was always a pretty good hand. Shot dead, an' he never had a chance."

Butler looked up. "Why, I wonder? Why would his own partner kill him?"

"Money. Moody held up Irwin an' killed him, but for all this second man knew, Moody was seen. But he didn't care. Moody pulled off the hold-up, now this second man has all the loot. He's got twelve thousand dollars and he's scot-free."

"And we don't know anything about him," Butler said.

"We know a couple of things. He's a dead shot with a pistol, and he's left-handed. Also, he was somebody who knew Jim Moody."

"Left-handed?" Robley asked.

"He sat with his back braced against that rock, waitin'. He smoked cigarettes. Now, you just take a look at those two stubs of cigarettes and the burned matches. They are on the left side of the fire. If he was right-handed, they would be on the right side.

"He waited, smokin', and he flipped the cigarette stubs an' matches into the fire. Some didn't make it.

"Somethin' here I don't understand. The killer took Moody's saddle. He was ridin' a bronc saddle with an undercut fork. That saddle was dropped right over yonder an' you can see where the fork butted into the wet sand. He also took the rifle Moody had."

"It figures," Butler agreed. "So far as I know, Moody never rode over this way. He rode for the Circle W away the other side of town. He never rode in except to see his girl. I doubt if he knew anything about this part of the country."

"Somethin' else that's curious. That mark to the right side of his right boot. That mark was made by a holster touching the sand. Now, if this gent is left-handed, why does he wear his gun on the right side?

"Unless . . . unless he wears it for a cross-draw? If he wore that gun in front of his right hip an' had his right side toward a man, he could draw almighty fast."

Tom Robley's head came up sharply, his eyes filled with a dawning realization. Bowdrie stared at him. "Tom, d'you know anybody like that?"

Robley flushed. "I ain't sure," he muttered. "I just ain't sure."

Bowdrie looked down at the dead man, but in his mind he was studying the young deputy. Robley had been acting very strange. His reaction to this situation was odd, and had been so from the beginning. Since they had found Jim Moody's body he had seemed upset, almost frightened.

What could Tom Robley know? Did he have a clue they did not possess? Always, in any criminal situation, human passions and feelings are involved, and Bowdrie knew too little of the townspeople and their relationships with each other.

Bowdrie mounted and began casting for a trail. He knew he had his work cut out for him. The killer did not intend to be followed and was using every trick in the book. He had brushed out the tracks where his horse had stood waiting, so there were no identifying tracks. Nearby there was a wide, rocky shelf several acres in extent where he would leave no tracks. Searching for the place where he left the rock shelf, Bowdrie found nothing.

After two hours of fruitless searching Bowdrie sat his saddle looking out over a waste of scattered tar bush, yeso, and tobosa. There was no trail.

Tom Robley suddenly broke the silence. "I'm headin' for town. Nothin' more to be done here." Without waiting for a reply, he turned back toward town.

Butler stared after him. "Now, what's eatin' that youngster? Never seen him cut up so."

Bowdrie was concerned with the matter at hand. Moody was dead and Robley would report it in town. But what did he know about the man they must now pursue? That he was utterly ruthless, left-handed, and knew this desert well. The rock shelf was no accident. The man had planned well. That was indicated by his choice of a meeting place. Bowdrie gestured toward Moody's body. "He was a tool, Butler. The real criminal is the man who killed him. He worked all this out ahead of time."

Bowdrie was searching for more than an obvious trail across the desert. He was trying to find the trail left by the man's secret thoughts. Each move the man made helped to outline his character. His cold-blooded planning indicated he did not intend to leave the country. If he had so planned, he would have paid less attention to his trail and just kept going.

He had been looking, looking . . . His eyes caught at something tangled in the cat claw. It was a low clump of the brush growing close to the ground. One of its vicious thorns had caught . . .

Burlap!

He held up the thin strand to Butler. "Wrapped his horse's hooves in burlap sacking so's it would leave no trail. No wonder we couldn't find where he left the rock shelf."

He swung to the saddle. "Sam, that gent, whoever he is, won't be wanderin' around. He won't travel fast with that sackin' on his horse's hooves. From here there's just three trails that lead to water. To Horse Thief Mesa, to Casa Piedras, or to someplace on the upper Cibolo."

"My guess would be either of the first two. He wouldn't be gettin' noplace goin' up to Cibolo."

Bowdrie agreed. "You take the Casa Piedras trail. I'll head for the mesa. Scout for some of that burlap fiber, or tracks. If you see any, holler or give a shot."

They separated and Bowdrie began painstakingly to search the desert, yet scarcely ten minutes had gone by when he heard a long cowboy yell from Butler. When he rode over to him Butler pointed out a thin thread of burlap caught on some prickly pear.

For an hour they followed at a walk, picking up occasional smudges or signs of passage. Suddenly the trail they followed merged with a cattle trail and the ground was torn by their passing.

Butler swore. "Lost him! Too many critters come this way."

"We'll follow along. He'll get rid of that burlap soon, I think."

A mile farther they found it, half-buried in hurriedly kicked-up sand. Bowdrie picked it from the sand, shook it out, and brought it along. From time to time as they rode he turned it over as if trying to read something from the sacking itself. Then he stowed it in one of his half-empty saddlebags.

In Casa Piedras Bowdrie called to a Mexican boy. "Want to feed and water these horses? Then bring them back and tie them here." He tossed the boy a bright silver dollar.

Bowdrie glanced at a horse hitched nearby as Butler joined him on the walk. "That steel-dust's wearing a bronc saddle with an undercut fork," he commented, "and the horse has been ridden hard."

"Let's eat," Butler suggested. "I'm hungry as a Panhandle wolf!"

It was boardinghouse style, and Bowdrie seated himself, turning a cup right-side-up, then reaching for the coffee. Another hand reached at the same time and only Chick's dexterity prevented the pot from being upset. Bowdrie looked around into a pair of frosty blue eyes. The man had reached for the pot with his left hand. Chick smiled.

"Help yourself!" he suggested. "Coffeepots are bad luck when they are upset."

Sam Butler nodded sagely. He speared a triple thickness of hotcakes and lifted them to his plate. "Sure is. Wust kind of bad luck."

The frosty eyes turned ugly. For an instant they flickered to the badge on Butler's chest, then shifted to Bowdrie.

"Uh-huh," Bowdrie agreed. "I knew a gent once who got drilled right through the heart whilst holding a coffeepot in his right hand. Never had a chance."

"Sho nuff?" A big blond cowhand at the end of the table glanced up. "A man surely couldn't let go of a pot fast enough, could he?"

"That's what the murderer figured," Bowdrie replied. "This just happened a few hours ago, over at Pistol Rock Springs."

The cowhand stared but the man with the frosty blue eyes continued to eat. "Been to those springs many a time," the cowhand said. "Who was it got hisself killed?"

"Name of Jim Moody. He robbed the stage station over yonder last night, shot John Irwin, then cut across country to the spring. His partner was waitin', an' the way he was ridin', I figure Moody expected his partner had a fresh horse waitin'. Instead of that he got lead for breakfast. This partner of his shot him, took the money, and lit out."

"Now, that's a dirty skunk if I ever heard of one!" the blond cowhand said. "He ought to be hung! Hell, I knew Jim Moody! He used to spark that Boling gal from over the way. Seen him at dances, many's the time." He turned to the man with the frosty blue eyes. "Sho, Al! I reckon you won't be none put out. I've heard tell there was a time you was sweet on that Boling gal yourself!"

Al shrugged. "Talked to her a few times, that's all. Same as you did."

Something clicked in Bowdrie's brain. Al . . . Al Harshman, a rancher. The ambitious one.

Al got to his feet. "I'll be ridin'," he said, to nobody in

particular. Then he asked, "How much did he get away with?"

"Twelve thousand," Bowdrie replied, his face inscrutable. Al was wearing his gun on the right side, butt forward, and pulled slightly to the front. "But he won't have it long, Harshman. He left a plain trail."

Harshman stiffened angrily and seemed about to reply, then turned toward the door. He glanced back. "I wouldn't want the job of trailin' him," he commented. "He might prove right salty if cornered."

"When a man is murdered without a chance," Bowdrie commented, "we Rangers make it a point of honor to hunt him down. A Ranger will get that killer if it is the last thing he ever does."

"Rangers can die."

"Of course, but we never die alone." Bowdrie smiled. "We always like to take somebody with us."

When he had gone outside, Butler glanced over at Bowdrie. "How'd you know his name was Harshman?"

"He looked like a harsh man," Bowdrie replied, smiling.

———

STROLLING TO THE porch outside, Bowdrie sat down on the bench after retrieving the burlap sacking from the saddle-bag. He began to go over it with painstaking care. The Mexican boy who had returned the horses stood watching, eyes bright with curiosity. "What you look for, *señor*?"

"Somethin' to tell me who the hombre was who used this sack. Nobody uses anything for long without leaving his mark on it."

The outside of the sacking was thick with damp sand; much more must have come off in his saddlebags, Bowdrie reflected unhappily. Stretching the fibers, he searched them with keen eyes. Suddenly the Mexican boy reached over and plucked a gray hair from the sacking, then another.

"So? He had a gray or steel-dust horse, Pedro?"

"The name is Miguel, *señor*," the boy protested, very seriously. He bent over the sack, pointing at a fragment of blue clay. "See? It is blue. The sack has lain near a well."

"Near a well, Pedro? Why do you say that?"

"The name is Miguel, *señor.* Because there is the blue clay. Always in this country there is blue clay in the hole of wells, *señor.* Always, it is so."

"Thanks, Pedro. You'd make a good Texas Ranger."

"I? A Texas Ranger? You think so, *señor*?" His expression changed. "But, *señor,* the name is not Pedro. It is Miguel. Miguel Fernández."

"All right, Pedro." Bowdrie stood up. "Just as you say."

He glanced once more at the sacking, and suddenly, in the crease near the seam, he noticed a tiny fragment of crushed, somewhat oily pulp. He took it out, studied it, then folded it into a cigarette paper.

"Wait for me," he said to Butler.

Swiftly he crossed the street to the store. A little old man with gold-rimmed spectacles looked up. Bowdrie asked him a question, then another. The old man replied, studying him curiously.

Bowdrie walked back to Butler. "Let's go. I think we've got our man. I only hope we'll be in time."

"In time?" Butler asked. "In time for what?"

The Mexican boy caught his hand. *"Señor!"* he pleaded. "If I am to be a Ranger, you must know my name! It is Miguel! Miguel Fernández!"

Bowdrie chuckled and handed him another dollar. "If you say so, Pedro! Miguel it is! *Adiós,* Pedro!"

He swung to the saddle and started out of town, Butler beside him. "In time for what?" he repeated.

"To prevent another killing," Bowdrie told him.

"Robley knew," Bowdrie continued. "He guessed it when he saw the dead man was Jim Moody. He knew who it was when I said the killer was left-handed. He was away ahead of us."

"You think it was Harshman? But how could he have known about the money? For that matter, how did Moody find out?"

The desert flat gave way to rising ground, the hillsides scattered with juniper. The sage had taken on a deeper color and there were clumps of grama grass. Chick dipped into an arroyo and skirted a towering wall of red sandstone, into a shaded canyon, then across another flat. The trail dipped again and they rode into the yard of a lonely ranch house. Nearby there were several pole corrals and three saddled horses.

Bowdrie dropped to the ground. As his feet touched the earth, Al Harshman stepped from the door. Narrow-eyed, faint perspiration showing on his brow, he looked from Butler to Bowdrie and back. "Huntin' somethin'?"

"You," Bowdrie said. "I am arrestin' you for the murder of Jim Moody and complicity in the robbery and murder of John Irwin."

Harshman took a step into the yard. He was smiling, a taunting smile.

"All you've got is suspicion. You can't prove nothin'. I ain't been away from here but that ride to town, where you saw me."

He smiled again. "You can't prove I was anywhere near Pistol Rock Spring. And how would I know about the money? How would Moody know?"

"I know how you knew about the money." Tom Robley stepped around the corner of the house. His eyes flickered to Bowdrie and back. "I'd have beat you here, but I was looking for the girl first."

"What girl?" Butler demanded.

"Mary Boling. It was she told them about the money. She with all her talk about New Orleans and fancy clothes. She put poor Jim Moody up to it. She's partly responsible for both Irwin an' Moody bein' dead. Me, I'm mostly responsible."

"You?" Butler exclaimed. "Now, Tom, you just—"

"Don't get me wrong. I'd nothin' to do with stealin' the money or the killing. It was my mouth. I was so busy tryin' to convince Mary what an important job I had that I just ran off at the mouth. Because of my loose tongue, two good men are dead."

Harshman laughed. "You think Mary had a hand in it? You're a fool, Tom Robley, a double-damned fool. Suppose you had told Mary? What could that mean to me?"

Chick Bowdrie stood listening and curious. Watching the scene, every sense alert, quick to hear every word, he was also aware that three saddled horses, packed for the trail, stood at the corral.

The big rancher wore a dark blue shirt, two of the front buttons unfastened. His boots were highly polished, and he looked quite the dandy. Bowdrie smiled, understanding a few things.

"You're pretty sure of yourself, Al, but Sam Butler and me, we trailed you. We know a left-handed man sat against a rock at Pistol Rock Spring and smoked cigarettes. He tossed the matches at the fire with his left hand.

"We trailed you from the spring, and it wasn't even hard. You wrapped your horse's hooves in burlap sacking so you wouldn't leave a trail. We have the sacks."

Harshman shrugged. "There are a lot of sacks around. Can you prove those sacks were mine? Don't be foolish! Those sacks could have belonged to anybody."

"I found gray horsehairs that will match your gelding, and there's blue clay on them, as there is around your well."

"So? There's blue clay around half the wells in the county, and as for horsehairs, how many gray horses are there?"

"We've got somethin' else, Al," Bowdrie said. "Folks told me you were ambitious. That you had brains. Mary spoke mighty highly of you back there at the dance.

"You were smart, all right. You had ideas. You decided to try something new, Al. You had some cottonseed shipped in here so you could try planting it."

"So? Is that criminal?"

"Not at all. You were away ahead of everybody else around this part of the country. You sent for cottonseed and you got it. Some of it came in that sack you used, Al. I found some of the cottonseed in the sack."

"Bowdrie!" Robley shouted. *"Look out!"* Robley's hand slashed down for a gun, and a shotgun roared from the window of the house and Tom Robley staggered, firing toward the house.

It was one of those breathtaking instants that explode suddenly, and Bowdrie saw Harshman grab for a gun—with his *right* hand!

The hand darted into the gaping shirtfront and the gun blasted, but a split second late. Bowdrie had palmed his six-gun and fired, then took a long step forward and right, firing again as his foot came down.

Al Harshman was on his knees, his face contorted with shock and hatred. Vaguely Bowdrie knew other guns were firing, but this was the man he had to get. Harshman had dropped the derringer hideout gun and was coming up with his other pistol.

Bowdrie held his fire and the gun slipped from Harshman's fingers.

Butler was at the cabin door, gun in hand. Robley was down, covered with blood.

Sam Butler turned to Bowdrie, his face gray. "I never killed no woman before," he muttered. "Dammit, Bowdrie, I—!"

"You did what you had to do. Anyway," he added practically, "it might have been Tom."

Robley was dying. Bowdrie knew it when he knelt beside him. "Mary? Wha . . . happened?"

"Mary's gone, Tom. She was killed. So is another man in there."

"Her brother," Butler said. "We didn't even know he was around."

"Mary . . . it was Al all the time," Robley was saying. "It wasn't Jim or me."

He lay quiet and Bowdrie got slowly to his feet. "Too bad," he said. "He was a good man."

"All because she was greedy. She couldn't be content with the looks she was born with an' clothes like the other gals had." Butler swore softly, bitterly.

"Me," Bowdrie said, "all I want is a good horse under me, the creak of a saddle, and a wind off the prairies in my face.

"An' maybe, Sam, just like you, maybe I want to make things a little more peaceful for other folks. A man can't build anything or even make a living when there's somebody ready to take it from him."

"Maybe that's it," Butler said. "Maybe you just said it. I never could figure why I took this job in the first place."

Butler walked to his horse, and Bowdrie followed. "Ain't more than six miles over to the Fernández place. She fixes the best *frijoles* anyplace around. We'll just ride over there an' hire him to haul these bodies into town."

"All right," Bowdrie said, "let's ride over an' see Pedro."

"Miguel," Sam Butler said. "The name is Miguel!"

BOWDRIE PASSES THROUGH

THERE WAS NO reason to question the authority of
the Sharps .50 resting against the doorjamb.

"Hold it right there, mister!"

The voice behind the Sharps was young, but it carried a
ring of command, and it does not require a grown man to pull
a trigger. Chick Bowdrie had lived this long because he knew
where to stop. He stopped now.

"I didn't know anybody was to home," he said agreeably.
"I was lookin' for Josh Pettibone."

"He ain't here." The youthful voice was belligerent.

"Might as well rest that rifle, boy. I ain't huntin' trouble."

There was no response from the house, and the gun muzzle
did not waver. Chick found the black opening of the muzzle singularly unattractive, but he found himself admiring the resolution of whoever was behind the gun.

"Where is Josh?"

"He's . . . they done took him off." Chick thought he
detected a catch in the boy's throat.

"Who took him off?"

"The law come an' fetched him."

"Now, what would the law want Josh Pettibone for?"

"Claimed he poisoned a horse of Nero Tatum's," the boy
said. "He done no such thing!"

"Tatum of the Tall T? You'd better put down that rifle, boy, an'
talk to me. I'm no enemy of your pa's."

After a moment of hesitation the rifle was lowered to the
floor and the boy stepped out. He wore a six-shooter thrust
into his waistband. He was towheaded, and wearing a shirt
that had obviously belonged to his father. He was probably
as much as twelve, and very thin.

Bowdrie studied him, and was not fooled. Young he might

be, but this boy was no coward and he was responsible. In Bowdrie's limited vocabulary, to be responsible was the most important word.

The boy walked slowly, distrustfully, to the gate, but he made no move to open it.

"Your pa poison that horse of Tatum's?"

"He did not! My pa would never poison no stock of anybody's!"

"Don't reckon he would," Bowdrie agreed. "Tell me about it."

"Nero Tatum, he hates Pa, and Pa never had no use for Tatum. He's tried to get Pa off this place two or three times, sayin' he didn't want no jailbirds nestin' that close to him."

When the boy said "jailbirds" he looked quickly at Bowdrie for his reaction, but Chick seemed not to notice.

"Then Pa got that Hereford bull off of Pete Swager, and that made Tatum madder'n ever. Tatum had sure enough wanted that Swager bull, and offered big money for it. Pete knowed Pa wanted it and he owed Pa a favor or two so he let Pa have it for less money. Pete was leavin' the country."

Chick Bowdrie knew about that favor. Pete Swager had gone to San Antonio on business and had come down sick. His wife and little boy were on the ranch alone, and two days after Pete left, they came down with the smallpox, too. Josh Pettibone had ridden over, nursed them through their illness, and did the ranch work as well. It was not a small thing, and Pete Swager was not a man to forget.

"Tatum's black mare up an' died, an' he accused Pa of poisonin' her."

"What have they got for evidence?" Bowdrie asked.

"They found the mare close to our line fence, an' she was dyin' when they found her, frothin' at the mouth an' kickin' somethin' awful.

"When she died, he accused Pa, and then Foss Deal, he claimed he seen Pa give poison to the mare."

"You take it easy, boy. We've got to think about this. You got any coffee inside?"

The boy's face flushed. "No, we ain't." Then, as Chick

started to swing down, he said, "There's nothin' in there to eat, stranger. You better ride on into town."

Bowdrie smiled. "All right if I use your fire, son? I've got a mite of grub here, and some coffee, and I'm hungry."

Reluctantly, and with many a glance at Bowdrie, the boy opened the gate. He glanced at the roan. "He's pretty fast, ain't he?"

"Like a jackrabbit, only he can keep it up for miles. Never seems to tire. There's been a few times when he really had to run."

The boy glanced at him quickly. "You on the dodge, mister? Is the law after you, too?"

"No, I've found it pays to stay on the right side of the law. A few years back I had a run-in with some pretty tough people, and for a spell it was like bein' on the dodge.

"Nothin' romantic about bein' an outlaw, son. Just trouble an' more trouble. You can't trust anybody, even the outlaws you ride with. You're always afraid somebody will recognize you, and you don't have any real friends, for fear they might turn you in or rob you themselves.

"The trouble with bein' an outlaw or any kind of criminal is the company you have to keep."

As they neared the house, Chick heard a slight stir of movement within, and when he entered, the flimsy curtain hanging over the door opening into another room was still moving slightly. It was growing dusk, so Chick took the chimney from a coal-oil lamp and lighted the wick, replacing the chimney.

The boy stared at him uneasily, shifting his eyes to the curtain occasionally.

"Tell your sister to come out. I won't bother her, and she might like to eat, too."

Hesitantly a girl came from behind the curtain. She might have been sixteen, with the same large, wistful eyes the boy had, and the same too-thin face, but she was pretty. Chick smiled at her, then began breaking kindling to build a fire.

Chick glanced at the boy. "Why don't you put up my horse, son? Take your sister along if you've a mind to, and when you come in, you might bring my rifle along."

While they were gone, he got the fire going, and finding a

coffeepot that was spotlessly clean, he put on some coffee. Then he dug into the haversack he had brought in for some bacon, a few potatoes, and some wild onions. By the time they returned, he had a meal going and the room was filled with the comforting smells of coffee and bacon.

"Tell me about your pa," he suggested, "and while you're at it, tell me your names."

"She's Dotty. I'm Tom," the boy said.

When Tom started to talk, Chick found there was little he did not already know. Three years earlier, Josh Pettibone had been arrested and had served a year in prison. Along with several other Rangers, Chick had always felt the sentence had not been deserved.

Pettibone had torn down a fence that blocked his cattle from water, and had been convicted for malicious mischief. Ordinarily no western jury would have convicted him, but this was a case where most of the jury "belonged" to Bugs Tatum, Nero's brother. The judge and the prosecuting attorney had been friends of the Tatums', and Josh, having no money, had defended his own case. Chick Bowdrie had not been judge and jury, but he knew what he believed.

"When does this case come up?" he asked.

"The day after tomorrow."

"All right, tomorrow you an' your sister put on your best clothes and get out the buckboard and we'll go into town together. Maybe we can help your pa.

"In the meantime," he added, "I'll ride out in the morning and look the situation over."

It was not only a Ranger's job to enforce the law and do what he could to protect the people, but in this thinly settled country where courts were few and of doubtful legality, they were often called upon to be judge and jury as well. They were advisers, doctors, in some cases even teachers. All too often the courts were controlled by a few big cattlemen for their own interests.

Chick Bowdrie knew Josh Pettibone was not a bad man. A stubborn man, fiercely independent, and often quick-tempered, he knew the fencing of that water hole had been pure spite. By fencing the draw, Tatum had fenced out only

Josh's cattle, allowing all other cattle to come and go as they wished. Bugs Tatum had wanted Josh's place, and while Josh was in prison, he got it.

On his release, Josh got his children from a relative who had cared for them and filed on a new claim. Here, too, he encountered a Tatum, for Nero owned a vast range north of Pettibone's new claim.

Foss Deal had also wanted that claim, but failed to file on it, and was angry at Pettibone for beating him to it.

Bowdrie was out before daylight and riding up the canyon. Young Tom had given him careful directions, so he knew where he was going. He found the dead horse lying near a marshy and reed-grown water hole in a canyon that branched off the Blue. It had been a fine mare, no question of that.

Thoughtfully he studied the situation. He eyed the rocks and the canyon walls, which were some distance away, and finally walked up to the pool itself and studied the plant growth nearby. In the loose soil at the pool's edge and among the rank grass were other plants, because of the permanent water supply.

Squatting on his heels, he tugged one plant from the earth, noting the divided leaves and tuberous root. When he returned to his horse, he stowed the plant in his saddlebags. He led the roan off a little distance, and keeping a hand near his gun, swung into the saddle.

He was almost back to Pettibone's ranch when he heard several gunshots, then the dull boom of the Sharps.

Spurring the roan into a run, he charged out of the branch canyon to see four riders circling the house, and heard a shrill cry from the stable. Lifting a hand high, he rode into the yard.

One of the men rode toward him. "Get movin', stranger! This is a private fight."

"Not 'stranger,'" Bowdrie said. "Ranger! Now, shove that gun back in the boot and call off your dogs or I'll blow you out of the saddle!"

The rider laughed contemptuously. "Why, I could—!"

Suddenly he was looking into a Colt. "Back off!" Bowdrie said. "Back off an' get out!"

A scream from the stable brought Bowdrie into action. Not daring to turn his back on the other man, he suddenly leaped his horse at him and slashed out with the barrel of his Colt, knocking him from the saddle. Wheeling his horse, he rode into the stable.

A man was grappling with Dotty, his face ugly with rage, blood running from a scratch on his cheek. When he glimpsed Bowdrie, he threw the girl from him and went for his gun, but the roan knew its business, and as Bowdrie charged into the stable, the roan hit the man with a shoulder, spilling him to the floor.

Bowdrie hit the dust beside him, grabbing him by the collar and knocking the gun from his hand with a slap of the pistol barrel, then laying him out with another blow, this one to the head.

He whipped the gunbelt from the man's waist and was just turning when he saw two men charging into the barn. He covered them. "Drop 'em! An' drop 'em fast!"

Gingerly, careful to allow no room for a mistake, they unbuckled their belts.

"Now, back up!"

Tom Pettibone stepped from the house, the Sharps up and ready.

"Cover them, Tom. If anyone so much as moves, blow him in two!"

"Hey, mister!" one of the men protested. "That kid might get nervous!"

"Suppose you just stand there an' pray he doesn't?" Bowdrie suggested.

He walked over to the man he had pistol-whipped, disarmed and tied him. When he got back to the stable, Dotty was guarding the man who had been attacking her, holding a pitchfork over him.

"Thanks, Dotty. I'll handle him."

Jerking the man to his feet, he tied his hands, then brought him into the yard.

"You've played hell!" one rider declared. "Nero Tatum will have your hide for this!"

"So you're Tatum's boys? No sooner is the father of these

youngsters in jail than you come over here. What are you doing here?"

"Wouldn't you like to know?" one of them sneered.

Chick smiled. "I will know. I intend to find out. Take a look at me again, boys. Does my face mean anything to you?"

"You look like a damned Apache!"

Chick smiled again. "Just think that over," he said. He waved a hand around. "We're a long way from anywhere, and I've just found you molesting a girl. Now, you know Texans don't like that sort of thing. You thought you could get away with it and nobody would know. Before I am through, you will not only have told me what I want, but Texas won't be big enough for you. Everybody in the state will know what a low-life bunch you are.

"Maybe," he added, "they'll hang you. I'm a Ranger and I'm supposed to stop that sort of thing, but I can look the other way. Of course, to an Apache, hangin' would be too good for you."

While Tom stood guard over the men with their hands and now their feet bound, Dotty brought up the buckboard.

Meanwhile Chick had gathered sticks and a little straw from the barn and had kindled a fire. Into the fire he placed a branding iron. The prisoners stared at him, then at the fire.

"Hey, now, what the devil do you think . . . ?"

"Be surprised how tough some men are," Bowdrie commented casually. "Why, sometimes you can burn two or three fingers off a man, or even an ear, before he starts to talk."

Bowdrie reached out suddenly and jerked to his feet the man who had attacked Dotty. "You, now. I wonder how tough you are."

He glanced at the others. "Does the smell of burnin' flesh make you fellers sick? It even bothers me, sometimes. But not right away. Takes a while."

"Now, see here . . . !" one man protested.

Chick glanced at the wide-eyed Tom. "If any of these men start to move, just start shootin'."

"Wait a minute." The man who spoke was mean-looking, short, and wiry. "I don't believe you'll do this. I don't believe you'll burn anybody, but if you take us in, will we have to stand up in court an'—"

"Tatum's got the court in his hip pocket," another sneered.

Bowdrie glanced at him. "I'll quote you. So will the youngsters. He won't have any court in his pocket. He will be in jail.

"I'm just one Ranger. If anything happens to me or if I need more, they'll come a-running. We started workin' on this case while Josh Pettibone was in jail, and we've got enough to hang every one of you, but the Tatums will be first."

The wiry man interrupted. "Like I say, I don't believe you'd burn anybody." He looked into Bowdrie's hard black eyes and shook his head. "Again, maybe you might. What I'm sayin' is, if I talk, can I get out of this? Supposin' I give you a signed statement? Will you give me a runnin' start?"

"I will."

"Laredo! For the Lord's sake—!"

"No, you boys do what you want! I'm gittin' out o' this! I ain't gonna have my neck stretched for nobody, and I surely ain't gonna stand up there in court."

"Dotty?" Bowdrie said. "Get pencil and paper, and what this man says, write down. Then we'll get him to sign it. But first"—with his left hand Bowdrie went into his saddlebags and brought out a small Bible—"we will just swear him in."

The others waited in silence. One of them twitched anxiously. "Laredo, think what you're doin'!"

"I am thinkin'. If I stand up in that court, somebody's goin' to recognize me. What did them Tatums ever do for me, that I should get hung for them? They paid me my wages, and I earned ever' cent. I got a few days comin', and they can have it."

Laredo began to speak. "We were sent to burn Pettibone out, and Tatum said he didn't care what happened to the youngsters, only he didn't want to be bothered with them. He said to drive 'em out of the country or whatever, that Josh wouldn't be comin' back anyway. That's what Nero Tatum told us."

Given the pad on which his statement had been written, he

signed it. Without a word, Bowdrie freed him and pointed at the horses. "Take yours an' get out!"

For a moment there was silence. "How about me?" The speaker was a rough-looking man whose shirt collar was ringed with dirt. "Can I sign that an' go free?"

"Dammit, Bud!" One of the other men lunged at him. His hands and feet were bound, so all he could do was to butt with his head. Bud shook him off.

"All right, Bud. Sign it and go, but you're the last one."

"What? That's not fair! Now, you see here, you—"

"You all had your chance. That chance is gone. You'll be in court."

———

MOST OF MESQUITE'S population of three hundred and fifty-two people were gathered in the street close to the dance hall that was to double as a courtroom. None of the gathering had seen the buckboard roll into town the night before. The cargo was unloaded in an abandoned stable, and Chick Bowdrie took his place as guard.

A few people who saw Bowdrie outside the stable wondered at the presence of the man in the flat-crowned hat, wearing twin six-shooters. He was joined by a lean red-haired cowhand who followed him on guard duty.

Rawboned Judge Ernie Walters, judge by grace of Nero Tatum and two other large ranchers, called the court to order. As was often the case in the earliest days, the conduct of courtroom proceedings was haphazard, depending much on the knowledge or lack of it on the part of the court officials.

Claude Batten, prosecuting attorney, was presenting the case against Pettibone.

Walters banged the gavel and glared around the room. "If any of you have ideas of lynchin', get 'em out of your heads. This here Pettibone is goin' to get a fair trial before we hang him. Court's in session!"

Batten began, "Your Honor, gents of the jury, and folks, this court's convened to hear evidence an' pass sentence on this no-account jailbird Josh Pettibone, who's accused of poisonin' that fine black mare of our good friend and fellow citizen Nero Tatum.

"Pettibone done time in jail, one year of it, sent to jail for a crime against Bugs Tatum, Nero's brother. When he got out, he come here an' grabbed off a piece of land alongside Nero Tatum an' waited until he had a chance to get even. He poisoned the best brood mare this side of San Antone!"

He glared around the room, his eyes hesitating only for an instant on the guileless countenance of Chick Bowdrie, a stranger.

"Foss Deal?" Batten ordered. "Take the stand!"

Deal came forward and seated himself. His hair was combed, plastered to his head with water, but he was unshaved. His cruel blue eyes focused on Pettibone and remained there.

"Foss, tell the court what you saw!"

Deal cleared his throat. "I was ridin' out huntin' strays and I seen Pettibone there poisonin' Tatum's Morgan mare. I seen him give her poison, and a few minutes later that hoss fell down an' died!"

There was a stir in the courtroom.

Batten glanced around. "Hear that? I reckon no more's necessary. Judge, I move you turn this case over to the jury!"

"Just a minute, your Honor!"

Bowdrie stood up. Walters, Batten, and Tatum had seen the lean, hard-faced young man and wondered who he was, as strangers were comparatively rare in Mesquite. It was off the beaten track, and they had not expected anyone to interfere in local affairs. So far, they had managed such things very successfully for themselves.

"Who are you? What right have you to interrupt this proceedin'?"

Bowdrie smiled, and with the smile his face lighted up, drawing an almost automatic response from many in the courtroom. "In this case, your Honor, I am acting as attorney for the defense.

"You spoke of giving Mr. Pettibone a fair trial. If that is true, he should get a chance to speak for himself and for his attorney to question the witnesses, and perhaps to offer evidence on behalf of the defendant."

Walters glanced uneasily at Nero Tatum. He was confused. Tatum had told him to make it look good, but there was something about this stranger that worried him and spoke of a little more courtroom experience than he had.

"What can he say?" Batten demanded. "Foss Deal saw him poison her!"

"That's the question. Did he see poison given to the mare?"

"I don't reckon we have to hear what you have to say," Walters said. "You set down!"

"In that case, gentlemen, I shall have to write a complete report of these proceedings for the governor of Texas!"

"Huh?" Walters was startled. The governor was a faraway but awesome power. He glanced at Nero Tatum, who was frowning. "Just who are you, young feller?"

"The name is Chick Bowdrie. I am a Texas Ranger."

Had he exploded a bomb, it would have caused no more excitement. Tatum caught Walters' eye and nodded. Claude Batten sat down, looking uneasily at Foss Deal. He had been against the procedure from the first, not from principle but simply because it was too obvious. Not for a minute did he trust Foss Deal, nor believe in the kangaroo-court procedure. He had tried to explain to Tatum that the time for such tactics was past.

"All right!" Walters grumbled. "Question the witness!"

Bowdrie strolled over to Deal, who glared at him belligerently. "What kind of poison was it?" he asked.

"Huh? What was that?"

"I asked what kind of poison it was."

"How should I know? I wasn't right alongside him."

"Then how do you know it was poison?"

"I reckon I know poison when I see it!"

"You're very lucky," Bowdrie said. He took two small papers from his pocket and opened them. Each contained a small amount of white powder. "Now, my friend, there are two papers. One contains sugar, the other holds a deadly poison. Suppose you decide which is which and then prove you are right by swallowing the one you have decided is not poison."

Foss Deal stared at the papers. He licked his lips with his tongue. His back was to Tatum, and he did not know what to do. He twisted in his chair, struggling for words.

"Come, come, Mr. Deal! You know poison when you see it. We trust your judgment."

Batten leaped to his feet. "What are you doing? Trying to poison the witness?"

"Of course not!" Bowdrie said. "There's no danger of that! Why, this witness just testified he could recognize poison from a distance of two hundred yards!"

"I never! I never done such a thing!"

"If you had ever even been near the place where the mare died, you would know there's no place where you could watch from cover within two hundred yards!"

"That's right!" The voice was from the audience. "I was wonderin' about that!"

"Order in the court!" Walters shouted angrily.

"Isn't it a fact," Bowdrie asked, "that you wanted Pettibone off that place so you could file on it yourself?"

"No such thing!"

"Then," Chick suggested, "if Pettibone is convicted, you will *not* file on it?"

Deal's face grew flushed. "Well, I—"

"Forget it," Bowdrie said. "Now, you said you saw Pettibone poison the mare? Or at least, you saw him give something to the mare?"

"That's right."

"He was alone?"

"Yeah, he was alone."

"Deal, where were you the previous night?"

"Huh?"

Deal glanced hastily at Batten, but got no help. Claude Batten was unhappy. A Texas Ranger was the last thing he had expected. Previously such cases had all been pushed through without any outward protest. Now what he wanted was to wash his hands of the case and get out. Nero Tatum had gone too far, for no matter how this case turned out,

Bowdrie had to write a report. In fact, if Batten understood correctly the Ranger procedure, the chances were that reports had already gone in or that he was acting upon orders.

"Where were you Friday night?" Bowdrie insisted.

"Why, I was . . . I don't exactly recall."

"I can believe that!" Bowdrie said. He turned to the jury. "Gentlemen, I am prepared to prove that the witness was nowhere near Mesquite or the Pettibone ranch on the day in question. I am prepared to produce witnesses who will testify that Deal was lying dead drunk in O'Brien's Livery Stable in Valentine!"

Deal sat up sharply, consternation written all over him.

"Do you deny," Bowdrie said, "that you were in O'Brien's stable last Friday night? Or that you ate breakfast at Ma Kennedy's the next morning?"

Foss Deal started to speak, stopped, then tried to twist around to catch Tatum's eye. Tatum avoided his glance. All he wanted now was to get out of this. He wanted out as quickly and quietly as possible. Batten had warned him something like this would happen sooner or later. He should have listened.

"Your Honor," Bowdrie said, "I want this man held on a charge of perjury."

Before anything more could be said, he stepped up to the table behind which the judge sat, and taking a paper from his pocket, he unwrapped it, displaying the plant he had picked from the edge of the pool where Tatum's mare had died.

"Your Honor, ladies and gentlemen, I don't know as much about legal procedure as I should. I came here because I wanted to see justice done, and there's more experienced Rangers who could have handled this better, but this plant I have here is called water hemlock. This came from the pool near where Tatum's mare died, and there's more of it out there.

"As most of you know, animals won't touch it, as a rule, but it's one of the few green things early in the spring. The leaves and fruit of this plant can be eaten by stock without much danger, but the roots of water hemlock are poisonous.

"Cattle suffer more from it than horses, but horses, like

Tatum's mare, have died from it, too. In the spring, when it's green and the soil's loose, the plant is easier pulled up. When an animal eats water hemlock, the first symptom is frothin' at the mouth, then convulsions with a lot of groanin', then the animal dies.

"Nobody poisoned Tatum's mare, and Foss Deal lied, as I have shown. The mare was poisoned by water hemlock, and if you open up the stomach you'll find some of it there. Unless Mr. Batten has more witnesses, I suggest this case be dismissed!"

Judge Ernie Walters looked uncertainly toward Tatum and Batten, who were whispering together.

"Nothing more," Batten said. "We will forget it."

As the rancher arose, Chick Bowdrie said, "Nero Tatum, you are under arrest!"

Tatum's face flushed. "Look here, young man, you're going too far! Now, I'll admit—"

"Mr. Tatum—"

"See here, young man, you're goin' too far. I've friends down at Austin. I'll have you fired!"

"No, you won't, Mr. Tatum. I am arrestin' you for incitin' to arson, for conspiracy, and a half-dozen other items. I have signed statements from some of your men and some others who want to turn state's evidence. You're going to jail."

Bowdrie stepped over to him, and before Tatum realized it, he was handcuffed. Then Bowdrie took him by the elbow and guided him down the street to the jail.

"Listen!" Tatum said when they reached the jail. "You've made your play. Now, let's talk this over. We'll forget about Pettibone. He can keep his place. As for you an' me, I've got some money, and—"

"No, Mr. Tatum. You're going to jail. You ordered Pettibone's ranch burned and told your men to get rid of those youngsters, and you didn't care how."

Bowdrie stepped outside. In his hurry to get Tatum locked up, he had forgotten Foss Deal. Now he must find him, for there were few worse crimes against the cause of justice than perjury.

He had been fortunate, there was no mistaking that, for

after bringing the Pettibone children into town, he had encountered Billy O'Brien, the bluff, goodhearted owner of a livery stable in Valentine, a town down the trail. When O'Brien heard about Deal's accusations, he had come at once to find Bowdrie. Deal had felt safe, for O'Brien rarely left Valentine and the town was some distance away.

With Tatum in jail, the place was crowded, but Bowdrie intended to add Foss Deal to the collection.

Crossing the street, he pushed through the batwing doors of the saloon. The bartender, long resentful of the bullying ways of the Tatum cowhands, greeted Bowdrie with pleasure.

"Have one on the house!" he said affably. As Chick accepted a beer, the bartender whispered, "Watch yourself. Deal's got a shotgun an' swears he'll kill you on sight."

Wiping a glass, he added, "When Foss has had a couple, he gets mean. Worst of it is, Bugs Tatum is in town. He declares he'll have your scalp and Pettibone's, too."

The door pushed open and Josh Pettibone walked in. "Bowdrie, I ain't had a chance to thank you, but Tatum an' Deal are huntin' you, and I've come to stand with you."

"You go to your youngsters and stay there. Foss Deal wouldn't be above killin' your kids to get even. This is my show, and I can handle it alone."

The town's one street had suddenly become empty. He knew western towns well enough to realize the word was out. He knew also that more depended upon this than the mere matter of handling two malcontents. Bugs Tatum and Deal were big cogs in the wheel of Nero Tatum's control over this corner of Texas, something the Rangers had long contemplated breaking up.

If he, Bowdrie, should be killed now, what had happened might die with him. Tatum had friends in important places and knew how to wield power, and Bowdrie was essential as a witness, despite whatever reports he had filed.

Bowdrie had lived long enough to know that killing was rarely a good thing, but in this town and this area, guns were the last court of appeal. He had appeared here in the name of Texas; now he had to make his final arrests.

He knew the manner of men they were, and he also knew that not only his life depended upon his skill with a gun, but also those of Josh and his children. The town was waiting to see which would triumph, Texas law or Tatum's law.

He stepped outside and moved quickly into the deeper shadow of the building, looking up and down the street. It was cool and pleasant here, for a little breeze came from between the buildings.

A man whom he did not recognize squatted near the hub of a wheel, his back toward Bowdrie. He was apparently greasing the axle. A door creaked but he did not move. He heard a footfall, then another. The sound seemed to come from the building on his right. As there were no windows on the side toward him, whoever was inside would have to emerge on the street before he could see Bowdrie.

Listening to catch the slightest sound, he saw that the man greasing the axle, if that was what he was doing, had turned his side toward Bowdrie.

A shadow moved in the space between two buildings across the street, and from inside the vacant store building beside him a board creaked. If he had to turn toward a man emerging from the empty store, he would be half-turning his back on the man by the wagon wheel.

The door hinge creaked and Bowdrie moved. Swiftly he ducked back through the batwing doors and ran on cat feet to the back of the saloon and outside. He ran behind the building where he had heard movement and came up on its far side.

As he neared the front, somebody said, "Where'd he go? Where is he?"

Chick stepped from behind the building. "Looking for me, gentlemen?"

The man who had come from the empty building and the one who had come up from between the buildings turned sharply around—Bugs Tatum and Foss Deal.

The situation was completely reversed from the way it had been planned, but as one man they went for their guns. Chick Bowdrie had an instant's advantage, the instant it took them to adjust to the changed situation. His draw was a breath faster, his hands steady, his mind cool.

His right-hand gun bucked, and Bugs Tatum died with his hand clutching a gun he had scarcely gripped. Bowdrie fired at Foss, felt a bullet whip by his face and another kick dust at his feet, fired by the man by the wagon wheel.

Bowdrie fired, and the bullet clipped a spoke of the wheel just over the man's head. The fellow flattened himself into the dust.

Foss Deal had been hit and was staggering, trying to get his gun up. Bowdrie sprang toward him and with a blow from the barrel of his gun sent Deal's gun spinning into the dust.

Bugs Tatum was flat on his face and unmoving. Deal was struggling to rise, but badly hurt. Walking toward him, Bowdrie glanced suddenly toward the man by the wagon. He was on his feet, gun in hand, the gun lifting. A shot came from the direction of the jail and the man by the wagon lifted on his toes, then pitched forward.

The red-haired man who had been guarding the prisoners walked out, rifle in hand.

"Thanks, McKeever," Bowdrie said.

"You moved too fast for me, Chick. It was almost over before I could get to the door."

"It was more important you hold the prisoners. I was afraid they'd try to bust them out."

"You goin' to write the report on this, or shall I?" McKeever asked.

"We'd both better write it up," Bowdrie said. "We will be in court on this one."

Josh Pettibone was standing over Deal. "This one will live, I'm afraid, but he won't be eatin' any side meat for a while!"

Dotty was standing in front of the store with her brother, Tom. "Mr. Bowdrie," she said, "I've got to ask you something. Would you have burned that man's hand off?"

He shrugged. "I don't imagine I would have, Dotty, but I didn't think I'd have to. A man with enough coyote in him to bother a nice girl like you wouldn't have enough sand in him to take it."

He reloaded his gun. There were things to be done, but all he wanted was to be back on the trail again. He wanted to be out there with the cloud shadows and the miles spread out around him. Folks said there were high mountains out yonder with snow on them, and forests no man had ever seen.

Well, no white man, anyway. The Indians had been everywhere. Someday, when all this sort of thing was over with, maybe he'd ride that way. Maybe even find a place for himself where he could feel the cool winds and look at distance.

WHERE BUZZARDS FLY

THE MEXICAN'S RIFLE lay over his horse's body, his pistol near his hand. He had gone out fighting, riddled with bullets. His flat, knife-scarred face was unforgettable, his eyes wide and unafraid, staring up to a brassy sky.

"Well, Zaparo," Bowdrie said aloud, "it looks like they've washed out your trail."

His eyes swept the narrow gray gravel-and-sand trail that lay along the bottom of the arroyo, littered now with the bodies of men and horses, all dead.

Fourteen men had gone out fighting, fourteen men killed in what must have been minutes. These had been hard, desperate men and they would not have gone easily. This had been an ambush, of course, carefully planned, perfectly timed.

He who conceived the idea had a mind to reckon with. He was cold, cruel, utterly ruthless. Walking slowly along the line of fallen men, Bowdrie stared bleakly at the litter of bodies scattered along three hundred yards of trail. Above, in slow, patient circles, the buzzards were waiting. They had seen such things before and knew their time would come.

Yesterday, probably in the late afternoon, there had been a moment here of blood-steeped inferno, flashes of gunfire, and the thunder of heavy rifles.

Zaparo had moved fast after his swift raid on the ranches and missions, moving along a preplanned route, but somebody had sold him out. Other men, more bloodthirsty than he, had waited with a welcome of gunfire. It was not a nice thing to see or to contemplate. In the hard world to which Bowdrie had been born and in which he lived, death was an old story, and the possibility of death by violence rode along with every traveler. The death of men in gun battles he could accept, but ambush and murder were another thing. In any event, it was his job.

When he had become a Ranger he had known what lay before him, but this was the worst he had seen. Unless he was failing to read the signs, the betrayer had himself been betrayed. That last man, who hung back behind the others, had left his gun in his holster, and he had been shot in the back at close quarters. Whoever planned this crime had not planned to trust the man who betrayed others. He lay dead along with the rest.

For three hours Bowdrie studied the scene, and he was stumped. There were those who said Bowdrie could trail a snake across a flat rock, but now he could find no evidence.

No cartridge shells remained that could have been left by the attackers, no cigarette butts. All had been gathered up with painstaking care. Every track had been brushed out with mesquite branches. Not one iota of evidence remained, nothing that might lead him to the perpetrators. Yet there is no such thing as a perfect crime. There are only imperfect investigators.

Seated on a flat rock, Chick brooded over the situation.

Obviously the killers had known well in advance, for the site had been well-chosen. There had been, Bowdrie calculated, at least seven men in the ambush party, and those seven must have been among the deadliest marksmen along the border. They had been facing fourteen Mexicans who could and would fight. Hence the seven, if there were that many, had to have been carefully picked. That, he decided, was his first clue.

If he could not trail the killers on the ground, he would trail them with his mind.

Seven dangerous, hard-as-nails men, all ready to kill. To lead them, a man would have to be harder, colder, even more dangerous. He would have to be able to handle the other six, and he would have to enjoy their confidence. Such men were rare.

Scanning in his mind the Rangers' fugitive list, he could find no man that fit. John Wesley Hardin might have been a possibility, but Hardin's killings had never been for profit but were a result of feuds or similar situations. Nor was he a planner such as this man had been.

First he must discover who had been involved. What men had been seen in the country around who might have been involved? He must locate one or two possibilities and track them back through the past few weeks to see if they had come together at any time.

Of course, there was another way.

The betrayer was dead, but his betraying need not be at an end. Mounting his roan, he walked back along the line of battle until he came to the body of the betrayer. Zaparo was no longer important. This man was.

Swinging down, Chick Bowdrie went through the dead man's pockets. Nothing had been taken from him. The man's name was Juan Pirón. It was hand-tooled on his belt. He was short and thick with a ragged scar over an eyebrow, and he had ridden a mouse-colored mustang with one white stocking. Pirón looked like a hard man to get along with.

If Juan Pirón had betrayed Zaparo, he had betrayed him to someone he knew, someone he believed could cope with the bandit chief. At some time in the past few weeks or months they had met, but at sometime in the past few days Pirón must have met the killer boss or one of his men to supply the information as to their route.

There lay a chance. To trail Juan Pirón, check with everyone he had known, to find out where he hung out, what he had been doing.

Mounting his hammerhead roan, Bowdrie let the long-legged horse turn back up the arroyo trail. The roan took his own pace, a shambling, loose-limbed trot, and the miles began to fall behind.

Zaparo's gang had looted two missions and some Mexican ranches of nearly one hundred and fifty thousand dollars in gold and money, most of this altar fixtures from the missions. They had fled across the border to the north, and the Rurales had alerted the Rangers.

The Rangers, as usual, had business of their own, and

McNelly detached Bowdrie to see what he could find. What he found was totally unexpected.

It was nearly dusk when Bowdrie rode into the wide ranch yard of Tom Katch's K-Bar. A couple of hands loafed in front of the bunkhouse, and Tom Katch himself, an easygoing man with friendly eyes, was sitting on the veranda. Rangers were always welcome at the K-Bar, and there was always coffee, a meal, and a bed.

"Howdy, Chick!" Katch leaned his massive forearms on the rail as Bowdrie stepped down from the saddle. "What brings you thisaway?"

"Zaparo."

"He on the rampage again? Somebody ought to round him up with a rope."

"Somebody has. With a bullet."

"Dead, is he? What happened?"

Bowdrie dropped into a chair beside Katch and accepted a cup of coffee from a Mexican girl. He dropped his hat on the floor and sipped coffee. Then he put his cup down and explained as briefly as possible, telling only about the ambush, fourteen dead bodies, and the dead horses.

"Clean job," Bowdrie added. "Not the least hint of a trail."

"Hey, boys!" Katch called out. "Zaparo's been killed!"

The hands trooped up to the porch. The first one seated himself on the steps, looking toward them. He was a hard-featured, wiry, and whipcord young man. "We ain't met," he said to Bowdrie. "My name's Ferd Cassidy."

Katch waved a hand at the others. "Hawkins, Broughten, Werner, and Cadieux. Top hands ever' man of them, Bowdrie, and on this outfit they'd better be."

Cassidy agreed. "He works the hell out of us. You're lucky to have a job that beats punchin' cows."

"Well, nobody much cares about a lot of Mexican outlaws," Hawkins commented. "Who d'you reckon did the killin'?"

Bowdrie shrugged. "No idea who did it. Must be a new outfit. But you're wrong about nobody caring. We care. And an outfit that kills like that might kill anybody. We don't hold with lawbreakers, no matter who they are or who they kill."

"Some other Mexican outfit could have trailed 'em," Broughten suggested, "or Apaches."

Bowdrie nodded. "Could be." He paused a moment. "Any of you hombres seen a short, stocky Mexican with a scar over one eye?"

Did Hawkins stiffen a little? Or was it imagination? "Can't say I have," he said, "but I never knowed many Mexicans, anyway."

"Got a pickup order on him," Bowdrie lied. "Some shootin' over Concho way. He prob'ly headed east, anyway."

"Lots of Mexican cowboys workin' this range," Katch suggested. "Right good hands, some of them."

AT DAYBREAK BOWDRIE rolled out of his bunk and poured water from a wooden bucket into a basin and bathed his face and hands. He threw out the water and refilled the bucket at the well.

He wiped the dust from his boots and the silver spurs given him long ago by a Mexican he had befriended. He dug a fresh shirt from his pack and donned it, a black-and-white-checked shirt. He wore a black neckerchief and black pants. He checked his Colts, returned each to its holster, and taking up his Winchester, he went outside.

"Better have some breakfast," Cassidy suggested as he walked past, headed for the corral.

Tom Katch was alone at the table when Bowdrie went inside. Katch was a big man, six-feet-four and weighing a good two hundred and thirty.

"If there's anything we can do, let us know. Cassidy is a good man on a trail and he likes a fight, but all of us are ready to take a hand if we're needed."

Katch talked while Bowdrie ate, sitting with a cup of coffee over the remains of his breakfast. "That Mexican you spoke of? Did he have a name?"

"We didn't have a name," Bowdrie said, "just a description. He was a horse thief who got caught and killed a man."

He was making up the story as he went along, not wanting to tip his hand too much. "I can't bother with him now. This ambush is the important thing."

———

ONCE HE WAS back on the trail, Bowdrie slowed the roan to a walk. He had little to work with aside from the knowledge that it would require a hard lot of men and the fact that he knew who had betrayed the Zaparo outfit. The loot had been taken away on the pack mules that carried it, and those mules must be somewhere around. He knew they were mules from the hoof-prints at the scene, and he had back-trailed the bandits for a mile or so.

The loot must be hidden for the time, and such a lot of men and mules could not travel far without being seen.

Mentally he shaped a map of the area, bounded on the south by the Rio Grande, and with the arroyo where the ambush occurred as the center. North and west of that arroyo was the range where the K-Bar ran their cattle, and south to the river it was rough, half-desert country where few men ventured. East there was twenty miles of rough country and then the small village of Pasamonte. There was something else. Not over eight miles from the arroyo was the cantina and roadhouse of Pedro Padilla.

The cantina was the favored stopping place for cowhands, wet Mexicans from the Rio Grande crossing, and all manner of wayfarers. Aside from Pasamonte it was the only place a man could buy a drink or a meal.

The cantina was built on the ruins of an old mission, a long, low, rambling building surrounding a stone-paved patio. It utilized two walls and the floor of the ancient building, three sides of which were the cantina, and the fourth was reserved for the Padilla family.

If any news was floating around, Pedro Padilla would have heard it. If any strangers had come into the country, he would know. If mules had passed, he would have seen them. The question was, would he tell a Ranger? Or anybody?

What must Bowdrie find out? Who was the leader of the attackers? Where had they gone from the arroyo? Where had

Juan Pirón met with the leader of the ambushers? How had he transmitted the final information as to route, and so on? By what route had the killers arrived at the arroyo?

All could turn on Pirón himself. He was the one link between the bandits and their murderers.

The cantina basked in the hot desert sun. Leaving his horse in the shade of some cottonwoods, Bowdrie entered the spacious, low-raftered room that was the cantina itself. Strings of peppers hung everywhere, and there were two ollas of fresh cold water, each with a gourd dipper. A dozen tables and a bar, a floor of freshly swept flagstones.

Padilla was a paunchy Mexican with a large black mustache and a wary eye, the latter no doubt because he had several attractive daughters. He wore a huge old-fashioned pistol, perhaps for the same reason.

He not only had daughters, Bowdrie perceived, but granddaughters as well, and a wife that would make two of him. Dropping into a chair, Bowdrie ordered a cold beer, suggesting to Padilla that he join him and have one himself.

A desultory conversation began, inhibited somewhat by the Ranger's badge on his vest, a conversation that covered the heat, the lack of rain, the condition of the range and its cattle, as well as the difficulties of conducting a business so far from the law.

"No doubt," Bowdrie suggested, "many bad men come as well as the good. You are close to the border."

"*Sí!* They come, they spend money, they go! I know none of them, and do not wish to know!"

One of Padilla's daughters was wiping a table nearby, and Chick watched her.

"Juan Pirón comes here often?" he asked casually, aware that she was listening.

"Pirón?" Padilla shrugged. "I do not know him. He is a vaquero?"

"That, too, maybe. . . . He is a *bandido,* I think."

Padilla's daughter had paused an instant at the name. She knew the name, he was sure. More likely that Padilla knew Zaparo.

"It is bad about Zaparo," he said thoughtfully. He took a swallow of the beer.

Padilla glanced at him, then away. "Zaparo? I have heard of him."

"*Sí.* It is a bad thing. To be killed is bad, to be ambushed—"

The broom handle hit the floor. Bowdrie's eyes went to the girl. She was staring wide-eyed at him. "Zaparo? He was killed? His men, too?"

"All," he replied, "all are gone. They never had a chance."

Padilla was staring, disbelief in his eyes. His daughter dropped to her knees, clasping her apron in her fingers. "Not the young one! Not he of the curly hair! Do not tell me the young one with the smile, the—!"

Bowdrie's memory was good, and no such Mexican had been among the dead. Yet, how could that be? An ambush with one man escaping? The sort of men he had been picturing would never let anyone escape. There was something wrong here, something . . .

"Fourteen men were dead on the ground, Chiquita," he explained.

"The Rurales?" Padilla asked.

"No, it was other *bandidos,* gringo *bandidos* perhaps. I do not know." His eyes studied the innkeeper. "Zaparo is dead, *señor,* and you were his friend, I think. Now it does not matter except that I must find those who killed him. A killing is an evil thing no matter who is killed, and his killers were evil men."

He paused. "I think this Juan Pirón betrayed Zaparo." He caught Padilla's wrist. "Do you know who that someone was, *amigo*? Have you seen Pirón talking to someone? Even here, perhaps?"

There was a brief flare of realization in Padilla's eyes, but he merely shrugged. "Perhaps he talks here. I do not remember."

Bowdrie glanced at the girl, still on her knees where she had fallen. "Chiquita, if your lover was a man of Zaparo, and if he looked as you have said, he was not among the dead. I remember each face, each man. He was not among them."

"Gracias, señor!" She got to her feet, eyes bright with happiness.

Padilla got up suddenly and left the room. Chick caught the girl's hand. "Chiquita, you can help me. Zaparo was not a good man, yet not so bad as some. He stole precious things from churches in Sonora. They must be found and returned. Your lover was not killed, so he will come to you, no? If he does, send him to me. He can help me."

"You would not betray him, *señor*? To the Rurales? We are to be married soon."

"I wish to speak to him, that is all. What he has done was in Mexico, but now he can change. Zaparo is dead, but those who killed him must be found. Your man can help me."

BOWDRIE AWAKENED SUDDENLY, hours later, lying across his bed above the cantina. Music sounded from below, but it was not that which awakened him. A dozen horses were tied at the hitching rail outside the gate of the patio. From where he lay he could see across the patio and into the lighted window opposite.

Ferd Cassidy suddenly appeared in the room, but moving as if he had just risen from a seat. Then Broughten came into the room with Hawkins. Only nine or ten miles from the K-Bar this was undoubtedly a hangout for the men from the ranch.

Bowdrie went to the basin, still in the half-light from the window opposite, and splashed cold water on his face. Then he combed his hair before picking up his hat. As he started for the door, a surreptitious movement arrested his attention and he froze in position, watching.

The Mexican girl, Chiquita, was leading a saddled horse toward the gate, obviously not wishing to be discovered. He waited an instant, then stepped out into the night. The girl was outside the gate, where she slipped into the saddle and started walking her horse along the trail.

At almost the instant she got into the saddle, the dark figure of a man showed against the lighted window opposite, then vanished. As Bowdrie started for the gate himself, he saw the man mount and ride after the girl. Where could she be going at such an hour? Who was following her?

Stepping quickly into the stable, Bowdrie saddled and bridled the roan. Gathering the reins, he stepped into the saddle and followed them down the trail, keeping to the grassy shoulder. Within a few minutes he glimpsed the man ahead; then he seemed to vanish.

Worried, Bowdrie reached the spot only to discover that the desert broke away into the steep bank of a wash. Starting down the side, he glimpsed the outline of a rider against the night, a rider some distance off, but who could only be Chiquita. What had become of the man following her?

Glancing right and left into the deeper shadows, he decided that rider must have ridden either up or down the wash, knowing perhaps that this wash intercepted the trail farther along. Bowdrie chose to follow Chiquita up the steep opposite bank. She rode straight on as though to a goal, and Chick had an idea of whom she planned to meet.

They rode for nearly an hour; then a faint glimmer of firelight showed. By now they were in a remote region of canyons and weird rock formations where such a fire could not be seen for any distance. Bowdrie, following warily, glimpsed it only occasionally when he topped out on high ground or when the rocks stood apart to offer greater visibility. Chiquita rode directly to the fire and slid from her horse.

Bowdrie studied the terrain. What had become of the rider who followed her? Had that rider realized Bowdrie was behind them?

Tying the roan to a mesquite bush, he crept through the cacti and mesquite until he could, from behind a rock, overlook the situation.

The young Mexican who held the girl in his arms could only be a henchman of Zaparo's. They were talking in Spanish but the air was clear and Bowdrie was close enough to hear every word.

"It is what you feared," she was saying. "Something has happened! Zaparo is dead! All of them are dead! They were attacked by other outlaws and killed! All of them!"

"*Zaparo?* But *how*? Who could have known their way?"

"The gringo with the black hat, the one who looks like an Apache, he says it was Juan Pirón who betrayed them."

"Ah? I am not surprised. But he was killed also?"

"The gringo says they are all dead, that they had no further use for Pirón, and did not trust him. And now they have the loot!"

"I care nothing for that!" he said indignantly. "But *Zaparo*! There was a man! He was my friend, also, and to be betrayed by such a man?"

"The gringo wishes to talk to you. He promises you no harm. He wishes only to find the gringo outlaws."

The Mexican shook his head. "I know nothing, Chiquita!"

Their voices became lower, and then after a quick kiss Chiquita gave him a package of food and got back into the saddle. Turning her horse, she rode into darkness.

Bowdrie was in a quandary. Here was his chance to talk to the young Mexican, and there might never be another. On the other hand, the unknown rider might follow Chiquita. Had he also overheard? Or had he come this far?

He made his decision quickly. He would do both.

He spoke, hoping his voice would carry no farther than the young Mexican. "Stand where you are! I am a friend!"

The Mexican rooted himself in his tracks, but turned slowly to face him.

"I am the gringo Chiquita mentioned, and I must talk with you, but we must ride also, for Chiquita is in danger."

"Chiquita? In danger? I will get my horse."

Warily Chick watched him go, then circled the fire beyond the reach of its light. He saw no good place where a watcher might have been, and if there had been one, he was gone.

"Leave the fire. There is nothing for it to burn and there is no time."

Bowdrie led the way; then the Mexican closed up beside him and Bowdrie explained about the follower he had glimpsed. Then he asked, "What do you know of Pirón?"

"He was cousin to Zaparo but I did not trust him. I followed once when he met with two men, but could not see their faces. Zaparo would not believe he was a traitor. He became very angry with me."

"How did it happen you were not with them?"

"My father, *señor,* he is ill. When he became better I rode to see Chiquita, but also hoping she could tell what happened to Zaparo. He had been gone too long, and at the cantina they hear everything."

Suddenly they heard a scream, quickly choked off. The young Mexican slapped spurs to his horse and was gone like a shot. Bowdrie could only follow.

He saw them suddenly, two struggling figures in the road, but at the sound of the rushing horses the man threw the girl from him and grabbed for his pistol. Chick drew and fired, and the man dropped his gun and staggered, dropping to his knees.

Bowdrie hit the ground on the run and saw the young Mexican go to Chiquita. She fell into his arms, moaning with fright, and Chick struck a match with his thumbnail. The wounded man was Hawkins.

"What did you jump me for?" Hawkins did not seem badly hurt, but it was too dark to see. "Can't a feller have a little fun without you hornin' in?"

"Not when the girl doesn't want him," Bowdrie replied.

"Huh! You'd help one of Zaparo's outlaws rather'n an American?"

The moon, rising now above the mountain ridge, provided small light. How, Bowdrie wondered, had Hawkins known the Mexican was one of Zaparo's gang? Such gossip might be going around, of course. Still . . .

"Mount up," he said. "We'll ride back to the cantina. And you, Hawkins, consider yourself my prisoner."

"Me?" Hawkins was startled. "A prisoner? What for?"

"Mount up," Bowdrie replied. "I think you're just the man I've been lookin' for."

Hawkins became suddenly quiet. "So?" he said. Nor did he utter another word during the ride back to the cantina. Bowdrie took him through a back way, guided by Chiquita, to one of Padilla's spare rooms, where he handcuffed him to the bed.

Bowdrie's hasty shot had done little damage. It had, judging from a quick examination, hit Hawkins's large belt buckle at an angle, glanced off, and ripped his shirt at the elbow, scratching the skin and momentarily numbing his arm and hand.

"You were lucky," Bowdrie said briefly, "or maybe you weren't, depending on whether you prefer a bullet to a rope."

"What's that mean?" Hawkins demanded.

Leaving him handcuffed, Bowdrie went into the cantina, where Broughten was watching a poker game and a half-dozen others were hanging about. One of them was Ferd Cassidy.

Chick nodded to him. "When you get ready to ride," he commented, "don't wait for Hawkins. He's under arrest."

Broughten turned sharply and Cassidy put his glass down on the table.

"What's he done?" Cassidy asked.

"He followed one of Padilla's girls into the desert and got rough with her." Bowdrie paused, then added, "While I have him, I'd better speak to him on some other matters."

"What matters?" Cassidy's eyes were cold and ugly.

There was a tenseness in the man that went beyond what could be expected. Suddenly Bowdrie was wondering. Why not the K-Bar outfit? A tough lot, close to the scene, yet so far as he knew, nothing of the kind had ever been held against them before. Of course, there was always the first time, and if they were tipped off to the amount of loot . . .

A man came in the door, glanced around, taking in the tableau with casual interest; then he sat down at a table near the door. He was young, blond, and wiry-looking. Nobody seemed to notice his arrival.

"Just a little investigation," Bowdrie replied. "Hawkins knew that Pablo, Chiquita's friend, was one of the Zaparo outfit. We're trying to learn all we can about Zaparo, and I'm curious as to how he knows."

The room was very still. Two Mexican cowhands who had been standing at the bar quietly left, and an older man with gray chin whiskers eased himself off his chair, and putting on his hat, went out a side door.

"Thought all of Zaparo's outfit were dead," Cassidy said.

"Looked like it," Bowdrie replied, "but it seems some of them were suspicious of Juan Pirón. They'd seen him talkin' with some gringos, and it didn't look good to them."

Cassidy shrugged. "Well, whatever, but don't hold him longer than you need to. We've got work to do."

The K-Bar boys left, mounted, and rode away. Bowdrie went to the bar and ordered a beer, turning the matter over in his mind. There was small chance the cowhand would talk, and a better-than-even chance he had nothing to tell. It might be nothing more than a cowhand going after a girl he believed might listen to him.

Bowdrie had an unhappy feeling that he was making a fool of himself. Certainly he would no longer be welcome at the K-Bar. Ranch hands were clannish, and a move against one of their number was a move against all. Yet he could not rid himself of the notion that he had a fingerhold on the problem.

Leaving his beer only half-finished, he went to his room, and was passing the spare room where he had left Hawkins when he heard a scurry of movement. Drawing his gun, he flung the door open and was just in time to see Hawkins going out the window. He grabbed for him with his left hand.

He caught the corner of a hip pocket and it ripped. The pocket tore away and something tinkled on the floor. Hawkins was out the window, sprawling on the ground. Scrambling to his feet, the bald-headed man started to run as Chick jumped through the window. As he hit the ground he thought he heard a low voice speaking to Hawkins; then a gun flashed and a bullet struck near him. Bowdrie fired in return at two indistinct riders. Two guns barked and a bullet nicked his arm, spoiling his last shot.

There was a pound of racing hooves, then silence. Moving with care, Bowdrie started toward where he had last seen Hawkins and saw the body of a man sprawled on the hard-packed earth in the pale, greenish light from the risen moon.

Waiting a moment, he listened but heard no sound. Kneeling, he struck a match.

The dead man was Hawkins. Hawkins had been wounded

in the exchange of gunfire, but despairing of getting him away, somebody had put a gun to his head and blown his brains out.

Now men were coming from the cantina. Padilla and Pablo came up. Bowdrie motioned to the dead man and the obvious powder burns. "Looks like they killed him so he couldn't talk," he commented.

Which was foolish of them, for their actions spoke as loudly and clearly as anything Hawkins might have said. Their killing of him implied Hawkins would or might have had something to say. It pointed a finger at his killers and at the K-Bar.

Once in the spare room, Bowdrie lighted a candle and looked around. Something had fallen from Hawkins's pocket to the floor, but the first thing he found was the handcuffs. The lock had been opened either with a key or a lock-pick.

A gleam caught his eye, and on his knees, he retrieved a bright object from under the edge of the bed. It was a gold ring with an amethyst setting. It was a ring described in the list of loot stolen by Zaparo.

Hawkins, evidently thinking of Chiquita, had held out the ring as a gift to her for favors he hoped to receive. Obviously he had not known of her commitment to Pablo.

Chick slipped the ring into his pocket. He must work fast now. He crossed the patio on the run. The blond newcomer was at the bar. He turned as Bowdrie entered.

"Rip! How many came with you?"

"Deming an' Armstrong. Ain't that enough?"

"Get 'em an' come on! I'm headed for the K-Bar. If there's a fight this time, it will be something to write your girl about, believe me."

Once in the saddle, he let the roan have his head. The hammerhead outlaw knew when his master was in a hurry and he could set his own pace.

The K-Bar outfit might try to bluff it out or they might not even expect trouble. What he was hoping was that they would try to move the loot or get to where it was. The ranch itself was the logical place, of course, as it was one of the few places the mules could be taken without arousing suspicion or interest. Pack animals in such numbers do not just vanish from sight.

Rip Coker would be along with the two Rangers accompanying him. Bowdrie had spotted him the moment he entered the cantina, and realized McNelly had sent them along to help.

When he drew near the K-Bar he slowed the roan to a walk, keeping to the soft shoulder of the road, hoping a hoof would not strike stone. The other Rangers were not far behind, but speed was of first importance.

There was activity near a stack of hay, and some mules with packsaddles were being loaded. Three men were in sight as he approached, and he could hear cursing. There were lights on in the house. Was Katch involved, too? Or was it only the ranch hands?

Chick Bowdrie stepped down from his horse. "You stand," he warned, "but if I yell, come a-runnin'."

The roan was already dozing, accustomed to such moments but prepared to take what rest he could get.

The other Rangers closed in and Bowdrie explained what he had in mind and then moved off, stepping softly and hoping his spurs would not jingle.

When he reached the back of the well-house, he took a quick glance about, then walked across to the back door of the ranch house. He had been in the house too many times before not to know his way. He crossed the kitchen, hearing a murmur of voices from the living room.

Walking softly behind the chairs in the big dining room, he reached the door and paused to listen. The door stood open but he was well back and out of sight.

"Forget it, Cassidy!" Katch was saying. "You're jumpy! If Hawkins is dead, he can't talk. That fool Ranger will think one of his own shots killed him. He likes to believe he's good with a six-shooter."

"Maybe you're right," Cassidy replied doubtfully, "but maybe he knows too much. After all, he knew about Pirón. How could he find out about him?"

"Don't get the wind up," Katch replied carelessly. "This is foolproof."

Katch got up and stretched. In the dim light he looked enormous.

"I told the boys to load the stuff so's we could move it," Cassidy said.

Katch brought his arms down slowly. "You *what*?" His tone was low but there was something so deadly in it that Bowdrie felt his scalp tighten.

"It seemed the thing to do. If they search the place, they'll find nothing."

Katch's tone was mild. "Ferd, if they did search, they'd never think to look in that haystack. Besides, the Rangers know me. I'm their friend. If that loot starts paradin' around in the moonlight, somebody is sure enough goin' to see it."

Cassidy had his hands flat on the table. "I'll go tell 'em to put it back," he said. "I guess I acted too fast."

"That's your trouble, Ferd. You're too jumpy. I don't like men who get jumpy, Ferd. You're a good man on a job, smooth as silk and cold as ice, but when we ain't workin' you're too easy to upset. Besides, I don't like men who give orders without consultin' me."

"I'm right sorry," Cassidy said. "You ain't mad, are you, boss?"

His features were sallow in the dim light, and suddenly Bowdrie knew what was about to happen. Big Tom Katch was playing with his lieutenant as a cat plays with a mouse. Katch knew that Cassidy was on edge. He led him on now, building him to a crisis.

"No, I'm not mad, Ferd. Not mad at all." Katch smiled. "I just don't need you anymore, Ferd."

The words fell softly in the room and for a moment there was utter silence as the words sank into Ferd Cassidy's brain. Realization hit him like a blow. His eyes seemed to flare and he went for his gun. And Tom Katch shot him.

He had held the gun at his side, turned half away, so Ferd Cassidy, expecting no trouble here, had not even noticed.

Bowdrie stepped softly into the room, so softly that Tom Katch did not hear it. The big man was staring at the dying Cassidy with amused contempt. Katch holstered his gun.

Then his eyes lifted and his peripheral vision seemed to catch a glimpse of Bowdrie. He turned his head.

Bowdrie saw the shock in Katch's eyes, then a slow smile. He had to admire the man, for it had taken only that instant to adjust to the changed situation.

"How are you, Chick? I've been havin' some trouble with my foreman, seems like. He and some of the boys been doin' some outside jobs I didn't know about."

"I don't buy it, Katch. You can't lay it on them alone. You're the boss here. Yours is the brain. From the beginning I knew there was something I should remember. Something that hung in the back of my mind trying to be remembered.

"It didn't come to me until I saw that those handcuffs had been opened with a lock-pick. Then I realized who Cassidy was. When I knew who he was, I knew who you were."

"Don't tell me I was on your Ranger list of wanted men. I never saw Texas until a few years back, and I've lived right here all that time."

"What about Missouri, Tennessee, Ohio, and Nebraska? Four big jobs, four clean jobs, except for one thing. The gent that saw you on the platform at the railroad station in Dodge City.

"It just happened that a little fat drummer was standin' there who had known you in Memphis. Big Tom Caughter, the smartest crook of them all, the man who never left a witness and always got away with the loot. Ferd Cassidy was Lonnie Webb, a Kansas boy with a gift for picking locks, other people's locks."

Katch was thinking. Bowdrie could almost see his mind working, and this was a shrewd, dangerous man. Always before he had gotten away with it. No trail, no witnesses, no evidence. Four big jobs, and this was to be the fifth.

Katch shrugged. "Well, I guess a man can't win 'em all. With the money I've got cached I can be out in a couple of years."

"Sounds easy, doesn't it?" Bowdrie said. "But what about the killings?"

"You mean Zaparo? You can't prove I was there. As a matter of fact, I wasn't. Anyway, no jury is going to hang me for killing a few Mexican outlaws."

"I wasn't thinking of Zaparo. I was thinking of Ferd Cassidy. That was a cold-blooded killing. I saw it."

"Oh? So that's the way it is?" Katch eyed him with a steady, assured gaze. "Then we don't need a witness. When you die, who else will know?"

"The Rangers are outside waitin' for my signal," Bowdrie said. "Your boys are already rounded up, and without a shot fired. I was waiting to hear, but there never was a one. Now I'll take you."

Katch flashed a hand for his gun, incredibly fast, only Bowdrie was already shooting.

Coker stepped into the door. "Get 'em all?" Chick asked.

"Yeah." He looked at the bodies. "Both of them yours?"

"Only the big one." He looked at Katch and shook his head. "Rip, that man had brains, some education, and nerve. Why can't they ever realize they can't beat the law?"

SOUTH OF DEADWOOD

THE CHEYENNE TO Deadwood Stage was two hours late into Pole Creek Station, and George Gates, the driver, had tried to make up for lost time. Inside the coach the five passengers had been jounced up and down and side to side as the Concord thundered over the rough trail.

The girl with the golden hair and gray eyes who was sitting beside the somber young man in the black flat-crowned hat and black frock coat had been observing him surreptitiously all the way from Cheyenne.

He had a dark, Indian-like face with a deep, dimplelike scar under his cheekbone, and despite his inscrutable manner he was singularly attractive. Yet he had not spoken a word since leaving Cheyenne.

It was otherwise with the burly red-cheeked man with the walrus mustache. He had talked incessantly. His name, the girl had learned with no trouble at all, was Walter Luck.

"Luck's my name," he stated, "and luck's what I got!"

The other blond was Kitty Austin, who ran a place of entertainment in Deadwood. Kitty was an artificial blond, overdressed and good-natured but thoroughly realistic in her approach to life and men. The fifth passenger had also been reticent, but it finally developed that his name was James J. Bridges.

"I want no trouble with you!" Luck bellowed. "I don't aim to cross no bridges!" And the coach rocked with his laughter.

The golden-haired girl's name, it developed, was Clare Marsden, but she said nothing of her purpose in going to Deadwood until Luck asked.

"You visitin' relatives, ma'am? Deadwood ain't no place for a girl alone."

"No." Her chin lifted a little, as if in defiance. "I am going to see a man. His name is Curly Starr."

If she had struck them one simultaneous slap across their mouths they could have been no more startled. They gaped, their astonishment too real to be concealed. Luck was the first to snap out of it.

"Why, ma'am!" Luck protested. "Curly Starr's an outlaw! He's in jail now, just waitin' for the law from Texas to take him back! He's a killer, a horse thief, and a hold-up man!"

"I know it," Clare said stubbornly. "But I've got to see him! He's the only one who can help me!"

She was suddenly aware that the dark young man beside her was looking at her for what she believed was the first time. He seemed about to speak when the stage rolled into the yard at Pole Creek Station and raced to a stop.

Peering out, they saw Fred Schwartz's sign—CHOICEST WINE, LIQUOR, AND CIGARS—as the man himself came out to greet the new arrivals.

The young man in the black hat was beside her. He removed his hat gracefully and asked, "If I may make so bold? Would you sit with me at supper?"

It was the first time he had spoken and his voice was low, agreeable, and went with his smile, which had genuine charm, but came suddenly and was gone.

"Why, yes. I would like that."

Over their coffee, with not much time left, he said, "You spoke of seein' Curly Starr, ma'am? Do you know him?"

"No, I don't. Only . . ." She hesitated, and then as he waited, she added, "He knows my brother, and he could help if he would. My brother is in trouble and I don't believe he's guilty. I think Curly Starr does know who is."

"I see. You think he might clear your brother?"

There was little about Curly Starr he did not know. Starr, along with Doc Bentley, Ernie Joslin, Tobe Storey, and a kid called Bill Cross had held up the Cattleman's Bank in Mustang, killing two men in the process. Billy Marsden, son of the owner of the Bar M Ranch, had been arrested and charged with the killing. It was claimed he was Bill Cross.

"I hope he will. I've come all the way from Texas just to talk to him."

"They'll be takin' him back to Texas," the young man suggested. "Couldn't you have waited?"

"I had to see him first! I've been told that awful gunfighting Ranger, Chick Bowdrie, is coming after him. He might kill Starr before he gets back to Texas."

"Now I doubt that. I hear the Rangers never kill a man unless he's shootin' at them. Have you ever met this Bowdrie fellow?"

"No, but I've heard about him, and that's enough."

Gates thrust his head in the door. "Time to mount up, folks! Got to roll if we aim to make Deadwood on time."

Clare Marsden hurried outside and Walter Luck stepped up beside her.

"Seen you talkin' with that young feller in the black hat. Did he tell you his name?"

"Why, no," she realized. "He did not mention it."

"Seems odd," Luck said as he seated himself. "We all told our names but him."

Kitty Austin drew a cigar from her bag and put it in her mouth. "Not strange a-tall! Lots of folks don't care to tell their names. It's their own business!"

She glanced at Clare Marsden. "Hope you don't mind the smoke, ma'am. I sure miss a cigar if I don't have one after dinner. Some folks like to chaw, but I'm no hand for it, myself. That Calamity Jane, she chaws, but she's a rough woman. Drives an ox team an' cusses like she means it."

Luck had a cigarette but he tossed it out of the window as the stage started.

The young man in the black hat reached into his pocket and withdrew a long envelope, taking from it a letter, which he glanced at briefly as they passed the last lighted window. He had turned the envelope to extract the letter, but not so swiftly that it missed the trained eye of Gentleman Jim Bridges. It was addressed, *Chick Bowdrie, Texas Rangers, El Paso, Texas.*

Bridges was a man who could draw three aces in succession and never turn a hair. He did not turn one now, although there was quick interest in his eyes. There was a glint in them as he glanced from Bowdrie to the girl and at last to Walter Luck.

"If you plan to see Starr, you'd better get at it," Luck suggested. "Texas wants him back and I hear they're sendin' a man after him. They're sendin' that border gunfighter, Chick Bowdrie."

"Never heard of him," Bridges lied.

"He's good, they say. With a gun, I mean. Of course, he ain't in a class with Doc Bentley or Ernie Joslin. That says nothin' of Allison or Hickok."

"That's what you say." Kitty Austin took the cigar from her teeth. "Billy Brooks told me Bowdrie was pure-Dee poison. Luke Short said the same."

"I ain't interested in such," Luck replied. "Minin' is my game. Or mine stock. I buy stock on occasion when the prospects are good. I don't know nothin' about Texas. Never been south of Wichita."

Bowdrie leaned back and relaxed his muscles to the movement of the stage. Clare Marsden aroused his sympathy as well as his curiosity, yet he knew that Billy Marsden was as good as convicted, and conviction meant hanging. Yet if his sister was right and Starr knew something that might clear him, he would at least have a fighting chance. How much of a chance would depend on what Starr had to say, if anything. The court would not lightly accept the word of an outlaw trying to clear one of his own outfit.

If he had even a spark of the courage it took to send his sister rolling over a thousand miles of rough roads, he might yet make something of himself.

Chick had himself made a start down the wrong road before McNelly recruited him for the Rangers. It had been to avenge a friend that he had joined the Rangers. It led to the extinction of the Ballard gang and the beginning of his own reputation along the border. Yet since he had ridden into that lonely ranch in Texas, badly wounded and almost helpless, he had never drawn a gun except on the side of the law.

It was easy enough for even the best of young men to take the wrong turning when every man carried a gun and when an excess of high spirits could lead to trouble. Chick Bowdrie made a sudden resolution. If there was the faintest chance for Billy Marsden, he would lend a hand.

Dealing with Curly Starr would not be simple. Curly was a hard case. He had killed nine or ten men, had rustled a lot of stock, stood up a few stages, and robbed banks. Yet so far as Bowdrie was aware, there were no killings on Starr's record where the other man did not have an even break. According to the customs of the country that spoke well for the man.

When the stage rolled to a stop before the IXL Hotel & Dining Room in Deadwood, a plan was shaping in Bowdrie's mind. He was the last one to descend from the stage and his eyes took in an unshaven man in miner's clothing who lounged against the wall of the IXL, a man who muttered something under his breath as Luck passed him.

Stooping, Bowdrie picked up Clare's valise with his left hand and carried it into the hotel. She turned, smiling brightly. "Thank you so much! You didn't tell me your name?"

"Bowdrie, ma'am. I'm Chick Bowdrie."

Her eyes were startled, and she went white to the lips. He stepped back, embarrassed. "If there's any way I can help, you've only to ask. I'll be stayin' in the hotel."

He turned quickly away, leaving her staring after him.

Bowdrie did not wait to see what she would do or say, nor did he check in at the hotel. He had sent word to Seth Bullock, and knew the sheriff would have made arrangements. He headed for the jail.

Curly Starr was lounging on his cot when Bowdrie walked up to the bars. "Howdy, Starr! Comfortable?"

Starr glanced up, then slowly swung his feet to the floor. "Bowdrie, is it? Looks like they sent the king bee."

Bowdrie shook his head. "No, that would be Gillette or Armstrong. One of the others.

"Anyway, I've a lot of work to do when I get you back, Curly. There's Bentley, Joslin, Tobe Storey to round up." And then he added, "We've got the kid."

Starr came to the bars. "Got any smokin'?"

Bowdrie tossed him a tobacco sack and some papers. "Keep 'em," he said.

"Curly," he said as Starr rolled his smoke, "the kid's going to get hung unless something turns up to help him."

"Tough." Curly touched his tongue to the paper. "We can go out together, if you get me back to Texas."

"I'll get you back, settin' a saddle or across one, but that kid's pretty young to die. If you know anything that would help, tell me."

"Help?" Starr chuckled. He was a big, brawny young man with a hard, square brown face and tight dark curls. "You're the law, Bowdrie. You'd hang a man, but I doubt if you'd help one."

"He's a kid. I'd give any man a break."

"He was old enough to pack a gun. In this life a man straddles his own horses and buries his dead. Nobody is lookin' for any outs for me. Besides, how do I know you ain't diggin' for evidence against the kid? Or all of us?"

Despite himself Bowdrie was disturbed as he walked back to the IXL. He was positive the man Luck had spoken to was Tobe Storey. He had had only a glimpse, but the man's jawline was familiar, and the Pecos gunman could have ridden this way.

What if they had all ridden this way? What if they planned a jailbreak? Curly Starr was the leader of the outfit and they had ridden together for a long time.

Later, in the dining room of the IXL, he loitered over his coffee. Deadwood was wide open and booming. Named for the dead trees along a hillside above the town, it was really a succession of towns in scattered valleys in the vicinity.

The Big Horn Store, the Gem Theater, the Bella Union Variety Theater, run by Jack Langrishe, and the Number Ten Saloon all were busy, crowded most of the time.

After leaving the jail, Bowdrie had drifted in and out of most of the places, alert for any of the Starr outfit. Now he sat over coffee for the same purpose, waiting, watching.

The door opened and Seth Bullock appeared. With him was Clare Marsden. As her eyes met Bowdrie's, she flushed. Bowdrie arose as they came to the table.

"Bowdrie, this young lady wants to talk to Curly Starr. I told her Starr was your prisoner and she would have to ask you."

"She can talk to him," Bowdrie replied. From the corner of his eye he glimpsed a man standing just inside the saloon, looking into the dining room. It was the man he believed was Tobe Storey.

"Tonight?" Clare asked.

Bowdrie hesitated. It was foolhardy to open the jail now unless necessary, but . . .

"All right. I'll go along."

As she turned toward the door, he hesitated long enough to whisper to Seth Bullock, "Tobe Storey's in town, and maybe the rest of that Starr outfit."

She walked along beside him without speaking, until suddenly she looked up at him. "I suppose you think I am a fool to come all this distance to help a man who is as good as convicted, even if he is my brother."

"No, ma'am, I don't. If you think there's a chance for him, you'd be a fool not to try, but if you've any reason for believing your brother wasn't involved, why not tell me?"

"But you're a *Ranger*!" The way she said it, the term sounded like an epithet.

"All the more reason. You've got us wrong, ma'am. Rangers don't like to jail folks unless they've been askin' for it. Out on the edge of things like this, if there weren't any Rangers there'd be no place for people like you.

"If your brother took money with a pistol, he's a thief and a dangerous man, and if he killed or had a part in killing an innocent man, he should hang for it.

"If he didn't, then he should go free, and if Starr has evidence that he's innocent, I'll do my best to clear him."

They turned a corner but a sudden movement in the shadows and the rattle of a stone caused Chick Bowdrie to swing aside, brushing Clare Marsden back with a sweep of his arm.

A gun flamed from the shadows and a bullet tugged at his shoulder. Only his sudden move had saved them, but his gun bellowed a reply.

He ran to the mouth of the alley, then stopped. It led into a maze of shacks, barns, and corrals, and there was nobody in sight. The ambusher was gone.

He walked back to Clare. She stared at him, pale and shocked. "That man tried to kill you!" she protested.

"Yes, ma'am. I am a Ranger and they know why I am in town."

"But why here? Deadwood is a long way from Texas!"

"I am here to take Starr back. They don't want him to go. If your brother was involved in that hold-up, the man who tried to kill me is his friend. Or an associate, at least."

"My brother wouldn't do any such thing!" she protested, but her voice was weak.

He had expected something of the kind. His eyes narrowed thoughtfully as they neared the jail, remembering something he had noticed earlier.

The deputy on guard opened the door cautiously, gun in hand, then opened it wider when he saw who was there.

Starr was sprawled on his bunk. A big man in a checked shirt, jeans stuffed into cowhide boots.

He swung his feet to the floor. "You again? Was that you they shot at?"

"Wouldn't you know?" Bowdrie saw Starr's eyes go to the tear in the shoulder of Bowdrie's shirt. "Close, that one. I reckon the boys aren't holdin' as steady as they should."

His eyes shifted to Clare, and he came quickly to his feet, surprise mingled with respect. He could see at a glance that she was a decent girl, and he had that quick western courtesy toward women. "How d'you do, ma'am?"

"Curly, this is Clare Marsden, sister of Billy Marsden. The law thinks he is Bill Cross. She hopes you can tell her somethin' that will get her brother off the hook."

Starr shrugged contemptuously. "Is this another trick, Bowdrie? I won't give evidence, not any kind of evidence. I don't know anybody named Marsden, or Cross either. I've nothing to say."

"You can't help me?" she pleaded. "If only Billy wasn't with you! Or if he was only holding the horses or something!"

Curly avoided her eyes. He looked a little pale but he was stubborn. "I don't know nothin' about it."

"You were seen an' identified by four men, Curly." Bowdrie's tone was gentle. "So was Tobe. Everybody in town knew Bentley. That leaves Joslin and the kid. We have no description of Joslin, but the kid was identified by one man and he was caught under suspicious circumstances. If you can save his neck, why not do it?"

She stared helplessly for a moment, then dropped her hands from the bars and turned away with a gesture of hopelessness that caught at Chick's heart.

"Starr, I knew you were a thief but I didn't think you were a damned louse! This won't do you any good."

"I'll do myself some good before we get to Texas. I'll have your hide, Bowdrie. It's a long road home and I'll get my break."

At the door of the IXL Bowdrie paused. "You'd best go home, ma'am. Most outlaws aren't like him. They are rough men but many of them are pretty decent at heart. I am sorry."

"Thank you, and I am sorry for what I said. You really tried to help me." Tears welled into her eyes and she turned away.

He stared after her, and swore under his breath.

———

THE WIND HAD a way of rippling the grass into long waves of gray or green, and it stirred now, rolling away over the sunlit prairie. Bowdrie, astride the appaloosa gelding he had bought in Deadwood, rode beside his prisoner.

Curly Starr, his chin a stubble of beard, stared bleakly ahead. "You won't get me much further! Ogalalla's ahead, an' I've friends riding the cattle trails."

"You talk too much. I've prob'ly just as many friends as you've enemies among those herds, too. You stole too many horses, Curly. I'll be lucky if I get you back to Texas unhung." He paused. "What happened to Tobe an' Doc?"

"How would they guess you'd ride fifty miles west out of Deadwood? That you'd ride fifty miles out of your way to keep me away from them? But you're back on the cattle trails now, an' they'll find us."

It had been a hard ride. On impulse Bowdrie had taken his prisoner out of Deadwood on the same night he left Clare Marsden at the door of the IXL. He headed due west, only later turning south and heading for the tall-grass country.

Ogalalla, which lay ahead, was a tough trail town and a dozen Texas herds were gathered nearby. Bowdrie had friends there, as did Starr. When things went well for him, the big outlaw was a friendly, easygoing man who had punched cows with many of the trail hands. Those friends would not forget.

Bowdrie kept his plans to himself. He had no intention of going into Ogalalla at all. He would camp at Ash Hollow, then head south again, keeping west of Dodge on a course roughly parallel to the proposed Nation Trail, until inside the Texas boundaries. At that time he would veer west toward Doan's Store and Fort Griffin.

"They'll be good hunters if they find us," Bowdrie commented. Starr looked at him, but said nothing. He had been watching the stars, and was puzzled.

At dusk they camped in a canyon where a few ash trees grew and which had been named Ash Hollow by Frémont. They made camp close to the spring, and then taking Starr with him, Bowdrie went down to a moist place in the brush where gooseberries and currants were growing. When they had picked a few to supplement their supper, they walked back.

"You takin' these irons off me? I'll sleep better if you do."

Bowdrie smiled. "And I'll sleep better with them on, so why don't you just settle down an' rest? Nobody is going to turn you loose unless you get a smart Texas lawyer."

Despite their continual bickering, the two men had come to respect and even like each other during the ride. Curly Starr was typical of a certain reckless, devil-may-care sort of puncher who often took to the bad trails when the country was wild. He was not an evil man, and under other circumstances in another kind of country he might never have become an outlaw.

Bowdrie was not fooled by his liking for the man. He knew that at the first chance Starr would grab for a gun or make a run for it. By now the outlaw knew something had gone awry with their planning. He kept staring around at the spring, then the ash trees.

"Hey?" he exclaimed. "This place looks like Ash Hollow, west of Ogalalla!"

"Go to the head of the class," Bowdrie replied.

"You're not goin' into Ogalalla?" Disappointment was written in his expression. "Ain't you goin' to give me any chance at all?"

"Go to sleep," Bowdrie said. "You've got a long ride tomorrow."

When he picketed the horses he took a long look around. Earlier he had glimpsed some distant riders who rode like Indians.

He slept lightly and just before daybreak rolled out of his blankets and got a small fire going. Then he went for the horses. He was just in time to see an Indian reaching for the picket pin. The warrior saw him at the same instant and lifted his rifle. Bowdrie drew and fired in one swift, easy movement. Grabbing the picket ropes, Bowdrie raced back for the shelter of the trees.

Curly was on his feet. "Give me a gun, Bowdrie! I'll stand 'em off!"

"Lie down, Starr! If it gets rough I'll let you have a gun. In the meantime, just sit tight."

A bullet clipped a leaf over his head, another thudded into a tree trunk. Chick rolled into a shallow place in the grass and lifted his Winchester.

An instant he waited; then he glimpsed a brown leg slithering through the grass and aimed a bit ahead of it and squeezed off his shot. The Indian cried out, half arose, then fell back into the grass. A chorus of angry yells responded to the wounding of the warrior.

Bowdrie waited. This was, he believed, just a small party on a horse-stealing foray, and two of their number were down. His position was relatively good unless the Indians decided to rush them. Which they promptly did.

Dropping his rifle as they broke from the brush and arose from the grass, Bowdrie drew both six-shooters. He opened fire, dropping the nearest Indian; then with his left-hand gun he got the man farthest on the right. Then they vanished, dropping into the grass and the brush. One warrior was slow in getting under cover and a rifle boomed behind Bowdrie and the Indian fell.

Bowdrie turned swiftly, covering Starr. The outlaw grinned at him. "Had to get in one shot!" he protested. Yet Bowdrie saw the man had started to swing the rifle to cover him. Only his quick turn with the pistol had stopped it.

He grinned again. "Hell, Bowdrie, you can't blame a man for tryin'!"

He nodded toward the area beyond their brush screen. "No real war party, just huntin' horses an' a few scalps."

An hour later they were on their way. It was short-grass country now and would be all the way back to Texas. There might be occasional belts of tall grass, but it was going to be scarce. Bowdrie kept them moving at a stiff pace, knowing Starr's followers would almost certainly figure out what had happened. He could not avoid them much longer.

Undoubtedly even now they were working their way west to cut his trail, and when they came, it would be fast.

When they did come, it was a surprise. Bowdrie had holed up in a deserted cabin in the upper Panhandle of Texas. Theirs had been a long, hard ride under blazing suns, cold nights, and sometimes showers of pounding rain. As they reached the cabin, Starr said, "You're goin' to a heap of trouble just to hang a man. Why don't you let me go?"

"Hangin' you isn't important," Bowdrie replied, "but I've got a job to do and you're part of it. The day has come when a man can no longer live by the gun. Two men were killed in that robbery of yours. Both of them had wives, one of them had two youngsters.

"Hangin' you won't bring back their father or that other woman her husband, but it might keep some other father or husband alive.

"Society is not taking revenge. It is simply eliminating someone who refuses to live by the rules."

Starr swore and spat into the dust. "Get me back to wherever you're takin' me, Bowdrie, or by the Eternal you'll have me converted! But keep them guns handy, boy. If I get a hand on one of 'em, I'll have a chance to be glad you aren't leavin' a widow!"

"Get busy an' pick up sticks. We'll need a fire for coffee."

On the edge of the hollow where the cabin lay, Chick paused and took a careful look at the surrounding country. His nerves were on edge, and in part it was due to the long ride with a man who was ready to kill him at any slight chance, a man with everything to gain and nothing to lose. Around the next hill or down the next draw his friends might be waiting.

Doc Bentley, Joslin, and the rest were all plainsmen and by now they would have figured out what he was doing and they would expect him to turn east, which he must do to deliver his prisoner. Also, they were on the edge of Kiowa-Comanche country.

Bowdrie studied the situation. The adobe cabin was built in a hollow in a rocky canyon with a spring close beside it. There were a few cottonwood trees, and a couple of huge tree trunks that lay near the cabin. The view from the door overlooked the trail and the approach to the spring. The cabin had often been a refuge for buffalo hunters and had figured in many a brush with Indians, judging by the bullet scars.

With an armful of wood on his left arm, Bowdrie walked back to the cabin. Working with the handcuffs on, Curly Starr had a fire going. He looked up, smiling.

"As long as they sent a Ranger after me, I'm glad they sent one who could cook. I believe I've gained weight on this trip."

Bowdrie built his fire of dry wood to eliminate smoke. Earlier, crossing the plains, he had killed an antelope. Now he cut steaks and began to broil them. He knew better than to relax.

"Always keepin' an eye out, aren't you?" Starr said. "I see you're pretty handy with a gun, too. You'll have to be if you ever tangle with Doc or Joslin.

"That Ernie's a pretty hand himself, you know. I had an idea he might try to cut me down someday. He wanted to boss the outfit himself, but he's too bloody.

"Between the two of us, it was Doc an' Joslin who did the

killin'. I led them to that bank and I wanted the money, but I never figured on no killin'."

"Then why don't you give the Marsden kid a clean bill, Curly? He's young enough, an' he might turn into a pretty decent man."

"Or he might turn into a country lawyer." Starr glanced at him. "That pretty sister of his must have sold you a bill of goods."

A quail called out in the tall grass beyond the cottonwoods. There was a shade of difference in Starr's tone when he added, "She seemed like a mighty fine girl, at that."

Bowdrie was squatted beside the fire. His ear caught the change in Starr's tone. It had come right after that quail called. He pushed the coffeepot against the glowing sticks, pushed others closer.

He glanced around casually. Starr was sitting up more and he had drawn one foot back so the knee was bent and the foot was flat on the ground. His hands, still in the cuffs, lay loosely on his right side. At an instant's warning he could roll over and make a run for it.

Bowdrie's mind raced. His rifle was twenty feet away, leaning against the wall of the adobe cabin. He was between it and Starr. Starr's best bet if Bowdrie was attacked was to run for the shelter of the cottonwoods, climb a horse, and get out of there. As for himself, he would never make the cabin. He would have to fight it out right here, behind that log.

There was no sound but the bubble of coffee in the pot. He tossed Starr a cup. "Here!" he said.

Curly grabbed it but his eyes sparked. Bowdrie knew where they would be, among the cottonwoods. The toss of the cup had put Curly off guard, but for the moment only.

Curly had but one thing to do. To get away. Bowdrie had to both keep his prisoner and fight off three gunmen.

Bowdrie heard a rustle among the leaves and he turned, drawing as he wheeled. He fired into the brush from which the movement came, and as he fired Starr dropped his cup and lunged to his feet. Bowdrie had anticipated the move and he swung back and down with the barrel of his pistol, stretching Starr unconscious beside the fire.

Bowdrie dropped behind the log and snapped a quick shot at a stab of flame from the brush. Rolling over, he crawled the length of the log, getting closer to the doorway and his rifle.

"Hold it, Bowdrie!" a voice called. "Turn Starr loose an' you can ride off!"

It was the moment he wanted, for they would be listening for his reply and not poised to shoot. With a lunge he was through the door and inside the adobe house. Two bullets struck the doorjamb as he went through.

"You boys come in with your hands up," he called, "and I'll see you get a fair trial!"

"You're a fool!" somebody grumbled. "You haven't a chance. We'll burn you out!"

"Anytime you're ready!"

The fire was blazing brightly and to approach the cabin they must make a frontal attack. He reached around the doorpost and got his Winchester.

In the corner of the adobe was a huge pile of sticks, part of it a pack rat's nest, part of it wood for the fireplace, left by nameless travelers. Taking up one of the sticks, he tossed it into the fire. As the fire blazed up, he detected a slight movement from Curly Starr.

"Curly," he spoke loud enough for the outlaw to hear, "don't make any sudden moves. If you try to escape, I'll kill you. I don't want to, so don't push your luck."

He waited, and all was still. Nobody wanted to rush him as long as the fire was burning brightly. He threw another stick into the fire. In the next half-hour three of the five sticks he threw landed in the fire. Yet it was a long time until morning.

Starr had witnessed the brief battle with the Indians and had no idea of taking the risk. He reached for the coffeepot, snared it and a cup, and calmly filled the cup.

"Thanks, Bowdrie. All the comforts of home!"

"I should have hit you harder," Chick replied cheerfully. "You've a thick skull."

"You hit me hard enough. My head feels all lopsided. Why don't you be smart and turn me loose?"

"They'd kill you," Chick said.

"Kill *me*? Are you crazy?"

Although the outlaws could hear him talking, they would not be able to distinguish the words.

"When the shootin' was goin' on, one of the bullets was aimed for you. Missed by mighty little."

"You're lyin'! Doc an' Tobe are my friends!"

"What about Joslin?"

Curly Starr was silent.

After a while he threw another stick into the fire and somebody shot at him, but the bullet was high. Later, he glimpsed the flickering light from a fire back in the trees, sixty or seventy yards away.

Starr spoke suddenly. "Did you mean that? About the shot?"

"It hit the log right over you, and couldn't have been aimed at me."

Bowdrie waited, studying the fire. He could barely see it flickering but decided to take a chance. Lifting his rifle, he fired three quick shots. He was shooting through underbrush, which might deflect a bullet, but at least one shot got through. Sparks shot up from the fire and somebody swore.

Later, he must have dozed, because he awakened with a start. Undoubtedly the outlaws were waiting until morning, not relishing an attack past the firelight.

Bowdrie crawled to the hole where the spring was. The old gourd dipper was probably dusty, but . . . He dipped up water and poured some over his head, then dipped again and drank.

The spring was right outside the wall, but the first resident or someone later had removed adobe bricks so the spring could be reached without going outside in case of an Indian attack. Suddenly Bowdrie got out his knife and began digging at a brick beside the hole. Carefully he removed several of the crumbling adobe bricks. Then he tossed a couple of sticks on the fire.

Returning, he slipped through the hole and flattened against the rock wall beyond the spring. He waited, but nothing moved.

Placing each foot with care, he moved away from the house. By the time he was close to the fire the sky was growing gray. One man was asleep, the other was placing fuel under the coffeepot. He was about to step out when the sleeping man opened his eyes and got to his feet suddenly. His eyes focused on Bowdrie, realization hit him, and he gave a startled yip and went for his gun. Bowdrie fired, but the man was weaving and his bullet missed.

A bullet whipped past his face, another hit his holster, half-turning him with its force. He fired again and Doc Bentley fell back against a tree.

Bowdrie swung his gun to Tobe, who, startled by Doc's surprised move, had shot too fast. Bowdrie's bullet caught Tobe Storey in the middle of the stomach and he stepped back and sat down. He started to lift his gun but could not. He fell sidewise and lay on his shoulder against the ground.

Bowdrie swung on Doc but the gunman lifted a shaky left hand. "Don't shoot! I've had it."

"Throw your gun over here. With your left hand."

The gun landed at his feet. "Where's Joslin?"

Doc made a feeble gesture with his left hand and, thumbing shells into his right-hand gun, Bowdrie ran into the woods. Suddenly he heard an outburst of firing at the cabin.

Ducking through the woods, he ran up to the fire. Ernie Joslin was standing over the fire. He was unsteady on his feet but he held a gun.

He turned toward Bowdrie, lifting his gun. Bowdrie fired. Joslin stood for an instant, then fell flat, all in one piece. Bowdrie walked over to him and kicked the gun from his hand.

Joslin was staring at him, his face against the ashes and earth. "If I'd known who you was there at first—"

"I knew who you were. I knew you by the cigarette. You threw it away too late. You said you'd never been south of Wichita, but folks around Deadwood don't smoke cigarettes. It's a Mexican habit, although it's workin' its way north, I expect. Men up Dakota, Montana way smoke cigars. Up north they think cigarettes are kind of ladylike."

He turned to Starr. "Take off . . . take off these damned cuffs," Starr pleaded. "I don't want to die with 'em on."

Starr coughed, and when the coughing was over and the cuffs were off, he asked, "You got him?"

"One of us did."

Folding his coat, he placed it under the head of the dying man. Then he opened Starr's shirt. There was nothing he could do.

"Got to your pack. Seen where you put my guns. I was figurin' on a break when Joslin come for me. He killed those men back yonder. Him an' Doc. I never went for killin' m'self. Joslin, he was a bad one. I knowed he didn't like me much, but . . ."

For a long time he was silent and then he whispered, "You write it. The boy . . . You say Bill Cross is gone. Dead. Buried. Put . . . it down."

Billy Marsden was not in my outfit. The man named Bill Cross was badly wounded and we buried him in the hills. The killing was done by Ernie Joslin and Doc Bentley. This is my dying statement.

Bowdrie wrote it, then read it to him. "Good!" He waited, gathering strength, then he signed his name. "You . . . you keep that kid . . . straight."

Bowdrie put wood on the fire. A glance at Joslin told him the man was gone. He hesitated to leave Starr, but he went back through the patch of woods.

As he came through the woods, he heard a shot. He hesitated, then went on. Tobe Storey lay where he had fallen.

Doc Bentley lay nearby. His right hand was horribly mangled from a bullet. He had taken Tobe's gun and shot himself.

"Maybe it's better than hangin'," Bowdrie said aloud; then, gathering up the weapons, he walked back to Starr.

"Joslin never liked me." Starr had wiped the blood from his face and had pulled himself into a sitting position. "Figured to have all that bank loot for himself. It's cached under a flat rock at Granite Spring."

He lay quite awhile, then said, "That Marsden girl? Sure pretty, wasn't she?" His voice trailed off and then he said,

"Chick? Bury my saddle with me, will you? Might have some mean broncs where I'm goin'. Man feels the need of . . . of his own . . . saddle."

"Want your boots off?"

There was a flicker of a smile on Curly's lips. "Lived with 'em on. I'll die with 'em, only don't cache me with him. Not with Joslin."

Bowdrie went for the horses and brought them in, and loaded them with the weapons of the fallen men. Suddenly he heard Starr choking and ran to him. He had thrown out a hand and was gripping the horn of his saddle as it lay on the ground.

"They got me, kid! Bowdrie . . . I'm pullin' leather!"

Bowdrie dropped beside him and put a hand on Starr's shoulder. His hand had been there for several minutes before he realized the man was dead.

In the cool of the morning with the sun on his shoulders, Chick Bowdrie headed south and east, carrying in his thoughts the memory of a man who died game, and in his pocket another man's chance for a new life.

TOO TOUGH TO BRAND

H E RODE INTO the ranch yard at sundown, and the big man standing in the door lifted a hand. " 'Light an' set! You come far?"

"Fort Griffin. How's for some grub?"

Two men lounged on the steps of the bunkhouse, both studying him with interest. "This is the O Bar O, isn't it?"

The man came down the steps. He was unshaved, and his lips were thin and cruel. Chick Bowdrie tried to keep his thinking unclouded, but this was a man it would be hard to like. "Are you the Ranger?"

"I am. Name of Chick Bowdrie."

"Heard of you. Figured you'd be an older feller."

"I'm old enough." Bowdrie was irritated. "Lead me to some grub an' tell me what happened."

"My name is Lee Karns," the big man said when they were seated. "I own this outfit. My foreman was Bert Ramey and he took off for town to bank money for a cattle sale. He skipped with it. It was fifteen thousand dollars."

A girl with a lonely, frightened face brought coffee to the table. She was a pretty girl, but now her cheeks were tearstained. He looked away hurriedly, not to make her self-conscious.

"Was all that money yours?" Chick glanced casually around the room. It was painfully neat. The dishes were clean, yet Karns himself was an untidy man.

"It was mine. Ramey had been with me six years, a steady, all-around man."

The door opened and a tall, slender young man came in. He was flashily dressed, but there was nothing dressy about the well-worn Colts in his holsters.

Karns indicated him. "Mark DeGrasse, my new foreman. This here's Chick Bowdrie, Mark."

DeGrasse threw Bowdrie a quick glance. It was the glance of a man sizing up a rival, and with inner excitement and a flick of warning in his brain, Chick realized this was one of those gunmen who can brook no rivals, a man who must always be top dog. He had met such men before, and they were dangerous.

DeGrasse dropped into a place at the table. He glanced at the girl. "You'd better eat. It won't bring your father back if you starve yourself."

Bowdrie glanced inquiringly at Karns, and the rancher said, "This is Karen Ramey, Bert's daughter. She's upset over what happened."

"How long has he been gone?" Bowdrie hated to continue with questions when Karen was unhappy, but he must have answers.

"Week. It's only a day's ride into Comanche. Bert went alone. We'd no reason to expect trouble, as nobody knowed he was carryin' money. When he never came back, we rode into town and found he'd never even gotten there. Looks like he just hightailed it out of the country."

"It isn't likely that he'd go off and leave his daughter!"

"That's just it," Karns said. "She ain't his daughter. She's just a girl his wife took in to raise, an' after his wife died, he was saddled with her."

Karen Ramey looked up resentfully. "He didn't think of me as a burden, and I thought of him as my own father! I'll never believe he ran off! I think he was murdered! *Somebody* knew he had that money!"

"There, there, honey!" Karns reached a hand for hers. "Don't fret none. You'll be took care of."

She sprang to her feet, eyes blazing. "I can take care of myself, thank you! I'll go into Comanche and get a job! Or . . ."—her eyes turned on DeGrasse—"I'll go to El Paso!"

The foreman's lips tightened. There was nothing pleasant in the way in which he looked at her. Bowdrie sipped his coffee and listened. There was something under the surface here, something strange going on. Why had DeGrasse reacted so oddly to Karen's reference to El Paso?

Turning abruptly, she went through a door into what was apparently her room, and for a time the men ate in silence.

"Can't blame her, bein' upset," Karns said smoothly. "Matter of fact, she can stay right here. She's a fine-lookin' girl, and a man could go a long ways to find a better wife."

Mark DeGrasse stared at Karns with thinly veiled contempt.

"Did anybody else know he was to be carryin' money?" Bowdrie asked.

"Al did, I suppose," DeGrasse said. "He's one of the punchers, and he was outside when Lee brought the saddlebags to Bert before he left for Comanche."

After further questioning, Karns and DeGrasse sat on the steps and talked in low tones. Chick loafed about, his eyes missing nothing. There was every evidence the ranch was in good shape, to judge by the area around the house. Judging by Karns's appearance, Bowdrie was willing to bet the condition of the place was due to Ramey.

The hands seemed to have liked Ramey, but they were not inclined to talk. Not even Al Conway, a hard-faced cowhand with a lean jaw and irritable eyes. Not until Bowdrie mentioned marriage between Karns and the girl.

Al spat disgustedly into the dirt. "If she was to marry anybody, it would be that snake in DeGrasse!"

One of the hands chuckled at the pun, but added, "Better keep your voice down, Al. You ain't the hand to buck him with a gun, and he's touchy, mighty touchy!"

"I ain't afraid of him." Al spoke coolly, and while Bowdrie doubted that Al was afraid, he also doubted that Conway wanted to tangle with DeGrasse.

Chick dropped his blanket roll near some cottonwoods not far from the house. He had no love for sleeping inside and wanted his horse near him. There was something about lying under the stars that was conducive to thought, and he had some thinking to do.

Bert Ramey was missing with fifteen thousand dollars, yet everything seemed to indicate he was not a man to steal. The fact remained that he was missing. Lee Karns, on the other hand, acted oddly in some respects, but that could be due to a good many things. There were undercurrents here that disturbed him.

Al Conway was a character to be considered as well. Obviously he was smoldering with resentment, the reason for which was not plain. If Ramey had been murdered, he left behind strange tensions on the O Bar O that stemmed from an unknown source. Perhaps they tied in with his disappearance, perhaps not.

It was very late and he must have just fallen asleep when movement awakened him. He glimpsed the girl standing in the shadows close by. "I have to talk to you!" she whispered.

"Anybody see you leave the house?"

"No, I am sure they did not. Oh, Mr. Bowdrie, I am sure my father didn't run off. He was such a good man! And there's something wrong here. Something terribly wrong!"

"Tell me about it," he whispered.

"It may have no connection, but a few days ago Father said he wanted to get me away from here, that something was going on behind his back. He said cattle were disappearing, that a good many had vanished while he was gone with the herd."

"Ramey sold the cattle? Who collected the money?"

"Father did. He took the drive to Julesberg, collected the money, and returned. Some of the money should have been his, too."

"How was that? What do you mean?"

"Karns never paid Father very much. The bank was after Karns for money, as all the stock was mortgaged to them, and he kept telling Dad he would pay him when the cattle were sold. Karns owed Father more than a thousand dollars, and he owed the bank a lot, because they loaned him the money to stock the ranch."

That altered the situation. Karns owed both his foreman and the bank, so if the money vanished, he could pay neither of them. From his standpoint that did not make sense, as he would then lose the ranch to the bank. Whatever happened, it did not seem likely that Karns was himself involved.

Nor did it make sense that Ramey, if he had that money as far away as Julesberg, would then bring it all the way back here before stealing it.

For an hour he questioned Karen, and long after she returned to her room he lay awake considering all aspects of the case.

Yet the following afternoon when he trotted the roan down the street of Comanche, he was no nearer a solution. The loss of fifteen thousand dollars, a very considerable sum, as well as the disappearance of a ranch foreman, was sure to be discussed in town, and the easiest way to learn was to listen and keep his mouth shut.

By midnight when he stretched out on his bed in his hotel room, Chick Bowdrie had learned a few things.

Lee Karns had mortgaged his stock and his headquarters land to the bank for seven thousand dollars, to be paid when the cattle were sold. The main reason the bank had loaned the money to him was because Bert Ramey was foreman. Bert was a known and respected stockman, and Ramey's last report had been that the increase had been a shade better than normal. Nobody wanted to believe Bert Ramey was a thief, yet many believed there was no alternative. Others, frankly skeptical, were waiting until all the evidence was in.

One definite lead had come from a big whiskery cowhand. He had recognized Chick and commented in a low tone, "Seen you over to Uvalde a couple of times. This here ain't none of my affair, but if I was huntin' Ramey, I'd ride up to the Canadian River country an' look up a brand called the Spectacles."

"Why that outfit?"

The puncher shrugged. "I don't know from nothin', only Ramey heard I'd ridden for an outfit up that way and he was curious about that Spectacle brand. A gent named Lessinger had owned it, but he sold out and went east."

Crossing the street to the hotel, Bowdrie saw DeGrasse standing on the steps of the saloon.

"Howdy!" The foreman smiled through a cloud of cigarette smoke. "Solved the crime yet?"

"Just sort of sashayin' about listenin' to folks. Tomorrow

will be soon enough. I guess Ramey's got clean out of the country. Wonder what he was plannin' on? Buyin' his own place, maybe? I hear he was interested in the Canadian River country."

DeGrasse stiffened sharply, and the smile left his face. "I wouldn't know about that," he replied. "We never talked much."

"He didn't like you around Karen, though, did he?" Bowdrie slipped the question into the conversation like a knife.

The gunman turned, flicking his cigarette into the dust. "That doesn't concern you, Ranger! You get on with your lawin' an' don't go nosin' into things that don't concern you. It was Lee Karns he had trouble with over Karen, not me. You just keep your nose out of my business!"

Bowdrie shrugged. "You may be right. I'll just look around a little."

As he turned away, obviously sidestepping a fight, he caught the hard triumph showing in the gunman's eyes. DeGrasse had him pegged as a four-flusher who would back down in a pinch.

As he stepped through the door of the hotel, Bowdrie glanced back. DeGrasse had disappeared, probably into the saloon, but he saw something else. A man stepped from the shadows near the saloon, and Bowdrie recognized him as Al Conway.

Later, Chick went to the telegraph office and sent two wires, then returned to the hotel and to bed. His needling of DeGrasse had brought out two facts. Mark knew something about the Spectacle Ranch on the Canadian, and there had been trouble with Ramey about Karen.

The Spectacle brand offered interesting possibilities, and a vague theory was beginning to take shape in Bowdrie's thinking. As yet it lacked any basis of probability, and the theory had a major flaw. What had become of Bert Ramey?

No crime could be proved without evidence, and the facts indicated Bert Ramey was the thief, yet evidence can be misleading. Ramey was gone, and the fifteen thousand dollars was gone. Bowdrie must find Ramey and the money. If Ramey did not have it, what about Lee Karns? Mark DeGrasse? And where did Al Conway fit in?

There were cattle missing, so there must be organized rustling, and a man who would steal cattle would steal money resulting from their sale.

Daylight found him on the return trip, but now he was riding warily and looking for a horse trail that would lead off across the sagebrush country. When another day was almost gone, he found what he was looking for.

He knew the trail at once, for he had taken the precaution of checking at the blacksmith shop in Comanche, learning that nearly all O Bar O horses were shod there. In most cases horses were shod right on the ranch, but the O Bar O had theirs shod in Comanche. Bowdrie had even found a set of shoes that had been recently removed from Ramey's horse. The smith had indicated the shoes with his hammer. "Always liked his horses well-shod, Mr. Ramey did. He knew my work and figured the little extry it cost was worth it." So Bowdrie knew Ramey's tracks when he saw them.

When it grew too dark to follow further, Bowdrie rode off the trail and made camp. He was on the verge of sleep when the idea came to him, and he believed he knew why Bert Ramey had left the trail.

Awakening before day broke, Bowdrie hastily built a fire, for the morning was chill. While waiting for the coffee, he considered what he knew and suspected, yet trying to view all the facts objectively and trying to avoid jumping to conclusions.

The trail Ramey had taken would lead him toward the Canadian. Had Ramey stolen the money so he could buy a ranch?

Supposing, however, that Ramey was honest, and that from that high point on the trail he had observed a distant moving herd of cattle? The O Bar O had been losing cattle, and Ramey as its foreman would be inclined to investigate any such movements.

The sound of a moving horse brought him to his feet. It was Karen Ramey, riding a gray gelding.

"Trailin' somebody?" he asked as he stepped into view.

"Yes, I am! You may think my father is a thief, but I do not.

He wouldn't run off and leave me on that ranch! He knew I hated Lee Karns and was afraid of Mark DeGrasse!"

"Maybe we should work together," Bowdrie suggested. "Wait until I throw my gear together." He started to turn away, then looked back. "Karen, you said something to Mark about El Paso. What did that mean?"

"It may be nothing at all, yet he talked to Karns about El Paso, and they were so secretive, I was curious."

"You made a good guess, I'm thinking. You wait here until I get my horse."

Striding swiftly through the piñons, he rolled up his bed and thrust it under his arm. He was kicking dust over the fire when a voice warned him: "Make a wrong move and I'll kill you!"

It was a man's voice, low and behind him. Chick was facing toward where Karen waited, so the man might have been lying in wait as he talked to her.

"What do you want?" Bowdrie started to turn.

"Hold it!" The hoarse whisper froze Bowdrie in place. "Ranger, you're buttin' your nose into things that don't concern you. I'm tellin' you now, light out of here an' keep goin'. Another sun sets on you here, an' you die!"

"You know I'm not goin'," Bowdrie replied quietly, "and if you kill me, there'll be others in my place."

There was no reply. He waited just an instant, then dodged into the brush from which the voice came. He found himself in a nest of boulders and more piñons. The man had disappeared.

He started away, disgusted. Then, on the ground near a boulder, he saw a small black book. It was a tally book such as many cattlemen carry to keep a tally of brands and cattle. Flipping over the front pages, he glanced at the owner's name. It was there, plainly seen: "BERT RAMEY. *O Bar O, Comanche.*"

"You were gone a long time," Karen said.

He held the book out to her. "Have you ever seen that before?"

"Why, that's Father's tally book! Where did you get it?"

"Found it." He turned his horse down trail. "Let's go,

shall we?" When the horses had walked a few steps, he glanced around at her. "Did you see anybody back there? Or hear anything?"

She shook her head, eyes curious. Bowrie scowled irritably and looked along the trail that wound down into the flats, leaving the piñon behind. The tracks of Ramey's horse, old tracks, were plain in the dust.

What of the voice from the rocks? The dropped tally book? Suppose Ramey had stolen the money and was hiding nearby? Would the tracks they followed lead them into a trap?

Chick studied the trail, lifting his eyes from time to time to scan the horizon and the country about them. Despite himself, he was growing prejudiced in favor of Ramey. This was a nice, decent girl, and she obviously loved the man. He had cared for her when his wife died, and before. He was a respected cattleman, trusted by the bank, liked by people until his disappearance. "I figure," he said aloud, "that he left the trail to check the movement of cattle."

"What did you say?"

He flushed. "Sorry, ma'am. When a man's much alone, he gets to talkin' to himself."

She glanced at him curiously. "You have no family?"

"No, ma'am. Comanches killed my folks when I was a youngster. I got nobody, nowhere." He paused. "Except the Rangers. They taken me on when I was about to take myself down the wrong trail."

"You must have a girlfriend."

"No, ma'am. Ranger work keeps me on the move. I've known a few ladies, but I guess I'm not their type. An' I don't have nothin' but a horse, a saddle, and a few guns. Ain't much on which to court a woman, especially when a man can end his days with a bullet in his hide."

"You're very good-looking."

Bowdrie blushed. He had to change the subject. He never had known what to say to a girl, and as for being good-looking, she was teasing him.

"No, ma'am, I'm just a *ree*formed cowhand, and no hand with women. Never could read their sign. This here's my life, ma'am, ridin' a trail through a big empty country with Injuns or outlaws around."

The horseman they followed had ridden at a fast canter, heading directly across the open country toward a deep cut in the hills. Sometime later, leading the way, Bowdrie rode up to the deep cut. The ground here was chewed up by the hooves of cattle driven through the cut a few days before.

She saw the tracks, too. "What do you think happened?" he asked.

"I think my father was murdered."

"Why?"

"I don't know. It is just a feeling I have. If he could have come back, he would have, long before this." She lifted her chin defiantly. "He loved me like he was my own father. I doubt if he ever thought of me as anything but his daughter. I know that when he got his money from Karns he was quitting. He told me so."

Chick let the roan move forward, taking his time. He drew up suddenly when crossing a bench. At the edge the earth had caved away, and when he looked to the ridge crest ahead, he saw a low, thick, gnarled juniper. An easy place for someone to wait with a rifle until a man rode through the cut. The distance was an easy rifle shot, not quite two hundred yards, and if the first shot missed, there was no place for the target-rider to go. He would be right out in the open, as Chick and Karen were now.

Leaving his horse, he went up to the juniper. Looking back, he saw Karen had her rifle in her hands.

There were the prints of boots, some cigarette butts. They had known Ramey was following. Perhaps they had intended that he should. They had not waited long, just long enough for the rifleman to smoke two cigarettes. Perhaps they had known Ramey was coming this way and had deliberately let him see the cattle.

Slowly he walked back to his horse, stood there for a moment, and then walked to the edge of the bench where the earth had caved in.

Karen had followed, and she was looking down. "Karen,"

he said gently, "you'd better go back to the horse. Remember him as he was. That's the way he'd want it to be."

Without a word she walked back to her horse. He waited a moment; then with his hands he moved some of the earth and rocks until he had exposed the face of a man whom he knew by description as Bert Ramey. He had been shot twice, at close range, by a rifle.

When he climbed back to the bench, he carried Ramey's pistol, a Winchester, and several letters. There was a small packet of bills and some change.

He handed it to her, but when she drew her hand away, he said, "Don't be foolish, Karen. You will need money, and who is more entitled to it? Consider it a gift from him. That's what he would want.

"As for the guns, I'll keep them for now. They are evidence. And I shall want to read these letters and study that tally book."

He stuffed the letters into his saddlebags and hung the gunbelt over his pommel. The Winchester he slipped under the binding on his blanket roll, drawing the knots a little tighter.

Who was the killer? *Who?*

"Mr. Bowdrie? Somebody is coming."

So intent on the problem had he been that although the sound registered, he had not been alerted. Yet Karen's rifle was ready.

The horseman rounded into view, then pulled up. It was Al Conway.

"Howdy! I didn't expect to see you here."

Chick's eyes went to the O Bar O brand on the black's hip. His eyes held on Conway's. "I found Ramey," he said. "He's been murdered."

Conway got out the makings and rolled a smoke. "Figured so," he said bluntly. "Ramey was no thief."

Digging into his pocket, he drew out two telegrams. "These are for you. I judged you'd like to see them before they fell into the wrong hands."

"Meaning?"

"Whatever you like. It was just an idea I had."

Bowdrie ripped open the messages, glanced at each, and then looked up at Conway. "You want to do something for me, Al?" He hesitated, thinking. "Ride back to the ranch and tell Karns that DeGrasse has bought him a ranch and registered a brand in his name alone."

Conway shrugged. "You know what you're doin', but I'm sure glad DeGrasse is in Comanche. I ain't up to a shoot-out with him. He's tellin' it all over the country that he backed down the famous Chick Bowdrie, that you're all bluff."

Bowdrie looked after Conway, his eyes cold with speculation. Conway had been on the scene almost too suddenly, and how had he found them? Had they been followed? Or had Conway come to cover the scene of the crime more thoroughly?

"You found Father . . ." Karen said. "Are you going to leave him there?"

"Nothing will bother him, ma'am. He never knew what hit him. Later, if you like, we can send a wagon for him."

Comanche was shadowed by late dusk when they fast-walked their horses down the street. Bowdrie sent the girl to the hotel and then took a stance across the street from the saloon when he saw Mark DeGrasse was inside.

He was worried by a vague impression of something overlooked, of some mistake or error in his calculations.

It was almost midnight when Mark DeGrasse left the saloon and went to the hotel.

Bowdrie sighed with relief. Had DeGrasse mounted and headed for the ranch, Bowdrie would have had to follow. Suddenly a vague thought that had lingered in his mind became stark and clear. He came to his feet and went down the street to the blacksmith shop. All was dark and still, the shop like an empty cavern.

There was a pile of old horseshoes. . . . He crossed to it, then knelt and began to strike matches. A footstep behind him sent a prickly chill up his spine.

"Hey!" It was the blacksmith. "What're you doin' here?"

Bowdrie straightened. "Have you got a lantern? I want to check something."

Grumbling, the blacksmith went into his home, adjoining the shop, and returned with a lantern.

"You told me which of the old shoes had belonged to Ramey's horse. Do you know any of the others in this pile?"

"There ain't a shoe I ever put on or took off that I don't remember."

"Good!" Chick placed a pair of worn shoes on the ground near the pile. "Who owned these?"

The shoes showed much hard travel, yet on each arm of the shoe was an arrow-shaped design.

The blacksmith picked up one of the shoes. "That's the first pair of shoes I replaced for Lee Karns. Right after he come into this country an' bought that ranch. That arrowhead's the mark Indian Joe Davis puts on his work. He's the blacksmith over at Monahan."

Bowdrie turned away. "Thanks. You've been a help, and I appreciate it."

When Chick Bowdrie walked into the hotel dining room for breakfast the next morning, his dark features seemed sharper, his eyes restless. Scarcely had he seated himself when he was joined by Karen.

"I saw Mark DeGrasse last night. I saw him in the hallway."

"Did he see you?"

"I'm sure he didn't. When I heard his step, I thought it might be you, with something to tell me, but I drew back and closed the door. Mr. Bowdrie? What's going to happen? This morning, I mean?"

Before he could reply, Al Conway entered and walked directly to their table. "Karns came into town early, Bowdrie. We met on the trail this side of the ranch."

"What did he say?"

"Not much, just glanced my way and mentioned some work that needed to be done. Soon as he was out of sight, I circled into the hills and came into town myself."

Conway turned his hat in his hand. "Bowdrie, I don't want you to come up with the wrong idea. I never killed Bert Ramey. He was a good man. One of the best."

"I know you didn't, Al. Although for a while I wasn't sure.

You've rustled a few head of stock here and there, Al, and if I were you I'd keep my rope on my saddle and get rid of that cinch ring. It shows too much evidence of bein' used in a fire."

"Thanks." Al hesitated. "But can I help? This here DeGrasse . . ."

"What about DeGrasse?" The gunman had walked up behind him. "What were you about to say, Al?"

"He was about to say," Bowdrie interrupted, "that you were a bad man with a gun, Mark. Won't you sit down?"

DeGrasse simply stared at him, contempt in his eyes. "You'd better," Bowdrie said, "because you're in this up to your neck."

DeGrasse shrugged carelessly. "D'you think I killed Ramey, is that it?"

"Sit down!" Bowdrie's voice boomed in the small room. "Sit down, Mark!"

Chick Bowdrie had a gun in his hand, and it had not been there a moment before. Mark's tongue touched his suddenly dry lips.

Mark eased into a chair, keeping his hands in sight. "You registered a brand in El Paso, the Spectacle brand. It was registered in your name. You moved cattle off the range here up to your ranch on the Canadian."

DeGrasse touched his tongue to his again dry lips. The pistol appearing from nowhere had destroyed his poise. He realized suddenly that he had no business touching a gun in the presence of Chick Bowdrie.

"That was for Karns. We did it together."

"But the brand was registered in your name only. And it is mighty easy to change an O Bar O to a Spectacle. Are you implying Karns would steal his own cattle?"

The door opened gently, and Bowdrie looked up into the eyes of Lee Karns. "I see you got him, Bowdrie. DeGrasse was plannin' to steal my ranch. He's been rustlin' my cows, and I never even guessed!"

His eyes turned to DeGrasse. "Where's the money you stole? I found the sack it was carried in . . . in your bunk!"

DeGrasse lunged to his feet. "You lie! I stole no . . . !"

He made a stab for his gun—too late!

Lee Karns had a gun in his hand, and he fired, then again. DeGrasse sank at the knees, tried to straighten up, his hand working to draw the gun that was suddenly too heavy. Then he fell to the floor, his lips struggling with words that refused to come.

There was an instant of silence and then Lee Karns looked over at Bowdrie. "There's your killer an' your case, all wrapped up."

Chick Bowdrie had sat very still; now he got to his feet. "Conway? Take Miss Ramey out of the room, will you?"

Bowdrie picked up his flat-brimmed, low-crowned hat and put it on. "You're right, Lee. My case is all wrapped up. I am arrestin' you for the murder of Bert Ramey, for conspiracy to defraud, and for the killin' of Ranger Tomkins in the robbing of the Valverde Bank."

"Are you crazy?" Karns protested. "What's this nonsense about Valverde?"

Chick faced Karns across the table, his left side toward him. Karns still held his gun in his hand, and the range was point-blank.

"You framed DeGrasse. You planted that money bag, expectin' me to find it. You had him register that brand, knowing it would be additional evidence, and all the while you were plannin' to gyp the bank of their money.

"You owed the bank money and you owed Ramey money, so you stole the fifteen thousand and murdered Ramey. The bank could go ahead an' foreclose, because you had already rustled your own stock and moved it to the Spectacle, on the Canadian.

"You intended me to find that Mark had registered the Spectacle, but you'd already registered it yourself, in Tascosa. I checked both places by telegraph.

"I still didn't have you pegged until I recalled a horseshoe I'd seen at the blacksmith shop. Then this whole rotten deal cleared up. It was the same deal you tried to work six years ago in Dimmit County. That went sour on you, so when you pulled out, you robbed the Valverde Bank and killed Tomkins."

Lee Karns held his gun on Bowdrie. "I killed one Ranger, and I can kill another!" he shouted.

Bowdrie had never holstered his own gun, holding it at his side away from Karns. As Karns spoke, Bowdrie lunged hard against the table, throwing Karns off balance. As Karns caught himself and straightened up, gun lifting, Chick Bowdrie shot him.

Karns stood still against the wall, staring at him. "I had it made," he said. "I was winning."

"You never had a chance, Karns," Bowdrie said. "You hurt too many people, an' you left too many tracks."

Karns slid slowly down the wall, leaving a bloody streak behind him.

Bowdrie ejected a shell, then reloaded the chamber. He dropped the pistol into its holster.

Karen came running into the room. "Are you all right, Chick? Are you hurt?"

"I'm all right. Let's get out of here!"

Seated in the sunlight in front of the hotel, Bowdrie slowly let the tension ease from his muscles. He closed his eyes for a minute.

"You've got some money comin'," he said to Karen. "We'll sell those cattle an' you'll get what you have comin'. Your pa was a good man."

He opened his eyes and leaned forward, resting his forearms on his knees. "I'd move away from here, if I were you," he suggested. "Go to San Antone or somewhere. This country is hard on women."

"I thought I'd buy some cattle and start ranching on my own. If I could—"

"Get Al Conway to help. He's rustled a few head, but he's really an honest man, and he wouldn't cheat a woman. Al could do it.

"Me," he added, "I never learned to live with folks. Most youngsters learn to live with people by playin' with other youngsters. I never had any of that. I never really belonged anywhere. I was a stranger among the Comanches an' a stranger among my own people when I got back. I never belonged anywhere. I'm like that no-account horse of mine.

"Look at him. He's got him a mean, contrary disposition, he spends his time lazin' around at that hitch rail, just layin' for a chance to kick the daylights out of you.

"He'll bite, too, given the chance. Just look at him! He's ugly as sin! Ugly inside an' out, but you know something? He can outrun a jackrabbit, and once started, he'll go all day an' all night.

"He can get fat on grass burs an' prickly pear, an' some other cowhand's saddle is frosted cake to him. He'd climb a tree if he wanted to or if you aimed him at it, and he could swim the Pacific if he was of a mind to. He doesn't like anybody, but he's game, an' nothin' this side of hell could whip him. He's my kind of horse."

Bowdrie got to his feet. "That Conway, ma'am? He's a good man. He'll build you a good ranch, given time, an' a nice girl like you could gentle him down to quite a man."

Later, with a few dusty miles behind him, Bowdrie commented, "That there's a fine girl. Horse, you reckon you an' me will ever settle down?"

The hammerheaded roan blew his disgust through his nostrils and pricked his ears. He, too, was looking toward the horizon.

CASE CLOSED—NO PRISONERS

O N THE THIRD day after the robbery, Sheriff Walt Borrow gave up and wired Austin. On the fifth day, late in the afternoon, a rider swung down at the hitch-rail in front of the saloon. Leaving the roan standing three-legged at the rail, he passed the saloon and went into the sheriff's office next door.

The rider was a young man, lean, and broad in the shoulders. Watchers glimpsed a hard brown face, wide at the cheekbones, a firm straight mouth, and a strong jaw. But it was the rider's eyes that stopped those who saw him face-on. They were intensely black, their gaze level and measuring. There was something about his eyes that made men uneasy, with a tendency to look quickly away.

"Looks like an Indian," Bishop commented. "Reminds me of Victorio, the Apache. I seen him once."

"I know him," Hardy Young said. "By sight, anyway. He's a Ranger from the Guadalupes."

Within the hour everybody within a radius of five miles knew that Ranger Chick Bowdrie was in town. What they did not know was that the saddle tramp who loafed in the Longhorn Saloon was Rip Coker, also a Texas Ranger.

Coker had drifted into town the day before, a grim, blond young man looking down-at-heel and broke. He let it be known that he was down to his last few dollars and ready for anything. With his horse for a stake he sat in a poker game and won enough for eating money. Most of the time he was just around, drinking a beer now and again and keeping his eyes and ears open.

The story of the robbery was being told around. Outlaws had hit the Bank of Kimble just before daylight to the tune of forty thousand dollars, and as Hardy Young commented to John Bishop, "That's a nice tune!"

Awakening as they did each morning, the townspeople had no idea what had taken place until Mary Phillips stopped Sheriff Borrow as he passed the Phillips home en route to breakfast and asked him to look for Josh.

"Ain't he to home, ma'am?" Borrow was mildly surprised. He had no idea that bankers got up so early.

"Somebody came to the door just before daylight and Josh answered it. He called back to me that he would be back in a minute, then he stepped out and I heard the door close. I dropped off to sleep and when I awakened he was still gone. That isn't like him."

Walt Borrow was undisturbed until he saw the bank's door ajar. Pushing it wider, he found Josh Phillips lying in a welter of gore, and the banker just managed to gasp out a few words before he died.

"Forced me!" he gasped, and lifted a hand horribly blackened by fire. "Threatened to burn . . . Mary, too!"

A question from Borrow elicited a few more words.

"Strangers! A . . . hawk . . ." His voice broke and he struggled for words. "Red!"

The town was enraged, but the rage was tempered by wonder, for there were no tracks, and nobody seemed to have seen anything. The outlaws had come and gone unseen, unheard. Only the body of Josh Phillips, the safe they forced him to open, and the forty thousand missing dollars proved their visit.

Stabling his horse in the livery stable an hour after his arrival, Bowdrie seemed not to notice the saddle tramp currying his horse in the next stall.

"Forty thousand was the most money the bank had in four months." Coker spoke softly. "How does that sound?"

"Like somebody was tipped off," Bowdrie agreed. "Keep your ears open."

John Bishop intercepted Bowdrie as he was entering the hotel with his saddlebags. Bishop was a tall young man with a crisp dark beard and an attractive smile.

"I led the posse that hunted for tracks," he said. "I'd be glad to help in any way."

"You found nothing?"

Bishop had a fine-featured but strong face. He looked like a man who knew what he wanted and how to get it. "Nothing I could swear to. There was some wind that night, and blown sand would make the tracks look older."

Bowdrie thanked him and went into the hotel. He wore a black flat-crowned, flat-brimmed hat, a black silk neckerchief, gray wool shirt, and black broadcloth trousers over hand-tooled boots with California spurs. His two guns were carried low and tied down, a style rarely seen. His eyes, as they slanted across the street, missed nothing.

Leaving his saddlebags in his room on the second floor, he returned to the lobby and passed through the connecting door into the restaurant adjoining. Only two tables were occupied, the nearest one by a man wearing a black suit, his hair plastered down on a round skull and parted carefully. His face was brick-red, his eyes a hard blue.

The girl who waited on Chick had red hair and a wide, friendly smile. She put down a cup of coffee in front of him.

"I always bring coffee to a rider," she said. "My pop taught me that."

"He must have been a wise man as well as an Irishman," Bowdrie said. "May I ask your name?"

"Ellen. And you are right about the Irish. My other name is Collins. My father was a sergeant in the cavalry."

A shadow loomed over the table. The big man in the black suit stood there, a napkin tucked under his chin, a cup of coffee in his hand.

"Howdy, suh! Mind if I join you?" Without waiting for a reply, he seated himself. "Name's Hardy Young. Cattle buyer. Ain't so young as I used to be, but just as hardy!"

He laughed loudly, then leaned over and whispered hoarsely, rolling his eyes from side to side as if to see who might be listening.

"Heard you was in town, suh! Frightful thing! Frightful! Always aim to help the law, that's what I say! Now, if there's anything you want looked into, you just ask Hardy Young! I know ever'body hereabouts!"

Bowdrie measured him for a cool half-minute before replying, and the hard blue eyes became uneasy. Hastily the man gulped a swallow of coffee.

"Thanks," Bowdrie replied. "This job will not take long."

Young stared, momentarily taken aback.

"None of them are very complicated," Bowdrie replied. "The ones planned so carefully are often the easiest. This case doesn't appear to be as difficult as many we get."

Hardy Young mopped his mustache with the back of his hand and sucked his teeth noisily. The blue eyes were round and astonished.

"That sounds like a Ranger!" he said. "It surely does!"

Bowdrie was irritated. He was nowhere near as confident as he sounded, but the man angered him. Yet he knew that once a job was complete, thieves were always somewhat worried. Had they been seen, after all? Had they forgotten some vital thing? In a robbery so carefully planned, the planner might have overlooked something. Hardy Young was obviously a busybody and a talkative man. If he repeated what Bowdrie had said, it might lead the thieves into some impulsive act.

If they acted suddenly, they might betray themselves, and without doubt they had a spy in the town. Somebody had informed them of the amount of money in the bank.

"Then you figure to close this case right up?"

Bowdrie shrugged. "No great rush. This is a nice little town and as soon as I report back to Austin they'll give me another job, maybe tougher than this.

"This case won't be tough. Their boss forgot one important item, and it will hang them all."

"*Hang* them?" Young looked startled.

"Phillips was killed, wasn't he? We'll hang them all—except," he added, "the man who gives us information. He'll get off easy."

Young clutched his knife and fork desperately. The food he had ordered brought to Bowdrie's table lay untouched before him.

He leaned forward. "There is such a man, then? You already know such a man?"

Purposely Bowdrie hesitated. "If there isn't," he said, "there will be. There's always one man who wants to dodge the noose."

After Young had left the table, Bowdrie lingered over his coffee. Something about the man disturbed him. At first he had believed him an irritating busybody; now he was not so sure.

Despite his comments to Young, Bowdrie had literally nothing upon which to work. Bishop had found no tracks, but as suggested, the wind might have wiped them out. Phillips's last words seem to imply the outlaws were strangers, and then there were his incomprehensible words about a "hawk . . . red."

The thieves had known when to strike and their clean escape seemed to indicate that they had covered the distance to their hideout under cover of darkness.

There seemed no answer to that, unless . . . It came to him with shocking suddenness. Unless they never left town at all!

Strangers, Phillips had said, and in a town the size of Kimble the banker would know everyone, and Sheriff Borrow had told him there were no strangers in town but the saddle tramp called Rip who had arrived after the robbery.

Ellen returned to his table with the coffeepot and sat down opposite him. "You should be careful," she warned. "Men who would rob a bank and torture a man as they did Mr. Phillips would stop at nothing."

"Thanks." He glanced at her thoughtfully. "You must see everything and hear everything in here. Have there been any strangers in town? They all come here to eat, don't they?"

"No, not all. But there was a man . . . I used to see him around San Antone when I was a little girl. His name was Latham, I think. He was here, but I saw him only once."

"What became of him? Did he have a horse?"

"I don't think so. He walked along the street, then he stopped outside and smoked a cigarette. After that he went around the corner and down the alley. I did not see him again."

Bowdrie's dark features revealed nothing, but his heart was pounding. This might be the first break.

Latham, the man she had seen, could have been Jack Latham, one of the Decker gang of outlaws.

Standing in front of the restaurant, he would have had a good chance to study the bank. Yet he had been on foot and he did not disappear in the direction of the livery stable or the town corral. Behind the double row of business buildings that faced Main Street there were only dwellings. If Latham had turned down an alley it could only have been to go to one of them.

Jack Latham was on the Fugitives List as a cattle rustler, a horse thief and killer. He was known to have worked with Comanche George Cobb and Pony Decker.

Ellen was right, of course. Such men would stop at nothing. They were utterly ruthless, dangerous men. Yet this robbery was unlike them. Behind this one was a different kind of intelligence, someone with new techniques, a new approach.

He talked for a while to Ellen, simply the casual conversation of the town, the restaurant, the people. He learned nothing new but did acquire some knowledge of the community, its thinking, and its ways.

Returning to his room, Chick dropped on the edge of the bed and pulled off his boots. Then he sat very still, thinking.

And in the stillness of the unlit room he heard a movement.

His eyes went left, then right. Nothing. The hair prickled on his scalp and then he felt rather than heard a stealthy movement.

He sprang from the bed and turned swiftly, gun in hand. The rising moon illumined the room, but he could see nothing. It was empty, ghostly in the moonlight.

Once more he glanced around the room; then very cautiously he lighted a lamp. He had started to move away when he detected a faint movement among the blankets on the bed. Gun in hand, he reached with careful fingers and jerked the blanket back.

There, in a tight, deadly S, lay a sidewinder, one of the

deadliest of desert rattlesnakes, a snake that does not coil but simply draws back its head and strikes repeatedly.

The snake's gaze was steady, unblinking. Man and reptile watched each other with deadly intensity. The room was on the second floor and the chance that such a snake had come there of its own choice was next to impossible.

Moving carefully, Bowdrie got a broom left standing in a corner, and a broken bed slat standing beside it. Using them as pincers, he lifted the snake and dropped it from the window. He heard the soft *plop* when it hit the ground.

After a careful examination of the room he undressed, got into bed, and went to sleep. He slept soundly and comfortably.

The sun was chinning itself on the eastern mountains when he awakened. His door was opening softly, stealthily. A big, carefully combed head was thrust into the room. Hardy Young found himself staring into the business end of a Colt.

"Stopped by t'see if you was havin' breakfast! I'm a-treatin', such! I was tryin' to be careful so's if you was still asleep I'd not wake you up."

The blue eyes roamed uneasily over the room. Chick sat up and reached for his pants with his left hand. "Mighty kind of you." He invited, "Come in an' set. I'll get dressed."

Young was manifestly uneasy and kept looking around as Chick dressed. "Sit down on the bed," Bowdrie suggested. "It's more comfortable."

He slung on his gunbelts and dropped the free gun into its holster. As he did so, he brushed lightly against Young, enough to make him stagger and drop to the bed.

His face gray, Young bounded to his feet as if stabbed.

Bowdrie smiled pleasantly. "What's the matter, Hardy? Scared of something? You needn't be. I threw it out of the window."

"Threw what out?" Young blustered. "I got no idea what you're talkin' about."

The man's guilt was manifest and Bowdrie gripped the front of his stiff collar and twisted hard. His fingers were inside the collar and as his hand turned, his fist pressed against Young's Adam's apple. He shoved Young hard against the wall, still twisting.

The man's eyes bulged, he gasped for breath, and his face began to turn blue. Bowdrie slowly relaxed his grip, letting Young catch his breath. Then with his free hand he slapped Young across the face.

"Who's in this with you, Young? Talk, or I'll skin you alive!"

Bowdrie relaxed his grip a bit more. Gasping hoarsely, the big man said, "I don't know what you're talkin' about! Honest, I don't!"

Bowdrie jerked him away from the wall and kicked him behind the knees, and let go. Hardy Young hit the floor with a crash that shook the building.

"You'd better talk while you can. If you don't, Latham or one of the others will!"

Young's hand was at his throat but at the mention of Latham's name a kind of panic went through him. Bowdrie could almost see the man's mind working. If Bowdrie knew about Latham, how much more did he know?

"Get up!" Bowdrie said. "Get up an' get out! You've got until four this afternoon to talk. After that you hang with the rest of them!"

He was pushing his luck, he knew, but he had a feeling that Hardy Young was genuinely frightened. If the man would talk, it would save time, much time. Had the snake been Hardy's own idea? Or had somebody else done it or put Hardy up to doing it?

By riding Young, he might force them into a revealing move. When such men moved suddenly, they often made mistakes. Obviously somebody was worried or they would not have tried to get him killed by a rattler. Undoubtedly they believed he knew more than he did, which had been nothing.

Following a hurried breakfast, Bowdrie saddled the roan and rode out of town. His theory of the previous day, that the outlaws were still in Kimble, was still valid. Yet it would be impossible for a group of men to remain hidden for long in such a small town. Certainly there could not have been sufficient food for more than a few days, and he suspected they had already been in town longer than planned.

Drawing rein under some trees on the slope near the edge of town, Bowdrie sat his saddle, studying the place. His view was a good one, and as he studied the layout his eyes turned again and again to a large ranch house almost hidden in a grove of cottonwoods.

A huge barn, several corrals, various outbuildings. The barn backed up to an arroyo that wound through the low hills on the edge of town.

It was very hot now and the air was breathless. Chick mopped his face and neck. Squinting against the glare, he used the trees as a screen and rode down, crossed the trail, and entered the arroyo. He found no tracks and scowled with disappointment.

Yet he knew no track could long endure in this sand.

He was riding along immersed in thought, and the sharp jerk at his shoulder almost failed to register until he heard the metallic slam of the gunshot.

A frail tendril of smoke lifted from a rocky knoll, and touching a spur to the roan's ribs, Bowdrie sent him up out of the arroyo and on a dead run for the knoll itself. Another rifle shot rang out but the bullet missed, and the roan went charging up the knoll. Bowdrie's gun was in his hand, but the knoll was empty!

Amazed and angry, he took a quick swing around among the rocks. If the shot had come from here, the marksman was gone.

Perplexed, he looked all around. The grass was disturbed but he found no distinguishable tracks. Horses and cattle had been on the knoll, and there was a confusion of tracks, scratches, and scuffed earth.

His shoulder was smarting by the time he reached town. The shot had merely split the fabric of his shirt and scraped the skin.

He swung down at the livery stable and glanced over at the two or three loafers. "Anybody want to make a half-dollar caring for a horse?"

Rip Coker was seated on a box. "How about me? They

cleaned me at poker, and a half a dollar would buy me a couple of meals."

They walked into the barn, Bowdrie giving instructions.

"Who owns the big house over by the wash?" he asked when they were alone.

"I thought of it, but that's the Bishop place. He's well off, and one of the leading citizens. He and his brother put up money to help build both the church and the school. John Bishop is the mayor."

"What's his brother do?"

"Red? He ranches down in Mexico. He's never here, and hasn't even been here so far as I know, even though the Bishops sort of regard this as their town, and always contribute to worthy causes."

Bowdrie outlined all that had happened and what little he had learned, adding what Ellen had told him about Latham.

"Sounds like him. From all I hear, that banker looked like a Comanche had worked on him. He was badly used."

Ellen came immediately to his table when Bowdrie seated himself in the restaurant a few minutes later. "Does Sheriff Borrow eat here?" he asked.

"He was in, looking for you, perhaps an hour ago. It might have been two hours. I've been pretty busy until now."

"Thanks. If he doesn't come in, I'll look him up."

The outer door opened and when he glanced up, the newcomer turned out to be John Bishop.

"Any luck, Bowdrie?" His eyes went to Chick's shoulder. "Don't tell me you've been shot?"

"I didn't tell you," Bowdrie said sharply. "It seems you're a good guesser. From where you stand, that could be a thorn scratch or a barbed-wire cut, but if you'd like to believe it was a shot, you've the choice."

"You seem to be touchy. Is the case getting on your nerves?"

"Of course not. You haven't been a Ranger, Bishop. Most cases are routine. All a man needs is a little time and patience. All this case needed was a fresh viewpoint. It's like I told Hardy Young, the boss in a case like this always overlooks something. That's a beginning. Then somebody gets scared and they talk so they won't have to hang like the rest of them."

"At least you're confident. That's more than Borrow can say."

"He doesn't know all that we know, and his experience in crime has been local. In the Rangers you run into everything. But even Young was surprised when I mentioned Jack Latham."

Without seeming to pay attention, Bowdrie was watching Bishop for a reaction. If there was any, it was well hidden.

Bishop's eyes were on him and Bowdrie felt a tide of recklessness welling up within him. He had no evidence at all, but regardless of what Coker had said of Bishop, that ranch was simply too well located for what had been happening. He pushed his luck.

"The well-planned crimes are often the simplest. A plan is a design like that of a weaver, and all you have to do is get hold of one of the threads and it all begins to unravel."

"And you've found the thread?"

Bishop's eyes reflected his skepticism, but under that lay something else. Apprehension, maybe?

"I've got two or three threads," Bowdrie said. "The trouble with well-planned crimes is that the planner is never content. He always wants to take another stitch here or there. The first thread was that this mysterious crime was simply too mysterious. It was overdone. Nobody saw anyone entering or leaving town and there were no tracks. The second thread was the hour of the crime and the way it was done.

"Then came the added touches. A snake in my bed that was intended to kill or scare me. The next touch was the shot somebody took at me, which indicates whoever did this crime is not sure of himself. Or somebody connected with it isn't sure.

"That was pure stupidity. I was sent alone on this job, but if I got killed you'd have a company of Rangers in here turning over every stone in town.

"It also proves what I suspected from the beginning: there were no tracks because the thieves never left town. They are here now, right in Kimble."

"That's absurd!" Bishop sounded angry. "This is a nice little town. Everybody knows everybody else. Why would they stay in a town with everybody hunting them? I was on the search myself and we found nobody."

"Exactly. Nobody thought of searching houses, merely of getting out on the trails. A thief would be running, so they would chase him. All the thieves had to do was sit tight, and with friends in town, that would be easy."

"Friends?"

"They had to have friends. Somebody had to tell them when there was enough money in the bank to make it worth-while."

"That doesn't make sense," Bishop said. "I am afraid you're going off on a tangent."

"It makes a lot of sense," Bowdrie persisted. "Whoever pulled this job is outsmarting himself. That shot today, for example. As a miss it was very revealing."

"Revealing? How do you mean?"

"How does a man vanish off the face of the earth? I don't believe in magic, Bishop. I am a practical man."

Bishop shrugged. "I know nothing of crime, so I hope you find the guilty men. We've tried very hard to build a law-abiding community here. Sheriff Borrow and I worked out a plan to protect the town from just this sort of thing."

"It was a good setup," Bowdrie replied mildly. "Sheriff Borrow told me about it."

"We've tried very hard to build a good community here. That's why we all contributed to the church and the school."

"That makes sense." Bowdrie smiled. "A good community is a prosperous one. One with money around."

John Bishop threw him a sharp glance, as if trying to see meaning behind the comment. Bowdrie's expression was innocent.

"You're ranching yourself, are you not?" Bowdrie inquired. "Horse ranching, I think? I've noticed some fine horses around town, some with plenty of speed."

Bishop did not reply. His fingers gripped the cup Ellen had brought him.

"By the way," Bowdrie continued. "What's Red doing now?"

The fingers on the cup tightened. Bishop looked up, and the pretended friendliness was gone from his eyes. "He's ranching in Sonora." Bishop pushed back his chair. "I'll see you later."

He stood up and turned to go, but Chick's voice stopped him. "By the way . . ." Bowdrie's tone was gentle. "Don't leave town, and tell your brother not to."

Bishop turned sharply around. "What do you mean by that? I told you . . ." He paused, gaining control of himself. "I am beginning to see what you have in mind, but it won't work, Bowdrie. Don't try to frame me or my brother."

Bowdrie got up and stepped past him to the counter where Ellen was standing. "Let me treat Mr. Bishop," he said cheerfully. "I enjoy doing it. In fact, I plan to arrange for all his meals . . . as long as he will need them!"

"Don't start anything you can't finish!" Bishop's eyes were mean. "I am a friend of the governor!"

Bowdrie smiled. "Perhaps, but is he your friend?"

Bishop slammed the door and Chick smiled at Ellen. "You know, I always did like a girl with freckles on her nose!"

He walked outside and glanced along the street. He was displeased with himself. He had not intended to push Bishop so far, although in his own mind he was sure he was merely a smooth crook. Under the guise of being a public-spirited citizen he could have planned and pulled off this robbery without being suspected. What the case had needed was a fresh viewpoint, someone from outside the town, unimpressed by Bishop.

The worst of it was that Bowdrie had pushed too far without a bit of proof. He was sure that Bishop and his brother had engineered the robbery and killed Josh Phillips. Moreover, he was sure they had tried to kill him, but he could prove nothing. Yet Bishop was worried; that much was obvious.

Coker was loafing in front of the saloon. "Get on your horse and light out of here," Chick advised. "The first telegraph station you hit, wire to McNelly. Ask him to come runnin'."

"You've been talkin' to Bishop?"

"He's our man, I'm sure of it."

"I've been thinkin'. It's possible. Nobody would notice extry horses over there, nor a few extry men around. He carries a stock of grub and he's the only place aside from the restaurant that could feed men for more than a day or two."

"I'm going to see Borrow, but you'd better get out fast. I've a hunch my talk with Bishop will blow the lid off. He's supposed to be smart, but doesn't have sense enough to just sit tight."

The sheriff's office door was closed, but Bowdrie turned the knob and stepped in. He stopped, the door half-closed behind him. Just beyond the corner of the desk and inside the bedroom door Bowdrie saw a pair of boot toes turned up.

He sprang past the desk and stopped with his hands on the doorjamb. On the floor, lying on his back, was Sheriff Walt Borrow, the manner of his death obvious. Under his breastbone was the haft of a knife.

Bowdrie stopped and touched the dead man's hand. It was cold. He straightened up and glanced around. The picture became clear when he saw the chair in the shadows near several coats hung from a clothes tree.

Crossing to the chair, Bowdrie seated himself. He was facing the doors but well back in the shadows. Whoever sat in the chair would see whoever came in from the street, but Borrow, coming in from the glare of the sun, would not have seen his killer.

Near the chair were three cigarette butts, lying where the killer had dropped them. Borrow, as did most men of the time and the area, smoked cigars. Cigarettes were a Mexican custom only beginning to cross the border, so these might have been smoked by someone living south of the border.

Here the killer had waited. There was no evidence of struggle, and Borrow had been a strong, tough man. The killer might have struck from his chair, but it was likely that he had risen as Borrow drew close and driven the knife upward to the heart. Soundless, abrupt, and final.

But why?

Bowdrie recalled the old man's kindly features at their first meeting. "I'm stumped," Borrow confessed. "The answer keeps naggin' at me. It's right on the trail edge of my thinkin', but I can't quite get it out into the open."

He had glanced at the blanket roll Chick was carrying. "Might's well leave that here. You won't need it at the hotel."

And the tight roll of his poncho and blankets still stood in the corner where he had left it, yet the roll was neither as tight nor was it rolled in quite the same way now. Why would Borrow, or anyone, open his blanket roll?

Dropping to his knees, he pulled the roll loose. As it opened, a fold of paper fell out. Taking it up, Bowdrie opened it for a quick look. It was all he needed. Instantly he was on his feet.

Hurriedly bundling the roll together, he tossed it into a corner. The door opened almost in his face, and Ellen, the freckles dark against the paleness of her face, stood there.

"Oh, Mr. Bowdrie! Please be careful! They're after you!"

"Who is?"

"They were talking out in back of the restaurant. They did not guess anyone was around. One of the men said they would get you when you left the office."

"Then they saw you come to the door. That's bad, Ellen!"

"I thought of that. If they ask, I'll tell them you forgot to pay for your meal and I came after you."

"Good!" He reached into his pocket and counted out some money. "There! That'll pay for what I ate and the next two meals, if I should forget again."

He put the money in her hand. "Now, do something for me. If you see that lantern-jawed blond drifter they call Rip, get to him and tell him what is happening. Tell him where I am but not to come here. Understand?"

She turned away quickly, clutching the money in her hand. She paused an instant, flashing him a quick, frightened smile. "Good luck, Chick!"

He listened to the click of her heels on the walk, hoping she would not be stopped. He watched her enter the restaurant, from which she would be able to watch the trail into town.

They would not wait long now. If he did not appear on the street, they would come here. They had proved themselves to be impatient men. Somehow they had discovered the sheriff had finally found the solution and had killed him. Now they must kill Bowdrie.

Chick took stock of his position. The sheriff's office was separated from the saloon by a gap of about thirty feet. On the other side there was nothing but an open slope.

The building comprised four rooms. Two solidly built cells on one side of a narrow hall, on the other the office itself, and farther along, the sheriff's living quarters.

Bending over the dead man, he removed his gunbelt and pistol. The pistol was fully loaded. From the gun rack he got down the sheriff's old Sharps and his Spencer as well as a double-barreled shotgun. From a drawer he took ammunition for these guns and arranged it in neat rows on the desk.

Then he took up the body and carried it to the bed, where he straightened it out and covered it with a blanket.

Bowdrie knew that in this situation he could not depend on Rip Coker. The Ranger would go through hell and high water to do his duty, but the telegraph operator might be a friend of the Bishops or of Young. He would undoubtedly send his message both to McNelly and to Major Jones, who was actually in charge in this area.

The wise course was to depend on neither. The problem was his, to be solved here and now. Even if the message got through, there was small chance they would arrive in time. If they did, an arrest might be made without a fight through sheer numbers, but considering the type of men he was facing, even that was doubtful. Chick Bowdrie preferred to make arrests without trouble, but such occasions were rare in a land where the border was so near, escape so possible.

Undoubtedly the robbery had been pulled off by Red Bishop and the Decker-Latham outfit. John Bishop and Hardy Young had no doubt planned it, knowing of the money in the bank and choosing the time. Riders would attract no attention on Bishop's ranch, and there was plenty of cover for going and coming.

Due to the sheriff's recollection, Bowdrie knew how the bandits had arrived as well as where the shot came from that was meant to kill him.

The afternoon was warm and still. No breath of wind stirred the thick dust in the long, hot street. The false-fronted buildings across the street looked parched and gray.

Bowdrie mopped sweat from his face, loosened his neckerchief, then sat down behind the desk. There was a bucket of water in the shadowed bedroom, but no food.

Food did not worry him. This fight would be history before he had a chance to be hungry again.

He hoped to kill no one, but he was alone against five or six desperate men who had shown their style in torturing Phillips.

Nor could he expect help from the town. None of them would believe Bishop was a thief. Nor did they know Borrow was murdered. There was a pot of coffee on the stove. Hot though it was outside, he poured a cup. It was strong and bitter, but he liked it.

Down the street he heard a few steps on the boardwalk, then silence. Well, if he got himself killed, he had no family to worry about it. He was a loner. His family was the Rangers, his world was his job.

Ellen . . . now there was a likely lass. But even if she were interested in him, how could he ask any girl to marry a man who might end up on a slab at any moment? Still, a lot of the Rangers were married, and happily, too.

Bowdrie walked back to the cells, and keeping his head from in front of the small window, he peered out. There was a pile of scrap lumber back there, and watching it, he saw the grass stir. So they had a man out there, too.

He walked back to the office, and at that moment Bishop called out, "Bowdrie? Step over here a minute, will you? I've got something to show you."

"Bring it over here, John," Chick called back. "I'm not going to make it that easy for you."

He was impatient for them to get on with it. He had lain for hours without moving when stalking someone, but when the chips were down, he disliked waiting.

"Whoever fired that shot from the rocks gave you away, John!" he called out. "I know all about that old watercourse now!"

Somebody swore and Bishop stepped back out of sight. Then there was silence.

Bishop was handling this all wrong. He had the total sympathy of the townspeople, but now they would begin to wonder. Why was John Bishop, their mayor and leading citizen, trying to kill a Texas Ranger? Bowdrie had yelled, hoping others would be listening, and wondering now.

In the midst of the stillness Bowdrie had a sudden inspiration. Taking a couple of rawhide riatas Borrow had hanging on the clothes tree, he knotted one over a nail over the door to the bedroom, and crawling across the floor, knotted the other end over a nail near the outside door.

Crawling back, he took a turn around the doorknob, rigging a crude pulley. Then he fastened the end of his riata through an armhole of Borrow's poncho in such a way that by pulling on the riata he could make it move by the window. The light was such that anyone outside would see movement but could not detect who or what it was unless standing right outside.

He pulled the poncho opposite the window, then pulled again. Instantly the poncho jerked and a rifle bellowed. Bowdrie was watching, and when the rifle flashed, he fired.

There was a crash of glass and a startled yelp. If he hadn't hit somebody, he had at least scared him. His shot was followed by a scattered volley that broke much of the front window.

Keeping the Spencer in his hands, Bowdrie waited. Sweat trickled down his chest under his shirt. He wiped his hands on his pants. A searching shot struck the wall over his head, but he knew they could not see him, although given time, they might figure out his position. Bishop and Young must both have seen the inside of this office many times.

He refilled his cup, sipped coffee, and sat back in his chair, waiting. He had two front windows and a side window, and the glass in the front windows was more than half gone. By now the people around town were wondering just what was going on.

He waited, not wanting to waste a shot and hoping they would believe he had been hit.

Nothing happened. Chick yawned. If they waited long enough, the Rangers would be here. Of course, they could not know that. Yet even if he left the office somehow he was handicapped in not knowing the men he was fighting.

A shot rang out and a bullet cut a furrow in the desk and buried itself in the wall. Another struck the floor and ventilated the wastebasket. They were probing with fingers of lead.

He reached for his cup and caught a glimpse of movement from the window on the second floor of the harness shop across the street. There was a curtain inside that window, but he could detect a reflection of movement.

A man was inching his way along the rooftop to fire from behind the false front of the building next to the harness shop and directly opposite. The man was getting into position to fire down into the office. He was out of sight behind the false front but dimly reflected in the window over the harness shop.

Bowdrie took a swallow of coffee, put the cup down, and took the Spencer from his lap. He studied the window and then the roof. Taking up the Spencer, he took careful aim, drew in a breath, and let it out slowly and then squeezed off his shot.

The heavy rifle leaped in his hands, firing right into the false front of the building. A pistol bullet would penetrate several inches of pine at that distance, and the .56-caliber Spencer would not be impeded by the half-inch boards on the front opposite.

He heard a rifle clatter and fall into the dirt; then a man slid to the roof edge, clawing madly to keep from sliding on the steep roof, then falling.

The man scrambled up, obviously hurt but moving. As he started to run, Bowdrie, with only the wide posterior for target, squeezed off another shot. There was an agonized yell and the man disappeared.

Bowdrie thumbed two shells into the Spencer, then hit the floor as a hail of bullets riddled the windows and the door. One bullet ripped through the desk, leaving a hole in a half-open drawer right in front of his face.

The shooting died down and he got up just in time to see a man sprinting across the street. Bowdrie fired and the runner drew suddenly to his tiptoes, then spilled over into the dust. "If you weren't one of them," Bowdrie said aloud, "you used damn poor judgment!"

He slipped down the hall to the back cell. There was still a man behind the lumber pile, but there was no chance for a shot.

Returning to the office, he stood well back in the room and searched the line of buildings opposite. He could see nothing.

He put down the Spencer, mopped his face, and reached for the gun. Dust stirred on the floor and he wheeled, his grasp closing on the shotgun. Comanche George Cobb stood in the side door, his pistol in his hand.

Bowdrie saw the man's eyes blaze, and the pistol thrust forward; he saw the man's thumb bend as it pulled the hammer back, and Bowdrie squeezed both triggers on the shotgun.

Cobb's body jerked as if kicked by a mule, and he took a staggering step backward before he fell, a spur hooking itself on the doorjamb.

"Two gone," he muttered, "and maybe one wounded."

He started to move, then froze in mid-stride as his nostrils caught the faintest smell of smoke.

Smoke, and then the crackle of flames!

Grabbing up shotgun shells, he jammed them into his pockets; then he reloaded the shotgun itself. Testing the sheriff's pistols for balance, he thrust them into his waistband.

Flames crackled outside and smoke began to curl up from the floor and into the windows. Evidently they had gotten under the building and set fire to it.

Outside, men waited to cut him down the minute he showed himself. He might get some of them, but they would surely get him.

Suddenly he remembered something seen earlier. He glanced up. A trapdoor to the loft over the office. Now, if there was only a second trapdoor to the roof, as was often the case when access was left for possible repairs . . .

Leaping atop the desk, he shoved the trap aside, and grasping the lip of the opening, he pulled himself up. Though smoke was gathering even there, Bowdrie made out the square framework of a trapdoor in the roof. Closing the trapdoor behind him, he raced along the joists, shotgun in hand, unfastened the hasp, and lifted himself to the flat roof.

The rooftop slanted down slightly to allow rain to run off. Bowdrie looked over the edge. There was no one in sight, as they evidently believed Comanche George was still there.

Swinging his legs over, he hung for a minute, then dropped, knees bent to absorb the shock. He hit the ground, staggered, recovered, looked quickly around, his shotgun poised for firing.

There was nobody in sight.

A quick dash and he was behind the Longhorn Saloon. Opening the back door, he stepped in. A half-dozen men stood near the wide front window, watching the street. Opposite, plainly visible in the window across the street, was John Bishop.

The bartender turned his head, and when he saw Bowdrie, his face paled. He drew back, his hands falling to his sides.

Bowdrie walked quickly to the front door. The fire destroying the sheriff's office could be plainly heard.

"Hope it don't burn the whole town!" somebody commented.

"What started Bishop on a rampage? Who're those fellers with him?"

"Don't know any of 'em. Strangers. Somebody said that Ranger killed Walt Borrow."

The roof of the building collapsed suddenly, and John Bishop stepped into the street, a red-haired man beside him. From down the street Hardy Young was approaching.

"Stand aside, men!" Bowdrie said, and as they turned, he said quietly, "Red Bishop robbed your bank. John Bishop murdered Borrow because your sheriff had found him out.

The dead man out there is Jack Latham, the outlaw. Keep out of this!"

He stepped into the street as Hardy Young came up to the Bishops. Where was Decker, the man Bowdrie had shot when he fell from the roof?

Bowdrie stepped off the walk. "Bishop! I arrest you for robbing the Bank of Kimble, for the murders of Josh Phillips and Walt Borrow!"

The three men turned, staring as if at a ghost. John Bishop had an instant of panic. "How in . . . !"

"Drop your guns. You will get a fair trial!"

"Trial, hell!" Red Bishop's gun started to lift, and Bowdrie fired the shotgun. One barrel, then the other. The group were close together, the distance no more than sixty feet.

Red Bishop was shooting when he took the shotgun blast. John Bishop caught a good half of a load of buckshot and toppled back against the hitching rail. He was fully conscious, fully aware.

Hardy Young was running away down the street. He was running, crazed with fear, when the horsemen rounded the corner into the street. He glimpsed them and tried to turn away, and they saw him and tried to rein in. Both were too late.

The charging horses ran him down and charged over his big body, trampling him into the dust.

Rip Coker was in the lead, McNelly right behind him. "Bowdrie? You all right?"

Automatically Bowdrie extracted the shells and reloaded the shotgun. "All right," he said. "Case closed—no prisoners."

"Where's Cobb? And Decker?"

Bowdrie explained in as few words as possible. "Borrow finally figured it out. There's a draw comes in from the south on Bishop's land. Riders could come right up from Mexico, then follow that draw right to his ranch. Nobody need see them at all.

"Once you forgot who Bishop was and just looked at the situation, it almost had to be him. Borrow left a note in my bedroll just in case. He should have the credit for this one.

"I think," Bowdrie added, "you'll find the bank's money in Bishop's house. If they aren't carrying it on their bodies."

"Good job, Bowdrie!" McNelly said. "Thanks!"

Bowdrie lifted a hand. "There's coffee waitin' for me inside. Come an' join me, if you're of a mind to."

He turned toward the restaurant, suddenly tired. It was cool inside, and Ellen was standing by a table with the coffeepot in hand.

Someday, he thought, someday he might find a town like this, a place where he could stop, get acquainted, and build something.

"Your family will be glad you're safe," Ellen said.

"I've got no family," he replied. "I've got nobody. Only the Rangers and a mean roan horse. That's all I got. Maybe it's all I'll ever have."

As he sat down, she was pouring his coffee, and he *was* tired. Very tired.

THE KILLER FROM THE PECOS

I T WAS EARLY afternoon, but the town was already up and sinning when Chick Bowdrie left his roan at the Almagre livery stable.

Every other door was a saloon or gambling house. Five different nickelodeons blared five different tunes into the street. The rattle and bang of the music was superimposed upon the crack of teamsters' whips, the rattle of chips, and the clink of glasses. Occasionally the tumult was punctuated by the exultant bark of some celebrant's six-shooter.

Almagre, born of a silver outcropping, exploded from nothing into hearty exuberance, a town born to live fast and die hard but smoking, with many of its citizens setting the example. At the age of ten months the town had planted thirty-three men on Boot Hill, led by a misguided newcomer who tried to fill an inside straight from a boot top.

The founder, a wiser man than those who followed, had raced a pack of yelling Comanches to the railroad and departed for the East with his scalp intact. Behind him all hell broke loose. Strangers who hit the town broke knew fifty ways to make money, all of them dishonest, and among the gentry who now kept the lid off the town was one Wiley Martin. It was his trail from Texas that brought Chick Bowdrie to Almagre.

The reason was simple. Martin—or supposedly Martin— had used his six-shooter at the Pecos Bank to withdraw six thousand dollars. In the process he had shot down in cold blood both the cashier and the president of the bank.

There was a catch in it, of course, as there nearly always was. There was no adequate description of the outlaw.

A description of sorts: a big man—and at first glance all

Almagre's citizens looked big—and he had a girl's head and the name "Marge" tattooed under his heart.

Standing on the street, Bowdrie eyed the passing crowds with disgust. "If you go to pulling the shirts off every man in town, you've bought yourself some trouble!"

It began to look like the goosiest of wild-goose chases. Aside from the vague description, the escaping outlaw had dropped a letter addressed to Wiley Martin, and he had left a trail of sorts. Few trained men could have followed the trail, but a good many Apaches could have, and Chick Bowdrie did.

He had taken but two steps toward the nearest and largest saloon when the batwing doors exploded outward and a man landed in the street on his shoulder blades. He came up with a lunge, grappling at his gun, but the doors slammed open again, revealing a bearded man with a gun. He fanned his six-shooter, and four shots exploded into a continuous roar. The first shot smashed a window four feet to the left of the man in the street, the second and third shots obliterated his belt buckle, and the fourth grazed the hip of one of the two broncs hitched to a buckboard.

The bronc leaped straight up and forward, coming down across the hitching rail, which splintered beneath it. The horse went down, threshing wildly in a snarl of harness and broken rail. Its mate backed away, snorting. The girl in the buckboard grabbed at the reins, and Chick lunged for the downed horse. A grizzled prospector moved in to lend a hand.

"Looks like a live town," Bowdrie commented.

"This one?" The old man spat expressively. "She's a lala-palooza! A real wingdingin' hot tamale!"

The wounded man in the street made a futile effort to rise, then sagged back. Nobody approached him, not sure the shooting was over. Bowdrie's quick estimate told him the girl was in more need of help than the unfortunate battler, for he had only a minute or two to live.

"That's only the first one today!" the old man said cheer-fully. "Wait until Bonelli gets in! Things'll pop then!"

"Who's Bonelli?"

"He makes big tracks, son." He gave a glance at Bowdrie's guns. "If you're huntin' a gun job, there's only two ways to go. You work for Bonelli or you become town marshal. The first job can last a lot longer. We just buried our third town marshal."

"Bonelli hires gunhands?"

"He surely does! He's revolutionized the cow business in this neck of the woods. He drove fifty head into the hills three months ago, and now they all have four or five three- to six-month-old calves!"

Bowdrie chuckled. "Sounds like an enterprising man. What the marshal's job pay?"

"A hundred a month, cabin, an' cartridges. Of course, you'd be sleepin' in a dead man's bed!"

They had the horse on his feet and quieted, so he broached his question: "Ever hear of a man named Wiley Martin?"

The old man put his pipestem between his teeth and started away on his short legs without another word. Mildly astonished, Bowdrie stared after him, then turned to help the girl from her buckboard. An older man, probably her father, was coming to help.

He looked like any other man except that he was freshly shaved and seemed prosperous. The girl could have been nobody else in the world, for they never made two like her.

"Thanks for helping to get my horse up," the older man said. "I am Jed Chapin. This is my daughter, Amy."

"Proud," Bowdrie said. "Folks call me Tex."

"I ranch south of here, JC brand. If you're down that way, drop in an' see us."

Bowdrie glanced again at Amy. "Might be. Right now I'm thinkin' of applying for the marshal's job."

"Don't do it. Marshals don't last long around here. Erlanger doesn't like 'em."

"Who is Erlanger?"

"Foreman for Bonelli. He and that prison-mean Hank Cordova make life a misery for folks."

"How about Wiley Martin?"

Chapin's face changed. "Get up in the buckboard, honey. It's time we went home."

Bowdrie's dark eyes met Amy's. For an instant she searched his eyes; then she spoke softly. "Don't ask that question. There's trouble in it."

"I've a message for him."

"Forget it. There will be no answer in Almagre."

"I'll be riding your way. Maybe we should talk."

Her eyes relented a little. Her eyes became warmer, even curious. "Maybe we should," she said. "Please come."

He crossed to the saloon. Three men played cards at a table near the wall. One of them had a narrow, triangular face with a crisp blond mustache, the ends drawn out to fine points. His eyes were gray and steady, and their expression when they glanced up at Bowdrie was direct and probing. One of the others was the bearded man who fanned his pistol.

Three men followed him into the room and came to the bar near Chick. The biggest man spoke, immediately placing all three of them for Bowdrie. "Get Chapin for me, Jeff. Bring him here."

"I think he just left town." The speaker was slender and dark, not the man addressed. "I saw the buckboard leavin'."

"Then go get him and bring him back, whether he likes it or not!" The big man was obviously Bonelli, his face like polished hardwood, his eyes bright and hard.

Erlanger went out, and Bowdrie leaned his elbows on the bar. In the mirror he caught Bonelli's sharp, inquiring glance. The air had an electric feel like something about to happen.

Two of the men at the card table cashed in their chips and left quietly. The bearded man exchanged a brief, questioning glance with Bonelli. The man with the gray eyes riffled the cards with agile fingers, then lighted a long black cheroot.

"Who's the mayor of this town?" Bowdrie's question was unusually loud in the quiet room. Bonelli glanced at him as if irritated, but did not reply.

Cordova looked at Chick. "What you want with the mayor?" he asked.

"I heard the town needed a marshal. I'm huntin' a job."

The man with the gray eyes took the cheroot from his teeth, glanced at it, then at Bowdrie. He seemed amused.

Bonelli turned sharply and looked Bowdrie up and down.

The skin around his eyes seemed to tighten a bit. Bowdrie's back was to the bar, his elbows resting on its edge. He returned Bonelli's look with a blank, hard stare.

"You'll do well to keep movin'," Cordova said. "That job doesn't need fillin'."

"Some folks might feel otherwise. I saw a man shot out there a bit ago. Men shouldn't carry guns in town. They might shoot the wrong people."

"I suppose you'd take 'em away?" Cordova commented contemptuously.

"I'd ask 'em to hang 'em up when they came in. If they didn't, I might have to take them away. There's decent folks in every town, and mostly they like it quiet."

A buckboard rattled to a stop before the saloon; then the doors pushed open and Chapin came in. He looked pale but angry; Erlanger was right behind him. "What's this mean, Bonelli?" Chapin demanded.

"It means that I am buyin' you out, Chapin. I'm offering five thousand dollars for your place and your stock."

"*Five* thousand?" Chapin was incredulous. "It's worth fifty thousand if a dollar! I am not selling!"

"Sure you are." Bonelli was enjoying himself. "My boys found some misbranded stock on the range today. My brand worked over to yours. We hang rustlers, you know."

"I never rustled a head of stock in my life!" Chapin's fury did not prevent him from speaking with care. "That's a put-up job, Bonelli. You're tryin' to force me to sell."

"Are you callin' me a liar?" Bonelli spoke softly. He stepped away from the bar. His intention was obvious.

Chapin knew he was marked for death if he said the wrong thing. He was a courageous but not a foolish man, and he had a daughter waiting in the buckboard outside. "I am not calling you a liar. I am not selling, either."

"Reilly said he wouldn't sell. Remember?"

"Look, Bonelli. I am not bothering you. Leave me alone."

The man with the gray eyes had stepped to the bar. His eyes caught Chick's, and he took something from his pocket and slid it along the bar. Chick covered it with his left hand. Neither of the men with Bonelli had noticed; all their attention was on Chapin, whom they apparently expected to kill. Chick Bowdrie pinned the badge to his vest, then hooked his left thumb in his shirt pocket so the palm covered the badge.

"You don't have to sell if you don't want to, Jed." He spoke quietly. "As for that rustling charge, Bonelli, you'd have to prove it."

Bonelli turned irritably. "Keep out of this!"

"This is my affair, Bonelli." His eyes were on Erlanger. "Get in your buckboard and go home, Chapin. Bonelli's through pushing people around. He isn't the big frog in any puddle. He only looked big for a little while because the water's mighty shallow. You go on home, now."

"You heard me," Bonelli said. "Stay out of this!"

Bowdrie moved his left hand, revealing the badge.

"I'm in, Bonelli. I've drawn cards."

Erlanger moved toward him. "I don't like marshals! I don't like the law!"

"Bonelli!" Bowdrie's tone was stern. "Take your boys and ride out of town. The next time you come in, check your guns at the marshal's office when you reach town. Otherwise, don't come to town at all."

Erlanger and Cordova both moved toward him, but Chick's reaction was swift. Grabbing Erlanger's wrist, he jerked the man toward him, pulling him off balance. As Erlanger staggered toward him, Bowdrie deftly kicked his feet from under him and shoved him into the other two. Then he stepped back quickly, drawing a gun.

"Next time you start something with me, Erlanger," Bowdrie said, "better fill your hand first. Now, you three get out of town and don't let me hear of you makin' trouble or I'll come for you."

Bonelli's astonishment had turned to fury. "Why, you cheap tinhorn! I'll run you out of town! I'll strip you and run you into the desert!"

"Erlanger! Cordova! Unbuckle your belts and drop your guns . . . *now*!"

With infinite care the two men unbuckled their gunbelts. "Now, get over there and face the wall. Be very, very careful! This here's a hair trigger an' you might make me nervous."

When they stood against the wall, hands above their heads, Bowdrie's eyes shifted to Bonelli. "All right, Bonelli. You just threatened to run me out of town. You're said to be a bad man with a gun. You want my hide and you've strutted around here runnin' roughshod over some good people. Now, right here in front of your bold bad men I'm going to give you a chance to see how mean you are. Now, I am goin' to holster my gun. I'm goin' to give you an even break." As he spoke, he dropped his gun into its holster. "Come on, Bonelli! Let's see what you're made of!"

Bonelli's hand started, then froze. Some sixth sense warned him. It had been a long time since anyone had dared challenge him, yet he was no fool. This man was a stranger, and there was something in that dark, Indian-like face that made him suddenly uncertain. He hesitated.

Chick waited. "Come on, Bonelli! You've convinced these people you're a hard man. You've even convinced those poor slobs who follow you. Let's see you try! Maybe you can beat me. *Maybe!*"

Bonelli's hands slowly relaxed. "Just wait," he said. "My time will come."

"Get out of town, Bonelli, and take your two errand boys with you. If you have guts enough to come to town again, check your guns."

Bowdrie walked to the door and watched them mount, then ride sullenly from town.

Jed Chapin was not gone. The rancher stood across the street with a Spencer rifle. "I wasn't going to run out on any man," Chapin said. "They'd have certainly killed me if you hadn't come in."

"It's over now. I'll be ridin' out to see you in a couple of days." He glanced at Amy. "I promise we'll have that talk."

When they were gone, he walked back into the saloon. The gray-eyed man was back at the card table, playing solitaire. "My name is Travis, Bob Travis. I am head of the Citizens' Committee."

Lying on his bed in the hotel much later, Bowdrie reviewed the situation. He was now the marshal of a cattle and mining town, but no nearer to capturing the Pecos killer. Nor had he any clue except for the curious silence whenever the name was mentioned. He could not decide whether that silence was born of fear or friendship. That he was in or near Almagre seemed certain. Beyond that, he knew nothing. Nor, he realized irritably, did he know that the man he sought was in fact the killer. Only that the name was somehow connected to the killer.

He might be one of the Bonelli outfit, even Bonelli himself. He knew that several of the outfit had been in Texas. The man who had robbed the Pecos Bank had been in town at least an hour before the hold-up, had bathed the dust from his chest, shoulders, and arms in the corral trough, eaten a meal, and loafed about near the bank.

It had been there that Bowdrie found the small grayish seeds. Hoary saltbush, or wingscale, did not grow in the vicinity. Their seeds were often gathered by the Zuni to grind into meal, or even eaten as they were collected.

Travis puzzled him. Was the man a public-spirited citizen who wanted law in Almagre, or had he some more devious purpose in giving the marshal's job to Bowdrie?

Did he want Bonelli killed? Or—and Chick became speculative—did he want Bowdrie himself killed? Travis was a big, well-set-up man. Could he be Wiley Martin?

Certainly one of the trails he had followed from Texas might have been that of Travis.

Bowdrie returned to the street and wandered about. People looked at the badge either with contempt, or pity, or irritation. He spotted a buffalo hunter whom he remembered from other towns, although the man seemed to have no memory of him. Buffalo Barton had always been a decent, law-respecting man, so he made him a deputy. Next he arrested a cowhand who objected to checking his guns.

Nobody could tell him anything about Wiley Martin, although he asked few people, and those few chosen discreetly, and he asked no direct questions. He did check records in the marshal's office and found no arrest record for such a man or for anyone answering to the description.

One thing was obvious. The town was waiting for him to be killed. A few, however, hearing about how he had faced

Bonelli and made him back down, were betting on him. No one wanted to be anywhere near him when things began to happen. That much was obvious.

Travis, he learned, kept a gray horse in the livery stable. The killer had ridden such a horse. If he could see the tracks, it might be evidence enough to tell him he was at least on the right trail.

As the evening wore on, the feeling that he was marked for death became stronger. It was not an unfamiliar feeling, but never a comfortable one. Yet the night passed quietly, and after he turned in, he slept comfortably.

At daybreak he made a quick check of the town, noticing the new horses in the livery stable and in the corrals. With a friendly warning he freed the cowhand he had arrested, then walked the streets again, paying close attention to horse tracks.

He was sitting over a late breakfast in an empty dining room when Amy Chapin entered. She came to his table. "I couldn't sleep, knowing you might be in trouble because of us."

"It would not be your fault. I came here hunting a man . . . Wiley Martin."

Her lips tightened and her eyes were grave. "Tex, you have friends here. You are admired for the way you made Bonelli back down. Why don't you forget about Martin?"

"Does he have that many friends?"

She hesitated. "Something like that. Tex," she said impulsively, "why don't you quit this job and come to work for Dad? He needs help, and with you beside him he wouldn't be afraid of Bonelli. We have good range, and it can be built into something. He needs help and he likes you."

"Especially," Bowdrie said, "if I stop hunting Wiley Martin?"

She flushed and half-started to rise, then sat down again. "My offer was sincere, and it comes from Dad."

"Amy? Do you know who Wiley Martin is?"

An instant of hesitation. "Not really." Her voice sank almost to a whisper. "I think I do."

"Do you know why I'm huntin' him?"

"No, I don't, only somebody is always hunting him, and he's a good man, Tex, a very good man."

"Amy, a man believed to be Wiley Martin or somebody he knew robbed a bank in Pecos and killed two honest, decent men. He left two widows and five orphans. Is that the kind of man you wish to protect?"

Her face was ashen. So she did know him, then! "I don't believe it! It simply can't be true!"

Three tough-looking men had stopped outside the door and were arguing loudly. All three were wearing guns.

From where Bowdrie sat, he could see out the window and across the street. Through the shutters of a closed saloon across the way he could see sunlight, a few threads of which showed through the shutters evidently from a back window. Twice in just a few minutes somebody or something had blocked off that sunlight, so somebody was inside the closed saloon, peering out through the shutters.

The setup was too pat, even amateurish. He was supposed to step outside to stop the argument and take the guns from the three men, and as he did, the man in the saloon would cut him down.

Excusing himself, he stepped to the door. One of the men glanced his way and threw his cigarette into the street.

A signal? Or just getting his hands free? Chick stepped out quickly and just as quickly moved to the left, putting one of the men between himself and the window.

His move was totally unexpected. That he had judged the trap correctly was obvious from the disconcerted expressions on the faces of the men.

"All right, shuck your guns! Let 'em drop! Right in the street!"

"Like hell!" It was the bearded killer of the previous day. As he spoke, he stepped quickly aside. Only Bowdrie's awareness saved him. As the bearded man moved, he caught a glint of sunlight on a gun barrel, and he palmed his gun and fired.

Two guns boomed with the same report, Bowdrie's a hair faster. Bowdrie felt the whip of a bullet past his face, but he swung his gun and shot at the bearded man, who was drawing his own pistol. Chick's bullet broke his arm, and he dropped his gun, backing off.

The action was so swift the two remaining men were caught by the surprise of the trap's failure. With a chopping blow from his gun barrel, Bowdrie dropped the nearest man into the dust, then jammed the muzzle of his gun into the third man's stomach.

"Shuck 'em! Or I'll let you have it!"

Trembling visibly, the third man unbuckled his belt with shaking fingers and let the guns fall. Spinning the man around, Bowdrie lined him up with the other prisoner.

On the walk, not fifty feet away, was Buffalo Barton with a shotgun. "Didn't see no call to step in, you handled it so fast." He glanced at Chick. "A man would think you'd done this afore."

"Take 'em down to the jail and throw 'em in. Get a doctor for that wounded one. If they give you any trouble, shoot to kill."

Walking across the street, his gun still in his fist, Bowdrie lifted his boot and kicked hard at the old-fashioned lock. It needed three sharp kicks with his boot heel to knock the door open. Then he stepped inside. After a moment the by-standers followed.

Hank Cordova lay sprawled on the floor, his Winchester lying beside him. The .44 slug had smashed through his throat, breaking his spine. He lay dead in a pool of his own blood.

Almagre awakened slowly from the shock of the shooting. Wherever men gathered, they were talking of it. The very least many expected was a raid by Bonelli to wipe out the new marshal. Others dissented. "Bonelli won't want any part of him."

The obvious fact was that Bowdrie had seen through the plot to kill him, and Bonelli had lost one of his best men. Three others were in jail, two of them disabled. One had a broken arm, the other a scalp laid open and a very aching head.

"I've seen that marshal somewheres before, but his name was nothing like Tex."

Bowdrie walked the streets, noting the horses, studying the people. It was a good town, a booming town with most of the rough stuff taking place on the wrong side of the tracks. They were having a pie supper at the Methodist Church, and two volunteers were painting the school.

He was not worried about a raid. That was the foolish talk of some alarmist. By now Bonelli would have heard that Cordova was dead and he would be doing some fast thinking. There was a chance that if he were not Martin himself he might surrender the man in exchange for Bowdrie leaving town.

Down the street, Amy Chapin was talking to Bob Travis. Bowdrie walked back to his desk. His job was not cleaning up boom mining camps but capturing men wanted in Texas. No doubt Hank Cordova would prove to have a long record of cattle theft in Texas, so it had not been a total loss. Still, that was not getting his job done.

"Saw you talkin' with that Chapin gal," Barton commented. "Mighty pretty youngster. Her pa's got a good spread out yonder, if only Bonelli will let him alone.

"He was mortgaged pretty heavy, but after he come back from Texas, visitin' his brother, he was able to pay it off, all eight thousand dollars of it."

Chick Bowdrie had been cleaning a gun. He glanced up at Barton. "Chapin was in Texas? Just recently?"

"Uh-huh. He's got a brother in Fort Griffin. Jed owed the bank down to Santa Fe, but his brother loaned him money. Now, if he can keep Bonelli off his back he should do something with that ranch.

"Bonelli wants him out of there, and partly I suspect because that ranch sits right astride Bonelli's rustlin' trail from the Panhandle."

So Jed Chapin had been to Texas and had returned with money?

"How about Travis? Has he been out of town lately?"

"He comes an' he goes. Nobody knows where, because Bob Travis isn't a talkin' man." He spat. "Shrewd . . . smart businessman. He owns the general store, the livery stable, the Silver Dollar Saloon, an' the hotel."

"Does he have trouble with Bonelli?"

"None that I know of. They sort of walk around each other. A fine man, that Travis. A finer one, you never met."

Chick Bowdrie walked down to the telegraph office and sent two wires. The operator stared down at them, then watched Bowdrie walk away. His eyes were speculative. Pausing at the corner, Bowdrie started to put his pencil away, and it slipped from his fingers.

Stooping to pick it up, he saw right before his eyes the unmistakable print of the hoof he had been looking for. To a skilled reader of sign a track once seen is as unmistakable as a signature. And this was the track Bowdrie had followed all the way from Texas. He straightened up, glancing around.

He stood in front of the general store, where not long before Amy Chapin had sat her horse talking to Bob Travis!

It was late before Bowdrie left the office. Buffalo Barton, who had been sleeping on a cot in the office, awakened to take over the task of keeping the peace.

No reply had come to his wires, and he had waited until the office closed. The street was empty, but there were several rigs still tied along the street, and a dozen saddle horses dozed at the hitching rails.

The streets were brightly lighted, there was a sound of tin-panny music, and up at the Silver Ledge Mine there were lights and sound. His black eyes swept the street, probing shadows, searching, estimating. He started to move down the street, making a last round, when he heard a rider coming from between the buildings.

It was Bonelli.

Bowdrie waited, watching. "Tex?" Bonelli spoke softly. "I'm not huntin' trouble."

"What's on your mind?"

"Look"—he leaned on the pommel—"I've got a nice thing here. Things goin' my way. You've no call to push me. You're a Texas man, Bowdrie."

"You know me?"

"Took me a while, but I figured it out. Then today I got a tip. You're huntin' Wiley Martin."

"I'm huntin' a killer from Pecos. He could be the man."

"Suppose you were to find Martin? You'd go back to Texas?"

Bowdrie hesitated. Bonelli was a tough enough man when faced with average men, most of whom wanted no trouble, but he had no stomach for bucking a really tough man. "If I find the man I want, of course I'll go back to Texas."

"I know where Martin is, and I know who he is."

"Who is Martin, then?" His eyes were on Bonelli's shadowed face. He saw Bonelli's hand go to his mouth and heard his teeth crunch.

In a lower tone Bonelli said, "Don't say where you heard it. I would rather it wasn't known that I told, but Wiley Martin is Bob Travis!"

"Thanks. I'll have a talk with him."

"You'll not take him now?" Disappointment was obvious. "He's your man! He just got back from Texas!"

"So did Jed Chapin. So did your man Jeff Erlanger. Maybe you, too, for all I know. I want to talk to Martin. I have some other evidence that will have to tie in."

When Bonelli was gone, Bowdrie walked down the dark street. Bob Travis was sitting at his usual table in the Silver Dollar, but Bowdrie did not enter. He had reached the end of the street when he saw a light in the telegraph office again.

Bowdrie crossed to the railroad-station platform, glanced around, and then pushed the door open and went in. The operator glanced up. "Any message?" Bowdrie asked.

The operator hesitated, started to say there was none, trying meanwhile to shuffle some papers to cover another lying there.

"All right," Bowdrie said, "let me have it. And after this, don't be running to Bonelli with stories, or you won't have a job!"

"You can't accuse me of that! Besides," the operator said, "how would you get messages without me?"

"I can handle one of those keys as well as you, and from the speed you were sending, I can do a lot better!"

"You're an operator?"

"When necessary. Learned it as a youngster, an' worked at it a mite. Too confining for me, so I quit."

Grudgingly the operator passed messages through the barred window. Bowdrie glanced at one page, then the other. "You know who I am." His black eyes pinned the operator. "Now destroy the copies."

"I can't! I don't dare!"

Bowdrie slapped a hard palm on the window ledge. "You heard me! Destroy them. I will be responsible. And if one word of this gets out, I'll be back. I'll take over that key and report to your headquarters just what has been going on here."

"Bonelli will pistol-whip me. He threatened it."

"Keep your doors locked. If there's a ruckus, I'll come running. Anyway, these messages don't concern Bonelli or you."

Chick took the mesages and walked back up the dark street, pausing briefly in the light of a window to read the messages again. The first presented no problem.

Jed Chapin's brother loaned him eight thousand. All regular. Impossible Chapin could reach Pecos in time.

The second message left Bowdrie a lot to think about.

Wiley Martin not wanted in Texas. Wanted in Missouri, Wyoming, and Nebraska for killings on Tom, Bench, and Red Fox. If he's your man, be careful! His real name Jay Burke. Will not be taken alive.

Jay Burke. The name was familiar. He was the last survivor of the Saltillo Cattle War that had taken place on both sides of the border. The Burke enemies had been the notorious Fox family of outlaws. The Fox outlaws had killed Jay Burke's father and destroyed his home. Jay Burke's pursuit of the outlaws was legend. He had followed them from state to state and killed them where he found them; all were killed in fair stand-up fights.

Bob Travis still sat at his table when Bowdrie walked into the saloon and seated himself across from him. Erlanger and Bonelli were present, and Bowdrie caught a dark, malicious gleam in Bonelli's eyes as he sat down.

His face inscrutable, the gray-eyed man faced Bowdrie, measuring him with careful attention. "You have made a good start on your job, Bowdrie."

"You know me, then?"

"The whole town knows. They also know—" he struck a match and lifted it to his cigarette—"what you're here for."

"Not many of them seem to want to talk," Bowdrie said.

Travis' eyes flickered to Bowdrie's. "Then somebody has?"

"Of course." Chick picked up the deck of cards and shuffled them. "There is always somebody who will." His eyes strayed to Bonelli, who was trying to conceal his interest.

"I see." Travis seemed uncertain, and Bowdrie's face indicated nothing. Travis, he was thinking, was a dangerous man, which was probably why Bonelli had left him alone.

On his part, Travis was studying Bowdrie and wondering about the next move. Bowdrie was known as a hard, relentless man, but rumor credited him with many acts of kindness. "What are you going to do?" he asked finally.

"Ask some questions. Where did you go in Texas?"

"To a ranch north of Pecos."

"Not to Pecos itself?"

"No. Although I passed within a mile of it."

"You rode your gray?"

"Why, yes, I did. Why? What's wrong?"

"I tracked that gray from in front of the Pecos Bank. The man who rode that horse killed two men while robbin' the bank."

Travis was white to the eyes, and Bowdrie reached a careful hand to his shirt pocket to bring forth the message that mentioned Burke. He handed it to Travis.

Travis glanced at it. "What you have here"—he indicated the message—"is true. You know from what it says here the kind of man I am. No Burke ever robbed a bank. No Burke ever lied. I did not ride into Pecos. I did not rob a bank. I have never killed anyone in Texas."

Bonelli was still watching them, but he was frowning

now, and impatient. Jeff Erlanger had moved to the bar and was standing with his back to it, glass in hand, watching Bowdrie.

"Travis, I would like to believe you, but today you talked to Amy Chapin in the street, and the tracks of your horse were the tracks of the horse the killer rode!"

"What?" He leaned forward. "Man, why didn't you say so? I rode a gray horse, all right, but not that horse. Today was the first time I've ridden him, although he's been in my corral back of the saloon for the past two months."

Bowdrie took the letter from his pocket, the letter addressed to Wiley Martin that had been found outside the bank after the robbery.

"This letter was dropped by the killer. It is addressed to you."

"Yes," Travis agreed, "that letter came to me. I do not recall seeing it again after receiving it."

"About those horses in the corral? Did anybody but you ever ride them?"

"Half the town did. I kept at least a dozen head there. My own riders rode them when they needed a fresh horse, but so did various people around town, but I can't imagine anybody actually taking one of them to Texas!"

Chick shoved back his chair. "Don't let it bother you, Travis, and just stick that message in your pocket. You aren't wanted in Texas, and I don't make arrests for anybody else. There were a few points I wanted to clear up. Now I know the answers."

He got to his feet, his eyes sweeping the room.

Erlanger lounged against the bar, watching him. Bonelli remained at his table, but he seemed uneasy now. Then the door opened and Jed Chapin came in. Buffalo Barton was with him.

"Tex," Chapin said, "I've got to see you!"

"Later," Bowdrie replied. "I've some work to do!"

Bonelli took something in his hand, glanced at it, then tossed it into his mouth.

"Bonelli, I am a Texas Ranger. I am arresting you for the robbery of the Pecos Bank and the murder of two men there!"

Bonelli got up. "That's a lot of hogwash! You've got the deadwood on Travis! Or Martin, if he wants to call himself that! You've got nothing on me!"

"You're wrong, Bonelli. I have all I need, even though you did all you could to implicate Travis, and so rid yourself of the one man you feared. You dropped that letter of Martin's where it would be found. You rode one of his horses, planning for the trail to lead to him."

Bonelli shrugged with apparent indifference. "Prove it! I've people will swear I was never out of the state, and you can't prove I was ever in Texas!"

"Bonelli, a few days ago I noticed a habit you have. You chew wingscale seeds, like some Zunis do. You're doing it now. You were chewing them tonight when I talked to you on the street, and you were chewing them when you waited across the street from the bank in Pecos. It isn't a common habit, Bonelli."

"That's no proof. That's no proof at all!"

"It's enough for me to ask you to take off your shirt, Bonelli. You bathed the dust off your upper body in the trough by the corral in Pecos, and some people there saw the tattoo under your heart. Will that be proof, Bonelli?"

"I didn't rob no bank!"

"Take off your shirt and show us. If you've no tattoo, I'll not only apologize but I'll stand treat for the house."

"All right! I'll show you! I'll prove you wrong!" His hands went to the buttons on his shirt and dropped to his gun butt.

The draw was fast, for when his hand went to the buttons it was already moving and within inches of the gun, but Bowdrie had expected it and his gun stabbed flame an instant faster.

At almost the same instant, Travis fired across the table-top, smashing Jeff Erlanger against the bar. His knees sagged and he went to the floor, but Bowdrie was watching Bonelli.

He was still on his feet, his lips twisted in a wry, unhappy grin. "Guess I wasn't cut out for . . . for this here game." He sank to the floor and spilled over on his face.

Gently Bowdrie turned him over. "I knew it was you," he muttered. "Had you spotted."

"No . . . no hard feelings?"

"No hard feelings. I'm only sorry you took the wrong turn in the trail."

"Yeah." Bonelli stared upward into the darkness near the ceiling. "Guess that was it. Had me a little ranch once, in Texas." He fumbled for words, but though his lips twisted, no sound came.

Bowdrie stood back, glanced around the room, then walked over to Travis' table and sat down.

He glanced at Erlanger's body, then at Travis. "Thanks," he said; then he added, "Bonelli gave himself away earlier. He told me I'd know the tracks of Travis' gray if I saw them, but the only way he could have known I got here by following the gray was by seeing me.

"For all he could have known, I'd gotten here by trailin' *you,* because your trail and his crossed each other now and again. A good tracker can tell a lot by the trail of the man he is followin'. You rode like a man with an easy conscience, but Bonelli spent a lot of time stoppin' from time to time to look down his back trail, and he kept under cover wherever he could."

"That's what I wanted to tell you about," Chapin said. "I located a man who saw Bonelli take that gray from the corral." He looked from Travis to Bowdrie. "Amy's outside, Tex."

Bowdrie went outside. Amy sat in the buckboard. "I'm glad you're all right," she said. "Now you know why I couldn't tell you about Wiley Martin."

"Everybody seemed to like him," Bowdrie admitted. "And I guess he was the only man standing between the Bonelli crowd and even more trouble."

"It wasn't only that, Tex. He's my uncle. You see, my mother's name was Burke, and my uncle's name was Robert Jay Burke. He used whatever name was handy when he was on the trail of the Foxes, and when he first located here, he was known as Travis. He just kept that name."

Amy glanced at Chick. "Are you going to accept Dad's offer? He does need help."

Bowdrie shook his head. "There's too much to do back in Texas, and I'm a tumbleweed, I guess."

"You can always come back, Tex." Then she said, "I shouldn't call you that, I guess. They say you are Chick Bowdrie." Then she laughed. "However did you get a name like Chick?"

He smiled. "My name was Charles. Most times Chuck is a nickname for Charles, but there was another boy in school who was called Chuck. He was bigger than I was, so they called me Chick." He chuckled. "I never minded."

When he was back in the hotel, he started thinking again about Amy. Maybe if he stayed on, worked for her father, and . . .

A RANGER RIDES TO TOWN

MORNING LAY SPRAWLED in sleepy comfort in the sunlit streets. The banker's rooster, having several times proclaimed the fact that he was up and doing, walked proudly toward the dusty street. The banker, his shirt-tail hanging out, was just leaving the front door accompanied by two men, both dusty from hard riding.

Outside the bank a rider clad in a linen duster sat astride a blood bay with his rifle across his knees and the reins of three other horses in his hands. The fourth man of the group leaned against a storefront some twenty yards away with a rifle in his hands.

The bank's door was already wide open and the banker and his escort disappeared within.

East of town the dry wash had been bridged and the sound of a horse's hooves on that bridge was always audible within the town. Now, suddenly, that bridge thundered with the hoof-beats of a hard-ridden horse, and the two men in the street looked sharply around.

Behind his house, Tommy Ryan, thirteen years old and small for his age, was splitting wood. He glanced around in time to see a man on a hammerhead roan, the horse's sides streaked with sweat, charge into the street. The man wore a black flat-crowned hat and the two guns in his hands were not there for fun.

The man in the linen duster was closest, and he hesitated, waiting to see who or what was approaching. When he saw a rider with pistols in his hand and a Ranger's badge on his chest, he lifted his rifle, but too late. The rider's bullet cut a long furrow the length of his forearm and smashed his elbow. The rifle fell into the dust. Numb with shock, the rider sat gripping his arm and staring.

The rifleman down the street caught the second bullet just as he himself fired. He stood for an instant, then turned and walked three steps and fell on his face. One spur rowel kept turning a moment after he fell.

When the shooting was over, one of the banker's escorts lay sprawled in the doorway, gun in hand, and the Ranger stood over him, gun in hand, staring into the shadowy precincts of the bank.

Another man with a badge pushed his way through the crowd that gathered. "Hi, Bowdrie! I'm Hadley, sheriff. I didn't know there were any Rangers in the country."

"Looks like I got here just in time," Bowdrie commented. He kept a pistol in his hand.

"Some shootin'," a bystander commented.

"Surprise," Bowdrie said. "They didn't expect anybody to come shooting. I had an edge."

Sheriff Hadley led the way into the bank. Two men lay dead on the floor, one of them the banker. He had been shot through the head at close range.

"He was a good man," Hadley said. "The town needed him." He glanced around. "You scored a clean sweep. You got 'em all."

"That's what it looks like," he agreed. His eyes swept the scene with a swift, all-seeing glance. Then he went past the bodies and into the private office of the banker. It was cool there, and undisturbed.

Bowdrie paused for a long minute, looking around, considering not only what he saw but what he had just seen. This room had been the seat of a man's pride, of his life's work. He had been a man who was building something, not only for himself and those who followed, but for his country. This man was putting down roots, enabling others to do the same.

Now he was dead, and for what? That some loose-gunned wastrels might have a few dollars to spend on whiskey and women.

He turned to look back into the bank, where Hadley was squatting beside the bodies. "No business today, Hadley. I want the bank closed."

"Young Jim Cane can handle it," Hadley said. "He's a good man."

"Nevertheless, I want the bank closed for business. I want to look around. Don't explain, just close it."

Tommy Ryan stared wide-eyed at the Ranger. He had been hearing stories of Chick Bowdrie but had never seen a real live Ranger before. Bowdrie's eyes wandered the street, studying the storefronts, the upstairs windows. Who might have been a witness? In a town of early risers, somebody must have seen what happened before the hold-up.

"Anything I can do?" The man was tall and well-set-up, with blond hair and friendly eyes. "I'm Kent Friede. I was a friend of Hayes's."

"Nothin' anybody can do, Kent. Hayes never had a chance. Shot right through the skull. Bowdrie here come in on 'em and made a cleanup. He got 'em all."

"No," Bowdrie said quietly, oblivious of the startled glances from Hadley and Friede. "I got three. But I didn't shoot at that man inside the bank and he didn't shoot Hayes."

"What?" Hadley turned on him. "Then who—?"

"There was a fifth man who never appeared in the operation. He killed both Hayes and the outlaw inside the bank."

"I don't follow," Friede said. "How could that be?"

Bowdrie shrugged. "Who runs the bank now? Is it this Jim Cane you mentioned?"

"If there's anything left to run. Lucky they didn't get away with any money."

"It's my guess they did get the money," Bowdrie said. "The fifth man got it, and it's my bet he knew where to look."

"You're implying it was an inside job?" Friede was obviously skeptical. "I don't believe that. Jim Cane's a fine young man. We all trust him."

Bowdrie waved a hand. "Close it up, Hadley, and give me the key. Some things don't fit, but they will before I'm through."

Yet as he walked along the street he was far from feeling confident. The outlaw with the broken arm had been taken to jail and must be questioned. Bowdrie had an idea he would know nothing. The man who planned this job would have been shrewd enough to communicate with only one man, undoubtedly the outlaw killed inside the bank. At least, that was how it looked now.

He believed there was a fifth man involved, but it was no more than a theory and one that might not hold water.

First, his own arrival had not been by chance. He had been tipped that a robbery was planned. Who had tipped him, and why? Who had thrown that note wrapped around a rock into his campsite only a few hours ago? A note that warned him of the hold-up and how it was to be carried out? At first glance he had seen that the banker had been killed from close up. Also, when he entered the bank there had been a thin blue tinge of tobacco smoke in the office air, and the smell of tobacco. None of the outlaws had been smoking, nor had the harried banker.

Nor was there any reason for them to enter the private office. The huge old safe was against the back wall some distance away, and it was before this safe that Hayes had been murdered. A man standing in the door of the private office could have fired that shot, yet all Bowdrie's man-hunting experience told him no outlaws would have been in that position. But suppose a man had already been hidden inside the bank?

A small boy stood nearby in bare feet and Bowdrie glanced down into the wide blue eyes and the freckled face. "Hi, podner! Is this your town?"

"Yup! My pa sank the first well ever dug in this county!"

"Rates him high in my book," Bowdrie said. "Any man who brings water to a dry country deserves credit."

"You stayin' in town?"

"For a little while, I guess. I've got to find the men who did this." He paused. "It was a dirty deal, son, because there was another man in on this. He not only shot Banker Hayes in the back, he double-crossed his own pals."

The boy nodded seriously. By his own standards as well as those of the country in which he lived, the two crimes were among the worst of which a man could be accused.

All was quiet at the jail when he arrived. The wounded outlaw was lying on his bunk staring at the ceiling. Reluctantly he sat up when Bowdrie came to the bars. "You should have killed me," he said bitterly. "I ain't cut out for no prison. I'll die in there."

"Maybe you won't have to go," Bowdrie said.

"What's that?"

"If you can tell me who was in on this job, you might go free. Who was waiting inside the bank?"

"Huh?" The outlaw was obviously surprised. "Inside? Nobody. The boys went after Hayes. He opened the bank door." He paused, frowning. "Come to think on it, the banker just walked in. The door was already unlocked. But how could anybody be inside?"

"You tell me." Bowdrie studied the man. The outlaw was surprised and disturbed. "Who planned this job?"

"I dunno. They come to me an' asked if I'd like to go as horse-holder. I'd done a few things with one of those boys before, so I went along. We wasn't to use no names. Nobody was supposed to ask questions. Him who was killed inside, he was ridin' herd on us. He set this up if anybody did."

"Where was the split to be made?"

"Well"—the outlaw hesitated—"it was to be made after. After we got away, I mean. Nothin' much was said about it. We done taken it for granted, like."

"The man who was killed down by the store. Did you know him?"

"Seen him around. He was rounded up, just like me. Those boys had a job planned and they needed help. We wasn't any organized outfit, if that's what you mean."

"Was there any talk about money?"

"Sure! That's why we done it. The big feller, the one who was killed inside, he said we'd make five hundred apiece from it, maybe more. That there's a lot of money for somebody like me. Hell, I on'y worked seven months last year, at thirty dollars a month. Stole a few head of stock here'n there, never made more than drinkin' money."

Chick Bowdrie went back to his horse, and mounting, rode out of town. That he was being watched, he knew. Out of curiosity? Or fear? Suspicion was growing, centering around young Cane, who would inherit whatever the banker left.

Easy as that solution was, and Bowdrie could think of a half-dozen reasons for believing it, that simple answer left him uneasy and unconvinced. Riding out of town, he circled around until he could pick up the incoming trail of the four outlaws.

They could have reached town no more than fifteen minutes before he himself. That meant they must have been camped not too far from town, and might have been visited by whoever the inside man had been.

Slowly, a pattern was beginning to shape itself in Bowdrie's mind, although he was careful to remember it was no more than a possibility.

The inside man had known there was money in the bank and he had made contact with an outlaw, perhaps somebody he had known before. At his suggestion that outlaw had rounded up a few men to pull off the job. None of them were to know anything. If captured they would be unable to tell anything because they knew nothing.

It was early and nobody had come over the trail since the arrival of the outlaws. He picked up their trail without difficulty. They had made no effort to hide their tracks, until suddenly, by intent or accident, their trail merged with that of a herd of horses. He was more than two hours in working out their trail.

At first it held to dry washes and then wove through mesquite groves higher than the head of a man on horseback. Almost an hour of riding brought him to a campfire of ashes and a few partly burned sticks. He stirred the ashes and found no embers, but when he felt the ash with his fingers, there was still warmth.

Dividing the camp into quarters, he searched each section with meticulous care. They had eaten here, and they had drunk coffee. There had been four men who were joined by a fifth man who sat with them. This man had sat on the ground, one leg outstretched. His spur had gouged the sand and there were faint scratches near the upper part of the boot.

Studying the situation carefully, he then mounted and rode in careful circles, ever-widening, around the camp. He drew up suddenly. Here, behind a clump of mesquite, a man had crouched, spying on the outlaw camp. Bowdrie muttered irritably. The roan twitched an ear and Bowdrie glanced up. The horse was looking toward the trail with both ears pricked and his nostrils expanding. Speaking softly to the horse, Bowdrie waited, ready.

A rider pushed through the mesquite and came toward them at a fast trot, but his eyes were on the ground and did not see Bowdrie until he was quite near. He drew up sharply. It was Kent Friede.

"Find anything?" Was there an edge to his tone?

"Not much. They camped back yonder, an' they had a visitor."

"Ah!" Friede nodded. "I suspected as much! Most likely Cane rode out here to give them information."

"What makes you suspect Cane? Anybody might have done it."

"Who else would gain by Hayes's death?"

Bowdrie shrugged, sitting easy on his horse. Something about Friede bothered him, and he decided he would not want to turn his back on him. It was just a feeling, and probably a foolish one. It was never wise to jump to conclusions. What he wanted was evidence.

"I've not met Cane. What's he like?"

"About twenty-five. Nice-looking man. He's been a cowhand, and he drove a freight wagon. Lately he's been working in a store."

"How'd he come to be Hayes's heir?"

"Hayes cottoned to him from the first time they met, and now he's about to marry Hayes's daughter. He works part-time in the bank, with Hayes. After the bank closes, he goes over to the store."

JIM CANE WAS in the Caprock Saloon with Hadley when they walked in. He was a rangy young man with dark red hair and a hard jaw. He looked more like a rider than a banker. Cane turned as they entered and his eyes slanted quickly from one to the other. Bowdrie felt his pulse skip a beat as he saw Cane. A few years had changed him a lot.

"Find anything?" Hadley asked. The sheriff was a stalwart man, a leather-hard face and cool, careful eyes. A good man to have on your side, a bad man to have on your trail.

"Not much." Bowdrie explained about the campfire and the visitor. He did not mention the unseen watcher, nor what he had found near the campfire.

"All right to get back to business at the bank?" Cane asked. There was a shade of belligerence in his tone. "I've ranchers coming in for their payroll money."

"Will you have the money they need?"

"I've sent to Maravillas for it. We lost eight thousand dollars," he added.

"Payroll money? Somebody must have known it would be there."

"Everybody knew. We've been supplying ranchers with payroll money for years."

"Eight thousand? That could hurt to lose. Can you make out?"

"You mean, will it break the bank? No, it won't. That bank belongs to Mary Jane now, and I won't let it break." He spoke with cool determination, yet there was something more in his tone. A warning?

"You should make out," Friede commented, "as long as no rumors get started. What if there was a run on the bank?"

Jim Cane turned his eyes to Friede. "You'd like that, wouldn't you? You'd like to see Mary Jane broke and me thrown out."

Bowdrie watched the two men. Hadley had tightened up, ready to avert trouble if it began. Out of such a quarrel might come something revealing.

Friede put down his glass. "I've no trouble with either of you. If Hayes wanted to take in a saddle tramp, that was his business, and if Mary Jane wants to marry a drifter, that's hers."

Cane balled his fists. "Why, you—!"

"Easy does it!" Hadley interrupted. "Kent, you watch your tongue. I've seen men killed for no more than that."

Friede shrugged contemptuously. His face was white and drawn, but not with fear. This man when cornered could be deadly. "Don't start anything, Cane, or I'll have my say. Some people don't like wet stock."

Jim Cane looked as if he had been slapped, but before he could reply Kent Friede turned away, an ugly triumph in his expression. Cane stared after him and his hand shook as it lifted to the bar as if to steady himself. Then without a word he walked out.

Hadley stared after them. "Now, what did he mean by that?" Hadley glanced at Bowdrie. "Friede seems to know more than he lets on."

Bowdrie made no comment, but behind his dark, Indian-like features his mind was working swiftly. The deep, dimplelike scar beneath his cheekbone seemed deeper, and his face had grown colder. Leaving Hadley in the saloon, he crossed to the bank.

There were things here he must check before the bank was permitted to reopen, but more than that he wanted to be alone, to think. Letting himself in, he closed and locked the door behind him, then stood looking around.

It was late afternoon and the sun was going down. Most of the townspeople were at home preparing for supper. Only hours before, two men had died here, killed by a man they trusted, but who was the man?

For almost an hour he sat in the banker's chair reconstructing the crime by searching through his experience and what little he had learned for the motivation. After a while he went to the old filing cabinet and rummaged through the papers there and in the desk. Finally he stepped out on the street, locking the door behind him.

The Hayes house was just down the street and he turned that way. In answer to his knock the door was opened by a slender, dark-haired girl with lovely eyes. Eyes red from crying. "Oh? You must be the Ranger? Will you come in?"

Bowdrie removed his hat and followed her through the ornate old parlor with its stiff-collared portraits of ancestors to a spacious and comfortable living room. He realized then that he had come to the wrong door. The parlor entrance or "front door" was rarely used in these houses. The kitchen door was the usual entrance. The table, he noticed as he glanced into the dining room, was set for three, although but one plate was in use.

"Please don't let me interrupt your supper," he protested.

She glanced at him quickly, embarrassed. "I . . . I set Dad's place, too. Habit, I guess."

"Why not? And the other is for Jim Cane?"

"Have you seen him? I've been so worried. He's taking this awfully hard. He . . . he loved Dad as much as I did."

Her voice was low and he caught the emotion in it and changed the subject.

"I hope to finish my work tomorrow and be riding on, but there are some things you could tell me. Was Kent Friede sweet on you? I mean, was he a suitor?" Bowdrie could not recall ever using the expression before, but believed it was the accepted one. There was so much he did not know about how people talked or conducted themselves. So much he wanted to know.

"Sort of. As much as he could be on anyone. Kent's mostly concerned with himself. Then . . . well, he's not the sort of man a girl would marry. I mean . . . he's killed men. He is very good with a gun. The best around here, unless it is Sheriff Hadley."

Bowdrie's black eyes met hers. His expression was mildly amused. "You wouldn't marry a gunfighter?"

She flushed. "Well, I didn't mean that . . . exactly."

Bowdrie smiled, and she was startled at how warm and pleasant it made him look. He had seemed somehow grim and formidable. Maybe it was because she knew who he was. "Your coffee's good." She had almost automatically filled his cup. "Even a gunfighter can enjoy it. But I know what you mean. You want to be sure when you cook supper there's somebody there to eat it."

The door opened suddenly and there was a jingle of spurs and Jim Cane stood framed in the opening. His face was drawn and worried. His eyes went sharply from Bowdrie to Mary Jane. "You here? Why can't you let this girl alone? She's lost her father, and—"

"Jim!" Mary Jane protested. "Mr. Bowdrie has been very

nice. We have been talking and sharing some coffee. Why don't you sit down and we will all have supper?"

"Maybe the Ranger won't be able to. There's been a killing. Kent Friede was found dead just a few minutes ago."

Bowdrie put down his cup. He had been looking forward to a quiet supper. It was not often he ate with people. "Who found him?"

"I did." Cane stared defiantly. "He was lying in the alley behind the bank, and if you think I killed him, you're dead wrong!"

"I didn't say . . ." Bowdrie got to his feet. "Thank you, Miss Hayes."

Kent Friede lay on his face in the alley back of the bank with a knife between his shoulder blades, a knife driven home by a sure, powerful hand. His body was still warm.

A half-dozen men stood around as Bowdrie made his examination. Chick was thinking fast as he got to his feet.

This was all wrong. Kent Friede was not the man to let another get behind him. Nor was there any cover close by. The alley was gravel and not an easy place to creep up on a man unheard. This was cold-blooded murder, but one thing he knew. It had not happened in this alley.

He withdrew the knife and studied it in the light of a lantern. He held it up. "Anybody recognize this?"

"It's mine!" Tommy Ryan's eyes were enormous with excitement. "It's my knife! I was throwin' it this afternoon. Throwin' it at a mark on that ol' corner tree!"

Bowdrie glanced in the direction indicated. The knife would have been ready to anyone's hand. He balanced the knife, considering the possibilities.

Kent Friede was dead, the body found by Jim Cane. Only a short time before, the two had almost come to blows before a dozen witnesses, and Friede had made his remark about wet stock. Bowdrie heard muttering in the gathering crowd, and Cane's name was mentioned.

Sheriff Hadley joined them. "This doesn't look good, Bowdrie. People are already complainin' that I haven't arrested Jim Cane for the bank robbery. Now this here is surely goin' to stir up trouble."

"Have you any evidence? Or have they? A lot of loose talk doesn't make a man guilty."

"No evidence I know of," Hadley agreed. "I'd never have suspected anything was wrong at the bank without you bringin' it up. What gave you the idea?"

"Tobacco smoke. Somebody was inside the bank before the outlaws got there. After tipping me off to the robbery and its time. Whoever it was figured I'd come a-shootin' and kill all or some of them and maybe get killed myself. In fact, I think he counted on that.

"Then during the gun battle outside he finished off the two inside and got away with the money. If I'd been killed too, there was just no way anybody could figure out what happened. He'd have the money and be completely in the clear."

"Looks like he is anyway," Hadley agreed ruefully. "This Friede, he might have known something."

"He knew a lot, a lot too much. You see, Sheriff, he knew who that other outlaw was. He knew the fifth man. He followed somebody to that outlaw camp and he crouched down in the mesquite and heard them planning it."

Bowdrie ARRANGED FOR the body to be picked up and then walked back to the hotel, where he had taken a room. In the hotel he bundled the bedding together to resemble the body of a sleeping man; then he unrolled his blankets and slept on the floor.

The gun's report and the tinkle of falling glass awakened him. The bullet had smashed into the heaped-up clothing on the bed, then thudded into the wall. He got up carefully and eased to a position near the door. Outside somewhere a light went on and he heard an angry voice. He looked into the alley. It was dark, empty, and still.

He waited. A few people came out on the street, and he heard more complaints about drunken cowboys and disturbed sleep.

He studied the line the bullet must have taken to break the window, penetrate the heaped-up bedding, and crash into the wall. It was, he reflected, the thud of the bullet into the wall that had awakened him, almost the instant of the report.

From beside the window he studied the situation. The bullet could have come from a dark corner of the livery stable, a place where a man might wait for hours without being seen. At night there was very little activity in town. Even the saloons closed by midnight.

Pulling on his clothing, he went into the street, moving toward the livery stable. The door gaped wide. There was a lantern hanging from a nail over the door, but nobody was around. A hostler slept in the tack room at the back of the stable during the busy times.

Stepping inside the door, he glanced around. He saw no cigarette butts, although when he squatted on his heels he detected a little ash. Taking a chance, he struck a match. There was some ash and a few fragments of tobacco. He scraped them together and put them in a fold of a sheet torn from his tally book.

Standing on the corner in the shadow of the barn, he saw he was no more than fifty yards from Jim Cane's cabin. He walked past the cabin, staying in the dust to make no sound. No light showed.

He walked past the sheriff's office and back to the hotel, passing the tree where young Tommy Ryan had been practicing throwing his knife.

———

MORNING DAWNED BRIGHT and clear. Bowdrie went out into the street, feeling good. He knew the killer was both puzzled and worried.

A well-laid plan had backfired. Too many things had gone wrong, and now the killer did not know but what something else, something he had not thought of, might also have gone wrong. One way out remained. To kill Bowdrie. The Ranger knew more than he was expected to know and at any moment he might achieve a solution that would mean the collapse of all the killer's schemes and his own arrest.

That he had been marked for death on the day he rode into town, Bowdrie was well aware. That he survived the initial shoot-out had been the first thing to go wrong. Of course, even before that, Kent Friede had spied on the outlaw camp, but of that the killer had no knowledge at the time, and that situation had been remedied. Bowdrie remained.

He walked across the dusty street to the restaurant. Every sense was alert. What happened must take place within the next few hours. His hands were never far from the butts of his pistols. When he reached the restaurant door he looked around. Jim Cane stepped out of an alley and crossed the street toward him.

Bowdrie went inside and sat down. He knew the killer. He knew just who the other outlaw was and what he had done. The difficulty was that he had no concrete evidence, only several intangible clues, things that weighed heavily with him, but nothing he could offer a jury.

Jim Cane pushed open the door and strode across to his table. "How about the bank? Hadley says it's okay to open."

"How about a cup of coffee?" Bowdrie suggested. Then, as Cane seated himself, he added, "Sure, you can open up, and good luck to you. However"—he leaned closer—"you might do something for me." He went on, whispering.

Cane stared at him, then swallowed his coffee and left the café. Chick Bowdrie stirred his coffee and smiled at nothing.

Tommy Ryan came to the door and peered in; then he crossed to the table. "Mr. Bowdrie," he said, "I got somethin' to tell you. I seen who took my knife."

Bowdrie glanced at him sharply. "Who have you told besides me?"

"Nobody. On'y Pa. He said—"

"Tell me later. Why don't you sit over at that table, drink a glass of milk and eat a piece of that thick apple pie? On me."

Sheriff Hadley entered. He was a strapping big man and as usual he walked swiftly, his gray hat pulled down, the old-fashioned mule-ear straps flapping against the sides of his boots.

He dropped into the chair across from Bowdrie. "Bowdrie, I figured it only right to talk to you first. I got to make an arrest. It's no secret who done it. I've got to arrest a thief and a killer."

"Why not leave it to me?" His thick forearms rested on the table and his black eyes met those of the sheriff. "You see, I've known almost from the start who the guilty man was. Things began to tie up when I first saw those bodies lyin' on the floor in the bank. That dead outlaw? That was Nevada Pierce."

"Pierce? You sure of that?"

"Uh-huh. You see, I sent him to prison once. And his description was in the Rangers' Bible. Lots of descriptions there, Hadley."

Their eyes clung. "You mean . . . you got Jim Cane's description, too?"

"Sure. I spotted him right off. Jim used to run stock across the Rio Grande. That was four, five years ago."

"You knowed he was a horse thief and you haven't arrested him?"

"That's right, Hadley. You see, we live on the edge of lawless times. Lots of men got their first stake branding unbranded cattle. It surely wasn't theirs, but nobody else could prove a claim to it either. Afterward some other boys came along later, so to even things up, they switched brands.

"Now, maybe that's stealin', Hadley. By the book I guess it is. Nowadays it would surely be stealin', for there's no unclaimed stock runnin' around. It all belongs to somebody. It hasn't always been easy to decide who was a crook and who wasn't.

"So you know what I do? I judge a man by his record. Suppose a man who's rustled a few head in the old days goes straight after that? The country is settlin' down now, so if a man settles down an' behaves himself, we sort of leave him alone. If we went by the letter of the law, I could jail half the old-time cattlemen in Texas, but the letter of the law isn't always justice. It was open range then, and two-thirds of the beef stock a man could find was maverick. If a man goes straight, we leave him alone."

"What do you mean?" Hadley kept his voice low. "You call robbin' banks an' killin' goin' straight?"

"Not a bit of it. If Cane had robbed a bank or killed anyone, I'd have arrested him. He had nothing to do with it."

Their eyes met across the table and Bowdrie said, "That Rangers' Bible of ours, it carries a lot of descriptions, like I said. It has descriptions of all the crowd who used to run with Pierce.

"There was one thing always puzzled Pierce, and that was how the Rangers always managed to outguess him. What he never knew was that we were always tipped off by one of his own outfit."

Hadley pushed his chair back, both hands on the table's edge. "You've got this man spotted, Bowdrie?"

"Sure. He had a record, just like Cane, but at first I held off. Maybe I was prejudiced because of his record. It might have been Cane or Kent Friede, so I waited."

Chick Bowdrie lifted his coffee cup and looked over it at Sheriff Hadley. "You shouldn't have done it, Hadley. You had a nice job. People respected you."

"With eight thousand dollars just waitin' to be picked up? And Jim Cane to lay it on?" His tone deepened and became ugly. "An' I'd have made it but for you."

"You tipped the Rangers to that Pierce hold-up, didn't you? We always wondered where the money got to. Now I know. The Rangers got him and you got the money, and now you've tried it again. You're under arrest, Hadley."

Hadley got to his feet, his hands hovering over his guns. "You make a move, Ranger, an' you die! You hear that?"

"Sure." Bowdrie still held his cup. "I hear."

Hadley backed through the door and ran across the street as Bowdrie got up and tossed a silver dollar on the table. "For the kid's grub, too," he said.

He glanced at the boy. "It was Hadley you saw, wasn't it?"

"Uh-huh. You lettin' him get away?"

"No, Tommy. I just didn't want any shooting in here. He won't get far, Tommy. You see, I planned it this way. There isn't a horse on the street, nor in the livery stable. Hadley won't go far this time."

Outside, the street was empty, yet people knew what was happening and they would be at the windows. Hadley was at his hiding place now, getting out the eight thousand dollars.

Soon he would discover there was no horse in his stable, so he would rush to the street to get one.

"Only he knew where the money was, Tommy. The bank has to have it back. He'll get it for us."

Bowdrie walked outside and away from the front of the café.

Hadley emerged from an alley, a heavy sack in his hand, a pistol in the other. When he saw no horses tied at the hitching rails, he looked wildly about.

"Hadley, you needn't look. There ain't a horse within a quarter of a mile."

"You! You set me up!"

"Of course I did. Just as you set up your partners, time after time.

"I didn't have enough proof, Hadley. Only that there were no cigarette butts, just ashes and sometimes burned matches. You smoke a pipe, Hadley.

"Also, Pierce's old partner was a knife-thrower, and the knife that killed Friede had to be thrown. At first I thought he'd been killed elsewhere, because nobody could have walked up behind Friede over that gravel.

"We just had a few facts, Hadley, never a full description of you, so you could have gone straight and nobody the wiser. You tied it all up nicely, Hadley, you yourself."

Hadley's gun came up and Bowdrie drew and fired before the gun came level. Flame stabbed from Bowdrie's pistol and the sheriff dropped the loot and tried to bring his gun into line. Something seemed to be fogging his vision, for when he fired again, he was several feet off the target.

Blood covered his shirt. He went to his knees. "A damn Ranger!" he said. Then he cursed obscenely. "It had to be a Ranger."

"Our job, Hadley, but you got yours in front, not in the back."

Hadley stared up at him; then his eyes glazed and the fingers on the pistol relaxed. Bowdrie bent down and took the gun from his fingers.

People came out on the street. Some lingered, shading their

eyes to see. Others came closer. Bowdrie indicated the sack. "There's your money, Cane."

"Thanks. I moved the horses like you said." Then he asked, "How did you know?"

Bowdrie thumbed shells into his gun. He told Cane what he had told Hadley, then added, "It was all of it together, along with those mule-ear straps on Hadley's boots. I saw the marks on the sand made by them when he sat talking in the outlaw camp. Some of those old-timey boots like Hadley wore had loose straps to pull on the boots. Nowadays they make them stiffer and they don't dangle.

"I had an idea what might have made those marks, but when I saw Hadley, I knew. I had to be around town a mite to see if anybody else around was outfitted like him. Nobody was.

"All along, he had you pegged for the goat. He even rode one of your horses out there to talk to the outlaws. Hadley said he didn't know I was in the country, but I happen to know headquarters told him I was ridin' this way. He was the only one who could have thrown that note tipping me to the raid."

"You'd have thought he would have been sensible enough to go straight, with a good job, and all."

"Yeah," Bowdrie said, smiling at Cane, "the smart ones do go straight."

"You got time for something to eat? Mary Jane's frying up some eggs and she makes the best griddle cakes in Texas!"

"Home cookin'! I always did have a weakness for home cookin'. Although," Bowdrie added, "I never see much of it."

RAIN ON THE MOUNTAIN FORK

LEW JUDD WAS a frightened man. His hands, white as those of a woman, gathered the cards from the table-top, and he touched his tongue to dry lips. Overhead the rain was increasing its roar, and within the stuffy warmth of the sod shanty the air was thick with mingled tobacco and wood smoke, overlaid by the odor of wet, steamy clothing, drying wood, and worn leather.

DeVant, Baker, and Stadelmann sat around the table. Peg Roper snored on a bunk against the wall, and Big Ed Colson, the stage driver, straddled a chair and leaned his hairy fore-arms on its back, watching the play. Judd was sure that Big Ed knew he wore a money belt, but whether the others knew, he could not guess.

"You think the next stage will get through?"

The question was important to Judd. If the stage came soon enough, he might get away, and he might get Nelly away. The stage on which they had come lay hub-deep in mire with a broken axle.

Colson shrugged. "Your guess is as good as mine. This is the worst storm I've seen in this country, an' I've seen a few."

Nelly Craig, Judd's niece, sat beside the fire. It was bad enough to have to escort a young girl through such country without having to stop over in a place like this. As a protector he felt woefully inadequate, yet he kept his face composed, trying to keep the others from realizing his fear.

"We might as well figure on spending the night here," Baker commented. "If the stage does come, it will not get here before morning."

Big Stadelmann turned and stared toward the fire. Judd felt his abdominal muscles tighten, knowing he was staring at Nelly. In the feeble glow of the fire and the kerosene lantern he looked monstrous and brutal, a great bear of a man, his face covered with a stubble of short beard.

DeVant was slender and sallow-faced with malicious yellow eyes, his agile fingers fondling the cards like a lover. All the men were armed, as was the sleeping man on the bunk, and there was a watchfulness about them that warned Judd these were dangerous men.

Colson was armed, but where he would stand, Judd did not know. A postal employee from Minnesota, Judd was new to the country, and although he carried a gun, he was clumsy with it.

The fire sputtered from rain falling down the chimney and in the interval that followed a roll of thunder, they distinctly heard the splash of a horse's hooves on the sloppy trail.

DeVant's head came up sharply, and Stadelmann's hands became still. All were listening. Ed Colson took the pipe from his mouth and turned his head.

"Who in blazes would be riding on a night like this?" Baker demanded. "No man in his right mind would ride in this rain."

They heard the subdued sounds of a man stabling a horse in the sod barn adjoining. Then footsteps splashed and the flames flickered as the door opened to reveal wet boots and above them the lower edge of a slicker as the man stood on the steps closing the slanting door behind him. Judd waited, apprehensive and hopeful at the same time. Baker's hand was in his lap and Judd knew it held a gun. What was he afraid of? What were they all afraid of?

The newcomer came on down the steps, but nothing could be seen of him because of his raincoat collar and his tilted hat brim. The hat was flat-crowned and black, the visible mouth was firm, the jaw strong. His rain-wet chaps were black leather and when he removed the raincoat, he was wearing a fringed buckskin jacket over a gray wool shirt.

He was, they all noted, wearing two guns, tied down.

When he removed his hat to slap the rain from it, they saw a dark, Indian-like face. His eyes swept the room, lingering a bit on Roper, stretched on the bunk. Under his cheekbone there was a deep scar, possibly a bullet wound.

"Who's the owner here?" His tone was casual.

After a moment, when nobody answered, Colson replied. "Place was empty. When the stage broke down, we took shelter. I was drivin' the stage."

Judd looked at him hopefully. "Did you see the other stage on the trail?"

The steady black eyes examined and judged him. "There won't be a stage. A landslide wiped out the trail. Take work to get it back in shape. A lot of work."

DeVant's mind, nimble as his too clever fingers, came up with the logical question. "How did you get here, if the road is closed?"

"I came from the west, but that trail's closed, too. I had to come over the mountain above the creek, but I circled to examine the other way out."

Colson took the pipe from his mouth. "You came over the *mountain*? You're lucky to be alive. I wouldn't have thought a goat could make it on a night like this."

"That second slide came while I was up there. Seemed like the whole mountain started to move, but mine's a good horse an' we made it."

Thunder muttered irritably back in the canyons. The rain seemed empowered by the sound and rose to a shattering roar. There was a slow drip of water from near the bunk where Roper slept.

"We're stuck then," DeVant said. "We might as well make the best of it." He glanced at Nelly, meeting her eyes boldly. "All the comforts of home."

Nelly turned her eyes away and added a stick to the fire. The flames reached for it hungrily, and the stranger moved nearer to the fireplace, aware of her fear. "You were on the stage?" He spoke softly.

There were shaded hollows of tiredness beneath her eyes, which were dark and large. "I am traveling with my uncle, Lew Judd. We are from Illinois."

That would be the slender man in the store-bought suit, a

feeble staff on which to lean on such a night, in such a place. She knew he would be of no help and she was frightened.

"Don't be afraid," the stranger said. "It will be all right."

The others heard the murmur of their voices but the words were inaudible. When the stranger looked up, DeVant's cat-like eyes were on him. "A man ridin' on a night like this must want to go somewhere mighty bad."

"You could be right." The black eyes held DeVant's and the man felt a distinct chill, which irritated even as it frightened him.

Stadelmann was watching him, eyes suddenly attentive. Peg Roper shifted and muttered on the bunk.

"You were all on the stage?"

Baker's eyes lifted from his cards. His was a narrow, rock-hard face with a clipped mustache on his broad upper lip. "Now you're asking questions?"

The black eyes shifted to Baker and held him an instant before moving on. "That's right. I am asking questions."

The challenge was understood by everyone listening, and for a minute or so there was no sound but the hissing of the raindrops in the fire.

Baker felt something cold and empty in his stomach and he fumbled the cards. The yielding of his eyes enraged him. Yet that voice had rung with the crisp sound of authority.

The stranger turned his attention to Colson. "You were the driver? How many were on that stage?"

"Only Judd, his niece, and DeVant. Stadelmann an' Roper were in the dugout when we got here. Baker came along after."

"Roper was fast asleep when I come in," Stadelmann said. "You got a reason for askin'?"

"Murder's my reason. Murder an' robbery. The killer is in this room. He just can't be anywhere else."

Nelly Craig's face was a blotch of white. Her eyes seemed even larger.

"You're sure he came this way?" Colson asked.

"You know this country. He had no choice. He could have been on the stage or he might have been one of the others."

"You've no description?" Baker asked.

DeVant's eyes lifted from his cards. "Who're you? Askin' all the questions?"

"I'm a Ranger. My name is Bowdrie."

There was a heavy silence in the room. Others here might be wanted men. All at that moment felt guilty, and their resentment was electric in the room.

"You should have kept still about it," Judd said. "Now there will be trouble."

"You can't avoid trouble in this case. One of you here is carryin' money an' the murderer knows it. The murder back yonder was not a planned thing, and the murderer did not get as much as he counted on. It was something he stumbled into."

A stick toppled over into the fire and sent a shower of sparks up the chimney. Nelly moved her wet feet closer to the blaze and Big Ed Colson got out his pipe and stoked it methodically. Peg Roper continued to sleep. Judd sat silent, keeping his palms pressed to the table so their trembling would not be observed. It was Stadelmann he was afraid of, Stadelmann and DeVant, yet he trusted none of them. Not even the Ranger.

"Anybody got any coffee?" Baker suggested. "We might as well wait in comfort."

Bowdrie squatted against the wall. No doubt the killer was the most composed of them all. He alone knew who he was. No betraying clue had been left. Not a clue, only a slight indication of character. Somehow he must lead the murderer to betray himself.

Surprisingly, Nelly seemed revived by the new element introduced by the Ranger's arrival. Attention had been turned from her and other thoughts occupied the minds of the men in the room. More than one might be carrying money, and each would be likely to think himself the intended victim. Any of these men, she reflected, could crush Lew Judd like an insect.

She arose and went to the box Judd had carried into the room and came away with coffee. Colson found a flat stone to be placed among the coals, and retrieved a blackened coffee-pot from a shelf. There was darkness back there, a darkness into which they could not see, and when Colson went that way, all eyes followed him. All hands were resting near their guns. Colson returned with the pot and Nelly went about making coffee.

Her quick, homey manner brought relief to the tension, and instead of fear there was a growing levity, as though each had become conscious that he held a seat at a very dramatic show. Underneath it all, however, there was the taut strain of nervous tension. Of them all, Nelly and the stage driver seemed the least affected.

Judd, his own danger alleviated for the moment, opened the case he had carried into the room along with the small box with the coffee, and brought out a mandolin. While they waited for water to boil, he sang, in a fair tenor, "Drill Ye Tarriers," a song sung by Irish railroad builders, and inspired a healthy applause. He then sang "Sweet Betsy from Pike" and "Jenny Jenkins." The listeners came up with requests and the singing continued.

Bowdrie remained quiet against the wall. More than the others possibly could, he realized his own inadequacy. He knew his skill with guns, and that few men were better on a trail, but here he had only the devious path of a man's thinking to follow. He was moving in the dark, only aware that the killer might give himself away. How that was to happen, he did not know. Later, he might ask more questions.

Somehow, tonight, within this shack, the issue would be decided. And it was a narrow place for shooting.

DeVant moved his chair against the wall, a position from which he could survey the room as well as Bowdrie, and from which he could move swiftly to attack, defend, or seek the doubtful shelter of the bunk's corner.

At this moment Peg Roper awakened and sat up, obviously confused by the singing, the smell of coffee, and the crackle of the fire. Swinging his feet to the floor, he caught one spur in the ragged blanket. Disengaging it with care, he sat up, blinking around him, his sleepy little boy's face oddly puzzled under his shock of unruly hair.

"What's comin' off?" Peg asked. "I go to sleep in a morgue and wake up in a party."

"Folks kept dropping in," Baker said. "We've a special guest, a Texas Ranger."

Roper looked uneasy, but said, "Well, he seems a quiet Ranger. Knows how to keep his place."

Bowdrie smiled and put his shoulders against the wall. It was a thick wall and it felt good, about the only security he was likely to enjoy.

Colson found several cups back in the darkness and brought them to the table. He rinsed them with rainwater from the barrel outside the door.

Stadelmann appeared to be dozing and probably was. A man could doze and still catch some of the talk, although nothing important was being said. In fact, everyone seemed to be keeping to casual talk between songs.

Baker changed all that. "How d'you expect to find your man?" he asked Bowdrie. "He ain't just goin' to walk up an' tell you, you know."

"No problem," Bowdrie replied. "Biggest thing in my favor is that he knows he's guilty. A guilty man is afraid of makin' mistakes, of givin' himself away."

Peg Roper's eyes went to the girl, sitting quietly by the fire, watching the coffee. They stayed on her as she took a cup and poured, taking it first to the Ranger. He thanked her while Roper watched them. Obviously he was curious about her, so strange to such surroundings. Roper rubbed his unshaved chin ruefully. He looked miserable to try to make a play for the girl, but from the looks of it the Ranger had the inside track. Although he did not appear to be doing anything about it. Maybe it was because the Ranger was protection.

Bowdrie tasted the coffee with real appreciation. He was vastly comfortable now, with the cup in his hands, hot coffee in his belly, and that wall behind him. When the side of that mountain had started to move back yonder, he had an awful, sinking feeling inside of him and he had been the most scared he'd ever felt. Only the fact that he was riding the roan, a once wild mustang, saved him. The bronc knew what to do, and did it.

Thunder growled in the canyons like a surly dog over a bone, and the fire blazed up, adding light to the room.

Bowdrie let his eyes go closed. One man here was a murderer, but which one? He was a man quick to make decisions, even impulsive. He was utterly ruthless, with a sharp, cold mind and a contempt for human feelings and life. If unmasked he would begin shooting, without warning if possible, and he would not care who got in the way. Yet Bowdrie did know a little about him.

The killer had washed his hands back there at the shack where he murdered the old man. He had washed the blood off the bench and hung up the pan. The old man would not have done that, as he was notoriously untidy.

Bowdrie opened his eyes. "The man I'm looking for," he said, "just stumbled across an old miner an' killed him, prob'ly thinkin' the old man had more'n he did have. He did this just along the way whilst followin' a man who he knew had money."

"You'll never get him," Baker said. "What do you have to go on?"

"Very little," Bowdrie admitted, "but we don't always need a lot. No man can escape the pattern of his habits. He leaves sign in the minds of people just as he would on a trail. People observe things and remember things they often don't recall until questioned or until the memory is stirred up in conversation."

"That wouldn't stand before a jury," DeVant said.

"No jury will ever get this case," Bowdrie said. "This gent makes up his mind on the sudden. I'll draw a pattern of sign to corral him, an' when he realizes I'm closin' in, he'll go to shootin.' Then he'll die."

"Or you will. Ever think of that, Ranger?"

"Of course. It is an accepted risk in my business, but Rangers are enlisted because they're fightin' men an' when they go out they don't go alone. When I go down that dark trail there'll be a man ahead of me."

"Killer or no killer," Colson said, "we're warm an' dry in here." He gathered up bits of moss and sticks fallen from the woodpile and tossed them into the fire. "Only, if you expect to get your killer, get him before we get the stage started. Shootin' frets my horses."

Bowdrie went to the fire to refill his cup, and felt their eyes upon him. Perhaps more than one man here had reason to fear a Ranger. Mentally he reviewed their faces, but none rang a responsive chord. His eyes avoided the fire, knowing the time it takes to adjust back to shadows after gazing into the flames. Time enough for a man to die.

He glanced at Roper. "Driftin'?"

"Sort of. I been punchin' cows on the Nueces. Figured I'd head for Mobeetie."

"Good place to stay shut of," Baker commented. "That black-headed two-gun marshal is poison."

"Not no more," Colson replied. "Killed by a drunken gambler who pulled a sneak gun on him."

Bowdrie glanced at him. "You boys on the stage lines get all the news."

"West-bound driver told me. Carried one to the other, news travels fast."

Stadelmann glanced at Roper. "If you're through with that bunk, I'd like a try at it."

"She's all yours." Roper moved closer to Bowdrie, studying him. Bowdrie was a man he had heard about.

Bowdrie was not eager to bring the matter to a head now, with the night before them. If he was correct and the killer would elect to shoot it out, this was no place for it. Some innocent person might be killed. Yet soon the light would be blown out and they would try to sleep, and the man with the money would be alone in the dark.

There were detached clues but they pointed in more than one direction, and somehow he must force the issue.

DeVant helped him, without realizing it. "Whoever he is, you've got him trapped. With both roads closed, there's no way out."

"There is, though." Bowdrie was casual. "There's a canyon runs north of here. Looks like a dead end when you ride into it, but she branches out right quick. It would take a rider with nerve and a good horse to make it. That canyon's prob'ly runnin' ten foot deep in water about now."

"That's not for me!" DeVant was emphatic. "I've seen those canyons after a cloudburst."

Ed Colson tamped the tobacco in his pipe and lighted up again. Bowdrie could feel Baker watching him but Big Stadelmann was looking at the girl again.

Lew Judd replaced the mandolin in its case, then moved nearer to Nelly. If there was only some way out! Some means of getting away. He was afraid for Nelly, and for himself. He must have been the man the killer was following, yet how could he have known he was carrying money?

"Need wood," Judd said suddenly. "I'll go after it."

He got up quickly and went out, and Bowdrie felt a twinge of impatience. Didn't the man realize how obvious he was? He must be going outside to cache the money belt. Or was it something else? Why cache the money belt when he would have to recover it again in broad daylight?

Stadelmann got up quickly. "I'll help him. He can't handle enough for all night."

Stadelmann lumbered toward the door and nobody looked at anybody else. As the door opened they all heard the rain and Colson walked over to the fire. Nobody spoke, but all were listening.

Nelly Craig's face was pale as death, and Bowdrie got up, reaching for his slicker. He saw the fear in her eyes and knew she was afraid to be left alone. Bowdrie glanced over at Roper. "If the lady needs anything, see that she gets it, will you?"

Outside the night was black, but for an instant the opening door sent a shaft of light into the rain-streaked darkness. The door closed behind him and Bowdrie stood still.

Somewhere he heard a footstep splash in a pool. He listened and heard no sound but the rain. Where were Judd and Stadelmann?

He turned toward the stable. The stage horses were there as well as his own and the horses ridden by those who had not arrived on the stage. He grinned into the night as he realized what would happen if somebody tried to mount his roan. The horse merely tolerated Bowdrie, but it turned into a fiend if anyone else tried to mount it.

Rain slashed at his face. The stable loomed before him. There was no sound from within, nor could he hear a sound from elsewhere that would lead him to believe anyone was gathering wood. Straining his eyes into the darkness, he suddenly saw starkly revealed in a flash of lightning a huge, looming figure!

Bowdrie sidestepped quickly but his boot came down on something that skidded from under him, and he fell, catching a ringing blow on the skull as he went down. Lights seemed to burst in his brain and he rolled over in the wet, struggling to rise. Another blow stretched him flat and then he rolled over and rain poured over his face. He heard the splash of what sounded like a horse's hoof, then silence.

He tried to rise and the move caused a rush of pain to his head and he blacked out. When he opened his eyes again he had the feeling minutes had passed. He struggled to his feet and stood swaying, his head throbbing with pain.

Who could have hit him? Only his hat and his slipping in the mud had saved him from a cracked skull. He fought back the pain in his head. He had stepped, slipped, and the man had hit him.

A big man . . . *Stadelmann!*

But he could not be certain. It might only have been somebody who looked large in the night, somebody with an enveloping raincoat.

He swung back the door and almost fell down the steps. They stared at him, amazed. Stadelmann, his big face stupid with surprise, DeVant, Baker, Judd . . .

"What happened?" Roper was on his feet. "You're all blood!"

"I got slugged. Somebody slugged me with a chunk of wood."

Nobody moved. Bowdrie's eyes went to Stadelmann. "You were outside."

"So was I." Baker smiled contemptuously. "So were Judd and DeVant, but nobody was out for long."

Nelly came to him with a hot damp cloth. "Here, let me fix your head."

Bowdrie sat as she bathed away the blood, trying to force

his thoughts through the foggy jungle of his brain. Were they all working together? Who could he suspect? Peg Roper and Stadelmann had been in the dugout before the stage arrived. Had they planned a hold-up? What of Baker? Where had he been? He had apparently come up after the stage arrived, but Bowdrie had seen no tracks on the road he had followed as far as the landslide. No rider had come over the mountain ahead of him.

He was a blockhead! Somewhere here a killer was lurking, ready to kill again. It was very likely that killer who had made an attempt on him a few minutes past, and had he not been fortunate enough to slip in the mud he would be lying out there now, dead as a man could be.

How could he be sure several of these men were not wanted? Or that they were not a gang, working in concert?

Peg Roper had acted strangely when he awakened, and Baker had taken pains to let Roper know there was a Ranger present. Had he been afraid Roper would make a break and give them away?

Bowdrie was angry. He did not like being slugged; he liked still less being made a fool. He wanted a trail he could follow, not this feeling around in the dark for an enemy he could not even see. He almost hoped it was Baker, for he had come to dislike the man.

"You know," Judd said, "I thought I heard a horse when I was outside."

Bowdrie's head came up so sharply he winced with pain. "You did," he said. "I heard it, too."

"Must be a horse missing, then." DeVant was cool. "What's the matter, Ranger? I thought you fellows had all the answers."

Bowdrie got to his feet again and put on his hat. His head had swelled and the hat fit poorly.

"Want some protection, Ranger?" Baker taunted.

Bowdrie turned at the steps. His black eyes were cold. "Stay here! All of you! I want nobody outside, and if I see anybody, I'll shoot!"

He went out into the night, and it seemed even darker than

before. Crossing to the stable, he struck a match and held it high.

The horses turned their heads and rolled their eyes at him. He counted them, struck a fresh match, and counted again. All were here.

Savagely he threw the match to the floor and rubbed it into the ground with his toe, stepping away quickly so as not to be standing where he had been when he held the match.

He had distinctly heard a horse, but no horses were missing, hence there must be some other rider around. Someone who was not inside the dugout.

He considered that. The shelter they had found was half a sod shanty, half a dugout in the side of a low hill. So far as he could see, there was no place to get in or out but the door. On the other hand, he had not examined the back of the room where Colson had found the coffeepot.

He had heard a horse, but Judd had not been robbed. If the killer was the kind of man Bowdrie believed, he would not leave without robbing Judd.

Bowdrie went back to the dugout. "No horses missing," he said.

"I heard a horse, too," Stadelmann said.

"Do you believe in ghosts, Ranger?" Baker smirked.

"Where's Colson?" he asked suddenly.

For the space of three breaths no one replied. Baker looked quickly around, frowning. DeVant got up uneasily. Nelly broke the silence. "Why . . . why, he's gone!"

"When did he go?" Judd asked. "I don't recall when I last saw him."

DeVant looked at Bowdrie. "Colson is a big man, Ranger, but why would he slug you?"

"Don't be foolish!" Baker interrupted angrily. "Why would he want to do that?"

Chick Bowdrie was very still, thinking. "Did any of you talk to him at the last station?"

They looked at each other, then shook their heads. Nobody had. Were there any stops between here and there? No stops.

Colson? Why had he not thought of him? Because he was,

or seemed to be, the stage driver. "If it was him," he muttered, "he had this better planned than I thought."

Baker smiled. "If it was him, Ranger, how did he get out of this dugout without being seen? And where did the horse come from?"

"He didn't go up the steps," Roper said. "I was settin' there all the time."

The coffeepot! Bowdrie stepped around Judd and went into the dark area behind the sideboard. There was a pool of water on the earthen floor from a leak in the roof. He held the lantern high. There was also a wrecked bunk and some old debris. Away from the firelight, the muddy space was damp and cheerless. He looked around; then suddenly they heard an irritated, half-uttered *"Damn!"* The light of the lantern disappeared.

He called back, "There's another room back here. It was where he kept his horse!"

They crowded to look. Beyond the dank, dark space there was a door, not to be seen from the front of the dugout, and the small room beyond it was tight-roofed and dry. There was hay on the floor and a crude manger. Beyond was a door that led outside.

DeVant peered through the peephole in the door. "He must have stood here and watched us at the woodpile. He could see us by lightning flashes, so he knew when to leave."

Judd shoved them aside and plunged past, opening the door to the outside, charging through the dwindling rain to the far side of the woodpile. "It's gone! My money's gone!" he wailed.

White and stricken, he stood over a hole in the woodpile where sticks had been hastily thrown aside. "You hid it here?" Bowdrie asked.

"And he must've stood by that peephole watching me hide it." He stared at Bowdrie. "It was all I had. All! And all she had, too!"

Ed Colson, then, had been here before. Instead of being spur-of-the-moment, this robbery had been part of a carefully conceived plan. Colson had robbed the prospector by taking advantage of an unexpected opportunity, but his appearance as a stage driver was deliberately planned. He must have lurked beside the trail, boarded the stage at some steep grade where it moved slowly, climbed over the back, then knifed or slugged the driver. He must then have taken the reins, gambling that in the darkness no one would know the difference.

The breakdown was undoubtedly deliberate, but the blocked trails and the arrival of Bowdrie had been no part of his plan.

Peg Roper threw wood on the fire and stepped back, watching the flames take hold. DeVant dropped back into his chair and gathered the cards into a stack. Baker smiled, looking around at Bowdrie. "Well, Ranger, now what happens?"

Chick Bowdrie studied a spot on the back of his hand with perplexed eyes. It was a round, red spot slightly fringed on the edges. It was blood. He ignored Baker and shifted his glance to Roper. "You were the first one here?"

"Yeah. The place was cold an' empty. I knew nothing about no back room. I just broke up some kindling an' got a fire goin'. Once she was burnin' pretty good, I put some chunks on the fire an' laid down. I was played out."

"You were next, Stadelmann?"

"Uh-huh. Roper there, he was asleep or pretendin' to be when I come in. I put more wood on the fire an' set down at the table. About that time other folks started arrivin'."

Bowdrie picked up his cup and Nelly filled it from the pot. He sat down in an empty chair with his back to the wall. Right from the start this had been a tough one. He had been searching for a man he had never seen and of whom he had no description. He had found himself among a group of people, any one of whom might be guilty. Now the least likely of them all seemed to be the man he must find. And that man was gone. Or was he?

"Roper? The way I understand it, you an' Miss Craig were in here all the time?"

"Uh-huh, only Baker never did go clear out. Just his head an' shoulders."

DeVant's yellow eyes followed Bowdrie with that same malicious gleam as his fingers riffled the pasteboards.

Nelly and Roper were near the fire. Judd, his face drawn and bitter with the loss of his life savings, stood nearby. Baker and Stadelmann were at the table with DeVant.

Finishing his coffee, Bowdrie took off his wet slicker and hung it on a nail. Then he dried his hands with infinite care, his dark Apache features inscrutable as he carefully thought out every move. What he would now attempt to do was fraught with danger.

He turned suddenly. "Stadelmann! Baker! Get up, will you, please?"

Puzzled, they got to their feet. Baker was on the verge of a sarcastic comment when Bowdrie said, "Now, if you will go into the back room and take the body of Ed Colson down from the rafters."

"What?" Stadelmann exclaimed.

Judd was staring, jaw hanging.

"Don't bring the body in here, just take it down."

DeVant was watching him, alert and curious. Lew Judd passed a shaking hand over his chin. "You . . . you mean he's *dead*?"

"Murdered and robbed after he had robbed you, Judd, by the only man who could have done it."

"What? What do you mean?" Baker demanded.

"Why, DeVant did it," Bowdrie said, and the two guns thundered at once.

Bowdrie stood still, his .44 Colt balanced easy in his hand, while DeVant sat perfectly still, a round hole over his right eye. Slowly he started to rise, then toppled across the table. Nelly Craig screamed.

White-faced, Baker stared from one to the other, unable to grasp what had happened. Bowdrie stepped over to the dead man, and unfastening his shirt, removed Lew Judd's money belt and passed it to him.

Judd grasped it eagerly. "Thank God!" His voice trembled. "I slaved half my life for that!"

Peg Roper stared at Bowdrie, and exclaimed, "Did you see him throw that gun? DeVant had his in his lap with his hand on it, an' Bowdrie beat him!"

"How could you know?" Baker asked. "How could you possibly know?"

Bowdrie fed a cartridge into his pistol and holstered it. "I should have known from the beginning. Ed Colson killed that prospector, and he probably killed the stage driver.

"Somehow, DeVant got wise. Maybe he actually heard or saw something back there on the grade. Maybe he was following Judd himself.

"Judd an' Stadelmann went after wood and I followed them. Colson had been to the back of the dugout before, and he went there again. He slipped out, tried to kill me, and robbed Judd's cache almost as soon as Judd hid it. He thought he pulled it off, but DeVant had seen him go.

"Probably DeVant knew who to watch. Naturally, Roper and Nelly were looking toward the dugout door where Baker had gone. DeVant was a quiet-moving man, anyway, who knew from card-cheating the value of doing things by misdirection. He got back there, knifed Colson when he came back with the money, and shoved the body across the rafters. Then he just quietly came back into the room. I doubt if the whole operation took him more than two or three minutes.

"Remember, nobody knew there was another room then. All he would seem to have done was to get up and move around."

"What about Colson's horse?"

"Turned it loose with a slap on the rump. DeVant had no reason to be suspected. He planned to ride out on the stage with the rest of you. It was cold, unadulterated gall, but he might have gotten away with it. Only when I was in that back room a drop of blood hit my hand.

"Figure it out. Who was missing? Only Colson. Where could that drop have come from except overhead? It had to be those low rafters. Who had the opportunity? DeVant.

"Baker said DeVant was outside, but he wasn't. That indicated to me that DeVant was moving around. Probably Baker *thought* he had gone out because he was not in sight, but he wasn't paying that much attention."

"I wasn't," Baker said. "I was expecting gunfire out there."

Nobody said anything for several minutes; then Lew Judd

sat down and looked at his niece, smiling. "We're going to make it now, honey," he said.

Stadelmann crossed to the bunk and stretched out on the hard boards. He was soon asleep. Roper hunkered down near the fire.

"It is almost morning," Baker said. "Maybe the stage will get through."

"I hope so," Judd said sincerely.

Chick Bowdrie said nothing at all. He was sitting against the wall, almost asleep.

DOWN SONORA WAY

DOWN ON HIS stomach in the sand behind his dead horse, Chick Bowdrie waited for the sun to go down. It was a hot Sonora sun and the nearest shade was sixty yards away in a notch of the Sierra de Espuelas, where Tensleep Mooney waited with a Winchester.

Bowdrie had scooped out sand to dig himself a few inches deeper below the surface, but a bullet burn across the top of his shoulder and two double holes in his black flat-crowned hat demonstrated both the accuracy and the intent behind Tensleep's shooting.

Five hundred miles behind them in Texas were two dead men, the seventh and eighth on the list of Mooney's killings, and Bowdrie was showing an understandable reluctance to become number nine.

The sun was hot, Bowdrie's lips were cracked and dry, his canteen was empty. A patient buzzard circled overhead and a tiny lizard stared at the Ranger with wide, wondering eyes. It was twenty miles to water unless some remained in the *tinaja* where Mooney was holed up, and twenty miles in the desert can be an immeasurable distance.

Neither man held any illusions about the other. Tensleep Mooney was a fast hand with a six-shooter and an excellent rifle shot. His courage was without question. His feud with the gunslinging Baggs outfit was a legend in Texas. Al Baggs had stolen Mooney's horse. Mooney trailed him down, and in the gun battle that followed, killed him, recovering his horse. The Baggs family were Tennessee feudal stock and despite the fact that killing a horse thief was considered justifiable homicide, a brother and a cousin came hunting Tensleep. Mooney took two Baggs bullets and survived. The Baggs boys took three of Mooney's slugs and didn't.

From time to time a Baggs or two took a shot at Mooney, and at least two attempts were made to trap him. Others were killed and the last attempt resulted in a woman being shot. Then Tensleep unlimbered his guns and went to work. Until then he had been rolling with the punches but now he decided if the Baggs clan wanted war, they should have it.

Gene Baggs, the most noted gunslinger of the outfit, was in San Antonio. One Tuesday night Mooney showed up and gave Gene Baggs his chance. The Variety Theater rang with gunshots and Gene died of acute indigestion caused by absorbing too much lead on an empty stomach.

Killings seven and eight had taken place near Big Spring, one of them a Baggs, the other an itinerant gunfighting cattleman named Caspar Hanna. Settling disputes with guns was beginning to be frowned on in Texas, so the Rangers got their orders and Bowdrie got his.

Mooney was tricky and adept at covering his trail. Cunning as a wolf, he shook off his trailers and even lost Bowdrie on two occasions. Irritated, Bowdrie followed him to the Mexican border and kept on going. Out of his bailiwick though it was, the chase had now become a matter of professional and personal pride.

So now they were in the dead heart of Apache country, stalemated until darkness. If Mooney escaped in the dark, Bowdrie was scheduled to walk home, the odds against his survival a thousand to one. If one left out the heat and lack of water, even the miles of walking in boots meant for riding, there were always the Apaches.

"Thirsty, Ranger?" Mooney called.

"I'll drink when I'm ready," Bowdrie replied. "You want to come out with your hands up? You'll get a fair trial."

"I'd never live for the trial. Without my guns in Baggs country? I wouldn't last three days."

"Leave that to the Rangers."

"Much obliged. I'll leave it to Mooney."

Neither man spoke again and the hour dragged on. Bowdrie tried licking dry lips with a dry tongue. The heat where he lay was not less than one hundred and twenty degrees. Shifting his position drew a quick bullet. Carefully he began to dig again, trying to get at the rifle scabbard on the underside of his horse.

Bowdrie had nothing but respect for Mooney. Under any circumstances but the present the two might have worked a roundup together. Tensleep was a tough cowhand from the Wyoming country that gave him his name, a man who had started ranching on his own, a man who had been over the cow trails to Montana from Texas, who had fought Indians and rustlers.

Bowdrie continued to dig, finally loosening the girth on the dead horse.

"Somethin' out there." Mooney spoke suddenly, and Chick almost looked up, then cursed himself for a fool. It was a trap.

"Somebody travelin' north." Mooney's voice was just loud enough for Bowdrie to hear.

"In this country? You've got to be crazy."

He lay quiet, thinking. There had been no faking in Mooney's tone, and travelers in this country meant, nine times out of ten, Apaches. They were in the middle of an area controlled by Cochise, with his stronghold just to the north in New Mexico. If those were Apaches out there, they were in trouble.

Silence, and then Mooney spoke again, just loud enough for him to hear. "Somebody out there, all right. Can't quite make 'em out. Three or four riders, an' I'd say one was a woman."

A woman in this country? *Now?* Bowdrie wanted to chance a look, but if he lifted his head, Mooney might kill him.

"Walkin' their horses." Mooney was a trifle higher than Bowdrie and could see better.

Both men were hidden, Bowdrie by cactus and rock, Mooney by a notch of rocks that hid both himself and his horse.

"The man's hurt, got his arm in a sling, bandage on his head. Looks like the woman is holdin' him on his horse."

Bowdrie had dug deep enough to pull the girth loose, and

now he pulled the saddle off and got at his Winchester. As he lifted the Winchester clear, it showed above the rocks.

"That won't do you no good, Bowdrie," Mooney said. "You lift your head to shoot an' I'll ventilate it."

"Leave that to me," Bowdrie replied cheerfully. "I'd rather take you in alive, because you'd keep better in this heat, but if I have to, I'll start shootin' at the rocks in back of you. The ricochets will chop you to mincemeat."

That, Mooney realized unhappily, was the plain, unvarnished truth. He rubbed a hand over his leather-brown face and narrowed his blue eyes against the sun's glare. He knew that Ranger out there, knew that behind that Apache-like face was as shrewd a fighting brain as he had ever known. No other man could have followed him this far. He peered through the rocks once more.

"Dust cloud." There was a silence while Bowdrie waited, listening. "Somebody chasin' the first bunch, I reckon. Quite a passel of 'em. The first bunch is comin' right close. Three horses, a man wounded bad, a woman an' two youngsters. The kids are ridin' double."

After a moment Mooney added, "Horses about all in. They've come fast an' hard."

"Comin' this way?"

"No, they'll pass us up."

A fly buzzed lazily in the hot afternoon sun and Bowdrie could hear the sound of the approaching horses. Hidden as he and Mooney were, there was not a chance they'd be seen.

"Should be water at Ojo de Monte." The man's voice was ragged with exhaustion. "But that's twenty miles off."

"After that?"

"Los Mosquitos, or the Casa de Madera, another thirty miles as the crow flies. You'll have to keep to low ground. I'll try to hold 'em off from those rocks up ahead."

"No!" The woman's voice was strong. "No, George. If we're going to die, let it be together!"

"Don't be a fool, Hannah! Think of the children! You might get through, you might save them and yourself."

Chick Bowdrie shifted his body in the sand. A cloud of dust meant a good-sized bunch of Apaches. A small bunch would make no dust. And they were sure of their prey, for this was their country, far from any aid.

If they kept on after the man and his family, they would never see Mooney or Bowdrie. Bowdrie was realist enough to realize all they had to do was lie quiet. The Indians would not see their tracks, as they had come in from the north and the Apaches were coming from the west. Moreover, they would be too intent on their prey to look for other tracks.

"Mooney?" He spoke just loud enough for the outlaw to hear. "Are we goin' to stand for this? I say we call off our fight and move into this play."

"Just about to suggest the same thing, Ranger. Call 'em back."

Chick Bowdrie got to his feet. The family were moving away, but within easy hailing distance.

"Hey! Come back here! We'll help you!"

Startled, they drew up and turned to stare. "Come over here! I'm a Texas Ranger. You'd never make it the way you're headin'!"

They rounded their horses and walked them closer. The man's face was haggard, the bandage on his head was bloody. The youngsters, hollow-eyed and frightened, stared at them. The woman, not yet thirty, had a flicker of hope in her eyes.

"What we can offer ain't much better," Bowdrie said, "but two more rifles can help. If he tried to hold 'em off, they'd just cut around him an' have you all with no trouble."

"They'd get you before you could say Sam Houston. You get down an' come into the rocks." Tensleep paused, grinning at Bowdrie. "But not where that in-curvin' rock is." He rolled his quid of chewing tobacco in his wide jaws. "The Ranger tells me that ain't safe."

The dust cloud was nearer now, and the Apaches, aware their quarry had elected to stop, were fanning out. Tensleep spat. "This here's goin' to surprise 'em some. They reckon they're only comin' up on a hurt man an' a woman with kids."

It was cooler in the shade of the big rocks, and a glance at the *tinaja* showed a couple of barrels of water, at least. There was shelter for their horses and it was a good place to make a stand. Trust Tensleep to choose the right spot to fight a battle.

The desert before them was suddenly empty. The dust cloud had settled. The buzzard overhead had been joined by a hopeful relative. The buzzards were neutral. No matter who won down there, they would win. They had but to wait. The lizard had vanished. Bowdrie had dragged his saddle and bridle back into the rocks. He worked himself into a hollow in the sand, found a place for his elbows, and waited.

Nothing.

That was expected. It was when you never saw Apaches that you could worry. They were confident but did not wish to risk a death to get the four they pursued.

The woman was washing the man's arm now, replacing the bandage. Tensleep rolled his quid in his jaws and spat upon an itinerant scorpion. The scorpion backed off, unhappy at the unexpected deluge of trouble.

"How many would you say?"

Mooney thought it over. "Maybe ten. No less'n that. Could be twice as many."

"Tough."

"Yeah."

Mooney shoved his canteen at Bowdrie. "What are you? A camel? Don't you ever drink?"

"Forgot how." Bowdrie took a mouthful and let it soak the dry tissues, then swallowed.

Both men understood their chances of getting out alive were so slim they weren't worth counting on. The children stared at them, wide-eyed. The girl might have been ten, the boy two or three years younger. Their clothes were ragged but clean as could be expected after a hard ride. Bowdrie dug into his saddlebag and handed each child a piece of jerky. He grinned at them and winked. The girl smiled warily but the boy was fascinated by Bowdrie's guns. "Can I hold one?" he asked.

"I need 'em, son. Guns are dangerous things. You use 'em when need be, but nobody plays with a gun unless he's a fool." He indicated the area out in front of them. "This is one time they're needed."

Nothing moved out there; there was only sun, sand, and sky, low brush, occasional cactus, and the buzzards who seemed to simply hang in the sky, scarcely moving their wings. A shoulder showed, and Bowdrie held his fire.

Mooney glanced at him. "You're no tenderfoot."

"I grew up with 'em," Bowdrie commented. "Them an' Comanches."

That exposed shoulder had been an invitation, a test to see where they were, and how many. Yet they believed they knew. They had been chasing a man, a woman, and children.

A half-dozen Indians came off the ground at once. It was as if they were born suddenly from the sand. Where they appeared there had been nothing an instant before.

The thunder of suddenly firing rifles smashed echoes against the rocks and the whine of ricocheting bullets sent shuddering sounds through the clear desert air. An instant, a smell of gunpowder, and they were gone. Heat waves danced in the still air.

An Apache lay on his face not ten feet away. Another was sprawled near a clump of greasewood. As Bowdrie looked, that Indian rolled over and vanished before Bowdrie could bring his rifle to bear. There was blood on the sand where he had fallen.

"How'd you make out?"

"One down an' a possible," Bowdrie replied.

"Two down here, an' a possible. What's the matter? Can't you Rangers shoot no better than that?"

"You light a shuck," Bowdrie replied complacently. "I can outshoot you any day and twice on Sunday."

"Huh," Mooney grunted, then glanced at the scorpion, who was getting ready to move again. He spat, deluging it anew. Then suddenly he fired.

"Scratch another redskin," he said.

Bowdrie lay still, watching the desert. They were doing some thinking out there now. The two rifles had surprised them, and an Apache does not like to be surprised. Their attack had seemed so easy. The Apache is an efficient, able fighting man who rarely makes a useless move, and even more rarely miscalculates. This easy attack had now cost them three or four men and some wounds.

The sky was a white-hot bowl above them, the desert a reflector, yet the sun had already started its slide toward the far-off mountains.

An Apache moved suddenly, darting to the right. Bowdrie had his rifle on the spot where he had seen him drop from sight. He was a young warrior, and reckless. As he arose and moved, Bowdrie squeezed off his shot and the warrior stumbled.

Instantly, several more leaped up. Behind him a third rifle bellowed. So the father was back in action now. Bowdrie's second shot was a clean miss as the Indian dropped from sight.

"Got one!" The father spoke proudly. He crept closer and Bowdrie wished he wouldn't. "Name is Westmore. Tried ranchin' down southwest of here. Mighty pretty country. They done burned us out whilst we was from home, so we run for it."

The shadows began to grow, the glare grew less. Bowdrie drank from the canteen. "I'd have had you tied to your saddle by now," he said.

Mooney chuckled. "Why, you track-smellin' soft-headed coyote! If these folks hadn't come along, you'd have been buzzard bait by now."

The woman looked surprised and curious. Westmore glanced from one to the other.

"Wished I could have got you without your guns," Bowdrie commented. "You're too good a man to shoot. I'd have been satisfied to take you in with my bare hands."

"You?" Mooney stared at him angrily. "Why, you long-horned maverick! I'd—!"

The Apaches tried it again, but this time it was cold turkey. Both men had spotted slight movements in the brush and were ready when they came up. Bowdrie got his before the Indian had his hands off the ground. Mooney fired at a rock behind where his Indian lay, dusting him with fragments.

"They'll wait until dark now," Mooney said. "I figure

we've accounted for maybe half of them. We been shot with luck, you know that, don't you?"

"I know," Bowdrie agreed. "They just ran into more'n they were expecting but they'll have figured it out by now. No wounded man and a woman could be makin' the stand we are."

"Look!" Westmore pointed. Three Apaches were riding off into the distance. "They've quit."

Westmore started to rise but Bowdrie jerked him down. "It's an old trick," he explained. "Two or three ride off and the rest wait in ambush. When you start movin' around, they kill you."

The sun slid down behind the mountains in the distance and the desert grew cool. It was ever so. There was nothing to hold the heat, and night cooled things off very quickly. Stars came out and a coyote yipped, a coyote with a brown skin and a headband. Bowdrie dug into his saddlebag and brought out a piece of jerky for each. It was dry and tough but it lasted a long time and was nourishing. They chewed in silence.

A faint gray lingered, disappeared and gave birth to stars. Chick tossed his saddle blanket to the youngsters. Westmore peered from behind the rocks.

"You reckon those that left will come back with more?"

"Could be. In fact, it's more than likely."

"My name's Westmore," the man repeated, looking from one to the other.

"I'm Tensleep Mooney. This here's a Texas Ranger named Bowdrie. He's been on my trail for weeks."

The woman was puzzled. "He wants to arrest you? Why?"

"This gent here," Bowdrie said, "is too handy with a gun. The governor wants more taxpayers and this gent has been thinnin' down the population somethin' awful."

"But you'll let him go now, won't you?"

Mooney chuckled. "This here Sou-wegian ain't got me yet, an' it'll be a cold day in Kansas before he does."

"Soon as we're rid of these Apaches," Chick said, "I'll hog-tie you and take you back. I'll give you about two drinks between here an' Austin." He turned his head toward

Westmore and his wife. "You know what this squatty good-for-nothin' did?

"He knows this country better than anybody. Knows ever' water hole. He passes one by, then swings back in the dark, gets him a drink, an' fills his canteen. Then he goes back to where I last saw him, lets me see him again, an' takes off in the dark. I have to follow him or lose him, so I've spent my days drier than a year-old buffalo chip!"

Talk died and they lay listening. There was no sound. Bowdrie turned to Mooney. "I'm goin' out there. There's at least one Apache out there, prob'ly more. I need a horse. When I get me a horse we'll light out. 'Paches don't like night fightin' an' we should make a run for it."

He dropped his gunbelts, then thrust one pistol into his waistband along with his bowie knife. He removed his spurs and jacket, then disappeared into the night.

The woman looked at Mooney. "Will he get back? How can he do this?"

"If anybody can do it," Mooney said, "he can. He's more Injun than many Injuns. Anyway, he's got no choice. He surely ain't goin' out of here a-foot."

There was a shallow arroyo nearby and Bowdrie found it and went down the sand bank to its bottom, then paused to listen.

He started on, paused again, hearing a faint sound he could not place, then went on. He was circling cautiously, feeling his way, when he heard a horse blow. He circled even wider, then dropped to the sand and crept nearer. He found them unexpectedly, six horses picketed in the bottom of the arroyo. Six horses did not necessarily mean six Indians, for some of the riders might already lie among the dead.

Try as he could, he saw no sleeping place, nor did he see any Indians or evidence of a fire, which they probably would not have, anyway.

Just as he was about to move toward the horses, an Indian arose from the ground and went to them. He moved around them, then returned to his bed on the sand a few yards away. When the Indian was quiet, Bowdrie moved to the horses. Selecting the nearest for his own, he drew the picket pins of all the horses, reflecting they must be stolen horses, for it was unlike Apaches to use picket pins, preferring the nearest bush or tree.

He moved to the horse he had chosen and swung to its back. The horse snorted at the unfamiliar smell and instantly there was movement from the Indian.

Slapping his heels to the horse, Bowdrie charged into the night, leading the other horses behind him. He turned at the flash of a gun and fired three quick shots into the flash.

Circling swiftly, he arrived at camp. "Roll out an' mount up!" he said. "We're leavin' out of here!"

He saddled swiftly, and they rode into the night. Three days later they rode into the dusty streets of El Paso. The Westmores turned toward New Mexico and the ranch of a relative. They parted company in the street and Mooney started for his horse. "Far enough, Mooney! Don't forget, you're my prisoner!"

"Your *what*?"

Mooney threw himself sidewise into an arroyo but Bowdrie did not move. "Won't do you a bit of good. Might as well give up! I've got you!"

"You got nothin'!" Mooney yelled. "Just stick your head around that corner and I'll—!"

"Be mighty dry where you're goin', Mooney. And you without a canteen."

"What? Why, you dirty sidewinder! You stole my canteen!"

"Borrowed it. You killed 'em all in fair fights, Mooney, so's you might as well stand trial. I'll ride herd on you so's you'll be safe whilst the trial's on.

"I've got the water, Mooney, and I have the grub, and the Baggs outfit has more friends here than you do. If you go askin' around, you'll really get your hide stretched. Looks to me like your only way is to come along with me."

There was silence and then Bowdrie said, "I will give you more than two drinks betwixt here an' Austin, Mooney. I was only makin' a joke about that."

There was no sound and Bowdrie knew what was happening. "If you're wise," he said loudly, "you'll come in an' surrender. No sense havin' an outlaw's name when you don't deserve it.

"I'll even testify for you. I'll tell 'em you were a miserable coyote not fit to herd sheep but that you're a first-class fightin' man."

Silence. Bowdrie smiled and walked back to his horse. By now Mooney was headed out of town, headed back to the boondocks where he came from, but he'd come in, Bowdrie was sure of it. Just give him time to think it over.

He had warned him about El Paso, and he was too good a man to be in prison. Maybe a day would come when a Ranger couldn't use his own judgment, but Bowdrie had used his and was sure ninety percent of the others would agree. By now Tensleep was on his way to wherever he wanted to go.

Bowdrie walked his horse back down the street from the edge of town. This wasn't a bad horse, not as good as his roan waiting for him back in Laredo, but better than the bay lying dead in Sonora. The spare Indian horses he had given to Westmore. After all, they were going to start over with all too little.

Bowdrie tied his horse to the hitch-rail and went inside to the bar and ordered a cold beer. Taking it, he walked to a table and sat down.

Well, maybe he was wrong. Maybe McNelly wouldn't agree with his turning Mooney loose, but—

"All right, dammit!" Tensleep dropped into the chair opposite. "Take me in, if it makes you feel better. I just ain't up to another chase like that one." He looked at Bowdrie. "Can I keep my guns until I get there?"

"Why not?" Bowdrie looked around. "Bartender, bring the man a beer."

They sat without speaking, then Tensleep said, "You notice something? Those youngsters back there? Never a whimper out of 'em, an' they must have been scared."

"Sure they were scared. I was scared." Bowdrie glanced at Mooney, a reflective glint in his eye. "You know, Mooney, what you need is a wife. You need a home. Take some of that wildness out of you. Now, I—"

"You go to the devil," Mooney replied cheerfully.

STRANGE PURSUIT

Y EARS HAD BROUGHT no tolerance to Bryan Moseley. Sun, wind, and the dryness of a sandy sea had brought copper to his skin and drawn fine lines around his pale blue eyes. The far lands had touched him with their silence, and the ways of men as well as the ways he had chosen brought lines of cruelty to his mouth and had sunk thoughts of cruelty deep into the convolutions of his brain, so deeply they shone forth in the flat light of his eyes.

"No, I don't know where he is. If I did know, I wouldn't tell you. Don't tell me I'm going to hang. I heard the judge when he said it. Don't tell me it'll relieve my soul because whatever burden my soul carries, it will carry to the end. I lived my life and I'm no welsher."

Chick Bowdrie sat astride the chair, his arms resting on the back, his black hat on the back of his head. He found himself liking this mean old man who would cheerfully shoot him down if he had a chance to escape.

"Your soul is your problem, but Charlie Venk is mine. I've got to find him."

"You won't find him settin' where you are."

"Known him long?"

"You Rangers know everything, so you should know that, too." The old outlaw's eyes flared. "Not that I've any use for him. He never trusted me an' I never trusted him. I will say this. He is good with a gun. He is as good as any of them. He was even better'n me. If he hadn't been I'd have killed him."

"Or was it because you needed him? You were gettin' old, Mose."

The old man chuckled without humor. "Sure, I could use him, all right. Trouble was, he used me."

"How was that?" Bowdrie took out a sack of tobacco and

papers and tossed them to the prisoner. "I figured you for the smartest of them all."

"Just what I figured." Mose took up the tobacco and began to build a smoke. "Don't think you're gettin' around me, I just feel like talkin'. Maybe it is time they hung me. I *am* gettin' old."

He sifted tobacco into the paper. "We had that bank down in Kelsey lined up. I done the linin'. Never did trust nobody to do that. The others always overlooked something. On'y thing I overlooked was Charlie Venk.

"You seen him? He's a big, fine-lookin' young man. Strong-made, but quick. I seen plenty of 'em come an' go in my time. Seen the James boys an' the Youngers. Cole, he was the best of that lot. Jesse, he had a streak of meanness in him, like the time he shot that schoolboy with his arms full of books. No need for it.

"Charlie reminded me of Cole. Big man, like Cole, an' good-lookin'. I never trust them kind. Always figure they're better'n anybody else. 'Cept maybe Cole. He never did.

"We got that bank job lined up. There was four of us in it. Charlie, Rollie Burns, Jim Sloan, an' me, of course. Burns an' Sloan, they were bad. Mean men, if you know what I mean, and they couldn't be trusted. Not that it mattered, because I never trusted anybody myself. An' nobody ever trusted me.

"Ever see Charlie sling a gun? I've heard you're fast, Bowdrie, but if you ever tangle with Charlie you'll go down. Not only is he fast but he can lay 'em right where he wants 'em, no matter how rough it gets.

"He was slick on a trail, too, but if you've already trailed him across three states, you know that. He was a first-rate horse thief. Given time, I'll tell you about that.

"Anyway, about noon we come down this street into town. No nice town like this'n. She was a dusty, miserable place with six saloons, two general stores, a bank, and a few odds and ends of places. We come in about noon, like I say. Sloan, he was holdin' the horses, so the rest of us got down an' went in.

"There was a woman an' two men in that bank. Two customers an' the teller. Rollie, he put his gun on the woman an' the man customer an' backed them into a corner, faced against the wall. At least, the man was. Rollie, he didn't pay much mind to the woman.

"Charlie, he pushed the teller over alongside of them an' vaulted the rail to start scoopin' money into a sack.

"Out front Sloan leans over to look into the bank an' he says, 'Watch it! The town's wakin' up fast!'

"Charlie, he was a smooth worker with no lost motion and he had cleaned up more cash than I had. We started for the door an' the teller, he takes a dive for his desk. Maybe he had a gun back there. Rollie backs his hammer to shoot an' Charlie says, 'Hold it, you fool!' An' he slaps the teller with his gun barrel an' the teller hit the floor cold as a wedge.

"Then we hit the leather and shot our way out of town. We rode like the devil for those first six miles, knowin' there would be a posse. Then we reached the grove where more horses were waitin'. It taken us on'y a moment to switch saddles. We rode out at a canter an' held it, knowin' the posse would almost kill their horses gettin' to that grove.

"We got away. Ten miles further we switched horses for the third and last time. By then the posse was out of the runnin' an' we doubled back in the hills, headed for our hangout. Rollie was ridin' a grouch an' Charlie, he was singin'. Nice voice, he had.

"Suddenly Rollie says, his voice kind of funny, 'Nobody calls me a fool!' We all look around an' he had the drop on Charlie. Had the gun right on him. Well, what d'you expect? Me an' Sloan, we just backed off. Whoever won, it was more money for the rest of us, an' Charlie had always figured he was pretty salty. He was, too. Right then we found out how salty.

" 'Aim to kill me, Rollie?'

" 'What d'you expect? I had that durned teller dead to rights.'

" 'Sure you did,' Charlie said, easy-like. 'Sure you did. But maybe that teller had a wife and kids. If you've got no thought for them, think of this. Nobody back there is dead.

All that's gone is the bank's money. Nobody will run us very far for that, but if we killed a family man they'd never quit.'"

"He was right," Bowdrie said.

"'You ain't talkin' yourself out o' this!' Rollie says. 'I aim to—'

"Charlie Venk shot him right between the eyes. That's right! Got him to talkin' an' off guard, then drew an' fired so fast we scarcely knowed what happened. Rollie, he slid from the saddle an' Charlie never looked at him. He just looked at us. He had that gun in his hand an' was smilin' a little. 'I wasn't askin' for trouble,' he said. 'You boys want to take it up?'

"'Hell no! Rollie always had a grouch on,' Sloan says. 'Leave him lay.'

"We camped that night at a good place Charlie knew. Three ways out, good water, grass an' cover. We ate good that night. Charlie, he was a good cook when he wanted to be, an' he really laid it on. Like a dumb fool, I ate it up an' so did Sloan. After all, none of us had et a good meal in a week. We et it up an' then Charlie outs with a bottle an' we had a few drinks. Charlie was a talker, an' he was yarnin' away that night in a low, kind of dronin' voice. An' we'd come a hard ride that day. Before we knew it, we were dozin'.

"Of a sudden I come awake an' it was broad daylight! Yessir, I'd fallen asleep right where I lay, boots an' all! What made me maddest of all was that I'd figured on gettin' up whilst the others were asleep an' skippin' with the cash.

"There was Sloan, still fast asleep. An' Charlie? You guessed it. Charlie was gone.

"He had hightailed. No, he didn't take our money but he did take Rollie's share, but that was half of it. Oh, yeah! He dipped into our share for a dollar each an' left a note sayin' it was for the extra grub an' the whiskey. Why, that—!"

Bowdrie chuckled. "You never saw him again?"

"Not hide nor hair." Mose got to his feet. "You catch up with him, you watch it. Charlie's got him some tricks. Slips out of cuffs, ropes, anything tied to his wrists. Mighty supple, he is. I seen him do it.

"Good at imitatin', too. He can listen to a man talk, then imitate him so's his own wife wouldn't know the difference."

———

ONE HUNDRED AND four miles north, the cowtown of Chollo gathered memories in the sun. Along the boardwalk a half-dozen idlers avoided work by sitting in the shade. Chick Bowdrie's hammerhead roan sloped along the street like a hungry hound looking for a bone.

Outside the livery stable a man kept his stomach on his knees by using a rope for a belt. When Bowdrie swung to the ground the flesh around what seemed to be one of the man's chins quivered and a voice issued, a high, thin voice.

"Hay inside, oats in the bin, water at the trough. He'p yourself an' it's two bits the night. You stayin' long?"

"Just passin' through." Bowdrie shoved his hat back on his head, a characteristic gesture, and watched the roan. Bowdrie lived with the roan the way Pete Kitchen had lived with Apaches. Safe as long as he watched them.

"Any strangers around?"

"Rarely is. Rarely."

"Ever hear of Charlie Venk?"

"Nope."

"Big gent, nice-lookin', an' prob'ly ridin' a black horse. Good with his gun."

Both eyes were wide open now, and the fat man peered at him with genuine interest. "We never knowed his name. Never saw him use a gun, but we know him. He's the gent that hung our sheriff."

"Hung your *what*?"

"Sheriff. Ed Lightsen." A fat middle finger pointed. "Hung him to that big limb on the cottonwood yonder."

"He hung the *sheriff*?"

A chuckle issued from the rolls of fat. "Uh-huh. He surely did! Best joke aroun' here in a year. The sheriff, he was aimin' to hang this gent, an' he got hung hisself. Funny part of it was, it was the sheriff's own rope."

The fat man leaned forward. There were rolls of fat on the back of his neck and shoulders.

"This gent you speak of. Venk, his name was? He come in here about an hour before sunset ridin' a wore-out bronc. He was carrying some mighty heavy saddlebags an' he was a big man himself, an' that bronc had been runnin'.

"Nobody has any extry horses in this town. All out on roundups. Stingy with 'em, anyway. This gent, he tried to buy one, had no luck a-tall, but he hung around. Split a quart with the boys over at the saloon. Sang 'em some songs an' yarned with 'em. Come sundown, he walked out of there an' stole the sheriff's sorrel.

"That's right, the sheriff's sorrel. Now, the sheriff had been makin' his brag that nobody but him could ride that horse. This here Venk, as you call him, he got astride an' he stayed astride for just one mile. Then he came head-on into ten of those hard-case riders of Fairly's. They recognized the horse and threw down on him before he even realized he was in trouble. They brought him back into town.

"Now, the sheriff was mighty sore. I don't know whether it was for stealin' the horse or because this here Venk actually rode him. 'You can put him in jail,' Webb Fairly says, but the sheriff was havin' none of it. 'Jail? For a horse thief? We'll hang him!'

"There was argyment, but not much. It looked to be a quiet time in town, so the boys figured a hangin' would liven things up a mite. Then this here Venk comes up with his own argyment.

"'Well, boys, you got me. I guess I've come to the end of my trail, but I'll be damned if I go out with money in my pocket. Nor should a man be hung with a dry throat. I don't favor that, an' I reckon you boys don't.

"'Actually, I feel sorry for you. Here you come to town for fun, now you've got to hang me. So let's go over to the saloon an' drink up my money.'"

The fat man hitched up that rope belt, which did no good, and shrugged. "Well, now. Who's to argy agin that? We all lit a shuck over to Bob's, an' this horse thief showed hisself a true-blue man. He had 'em set out eight bottles. That's right, *eight*!

"Webb Fairly, he said, 'Stranger, if there was ary thing to

do in town tonight, we'd not hang you! But you know how it is?'

"Those eight bottles went quick, and that stranger bought four more. By that time ever'body was palooted, but nobody had forgot the hangin'. This here was a story to tell their grandchildren! It was almighty dark, but this Venk, as you say his name was, he told us, 'Boys,' he says, 'when I was a youngster I played under cottonwood trees. I noticed a big ol' cottonwood down the street by the blacksmith shop, an' if you'd hang me from that tree I'd be almighty proud!'

"Why not? We agreed. It isn't ever' day a man gits hung, an' it ain't ever' day we hang a gent who stages his own wake, sort of.

"It was little enough to do. Now, that there cottonwood was in the darkest place in town and we rode over there. We felt this feller was gettin' mighty sad, as he sort of choked up an' we heard what we figured was sobbin'.

"Nobody likes to hear a growed man cry, least of all a dead-game sport like this stranger, so we turned our faces away, slung a rope over the branch, and the sheriff—at least we figured it was the sheriff—he puts the noose over this man's head an' says, 'Let 'er go, boys!' an' the sorrel jumped out from under him and that gent was hangin' right where he wanted it. We watched him kick a mite an' then the sheriff says, 'Drinks are on me, boys, an' the last one into the saloon's a greenhorn!'

"We taken out on the run for the saloon and it was not until two drinks later we realized the sheriff wasn't with us.

"Nobody paid it much mind, 'cept one o' the boys did speak up an' say, 'You know? He must take to hangin', because that's the first time the sheriff ever bought anybody a drink!'

"Come daylight, those of us who could walk started for home, an' when we seen that gent hangin', we went over for a last look, an' what d'you think? We'd hung the sheriff!"

The fat man slapped his thigh and chuckled. "Funniest thing happened around here in years! That gent sure had him a sense of humor! Somehow he'd got those ropes off his wrists an' he must have slugged an' gagged the sheriff. Then he slipped that noose over . . .

"But I'd have sworn that was the sheriff! I heard him plain! He—"

"Charlie Venk is a good mimic," Bowdrie commented. "Did you try to trail him?"

"What for? We figured it was a good joke on the sheriff, an' he wasn't much account, anyway."

THERE WAS A trail when Bowdrie left town, a good clean trail, as the sorrel had a nice stride. Bowdrie followed the trail into an area of small rolling hills, across slabs of rock that left but indistinct white scars to mark Venk's passing, and when Bowdrie rode up to the next water hole there was a message scratched in the mud.

Whoever's trailin' me better light a shuck. I ain't foolin'.

Bowdrie glanced at it, then drank and filled his canteen and led the roan to drink. As the horse drank, Bowdrie's eyes kept moving, and when he was again in the saddle he continued his searching of the hills. His dark features were somber, for he had no illusions about the man he trailed. Charlie Venk watched his back trail, and Venk would be either seeing him now or at some time within the next few minutes. From here on it would be tough, and the advantage lay with Venk in that he knew where he was going and could choose the ground. If he wanted a battle, he could also choose the place.

Four years now Bowdrie had been riding with the Rangers, and if they wanted a man, they got him. If not now, later, but get him they would.

The odds were all against the criminal, for the law had time, and the law was tireless. An outlaw might scoff and claim that he was "smarter than any dumb Ranger." Even that was doubtful, but was he smarter than fifty Rangers? And the thousands of citizens who had eyes in their heads and could remember?

Very few things that people do remain unnoticed by somebody. All the law has to do is find that somebody who saw or heard something. Not always easy, but always possible.

Bowdrie rode on into the dancing heat waves where the dust devils did their queer, dervishlike dances out upon the white bottoms where no water was. Blue lakes appeared and vanished. Again and again he lost the trail. Again and again he found it.

He followed the man on the sheriff's sorrel where the only trace was left by the wind, and he followed him where the wind died and curled itself in sleep among the dead hills or against the hot flat faces of the cliffs. By desert, ridge, and mountain, by alkali sink and timberline, by deep green forest and bald hill, through lands where the ghosts of long-dead Apaches rode, and to the trails where the stages followed their rutted routes.

He ate where Venk had eaten, slept where he had slept, and came to know his little ways and how he thought and acted. He drank with men who had drunk with Venk, and four times he found places where Venk had circled back to get a look at the strange dark rider who followed him. Then the trail disappeared. It ended at the edge of an alkali lake and there was nothing . . . not a track, not a wisp, simply nothing at all.

Yet the trail of a man is not left on sand alone or on the broken twigs or the scars upon rock. The trail of a man is worked into the way he thinks and in what he wants, so the silent Ranger rode on, his mind reaching out ahead of his horse. His thoughts crossed ridges and searched out in memory of towns he knew and of talk among Rangers as to places and possibilities, and one Saturday afternoon Bowdrie rode into a quiet little cowtown.

He was, he believed, four days behind the sheriff's sorrel, but he had noticed the stride was shorter. Occasionally the sorrel stopped; there had been places where it was almost too tired to graze. The sorrel was going to have to stop or fall dead in its tracks. The roan was unchanged. It was just as tireless and just as mean as ever.

When Bowdrie rode into town, almost the first thing he saw was the sorrel, standing head hanging, in a corral. When he rode closer, he could see the horse had been curried, cared for. He rode his own horse to a livery stable, led it to a stall, fed, watered, and curried it. Few western horses were used to being curried. The roan was, and it liked it, but had no intention of letting its rider know. Twice the roan tried to kick, and once it reached around to nip the Ranger. Bowdrie skillfully avoided the nip with a skill born of long experience, cuffed the roan lightly on the nose, and walked to a bench.

He sat down on the bench, and one at a time, keeping one always loaded and ready for use, he cleaned his guns.

There were nine saloons in town, and the usual assortment of subsidiary structures. The town was like other such towns in other such places. The same horses dozed at the hitching rails, the same dogs slept in the dust, and their tails slapped the dust or the gray boards as he approached with the pleasant acknowledgment that all was friendly in this sunny, dusty world and all they wanted was to be left alone.

Chick Bowdrie pushed through the batwing doors and walked to the bar. He accepted the rye whiskey pushed toward him and downed a glass, then filled it again. His eyes kept to the bar, then lifted to the mirror behind it. His mind spelled out the faces in the room. The man he wanted was not present, but he had not expected him to be.

An aging cowhand in faded blue denim with a tobacco tag hanging from his breast-pocket, his face seamed with years, weather, kindness, and irony. The town drunk; his face was a mirror for lost illusions, his eyes hungry with hope, his boots worn, and the old hands trembling. The solid, square-built rancher with new heels on his boots and an air of belligerent prosperity and affluence. The bartender, slightly bald back of the plastered black hair above a smooth, ageless face and brow. The wise, cold eyes and the deft, active hands.

They were types, men without names, faces from a page of life he had turned many times, and faces he had often seen, like the husky young cowboy at the end of the bar who had a split lip and a welt on his cheekbone.

A movement stirred beside him and Bowdrie's muscles relaxed like those of a cat, relaxed to a poised alertness that preceded movement.

In the mirror he saw it was the drunk. Sober now, but hopeful.

"Howdy, stranger." He looked at Bowdrie in the mirror. "I could use a dollar."

Bowdrie's expression did not change. "If I gave you a dollar, how do I know you wouldn't spend it for food?"

For a moment the drunk simply blinked. Then he drew himself up and with great dignity replied, "Sir, I assure you that no such idea ever crossed my mind."

Bowdrie's eyes wrinkled at the corners. "I'm in a good mood. I'll buy you a drink, and then you can show me where the best restaurant is and we'll eat. Both of us. After that, I'll buy you another drink."

They had their drink. "A quiet town," Bowdrie suggested. "A good place to sleep."

"You should have seen it last night. See that gent with the split lip? He got himself into an argument with a big stranger. He had two partners to help, but this stranger, he whipped all three."

"Is he still around?"

"Seemed like he was in a hurry when he came into town, but that was before he saw Lucy Taylor."

"What was the argument about?"

"Whether Tuscaloosa was in Alabama or Arkansas." The drunk looked regretfully at his empty glass, but Bowdrie was starting for the door. He was tired of fixing his own grub and he was a lousy cook, anyway. The drunk followed him, talking. "This here stranger said it was in Arkansas. One word led to another, and they started to slug it out. Mister, that stranger was hell on a bicycle! He whipped the three of them."

"Who is this Lucy Taylor you mentioned?"

"Purtiest gal in these parts. Or any parts, for that matter. Lives yonder by the creek where you see all those cherry blossoms. That big stranger, he seen her an' fell like a ton of bricks, and, mister, if that gent can court like he can fight, he's top man around here now, although Lucy is mighty hard to get."

"Who did he fight with? Local men?"

"You know, I been thinking about that. All three of those gents were courting Lucy. He simply wiped out all the competition at one stroke."

Chick smiled. "Want to know something? That man who did the fighting was born in Alabama. In Tuscaloosa."

"But he claimed it was Arkansas!"

"Know any better way of startin' a fight than by insistin' a man is dead wrong when he *knows* he's right?"

"He started that fight a-purpose?"

"They were courtin' this Lucy you speak of. He fell for Lucy. If they get beat up, they can't go callin' for days. So how does that brand read?"

―――――

AMONG THE CHERRY trees was a house built of native stone, vine-clad and lovely. Nearby was a stream shaded by willows and cottonwoods, and one big cottonwood loomed over the back porch of the house and the yard before it. A girl in a clean, starched gingham dress was hanging clothes on the line.

Her hair was strawberry blond, over a very cute nose a few freckles were scattered, and when she stood on tiptoe to pin clothes on the line, Bowdrie noticed she had very pretty legs.

Removing his hat after a careful glance around, he said, "Good mornin', ma'am."

She turned quickly, with three clothespins in her mouth. He laughed and she hastily removed the clothespins. Then she laughed, too. She *was* pretty!

"You surprised me. Are you looking for Dad?"

"Who would look for your father when you're here?"

"Wait until I get these things hung out to dry and I'll get you some coffee. Are you the one who is looking for Charlie Venk?"

Surprised, he said, "Why, yes. Were you expectin' somebody?"

"He told me you'd be along. Said to treat you real nice. He said you'd had a long, hard ride and were probably all worn out. He said age was catching up with you, and long rides were hard on you."

"I'm no older than he is," Bowdrie protested. "Is he still around?"

She hung the last garment. "Come inside. The coffee should be ready by now." She led the way, speaking over her shoulder. "You're here two days earlier than Charlie expected."

"Known him long?"

"Only one day. It seems like I've known him forever." She blushed a little. "He's very handsome." She filled the cup. "And he's not like the boys around here."

"No, I reckon he ain't," Bowdrie said dryly.

"He said you were probably a Texas Ranger."

"I reckon he was right, ma'am." Bowdrie glanced at the rows of books on the shelves behind her. Many of the titles were foreign, some French, some German. "You folks keep a lot of books. I never had a chance to get much schoolin'."

"My father taught me. He was a college man. He is a lawyer."

They talked idly and drank coffee. Finally she went to the sideboard and cut a piece of pie for him. He ate it with appreciation.

"You sure can cook, bake, or whatever," he said. "No wonder Charlie was taken with you. Although," he added, "I don't think it was just the cookin'." He paused. "A right curious kind of man, that Charlie Venk."

"I think he's a fine man!" she insisted indignantly. "He said you began chasing him because of a horse he borrowed. Why didn't you give him time to explain?"

Bowdrie looked as meek as he could and said nothing.

"I think it's a shame! You turn a nice young man like that into a criminal! And over nothing!"

Chick Bowdrie looked regretfully into his empty cup. "Trouble was," he replied mildly, "there was a man settin' on that horse he wanted to borrow."

"On it?" She was puzzled.

"Yes, ma'am. Charlie was in a sort of hurry to leave be-

cause of some other problems he had, and he needed a horse
right bad and this gent objected."

"Well?"

"Charlie shot him out of the saddle."

"I don't believe it!"

"No, ma'am. I don't reckon you do. If a man is young and
nice-lookin' and is somebody you know, you just don't believe those things about him, but the State of Texas believes
it, ma'am, an' that's why I'm here."

He got up from the table just as a tall older man came into
the room. He nodded at Bowdrie.

"Good evening, sir."

The older man turned to Lucy and spoke quickly in French.
She glanced at Bowdrie, who was staring at the books on the
shelf. He took one down that was printed in English. It was a
copy of Plutarch's *Lives of Illustrious Men*. The girl's father
noticed it.

"You must have a gift for choosing the best. Are you familiar with this book?"

"Carried it in my saddlebags for two years. Gent gave
me a copy when I was fourteen. Took me a while to read it."
He glanced at the older man. "I never got much schoolin'.
Learned to read some, an' cipher. But Plutarch, I grew up
with that book. Used to set by the campfire an' study over it,
tryin' to make out what was meant. I finally got around to it."

He glanced from the man to Lucy. "This time it just sort of
fell open to the part about Alcibiades. Now, there was a nice-
seeming young fellow who came from a good family, had
good education, just about everything. But he turned out to
be a traitor and worse.

"Just goes to show you. A man may be good in some respects, no good in others."

Lucy Taylor flashed her eyes at him, then glanced away.
Chick Bowdrie picked up his hat and turned to go. "Reckon
I better be gettin' on. I don't want Charlie to get too much
lead on me."

"What?" Lucy turned swiftly. "What do you mean?"

Bowdrie's slow smile gathered around the corners of his
eyes and then he spoke in French. "I heard what your father

said, and your reply, so I know that Charlie saw me and has gone. I know he was hidden not far away when I arrived. And you knew it."

"You speak French! You told me you had not been to school!"

"Ma'am, I grew up down Castroville way, around there an' D'Hanis. Now, when I was a youngster most folks around there spoke both French and German. I learned to speak those languages as soon as I did English.

"You should take no more for granted from an officer of the law than from a horse thief. Both parties might conceal more than they tell."

Charlie Venk had ridden west, then north. Bowdrie knew a showdown was approaching and he was almost sorry. Trailing Venk had been a rare experience. In a time when many men lived by the gun, some of them were men of education and background. John Ringo and Elza Lay, for example, were men of considerable reputation. Charlie Venk was another, yet whatever else he was, he was a killer and a thief.

All that day and much of the next he followed Venk through a maze of tracks. He lost the trail, then found it again. It led across bare hillsides where Venk could proceed swiftly but Bowdrie, for fear of an ambush, must move slowly. He had to ride with extreme care for he was sure that Venk had made up his mind. He was through running.

Venk knew every trick, and he tried them all. Then Bowdrie came on a wagon loaded with household goods. The driver and a woman sat on the wagon seat; a small child peered between their shoulders.

"Hi!" The driver drew up. "You're ridin' the wrong way! Apaches raidin'! Killed a couple of prospectors night before last and burned some folks out! Better head back t'other way!"

Bowdrie smiled. "Thanks. Have you seen a big man? Ridin' a sorrel horse? Nice-lookin' man, headed the same way I am?"

"Sure did! He he'ped me fix a busted wheel. Bought some ca'tridges from me. You a friend o' his'n?"

"You might put it that way."

"He said he had a friend foller'n him an' he aimed to take that friend right through the middle of Apache country. Said he'd take him right back to Texas if he had the nerve to foller!"

Chick Bowdrie looked south and west. "I imagine he expected you'd tell me that. See you."

He continued north, but now he rode with greater caution, avoiding skylines and studying country before trusting himself to cross open places. Off to the northwest there was a thin column of smoke. It was not a signal. Something was burning.

Bowdrie turned the roan toward it.

Venk, Bowdrie reflected, was a strange combination. He had rustled cattle, stolen horses, robbed banks, and had killed several men, most of them in gun battles. As to the killing that started Bowdrie on his trail when he shot the man off the horse, all the evidence was not in. There might be more to it than the cold-blooded killing it seemed to be.

He was shrewd and intelligent. He could be friendly, and he could be dangerous. He could smile right into your eyes and shoot you dead in your tracks. Whatever else he was, to ride into Apache country meant he had to be either a very brave man or a fool. Or both.

For Bowdrie to follow him was equally foolish. Yet Charlie thought he was playing his ace in taking the risk. Desperate the man might be, but he also knew something about Chick Bowdrie by now.

He could not shake Bowdrie from his trail. Venk had tried every ruse used in wild country. This would be his last attempt.

They were now in northern Arizona. It was the home country of the Mogollon and White Mountain Apache, a rough, broken country of mountains, cliffs, and canyons. Not many miles from here was a pine forest of considerable extent. Bowdrie would have to think and move carefully, for the Apaches were more to be feared than Venk.

Venk was no fool, and in saying he was returning to Texas, he might do just that. He might also weave a trail through raiding Apache bands, then circle back to pay another visit to

Lucy Taylor. Lingering in this country was a foolhardy matter, but better to linger than to act and blunder.

———

TEN MILES AHEAD of Bowdrie was Charlie Venk. Always before he had been able to talk or laugh himself out of a situation or his skills had been great enough to elude pursuit. He now knew the identity of his pursuer, and he could not have missed knowing something about Bowdrie.

He could find no way of eluding his pursuer, and good with a gun as he was, he knew that in any gun battle many things might happen, and Bowdrie would not die easily. He might kill Bowdrie, but he might also be killed. And Charlie Venk loved life.

He was fresh out of tricks. Several times he believed he had lost the Ranger, but always Bowdrie worked out the trail and kept coming. It was getting on Venk's nerves. He no longer felt like laughing. Twice lately he had awakened in a cold sweat, and he found himself looking over his shoulder constantly. Once he even shot into a shadow. He had not had a good night's sleep in weeks.

Now he was riding into Apache country. There was no mercy in Charlie Venk. He was a good fellow as long as it cost him nothing. Could he have killed Bowdrie without danger to himself, he would have done it.

Nowhere in sight was there movement. Hot sun lay down the valley, but it was cool in the shade and the trail was visible for miles. Cicadas sang in the brush, and somewhere not far off a magpie fussed and worried over something. Charlie Venk needed rest, and this was as good a place as he was apt to find. He would just—

A brown arm slipped from behind and across his throat. Hands seized his arms and he was thrown to the ground. Other Apaches moved in, and he was a prisoner. His arms were bound, his guns taken away.

Blankly he stared into the cruel dark faces around him. He could talk, but his words would fall on unheeding ears. He could laugh, but they would not comprehend. His guns were gone, his muscles bound, his gift of tongue useless.

Charlie Venk stared into the sunlit afternoon realizing the heart-wrenching truth that he was through. He, the handsome, the strong, the ruthless, the untouchable. He who had ridden wild and free was trapped.

He was too wise in the ways of his country not to know what awaited him. Fiendish torture, burning, shot full of arrows or staked to an anthill.

CHICK BOWDRIE FOUND the spot where the capture took place, not two hours after Venk was taken. He found the stubs of three cigarettes, a confusion of tracks, mingled moccasins and boots. He found the trail that led away, several unshod horses and one shod. There was no blood on the ground. No stripped and mutilated body. Charlie Venk had been taken alive.

It was after nightfall when he found the Apache camp. His horse was tied in a thicket a half-mile away, and Bowdrie had changed to the moccasins he carried in his saddlebags. He was among the rocks overlooking the Apache camp.

Below him a fire blazed and he could see Venk tied to a tree whose top had been lopped off. As Chick watched, an Apache leaped up and rushed at Venk, striking him with a burning stick. Another followed, then another. This was preliminary; the really rough stuff was still to come. There were at least twenty Apaches down there, some of them women and children.

Bowdrie inched forward, measuring the risk against the possibilities. Coolly he lifted his Winchester. His mouth was dry, his stomach hollow with fear. Within seconds he would be in an all-out fight with the deadliest fighters known to warfare.

His greatest asset aside from his marksmanship was surprise. What he must do must be done within less than a minute.

He fired three times as fast as he could lever the shots. The range was point-blank. The first bullet was for a huge warrior who had jumped up and grabbed a stub of blazing wood and started for Venk. The bullet caught the Indian in mid-stride.

Bowdrie swung his rifle and another Apache dropped, a third staggered, then vanished into the darkness.

Instantly he was on his feet. If he was to free Venk, it must be done now! Once the panic inspired by the sudden attack was over, he would have no chance at all.

A move in the shadows warned him, and he fired. Venk was fighting desperately at the ropes that bound him. Behind the tree, Bowdrie could see the knot. He lifted the rifle and fired, heard the solid *thunk* of the bullet into the tree, and then, as he was cursing himself for his miss, he saw Venk spring away from the tree, fall, then roll into the shadows.

His bullet, aimed at the knot, had cut a strand of the rope!

The Apaches had believed themselves attacked by a number of men but would recover swiftly, realizing it could not be so. Warned by the fact that nobody had rushed the camp, they would be returning.

Bowdrie worked his way to where the horses were. He heard a sliding sound and a muffled gasp of pain.

"Venk?"

"Yeah." The whisper was so soft he scarcely heard it. "And I got my guns!"

A bullet smashed a tree near them, but neither wasted a shot in reply. They were thinking only of the horses now. The Apaches would think of them also. Suddenly Venk lifted his pistol and shot in the direction of the horses. Bowdrie swore, but the shot struck an Indian reaching for the rope that tied them. Startled by the firing, the horses broke free and charged in a body.

Bowdrie had an instant to slip his arm and shoulder through the sling on his rifle, and then the horses were on them.

He sprang at the nearest horse. One hand gripped the mane and a leg went over the back. Outside camp they let the horses run, a few wild shots missing them by a distance. They circled until they could come to where Bowdrie's horse was tied.

Daybreak found them miles away. Bowdrie glanced over at the big, powerfully muscled man lying on the ground near the gray horse. That it had once been a cavalry horse was obvious by the "US" stamped on the hip.

Naked to the waist, Venk's body was covered by burns. There was one livid burn across his jaw.

Venk looked over at him. "If anybody had told me that could be done, I'd have said he was a liar!"

Venk had two guns belted on, and in his wild escape from camp he had grabbed up either his own or an Indian's rifle.

"That was a tough one," Bowdrie admitted.

"You Rangers always go that far to take a prisoner?"

"Of course," Bowdrie said cheerfully, "I could have saved Texas a trial and a hanging or a long term in prison by just letting them have you."

"I guess," Venk suggested, "we'd better call it quits until we get back among folks. No use us fightin' out here."

Bowdrie shrugged. "What have we got to fight about? You're my prisoner."

"Determined cuss, aren't you?" He put a cigarette in his mouth. "Oh, well! Have it your own way!" He took a twig from the fire to light his smoke; then he said, holding the twig in his fingers, "I might as well go back with you. You saved my life. Anyway—" he grinned—"I'd like to stop by and see that Lucy gal! Say, wasn't she the—!"

He jumped and cried out as the twig burned down to his fingers, but as he jumped his hand dropped for his gun in a flashing draw!

The gun came up and Bowdrie shot him through the arm. Charlie Venk dropped his gun and sprang back, gripping his bloody arm. He stared unbelieving at Bowdrie.

"You beat me! You beat me!"

"I was all set for you, Charlie. I've used that trick myself."

"Why didn't you kill me? You could have."

"You said you wanted to see Lucy again. Well, so do I. I'd hate to have to go back and tell her I buried you out here, Charlie.

"Now, you just unbuckle that belt and I'll fix up that arm before you bleed to death. We've a long ride ahead of us."

STRAWHOUSE TRAIL

H E LOOKED THROUGH his field glasses into the eyes of a dying man.

A trembling hand lifted, the fingers stirred, and the dying lips attempted to form words, trying desperately to tell him something across the void, to deliver a final message.

Chick Bowdrie stared, struggling to interpret the words, but even as he stared he saw the lips cease their movements and the man was no longer alive.

Lowering his glasses, Chick studied the wide sweep of the country. Without the glasses he could see only the standing horse that had first attracted his attention. The canyon between them was deep, but the dead man lay not more than one hundred yards away.

Mounting his hammerheaded roan, Chick Bowdrie swung to the trail again and started down the steep path into the canyon. By this route the man must have come. Had he been dying then? Or had he been shot as he reached the other side? There had been a dark blotch on the man's side that must be blood.

Twenty minutes later he stood beside the dead man. No tracks but the man's own. Falling from his horse, the fellow had tried to rise, had finally made it, struggled a few steps, and then fallen, to rise no more.

Chick knelt beside the dead man. About fifty-five, one hundred and thirty pounds, and very light-skinned for a western man, which he obviously was. He had been shot low down on the left side.

No . . . that was where the bullet had come *out*. The bullet had entered in the man's back near the spine.

Nothing in the pockets, no letters, no identification of any kind . . . and only a little money.

The jeans and shirt were new. The boots also. Only the gun belts, holster, and gun were worn. They showed much use, and much knowing care. The trigger was tied back . . . the man had been a slip-shot.

The dead man's hands were white and smooth. Not the hands of a cowhand, yet neither was the man a gambler. Getting to his feet, Chick walked to the horse. A steel-dust and a fine animal, selected by a man who knew horseflesh. The saddle was of the "center-fire" California style, of hand-worked leather and with some fine leather work on the tapaderos. The rope was an easy eighty feet long, and new.

No food, which indicated the man expected to reach his goal before night. He had been shot not more than two hours before dusk, which implied his destination could not be far off. Surely not more than fifteen miles or so.

A new Winchester rifle with a hundred rounds of ammunition. An equal amount for a pistol, and then, curiously enough, a box of .32-caliber pistol ammunition.

Returning it all to the saddlebags and a pack under the slicker, Bowdrie slung the body over the dead man's saddle, then mounted his own horse.

Four miles from where the body had been found, the tracks of a shod horse turned into the trail. Chick swung down and studied them. The shoes were not new and were curiously worn on the outside. Stepping back into the leather, Chick rode on.

Valverde came to life when Chick rode down the street. A man got up from a chair in front of the livery stable, another put down his hammer in the blacksmith shop. A girl came from the general store. As one person, they began to move toward the front of the Border Saloon, where Chick Bowdrie had stopped.

"Deputy sheriff here? Or marshal?"

A bulky man with a star came from the saloon. "I'm Houdon, I'm the marshal."

"Found him on the trail." Bowdrie explained as the marshal examined the body, yet as he talked Chick's eyes strayed to the faces of the crowd. They revealed nothing. Behind him, there was a click of heels on the boardwalk, a faint perfume, then a gentle breathing at his shoulder.

The girl who had come from the store looked past him at the body. There was a quick intake of breath and she turned at once and walked away. Because she had seen a body? Or because she knew the man?

After answering questions, Bowdrie walked into the saloon. The bartender shoved the bottle to him and commented, "Eastern man?"

"California," Bowdrie replied. "Notice his rig?"

The bartender shrugged, making no reply. Chick downed his drink, filled his glass again, and waited, listening to the discussion in the bar.

There was, he learned, no trouble in the vicinity, and jobs were scarce. Occasionally he helped the conversation along with a comment or a question. Most local cowhands worked years for the same outfit, and most of them were Mexicans. The Bar W had let two hands go, but that was an exception. The Bar W was in old Robber's Roost country, over against the Chisos Mountains.

"That trail I was followin'," he commented idly, "wasn't used much."

"It's the old Strawhouse Trail. Smugglers used it, a long time back. Only the old-timers know it."

But the dead man had been riding it. Was he an old-timer returning? Chick threw down his cigarette and crossed to the restaurant.

Pedro opened one eye and looked at Bowdrie. A fat, jolly Mexican woman came from the kitchen. She jerked her head at the man. "He is the sleepy one! Good for nothing!"

Pedro opened the eye again. "Juana have nice restaurant, six leetle ones. Good for nothing! Hah! What can we get you, señor?"

"How about *arroz con pollo*?"

Chick Bowdrie dropped to a bench beside the table, considering the situation. A man had bought an outfit, then loaded for bear, he had come to the border, a man who knew the old trails and who probably had been here long before.

From his age, however, the sort of man who would not lightly return to the saddle.

He was eating when the girl came in and stopped near his table. She hesitated, then abruptly, she sat down. She put her hands on the table before her and he glanced at them, carefully kept hands, yet western hands.

"That man . . . did he say anything? I mean, was he still living when you found him?" She was very lovely, tall, with blond hair bleached by the sunlight.

"He was alive when I first saw him through my field glasses, but by the time I had crossed the canyon, he was dead." He tasted his coffee. It was cowpuncher coffee, black and strong. "Did you know him?"

"No." The suit she wore was not new. Excellent material and beautifully tailored, but growing shabby now. "I . . . I thought he might be coming to see me. I'm Rose Murray."

The RM. He knew the ranch; from what he had heard earlier, he had ridden over part of it on his way into town. He waited for her to continue, and after a minute she said, "I'd never seen him. He . . . he knew where something was, something that belongs to my family. He was coming to get it for us."

Gradually, she told him the story. Her ranch had steadily lost money after the death of her father. Rustlers, drought, and the usual cattle losses had depleted her stock. With only a few hands left and badly in debt, a letter came from out of nowhere.

Long ago an outlaw band had roamed the area and they had raided the hacienda, stealing several sacks of gold coins, a dozen gold candlesticks, a gold altar service from the chapel, and a set of heavy table silver by a master craftsman. Owing to the weight of the treasure and the close pursuit, the thieves had been compelled to bury the loot. Taking only what gold coins they could safely carry, they had scattered.

Two of the six had been slain in a gun battle with the posse and another had been shot down on a dark El Paso street a few weeks later. The writer of the letter, who had not given his name, had gone west. He had fallen in love, married, and gone straight.

Hearing of the collapse of the once great fortune and the dire straits of the girl, his conscience troubled him.

His own wife had died and he was once more alone. Some word had come to him from Texas that worried him, so he had written the girl that he was coming to her.

"He mentioned no children?"

"There was a son."

When Rose had gone, Chick crossed to the stable for his horse. The hostler walked back with him. "Ain't you that Castroville Ranger? Name of Bowdrie?"

Bowdrie nodded, waiting.

The old man nodded wisely. "Figured so. Gent comes in askin' who your hoss belonged to. Seemed mighty interested. I told him I didn't know."

"What did this fellow look like?"

"Oldish feller, shabby kind of. Thin hair, gray eyes. No color to him but his guns. They seen plenty of use."

The hostler pointed out the inquirer's horse. Chick looked it over thoughtfully. Dusty and tired. He put a hand on the horse. "So, boy," he said gently, "so . . ." The horse was too tired to resent his hand as he picked up the hoof. Holding it an instant to let the horse get used to it, he turned it up and examined the shoe. It was badly worn on the outside. So were the others.

Bowdrie straightened. "Thanks. Do you a favor some time."

––––––

AT DAYLIGHT HE was out of town and riding for the border. Crossing the river, he pulled up at the house of an old Mexican he knew in Boquillas.

Miguel watched Bowdrie as he came up the walk from the gate where he had tied his horse. He started to rise, but Chick put a hand on his shoulder. "Don't get up, my friend. I have come to talk to the one who remembers all."

"You flatter an old man, señor. What is it you wish to know?"

When he explained the old man nodded. "*Sí*, I have not forgotten, but it was long ago." He leaned forward. "It was the Chilton gang, amigo. There were six, I was among those who fought the two who were killed. Before one died he told us one of the others was Bill Radcliff."

"The Chilton gang . . ."

Bowdrie remembered them from the files of the Rangers. Dan Chilton, Bill Radcliff, and Andy Short had been the core of the group. Robbing payrolls had been their game, at ranches, mines, and the railroad. "One was killed in El Paso," he said.

"Radcliff." Miguel lighted a fresh cigarette. "The killer was never known. Some thought John Selman. He was marshal then. I do not think so."

"Chilton?"

Miguel shrugged. "Who knows? He was the best of them. Wild, but a good man. My brother knew him. Short was the worst. A killer."

They talked into the hot afternoon about the border and bad men and Indians and wars. It was only with great reluctance that Bowdrie got up to leave.

"Vaya con Dios."

"Adios, amigo. Till next time . . ."

BOWDRIE RODE TOWARD Glen Springs Draw. He thought again of Andy Short . . . it could have been the name the dead man had been saying, shaping the name with his lips as he died.

Sunlight flashed on a distant hillside, and instantly Chick Bowdrie reined the roan over and slapped spurs to his ribs. The horse jumped just as the bullet whiffed past Bowdrie's head, but the roan was startled and the second bullet missed by yards. Only the sunlight on a rifle barrel had saved his life.

The shot had come from the slopes of Talley Mountain, and Chick kept the roan running, dodging from arroyo to arroyo and swinging back toward the mountain whence the bullet had come. Suddenly he eased to a canter, then a walk.

Dust in his nostrils, a settling of dust in the road, and the tracks of a horse . . . with shoes worn on the outside!

Making no attempt to follow, he turned his horse into the trail that led to the Bar W and the RM. Both outfits had headquarters beyond the ridge, and the trail swung suddenly left into a narrow cut. Hesitating only briefly, Bowdrie started into the opening. The sheer walls offered no place for a sniper, and the low rocks within the cut gave no shelter. He rode slowly, however, his six-gun in hand, and suddenly drew up, aware of a clicking. The sound stopped, and he started on. It began again. Suddenly he smiled ruefully. His horse's hooves were scraping against the eroded stones that lined the base of each wall. . . .

Shortly before sundown he walked the roan into the yard of the Bar W. The old adobe house, the pole corrals, the sagging roof of the barn gave no evidence of life. Then a rusty hinge creaked and Bowdrie saw a man step from the barn.

He saw Bowdrie in the same instant, and for a moment he hesitated, as if half-inclined to drop the bucket he was carrying and grab for a gun.

Unshaven, big and rough, his shirt was dirty and he had a narrow-eyed look like a surly hound.

There were, Bowdrie noted, six mules in the corral, and several fine horses . . . he took out the makings.

"Howdy"—his voice matter-of-fact—"takin' on any hands?"

"No." He jerked his head. "Go try the RM."

Bowdrie continued working with his smoke, taking his time. "Old place," he commented, "could stand some work. Figured there might be a job."

"You figured wrong."

"Don't rush me, amigo. I'm interested in old places. Why, I'd bet this one was here in the days o' the Chilton gang."

The name brought no reaction. "Never heard of 'em."

"Some years back. Nobody ever did find all that loot."

The big man was interested now. He walked toward Chick. "What loot?"

It was possible, Bowdrie decided, to drop a pebble in this pool and see what happened to the widening ripples. It might cause dissension in the ranks of the enemy. Or create a diversion. "A quarter of a million in gold and jewels," he said carefully. "It was cached. Somebody right close about knows where it is."

"You don't say!" The man was interested now. "So, what's the yarn?"

Bowdrie explained, then added, "Ticklish business, huntin' for it. Two of the outlaws must be still alive."

The man was greedy and interested, but obviously a hired hand who knew nothing. Chick reined his horse around. "Your boss prob'ly knows the story. Oldish man, isn't he?"

"Not more'n twenty-six or seven." The big man grinned maliciously. "An' pure D poison with a six-gun. You maybe heard of Rad Yates."

Bowdrie had . . . no definite record. Bought and sold cattle, gambled a good bit, usually consorting with outlaws and men along the fringe. He had killed, according to report, nine men. All had been in what were apparently fair fights.

Yates was not old enough to have been one of the Chilton gang, but the Strawhouse Trail pointed right at the Bar W . . . or the RM. Scowling, Bowdrie considered that as he headed off, down the trail.

Somebody had attempted to dry-gulch him, and that somebody rode a horse with worn shoes, as had the killer of the man in Venado Canyon. That somebody had come from this direction.

Tracks in the dust stopped him. Again the worn shoes . . . and the tracks were fresh!

He skirted wide around a clump of mesquite, then spotted the rider ahead of him, just disappearing down a slight declivity. Swinging wide again, he took the roan at a run toward the wash. Sliding into it, he put the horse up the far side along a trail cattle had taken. Dust hung in the air, and it followed the rider he was seeking. He swung around and drew up at the trailside. There were no tracks . . . and then he heard the hoofbeats of a cantering horse.

The rider rounded a low knoll, and Bowdrie stepped his horse forward, gun in hand. "All right. Get your hands up!"

He stared into the astonished eyes of Rose Murray.

His astonishment matched hers, but he was quick to note the rifle in her scabbard. After all, what did he know about her? She had been curious about the dead man, and a woman can squeeze off a shot as well as a man. He lowered his gun.

"Can I lower my hands?" Bowdrie nodded. "Who did you expect to see?"

"Not you . . ." He hesitated only briefly. "Riding home?"

As they rode he explained about the mysterious rifle shots and his visit to the Bar W.

"Rad Yates seems very nice," Rose said. "He's called at the ranch."

They rode into the yard and swung down. Bowdrie caught a vague movement up the mountainside. There was a man there, his clothing blending perfectly with the background. Only his movement had betrayed him. Rose had just stepped inside, so he followed, getting a corner of the barn between the hill and the door as he reached it.

A Mexican woman brought coffee, and after a few minutes Bowdrie asked, casually, "Had that horse long? The one you were riding?"

"He was born from one of my mares. Nobody has ever ridden him but me."

There had been her chance and she had passed it up. She seemed to have no suspicion of his reason for asking the question. In fact, she was not suspicious as a guilty person should be.

A drum of hooves and a hail. The Mexican woman answered the door and a moment later a big young man walked in. He had brown hair and a bold, handsome face. He walked with a casual swagger and his guns were tied down.

This would be Rad Yates. He was not the man on the hill; his clothing was bright and colorful. He grinned when he saw Bowdrie. "Heard you were out at the place," he said. He turned and spoke to Rose, and Chick moved where he could see Yates's horse. It was a flashy paint.

Rose came over to him, followed by Yates. "We're going towards Rad's place to start a tally on the cattle in those canyons," she said. "I'm sorry I can't stay to entertain you. Would you like to come along with us?"

Chick Bowdrie looked thoughtfully from one to the other.

His dark eyes showed one of their rare flashes of amusement. The pieces were beginning to fall into place now. "Maybe," he said. Then he shifted to the attack. "Sure he's got himself in place yet, Yates?"

Rad Yates tightened and his head lowered a little. His smile remained, but became set and hard. "What're you talkin' about?"

"That gent up on the mountain with the rifle."

Yates was caught flat-footed. "What gent? I don't know what you're talking about."

Bowdrie's hands were on his hips, only inches from his guns. "Your first name is Radcliff, isn't it? Maybe the son of Bill Radcliff? Or his nephew?"

"And if it is?"

"Well, it's an interesting point, Yates. But even more interesting if you and the gent up the hill get what you're lookin' for. Then what happens? You shoot it out?"

Rose was looking from one to the other, frankly puzzled. "What are you two talking about?"

Bowdrie smiled. "Why, Rose, we're talkin' about the loot from this ranch stolen and buried by the Chilton gang. Andy Short was one of them and Bill Radcliff another. Unless I miss my guess, that's Andy up there on the mountain right now, waitin' for me with a rifle."

Yates had recovered himself. "Rose, I reckon these Rangers are suspicious of ever'body. We'd better forget the ride. All right if I come over tomorrow?"

"Of course, Rad." Her voice chilled. "But I expect that Mr. Bowdrie will be leaving now."

She turned on him when they were alone. "You've no right to accuse on so little evidence. Rad is one of my best friends."

"Yes, ma'am," Bowdrie said. "But I would bear in mind that a man's been murdered for coming to help you. You should be careful."

RAD YATES WAS frankly stumped. When they learned a Ranger had come upon the body of the dead man, they were worried. For the first time an unforeseen element had intruded upon what seemed a perfect plan.

Almost a year before, Andy Short, only recently released from prison, had come upon Yates in an El Paso saloon. A casual word had told Yates who Short was, and he was disappointed to discover that Short did not know the whereabouts of the loot. Only Dan Chilton actually knew . . . and nobody knew where Dan Chilton was.

Yet Andy Short had an idea. Using Yates's place as a base, he had searched the hills to no avail. He could not locate the hidden loot. But on a casual visit to the RM, Rad Yates had seen the letter from the mysterious man in California and had gone at once to Short.

Short, a slender man, gray of face and cold of eye, had been immediately excited. "Chilton!" He slammed his fist on the table. "He's comin' to give that loot back! He was always a namby-pamby!"

Chilton had had a map. Short took it from the body after the shooting, mounted his horse, and rode off. From the side of a distant hill he glanced back and suddenly he was frightened.

Dan Chilton's body was gone!

Swinging back, he had seen the bloodstains and the tracks of a staggering man. Somehow, Chilton was still alive, and he had gotten into the saddle again.

Short had gone after him, but Chilton had disappeared. When he saw him again it was in the streets of Valverde and Chick Bowdrie was explaining to Houdon.

Had Chilton lived to talk?

Carefully, they remained away from the location of the loot, waiting to let the Ranger move first. He would show his hand if he knew anything. If he came after the loot, they could kill him. They watched and waited, and then, on Bowdrie's return from Mexico, they had tried and failed.

Now he was here. And he had known, somehow, about Andy Short being on the mountain.

The plan had been simple enough. Yates would get him out on the mountainside, Short would do the shooting, then Rad would make a show of chasing the killer. He'd impress

Rose and then he and Andy Short would go dig up the loot. But the Ranger was onto them, somehow, and he had posed a disturbing question. What would happen when they got the money? Was he ready to kill to get it all? Was he ready to kill simply to keep his part of it?

———

WHEN CHICK BOWDRIE had scouted the area to be sure he was not to be the target of a hidden marksman, he rode away and took back trails for town. His warnings to Rose Murray had gone unheeded. That she liked Rad Yates was obvious, that she did not appreciate Bowdrie's seemingly unfounded suggestions was equally obvious.

The existence of at least two sets of shoes worn in an identical manner damaged what little case he had and left him without evidence. For a supposedly abandoned route, the section of the Strawhouse Trail through the sandstone bottoms got more use than he would have expected. The horse Rose Murray had ridden was not the horse he had seen in town. Neither was the horse ridden by Yates.

Valverde was somber with darkness when he dismounted at the stable. The hostler took his horse. "I'll give him a bait of oats," he offered. Pausing, he added, "Stranger in town. Tall young feller. Askin' about the dead man."

Over a late supper, Chick pondered his problems. He had stumbled upon the body of a murdered man, yet he was no further along than in the beginning. Andy Short could be the killer. If he was actually around. On the other hand, so could Rad Yates. And Rose? That was still an open question. There might be more to this than appeared on the surface.

A quicker solution might be reached if he found the loot. The outlaws had been hotly pursued. Implying little time to conceal the treasure. No time to dig a deep hole. If it had not been recovered by the surviving members of the gang—and he was positive it had not—then that implied a place not too easy of access or too easy to guess.

The outlaws' line of flight had been from the hacienda through the Chisos Mountains, but by the time they reached Rough Run the loot had already been cached. That left many miles of country to be searched. Yet, there could not be too many possible hideaways on that route.

The door opened and he looked up. A tall young man had entered the room. He was blond and deeply tanned. "You're Mr. Bowdrie?"

"And you'll be Dan Chilton's son."

The blond young man was surprised. "Why, yes. As a matter of fact, that's my name, too. I didn't expect you to know me."

Chick Bowdrie was thinking swiftly. Chilton was an attractive young man, and more attractive, if he was any judge, than Rad Yates. He grinned suddenly. "Look," he said, "your father was trying to do a good deed out here, that's what got him killed . . ." Bowdrie carefully explained to the young man what he knew and what he suspected. He ended by asking for young Dan Chilton's help. "Rad Yates is involved somehow, and he's currying favor with Rose Murray. You go down there, and no matter what happens, stick close to her. I don't know what his scheme is, but you'll be in his way."

Chilton nodded. "And what excuse will I give? The son of the man who robbed her family?"

"Just that. You want to atone for what your father did. He was returning to help her; you want to carry on. She'll listen."

He hesitated, trying his coffee. "Can you use a gun?"

"I have one. A thirty-two Smith & Wesson."

That explained the ammunition. Bowdrie nodded. "It's small, but it will have to do. Don't use it unless you have to." He explained about Yates, who and what he was. Chilton nodded, offering no comment.

In their conversation Chilton had been able to tell him very little, but Bowdrie sat alone over his coffee in the now silent town and pieced that little together with what he knew.

The searchers, old Dan had told his son, had all looked in the Chisos Mountains, and that was the wrong place. This narrowed the distance by more than half. The old trail led from Oak Spring at the foot of the mountains to the Rock Hut at the base of Burro Mesa. I'll lay two to one it wasn't cached far from that Rock Hut, he told himself.

One thing he decided. If, as he believed, the presence of

Chilton at the RM would keep Rad Yates around Rose's ranch, it would leave him free to hunt down Andy Short. For he no longer had any idea of waiting to be shot at. Now he was going to hunt the hunter.

Finishing his coffee, he got up and walked to the door. Pedro and his spouse had long since retired, so he merely blew out the light and turned the knob. For several minutes he waited, listening to the night sounds in the empty street of Valverde.

A sign creaked rustily in the vague wind. A paper brushed along the street. All was still.

Suddenly a horseman appeared at the end of the street and started forward, coming along toward the saloon. Bowdrie stepped through the door and eased it shut behind him. Then he shifted away from the door and stood flat against the building.

The rider reached the marshal's office near the saloon and drew up. His saddle creaked as he swung down. Chick strained his eyes in the dim light and could see only that this was a big man, vaguely familiar.

Taking a careful look around, the man eased his gun in his holster and moved forward, and suddenly Chick knew him. It was the big cowhand from the Bar W!

Frowning, Chick waited. This . . . it simply did not fit. Unless the man had discovered something.

Opposite the door of the marshal's office, the big man paused. The man was in the darker shadow now, away from the gray of the street, and Chick only knew he was there, he could see nothing.

A flicker of movement drew Bowdrie's eyes and suddenly he realized there was another person—man or woman—in the space between the saloon and the office. Chick Bowdrie, suddenly comprehending, stepped out of the shadow and started forward.

Even as he moved he saw the big man, warned by some vague sound, grab frantically for his gun. Another gun boomed heavily between the buildings and the big man staggered, then fell back off the boardwalk. He tried to get up, and a shot nailed him to the spot. Chick tried a fast shot at the darkness whence the gun flashes had come, and a return shot whipped past his face.

Running, he dashed forward, hearing a door slam open and a shouted question. He reached the alleyway and plunged recklessly into it. At the far end of the dark alley a horse and rider lunged suddenly, running away behind the buildings. When Chick reached the spot, the rider was gone . . . out of sight. Only a drum of running hooves fading in the night.

Breathing hard, he walked back. It was utterly impossible, yet the gunman had somehow outdistanced him. He turned again, looking down the long alley.

Rad Yates?

It simply could not have been Andy Short. No man of the age he had to be could sprint sixty feet while Chick Bowdrie was covering less than thirty. And yet the man was gone.

Several men were gathered around the body and one had lighted a match to examine him. Pedro came from the back door of the restaurant, stuffing his shirt into too tight jeans. Closer by, Houdon came from his office, buckling his belt.

Without doubt the big cowhand had learned something, and he had come to town with it. Someone had followed him, not wanting him alive to repeat what he knew.

Easing away from the circle of talkers around the body, Chick walked back through the alley to where he had seen the horse. Distance was hard to estimate, and the horse might have been right behind the saloon. Yet when he reached the spot, two struck matches revealed nothing.

Not far away was a huge cottonwood, and near it, several smaller trees. It was the logical place. Here Chick found more hoof tracks than he had expected. He also found five cigarette butts. Here a man had waited, at least an hour . . . for what?

This man was here *before* the big cowhand arrived in town. He must have been here most of the time Chick was in the restaurant. Could he have followed him there? But that did not make sense, because from under the trees the watcher could not have seen the café.

What, then, had he waited for? And the tracks were those of a horse with shoes worn on the outside.

Houdon was waiting for him when he walked back to the street. The body of the man had been moved. The marshal jerked his head toward the street. "What did Jake want at this time of night?"

Houdon was unshaven and he looked tired and irritable. He stared at Chick and absently scratched his stomach. Briefly, Bowdrie outlined the situation, identifying himself to the marshal for the first time. Nothing seemed to arouse the marshal until Bowdrie mentioned the man who had lurked under the cottonwoods.

"Somebody else," he said, nodding his big head ponderously. "After me, I betcha. Man makes enemies in this here job." He looked shrewdly at Bowdrie. "Folks sometimes don't take kindly to the law."

"I think," Chick suggested, "it was Andy Short."

The scratching fingers paused momentarily. Other than this there was no reaction. Houdon shrugged. "Ain't from around here, I reckon. You see him, you let me know."

At daylight Bowdrie was getting a quick cup of coffee and some breakfast at Pedro's. The fat Mexican leaned his big elbows on the oilcloth-covered table. "You savvy Burro Mesa?" he asked suddenly.

Startled, Bowdrie looked up. Pedro glanced around, yawned widely, and put a stubby finger on a spot on the oilcloth. "Here," he said, "is the Rock Hut. And here is the trail across the mesa. On the west side is another spring. My compadre, he ride in last night. He say a man camps in the brush near that spring."

———

IT WAS HIGH noon when Bowdrie rode the hammerheaded roan into the scrub near Oak Spring. Burro Mesa loomed on the skyline only a short distance ahead. The morning ride had been a long one and both horse and man were tired.

Well back in the brush, Bowdrie made a fire of dry sticks that gave off no smoke, and prepared a meal of coffee, bacon, and sourdough flapjacks. He stretched out after eating and lighted a smoke. Above him a pin oak was shelter from the blazing sun.

Half-asleep and completely relaxed, some half hour later, he heard a horse approaching. Instantly he was alert. His hand touched the roan and the horse relaxed slowly. He waited, listening. The horse was coming through the pass from the Chisos.

It slowed . . . a saddle creaked . . . with a warning signal to the roan, Chick eased himself forward on cat feet.

The horse was drinking at the spring, and as he watched, the rider got up from the ground. It was Rose Murray. She wiped the water from her mouth and looked carefully around.

What was *she* doing here? And where were Yates and Chilton?

He watched her step into the leather and turn west, then mounted his own horse. Was she involved in the plotting? Or had she come upon some clue?

Holding a course that kept him inside the brush, he worked his way along the mountainside in the direction Rose had chosen. Suddenly he drew up.

A horse with shoes badly worn on the outside had come off the mesa from the west. A blade of grass in one of the hoofprints was just springing into place. This could be the mysterious camper in the brush of whom Pedro had told him.

Chick Bowdrie followed on, but slowly. He had good reason to know the skill and trickiness of Andy Short. The quiet, gray-faced man in the nondescript clothes, described to him by the hostler, but whom he had never seen. That the man was a gunman, Bowdrie knew from the Rangers' Bible—his agency's file of outlaws.

At the edge of the pin oaks he drew up, scanned the empty country before him, then moved ahead, alert for trouble. His eyes roved, and suddenly held.

The Rock Hut.

And two horses standing near a mesquite tree. One was the horse Rose had ridden. The other was the horse he had seen once before, the horse of the mysterious rider.

He waited, studying the lay of the land. There was a door,

obviously, from the path, leading from the front of the building toward where the horses stood. There was no window on this side, but there was a window behind. A small window.

Swinging down, he moved carefully, closing in. From the window came half-heard voices.

"So, you trailed young Radcliff. What a joke! He's back at your place taking care of Chilton's greenhorn son."

The girl spoke, too softly.

"You just sit there, Missy. We'll figure out . . ." The man's voice dissolved into a murmur.

Chick started to move closer, then he dropped to his haunches behind a boulder and some brush. A hard-ridden horse was coming down the trail. It was Rad Yates.

Chick moved away then stepped out from the brush as Yates slid his horse to a stop. His face was a study in cold fury. Bowdrie knew how tricky the situation was. "Rad." He spoke quietly, striving to keep his voice casual and calm on the other man. "Whatever you're figurin' on, don't do it." Yates's head snapped around.

Before Rad could speak, he continued, "Think now! You're clean. Nobody has anything on you. We have plenty on Short. Why butt into something where you're not wanted? Turn around and ride out of here a free man. Stay, and you become an outlaw."

The view was so eminently reasonable that Rad Yates hesitated. What Bowdrie said was true. He was still on the right side of the law. If he went ahead, there would be no return trail.

But the lure of the gold was strong. "No." He spoke slowly. "I've come too far—waited too long." He swung to the ground. As he turned he drew.

Whatever he planned failed to materialize. In the instant he swung down, Bowdrie had closed in. As Rad turned, his gun coming up, Bowdrie slapped the gun aside and down and hit him on the chin.

It was a short, wicked blow. Yates tottered and stumbled against his horse, the startled bronc moved, and Yates lost his balance and fell. As he hit ground, Bowdrie kicked the gun from his hand.

Yates came up fast and Bowdrie was too close to chance a draw. But Yates's rising lunge met the battering ram of Bowdrie's rock-hard fist and the bone in Yates's nose crushed under the impact, showering him with blood. The man was game, and shaking his head, he got up. Bowdrie let him rise, taking time for one quick glance toward the Rock Hut. No sign of life there at all.

The idea of Short discovering them frightened him and he stepped in quickly. For all his size, Rad was no fistfighter. He threw a long swing and Bowdrie went inside with a wicked right to the chin that dropped Yates. Grabbing the man's gun and taking his rifle, he threw them, whirling, high over the brush. Then he ran for the Hut.

He was running on soft ground and he heard voices, then stopped. "How come you knowed about this place?"

"I heard you tell Rad you'd meet him here today. Then I realized this *might* be the place."

Chick heard the chink of metal on metal. "You're hard luck, kid, you shouldn't have come here."

Andy Short came through the door, his hands and pant legs dusted with dirt, dragging a sack. His eyes went wide and he swung up the gun he carried in his right hand, and fired. The shot was too quick, a startled response to the unexpected sight of the Ranger. It missed.

Chick Bowdrie palmed his Colt and fired, but Short had dropped low and the bullet took him through the shoulder. It knocked him around and his second shot missed, and then Bowdrie put two fast bullets into him.

Bowdrie stepped back, his dark, Apache-like face grim and lonely. He began to shove out the shells for reloading when from behind him he heard Yates's voice. But it was a warning, not a threat.

"Bowdrie! Look out!"

Chick turned . . . another rider sat his horse, and he held a four-shot Roper revolving shotgun in his hands. It was Houdon, the marshal.

Bowdrie could see Yates, blood still streaming from his nose, and Yates had another cut now—on his skull. But he was not out.

Houdon's face was grizzled and old, his jowls heavy, his small eyes no longer looked dopey or sullen. Now they held amusement, and cunning.

"Killed Andy, did you? Can't say I'm sorry. Andy there could be right slick with a gun."

Bowdrie watched the man carefully. Slowly, things began to fit together.

"You're the sixth man," he said suddenly. "You're the last survivor of the Chilton gang."

Houdon did not change expression for a moment, then he chuckled. It was a slow, fat, easy chuckle. "Yep, an' I'm the one killed Dan. It wasn't Andy, like you prob'ly figured. I took Andy's horse from the livery, knowin' a body could track them shoes. I think that might've turned him against me, what d'you think?"

"You were all trying to find the treasure?"

"We were gonna be partners. But now . . . well, the deal's off. Knowed I had to move quick when you told me Andy had been layin' for me back o' the saloon.

"I killed that cowpoke, too. Heard he was huntin' around up here."

Bowdrie was thinking. He held his six-shooter and it was still partly loaded. Did Houdon know that? Or did he think because he had pushed out two shells that the gun was empty? But where were the loads? For the life of him, he could not recall. There should be one empty under the hammer, but was it there, or just above the loading gate?

"How'd you get away? I ran right into that alley," he asked.

Houdon chuckled. "The office is raised up, maybe two feet off the ground. I went under it, up into the trapdoor. I made that so's I could sweep right out and not have to use no dustpan. Pays to be a lazy bachelor, sometimes."

He nodded at the gold. "Old Dan never guessed when we made that strike at the RM that I'd wind up with it all. He sure didn't."

This was the last of the outlaws—what had his name been? Hopper? He had murdered Chilton in cold blood. Had killed two in gunfights, but he was a sure-thing killer, the kind who never gave anyone a break.

Chick Bowdrie smiled suddenly. He was a Ranger and this was his job. He felt the skin drawing tight over his wide cheekbones. He lifted his left hand and moved his hat back on his head. "You know, Hop, I think—" He threw himself in a wild lunge, low down and straight at the horse!

The startled bronc gave a leap, snorting. The shotgun blasted and dust kicked into Chick's face. Then he came up to his knees as Houdon fought the frightened horse and swung up his gun.

Houdon saw it coming, and left the saddle in a leap of agility surprising in a man of his years. He hit the ground in a crouch and triggered the shotgun, but the muzzle was high and the charge of shot blasted by, high and to the right.

Bowdrie's gun clicked on an empty chamber, then fired, then he threw himself into a roll, came up, and fired again.

Houdon took the shot right along the top of the shotgun. Smashing into his chest. He tried to come up, gasping, and Bowdrie shot into him again.

He fell, staring for one awful instant into Bowdrie's face, and then lay stretched out, choking horribly, his fingers working.

Chick Bowdrie turned away and walked to Rose. She stood in the Rock Hut door, her face in her hands.

He looked over his shoulder at Rad Yates. "Can you ride?"

Yates got slowly to his feet. His nose was smashed, and the cut on his head still bled.

"I can ride."

"Then get on your horse and get out of here. Don't stop until you're somewhere else."

Rad Yates wiped blood from his face. He started for his horse, then halted. "That Chilton kid . . . you'll find him in the smokehouse with a headache. He wasn't man enough for the job."

"Beat it," Bowdrie said.

Rad Yates walked his horse away, and after a minute Chick told Rose, "Get your horse. I'll load up the gold, then follow."

"There's blood on it," she said, dazed.

"Yeah"—Bowdrie's voice was dry—"but it'll buy cows."

KEEP TRAVELIN', RIDER

WHEN TACK GENTRY sighted the weather-beaten buildings of the G Bar, he touched spurs to the buckskin and the horse broke into a fast canter that carried the cowhand down the trail and around into the ranch yard. He swung down.

"Hey!" he yelled happily, grinning. "Is that all the welcome I get?"

The door pushed open and a man stepped out on the worn porch. The man had a stubble of beard and a drooping mustache. His blue eyes were small and narrow.

"Who are yuh?" he demanded. "And what do yuh want?"

"I'm Tack Gentry!" Tack said. "Where's Uncle John?"

"I don't know yuh," the man said, "and I never heard of no Uncle John. I reckon yuh got onto the wrong spread, youngster."

"Wrong spread?" Tack laughed. "Quit your funnin'! I helped build that house there, and built the corrals by my lonesome, while Uncle John was sick. Where is everybody?"

The man looked at him carefully and then lifted his eyes to a point beyond Tack. A voice spoke from behind the cowhand. "Reckon yuh been gone a while, ain't yuh?"

Gentry turned. The man behind him was short, stocky, and blond. He had a wide, flat face, a small broken nose, and cruel eyes.

"Gone? I reckon yes! I've been gone most of a year! Went north with a trail herd to Ellsworth, then took me a job as segundo on a herd movin' to Wyoming."

TACK STARED AROUND, his eyes alert and curious. There was something wrong here, something very wrong. The neatness that had been typical of Uncle John Gentry was gone. The place looked run-down, the porch was untidy, the door hung loose on its hinges, even the horses in the corral were different.

"Where's Uncle John?" Tack demanded again. "Quit stallin'!"

The blond man smiled, his lips parting over broken teeth and a hard, cynical light coming into his eyes. "If yuh mean John Gentry, who used to live on this place, he's gone. He drawed on the wrong man and got himself killed."

"What?" Tack's stomach felt like he had been kicked. He stood there, staring. "He *drew* on somebody? *Uncle John?*"

Tack shook his head. "That's impossible! John Gentry was a Quaker. He never lifted a hand in violence against anybody or anything in his life! He never even wore a gun, never owned one."

"I only know what they tell me," the blond man said, "but we got work to do, and I reckon yuh better slope out of here. And," he added grimly, "if yuh're smart yuh'll keep right on goin', clean out of the country!"

"What do yuh mean?" Tack's thoughts were in a turmoil, trying to accustom himself to this change, wondering what could have happened, what was behind it.

"I mean yuh'll find things considerably changed around here. If yuh decide not to leave," he added, "yuh might ride into Sunbonnet and look up Van Hardin or Dick Olney and tell him I said to give yuh all yuh had comin'. Tell 'em Soderman sent yuh."

"Who's Van Hardin?" Tack asked. The name was unfamiliar.

"Yuh been away all right!" Soderman acknowledged. "Or yuh'd know who Van Hardin is. He runs this country. He's the ramrod, Hardin is. Olney's sheriff."

Tack Gentry rode away from his home ranch with his thoughts in confusion. Uncle John! Killed in a gunfight! Why, that was out of reason! The old man wouldn't fight. He never had and never would. And this Dick Olney was sheriff!

What had become of Pete Liscomb? No election was due for another year, and Pete had been a good sheriff.

There was one way to solve the problem and get the whole story, and that was to circle around and ride by the London ranch. Bill could give him the whole story, and besides, he wanted to see Betty. It had been a long time.

The six miles to the headquarters of the London ranch went by swiftly, yet as Tack rode, he scanned the grassy levels along the Maravillas. There were cattle enough, more than he had ever seen on the old G Bar, and all of them wearing the G Bar brand.

He reined in sharply. What the . . . ? Why, if Uncle John was dead, the ranch belonged to him! But if that was so, who was Soderman? And what were they doing on his ranch?

Three men were loafing on the wide veranda of the London ranch house when Tack rode up. All their faces were unfamiliar. He glanced warily from one to the other.

"Where's Bill London?" he asked.

"London?" The man in the wide brown hat shrugged. "Reckon he's to home, over in Sunbonnet Pass. He ain't never over here."

"This is his ranch, isn't it?" Tack demanded.

All three men seemed to tense. "His ranch?" The man in the brown hat shook his head. "Reckon yuh're a stranger around here. This ranch belongs to Van Hardin. London ain't got a ranch. Nothin' but a few acres back against the creek over to Sunbonnet Pass. He and that girl of his live there. I reckon though," he grinned suddenly, "she won't be there much longer. Hear tell she's goin' to work in the Longhorn Dance hall."

"Betty London? In the Longhorn?" Tack exclaimed. "Don't make me laugh, partner! Betty's too nice a girl for that! She wouldn't . . ."

"They got it advertised," the brown-hatted man said calmly.

An hour later a very thoughtful Tack Gentry rode up the dusty street of Sunbonnet. In that hour of riding he had been doing a lot of thinking, and he was remembering what Soderman had said. He was to tell Hardin or Olney that Soderman had sent him to get all that was coming to him. Suddenly, that remark took on a new significance.

Tack swung down in front of the Longhorn. Emblazoned on the front of the saloon was a huge poster announcing that Betty London was the coming attraction, that she would sing and entertain at the Longhorn. Compressing his lips, Tack walked into the saloon.

Nothing was familiar except the bar and the tables. The man behind the bar was squat and fat, and his eyes peered at Tack from folds of flesh. "What's it for yuh?" he demanded.

"Rye," Tack said. He let his eyes swing slowly around the room. Not a familiar face greeted him. Shorty Davis was gone. Nick Farmer was not around. These men were strangers, a tight-mouthed, hard-eyed crew.

Gentry glanced at the bartender. "Any ridin' jobs around here? Driftin' through, and thought I might like to tie in with one of the outfits around here."

"Keep driftin'," the bartender said, not glancing at him. "Everybody's got a full crew."

One door swung open and a tall, clean-cut man walked into the room, glancing around. He wore a neat gray suit and a dark hat. Tack saw the bartender's eyes harden and glanced thoughtfully at the newcomer. The man's face was very thin, and when he removed his hat his ash blond hair was neatly combed.

He glanced around, and his eyes lighted on Tack. "Stranger?" he asked pleasantly. "Then may I buy you a drink? I don't like to drink alone, but haven't sunk so low as to drink with these coyotes."

Tack stiffened, expecting a reaction from some of the seated men, but there was none. Puzzled, he glanced at the blond man, and seeing the cynical good humor in the man's eyes, nodded.

"Sure, I'll drink with you."

"My name," the tall man added, "is Anson Childe, by profession, a lawyer, by dint of circumstances, a gambler, and by choice, a student.

"You perhaps wonder," he added, "why these men do not

resent my reference to them as coyotes. There are three reasons, I expect. The first is that some subconscious sense of truth makes them appreciate the justice of the term. Second, they know I am gifted with considerable dexterity in expounding the gospel of Judge Colt. Third, they know that I am dying of tuberculosis and as a result have no fear of bullets.

"It is not exactly fear that keeps them from drawing on me. Let us say it is a matter of mathematics, and a problem none of them has succeeded in solving with any degree of comfort in the result. It is: how many of them would die before I did?

"You can appreciate, my friend, the quandary in which this places them, and also the disagreeable realization that bullets are no respecters of persons, nor am I. The several out there who might draw know that I know who they are. The result is that they know they would be first to die."

Childe looked at Tack thoughtfully. "I heard you ask about a riding job as I came in. You look like an honest man, and there is no place here for such."

Gentry hunted for the right words. Then he said, "This country looks like it was settled by honest men."

Anson Childe studied his glass. "Yes," he said, "but at the right moment they lacked a leader. One was too opposed to violence, another was too law abiding, and the rest lacked resolution."

If there was a friend in the community, this man was it. Tack finished his drink and strode to the door. The bartender met his eyes as he glanced back.

"Keep on driftin'," the bartender said.

Tack Gentry smiled. "I like it here," he said, "and I'm stayin'!"

He swung into the saddle and turned his buckskin toward Sunbonnet Pass. He still had no idea exactly what had happened during the year of his absence, yet Childe's remark coupled with what the others had said told him a little. Apparently, some strong, resolute men had moved in and taken over, and there had been no concerted fight against them, no organization and no leadership.

Childe had said that one was opposed to violence. That would have been his Uncle John. The one who was too law abiding would be Bill London. London had always been strong for law and order and settling things in a legal way. The others had been honest men, but small ranchers and individually unable to oppose whatever was done to them. Yet whatever had happened, the incoming elements had apparently moved with speed and finesse.

Had it been one ranch, it would have been different. But the ranches and the town seemed completely subjugated.

The buckskin took the trail at an easy canter, skirting the long red cliff of Horse Thief Mesa and wading the creek at Gunsight. Sunbonnet Pass opened before him like a gate in the mountains. To the left, in a grove of trees, was a small adobe house and a corral.

Two horses were standing at the corral as he rode up. His eyes narrowed as he saw them. Button and Blackie! Two of his uncle's favorites and two horses he had raised from colts. He swung down and started toward them, when he saw the three people on the steps.

He turned to face them, and his heart jumped. Betty London had not changed.

Her eyes widened, and her face went dead white. "Tack!" she gasped. "Tack Gentry!"

Even as she spoke, Tack saw the sudden shock with which the two men turned to stare. "That's right, Betty," he said quietly. "I just got home."

"But—but—we heard you were dead!"

"I'm not." His eyes shifted to the two men—a thick-shouldered, deep-chested man with a square, swarthy face and a lean rawboned man wearing a star. The one with the star would be Dick Olney. The other must be Van Hardin.

Tack's eyes swung to Olney. "I heard my Uncle John Gentry was killed. Did yuh investigate his death?"

Olney's eyes were careful. "Yeah," he said. "He was killed in a fair fight. Gun in his hand."

"My uncle," Tack replied, "was a Quaker. He never lifted a hand in violence in his life!"

"He was a might slow, I reckon," Olney said coolly, "but he had the gun in his hand when I found him."

"Who shot him?"

"Hombre name of Soderman. But like I say, it was a fair fight."

"Like blazes!" Tack flashed. "Yuh'll never make me believe Uncle John wore a gun! That gun was planted on him!"

"Yuh're jumpin' to conclusions," Van Hardin said smoothly. "I saw the gun myself. There were a dozen witnesses."

"Who saw the fight?" Gentry demanded.

"They saw the gun in his hand. In his right hand," Hardin said.

Tack laughed suddenly, harshly. "That does it! Uncle John's right hand has been useless ever since Shiloh, when it was shot to pieces tryin' to get to a wounded soldier. He couldn't hold a feather in those fingers, let alone a gun!"

Hardin's face tightened, and Dick Olney's eyes shifted to Hardin's face.

"You'd be better off," Hardin said quietly, "to let sleepin' dogs lie. We ain't goin' to have yuh comin' in here stirrin' up a peaceful community."

"My Uncle John was murdered," Gentry said quietly. "I mean to see his murderer punished. That ranch belongs to me. I intend to get it back!"

Van Hardin smiled. "Evidently, yuh aren't aware of what happened here," he said quietly. "Your Uncle John was in a noncombatant outfit durin' the war, was he not? Well, while he was gone, the ranch he had claimed was abandoned. Soderman and I started to run cattle on that range and the land that was claimed by Bill London. No claim to the range was asserted by anyone. We made improvements, and then durin' our temporary absence with a trail herd, John Gentry and Bill London returned and moved in. Naturally, when we returned the case was taken to court. The court ruled the ranches belonged to Soderman and myself."

"And the cattle?" Tack asked. "What of the cattle my uncle owned?"

Hardin shrugged. "The brand had been taken over by the new owners and registered in their name. As I understand it, yuh left with a trail herd immediately after yuh came back to Texas. My claim was originally asserted during yore uncle's absence. I could," he smiled, "lay claim to the money yuh got from that trail herd. Where is it?"

"Suppose yuh find out?" Tack replied. "I'm goin' to tell yuh one thing: I'm goin' to find who murdered my uncle, if it was Soderman or not. I'm also goin' to fight yuh in court. Now, if yuh'll excuse me," he turned his eyes to Betty who had stood wide-eyed and silent, "I'd like to talk to Bill London."

"He can't see yuh," Hardin said. "He's asleep."

Gentry's eyes hardened. "You runnin' this place, too?"

"Betty London is going to work for me," Hardin replied. "We may be married later, so in a sense, I'm speaking for her."

"Is that right?" Tack demanded, his eyes meeting Betty's. Her face was miserable. "I'm afraid it is, Tack."

"You've forgotten your promise, then?" he demanded.

"Things—things changed, Tack," she faltered. "I—I can't talk about it."

"I reckon, Gentry," Olney interrupted, "it's time yuh rode on. There's nothin' in this neck of the woods for yuh. You've played out your hand here. Ride on, and you'll save yourself a lot of trouble. They're hirin' hands over on the Pecos."

"I'm stayin'," Gentry said flatly.

"Remember," Olney warned, "I'm the sheriff. At the first sign of trouble, I'll come lookin' for yuh."

GENTRY SWUNG INTO the saddle. His eyes shifted to Betty's face, and for an instant, she seemed about to speak. Then he turned and rode away. He did not look back. It was not until after he was gone that he remembered Button and Blackie.

To think they were in the possession of Hardin and Olney! The twin blacks he had reared and worked with, training them to do tricks, teaching them all the lore of the cow-country horses and much more.

The picture was clear now. In the year in which he had

been gone these men had come in, asserted their claims, taken them to carpetbag courts, and made them stick. Backing their legal claims with guns, they had taken over the country with speed and finesse. At every turn, he was blocked. Betty had turned against him. Bill London was either a prisoner in his own house or something else was wrong. Olney was sheriff, and probably they had their own judge.

He could quit. He could pull out and go on to the Pecos. It would be the easiest way. It was even what Uncle John might have wished him to do, for John Gentry was a peace-loving man. Tack Gentry was of another breed. His father had been killed fighting Comanches, and Tack had gone to war when a mere boy. Uncle John had found a place for himself in a noncombatant outfit, but Tack had fought long and well.

His ride north with the trail herd had been rough and bloody. Twice they had fought off Indians, and once they had mixed it with rustlers. In Ellsworth, a gunman named Paris had made trouble that ended with Paris dead on the floor.

Tack had left town in a hurry, ridden to the new camp at Dodge, and then joined a trail herd headed for Wyoming. Indian fighting had been the order of the day, and once, rounding up a bunch of steers lost from the herd in a stampede, Tack had run into three rustlers after the same steers.

Tack downed two of them in the subsequent battle and then shot it out with the other in a daylong rifle battle that covered a cedar- and boulder-strewn hillside. Finally, just before sundown, they met in a hand-to-hand battle with bowie knives.

Tack remained long enough to see his old friend Major Powell, with whom he had participated in the Wagon Box Fight, and then had wandered back to Kansas. On the Platte he joined a bunch of buffalo hunters, stayed with them a couple of months, and then trailed back to Dodge.

Sunbonnet's Longhorn Saloon was ablaze with lights when he drifted into town that night. He stopped at the livery stable and put up his horse. He had taken a roundabout route, scouting the country, so he decided that Hardin and Olney were probably already in town. By now they would know of his call at the ranch and his meeting with Anson Childe.

He was laboring under no delusions about his future. Van Hardin would not hesitate to see him put out of the way if he attempted to regain his property. Hardin had brains, and Olney was no fool. There were things Gentry must know before anything could be done, and the one man in town who could and would tell him was Childe.

Leaving the livery stable, he started up the street. Turning, he glanced back to see the liveryman standing in the stable door. He dropped his hand quickly, but Gentry believed he had signaled someone across the street. Yet there was no one in sight, and the row of buildings seemed blank and empty.

Only three buildings were lighted. The Longhorn, a smaller, cheaper saloon, and the old general store. There was a light upstairs over the small saloon and several lights in the annex to the Longhorn, which passed as a hotel, the only one in Sunbonnet.

Tack walked along the street, his bootheels sounding loud in the still night air. Ahead of him was a space between the buildings, and when he drew abreast of it he did a quick side-step off the street, flattening against the building.

He heard footsteps, hesitation, and then lightly running steps, and suddenly a man dove around the corner and grated to a stop on the gravel, staring down the alleyway between the buildings. He did not see Tack, who was flattened in the dense shadow against the building and behind a rain barrel.

The man started forward suddenly, and Tack reached out and grabbed his ankle. Caught in midstride, the fellow plunged over on his head and then lay still. For an instant, Gentry hesitated; then struck and shielded a match with his left hand. It was the brown-hatted man he had talked to on the porch of London's ranch. His head had hit a stone, and he was out cold.

Swiftly, Tack shucked the fellow's gun and emptied the shells from it and then pushed it back in his holster. A folded paper had fallen from the unconscious man's pocket, and Tack picked it up. Then, moving fast, he went down the alley until he was in back of the small saloon. By the light from a back window, he read the note.

"This," he muttered, "may help!"

Come to town quick. Trouble's brewing. We can't have anything happen now. V. H.

Van Hardin. They didn't want trouble now. Why, *now*? Folding the note, he slipped it into his pocket and flattened against the side of the saloon, studying the interior. Only two men sat in the dim interior, two men who played cards at a small table. The bartender leaned on the bar and read a newspaper. When the bartender turned his head, Tack recognized him.

Red Furness had worked for his father. He had soldiered with him. He might still be friendly. Tack lifted his knuckles and tapped lightly on the window.

At the second tap, Red looked up. Tack lighted a match and moved it past the window. Neither of the cardplayers seemed to have noticed. Red straightened, folded his paper, and then picking up a cup, walked back toward the window. When he got there, he dipped the cup into the water bucket with one hand and with the other, lifted the window a few inches.

"This is Tack Gentry. Where does Childe hang out?"

Red's whisper was low. "Got him an office and sleepin' room upstairs. There's a back stairway. Yuh watch yoreself."

Tack stepped away from his window and made his way to the stairway he had already glimpsed. It might be a trap, but he believed Red was loyal. Also, he was not sure the word was out to kill him. They probably merely wanted him out of the way and hoped he could be warned to move on. The position of the Hardin group seemed secure enough.

Reaching the top of the stairs, he walked along the narrow catwalk to the door. He tapped softly. After an instant, there was a voice. "What do you want?"

"This is Tack Gentry. Yuh talked to me in the saloon!" The door opened to darkness, and he stepped in. When it closed, he felt a pistol barrel against his spine.

"Hold still!" Childe warned.

Behind him a match struck, and then a candle was lighted. The light still glowed in the other room, seen only by the crack under the door. Childe grinned at him. "Got to be careful," he said. "They have tried twice to dry-gulch me!

"I put flowers on their graves every Monday!" He smiled. "And keep an extra one dug. Ever since I had that new grave dug, I've been left alone. Somehow it seems to have a very sobering influence on the local roughs."

He sat down. "I tire quicker than I once did. So you're Gentry! Betty London told me about you. She thought you were dead. There was a rumor that you'd been killed by the Indians in Wyoming."

"No, I came out all right. What I want to know, rememberin' yuh said yuh were a lawyer, is what kind of a claim they have on my ranch?"

"A good one, unfortunately. While you and your uncle were gone, and most of the other men in the locality, several of these men came in and began to brand cattle. After branding a good many, they left. They returned and began working around, about the time you left, and then they ordered your uncle off.

"He wouldn't go, and they took the case to court. There were no lawyers here then, and your uncle tried to handle it himself. The judge was their man, and suddenly a half dozen witnesses appeared and were sworn in. They testified that the land had been taken and held by Soderman, Olney, and Hardin.

"They claimed their brands on the cattle asserted their claim to the land, to the home ranches of both London and Gentry. The free range was something else, but with the two big ranches in their hands and the bulk of the free range lying beyond their holdings, they were in a position to freeze out the smaller ranchers. They established a squatter's right to each of the big ranches."

"Can they do that?" Tack demanded. "It doesn't seem fair!"

"The usual thing is to allow no claim unless they have occupied the land for twenty years without hindrance, but with a carpetbag court, they do about as they please. Judge Weaver is completely in Van Hardin's hands, and your Uncle John was on the losing side in this war."

"How did Uncle John get killed?" Tack asked.

Childe shrugged. "They said he called Soderman a liar and Soderman went for his gun. Your uncle had a gun on him when they found him. It was probably a cold-blooded killing because Gentry planned on a trip to Austin and was going to appeal the case."

"Have yuh seen Bill London lately?"

"Only once since the accident."

"Accident?"

"Yes, London was headed for home, dozing along in the buckboard as he always did, when his team ran away with him. The buckboard was overturned and London's back was injured. He can't ride anymore and can't sit up very long at a time."

"Was it really an accident?" Tack wanted to know.

Childe shrugged. "I doubt it. We couldn't prove a thing. One of the horses had a bad cut on the hip. It looked as if someone with a steel-tipped bullwhip had hit the animal from beside the road."

"Thorough," Tack said. "They don't miss a bet."

Childe nodded. Leaning back in his chair he put his feet on the desk. He studied Tack Gentry thoughtfully. "You know, you'll be next. They won't stand for you messing around. I think you already have them worried."

Tack explained about the man following him, and then handed the note to Childe. The lawyer's eyes narrowed. "Hmm, sounds like they had some reason to soft-pedal the whole thing for a while. Maybe it's an idea for us. Maybe somebody is coming down here to look around, or maybe somebody has grown suspicious."

Tack looked at Childe thoughtfully. "What's your position in all this?"

The tall man shrugged, and then laughed lightly. "I've no stake in it, Gentry. I didn't know London or your Uncle John, either. But I heard rumors, and I didn't like the attitude of the local bosses, Hardin and Olney. I'm just a burr under the saddle with which they ride this community, no more. It amuses me to needle them, and they are afraid of me."

"Got any clients?"

"Clients?" Anson Childe chuckled. "Not a one! Not likely to have any, either! In a country so throttled by one man as this is, there isn't any litigation. Nobody can win against him, and they are too busy hating Hardin to want to have trouble with each other."

"Well, then," Tack said, "yuh've got a client now. Go down to Austin. Demand an investigation. Lay the facts on the table for them. Maybe yuh can't do any good, but at least yuh can stir up a lot of trouble. The main thing will be to get people talking. They evidently want quiet, so we'll give them noise.

"Find out all you can. Get some detectives started on Hardin's trail. Find out who they are, who they were, and where they came from."

Childe sat up. "I'd like it," he said ruefully, "but I don't have that kind of money." He gestured at the room. "I'm behind on my rent here. Red owns the building, so he lets me stay."

Tack grinned and unbuttoned his shirt, drawing out a money belt. "I sold some cattle up north." He counted out one thousand dollars. "Take that. Spend all or any part of it, but create a smell down there. Tell everybody about the situation here."

Childe got up, his face flushed with enthusiasm. "Man! Nothing could please me more! I'll make it hot for them! I'll—" He went into a fit of coughing, and Tack watched him gravely.

Finally Childe straightened. "You're putting your trust in a sick man, Gentry!"

"I'm putting my trust in a fighter," Tack said dryly. "Yuh'll do!" He hesitated briefly. "Also, check the title on this land."

They shook hands silently, and Tack went to the door. Softly, he opened it and stepped out into the cool night. Well, for better or worse the battle was opened. Now for the next step. He came down off the wooden stair and then walked to the street. There was no one in sight. Tack Gentry crossed the street and pushed through the swinging doors of the Longhorn.

The saloon and dance hall was crowded. A few familiar faces, but they were sullen faces, lined and hard. The faces of bitter men, defeated, but not whipped. The others were new faces, the hard, tough faces of gunhands, the weather-beaten punchers who had come in to take the new jobs. He pushed his way to the bar.

There were three bartenders now, and it wasn't until he ordered that the squat, fat man glanced down the bar and saw him. His jaw hardened and he spoke to the bartender who was getting a bottle to pour Gentry's rye.

The bartender, a lean, sallow-faced man, strolled back to him. "We're not servin' you," he said. "I got my orders!"

Tack reached across the bar, his hand shooting out so fast the bartender had no chance to withdraw. Catching the man by his stiff collar, two fingers inside the collar and their knuckles jammed hard into the man's Adam's apple, he jerked him to the bar.

"Pour!" he said.

The man tried to speak, but Tack gripped harder and shoved back on the knuckles. Weakly, desperately, his face turning blue, the man poured. He slopped out twice what he got in the glass, but he poured. Then Tack shoved hard and the man brought up violently against the backbar.

Tack lifted his glass with his left hand, his eyes sweeping the crowd, all of whom had drawn back slightly. "To honest ranchers!" he said loudly and clearly and downed his drink.

A big, hard-faced man shoved through the crowd. "Maybe yuh're meanin' some of us ain't honest?" he suggested.

"That's right!" Tack Gentry let his voice ring out in the room, and he heard the rattle of chips cease, and the shuffling of feet died away. The crowd was listening. "That's exactly right! There were honest men here, but they were murdered or crippled. My Uncle John Gentry was murdered. They tried to make it look like a fair and square killin'—they stuck a gun in his hand!"

"That's right!" A man broke in. "He had a gun! I seen it!"

Tack's eyes shifted. "What hand was it in?"

"His right hand!" the man stated positively, belligerently. "I seen it!"

"Thank you, pardner!" Tack said politely. "The gun was in John Gentry's right hand—and John Gentry's right hand had been paralyzed ever since Shiloh!"

"Huh?" The man who had seen the gun stepped back, his face whitening a little.

Somebody back in the crowd shouted out, "That's right! You're durn tootin' that's right! Never could use a rope, 'count of it!"

Tack looked around at the crowd, and his eyes halted on the big man. He was going to break the power of Hardin, Olney, and Soderman, and he was going to start right here.

"There's goin' to be an investigation," he said loudly, "and it'll begin down in Austin. Any of you fellers bought property from Hardin or Olney better get your money back."

"Yuh're talkin' a lot!" The big man thrust toward him, his wide, heavy shoulders looking broad enough for two men. "Yuh said some of us were thieves!"

"Thieves and murderers," Tack added. "If yuh're one of the worms that crawl in Hardin's tracks, that goes for you!"

The big man lunged. "Get him, Starr!" somebody shouted loudly.

———

TACK GENTRY SUDDENLY felt a fierce surge of pure animal joy. He stepped back and then stepped in suddenly, and his right swung low and hard. It caught Starr as he was coming in, caught him in the pit of the stomach. He grunted and stopped dead in his tracks, but Tack set himself and swung wickedly with both hands. His left smashed into Starr's mouth, and his right split a cut over his cheekbone. Starr staggered and fell back into the crowd. He came out of the crowd, shook his head, and charged like a bull.

Tack weaved inside of the swinging fists and impaled the bigger man on a straight, hard left hand. Then he crossed a wicked right to the cut cheek, and gore cascaded down the man's face. Tack stepped in, smashing both hands to the man's body, and then as Starr stabbed a thumb at his eye, Tack jerked his head aside and butted Starr in the face.

His nose broken, his cheek laid open to the bone, Starr staggered back, and Tack Gentry walked in, swinging with both hands. This was the beginning. This man worked for Hardin and he was going to be an example. When he left this room Starr's face was going to be a sample of the crashing of Van Hardin's power. With left and right he cut and slashed at the big man's face, and Starr, overwhelmed by the attack, helpless after that first wicked body blow, crumpled under those smashing fists. He hit the floor suddenly and lay there, moaning softly.

A man shoved through the crowd, and then stopped. It was Van Hardin. He looked down at the man on the floor; then his eyes, dark with hate, lifted to meet Tack Gentry's eyes.

"Lookin' for trouble, are yuh?" he said.

"Only catchin' up with some that started while I was gone, Van!" Tack said. He felt good. He was on the balls of his feet and ready. He had liked the jarring of blows, liked the feeling of combat. He was ready. "Yuh should have made sure I was dead, Hardin, before yuh tried to steal property from a kindly old man!"

"Nothing was stolen," Van Hardin said evenly, calmly. "We took only what was ours, and in a strictly legal manner."

"There will be an investigation," Gentry replied bluntly, "from Austin. Then we'll thrash the whole thing out."

Hardin's eyes sharpened and he was suddenly wary. "An investigation? What makes you think so?"

Tack was aware that Hardin was worried. "Because I'm startin' it. I'm askin' for it, and I'll get it. There was a lot you didn't know about that land yuh stole, Hardin. Yuh were like most crooks. Yuh could only see yore side of the question and it looked very simple and easy, but there's always the thing yuh overlook, and *you* overlooked somethin'!"

The doors swung wide and Olney pushed into the room. He stopped, glancing from Hardin to Gentry. "What goes on here?" he demanded.

"Gentry is accusin' us of bein' thieves," Hardin said carelessly.

Olney turned and faced Tack. "He's in no position to accuse anybody of anything!" he said. "I'm arrestin' him for murder!"

There was a stir in the room, and Tack Gentry felt the sudden sickness of fear. "Murder? Are yuh crazy?" he demanded.

"I'm not, but you may be," the sheriff said. "I've just come from the office of Anson Childe. He's been murdered. Yuh were his last visitor. Yuh were observed sneaking into his place by the back stairs. Yuh were observed sneaking out of it. I'm arresting yuh for murder."

The room was suddenly still, and Tack Gentry felt the rise of hostility toward him. Many men had admired the courage of Anson Childe; many men had been helped by him. Frightened themselves, they had enjoyed his flouting of Hardin and Olney. Now he was dead, murdered.

"Childe was my friend!" Tack protested. "He was goin' to Austin for me!"

Hardin laughed sarcastically. "Yuh mean he knew yuh had no case and refused to go, and in a fit of rage, yuh killed him. Yuh shot him."

"Yuh'll have to come with me," Olney said grimly. "Yuh'll get a fair trial."

Silently, Tack looked at him. Swiftly, thoughts raced through his mind. There was no chance for escape. The crowd was too thick, and he had no idea if there was a horse out front, although there no doubt was, and his own horse was in the livery stable. Olney relieved him of his gun belt and they started toward the door. Starr, leaning against the doorpost, his face raw as chewed beef, glared at him evilly.

"I'll be seein' yuh!" he said softly. "Soon!"

———

SODERMAN AND HARDIN had fallen in around him, and behind them were two of Hardin's roughs.

The jail was small, just four cells and an outer office. The door of one of the cells was opened and he was shoved inside. Hardin grinned at him. "This should settle the matter for Austin," he said. "Childe had friends down there!"

Anson Childe murdered! Tack Gentry, numbed by the blow, stared at the stone wall. He had counted on Childe, counted on his stirring up an investigation. Once an investigation was started, he possessed two aces in the hole he could use to defeat Hardin in court, but it demanded a court uncontrolled by Hardin.

With Childe's death he had no friends on the outside. Betty had barely spoken to him when they met, and if she was going to work for Hardin in his dance hall, she must have changed much. Bill London was a cripple and unable to get around. Red Furness, for all his friendship, wouldn't come out in the open. Tack had no illusions about the murder. By the time the case came to trial, they would have found ample evidence. They had his guns and they could fire two or three shots from them, whatever had been used on Childe. It would be a simple thing to frame him. Hardin would have no trouble in finding witnesses.

He was standing, staring out the small window, its lower sill just on the level of his eyes, when he heard a distant rumble of thunder and a jagged streak of lightning brightened the sky, followed by more thunder. The rains came slowly, softly, and then in steadily increasing volume. The jail was still and empty. Sounds of music and occasional shouts sounded from the Longhorn; then the roar of rain drowned them out. He threw himself down on the cot in the corner of the room, and lulled by the falling rain, was soon asleep.

A long time later, he awakened. The rain was still falling, but above it was another sound. Listening, he suddenly realized what it was. The dry wash behind the town was running, probably bank full. Lying there in the darkness, he became aware of still another sound, of the nearer rushing of water. Lifting his head, he listened. Then he got to his feet and crossed the small cell.

Water was running under the corner of the jail. There had been a good deal of rain lately, and he had noted that the barrel at the corner of the jail had been full. It was overflowing, and the water had evidently washed under the corner of the building.

He walked back and sat down on the bed, and as he listened to the water, an idea came to him suddenly. Tack got up and went to the corner of the cell. Striking a match, he studied the wall and floor. Both were damp. He stamped on the stone flags of the floor, but they were solid. He kicked at the wall. It was also solid.

How thick were those walls? Judging by what he remembered of the door, the walls were all of eight inches thick, but how about the floor? Kneeling on the floor, he struck another match, studying the mortar around the corner flagstone.

Then he felt in his pockets. There was nothing there he could use to dig that mortar. His pocket knife, his bowie knife, his keys—all were gone. Suddenly, he had an inspiration. Slipping off his wide leather belt, he began to dig at the mortar with the edge of his heavy brass belt buckle.

The mortar was damp, but he worked steadily. His hands slipped on the sweaty buckle and he skinned his fingers and knuckles on the rough stone floor, yet he persevered, scraping, scratching, digging out tiny fragments of mortar. From time to time he straightened up and stamped on the stone. It was solid as Gibraltar.

Five hours he scraped and scratched, digging until his belt buckle was no longer of use. He had scraped out almost two inches of mortar. Sweeping up the scattered grains of mortar, and digging some of the mud off his boots, he filled in the cracks as best he could. Then he walked to his bunk and sprawled out and was instantly asleep.

———

EARLY IN THE morning, he heard someone stirring around outside. Then Olney walked back to his cell and looked in at him. Starr followed in a few minutes, carrying a plate of food and a pot of coffee. His face was badly bruised and swollen, and his eyes were hot with hate. He put the food down, and then walked away. Olney loitered.

"Gentry," he said suddenly, "I hate to see a good hand in this spot."

Tack looked up. "I'll bet yuh do!" he said sarcastically.

"No use takin' that attitude," Olney protested, "after all, yuh made trouble for us. Why couldn't yuh leave well enough alone? Yuh were in the clear, yuh had a few dollars apparently, and yuh could do all right. Hardin took possession of those ranches legally. He can hold 'em, too."

"We'll see."

"No, I mean it. He can. Why don't yuh drop the whole thing?"

"Drop it?" Tack laughed. "How can I drop it? I'm in jail for murder now, and yuh know as well as I do I never killed Anson Childe. This trial will smoke the whole story out of its hole. I mean to see that it does."

Olney winced, and Tack could see he had touched a tender spot. That was what they were afraid of. They had him now, but they didn't want him. They wanted nothing so much as to be completely rid of him.

"Only make trouble for folks," Olney protested. "Yuh won't get nowhere. Yuh can bet that if yuh go to trial we'll have all the evidence we need."

"Sure. I know I'll be framed."

"What can yuh expect?" Olney shrugged. "Yuh're askin' for it. Why don't yuh play smart? If yuh'd leave the country we could sort of arrange maybe to turn yuh loose."

Tack looked up at him. "Yuh mean that?" Like blazes, he told himself. I can see yuh turnin' me loose! And when I walked out yuh'd have somebody there to smoke me down, shot escaping jail. Yeah, I know. "If I thought yuh'd let me go—" he hesitated, angling to get Olney's reaction.

The sheriff put his head close to the bars. "Yuh know me, Tack," he whispered. "I don't want to see you stick yore head in a noose! Sure, yuh spoke out of turn, and yuh tried to scare up trouble for us, but if yuh'd leave, I think I could arrange it."

"Just give me the chance," Tack assured him. "Once I get out of here I'll really start movin'!" And that's no lie, he added to himself.

Olney went away, and the morning dragged slowly. They would let him go. He was praying now they would wait until the next day. Yet even if they did permit him to escape, even if they did not have him shot as he was leaving, what could he do? Childe, his best means of assistance, was dead. At every turn he was stopped. They had the law, and they had the guns.

His talk the night before would have implanted doubts. His whipping of Starr would have pleased many, and some of them would realize that his arrest for the murder of Childe was a frame. Yet none of these people would do anything about it without leadership. None of them wanted his neck in a noose.

Olney dropped in later and leaned close to the bars. "I'll have something arranged by tomorrow," he said.

Tack lay back on the bunk and fell asleep. All day the rain had continued without interruption except for a few minutes at a time. The hills would be soggy now, the trails bad. He could hear the wash running strongly, running like a river not thirty yards behind the jail.

Darkness fell, and he ate again and then returned to his bunk. With a good lawyer and a fair judge he could beat them in court. He had an ace in the hole that would help, and another that might do the job.

He waited until the jail was silent and he could hear the usual sounds from the Longhorn. Then he got up and walked over to the corner. All day water had been running under the corner of the jail and must have excavated a fair-sized hole by now. Tack knelt down and took from his pocket the fork he had secreted after his meal.

Olney, preoccupied with plans to allow Tack Gentry to escape and sure that Tack was accepting the plan, had paid little attention to the returned plate.

On his knees, Tack dug out the loosely filled in dust and dirt and then began digging frantically at the hole. He worked steadily for an hour and then crossed to the bucket for a drink of water and to stretch, and then he returned to work.

Another hour passed. He got up and stamped on the stone. It seemed to sink under his feet. He bent his knees and jumped, coming down hard on his heels. The stone gave way so suddenly he almost went through. He caught himself, withdrew his feet from the hole, and bent over, striking a match. It was no more than six inches to the surface of the water, and even a glance told him it must be much deeper than he had believed.

He took another look, waited an instant, and then lowered his feet into the water. The current jerked at them, and then he lowered his body through the hole and let go. Instantly, he was jerked away and literally thrown downstream. He caught a quick glimpse of a light from a window, and then he was whirling over and over. He grabbed frantically, hoping to get his hands on something, but they clutched only empty air. Frantically, he fought toward where there must be a bank, realizing he was in a roaring stream all of six feet deep. He struck nothing and was thrown, almost hurtled, downstream with what seemed to be overwhelming speed. Something black loomed near him, and at the same instant the water caught at him, rushing with even greater power. He grabbed again at the blob of blackness, and his hand caught a root.

Yet it was nothing secure, merely a huge cottonwood log rushing downstream. Working his way along it, he managed to get a leg over and crawled atop it. Fortunately, the log did not roll over.

Lying there in the blackness, he realized what must have happened. Behind the row of buildings that fronted on the street, of which the jail was one, was a shallow, sandy ditch. At one end of it the bluff reared up. The dry wash skirted one side of the triangle formed by the bluff, and the ditch formed the other. Water flowing off the bluff and off the roofs of the buildings and from the street of the town and the rise beyond it had flooded into the ditch, washing it deeper. Yet now he knew he was in the current of the wash itself, now running bank full, a raging torrent.

A brief flash of lightning revealed the stream down which he was shooting like a chip in a millrace. Below, he knew, was Cathedral Gorge, a narrow boulder-strewn gash in the mountain down which this wash would thunder like an express train. Tack had seen such logs go down it, smashing into boulders, hurled against the rocky walls, and then shooting at last out into the open flat below the gorge. And he knew instantly that no living thing could hope to ride a charging log through the black, roaring depths of the gorge and come out anything but a mangled, lifeless pulp.

The log he was bestriding hit a wave, and water drenched him. Then the log whirled dizzily around a bend in the wash. Before him and around another bend he could hear the roar of the gorge. The log swung, and then the driving roots ripped into a heap of debris at the bend of the wash, and the log swung wickedly across the current. Scrambling like a madman, Tack fought his way toward the roots, and then even as the log ripped loose, he hurled himself at the heap of debris.

He landed in a heap of broken boughs, and felt something gouge him, and then scrambling, he made the rocks and clambered up into their shelter, lying there on a flat rock, gasping for breath.

————

A LONG TIME later he got up. Something was wrong with his right leg. It felt numb and sore. He crawled over the rocks and stumbled over the muddy earth toward the partial shelter of a clump of trees.

He needed shelter, and he needed a gun. Tack Gentry knew that now that he was free they would scour the country for him. They might believe him dead, but they would want to be certain. What he needed now was shelter, rest, and food. He needed to examine himself to see how badly he was injured, yet where could he turn?

Betty? She was too far away and he had no horse. Red Furness? Possibly, but how much the man would or could help he did not know. Yet thinking of Red made him think of Childe. There was a place for him. If he could only get to Childe's quarters over the saloon!

Luckily, he had landed on the same side of the wash as the town. He was stiff and sore, and his leg was paining him grievously. Yet there was no time to be lost. What the hour was he had no idea, but he knew his progress would be slow, and he must be careful. The rain was pounding down, but he was so wet now that it made no difference.

How long it took him he never knew. He could have been no more than a mile from town, perhaps less, and he walked, crawled, and pulled himself to the edge of town and then behind the buildings until he reached the dark back stairway to Anson Childe's room. Step by step he crawled up. Luckily, the door was unlocked.

Once inside, he stood there in the darkness, listening. There was no sound. This room was windowless but for one very small and tightly curtained window at the top of the wall. Tack felt for the candle, found it, and fumbled for a match. When he had the candle alight, he started pulling off his clothes.

Naked, he dried himself with a towel, avoiding the injured leg. Then he found a bottle and poured himself a drink. He tossed it off and then sat down on the edge of the bed and looked at his leg.

It almost made him sick to look at it. Hurled against a root or something in the dark, he had torn a great, mangled wound in the calf of his leg. No artery appeared to have been injured, but in places his shinbone was visible through the ripped flesh. The wound in the calf was deeper. Cleansing it as best he could, he found a white shirt belonging to Childe and bandaged his leg.

Exhausted, he fell asleep—when, he never recalled. Only hours later he awakened suddenly to find sunlight streaming through the door into the front room. His leg was stiff and sore, and when he moved, it throbbed with pain. Using a cane he found hanging in the room, he pulled himself up and staggered to the door.

The curtains in the front room were up and sunlight streamed in. The rain seemed to be gone. From where he stood he could see into the street, and almost the first person he saw was Van Hardin. He was standing in front of the Longhorn talking to Soderman and the mustached man Tack had first seen at his own ranch.

The sight reminded him, and Tack hunted around for a gun. He found a pair of beautifully matched Colts, silver plated and ivory handled. He strapped them on with their ornate belt and holsters. Then, standing in a corner, he found a riot gun and a Henry rifle. He checked the loads in all the guns, found several boxes of ammunition for each of them, and emptied a box of .45s into the pockets of a pair of Childe's pants he pulled on. Then he put a double handful of shotgun shells into the pockets of a leather jacket he found.

He sat down then, for he was weak and trembling.

His time was short. Sooner or later someone would come to this room. Either someone would think of it, or someone would come to claim the room for himself. Red Furness had no idea he was there, so would probably not hesitate to let anyone come up.

He locked the door, and then dug around and found a stale loaf of bread and some cheese. Then he lay down to rest. His leg was throbbing with pain, and he knew it needed care, and badly.

When he awakened, he studied the street from a vantage point well inside the room and to one side of the window. Several knots of men were standing around talking, more men than should have been in town at that hour. He recognized one or two of them as being old-timers around. Twice he saw Olney ride by, and the sheriff was carrying a riot gun.

Starr and the mustached man were loafing in front of the Longhorn, and two other men Tack recognized as coming from the old London ranch were there.

He ate some more bread and cheese. He was just finishing his sandwich when a buckboard turned into the street, and his heart jumped when he saw Betty London was driving. Beside her in the seat was her father, Bill, worn and old, his hair white now, but he was wearing a gun!

Something was stirring down below. It began to look as if the lid was about to blow off. Yet Tack had no idea of his own status. He was an escaped prisoner and as such could be shot on sight legally by Olney or Starr, who seemed to be a deputy. From the wary attitude of the Van Hardin men he knew that they were disturbed by their lack of knowledge of him.

Yet the day passed without incident, and finally he returned to the bunk and lay down after checking his guns once more. The time for the payoff was near, he knew. It could come at any moment. He was lying there thinking about that and looking up at the rough plank ceiling when he heard steps on the stairs.

He arose so suddenly that a twinge of pain shot through the weight that had become his leg. The steps were on the front stairs, not the back. A quick glance from the window told him it was Betty London.

What did she want here?

Her hand fell on the knob and it turned. He eased off the bed and turned the key in the lock. She hesitated just an instant and then stepped in. When their eyes met, hers went wide, and her face went white to the lips.

"You!" she gasped. "Oh, Tack! What have you been doing! Where have you been!"

She started toward him, but he backed up and sat down on the bed. "Wait. Do they know I'm up here?" he demanded harshly.

"No, Tack. I came up to see if some papers were here, some papers I gave to Anson Childe before he was—murdered."

"Yuh think I did that?" he demanded.

"No, of course not!" Her eyes held a question. "Tack, what's the matter? Don't you like me anymore?"

"Don't I like yuh?" His lips twisted with bitterness. "Lady, yuh've got a nerve to ask that! I come back and find my girl about to go dancin' in a cheap saloon dance hall, and—"

"I needed money, Tack," Betty said quietly. "Dad needed care. We didn't have any money. Everything we had was lost when we lost the ranch. Hardin offered me the job. He said he wouldn't let anybody molest me."

"What about him?"

"I could take care of him." She looked at him, puzzled. "Tack, what's the matter? Why are you sitting down? Are you hurt?"

"My leg." He shook his head as she started forward. "Don't bother about it. There's no time. What are they saying down there? What's all the crowd in town? Give it to me, quick!"

"Some of them think you were drowned in escaping from jail. I don't think Van Hardin thinks that, nor Olney. They seem very disturbed. The crowd is in town for Childe's funeral and because some of them think you were murdered once Olney got you in jail. Some of our old friends."

"Betty!" The call came from the street below. It was Van Hardin's voice.

"Don't answer!" Tack Gentry got up. His dark green eyes were hard. "I want him to come up."

Betty waited, her eyes wide, listening. Footsteps sounded on the stairway, and then the door shoved open. "Bet—" Van Hardin's voice died out and he stood there, one hand on the doorknob, staring at Tack.

"Howdy, Hardin," Tack said, "I was hopin' yuh'd come."

Van Hardin said nothing. His powerful shoulders filled the open door, his eyes were set, and the shock was fading from them now.

"Got a few things to tell yuh, Hardin," Tack continued gently. "Before yuh go out of this feet first I want yuh to know what a sucker yuh've been."

"A sucker I've been?" Hardin laughed. "What chance have yuh got? The street down there is full of my men. Yuh've friends there, too, but they lack leadership. They don't know what to do. My men have their orders. And then I won't have any trouble with yuh, Gentry. Yore old friends around here told me all about yuh. Soft, like that uncle of yores."

"Ever hear of Black Jack Paris, Hardin?"

"The gunman? Of course, but what's he got to do with yuh?"

"Nothin', now. He did once, up in Ellsworth, Kansas. They dug a bed for him next mornin', Hardin. He was too slow. Yuh said I was soft? Well, maybe I was once. Maybe in spots I still am, but yuh see, since the folks around here have seen me I've been over the cattle trails, been doin' some Injun fightin' and rustler killin'. It makes a sight of change in a man, Hardin.

"That ain't what I wanted yuh to know. I wanted yuh to know what a fool yuh were, tryin' to steal this ranch. Yuh see, the land in our home ranch wasn't like the rest of this land, Hardin."

"What do yuh mean?" Hardin demanded suspiciously.

"Why, yuh're the smart boy," Tack drawled easily. "Yuh should have checked before takin' so much for granted. Yuh see, the Gentry ranch was a land grant. My grandmother, she was a Basque, see? The land came to us through her family, and the will she left was that it would belong to us as long as any of us lived, that it couldn't be sold or traded, and in case we all died, it was to go to the state of Texas!"

Van Hardin stared. "What?" he gasped. "What kind of fool deal is this yuh're givin' me?"

"Fool deal is right," Tack said quietly. "Yuh see, the state of Texas knows no Gentry would sell or trade, knowin' we couldn't, so if somebody else showed up with the land, they were bound to ask a sight of questions. Sooner or later they'd have got around to askin' yuh how come."

Hardin seemed stunned. From the street below, there was a sound of horses' hooves.

Then a voice said from Tack's left, "Yuh better get out, Van. There's talkin' to be done in the street. I want Tack Gentry!"

Tack's head jerked around. It was Soderman. The short, squinty-eyed man was staring at him, gun in hand. He heard Hardin turn and bolt out of the room, saw resolution in Soderman's eyes. Hurling himself toward the wall, Gentry's hand flashed for his pistol.

A gun blasted in the room with a roar like a cannon, and Gentry felt the angry whip of the bullet, and then he fired twice, low down.

Soderman fell back against the doorjamb, both hands grabbing at his stomach, just below his belt buckle, "Yuh shot me!" he gasped, round eyed. "Yuh shot—me!"

"Like you did my uncle," Tack said coolly. "Only yuh had better than an even break, and he had no break at all!"

Gentry could feel blood from the opened wound trickling down his leg. He glanced at Betty. "I've got to get down there," he said. "He's a slick talker."

Van Hardin was standing down in the street. Beside him was Olney and nearby was Starr. Other men, a half dozen of them, loitered nearby.

Slowly, Tack Gentry began stumping down the stair. All

eyes looked up. Red Furness saw him and spoke out, "Tack, these three men are Rangers come down from Austin to make some inquiries."

Hardin pointed at Gentry. "He's wanted for murdering Anson Childe! Also for jailbreaking, and unless I'm much mistaken he has killed another man up there in Childe's office!"

The Rangers looked at him curiously, and then one of them glanced at Hardin. "Yuh all the hombre what lays claim to the Gentry place?"

Hardin swallowed up quickly, and then his eyes shifted. "No, that was Soderman. The man who was upstairs."

Hardin looked at Tack Gentry. With the Rangers here he knew his game was played out. He smiled suddenly. "Yuh've nothin' on me at all, gents," he said coolly. "Soderman killed John Gentry and laid claim to his ranch. I don't know nothin' about it."

"Yuh engineered it!" Bill London burst out. "Same as yuh did the stealin' of my ranch!"

"Yuh've no proof," Hardin sneered. "Not a particle. My name is on no papers, and yuh have no evidence."

Coolly, he strode across to his black horse and swung into the saddle. He was smiling gently, but there was sneering triumph behind the smile. "You've nothin' on me, not a thing!"

"Don't let him get away!" Bill London shouted. "He's the wust one of the whole kit and kaboodle of 'em!"

"But he's right!" the Ranger protested. "In all the papers we've found, there's not a single item to tie him up. If he's in it, he's been almighty smart."

"Then arrest him for horse stealin'!" Tack Gentry said. "That's my black horse he's on!"

Hardin's face went cold, and then he smiled. "Why, that's crazy! That's foolish," he said. "This is my horse. I reared him from a colt. Anybody could be mistaken, 'cause one black horse is like another. My brand's on him, and yuh can all see it's an old brand."

Tack Gentry stepped out in front of the black horse. "Button!" he said sharply. "Button!"

At the familiar voice, the black horse's head jerked up. "Button!" Tack called. "Hut! Hut!"

As the name and the sharp command rolled out, Button reacted like an explosion of dynamite. He jumped straight up in the air and came down hard. Then he sunfished wildly, and Van Hardin hit the dirt in a heap.

"Button!" Tack commanded. "Go get Blackie!"

Instantly, the horse wheeled and trotted to the hitching rail where Blackie stood ground hitched as Olney had left him. Button caught the reins in his teeth and led the other black horse back.

The Ranger grinned. "Reckon, mister," he said, "yuh done proved yore case. The man's a horse thief."

Hardin climbed to his feet, his face dark with fury. "Yuh think yuh'll get away with that?" His hand flashed for his gun.

Tack Gentry had been watching him, and now his own hand moved down and then up. The two guns barked as one. A chip flew from the stair post beside Tack, but Van Hardin turned slowly and went to his knees in the dust.

At almost the same instant, a sharp voice rang out. *"Olney! Starr!"*

Olney's face went white and he wheeled, hand flashing for his gun. *"Anson Childe!"* he gasped.

Childe stood on the platform in front of his room and fired once, twice, three times. Sheriff Olney went down, coughing and muttering. Starr backed through the swinging doors of the saloon and sat down hard in the sawdust.

Tack stared at him. "What the—"

The tall young lawyer came down the steps. "Fooled them, didn't I? They tried to get me once too often. I got their man with a shotgun in the face. Then I changed clothes with him and lit out for Austin. I came in with the Rangers and then left them on the edge of town. They told me they'd let us have it our way unless they were needed."

"Saves the state of Texas a sight of money," one of the Rangers drawled. "Anyway, we been checkin' on this here Hardin. On Olney, too. That's why they wanted to keep things quiet around here. They knowed we was checkin' on 'em."

The Rangers moved in and with the help of a few of the townspeople rounded up Hardin's other followers.

Tack grinned at the lawyer. "Lived up to your name, pardner," he said. "Yuh sure did! All yore sheep in the fold, now!"

"What do you mean? Lived up to my name?" Anson Childe looked around.

Gentry grinned. "And a little Childe shall lead them!" he said.

NO MAN'S MESA

IT DOMINATED THE desert and the slim green valleys that lay between the peaks or in the canyon bottoms. It was high—over six hundred feet.

The lower part was a talus slope, steep, but it had been climbed. The last three hundred feet was sheer except upon one corner where the rock was shattered and broken edges protruded. This, it was said, was the remnant of the ancient trail to the flat top of the mesa.

There was, legend said, a flowing spring atop the mesa, there were trees and grass and an ancient crater, but all this was talk, for no living man had seen any of it.

The place fostered curious stories. After the Karr boys tried to climb it, there was no rain in the country for two months. After Rison fell from the remnant of the path, there was no rain again. Cattle seemed to shun the place, and people avoided it. The few horses and cattle that did wander to the mesa were soon seen stumbling, vacant-eyed and lonely, losing flesh, growing shaggy of coat, and finally dying. Their whitened bones added to the stories. "This," Old Man Karr often said, "wouldn't be a bad country if it wasn't for Black Mesa."

Matt Calou rode up to Wagonstop in a drenching downpour. When his mount was cared for he sloshed through the rain to the saloon.

"Some storm!" Calou glanced at the four men lining the bar. "Unseasonal, ain't it?"

"Floodin' our gardens." The man jerked his head westward. "It's Black Mesa, that's what it is."

"What's that got to do with it?"

They shrugged. "If you lived in this country you wouldn't have to ask that question."

He took off his slicker and slapped rain from his hat. "Never heard of a pile of rock causin' a rainstorm."

They disdained his ignorance and stared into their drinks. Thunder rumbled, and an occasional lightning flash lit the gloom. Old Man Karr was there, and Wente, who owned the Spring Canyon place. And two hard-case riders from the Pitchfork outfit, Knauf and Russell. Dyer was behind the bar.

Calou was a tall man with a rider's lean build. His face was dark and narrow with an old scar on the cheekbone.

"Lived here long?" he asked Dyer.

"Born here."

"Then you can tell me where the Rafter H lies."

All eyes turned. Dyer stared, then shrugged. "Ain't been a soul on it in fifteen years. Ain't nothin' there but the old stone buildin's and bones. Not even water."

Old Man Karr chuckled. "Right under the edge of Black Mesa, thataway, you couldn't give it to anybody from here. It's cursed, that's what it is."

Matt Calou looked incredulous. "I never put no stock in curses. Anyway, I'm goin' to live there. I bought the Rafter H."

"*Bought* it?" Dyer exploded. "Man, you've been taken. Even if it wasn't near Black Mesa, the place is without water an' overgrown with loco weed."

"What happened? Didn't they used to run cattle there?"

Dyer filled Calou's glass. "Friend," he said quietly, "you'd best learn what you're up against. Twenty-five years ago Art Horan started the Rafter H. Folks warned him about Black Mesa but he laughed. His cattle went loco, his crops died, an' then his well dried up. Finally, he sold out an' left.

"Feller name of Litman took over. Nobody saw him for a few days, an' then a passin' rider found him dead in the yard. Not a mark on him."

"Heart failure, maybe."

"Nobody knows. Litman's nephew came west, but he never liked to stay there at night. Used to spend all his time here, and sometimes he'd camp on the range rather than go near Black Mesa at night.

"Finally, he rounded up a few head of stock, sold 'em, an'

drifted. That's one funny part, stranger. Over two thousand head of stock driven to the place, an' never more than five hundred came of it." Dyer nodded his head. "Never seen hide nor hair of 'em."

"Tell him about Horan," Karr suggested. "Tell him that."

"Nobody ever figured that out. After Horan sold out an' then Litman died an' the nephew left, nobody went near the place. One night Wente here, he rode past Black Mesa—"

"I'll never do it again!" Wente stated emphatically. "Never again!"

"He was close to the cliff when he heard a scream, fair make a man's blood run cold, then a crash. He was takin' off when he heard a faint cry, then moanin'. He rode back, an' there on the rocks a man was layin'. He looked up at Wente an' said, 'It got me, too!' an' then he died. The man was Art Horan. Now you figure that out."

"Nobody has lived there since?"

"An' nobody will."

Calou chuckled. "I'll live there. I've got to. Every dime I could beg, borrow, or steal went into that place. I'm movin' in tomorrow."

———

THERE WAS ANIMOSITY in their eyes. The animosity of men who hear their cherished superstitions derided by a stranger. "You think again," Karr replied. "We folks won't allow it. It'll bring bad luck to all of us."

"That's drivel!" Calou replied shortly. "Let me worry about it."

Karr's old face was ugly. "I lost two boys who tried to climb that mesa, an' many a crop lost, an' many a steer because of it. You stay away from there. There's Injun ha'nts atop it, where there was a village once, long ago. They don't like it."

Knauf looked around. "That goes for the Pitchfork, too, mister. Move onto that place an' we'll take steps."

"Such as what?" Calou asked deliberately.

Knauf placed his glass carefully on the bar. "I don't like the way you talk, stranger, an' I reckon it's time you started learnin'."

He was stocky, with thick hands, but when he turned toward Matt Calou there was surprising swiftness in his movements. As he stepped forward he threw a roundhouse right. Matt Calou was an old hand at this. Catching the swing on his left forearm, he chopped his iron-hand left fist down to Knauf's chin, then followed it with a looping right. Knauf hit the floor and rolled over, gagging.

"Sorry," Calou said. "I wasn't huntin' trouble."

Russell merely stared, then as Calou turned he said, "You'll have the Pitchfork on you now."

"He'll have the whole country on him!" Old Man Karr spat. "Nobody'll sell to you, nobody'll talk to you. If you ain't off this range in one week, you get a coat o' tar an' feathers."

The rain had slackened when Matt Calou rode down into a shallow wash. Water was running knee-high to his horse, but it was not running fast. He crossed and rode through the greasewood of the flat toward the buildings glimpsed in occasional flashes of lightning. Beyond them, dwarfing the country, loomed the towering mass of Black Mesa. When he was still a mile from the house he found the first whitened bones. He counted a dozen skeletons.

Rain pattered on his slicker as he rode into the yard and up to the old stone house. There was a stable, smokehouse, and rock corrals, all built from the talus of the mesa.

Leaving his horse in the stable where it was warm and dry, Matt spilled a bit of grain from a sack behind the saddle into a feed box. "You'll make out on that," he said. "See you in the mornin'."

Rifle under his slicker, he walked to the house. The backdoor lock was rusted, and he braced his foot against the jamb and ripped the lock loose. Once inside, there was a musty smell, but the house floors were solid and the place was in good shape. Opening a window for air, he spread his soogan on the floor and was soon asleep.

It was still raining when he awakened, but washing off the dusty pots and pans, he prepared a hasty breakfast, then saddled up and rode toward the mesa. As he skirted the talus slope he heard water trickling, but when he reached the place where it should have been, there was none. Dismounting, he climbed the slope.

At once he found the stream of runoff. Following it, he found a place where the little stream doubled back and poured into a dark hole at the base of the tower. Listening, he could hear it falling with a roar that seemed to indicate a big, stone-enclosed space. He walked thoughtfully back to his horse.

"Well, what did you find?"

Startled at the voice, Matt looked around to see a girl in a rain-darkened gray hat and slicker. Moreover, she had amazingly blue eyes and lovely black hair.

She laughed at his surprise. "I haunt the place," she said, "haven't you heard?"

"They said there were ghosts, but if I'd known they looked like you I'd have been here twice as fast."

She smiled at him. "Oh, I'm not an official ghost! In fact, nobody is even supposed to know I come here, although I suspect a few people do know."

"They've been trying to make the place as unattractive as possible," he said, grinning. "So if they did know, they said nothing."

"I'm Susan Reid. My father has a cabin about five miles from here. He's gathering information on the Indians—their customs, religious beliefs, and folklore."

"And this morning?"

"We saw somebody moving, and Dad's always hoping somebody will climb it so he can get any artifacts there may be up there."

"Any what?"

"Artifacts. Pieces of old pottery, stone tools, or weapons. Anything the Indians might have used."

Together, they rode toward the ranch, talking of the country and of rain. In a few minutes Matt Calou learned more about old Indian pottery than he had imagined anybody could know.

AT THE CROSSROADS before the Rafter H, they drew up. The rain had ceased, and the sun was struggling to get through. "Matt," she said seriously, "you've started something, so don't underrate the superstition around here. The people who settled here are mostly people from the eastern mountains and they have grown up on such stories. Moreover, some strange things have happened here, and they have some reason for their beliefs. When they talk of running you out, they are serious."

"Then"—he chuckled—"I reckon they'll have to learn the hard way, because I intend to stay right where I am."

When she had gone he went to work. He fixed the lock on the back door, built a door for the stable, and repaired the water trough. He was dead tired when he turned in.

At daybreak he was in the saddle checking the boundaries of his land. There was wild land to the north, but he could check on that later. Loco weed had practically taken over some sections of his land, but he knew that animals will rarely touch it if there is ample forage of other grasses and brush. Several of the locoweed varieties were habit-forming. Scarcity of good forage around water holes or salt grounds was another reason. Most of the poisonous species were early growing and if stock was turned on the range before the grass was sufficiently matured, the cattle would often turn to loco weed.

It was early spring now, but grass was showing in quantity. There was loco weed, but it seemed restricted to a few areas. He had learned in Texas that overgrazing causes the inroad of the weed, but when land is ungrazed the grasses and other growths tend to push the loco back. That had happened here.

The following days found him working dawn until dark. He found some old wire and fenced off the worst sections of weed. Then he borrowed a team from Susan's father and hitched it to a heavy drag made of logs laden with heavy slabs of rock. This drag ripped the weed out by the roots, and once it was loose he raked it into piles for burning.

During all of this time he had seen nobody around. Yet one morning he saddled up, determined to do no work that day. His time was short, as the week they had given him was almost up, and if trouble was coming it might start the following day. He rode north but was turned back by a wall of chaparral growing ten to fifteen feet high, as dense a tangle as he had ever seen in the brush country on the Nueces.

For two miles he skirted the jungle of prickly pear, cat claw, mesquite, and greasewood until he was almost directly behind Black Mesa.

Looking up, he was aware that he was seeing the mesa from an unusual angle. The area was a jumble of upthrust ledges and huge rock slabs and practically impenetrable, yet from where he sat he could see a sort of shadow along the wall of the mesa. Working his way closer, he could see that it was actually an undercut along the face of the cliff. It was visible only because the torrential rains had left the rock damp in the shadow of the cliff. It might be that it had never been seen under these circumstances and from this angle before.

FORCING HIS HORSE through a particularly dense mass of brush, he worked a precarious way through the boulders until he was within a few feet of the wall, and near it, of a gigantic earth crack. In the bottom of this crack was a trickle of water, but it was running *toward* the mesa!

Leaving his horse, he descended to the bottom of the crack. At the point where he had left his horse it was all of thirty feet wide, but at the bottom, a man could touch both walls with outstretched arms.

All was deathly still. Only the faint trickle of the water and the crunch of gravel under his boots broke the stillness. Yet he was aware of a distant and subdued roar that seemed to issue from the base of Black Mesa itself!

He came suddenly to a halt. Before him was a vast black hole! Into this trickled the stream he had been following, and far below he could hear the sound of the water falling into a pool. Recalling the small hole on the opposite side, he realized that under Black Mesa lay a huge underground pool or lake. By all reason the water should have been flowing away from the mesa, but due to the cracks and convulsions of the earth, the water flowed downward into some subterranean basin of volcanic formation.

But if it did not escape? Then there would be a vast reservoir of water, constantly supplied and wholly untapped!

When he emerged, he looked again at the shadow on the wall, revealing a wind- and rain-hollowed undercut that slanted up the side of the mesa. And while he looked he had an idea.

The following day he rode north again, seeking a way through the chaparral. Beyond the belt of brush Sue had told him the green petered out into desert. Although she had not seen it herself, she also told him that only one ranch lay that way, actually to the northwest of Black Mesa, and that was the Pitchfork.

Suddenly he came upon the tracks of two horses. They were shod horses, walking west, and side by side.

The tracks ended abruptly as they had begun, at an uptilted slab of sandstone, but seeing scratches on the sandstone, he rode up himself. It was quite a scramble, but the ledge broke sharply off and a crack, bottomed with blown sand, showed horse tracks.

When he reached the bottom he was in a small meadow and the belt of chaparral was behind him except for scattered clumps. The riders had worked here—he puzzled out the tracks—rounding up a few head of cattle and starting them northwest up the edge of the watery meadow.

Realization flooded over Matt Calou like a cold shower. Wheeling his horse, he started back up the meadow and had gone only a short distance when he came upon a Slash D steer! That was the brand of Dyer, the saloon keeper. Farther along he found another Slash D and three KRs. Grinning with satisfaction, he retraced his steps and rode back to his own ranch.

———

SUE WAS IN the kitchen and a frying pan was sizzling with bacon and eggs when he returned.

"Eggs!" He grinned at her. "Those are the first eggs I've seen in months!"

"We keep a few chickens," she replied, "and I thought I'd surprise you." She dished up a plate of the eggs and bacon, then poured coffee. "You'd better get ready to leave, young man. Foster, of the Pitchfork, is coming over here with his crowd and the crowd from Wagonstop. They say they'll run you out of the country!"

Calou chuckled. "Let 'em come! I'm ready for 'em now!"

"You look like the cat that swallowed the canary," she said, studying him curiously. "What's happened?"

"Wait an' see!" he teased. "Just wait!"

"You've been working," she said. "What are you going to do with that pasture you dragged?"

"Plant it to crops. After a few years of that I'll let it go back to grass. That will take care of the loco weed."

"Crops take water."

"We'll have lots of water! Plenty of it! Enough for the crops, all the stock, an' baths every night for ourselves and the kids."

She was startled. "Ourselves?"

"My wife and myself."

"You didn't tell me you had a wife!" She stared at him.

"I haven't one, but I sure aim to get one now. I've got one in mind. One that will be the mother of fifteen or twenty kids."

"*Fifteen or twenty?* You're crazy!"

"I like big families. I'm the youngest of twelve boys. Anyway, I got a theory about raisin' 'em. It's like this—"

"It will have to wait." Sue put her hand on his arm. "Here they are."

Matt Calou got to his feet. He was, she realized suddenly, wearing a tied-down gun. His rifle was beside the front door and standing alongside it was a shotgun.

Outside she could see the tall, lean figure of Foster of the Pitchfork and beside him were Russell, Knauf, and a half dozen others. Then, coming up behind them, she saw Old Man Karr, Dyer, and Wente. With them were a dozen riders.

Matt stepped into the door. "Howdy, folks! Glad to have visitors! I was afraid my neighbors thought I had hydrophobia!"

There were no answering smiles. "We've come to give you a start out of the country, Calou!" Foster said. "We want nobody livin' here!"

Calou smiled, but his eyes were cold as they measured the tall man on the bay horse. "Thoughtful of you, Foster, but I'm stayin', an' if you try to run me off, you'll have some empty saddles, one of which will be a big bay.

"Fact is, I like this place. Once I get a well down, I'll make an easier livin' than you do, Foster."

Something in his tone stiffened Foster and he looked sharply at Matt Calou. Russell moved up beside him and Knauf faded to the left, for a flanking shot.

———

FOR A MOMENT there was silence, and Matt Calou laughed, his voice harsh. "Didn't like the sound of that, did you, Foster? I don't reckon your neck feels good inside of hemp, does it? I wonder just what did kill Art Horan, Foster? Was it you? Or did he just get suddenly curious an' come back to find out what happened to all the lost cattle?"

Dyer stared from Calou to Foster, obviously puzzled. "This I don't get," he said. "What's all this talk?"

"Tell him, Foster. You know what I mean."

Foster was trapped. He glanced to right and left, then back to the author of his sudden misery. This was what he had feared if Matt Calou or anyone lived on the Rafter H. His fingers spread on his thigh.

Sue spoke suddenly from a window to the right of the door. "Knauf," she said, "I know why you moved, an' I've got a double-barreled shotgun that will blow you out of your saddle if you lay a hand on your gun!"

"What's goin' on here?" Old Man Karr demanded irritably. "What's he talkin' about, Foss?"

"If he won't tell you"—Matt Calou suddenly stepped out of the door—"I will. While you folks have been tellin' yourselves ghost stories about Black Mesa, Foster has been bleedin' the range of your cattle."

"You lie!" Foster roared. "You lie like—!" He grabbed for his gun and Matt Calou fired twice. The first shot knocked the gun from Foster's suddenly bloody hand, and the second notched his ear. It was a bullet that would have killed Foster had he not flinched from the hand wound.

Russell's face was pale as death and he gripped the pommel hard with both hands.

Dyer's face was stern. "All right, Calou! You clear this up an' fast or there'll be a necktie party right here, gun or no gun."

"Your cattle," Matt explained coolly, "hunted water an' found it where nobody knew there was any. Then Foster found your cattle. Ever since then he's been sweepin' that draw ever' few days, takin' up all the cattle he found there, regardless of brand. You lost cattle, but you saw no marks of rustlin', no tracks, no reason to suspect anybody. An' you were all too busy blamin' Black Mesa for all your troubles. Your cattle drifted that way an' never came back, an' Foster was gettin' rich. All he had to do was ride down that draw back of Black Mesa, just beyond the chaparral.

"As for Black Mesa, the reason you thought you saw something movin' up there was because you did see something. The cows that they originally had on the Rafter H are up there, I imagine."

"That ain't possible!" Old Man Karr objected. "Not even a man could climb that tower!"

"There's a crack on the other side, an undercut that makes a fairly easy trail up. Cattle have been grazin' up there for years, an' there's several square miles of good graze up there."

Foster got clumsily from the saddle and commenced to struggle with his hand. One of the men got down to help him. Old Man Karr chewed angrily at his mustache, half resenting the exploded fears of the mountain. Dyer hesitated, then looked down at Matt. "Guess we been a passel o' fools, stranger," he said. "The drinks are on us."

Dyer looked down at Foster. "But I reckon it's a good thing we brought along a rope."

Foster paled under his deep tan. "Give me a break, Dyer!" he pleaded. "I'll pay off! I got records! Sure, I done it, an' I was a fool, but it was an awful temptation. I was broke when I started, an' then—"

"We'll have an accounting," Wente said stiffly, "then we'll decide. If you can take care of our losses, we might make a deal."

Together, Matt and Sue watched them walk away. "If you didn't want fifteen or twenty children," she suggested tentatively, "I know a girl who might be interested."

Matt grinned. "How about six?"

"I guess that's not too many."

He slipped his arm around her waist. "Then consider your proposal accepted."

Sunlight bathed the rim of Black Mesa with a sudden halo. A wide-eyed range cow lowed softly to her calf, unaware of mystery. The calf stumbled to its feet, brushing a white, curved fragment, fragile as a leaf.

It was the weathered lip of an ancient baked clay jar.

THE PASSING OF ROPE NOSE

TO ERR IS human, and Bill McClary was all too human, which accounted for the fact that the six-shooter pride of the Big Bend lay flat on his face in the bottom of a sandy draw with a hole in his head.

McClary was a reckless and ambitious young man known from Mescal to Muleshoe as fast on the draw, and finding that punching cows failed to support him in a style to which he wanted to become accustomed, he acquired a proclivity for cashing in his six-shooter at various cow country banks. To say that this practice was frowned upon by the hardworking sons of the sagebrush was putting it mildly, and Ranger Johnny Sutton had been called upon to correct McClary's impression that the country owed him a living.

Now the Big Bend of the Rio Grande has spawned some tough characters, and during his brief hour in the sun Bill McClary had been accounted by all, including himself, as one of the toughest. For a long time McClary had been hearing of Sutton, and had memorized descriptions of him until he knew he would recognize the Ranger at once. He had long entertained the idea that Johnny Sutton was an overrated four-flusher, an impression he was determined to substantiate.

He had dismounted in that draw south of Nine Point Mesa and waited, smoking a cigarette in cheerful anticipation of the early demise of one Texas Ranger.

Sutton appeared, riding a zebra dun that had an eye full of hell and alkali, and McClary duly informed him that he was going to blow his head off, and would he dismount and take it on the ground?

Johnny, being in an agreeable mood and aware that a fool must follow his natural bent, dismounted. Bill McClary dropped his cigarette, pushed it into the sand with a boot toe, and then with the cheerful smile for which he had been noted, reached for his gun.

The debate was brief, definite, and decisive. Johnny Sutton's Peacemaker put a period to the discussion, and Bill McClary paid for his mistake, cashing in his chips with a memory engraved on his mind of a Colt that appeared from nowhere and the realization, too late, that being the fastest man in the Big Bend did not make him the fastest in Texas.

As a result of the affair in the draw, Ranger Sutton found himself in possession of two saddlebags stuffed with gold coin and bills to the tune of seven thousand dollars, which is a nice tune on any sort of instrument. It is also a sum for one hundredth of which a man could be murdered in any yard of the miles between the Rio Grande and the Davis Mountains.

Moreover, there were in the vicinity several hard customers who knew what McClary had been packing, and would guess what Sutton was bringing back in those extra-heavy saddlebags. Due north of him, and awaiting with keen anticipation any well-heeled passing stranger, was the outlaw town of Paisano. In the choice between a hot meal in Paisano to a cold night among the cat claw and prickly pear, Paisano won hands down, and late in the day Johnny Sutton rode into the dusty main street.

To Rope Nose George, proprietor of the Mustang Saloon, the arrival of Johnny Sutton posed a problem of the first order. Rope Nose was unofficial boss of Paisano, the official boss being Pink Lucas, but Lucas was below the border on a raid. Rope Nose was disturbed, for he recognized Sutton the moment the dun stopped in front of the saloon, and he guessed what he carried. Now the guns of a Ranger are feared, yet seven thousand dollars has been known to turn many a yellow streak into the deep red of battle lust. This Rope Nose realized, and with misgivings.

He was aware that the town of Paisano existed solely because the Rangers had ignored it, being busy with immediate problems, but he was quite sure that if a Ranger were killed in Paisano the town would instantly be awarded first place on the list of Ranger business. In fact, even those not given to superstition in any form were willing to testify that killing a Ranger was bad luck.

Johnny Sutton carried his saddlebags when he came through the doors. With scarcely a glance at the hangers-on, he stepped to the bar. "Howdy, George! Mine will be rye, a meal, and a bed. How about it?"

"Sure thing! Surest thing you know, Mr. *Sutton*." George spoke that name loud enough so anyone in the room would know who had arrived and be hesitant to start anything. Seven thousand or no seven thousand, Rope Nose wanted nothing so much as to get the Ranger out of town.

Hurriedly, he put the glass on the bar, and a bottle beside it. "There's a good room right at the head of the stairs," he whispered confidentially. "You'll like it there." He hesitated, his curiosity struggling with his better judgment, and the better judgment lost in one fall. "You . . . you run into Bill McClary?"

John Sutton's black, steady eyes centered on Rope Nose and the saloonkeeper felt a little chill go up his spine. He'd heard about the feeling those eyes inspired and now he was a believer. "Yeah," Johnny said. "I saw him."

"He . . . he rode on south?" Rope Nose asked hopefully. Personally, he had liked McClary, the most cheerful of a bad lot of bad men, most of them a humorless crowd. "He was goin' on?"

"When I last saw him," Johnny replied, "he didn't give the impression that he was goin' anywhere. Fact is," he added, "I suspect he's right where I left him."

Perk Johnson edged along the bar. "You must be some slick with that gun," he said admiringly. "Bill always said he aimed to try you on."

Sutton's gaze was frosty. "Bill McClary," he said, "was a mighty good man with damn bad judgment. I hope bad judgment ain't contagious around here."

The swinging doors smashed open and a little brown bobcat in the shape of a girl rushed through the door. Her eyes were flashing and gray, startling against the deep brown of her face. Her dress was torn and she held a shawl about her shoulders. "Are you the Ranger?" she demanded of Sutton.

"If you are, come an' help me! Some thieves got my pa in the place next door, skinnin' him in a card game, an' I found another goin' through my wagon!"

There was no maidenly shyness about her. "Well, come on!" she said angrily. "Don't just stand there!"

"If your father's in a poker game he went into it of his own free will, and," Johnny added, "if he's your father I figure he's man enough to take care of himself. No coyote spawned a wildcat."

Her eyes flashed. "Are you another of these no-good loafin' cowhands, or are you a Ranger? They've got my pa drunk an' he can't see to hold his cards. I went to get him an' they nearly tore my dress off. You come help me or I'm goin' back in there with a horsewhip!"

Sutton tossed off his drink. "Hold that grub, George," he advised, "an' open your safe an' put these saddlebags in it." As Rope Nose George's eyes bulged, Sutton added, "And don't get any ideas. I know just how much there is in there an' you're personally accountable for every dime of it!" George's heart pounded. Seven thousand dollars was the stuff outlaw dreams were made of. He was a notorious coward who lived in fear of both the law and the other men in Pink Lucas's gang, but this was sorely tempting.

Sutton watched him stow the bags carefully into the safe, and when the door was closed he turned and followed the girl outside. She said nothing more but walked toward the light from the next door with a free swinging stride.

She pushed open the door and instantly there was a yell of enthusiasm and a rush. "She's back, boys! She's back! Let's teach that filly a—!"

The rush stopped so suddenly that one man almost fell down, for Johnny Sutton had stepped through the door after the girl. "Go back an' sit down!" he ordered. "An' damn you for a lot of mangy coyotes!"

Four men sat at a card table. The girl's father was obvious enough. He was not only so drunk he couldn't see, but two men were holding him upright in his chair and one of them was playing his cards. Johnny crossed the room and looked them over cynically. The redhead behind the drunken man looked up sheepishly. "Is he winnin'?" Johnny asked dryly.

The redhead's flush was deeper. "Well," he said guiltily, "he ain't been holdin' much. Right now he's losin'."

"How much has he lost?"

Red hesitated, then swallowed. "Right at a thousand dollars," he confessed, "maybe a mite over."

Johnny Sutton's right eyebrow tightened. The man did not look like he had a thousand cents, much less dollars. "Did he have that much, little lady?"

"You bet he did!" the girl flashed back at him. "And more, if these blisterin' pickpockets haven't stole it off him!"

Red looked abused, and he let go of the drunken man who slumped over on the table.

"Whose deal is it?" Johnny asked suddenly.

Their eyes were puzzled and wary. "Mine." The speaker was a lean-faced man marked with evil and crookedness.

"All right," Johnny said calmly, "you boys like this game. You started it. Now deal, and don't let any of your mistakes keep him from winning back his money."

"Now, look here—!" The tall man started to rise but Johnny's left hand dropped to his shoulder and slammed him back in his chair.

"Deal!" Sutton insisted. If he chose to make a fight of it, the result might mean a lot less crime in that part of Texas.

Grudgingly, the man began to deal. It was noteworthy that from that moment the drunken man began to win. Red, devilish in his glee and enjoyment of the reversed situation, bet the old man's hands recklessly. When thirty minutes had passed the tall man glanced at Sutton. "There, now. He's won it all back!" He dropped his hands to the table and started to push back.

"Deal." Johnny's voice was flat and dangerous. "Deal those cards. An' Red, you bet 'em like you see 'em! I like the way you play poker."

"He's got all his money, I tell you!" The tall man's face was wolfish. "I'll be damned if I—!"

Johnny Sutton's eyes fastened on the man, and they seemed to grow flat and lose their shine. With his free hand he reached out and swept all the money from in front of the players into the middle of the table. "You shuffle the cards, fast boy. You like it that way. Shuffle the cards, then you cut for high card with him. Winner takes all!"

"Don't do it, Chiv!" The speaker was a bearded man with a hard set to his jaw. "He can't get away with this!"

"You open your face again," Johnny said calmly, "an' you'll have a mouthful of loose teeth. Shuffle those cards, Chiv. This will teach all of you a lesson you'll remember next time you try to take a harmless old man who's just passin' through! Shuffle an' cut!"

The man looked at the cards with sudden distaste, then, belligerently, he looked up at Sutton. "This time I cut as I want, and it's on the level," he said. "If the old man wins he gets it all, an' if I win, I do."

The girl started forward with a cry of protest, but Sutton waved her back. "All right," he agreed, "but with your permission I'll cut for him." Sutton jerked a thumb toward the old man.

The gambler looked up and his hard eyes brightened with malice. "Why, sure! You cut for him!" He gathered the cards and shuffled them briefly, then slapped the deck on the table and took hold with his thumb and middle finger. "Okay?" he asked, and at Johnny's nod, he cut the cards and showed a queen of hearts, and smiled.

Johnny leaned over and shaped the deck with his fingers, then struck them slightly and split the deck.

At the cut, the gambler's face went white with fury and he grasped the arms of his chair, staring at the ace of clubs Sutton was showing. "Your own deck," Sutton said quietly.

"Lady," Sutton slid suddenly to his feet and stepped back from the table, "pick up the money. Tie it up in something and we'll leave." His black eyes held the gambler's. "Next time," he advised, "don't use a deck with slick aces."

The gambler stared at him, his face taut with hatred and pent-up fury.

As the girl moved toward the door, Johnny Sutton looked the room over, letting each man feel the weight of his attention. "If that girl is bothered again, or if there is any more trouble during my stay in this town, I'll burn the place to the ground, and the ones who are lucky will go to jail."

Deliberately, he turned his back and walked out through the doors. At the wagon the girl turned. "My name is Stormy," she said, "and thanks. I guess Pa an' me ain't much, but we're grateful."

Sutton shrugged. "I was glad to help. If you need me, scream." He pointed toward the window of the room assigned to him. "I'll be up there."

————

THE MOON FLOATED lazily above the serrated ridges of the scarred landscape below it. A coyote protested its troubles, and then as the moon slid down the sky, the coyote trotted off into the shadows in pursuit of food. Day edged its first skirmishing lines of light along the ridges and Rope Nose George turned over in his sleep and awakened.

All was dark and still but the window showed the first gray that preceded the dawn. Rope Nose George was suddenly wide awake, remembering the seven thousand dollars in the safe and three thousand more, or so it was rumored, in the old man's wagon. Most of this last had been realized from the sale of cattle, the rest from the poker game. Ten thousand dollars was more money than Rope Nose had ever seen. It was also more than had ever been in Paisano at any one time.

And then he heard the horses.

They were walking, and there were more than two of them. With a start, he sat up, realizing on the instant that it was Pink Lucas returning. Vastly disturbed, Rope Nose swung his legs out of bed and felt for his boots. Terrified, he knew he must inform Pink at once about the presence of the Ranger. He also knew that Pink would try to steal the money and that meant killing Sutton, an act which, he was sure, would put him out of business. Tumbling around in the back of his brain was the idea that he could somehow get his hands on the ten thousand dollars if he could only figure out how to keep from being caught by the Ranger or Pink Lucas.

He got his boots on, struggled into his pants, and hastened to the door. Then he stopped abruptly. *The wagon was gone!*

For a minute he stared, unmindful of the approaching riders, thinking only of the missing wagon. Then he thought of Chiv Pontious. If the gambler had—!

He turned for the stairs to the Ranger's room. He scrambled, panting up the stairs, clutching his unbelted pants with one hand. The Ranger's door stood open and on the rumpled bed was a note.

Sorry to leave like this. I got my money.

Got his money? But? . . . ! Turning, Rope Nose stumbled down the steps and into the saloon. The room was dark and still, and the safe was closed. Hurriedly, he spun the dial and opened the safe. Where the money had been placed was another note.

You should be more careful. I read the combination when you opened the safe for me. I've taken my money and you had better keep your boys home.

The door rattled, and he went to it. Opening it, he found himself pushed aside by Pink Lucas. The big outlaw swaggered to the bar and picked up the bottle left there by Sutton. Pouring a drink, he turned on George. "All right, where is it?"

"Where's what?"

Chiv Pontious had come into the room behind Lucas. He smiled now. "I told you he was scared, Pink. The money's in the safe."

"No, it ain't." George shoved the note at them. "Sutton took it and he's gone, the wagon with him."

"Ten thousand!" Chiv said aloud. "Think of it, Pink! Ten thousand dollars, for the taking!"

Pink slammed the glass down on the bar. "Get fresh horses!" he yelled. "Get 'em fast! We'll have that money! He can't go far with a wagon!"

In the distance, thunder rumbled.

Rope Nose George examined Lucas with heavy-lidded,

crafty eyes. "You're right, Pink. They're headed up toward the hills. Let's go get 'em."

"Not you, fat man," Pink said as a clatter of hooves announced the arrival of the remounts. "You're stayin' here, an' keepin' your mouth shut. Come on, men!"

———

SIX MILES TO the west, Johnny Sutton was leading the wagon into the rough country beyond Tornillo Creek. It was a country cut by many draws that in wet weather ran bank full with roaring water, and it was sprinkling even now. That is, it was sprinkling where Sutton rode. Over the mountains around Lost Mine Peak, heavy thunderheads were losing their weight of water upon the steep slopes of the mountains. Johnny Sutton knew the gamble he was taking and the risk he was running, but to get where he wanted to go he must cross at least two more of the deep draws that cut into the slope leading down into the bottom of Tornillo Flat. There was high ground there where they would be safe, and if his idea worked, it would not only prove safe for him and the Knights, but a trap for any who followed them.

The rain was increasing. Lightning flashed continually. Wheeling his horse, he rode back. "Whoop it up, Pa!" he yelled above the storm. "We've got two more draws to cross!"

Pale-faced, the older man stared at him. "We'll never make it! Look at the rain in those mountains!"

"We've got to!" Sutton replied. "Let's go!"

The horses strained into the harness and gathered speed. The wagon was not heavily loaded, and back along the way they had already thrown out several pieces of furniture. Each one had meant a battle with Stormy, but each time it was a battle Sutton won.

Ahead of them, a deep gash broke the face of the plain, and without hesitation he rode into it. A thin stream trickled along the bottom, but that was merely the result of local rain. What was coming was back up there in those rock-sided mountains, where nothing stopped the weight of rushing water. Whooping and yelling they raced across the draw and the horses lunged up the opposite side. Far off they heard a low roar. Stormy looked quickly at Sutton. "Can't we stop here?" she pleaded.

"Not unless you feel you can hold off a dozen men!" he replied. "Get rollin', old man!"

The team lunged into their collars and the four horses started the wagon moving. It was no more than a half mile to the next draw but the race was on in earnest. Johnny Sutton rode alongside the horses, whooping it up and slapping them with his rope.

Before them loomed the other draw, all of sixty yards across and the trail showing dimly up the far side. Now the roar filled their ears, but whipping up the horses, Sutton slapped his dun and lunged on ahead. Down the bank he went at a dead run with the wagon thundering behind him. The draw was straight away to the west for all of two hundred yards, and as they hit bottom they saw the water.

It was a rolling gray-black wall at least ten feet high! It was rolling down upon them with what seemed to be the speed of an express train. Sutton whipped the horses and, racing beside them, rushed for the trail. The frightened horses hit the trail up the bank and the wagon bounded like a chip as it struck a stone. Then they were up, and almost in the same instant the water swept by, thundering behind them.

"All right!" Sutton yelled. "Pull up an' give 'em a blow!"

Knight drew up on the lines and the horses quartered around. The draw was running bank full behind them. Then, standing in his stirrups, Sutton pointed.

Behind them, trapped between the two draws, was a small band of horsemen! Rain lashing his face, he laughed grimly. "Got 'em!" he said. "I figured they were close behind!" He rode in close to the wagon and leaned over. "Keep goin', but you can take it easy now. Head for the ranch at Paint Gap. You'll be safe there."

Stormy stood up. "What about you?" she demanded.

"I'm waiting here. I want to watch those hombres. There's one in particular I want to talk to!" He swung the dun and rode away through the rain. Stormy stared after him, then sat down abruptly, her eyes somber.

Johnny Sutton liked the feel of the rain. He was wearing

his slicker, but otherwise was thoroughly wet and enjoying it. He rode back toward the draw. The riders had turned and were headed upstream. He grinned, having foreseen that possibility and knowing well what awaited them. As a boy of sixteen he had been punching cattle in this area and had been trapped in the same way. He turned his own horse and followed them. Suddenly, they drew up. The place where they had stopped had been made an island by the two draws running bank full. By the look of the rain they would have no choice but to sit there and wait until the two draws went down, which would be four or five hours by the way the rain was continuing.

They had stopped at the foot of a steep red and grassless slope that led up the sides of a low mesa. The top of that mesa, the last twenty feet, was sheer rock extending from one draw to the other. A horse might scramble up that slope, but nothing could surmount that cliff at the top. Johnny Sutton sat on his horse and chuckled.

From where they sat they could see him plainly and he waved to them. One of the men threw his rifle to his shoulder and fired a shot, but the distance was far too great for it to be effective. Sutton rode forward, not certain whether he would find what he sought or not, but when he came to the bridge of stone, he grinned with satisfaction.

He was now well beyond the mesa that blocked the westward ride of the outlaws, and this stone ledge under which the water ran was in fact a part of that same mesa. Here the water had undermined the solid rock of the ledge and left a natural bridge some fifty feet wide and at least twenty yards along, ample to bridge the draw at that point. Johnny rode across the stone bridge and walked his horse through the rain to the top of the mesa. On this northern side it broke sharply off and was easy of access in several places, as it was from the west, although inaccessible for a rider from either the south or east.

When within some forty yards of the rim below which the horsemen were trapped, Johnny Sutton swung down and drew his rifle from its scabbard, keeping the weapon back under his slicker. He walked up behind some boulders and looked down on the riders standing below. He chuckled, then fired a shot into the ground at their horses' feet. Several animals started to buck. All heads swung around and guns came up.

"Drop 'em, Pink!" he called out. "All of you! I've got you under my gun and I can pick you off like ducks in a barrel! You," Sutton motioned to one of the men, "collect all the guns, an' I mean *all*!"

They sat dead still, staring up at him. Before and behind were roaring rivers, impassable for many hours. East, the ground fell away into a vast flat covered with a stand of water, much of it now treacherous with quicksand. On foot they might climb the stone wall before them; otherwise, there was no escape. Nor was there escape from the deadly rifle that covered them. They were caught in the open and helpless.

"No waiting!" Sutton ordered. "Collect the guns!"

Reluctantly, the outlaw went from man to man, gathering the weapons. Sutton had brought his rope, and now he lowered the end down the wall. "Tie 'em on!" he commanded.

When this was done he hauled the weapons up to him, worked with them a few minutes, and then went back to the rim. "All right, leave your horses and climb up here, one by one!"

"Leave our horses?" Lucas protested. "What becomes of them? How do we travel?"

"On foot."

A burst of profanity answered him, and one man shouted a refusal. Wheeling his horse he dropped low in the saddle and jumped the horse away toward the flat. Yet the horse had taken not even two full jumps when Sutton fired. The man swung loose in the saddle and dropped. Then he struggled to his feet, clutching his bloody shoulder and swearing.

"One at a time!" Sutton repeated. "Start climbin'!"

One by one they climbed up, and one by one he tied their hands behind them, patting them down for knives and other weapons. The last man to come up was Pink Lucas, his red face redder still, his eyes ugly. "I'll kill you for this!" he told Sutton.

Shrugging, Johnny Sutton started them walking northwest through the steady fall of the rain. An hour later he paused and allowed them fifteen minutes' rest. By that time the rain had slowed to a mere drizzle and gave signs of clearing. Then he started them again. Four hours later, wet, bedraggled, and weary, they stumbled into the Paint Gap Ranch yard, and were met by an astonished gathering of cowhands headed by their boss, Charlie Warner, and by Pa and Stormy Knight.

"Well, I'll be forever damned!" Warner stared. "Pink Lucas an' his crowd! How in the thunder did you ever get this bunch?"

Johnny Sutton shrugged wearily. "They got tired of livin' lives of wickedness and decided they would surrender. Isn't that right, Pink?"

Pink Lucas answered with a burst of profanity. Chiv Pontious only stared at Sutton, his eyes evil with murderous desire for a weapon.

Johnny Sutton looked at Stormy, and met her eyes. "You'd better eat something," she said. "You're cold and wet."

"That ain't all," Pink Lucas threatened. "He'll stay cold an' wet."

Johnny Sutton herded the men into the barn and left a cowhand to watch them. There had been no sign of Red, and secretly he was pleased. He had liked the way Red played Knight's hand the night before. At least, he liked the way he had played it after he, Sutton, moved in.

Sutton walked to the house and dropped the saddlebags against the wall. "I needed Lucas," he said, looking around at Warner. "He's been raiding across the border. I'd been trailing him when I ran into McClary. And that Pontious—he's wanted in New Orleans and Dallas, both places for murder."

"The rain has stopped," Stormy said suddenly. "Maybe we can go on tomorrow."

The rain had stopped. Johnny listened for it, and heard no sound, but he heard another sound—the faint clop, clop of a walking horse. "Somebody coming in?" he asked, turning his head. "Maybe one of your boys?"

"Maybe. There's two still out." Warner got up. "I'll see."

The big rancher turned toward the door. Suddenly he started backing toward them, and Rope Nose George was standing in the door with a shotgun in his hand. He wore two six-shooters, but it was the double-barreled shotgun that stopped Johnny Sutton. "Don't be a fool, George," he said, "you've been out of this."

"I know that," Rope Nose replied solemnly. "I was well out of it, an' then I got to thinkin'. Ten thousand dollars— why, that's a lot of money! It would keep a man a long time, if he used it right, especially down in one o' them South American countries. I just couldn't forget it, so I asked myself, 'where will Sutton go?' And I guessed right."

"George," Sutton said patiently, "you get out of here now and I'll forget this ever happened."

"That's fair. That's mighty fair, ain't it, Mr. Warner? Not many would give a man a break like that. Nevertheless, I ain't a-goin' to do it. Ten thousand—why, I never see that much money! I'll never have me another chance at it. I ain't nervy like that Pink Lucas is. I'm a yaller dog. I know that, Sutton. I always been afeard o' Pink an' his crowd, but why should I set in that durned bar when I could be settin' on a wide piazza down Guatemala way? I know a gent onct who come from Guatemala. He said . . ."

His voice trailed off and stopped. "You!" He pointed at Stormy. "I know that money you got is in that sack. Set it over here. Then get those saddlebags. Then I'll tie you all up an' drag it."

He chuckled. "I figured you'd come here, so I never went across that Tornillo Flat. I rode straight west without comin' north at all, then dropped south an' crossed the crick afore she got a big head up."

"Better think it over, Rope Nose," Sutton suggested mildly. "We'll get you."

"I done thought it over. I'm takin' two o' Warner's blacks. Nothin' around here will outrun them horses. I'll switch from one to the other an' ride hard to the border. It ain't far, an' once across I'll make the railroad an' head for Guatemala or somewheres. You'll never see hide nor hair o' me again."

With his left hand he gathered up the sacks. The shotgun

rested on the back of a chair with the muzzles pointed at Sutton, not ten feet away.

"Now," he waved to Stormy, "you tie these gents up. Tie 'em good an' tight because I'll look 'em over after. Then I'm takin' out. Sure do hate to take your money, young lady, but I'll need it, an' you're young."

Johnny Sutton was the last one tied. The girl drew the ropes about him, then tied a knot and, opening Johnny's hand, placed the end of the rope in it. Instantly, he realized what she had done. She had gambled and tied a slip noose!

Rope Nose called her over and proceeded to tie her hands. Then he picked up the sacks and, with the shotgun, backed to the door. As the door closed after him, Sutton jerked on the rope. His wrists were tied, and he could only pull a little at a time. Sweat broke out on his face and body but he fought with his fingers, struggling to pull the knot loose. He heard a horse walking, then another. He heard one of the outlaws call out from the barn, and Rope Nose replying.

Suddenly the noose slipped, and then he was jerking his arms and shaking loose the loops of rope about his wrists. Swiftly he untied his feet and grabbed for his gun belts. Whipping them about him, Johnny rushed to the door. Rope Nose had both blacks saddled. He hung the saddlebags and sack on one, then swung to mount the other.

Johnny heard Lucas swearing from the barn, and heard the refusal of Rope Nose to give them aid. Then Johnny stepped out and let the door slam behind him. Rope Nose whirled as if stabbed, the shotgun in his hands. He was all of fifty yards away and his mouth was wide, his eyes staring with incredulous horror.

Suddenly he shouted, almost screamed, "No! No, you ain't goin' to stop me!" He stepped forward and fired the shotgun waist high, and then Sutton fired. The widely scattered pellets of the shotgun clicked and pattered about him as he fired. He shot once, twice.

Rope Nose staggered, dropping the shotgun as the second barrel of shot plowed up earth. Sutton could see the man's fat stomach bulging over his leather belt. He saw the sudden whiteness in the man's face. Saw him step forward, hauling clumsily at a belt gun. He got it out, his eyes wide and staring.

"Drop it!" Sutton shouted. "Drop it, George!"

"No!" the fat man gasped hoarsely now. "No, I won't . . . !"

The gun came waist high and he began to shoot. The first shot went wild, the second kicked up earth at Sutton's feet, and then he saw the muzzle was dead on him, and Johnny Sutton fired a third shot. Rope Nose took a short step forward and kept falling until he hit the hard ground on his face. Then he rolled over and lay staring up at the sky, a spot of mud on his nose.

Sutton ran to him. The man was still alive. His eyes met Sutton's. "Should of knowed I'd . . . I'd never make it," he whispered, "but me, an' I'm a yaller dog, killed in a gun . . . gunfight with Ranger Johnny Sutton!" He breathed hoarsely. "Yessir, let 'em say I was yaller! Let 'em say that! But let 'em remember I faced up to Sutton with a six-gun! Let 'em remember, I died . . . game."

Johnny Sutton stared down at him, a fat, untidy man who had rolled over in the mud. The florid features were pale and the spot of mud might have made him ludicrous, only somehow he was not. It was simply that in this last minute, this moment of death, by his own shady standards at least, he had acquired a certain nobility.

Stormy Knight came up beside Sutton and took his arm. He put his hand over hers and turned away. Why didn't men like this ever learn that it wasn't money in the long run? It was contentment. Or had Rope Nose found contentment in that last moment when he knew he had faced a gun and stood up to it?

"You think it will be all right for us to go on tomorrow?" Stormy was trying to make conversation.

"Sure," Sutton replied, "I think it will. When you get that ranch, you might write me. I'll come calling."

"I'd like that," Stormy said, and when she smiled, Johnny knew she meant what she said.

TRAIL TO PIE TOWN

DUSTY BARRON TURNED the steel-dust stallion down the slope toward the wash. He was going to have to find water soon or the horse and himself would be done for. If Emmett Fisk and Gus Mattis had shown up in the street at any other time it would have been all right.

As it was, they had appeared just as he was making a break from the saloon, and they had blocked the road to the hill country and safety. Both men had reached for their guns when they saw him, and he had wheeled his horse and hit the desert road at a dead run. With Dan Hickman dead in the saloon it was no time to argue or engage in gun pleasantries while the clan gathered.

It had been a good idea to ride to Jarilla and make peace talk, only the idea hadn't worked. Dan Hickman had called him yellow and then gone for a gun. Dan was a mite slow, a fact that had left him dead on the saloon floor.

There were nine Hickmans in Jarilla, and there were Mattis and three Fisk boys. Dusty's own tall brothers were back in the hills southwest of Jarilla, but with his road blocked he had headed the steel-dust down the trail into the basin.

The stallion had saved his bacon. No doubt about that. It was only the speed of the big desert-bred horse and its endurance, that had got him away from town before the Hickmans could catch him. The big horse had given him lead enough until night had closed in, and after that it was easier.

Dusty had turned at right angles from his original route. They would never expect that, for the turn took him down the long slope into the vast, empty expanse of the alkali basin where no man of good sense would consider going.

For him it was the only route. At Jarilla they would be watching for him, expecting him to circle back to the hill country and his own people. He should have listened to Allie when she had told him it was useless to try to settle the old blood feud.

He had been riding now, with only a few breaks, for hours. Several times he had stopped to rest the stallion, wanting to conserve its splendid strength against what must lie ahead. And occasionally he had dismounted and walked ahead of the big horse.

———

DUSTY BARRON HAD only the vaguest idea of what he was heading into. It was thirty-eight miles across the basin, and he was heading down the basin. According to popular rumor, there was no water for over eighty miles in that direction. And he had started with his canteen only half full.

For the first hour he had taken his course from a star. Then he had sighted a peak ahead and to his left and used that for a marker. Gradually, he had worked his way toward the western side of the basin.

Somewhere over the western side was Gallo Gap, a green meadow high in the peaks off a rocky and rarely used pass. There would be water there if he could make it, yet he knew of the gap only from a story told him by a prospector he had met one day in the hills near his home.

Daybreak found him a solitary black speck in a vast wilderness of white. The sun stabbed at him with lances of fire and then rising higher bathed the great alkali basin in white radiance and blasting furnace heat. Dusty narrowed his eyes against the glare. It was at least twelve miles to the mountains.

He still had four miles to go through the puffing alkali dust when he saw the tracks. At first he couldn't believe the evidence of his eyes. A wagon—here!

While he allowed the steel-dust to take a blow, he dismounted and examined the tracks. It had been a heavy wagon pulled by four mules or horses. In the fine dust he could not find an outlined track to tell one from the other.

The tracks had come out of the white distance to the east and had turned north exactly on the route he was following.

Gallo Gap, from the prospector's story, lay considerably north of him and a bit to the west.

Had the driver of the wagon known of the gap? Or had he merely turned on impulse to seek a route through the mountains? Glancing in first one and then the other direction, Dusty could see no reason why the driver should have chosen either direction. Jarilla lay southwest, but from here there was no indication of it and no trail.

Mounting again, he rode on, and when he came to the edge of the low hills fronting the mountains, he detected the wagon trail running along through the scattered rocks, parched bunch grass, and greasewood. It was still heading north. Yet when he studied the terrain before him he could see nothing but dancing heat waves and an occasional dust devil.

The problem of the wagon occupied his mind to forgetfulness of his own troubles. It had come across the alkali basin from the east. That argued it must have come from the direction of Manzano unless the wagon had turned into the trail somewhere further north on the road to Conejos.

Nothing about it made sense. This was Apache country and no place for wagon travel. A man on a fast horse, yes, but even then it was foolhardy to travel alone. Yet the driver of the wagon had the courage of recklessness to come across the dead white expanse of the basin, a trip that to say the least was miserable.

Darkness was coming again, but he rode on. The wagon interested him, and with no other goal in mind now that he had escaped the Hickmans, he was curious to see who the driver was and to learn what he had in mind. Obviously, the man was a stranger to this country.

It was then, in the fading light, that he saw the mule. The steel-dust snorted and shied sharply, but Dusty kneed it closer for a better look. It had been a big mule and a fine animal, but it was dead now. It bore evidence of that brutal crossing of the basin, and here, on the far side, the animal had finally dropped dead of heat and exhaustion.

Only then did he see the trunk. It was sitting between two rocks, partly concealed. He walked to it and looked it over. Cumbersome and heavy, it had evidently been dumped from the wagon to lighten the load. He tried to open it, but could not. It was locked tight. Beside it were a couple of chairs and a bed.

"Sheddin' his load," Dusty muttered thoughtfully. "He'd better find some water for those other mules or they'll die, too."

Then he noticed the name on the trunk. D.C. LOWE, ST. LOUIS, MO.

"You're a long way from home," Dusty remarked. He swung a leg over the saddle and rode on. He had gone almost five miles before he saw the fire.

————

AT FIRST, IT might have been a star, but as he drew nearer he could see it was too low down, although higher than he was. The trail had been turning gradually deeper into the hills and had begun to climb a little. He rode on, using the light for a beacon.

When he was still some distance off he dismounted and tied the stallion to a clump of greasewood and walked forward on foot.

The three mules were hitched to the back of the wagon, all tied loosely and lying down. A girl was bending over a fire, and a small boy, probably no more than nine years old, was gathering sticks of dried mesquite for fuel. There was no one else in sight.

Marveling, he returned to his horse and started back. When he was still a little distance away he began to sing. His throat was dry and it was a poor job, but he didn't want to frighten them. When he walked his horse into the firelight the boy was staring up at him, wide-eyed, and the girl had an old Frontier Model Colt.

"It's all right, ma'am," he said, swinging down, "I'm just a passin' stranger an' don't mean any harm."

"Who are you?" she demanded.

"Name of Dusty Barron, ma'am. I've been followin' your trail."

"Why?" Her voice was sharp and a little frightened. She could have been no more than seventeen or eighteen.

"Mostly because I was headed thisaway an' was wonderin' what anybody was doin' down here with a wagon, or where you might be headed."

"Doesn't this lead us anywhere?" she asked.

"Ma'am," Dusty replied, "if you're lookin' for a settlement there ain't none thisaway in less'n a hundred miles. There's a sort of town then, place they call Pie Town."

"But where did you come from?" Her eyes were wide and dark. If she was fixed up, he reflected, she would be right pretty.

"Place they call Jarilla," he said, "but I reckon this was a better way if you're travelin' alone. Jarilla's a Hickman town, an' they sure are a no-account lot."

"My father died," she told him, putting the gun in a holster hung to the wagon bed, "back there. Billy an' I buried him."

"You come across the basin alone?" He was incredulous.

"Yes. Father died in the mountains on the other side. That was three days ago."

Dusty removed his hat and began to strip the saddle and bridle from the stallion while the girl bent over her cooking. He found a hunk of bacon in his saddle pockets. "Got plenty of bacon?" he asked. "I most generally pack a mite along."

She looked up, brushing a strand of hair away from her face. She was flushed from the fire. "We haven't had any bacon for a week." She looked away quickly, and her chin quivered a little and then became stubborn. "Nor much of anything else, but you're welcome to join us."

He seated himself on the ground and leaned back on his saddle while she dished up the food. It wasn't much. A few dry beans and some corn bread. "You got some relatives out here somewheres?"

"No." She handed him a plate, but he was too thirsty to eat more than a few mouthfuls. "Father had a place out here. His lungs were bad and they told him the dry air would be good for him. My mother died when Billy was born, so there was nothing to keep us back in Missouri. We just headed west."

"You say your father had a place? Where is it?"

"I'm not sure. Father loaned some man some money, or rather, he provided him with money with which to buy stock.

The man was to come west and settle on a place, stock it, and then send for Dad."

Dusty ate slowly, thinking that over. "Got anything to show for it?"

"Yes, Father had an agreement that was drawn up and notarized. It's in a leather wallet. He gave the man five thousand dollars. It was all we had."

When they had eaten, the girl and boy went to sleep in the wagon box while Dusty stretched out on the ground nearby. "What a mess!" he told himself. "Those kids comin' away out here, all by themselves now, an' the chances are that money was blowed in over a faro layout long ago!"

IN THE MORNING Dusty hitched up the mules for them. "You foller me," he advised, and turned the stallion up the trail to the north.

It was almost noon before he saw the thumblike butte that marked the entrance to Gallo Gap. He turned toward it, riding ahead to scout the best trail and at times dismounting to roll rocks aside so the wagon could get through.

Surmounting the crest of a low hill, he looked suddenly into Gallo Gap. His red-rimmed eyes stared greedily at the green grass and trees. The stallion smelled water and wanted to keep going, so waving the wagon on, he rode down into the gap.

Probably there were no more than two hundred acres here, but it was waist deep in rich green grass, and the towering yellow pines were tall and very old. It was like riding from desolation into a beautiful park. He found the spring by the sound of running water, crystal clear and beautiful, the water rippling over the rocks to fall into a clear pond at least an acre in extent. Nearby, space had been cleared for a cabin and then abandoned.

Dusty turned in the saddle as his horse stood knee deep in the water. The wagon pulled up. "This is a little bit of heaven!" he said, grinning at the girl. "Say, what's your name, anyway?"

"Ruth Grant," she said, shyly.

All the weariness seemed to have fled from her face at the sight of the water and trees. She smiled gaily, and a few minutes later as he walked toward the trees with a rifle in the crook of his elbow he heard laughter and then her voice, singing. He stopped suddenly, watching some deer feeding a short distance off, and listening to her voice. It made a lump of loneliness rise in his throat.

That night, after they had eaten steaks from a fat buck he'd killed, their first good meal in days, he looked across the fire at her. "Ruth," he said, "I think I'll locate me a home right here. I've been lookin' for a place of my own.

"I reckon what we better do is for you all to stay here with me until you get rested up. I'll build a cabin, and those mules of yours can get some meat on their bones again. Then I'll ride on down to Pie Town and locate this hombre your father had dealin's with an' see how things look."

That was the way they left it, but in the days that followed Dusty Barron had never been happier. He felled trees on the mountainside and built a cabin, and in working around he found ways of doing things he had never tried before. Ruth was full of suggestions about the house, sensible, knowing things that helped a lot. He worked the mules a little, using only one at a time and taking them turnabout.

He hunted a good deal for food. Nearby he found a salt lick and shot an occasional antelope, and several times, using a shotgun from the wagon, he killed blue grouse. In a grove of trees he found some ripe black cherries similar to those growing wild in the Guadalupe Mountains of west Texas. There was also some Mexican plum.

When the cabin was up and there was plenty of meat on hand he got his gear in shape. Then he carefully oiled and cleaned his guns.

Ruth noticed them, and her face paled a little. "You believe there will be trouble?" she asked quickly. "I don't want you to—"

"Forget it," he interrupted. "I've got troubles of my own." He explained about the killing of Dan Hickman and the long-standing feud between the families.

He left at daybreak. In his pocket he carried the leather

wallet containing the agreement Roger Grant had made with Dick Lowe. It was a good day's ride from Gallo Gap to Aimless Creek, where Dusty camped the first night. The following day he rode on into Pie Town. From his talks with Ruth he knew something of Lowe and enough of the probable location of the ranch, if there was one.

———

A COWHAND WITH sandy hair and crossed eyes was seated on the top rail of the corral. Dusty reined in and leaned his forearm on the saddle horn and dug for the makings. After he had rolled a smoke he passed them on to the cross-eyed rider.

"Know anything about an hombre name of Dick Lowe?" he asked.

"Reckon so." They shared a match, and looking at each other through the smoke decided they were men of a kind. "He's up there in the Spur Saloon now."

Dusty made no move. After a few drags on the cigarette, he glanced at the fire end. "What kind of hombre is he?"

"Salty." The cowhand puffed for a moment on his cigarette. "Salty an' mean. Plumb poison with a shootin' iron, an' when you ride for him, he pays you what he wants to when you quit. If you don't think you got a square deal you can always tell him so, but when you do you better reach."

"Like that, huh?"

"Like that." He smoked quietly for a few minutes. "Four hombres haven't liked what he paid 'em. He buried all four of 'em in his own personal boothill, off to the north of the ranchhouse."

"Sounds bad. Do all his own work or does he have help?"

"He's got help. Cat McQuill an' Bugle Nose Bender. Only nobody calls him Bugle Nose to his face."

"What about the ranch? Nice place?"

"Best around here. He come in here with money, had near five thousand dollars. He bought plenty of cattle an' stocked his range well."

The cross-eyed cowhand looked at him, squinting through the smoke. "My name's Blue Riddle. I rode for him once."

"I take it you didn't argue none," Barron said, grinning.

"My maw never raised no foolish children!" Riddle replied wryly. "They had me in a cross fire. Been Lowe alone, I'd maybe of took a chance, but as it was, they would have cut me down quick. So I come away, but I'm stickin' around, just waiting. I told him I aimed to have my money, an' he just laughed."

Dusty dropped his hand back and loosened his left-hand gun. Then he swung his leg back over the saddle and thrust his toe in the stirrup. "Well," he said, "I got papers here that say I speak for a gal that owns half his layout. I'm goin' up an' lay claim to it for her."

Riddle looked up cynically. "Why not shoot yourself and save the trouble? They'll gun you down."

Then he sized Barron up again. "What did you say your name was?"

Dusty grinned. "I didn't say, but it's Dusty Barron."

Blue Riddle slid off the corral rail. "One of the Barrons from Castle Rock?" He grinned again. "This I gotta see!"

Dusty was looking for a big man, but Dick Lowe, whom he spotted at once on entering the saloon, was only a bit larger than himself, and he was the only small man among the Barrons.

Lowe turned to look at him as he entered. The man's features were sharp, and his quick eyes glanced from Dusty Barron to Riddle and then back again. Dusty walked to the bar, and Riddle loitered near the door.

The man standing beside Lowe at the bar must be Cat McQuill. The reason for the nickname was obvious, for there was something feline about the man's facial appearance.

"Lowe?" Dusty inquired.

"That's right," Lowe turned toward him slowly. "Something you want?"

"Yeah," Dusty leaned nonchalantly on the bar and ordered a drink. "I'm representin' your partner."

Dick Lowe's face blanched and then turned hard as stone. His eyes glinted. However, he managed a smile with his thin lips. "Partner? I have no partner."

Dusty leaned on the bar watching his drink poured. He took his time.

———

LOWE WATCHED HIM, slowly growing more and more angry. "Well," he said sharply, "if you've got something to say, say it!"

Dusty looked around, simulating surprise. "Why, I was just givin' you time to remember, Lowe! You can't tell me you can draw up an agreement with a man, have it properly notarized, and then take five thousand dollars of his money to stock a ranch and not remember it!"

Dusty was pointedly speaking loudly, and the fact angered Lowe. "You have such an agreement?" Lowe demanded.

"Sure I got it."

"Where's the party this supposed agreement belongs to? Why doesn't he speak for himself?"

"He's dead. He was a lunger an' died on his way west."

Lowe's relief was evident. "I'm afraid," he said, "that this is all too obvious an attempt to get some money out of me. It won't work."

"It's nothing of the kind. Grant's dead, but he left a daughter and a son. I aim to see they get what belongs to 'em, Mr. Lowe. I hope we can do it right peaceable."

Lowe's face tightened, but he forced a smile. He was aware he had enemies in Pie Town and did not relish their overhearing this conversation. He was also aware that it was pretty generally known that he had come into Pie Town with five thousand in cash and bought cattle when everyone on the range was impoverished.

"I reckon this'll be easy settled," he said. "You bring the agreement to the ranch, an' if it's all legal I reckon we can make a deal."

"Sure!" Dusty agreed. "See you tomorrow!"

On the plank steps of the hotel he waited until Riddle caught up with him. "You ain't actually goin' out there, are you?" Blue demanded. "That's just askin' for trouble!"

"I'm goin' out," Dusty agreed. "I want a look at the ranch myself. If I can ride out there I can get an idea what kind of stock he's got and what shape the ranch is in. I've got a hunch if we make a cash settlement Lowe isn't goin' to give us much more chance to look around if he can help it.

"Besides, I've talked in front o' the folks here in town, and rough as some of them may be they ain't goin' to see no orphans get gypped. No western crowd would stand for that unless it's some outlaws like Lowe and his two pals."

Riddle walked slowly away shaking his head with doubt. Dusty watched him go and then went on inside.

He was throwing a saddle on the steel-dust next morning when he heard a low groan. Gun in hand he walked around the corner of the corral. Beyond a pile of poles he saw Blue Riddle pulling himself off the ground. "What happened?" Dusty demanded.

"Bender an' McQuill. They gave me my walkin' papers. Said I'd been in town too long, which didn't bother Lowe none till I took up with you. They gave me till daybreak to pull my freight."

He staggered erect, holding a hand to his head. "Then Bender bent a gun over my noggin."

Barron's eyes narrowed. "Play rough, don't they?" He looked at Riddle. "What are you goin' to do?"

"You don't see me out there runnin' down the road, do you?" Riddle said. "I'm sittin' tight!"

"Wash your face off, then," Dusty suggested, "an' we'll eat!"

"You go ahead," Riddle replied. "I'll be along."

Dusty glanced back over his shoulder as he left and saw Blue Riddle hiking toward the Indian huts that clustered outside of Pie Town.

———

WHEN HE RODE out of town an hour later Dusty Barron was not feeling overly optimistic. Riddle had stayed behind only at Dusty's insistence, but now that Dusty was headed toward Lowe's ranch he no longer felt so confident. Dick Lowe was not a man to give up easily, nor to yield his ranch or any part of it without a fight. The pistol-whipping of

Riddle had been ample evidence of the lengths to which he was prepared to go.

The range through which Dusty rode was good. This was what he had wanted to see. How they might have bargained in town he was not sure. He doubted if anyone there would interfere if a deal was made by him. It was his own problem to see that Ruth and Billy Grant got a fair deal, and that could not be done unless he knew something, at least, of the ranch and the stock.

Dusty was quite sure now that Lowe had never expected the consumptive Roger Grant to come west and claim his piece of the ranch. Nor had he planned to give it to him if he had. He knew very well that he himself was riding into the lion's mouth, but felt he could depend on his own abilities and that Lowe would not go too far after his talk before the bystanders who had been in the saloon. By now Lowe would know that the story would be known to all his enemies in Pie Town.

Cat McQuill was loafing on the steps when Dusty rode up, and the gunman's eyes gleamed with triumph at seeing him. "Howdy!" he said affably. "Come on in! The boss is waitin' for you!"

Bugle Nose Bender was leaning against the fireplace and Lowe was seated at his desk. "Here he is, Boss!" McQuill said as they entered.

Lowe glanced up sharply. "Where's the agreement?" he asked, holding out his hand.

Barron handed it to him, and the rancher opened it, took a quick look, and then glanced up. "This is it, Cat!"

Too late Dusty heard the slide of gun on leather and whirled to face McQuill, but the pistol barrel crashed down over the side of his head and he hit the floor. Even as he fell he realized what a fool he had been, yet he had been so sure they would talk a little, at least, try to run a blazer or to buy him off cheap.

Bender lunged toward him and kicked him in the ribs. Then Lowe reached over and jerking him to his knees, struck him three times in the face. The pistol barrel descended again and drove him down into a sea of blackness.

How long they had pounded him he had no idea. When he opened his eyes, he struggled, fighting his way to a realization of where he was. It took him several minutes to understand that he was almost standing on his head in the road, one foot caught in the stallion's stirrup!

The steel-dust, true to his training, was standing rigid in the road, his head turned to look at his master. "Easy boy!" Dusty groaned. "Easy does it!" Twisting his foot in the stirrup, he tried to free it, but to no avail.

He realized what they had planned. After beating him they had brought him out here, wedged his foot in the stirrup, struck the horse, and when he started to move, ridden hastily away before they could be seen. Most horses, frightened by the unfamiliar burden in the stirrup, would have raced away over the desert and dragged him to death. It had happened to more than one unwary cowhand.

They had reckoned without the steel-dust. The stallion had been reared by Dusty Barron from a tiny colt, and the two had never been long apart. The big horse had known instantly that something was radically wrong and had gone only a little way and then stopped. His long training told him to stand, and he stood stock still.

Dusty twisted his foot again but couldn't get loose. Nor could he pull himself up and get hold of the stirrup and so into the saddle. He was still trying this when hoofbeats sounded on the road.

He looked around wildly, fearful of Lowe's return. Then a wave of relief went over him. It was Blue Riddle!

"Hey!" Blue exclaimed. "What the heck happened?" He swung down from his horse and hastily extricated Dusty from his predicament.

Barron explained. "They wanted me killed so it would look like I was dragged to death! Lucky they got away from here in a hurry, afraid they might be seen!"

"But they got the agreement!" Riddle protested.

"Uh-uh." Barron grinned and then gasped as his bruised face twinged with pain. "That was a copy. I put the agreement down an' traced over it. He took a quick look and thought it was the real thing. Now we got to get to town before he realizes what happened."

———

DESPITE HIS BATTERED and bruised body and the throbbing of his face, Dusty crawled into the saddle and they raced up the road to Pie Town.

Two men were standing on the hotel porch as they rode up. One of them glanced at Dusty Barron. "Howdy. Young woman inside wants to see you."

Dusty rushed into the lobby and stopped in surprise. Facing him was Ruth Grant, holding Billy by the hand, but her smile fled when she saw his face. "Oh!" she cried. "What's happened to you?"

Briefly, he explained. Then he demanded, "How'd you get here?"

"After you left," Ruth told him, "I was worried. After Father's death and the trouble we had before you came, there was no time to think of anything, and I had to always be thinking of where we would go and what we would do. Then I remembered a comment Father made once.

"You see, Mr. Lowe left a trunk with us to bring west or send to him later. It wasn't quite full, so Father opened it to pack some other things in it. He found something there that worried him a great deal, and he told me several times that he was afraid he might have trouble when we got out here.

"From all he said I had an idea what he found, so after you were gone we searched through the trunk and found some letters and a handbill offering a five-thousand-dollar reward for Lowe. Why he kept them I can't imagine, but the sheriff says some criminals are very vain and often keep such things about themselves."

"And then you rode on here?"

She nodded. "We met two men who were trailing you, and as they had extra horses with them so they could travel fast, we joined them."

Dusty's face tightened. "Men looking for me?"

Riddle interrupted. "Dick Lowe's ridin' into town now!"

Dusty Barron turned, loosening his guns. He started for the door.

"I'm in on this, too!" Riddle said, trailing him.

They walked out on the porch and stepped down into the street, spreading apart. Dick Lowe and his two henchmen had dismounted and were starting into the saloon when something made them glance up the street.

"Lowe!" Dusty yelled. "You tried to kill me, an' I'm comin' for you!"

Dick Lowe's hard face twisted with fury as he wheeled, stepping down into the dust.

He stopped in the street, and Cat McQuill and Bender moved out to either side.

Dusty Barron walked steadily down the street, his eyes on Dick Lowe. All three men were dangerous, but Lowe was the man he wanted, and Lowe was the man he intended to get first.

"This man's an outlaw!" he said, speaking to Bender and McQuill. "He's wanted for murder in St. Louis! If you want out, get out now!"

"You're lying!" Bender snarled.

Dusty Barron walked on. The sun was bright in the street, and little puffs of dust arose at every step. There were five horses tied to the hitch rail behind the three men. He found himself hoping none of them would be hit by a stray shot. To his right was Blue Riddle, walking even with him, his big hands hovering over his guns.

———

HIS EYES CLUNG to Dick Lowe, riveted there as though he alone lived in the world. He could see the man drop into a half crouch, noticed the bulge of the tobacco sack in his breast pocket, the buttons down the two sides of his shirt. Under the brim of the hat he could see the straight bar of the man's eyebrows and the hard gleam of the eyes beneath, and then suddenly the whole tableau dissolved into flaming, shattering action.

Lowe's hand flashed for his gun and Dusty's beat him by a hair-breadth, but Dusty held his fire, lifting the gun slowly.

Lowe's quick shot flamed by his ear, and he winced inwardly at the proximity of death. Then the gunman fired again and the bullet tugged impatiently at his vest. He drew a long breath and squeezed off a shot, then another.

Lowe rose on tiptoes, opened his mouth wide as if to gasp for breath, seemed to hold himself there for a long moment, and then pitched over into the street.

Dusty's gun swung with his eyes and he saw Bender was down on his knees, and so he opened up on McQuill. The Cat man jerked convulsively and then began to back away, his mouth working and his gun hammering. The man's gun stopped firing, and he stared at it, pulled the trigger again, and then reached for a cartridge from his belt.

Barron stood spraddle-legged in the street and saw Cat's hand fumble at his belt. The fingers came out with a cartridge and moved toward the gun, and then his eyes glazed and he dropped his iron. Turning, as though the whole affair had slipped his mind, he started for the saloon. He made three steps and then lifted his foot, seemed to feel for the saloon step, and fell like a log across the rough board porch.

Blue Riddle was on his knees, blood staining a trouser leg. Bender was sprawled out in the dust, a darkening pool forming beneath him.

Suddenly the street was filled with people. Ruth ran up to Dusty and he slid his arm around her. With a shock, he remembered. "You said two men were looking for me. Who?"

"Only us."

He turned, staring. Two big men were facing him, grinning. "Buck and Ben! How in tarnation did you two find me?"

Buck Barron grinned. "We was wonderin' what happened to you. We come to town and had a mite of a ruckus with the Hickmans. What was left of them headed for El Paso in a mighty hurry—both of 'em.

"Then an Injun kid come ridin' up on a beat-up hoss and said you all was in a sight of trouble, so we figgered we'd come along and see how you made out."

"An Injun?" Dusty was puzzled.

"Yeah," Riddle told him, "that was my doin'. I figgered you was headed for trouble, so I sent an Injun kid off after your brothers. Heck, if I'd knowed what you was like with a six-gun I'd never have sent for 'em!"

Ben Barron grinned and rubbed at the stubble of whiskers. "An' if we'd knowed there was on'y three, we'd never have come!" He looked from Dusty to Ruth. "Don't look like you'd be comin' home right soon with that place at Gallo Gap an' what you've got your arm around. But what'll we tell Allie?"

"Allie?" Ruth drew away from him, eyes wide. "Who's Allie? You didn't tell me you had a girl!"

Dusty winked at his brothers. "Allie? She's war chief of the Barron tribe! Allie's my ma!"

He turned to Riddle. "Blue, how's about you sort of keepin' an eye on that gap place for me for a week or so? I reckon I'd better take Ruth home for a spell. Allie, she sure sets a sight of store by weddin's!"

Ruth's answering pressure on his arm was all the answer he needed.

THE DRIFT

SMOKE LAMSON CAME into the bunkhouse and Johnny Garrett cringed. The big foreman rolled his tobacco in his jaws and looked slowly around the room.

Nobody looked up. Nobody said anything. It was a wicked night, blowing snow and cold, so it was a foregone conclusion who was going to night-herd.

"You"—he turned suddenly to Johnny—"saddle up and get out there. An' remember, if they start to drift, make 'em circle."

Johnny swung his feet to the floor. "Why me?" he protested. "I've been on night ridin' every night this week."

Lamson grinned. "Good for you, kid. Make a man out of you. Get goin'."

An instant, Johnny Garrett hesitated. He could always quit. He could draw his time. But how long would forty dollars last? And where else could he get a job at this time of the year? Moreover, if he left the country he would never see Mary Jane again.

He drew on his boots, then his chaps and sheepskin. He pulled the rawhide under his chin and started for the door.

Lasker rolled over on his bunk. "Kid, you can take my Baldy if you want. He's a good night horse."

"Thanks," Johnny said. "I'll stick to my string. They might as well learn."

"Sure." Smoke Lamson grinned and started to build a smoke. "Like you, they gotta learn."

Johnny opened the door, the lamp guttered, and then he was outside, bending his head into the wind. By now he should be used to it.

HE HAD COME to the Bar X from Oregon, where he had grown up in the big timber, but he came to Arizona wanting to punch cows. After a couple of short jobs he had stumbled into the Bar X when they needed a hand. The boss hired him, and Lamson did not like that, but he had said nothing, done nothing until that night in town.

Everybody on the Bar X knew that Smoke was sweet on Mary Jane Calkins. Everybody, that is, but Johnny Garrett. And Johnny had seen Mary Jane, danced with her, talked with her, and then walked out with her. Looking for Mary Jane, Smoke had found them in a swing together.

He had been coldly furious, and Mary Jane, apparently unaware of what she was doing, told Smoke that Johnny was going to be a top hand by spring. "You wait an' see," Johnny had said.

And Smoke Lamson looked at Johnny and grinned slowly. "You know, Mary Jane," he said meaningfully, "I'll bet he is!"

That started it. Every tough and lonely job fell to Johnny Garrett. Morning, noon, and night he was on call. Everybody in the bunkhouse could see that Smoke was riding Johnny, driving him, trying to make him quit. "Want to be a top hand, don't you?" he would taunt. "Get on out there!" And Johnny went.

He mended what seemed to be miles of fence, and if Lamson did not think it was well done, it was done over. He cut wood for the cook, the lowest of cow ranch jobs; he hunted strays in the wildest and roughest country; he used a shovel more than a rope, cleaning water holes, opening springs. He did more night riding than any three men in the outfit. He worked twelve and fourteen hours a day when the others rarely did more than seven or eight in the fall and bitter winter.

Smoke Lamson was big and he was tough. It was his boast that he had never been bested in a rough-and-tumble fight, and although he outweighed Johnny by forty pounds, he seemed to be trying to tempt the smaller man to try his luck.

As the months went by it grew worse. As if angered by

his failure to force Johnny to quit, Lamson became tougher. Even Lasker, a taciturn man, attempted to reason with Smoke. "Why don't you lay off the kid?" he demanded. "He's doin' his job."

"My business, Dan." Smoke was abrupt. "When he's as good a hand as you or me, I'll lay off."

———

JOHNNY GOT THE saddle on his dun and rode out of the big barn, ducking his head under the door. From the saddle he swung the door shut, then turned the horse into the wind and headed toward the west range.

Ice was already forming and the ground had white patches of snow, but there was more in the air, blowing as well as falling, than on the ground. It was blowing cold and bitter from the north, and if the cattle started to drift and got any kind of a start, there would be no stopping them. Not far below the valley where he would be riding was Sage Flat, fifty miles wide and half again that long, and nothing to stop them in all that length but a forty-foot arroyo. If they started south ahead of the wind, they would be half-frozen by the time they reached that arroyo and would walk off into it.

Johnny had heard about a drift. He had never seen it, but his imagination was good.

He had been in the saddle over an hour when he saw the first steer, a big roan steer, heading toward him, plodding steadily. Behind him there was another, then another . . . and for the first time, he knew panic.

Deep inside he knew that nobody had ever expected this. The upper end of the valley he patrolled was fenced, and Smoke had sent him here just for safety's sake or out of pure cussedness, but the fence must be down, must have been pushed over, and they were coming.

There was no time to go for help. He drew his pistol and fired into the air, partly hoping to stop the drift, partly to call for help. It did neither. Desperately, he tried to turn the cattle, and they would not turn. When he got one half-turned into the storm, others would go by him.

And from up the valley came more, and more, and more.

Then he realized the full enormity of what was happening. The whole herd, more than a thousand head, would be drifting ahead of the norther. Unless stopped they would drift into the arroyo, winding up at the bottom either dead or with broken legs, helpless, for the cold to kill. A few would survive, of course, but not many. A forty-foot fall into a rocky ravine is not calculated to do either man or animal any good.

The dun worked hard. Johnny yelled, fired more shots, tried everything. The cattle kept coming. He had forgotten Smoke Lamson, who had sent him here. He had forgotten everything but the cattle and the kindly old man, old Bart Gavin, who had hired him when he was broke.

He drew up, staring into the storm. Ice was forming on the scarf over his chin. His toes were numb from inactivity, and the cattle drifted. It was four miles to the gate, four more to the bunkhouse. To go there and get back with the hands—for they must all dress and saddle up—would let too many cattle go by. And what could be done when they got here?

By daybreak a thousand head of beef steers would be piled up along a mile or so of that arroyo. Unless . . . unless he could force them over. If he could push them east to the flank of Comb Ridge, start them down along the ridge until they got between the ridge and Gavin Fault, he might force them to pile up in one place. Some would be lost but the fall of the others would be cushioned . . . An idea clicked in his mind.

Swinging the startled dun, he slammed the spurs to the mustang and raced south. He passed steer after steer, plodding steadily, methodically on, hypnotized by their movement and driven by the howling norther behind them. Racing on at breakneck speed over the frozen ground, he was soon beyond them. As he raced, he was thinking. They were traveling slow, the usual slow walk of a drift herd. There would be, with luck, time enough.

Soon he was passing the straggling leaders, strung out for a quarter of a mile, and then he was racing alone into the night and the south, away from the herd, toward the arroyo. Yet, when a few miles were behind him he swung off west and rode hard. Suddenly he saw a shoulder of Gavin Fault, a huge upthrust of sandstone. Keeping it close on his left, he rode down it until against the night he caught the square shoulder of Rock House. He swung the dun into the lee of the house and got out of the saddle.

The door opened when he lifted the latch and shoved. He got in quickly and struck a match. Against the wall were piled four boxes of powder. He stuffed it into sacks, caught up a roll of fuse, and ran from the shack, closing the door after him.

Putting the giant powder behind the saddle, he got up himself, and, the fuses around his arm, heedless of risk, he rode on south. If the dun stumbled and fell—well, there would be a mighty big hole in the grass!

The dun liked to run, and it was bitter cold now. How cold he did not know, but getting down there. He raced onward until suddenly he saw ahead of him the black line of the arroyo. He swung from the dun and led the horse into the shelter of a rocky projection and hurried to the edge. Carefully, he clambered down.

He knew that spot. He had slipped away and hidden from Lamson to catch a quiet smoke on several occasions. It was cracked and honeycombed with holes. Working swiftly, he stuffed the cracks with powder, jammed bunches of sticks into holes, and worked his way from the lip almost to the bottom. He had been working for more than a half hour before he saw the first steer. It had brought up against a rock some distance off and stood there, befuddled. It would soon come on.

Sheltered from the wind that blew over the lip above him, Johnny ran along, hastily spitting his fuses. When all were lighted that he could see, he scrambled back up and grabbed his horse. He was riding into the teeth of the wind when he heard the blast. There was no time to go back. It had to work. It must work.

North he rode until he saw the cattle. They were coming now in droves, and soon he was past the end of the fault. Channeled by the valley from which they had come, the animals plodded steadily ahead. Only a few seemed inclined to stray west, and these he pushed back. He could move them east or west, but no power on earth could now prevent them from going south.

How long he worked he did not know. Every move might be futile. Once the dun fell, but scrambled gamely up. Soon Johnny found a place from which he could watch for some distance. The snow was letting up, the ground was white, and visibility not bad. He worked more slowly, half-dead in the saddle, and then the last of the cattle drifted by and he turned his horse and walked slowly back to the ranch.

Half-dead with weariness, he stripped the saddle from his horse and then went to work. For half an hour he worked hard over the dun, and then he blanketed the horse to allow him to conserve as much heat as possible. Stumbling, he got into the bunkhouse and crawled into bed. His feet were numbed and for a while he held his toes, trying to warm them. And then he fell asleep.

A hand on his shoulder awakened him. It was Dan Lasker. "Better crawl out, kid. Lamson's on a tear this mornin'."

He was the last one to reach the breakfast table. He came into the room and stopped abruptly. Sitting with Bart Gavin was a girl . . . and what a girl!

Her hair was dark and thick, her eyes bright, her lips slightly full and red. In a daze he got into a chair and hitched close to the table. The hands were tongue-tied. No conversation this morning. In front of the radiant creature beside Bart they were completely at a loss. Even Smoke Lamson was speechless.

Suddenly, she spoke. "Why is it that only one of the horses has a blanket on him? It was so cold last night!"

"Blanket?" Gavin looked around. "Blanket on a horse?"

The hands looked around, astonished. The tough western cow ponies were unaccustomed to such treatment. Even Smoke Lamson was surprised. Suddenly he turned on Johnny, seeing a chance to have some fun. "Maybe it was the Top Hand here. That sounds like him."

The dark and lovely eyes turned to Johnny and he blushed furiously.

"Did oo w'ap up the po' itto hossie?" Lamson said, glancing at the girl to see if his wit was appreciated, and chuckling.

Gavin looked at Johnny sharply. Feeling some explanation necessary, Johnny said feebly, "He was pretty wore out. It was near to daybreak before I got in."

Gavin put his fork down. "Daybreak?" He was incredulous. "What were you doing out last night?"

It was Lamson's turn to grow confused. He hesitated. Then he said, "I figured somebody better watch in case of a drift."

"A *drift*?" Gavin's voice was scornful. "With that fence? It's horse high and bull strong! Anyway"—his voice was biting—"what could one man do against a drift?"

Smoke Lamson stuttered, hesitated, and finally tried a feeble excuse. The girl looked from him to Johnny, and then at the other hands. Bart Gavin was no fool. He was beginning to realize something he had not realized before.

"The cows are all right." Johnny found a voice. "I was there when the drift started. They are in the arroyo."

"What?" Bart Gavin came out of his seat, his face shocked and pale.

All eyes were on Johnny now. "I never did figure out what happened to the fence. I was ridin', then all of a sudden I seen 'em comin'. I shot off my gun an' yelled, but nobody heard me, an' it didn't have any effect on the cows."

Lamson was hoarse. "You mean . . . there was a drift? They got through the fence?"

"Yeah," Johnny said, "but they are all right."

"What do you mean"—Gavin's voice was icy—"all right? You mean I've got forty thousand dollars' worth of cattle piled up in the arroyo?"

"They ain't piled," Johnny explained. "Not many, at least. I seen—saw—what was goin' to happen, so I got that powder out of the Rock House and blowed—I mean, I blew the edge of the arroyo. I figure they couldn't go no further, so they are probably scattered up an' down it."

There was a long moment of deathly silence. Lamson was pale, the others incredulous. Gavin stared at Johnny, and after a minute he picked up his fork and started to eat. "Let me get this straight," he said. "You got ahead of the herd, blew off the edge of the arroyo, then got back and worked all night pointing those cattle toward the break?"

"It wasn't much." Johnny was sheepish. "I had 'em narrowed down by the valley, so I just had to keep 'em that way."

"I think that was wonderful!" the girl with the dark eyes said. "Don't you, Uncle Bart?"

"It saved me the best part of forty thousand dollars, is all." Gavin was emphatic. "Lamson, I want to talk to you. First, we'll take a look."

Of the more than a thousand cattle that drifted south, only six were lost. Despite the hurry and the darkness, Johnny had chosen his spot well and the powder had been well planted. Knowing the arroyo, he had known how many cracks were in the rocky edge, and how honeycombed it was with holes eroded by wind and water.

Gavin found his cattle scattered along the bottom of the arroyo, feeding on the rich grass that grew there where water often stood. He studied the blasted edge, glancing sharply at Johnny. "You knew something about powder, son," he said. "Those shots were well placed."

"My dad had a claim up in Oregon," Johnny explained. "I helped him some, doin' assignment work."

WHAT BART GAVIN said to Lamson none of them knew, but for a few days his driving of Johnny ceased, although some sneering remarks about "pets" were made. And then gradually the old way resumed. It was Johnny Garrett who drew the rough jobs.

When there was to be a dance at Rock Springs Schoolhouse, where Johnny might have seen Mary Jane, he was sent to a line-camp at Eagle Rest.

It was a rugged, broken country, heavily timbered like his native Oregon, but riven by canyons and peaks, and cut here and there by lava flows and bordered on the east by the *malpais,* a forty-mile-wide stretch of lava where no horse could go and where a man's boots would be cut to ribbons in no time. Supposedly waterless, it was a treacherous area. There were stretches of flat, smooth lava, innocent in appearance, but actually that seemingly solid rock was merely the thin dome over a lava blister. Stepping on it, a man could plunge fifteen to fifty feet into a cavernous hole whose sides were slick and impossible to climb.

The few openings into this *malpais* were fenced, and the fences had to be kept up. At places the lava rode in a wall of basaltic blocks.

After the water holes were cleaned, salt scattered, and the fences checked, there was little to do. Johnny had a Colt and a Winchester, and he did a lot of shooting. He killed two mountain lions and a half-dozen wolves, skinning them and tanning the hides.

A week later Lasker rode in with two pack horses of supplies. Lasker was a tall, rawboned man who had punched cows for fifteen years.

He noticed the hides but made no comment. Hunkered down by the wall in the morning sun, he said, "Old man's worried. The tally fell off this year. He's losin' cows."

"You seen Mary Jane?"

"She was at the dance with Smoke," Lasker said, started to say something further, but stopped. Then he said, "'Member that niece of Gavin's? She's livin' at the ranch. Her name is Betty."

"Too high-toned for any cowpunch."

"Can't tell about a woman," Lasker said. "Some of the high-toned ones are thoroughbreds."

———

TWO DAYS LATER Johnny found a dead cow. Wolves had torn it, but the cow had been shot in the head . . . the carcass not even a week old. Nobody had been around but Lasker and himself.

It was a Gavin cow. The only reason to shoot a cow was because she followed a rustled calf. Johnny was woods-bred and he spelled out the trail. A dozen head of young stuff had been taken through the timber into high country. He followed the scuffed trail through the pine needles, then lost it at the rim of a high canyon about the *malpais*.

For a week he scouted for sign, keeping up the pretense of

only doing his work. Once, he cut the trail of a shod horse but lost it. Back at the cabin he began to sketch a crude map on brown wrapping paper, incorporating all he knew of the country, marking ridges, arroyos, and streams.

Three small streams disappeared in the direction of the lava beds, and nobody had ever followed those streams to see where they went. Both streams were shallow—no water backed up anywhere.

The first stream, he discovered, veered suddenly south and dropped from sight in a deep cavern under the lava. Two days later, mending fence, he checked the next stream. It ended in a swamp.

Lasker and Lamson rode in the following day. Lasker was friendly and noticed the fresh wolf hide. "Good huntin'?"

"Yeah, but not enough time."

Smoke Lamson said nothing, but looked around carefully, and several times Johnny found Smoke watching him intently. It was not until they were about to leave that Lamson turned suddenly. "Seen anybody? Any strange riders?"

"Not a soul," Johnny told him, and after they were gone he swore at himself for not mentioning the tracks. And the cow.

ON THE THIRD day after that, he circled around to trace the source of the one unexplored stream. When he found it he rode into the water and had followed it downstream more than a mile when he heard voices. He could distinguish no words, but two men were talking. Through a veil of brush he saw them ride out of the trees. One was a fat, sloppy man in a dirty gray shirt. The other was lean and savage; his name was Hoyt, and Johnny had seen him in town. He was said to be dangerous. After they were gone, Johnny followed cautiously.

The stream's current increased. It was dropping fast, and suddenly he found himself about to enter a sheer-walled canyon. Climbing his dun out of the water, he followed along the rim for more than an hour as the canyon grew deeper, until the riders were mere dots.

In a clearing atop the mountain, Johnny took his bearings.

To north, south, and east lay the *malpais,* spotted with trees and brush that concealed the razorlike edges of broken lava. Suppose there was, far out there where the stream flowed, a grassy valley where stolen cattle were held?

Back at the cabin he made his decision. It was time to talk to Bart Gavin. Switching horses he rode back, arriving long after dark. It would take another day to return, but he must see the rancher. "Nobody home," the cook told him. "All gone to dance. Only Dan, he here."

Lasker sat up when Johnny walked into the bunkhouse. "Hey, what's up?" The sleep was gone from his eyes.

"Needed tobacco," Johnny lied glibly. He sat down. "A dance in town?"

Lasker relaxed. "So that's it? Kid, you'll get Lamson sore. You shouldn't oughta have come in."

"Aw, why not? Climb into your duds an' we'll ride. I want to see Mary Jane."

Riding into the outskirts, Lasker said, "That's a staked claim, kid. Better lay off." Then he added, "He's a fighter."

"So'm I. I grew up in lumber camps."

As they tied their horses, Lasker said again, "Stay away from Mary Jane. She ain't for you, kid, an'—"

Johnny turned to face him. "What's wrong with her?"

Lasker started to speak, then shrugged. "Your funeral."

Mary Jane squealed excitedly when she saw him. "Why, Johnny! I thought you were 'way up in the woods. What brought you back?"

"I had a reason." He liked being mysterious. "You'll know soon enough."

During the second dance she kept insisting. "What reason, Johnny? Why did you come back?"

"Secret," he said. "You'll know before long."

"Tell me. I won't tell anybody."

"It's nothing." He shrugged it off. "Only I found some rustlers."

"You *found* them?" Her eyes were bright. "Why, John—!"

A big hand fell on his shoulder and he was spun into a hard fist crashing out of nowhere. He started to fall, but the second blow caught and knocked him sprawling.

Johnny's head was buzzing but he rolled over and got up swiftly. Smoke Lamson, his face hard and angry, swung wickedly, and Johnny clinched. Lamson hurled him to the floor, and before Johnny could scramble to his feet, Smoke rushed in and swung his leg for a kick. Johnny threw himself at Lamson's legs and they hit the floor in a heap. Coming up fast they walked into each other, punching with both hands. Johnny had the shorter reach but he got inside. He slammed a right to the ribs and Lamson took an involuntary step back. Then Johnny smashed a left to his face and, crouching, hooked a right to the body.

Around them the crowd was yelling and screaming. In the crowd was Mary Jane, her face excited, and nearby another face. That of the fat, sloppy man from the canyon!

Lamson rushed, but, over his momentary shock from the unexpected punch, Johnny was feeling good. Due to the brutally hard labor of the preceding fall and winter he was in fine shape. He was lithe as a panther and rugged as a Texas steer. He ducked suddenly and tackled Lamson. The big man fell hard and got up slowly. Johnny knocked him down. Lamson got up and Johnny threw him with a rolling hiplock, and when the bigger man tried to get up again, Johnny knocked him down again.

His face bloody, Lamson stayed down. "Awright, kid. You whupped me."

Johnny backed off and then walked away. Mary Jane was nowhere in sight. Disappointed, he looked around again. Across the room he saw Gavin and his niece. Betty was looking at him, and she was smiling. He started toward them when something nudged his ribs and a cool voice said, "All right, kid, let's go outside an' talk."

"But I—"

"Right now. An' don't get any fancy ideas. You wouldn't be the first man I killed." The man with the gun in his back was Hoyt, the gun held so it could not be seen. They walked from the hall, and Betty looked after them, bewildered.

The fat rustler was waiting. He had Johnny's horse and theirs. Johnny moved toward his horse, remembering the pistol he had thrust into the saddlebag and the rifle in the scabbard. He reached for the pommel and a gun barrel came down over his skull. He started to fall, caught a second glancing blow, and dropped into a swirling darkness.

The lurching of the horse over the stones of the creek brought him to consciousness. The feel under his leg told him the rifle was gone. His ankles were tied, and his wrists. Was the pistol still in the saddlebag?

Pain racked his skull, and some time later he passed out again, coming out of it only when they took him off his horse and shoved him against the cabin wall. He was in a long grassy valley, ringed with *malpais,* but a valley of thousands of acres.

A third man came from the cabin. Johnny remembered him as cook for one of the roundup outfits, named Freck. "Grub's on," Freck said, nodding briefly at Johnny.

They ate in silence. Hoyt watched Johnny without making a point of it. Freck and the fat man ate noisily. "You tell anybody about this place?" Hoyt demanded.

"Maybe," Johnny said. "I might have."

"Horse comin'," Hoyt said suddenly. "See who it is, Calkins."

Johnny stiffened. Calkins . . . Mary Jane's father. Something died within him. He stared at his food, appetite gone. It had been Mary Jane, then, who told the rustlers he had found the cattle and the hideout. No wonder she had been curious. No wonder they had rushed him out before he could talk to Gavin.

Calkins stood in the door with a Winchester. Turning his head, he said, "It's the boss."

A hard, familiar voice called, then footsteps. Johnny saw Dan Lasker step into the door. Lasker's smile was bleak. "Hello, Johnny. It ain't good to see you."

"Never figured you for a rustler."

"Man can't get rich at forty a month, Johnny." He squatted on his heels against the wall. "We need another man." Lasker lit a smoke. He seemed worried. "You're here, kid."

It was a way out and there would be no other. And Lasker wanted him to take it. Actually speaking, there was no choice.

"Are you jokin'?" Johnny's voice was sarcastic. "Only

thing I can't figure is why you didn't let me in on it from the start." And he lied quietly: "I was figurin' to moonlight a few cows myself, only I couldn't find a way out of the country."

Lasker was pleased. "Good boy, Johnny. As for a way out, we've got it."

Hoyt shoved back from the table. "All I can say is, one wrong move outa this kid, an' I'll handle it my own way!"

"All right, Hoyt." Lasker measured him coolly. "But be double-damned sure you're right."

They had over four hundred stolen cattle and were ready for a drive. But they did not return Johnny's guns. Nor did he make as much as a move toward his saddlebags.

———

CALKINS CAME IN midway of the following afternoon. He was puffing and excited. "Rider comin'. An' it's that young niece of Gavin's!"

Hoyt got up swiftly. "Dan, I don't like it!"

Freck walked to the door and waited there, watching her come. "What difference does it make? She's here, an' she ain't goin' back. Nobody ever found this place, and it's not likely they have now."

"What I want to know," Hoyt said bitterly, "is how she found it."

"Probably followed the kid." Lasker was uneasy and showed it. "She's sweet on him."

Betty Gavin was riding a black mare and she cantered up, smiling. "Hello, Johnny! Hello, Dan! Gee, I'm glad I found you! I thought I was lost."

"How'd you happen to get here?" Lasker inquired. He was puzzled. She seemed entirely unaware that anything was wrong. But being an eastern girl, how could she know? On the other hand, how could an eastern girl have got here?

"Uncle Bart was at the old place on Pocketpoint, so I decided I'd ride over and surprise Johnny. I lost my way, and then I saw some horse tracks, so I followed them. When I got in that canyon I was scared, but there was no way to get out, so I kept coming."

She looked around. "So this is what Eagle's Nest is like?"

Johnny Garrett was appalled. Calkins was frowning. Hoyt was frankly puzzled, as was Lasker. Yet Lasker looked relieved. He was not a murderer nor a man who would harm a woman, and this offered a way out. If Betty did not know the difference—

She came right up to Johnny, smiling. "My, but you're a mess!" she said. "Straighten your handkerchief." She reached up and pulled it around and he felt something sharp against the skin of his neck under the collar. It was a fold of paper. "Are you going to take me back to Pocketpoint?"

"Can't," he said. "But maybe Dan will. I'm busy here."

He scratched his neck, palmed the paper, and when an opportunity offered, he got a glimpse of it. The paper was the brown wrapping paper upon which he had worked out his first map of the streams and the probable route into this valley, with his notes.

She had lied then. She had come from Eagle's Nest following his own map, and she knew exactly where she was! He looked at her in astonishment. How could she be so cool? So utterly innocent?

He began to roll a smoke, thinking this out. Lasker might take her out of here. He could be trusted with a woman, and the others could not. Out of the corners of his eyes, he measured the distance to the saddlebag. No good. They'd kill him before he got it open. Unless . . . He hesitated. Unless he was very careful about it—

———

LASKER, CALKINS, AND Hoyt had moved off to one side and were talking. Betty glanced at Johnny. "I was afraid I wouldn't find you," she said, low-voiced.

Freck could hear them, but there were two meanings here.

"Won't Bart be worried?"

"Yes, he probably will. I"—she looked right at him— "left a note at the cabin." *A note at the line cabin!* Then there was a chance!

Suddenly, Freck was speaking. "Hoyt," he said, "we better look at our hole card. That gal's got red mud on her boot.

Ain't no place got red mud but around the cabin at Eagle's Nest."

Johnny felt his mouth go dry. He saw Betty's face change color, and he said quietly, "You don't know what you're sayin', Freck. There's red mud behind the cabin at Pocket-point."

Hoyt looked at Calkins. "Is there? You been there?"

"I been there. Dogged if I can recall!"

Hoyt's eyes were suddenly hard. He turned a little so his lank body was toward Lasker. Almost instinctively, Calkins drew back, but Freck's loyalty to Hoyt was obvious.

"Got a present for you, Betty." Johnny spoke into the sudden silence. His voice seemed unusually loud. "Aimed to bring it down first chance I got. One of those agates I was tellin' you about."

He walked to his saddlebag, and behind him he heard Hoyt say, "We can't let that girl leave here, Dan."

"Don't be a fool!" Lasker's anger was plain. "You can steal cattle and get away with it. Harm a girl like this and the West isn't big enough to hide us!"

"I'll gamble. But if she goes out, we're finished. Our work done for nothin'."

"Keep her," Freck said. "She'd be company." He winked at Lasker.

All eyes were watching Hoyt. It was there the trouble would start. Johnny ran his hand down into the saddlebag and came up with the .44 Colt. He turned, the gun concealed by his body.

"She goes," Lasker said, "cattle or no cattle."

"Over my dead body!" Hoyt snapped, and his hand dropped for his gun.

Freck grabbed iron, too, and Johnny yelled. The cook swung his head and Johnny's pistol came up. Johnny shot and swung his gun. Calkins backed away, hands high and his head shaking.

Guns were barking, and Johnny turned. Lasker was down and Hoyt was weaving on his feet. Hoyt stared at Lasker. "We had him, Freck an' me, just like we figured! Had him boxed, in a cross-fire! Then you—!" His gun came up and

Johnny fired, then fired again. Hoyt went down and rolled over.

Johnny wheeled on Calkins. "Drop your belt!" His voice was hard. "Now get in there an' get some hot water!"

He moved swiftly to Betty. "Are you all right?"

Her face was pale, her eyes wide and shocked. "All right," she whispered. "I'll be all right."

Johnny ran to Lasker. The cowhand lay sprawled on the ground and he had been shot twice. Once through the chest, once through the side. But he was still alive . . .

———

BART GAVIN AND four hands rode in an hour later. Gavin stopped abruptly when he saw the bodies, then came on in. Betty ran to him.

Johnny came to the door. "Me an' Dan," he said, "we had us a run-in with some rustlers. In the shootout Dan was wounded. With luck, he'll make it."

Bart Gavin had one arm around his niece. "Betty saw Hoyt take you out, but we thought she was imagining things, so when she couldn't make us believe, she took off on her own. Naturally, we trailed her . . . and found her note and your map, traced out."

Gavin saw Calkins. His face grew stern. "What's he doin' here?"

Johnny said quietly, "He stayed out of it. He was rustlin', but when it came to Betty, he stayed out. I told him we'd let him go."

Inside the cabin they stood over Lasker. He was conscious, and he looked up at them. "That was white, mighty white of you."

"Need you," Johnny said quietly. "Gavin just told me he fired Lamson. He said he'd been watchin' my work, an' I'm the new foreman. You're workin' for me now."

"For us," Betty said. "As long as he wants."

Lasker grinned faintly. "Remember what I said, kid? That some of the high-toned gals were thoroughbreds?"

About Louis L'Amour

"I think of myself in the oral tradition—as a troubadour, a village tale-teller, the man in the shadows of the camp-fire. That's the way I'd like to be remembered—as a storyteller. A good storyteller."

IT IS DOUBTFUL that any author could be as at home in the world re-created in his novels as Louis Dearborn L'Amour. Not only could he physically fill the boots of the rugged characters he wrote about, but he literally "walked the land my characters walk." His personal experiences as well as his lifelong devotion to historical research combined to give Mr. L'Amour the unique knowledge and understanding of people, events, and the challenge of the American frontier that became the hallmarks of his popularity.

Of French-Irish descent, Mr. L'Amour could trace his own family in North America back to the early 1600s and follow their steady progression westward, "always on the frontier." As a boy growing up in Jamestown, North Dakota, he absorbed all he could about his family's frontier heritage, including the story of his great-grandfather who was scalped by Sioux warriors.

Spurred by an eager curiosity and desire to broaden his horizons, Mr. L'Amour left home at the age of fifteen and enjoyed a wide variety of jobs, including seaman, lumberjack, elephant handler, skinner of dead cattle, and miner, and was an officer in the transportation corps during World War II. During his "yondering" days he also circled the world on a freighter, sailed a dhow on the Red Sea, was shipwrecked in the West Indies and stranded in the Mojave Desert. He won fifty-one of fifty-nine fights as a professional boxer and worked as a journalist and lecturer. He was a voracious reader and collector of rare books. His personal library contained 17,000 volumes.

Mr. L'Amour "wanted to write almost from the time I could talk." After developing a widespread following for his many frontier and adventure stories written for fiction magazines, Mr. L'Amour published his first full-length novel, *Hondo,* in the United States in 1953. Every one of his more than 120 books is in print; there are more than 300 million copies of his books in print worldwide, making him one of the bestselling authors in modern literary history. His books have been translated into twenty languages, and more than forty-five of his novels and stories have been made into feature films and television movies.

His hardcover bestsellers include *The Lonesome Gods, The Walking Drum* (his twelfth-century historical novel), *Jubal Sackett, Last of the Breed,* and *The Haunted Mesa.* His memoir, *Education of a Wandering Man,* was a leading bestseller in 1989. Audio dramatizations and adaptations of many L'Amour stories are available from Random House Audio.

The recipient of many great honors and awards, in 1983 Mr. L'Amour became the first novelist ever to be awarded the Congressional Gold Medal by the United States Congress in honor of his life's work. In 1984 he was also awarded the Medal of Freedom by President Reagan.

Louis L'Amour died on June 10, 1988. His wife, Kathy, and their two children, Beau and Angelique, carry the L'Amour publishing tradition forward.

FORGET THE LAW OF THE JUNGLE...

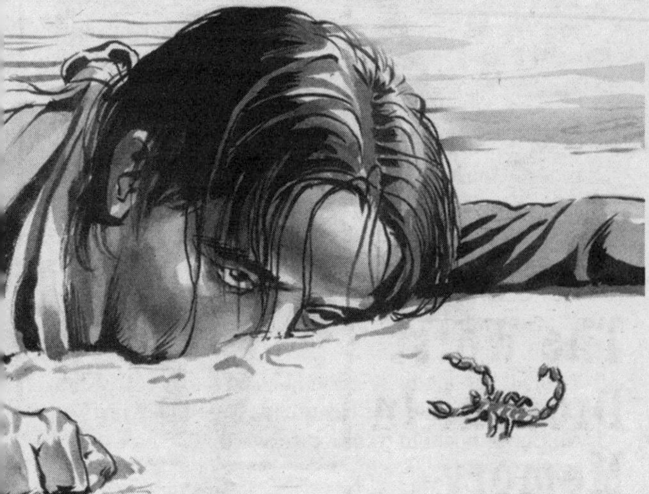

The Worst
Drought In
Memory . . .

In Louis L'Amour's
classic tale
of loyalty
and betrayal . . .

BASED ON THE STORY BY
LOUIS L'AMOUR
LAW OF THE DESERT BORN
A GRAPHIC NOVEL
Adapted by CHARLES SANTINO
Script by BEAU L'AMOUR
and KATHERINE NOLAN
Produced by BEAU L'AMOUR
Illustrated by
THOMAS YEATES